KNIGHTS-ERRENT

By DL Simmill

Published 2007 by arima publishing

www.arimapublishing.com

ISBN: 978 1 84549 163 5

© Donna Simmill 2007

All rights reserved

This book is copyright. Subject to statutory exception and to provisions of relevant collective licensing agreements, no part of this publication may be reproduced, stored in a retrieval system, or transmitted in any form or by any means, without the prior written permission of the author.

Printed and bound in the United Kingdom

Typeset in Garamond 10.5/14

This book is sold subject to the conditions that it shall not, by way of trade or otherwise, be lent, re-sold, hired out, or otherwise circulated without the publisher's prior consent in any form of binding or cover other than that which it is published and without a similar condition including this condition being imposed on the subsequent purchaser.

In this work of fiction, the characters, places and events are either the product of the author's imagination or they are used entirely fictitiously. Any resemblance to actual persons, living or dead, is purely coincidental

Swirl is an imprint of arima publishing.

arima publishing
ASK House, Northgate Avenue
Bury St Edmunds, Suffolk IP32 6BB
t: (+44) 01284 700321

www.arimapublishing.com

I would like to dedicate this book to my loving husband Rob, who spent many hours supporting, motivating and listening. Also to my mother in law, Sandra, my mum, dad, brother Peter and my Nan Alma, with thanks to their constant support and encouragement, this book has been made possible. Thank you.

I would also like to thank my high school English teacher Mrs Taylor-hope, without her, I would have possessed passion but not the skill and also my friends Patrick, Stacy, Peter, Tripti and Chrissie for their encouragement.

In loving memory of my Granddad Tom and Jack, and Uncle John who are sadly not here to see my dream realised

Chapter one

Acha lived a simple life, unaware of the uncertain future that awaited her, unaware of the horrors that loomed in her not so distant future as she sat daydreaming tending to their small plot of land in her father's place, but things were about to change, she was about to be cast into a world she should never have seen, the reason? Her father's ambitions. Her father had great plans to reclaim that which he once lost, that which he spoke of to no one, and finally, the preparations were complete. When his plan was fulfilled he would once more become a force to be feared, a force that would make even the earth tremble with fear. He had waited countless years, never losing his cold and calculating anger, his entire life was nothing more than a charade, a plan to obtain that which he so desperately needed, a body. A body in which to transfer the soul of Metis, a deal done by the divine word of the new lord of the underworld, Hades, in return, he would be granted eternity once again, he would reclaim his immortality. He had to be careful, if people, or even the Gods, suspected his ambitions it would jeopardise his plan, it was just as well his wife bore him a child that grew to fit his needs perfectly. He had never cared for either of them, they had just been pawns in his game of life, but sometimes, a pawn's role, and a pawn's sacrifice could be that which won the game.

"Acha, your father has requested your presence." Her mother's gentle voice called her back from her dreams, she looked towards her, the setting sun made her image appear nothing more than a silhouette, but even so squinting against the light Acha could see her arm pointing her in the direction of the forest, she nodded, it was an unusual request, her father was as a stranger to her, they rarely spent time in each others company, yet he was her father and she would obey his requests right to the end, for that was her duty, she stood dusting herself down before she ventured into certain doom.

Little did she know, as she entered the forest, that the next time she looked to the place her home stood, it would be nothing more than dust that the place she called home would have vanished completely.

The last thing she felt was an intense pain to the back of her head as a light exploded behind her eyes, she fell to the floor, unable to see her father standing behind her, a large branch gripped within his hands. It was all over within a matter of moments, the incantations, the offerings, all went according to *his* plan, his daughter's body twitched and slowly rose from the ground, the change to *his* eyes was obvious, yet to others, she would appear the same as always, this was a crucial to the plan. The life-force Hades had sent had finally arrived, after over twenty years of waiting and careful planning, the agreement was complete and he was granted immortality once again.

Darkness surrounded her, she found the fight to move one she could not win, trapped in the darkness she was vaguely aware of her father's voice and the tone of excitement rang within it. For a second, she could have sworn she heard her own voice reply, but she knew it couldn't have been, she was dying, the voice grew distant, muffled as she lay paralysed in the darkness, she came to an understanding, all her father's long nights, the strange items that lay hidden within his room, she knew he had been dabbling with the arts, but it wasn't until this moment it made sense, he had greater ambitions than to become the next Shaman, the magic he fooled with was darkness itself, and her soul had been offered to it. At the same time, somehow, she knew something was wrong, had his spell, the spell that should have sent her to Hades to take the place of the one he summoned, been incomplete? She vaguely remembered the words; they had been so loud within her throbbing head as he struck her down… something about a kind of placement or something. If only she could remember the words, she was sure they would offer some guidance on what had happened, perhaps by knowing them she could even find the answer to breaking the spell. Her optimism faded as two things became clear, she could neither remember the words that were spoken, nor did she possess any form of power to try to escape if she could, she was simply trapped in this perpetual darkness, she could only hope that somehow, someone would rescue her before the silence drove her to insanity.

'Fear not his spell was incomplete, he was, until now, only mortal after all. Your life-force shall remain yours to walk the path of light. You must rest now, rest to awaken when the chosen are to be united.' A soft voice whispered through the silence, when first she heard it, she was sure it had been an illusion created by her mind, could it be someone else shared this space with her, perhaps they could help, she had to ask them, but to ask she first needed to find a voice, she fought the growing tiredness, trying desperately to speak, but sleep descended upon her she struggled to fight it, staying awake was surely her only hope, she fought and fought, but to no avail.

Her father would not know the consequences of his actions, he would not know that a mortal conducting the rites of a God would have effects slightly different to those he had planned, after all, such power belonged to the Gods and although he was one once again, the caster had not been, and such, the spell had been imperfect. He would never know that the place of his victory, the place he now stood with Métis, was also the place his daughter's life-force slept, awaiting the time of awakening, beneath his feet an artefact of an old Shaman lay buried, an amulet with powers and traits lost through time, just like the charm itself, but it did not want to remain lost. Acha's soul transferred as he desired, but the spell had been incomplete, not by the words but by the power, or lack of, instead of her life-force entering the domain of Hades, it found the closest unoccupied space that possessed the power to contain it, a conveniently placed talisman under the ritual area.

A young girl enters the scene her hair as dark as the mighty oak, her eyes as rich as the earth itself. From her clothes we see much time has past since the modest clothing of Acha's time, for she is wearing slim fit leather trousers and a v neck shirt, dirt encrusted down the front, her body bleeding and torn where someone or something has grabbed at her ripping her clothes and flesh, she glanced behind her panic in her eyes as the tears stream down her muddy face, the howls of approaching men are not far from where she falls, her legs no longer able to hold her weight, she has been running so long, the fatigue robbing her now of the ability to save herself, she knew if she is to live, her only hope is to find a safe haven, a town, a traveller, but it seems her luck just ran out, the area was nothing more than a dusty wasteland, the occasional shrub and bush lining the open plain, she had hoped to lose them in the forest, but they had gained the upper hand leaving her no choice but to flee onto the open plains leaving her fate in the hands of the Gods, the only town on the island was still miles away, why had she thought it a good idea to walk the path of the priestess Sandra alone? Why had she been so desperate to travel the world, to prove to those back home that she could accomplish something more than her family would allow her? Why had it bother her that they thought her to be so useless that even the temple refused her training as a priestess unless she could complete the rite of the high priestess? And now, because she was so eager to prove them wrong, she was going to die.

'*Awaken.*'

Her fingers clawed at the floor her fingernails broken and bloody as she tries to pull herself into the cover of the near by bushes, hoping that somehow they will provide her with enough cover to hide. Her fingers scrape around a metallic object.

'Let it be a weapon, if I am to die let me take them with me.' She begged the listening forces, yet it seemed once more they had dealt her a poor hand, for within her grasp she held not a weapon, but an ancient charm of some form, a talisman from eras past.

'*Awaken*'

A sudden explosion of light surrounded the girl, a force that seems to radiate from the talisman itself, surrounding her in a foggy haze, could this charm be the tool of her salvation? No, it seemed not, for the light began to fade, she found herself looking upon her body as it lay besides her on the floor, for an instant she thought she saw it move, regardless the men were nearly upon it now, and Hades had sent an escort, she took her mother's hand and walked away.

Acha's eyes shot open, since she had slept so much had changed, yet somehow in a strange way, so much remained the same, just as her eyes had opened the life of the body she took flashed before her, the town she once called home was now less than dust as the passing years had taken their toll. Although much time had passed the villages now, were not too dissimilar from those she knew, although more settlements had appeared, the world itself was still filled with ancient splendour, she could do nothing but watch as the images of this new world passed before her, amazed at really how little had changed considering.

Each town still possessed the old dirt tracks created only by the wear of footsteps, the forests, although smaller now, still shone with magic. The single storey houses were still built from wood or brick, whichever material was in abundance within the settlement's area, yet somehow the houses appeared more stable. Her host had spent much time within a city, where those that built it had somehow balanced one or even two buildings on top of each other to create a multi-storey effect. She also noticed through this girl's vision a strange new substance, like nothing she has seen before, it seemed to cover some of the old dirt tracks as if a solid long stone was placed upon the ground, she also noted it had appeared in a few of the houses seen by this girl as flooring instead of common place wood.

Throughout the paths of the city tall wooden objects towered, at night they would come a glow as the stone cylinder was filled with oil and set alight illuminating the streets with the power of a hundred candles, it seemed this 'light' had worked its way inside on a lesser scale, the houses had small versions that hung from the ceilings, these however contained a small lid no doubt to remove the oxygen when it was time to extinguish the flame. From glass, they had also made lamps working on the same principal as cloth soaked the fluid and was burned to make portable light, it was incredible, all this new technology, yet with little of the external change she had expected.

Now aware of the events that had transpired while she had slept, retaining the knowledge of this girl she felt ready to face this strange new time. Fate had found her a soul to replace, yet, at the same time, would her fate not meet that of the girls? Here, now, she knew this girl and through her knew this world, she knew the fate that was to become her and was still as powerless as the one who died to fend off her attackers, her muscles ached her skin throbbed, moving was almost impossible… but to lie here, to die as that girl would have… surely that can not be fates plan. The girl's pursuers were upon her now their foul breath and sweat stained the air stifling her. Her eyes swam with darkness, she never saw the face of her attacker, she just felt his coarse hands upon her cool skin as he lifted her limp body to her feet, she tried to struggle, to fight, but her entire body seemed so heavy.

An agonising cry filled the air, at first she thought it was her own, but then things became clear, a small amount of resistance renewed within her body. The screams were that of a man, the one who gripped her tightly to be exact, he howled as though her touch burned… images rose to mind, unfamiliar ones, she couldn't make out, strange pictures that passed so quickly she couldn't distinguish one from another and then she saw one final image, him reaching out his hand to grab her, then, it was over, his hands fell from her as the weight of his body pulled him down. Could this strange force be yet another side effect from her father's incomplete incantation?

"What have you done to him?" Another man stepped forwards only to be stopped by her third attacker, if she could have seen through the dancing swarms of darkness; she would have seen the two figures looking to her in paralysed horror, one standing with his arm outstretched before the other preventing his advance.

"Didn't you see what she just did?" He whispered panic seemed to flood the air around them, "she killed him! She didn't even touch him!" She heard their running footsteps vanishing quickly into the distance, but the dancing blackness that covered her eyes made seeing almost as impossible as standing, there was a slight whimper that sounded around her head for some time as her legs gave beneath her. The dark patches within her vision swam and grew until she felt the soft arms of the earth supporting her weight… she would rest… just a little.

**

A year or so had passed since Elly planned and fulfilled Marise's escape. Each day that his troops would return empty handed, no sightings, no violence, Elly's heart would heave a sigh of relief, it seemed she had done an admiral job of hiding her. Although she longed with all her soul to be with her, until the time came it would be too dangerous, for now, she knew she would have to wait and even then, when they did meet, she could only hope Marise would see sense, hope she would understand why she had to do what she did. The time was growing closer, she felt it even as she sat an idea was blooming in the lord's mind, a guard already making his way to Elly's quarters, an idea that had been put there by her true employer, her waiting was almost over.

"The lord has requested your presence immediately." Ordered the guard as he flung open Elly's door without so much as a knock, he backed away from her angry stare. "Please, forgive the intrusion." He added seeing the annoyance on her face.

"Very well inform him I am on my way." A slight smile crossed her lips as she smartened her appearance, she knew it was time.

"You requested me my lord?" She gave a half-hearted bow as she approached, more than anything it was an action to satisfy his ego, for now it was vital she kept him believing she was one of his loyal employees.

"Elaineor." He acknowledged her presence and sat in silence for what seemed like an eternity, she stood in silence, a nervous anticipation of what was to follow washing over her as the silence was once more broken. "I miss her you know, my battle angel, I've tried almost everything to find her, but each effort has returned in vain." The silence descended once more. "I was thinking that surely someone must know where she is, and then it dawned on me, you."

"Me my lord?" She felt her heart pounding against the walls of her chest so hard she swore he would hear, could it be he knew the truth? Of course, on the inside she was concerned, but looking at her, there were no signs of such feelings.

"Yes, after all you were very close; she spoke to you in ways none of us ever knew. I believe given the chance you could find her after all..." He paused once more "You were best friends were you not? I worry Elaineor, what could have happened? Could it be she met a foe stronger than herself? Was she injured and could not return? That I doubt, I think it's something else, you noticed the changes in her to before she left, I think whatever is happening is preventing her returning home, to me"

"So what do you have in mind my lord, you know I, as much as anyone, long to see her again." Elly sighed, it was true, only Marise could truly appreciate her skills, she was the only person ever worthy of travelling besides her.

"Indeed, that is why I want you to find her."

"Me? My lord? Why?" A performance of surprise that would have had many travelling theatres asking for her skills rang in her voice.

"Well you had a special connection; I am unsure why I failed to think of it before."

"Very well my lord I shall leave immediately." Her hand almost rested upon the door when his voice stopped her once again.

"Bring *her* back with you Elaineor." His voice oozed with threat, although low and almost silent, his words screamed into her soul. With his warning she departed. "Eiji, I take it you understand your task?" From behind the curtains emerged a young man of about twenty-six, his blond hair ruffled as though his hand had passed through it many times, he looked to the figure, did he really have to go through with this? For his master's sake he knew the answer, if he wished to see him alive again, he had no choice but to do what this figure requested.

"My lord." Unlike Elly, he did not bow, his very morals disallowed it.

"You will report back as soon as she finds the girl."

"And my master?"

"It is early days to deal, you see to your side first. Now be gone."

***

"Zo." The pure panic in Daniel's voice startled her. "Zo, Zo." Finally he saw her; she was already rushing towards the sounds of his cries, her trowel still clutched within her muddy hands. "…Dad…found…need…" He gasped, swallowing gulps of air between barely audible words; she stood before him now, his face flushed as he fought for breath.

"Take a breath, slow down." She placed her hand on his back as he leaned forwards his hand resting upon his knees as he breathed deeply.

"Dad's found a girl… she's really hurt…" Halfway through his words Zo vanished into the hut emerging with her battered cloth satchel slung over her shoulder he had just about recovered when she reappeared before him. "Mum's done what she can but…"

"Show me." Daniel grabbed her hand to stop her falling behind, as he took off in a run, although by now he should have known better. Whoever this girl was before her arrival here, she sure could run, maybe some kind of athlete, then again it seemed more likely she was a trained alchemist.

Recently he had found himself thinking back to how they first met, how his life would have turned out had she not appeared on that day…

…Arriving home at Crowley port Daniel had found himself distracted, although he had said he would be straight home with the herbs for his mother ready for her to sort, he found himself wandering through the forest, it was something his mother had grown to expect, although she was training him in medicine in his spare time, she understood the importance of him having time alone, she was grateful for the days he came home late, it meant he was doing something else other than burying his head and emotions in study.

It had been a few weeks now since he had ventured here, it was his place of inspiration. Every day at the end of term he would find himself here mulling over the work that had been set, even now, as he entered Crowley forest, his head was buried deep in a book. It was a short walk from the forest to his home, a town sharing the name as the island on account of it being the only town on the island, yet despite this close proximity, it felt as if there was no one for miles, no one seemed to venture here anymore.

He buried his head deeper into the book, knowing each turn of the forest without the need to look, leaving his mind free to study the examples of ancient writings that had been found in the last decade in some underground ruins, it was said the art of this language had been long forgotten when the Hectarian power faded, so too did the ability of magical readings from the text of the ancients.

Daniel was forced to a stop as his path unexpectedly collided with something, his books falling from his hands from the impact as he looked to see what had brought him to such an abrupt stop.

"I'm sorry." Daniel apologised finding he was no longer alone within these woods, he looked down at the girl now sitting on the floor following their collision, his eyes growing wide with fear as he stepped back, his mind taking him back to that event of years ago, a memory causing him to freeze unable to move or utter another word. He could do nothing but stare reliving the fear he felt then. He simply stood there, staring at a girl no older than himself until his panic slowly began to subside, seeing more of reality than the illusion created by his fear as the girl herself sat staring back, her eyes wide with dear like shock at having been discovered. Daniel's mind was still reasoning with him, trying to encourage him to say something else, trying to make him break his fear locked gaze on the figure, surely this couldn't be who he thought it was, the resemblance was there true enough, but her hair was redder and weren't her eyes a different colour? The sensible side of him reasoned and surely she was much taller than the brown haired girl that sat before him, she moved slowly picking his books from the floor stopping a moment to study one as she stood.

"You're reading about Metiseous legends?" She questioned softly her eyes skimming down the page before passing him the books; he glanced down to the ancient writing and back to her.

"You can read this?" He questioned doubtfully.

"Can't you?" She questioned almost timidly as she took a slight step back. "With it being in your book… I thought…" Daniel having now completely forgotten his fears, took his bearings, glancing around for the first time to find himself in the small clearing he always visited, looking around now, it was clear she had been staying here for some time, there was a makeshift camp and a scorched stone circle where she built her fire.

"You aren't from around here are you?" He questioned when what he really wanted to ask was, 'who are you? What are you doing here? And how can you claim to read a long forgotten text?'

"I don't think so." She answered slowly as if thinking carefully about her answer, all the time she watched him cautiously. "I just kind of, woke up here"

"No… this is a small island… everyone knows everyone if you know what I mean." He smiled gently before he looked down to the ancient text once more. "What do you mean woke up here?" He asked approaching her slowly

"Well… I don't remember much before, I think I remember leaving for school… but everything's a blank, and I think, that was over ten years ago." She answered.

"Ten years ago?" He questioned in disbelief. "I think you should come to meet my mum, she's a doctor." He added after the curious stares. "She has a lot of contacts, I'm sure she'll find your home, you must have a family somewhere." She smiled at him lifting the book from his hands.

"So are you studying Metiseous legends… or magic?" She questioned quickly changing the subject giving herself time to think over his proposition.

"Mythology and supernatural studies, amongst other things." He answered.

Above the forest the sky began to darken, Daniel suddenly realised how late it was getting, his mother was bound to worry if he was not back soon, yet at the same time, he felt compelled to stay, to find out more about this stranger, that in itself was uncharacteristic, he wasn't a very sociable person unless needs dictated him to be. "So you can really read this?" He questioned again moving to sit besides her as she perched herself on a fallen tree, one that Daniel had used himself for many years.

"This? Sure." She smiled. "It tells the story of Metis, of how she and Zeus bore a child, the profits said if ever she were to bare another it would be a boy and would overthrow Zeus like he had his father before, this troubled Zeus so before the prophecy could be realised he ate Metis still pregnant with his first child, it goes on to say later his head was cracked open so the child he devoured in Metis was born, there's a lot of hearsay, but that's about the idea of it" she passed the book back to him "what did you say your name was?" She stood gathering some wood from a nearby pile ready to build a fire as the air began to chill, Daniel stood helping her

"Sorry." It was only now he realised he had failed to introduce himself. "I'm Daniel, Daniel Starfire, and you are?" He questioned apologetically.

"Zodiac Althea…Zo." She corrected, despite everything her name was one thing she remembered clearly, Daniel helped to stack the wood and offered her a light she looked at him questioningly before accepting, as he leaned towards the firewood he stopped suddenly.

"Is that… camomile?" He questioned approaching a small area of greenery.

"Yes, I grew it myself." She smiled looking towards the small herb plantation, when she had awoke she had found herself with many herbs and seeds, most of which she planted.

"It's nearly impossible to grow in these soils." He stated, a new thought dawning in his mind as he moved the light from the fire leaving it unlit. "My mum has this cabin a little outside the town, she use to have an incredible herb garden… but it has long seen better days, I'm sure you could stay there, just until we find someone who knows you. In return, perhaps you could tend the garden?" He questioned wandering how it could be she was not only skilled with botany but could read a language that for years now none had been able to decipher.

"Ok." Zo answered cautiously, yet at the same time, there was a strange aspect of familiarity about the boy that stood before her, something about him that almost made her remember something, she stared at him intently, she couldn't place the feeling or the forgotten memory, but this strange familiarity told her she could trust him, besides it may be her only chance to find someone who knew her, to find her home, Daniel sprung to his feet to lead the way…

…They had barely arrived at the door of his home when his mum, Angela, hustled them quickly inside returning Daniel from his thoughts of last year.

"Zodiac thanks the Gods I did all I could but… she's not responding at all I hoped…" Zo nodded in silent understanding, it was clear Angela had been with the girl some time, her long blond hair spilled out from her pony tail, her deep blue eyes alive yet so very tried. Finally she rested, sitting in the chair facing the stained glass window, the coloured light from its finely patterned glass spilled into the room dancing across the wooden floor, she knew the girl would be in safe hands, even if Zodiac was the same age as her son she had skills with herbs and alchemy that defied her age, she could rest easy knowing Zo was with her.

Zo slowly climbed the wooden stairs followed by Daniel. Over the last year this place had become a second home to her, she found it almost second nature navigating through the twisting corridor, past the three major bedrooms, each door now tightly closed, a turn to the right and finally she was there the end room, the door lay open, light spilled out from it.

Inside Daniel's father, Jack, watched the girl sleeping his brow crinkled in a frown. As his vision rested upon the visitors his brown eyes softened a little as he ruffled a hand through his pepper hair. He exited after greeting them closing the door behind them, there was something different about that girl, he feared to stay in case he found out what it was. After all he had already misjudged her once, mistaking her for someone she was so different to, but he had a family to protect and the likeness between her and that killer was so unmistakable. But he soon learnt the likeness to be only skin deep, never had he met a more loving, nurturing child and besides Daniel thought the world of her. He and always feared his son would end up alone, before meeting her, he was withdrawn, alone, burying himself in his studies his social life was none existent, but this girl stirred something in him, changed him, brought him to life so to speak, he feared knowing what was so different about his son's closest friend would change his view on her forever. She was just too good, after all, she turned a dying garden into a flourishing abundance of life in little more than a fortnight and as for her gifts with herbs, well what more can he say apart from that his wife, Angela, had thought of taking her on as a her apprentice. But it seems she had more to learn from her when it came to botany, whenever a case was past her skills, Zo always knew just what to do, she certainly was an amazing girl, he was surprised that such a person could remain missing so long without someone looking for her, she was clearly well educated, surely someone, somewhere was looking for her.

He looked at Angela sleeping in her favourite chair, it wasn't surprising, she arrived home early hours of the morning after being called out for the birth of Mrs Hamisley's first child, a painful labour that lasted into early hours of the morning but finally resulted in the birth of a healthy baby boy. He covered his wife with the blanket usually draped over the back of the chair back taking a moment to watch her sleeping.

***

Zo knelt besides the girl, resting her hand delicately on her forehead, moments later Daniel grabbed the mortar and pestle as she rummaged through her satchel removing three small bags of herbs indicating how much to apply and the order to be mixed. Daniel sat with his back to the bed, giving the girl respectful privacy while Zo examined her. Some of her wounds were deep, but the blood she lost was not sufficient to cause the lapse of consciousness she suffered, she looked harder, not with her eyes but deep within her mind, her hand resting lightly now on the girl's chest.

"I can't see it." She whispered Daniel stopped, resisting the urge to turn to look at her

"What do you mean?" Concern was etched in his voice, she always saw *it*, that's what made her so good, she always pinpointed the exact problem within moments of applying her special methods.

"Her wounds are not sufficient to cause this deep a receding in her conscience." Zo gave a sigh as Daniel handed her the pureed powder, she added water from the jug by the bed making it into a thick paste before applying it to the wounds and bandaging them gently "maybe she can tell me something…" Zo muttered

"Huh?"

"Never mind." Zo smiled, in theory her mind knew the routine, she was familiar with it, but it had been so long, at least eleven years before she recalled even attempting it, then again the eleven year gap in her life did not mean her talents went unused, she remembered briefly her arrival here, at that point there was nothing but darkness stretching behind her. Yet over the last year she had began to remember, still nothing past the age of twelve, but now she knew her mother's face, the face of her trainer and friend, Amelia, she knew against all odds she used Hectarian magic and back then when she was young she was taught how to, yet she never recalled the place of her home. From that point she remembered nothing, but would think herself a fool if she hadn't used he talents within that time.

Steadying her breath she ran her fingers across the girl's forehead, Daniel listened intently committing the words she spoke to memory, he always did whenever she used her skills, the words themselves spoken in an ancient tongue, well some of the time, usually when the skill she used required the most concentration, the easier spells she spoke in plain language summoning forth her powers, he sometimes wondered in these cases if words were at all necessary, even though he found this fascinating, he knew better than to disturb her, chances were it would have serious repercussions.

A stabbing pain shot up Zo's arm causing a slight cry to leave her lips as she gritted her teeth against the resistance, he was at her side in a flash hovering unsure what to do even should she be in danger. Then she was somewhere else, watching, a girl's life-force identical to the body laying before her the forest surrounded her as the girl looked upon herself, she felt Daniel's hand touch her lightly, feeling his concern she spoke.

"I don't understand... is she... dead?" Zo opened her eyes looking to him, he seemed to relax slightly pulling away his hand, for a moment there she had looked like she was ready to collapse, he had been unable to do anything but watch as her pallor grew paler.

"I read once about an immortal who had the ability to take the body of another soul displacing the soul of the occupant and sending them to Hades, it's rumoured, he continued to do so until he had enough power to regain his own form, of course it's only speculation, nothing like this I'm sure." He stated, Zo gasped as suddenly the resistance stopped, her knees gave beneath her as the girl's eyes opened as she sprung quickly to a sitting position, Daniel stood besides her ensuring she was alright, he'd never seen her look so tired, her hand still clasped the girl's tightly as she struggled to stand up as the girl's eyes searched the room fearfully.

"It's alright; you don't need to be afraid." Zo said comfortingly as she met the girl's brown eyes for but a moment until she moved her gaze quickly to her hand which was being grasped so tightly by the stranger who was still speaking to her. "Do you have any family? Any one that needs to know you're here?" The girl shook her head stifling a cry. "Well, I have plenty of room if you'd like to stay a while, I could do with the company." She smiled reassuringly. "I could do with watching those wounds as well; they'll need several more applications before they heal." The girl looked at her bandaged wounds then back to Zo and nodded slowly before speaking.

"What's your name?" She asked shakily, it was one of many questions she had, but this was the first, she knew much about the time she was in, she knew the when and most of the where, so this seemed to be the most important question of all.

"Sorry, I'm Zodiac, Zo." She smiled. "And my friend here is Daniel." Daniel offered his hand, their skin had barely touched when they felt it, she pulled away quickly removing her hand from Zo's embrace.

"I'm sorry I didn't mean it... I didn't ... I thought..." She gave a frustrated sigh moving her hands to cradle her head.

"It's just as I thought Zo, she can occupy any chosen soul, changing with a touch, yet for some reason she has no control over it...." He looked at the girl. "There was only one other person with your skill but that is nothing more than a legend, but your body seems to be protecting you, by touching people you take their life-force ultimately killing them." Daniel's eyes sparkled

"By the Gods I didn't mean to hurt you." She cradled her head in her hands sobbing gently as she did so, Zo frowned at him.

"Daniel, stop scaring her." Zo took her hand again waiting for the sobs to subside before taking Daniel outside it was clear he had something to say, but it was not suitable for him to say such things in front of the already terrified girl.

"Don't you see?" His voice was hushed. "What you said about her being dead… there's a few things I still don't understand but from what I can gather she's like that God I mentioned earlier, but for some reason has no control over her power, so should anyone touch her, and this is the part I don't get, should anyone touch her she drains the life from them ultimately killing them, yet for some reason you seem to be immune, I can only assume one of two things, you're not a suitable host or more likely something you did effected her power on a deeper level allowing you to be unaffected… what exactly did you do?"

"I gave her what she needed to wake." Daniel watched Zo aware of her using the wall to support her weight, it was almost as if she was barely remaining upright although supported by the wall her body seemed to sway slightly, Daniel thought it best to ask no more questions.

"Shall I ready the carriage for your departure?" Jack walked slowly to the bottom of the stairs. "I assume you wish to monitor her for a while." Daniel looked at his father searchingly, it was clear from his posture, his calm tones; he had not heard their conversation.

"If you would be so kind." She smiled gently at Jack, he had always seemed a little cautious around her, yet never could she figure out why. He always had some pressing issues to be addressed whenever she was near, she tried to tell herself she was paranoid, only it truly seemed that way, even should she stay for dinner conversation at best was strained.

"You look tired; I'll have Daniel take you back." He smiled before disappearing from view; she shot a concerned look to Daniel.

"He properly just heard our voices." Daniel reassured her knowing his father's reaction would be much different, had he the slightest inkling of what had just transpired.

***

Daniel helped Zo as she placed the last of the fire wood in the furnace under the bathroom outside of the house, this bath system was ground breaking, as it was the first to use wood to heat the water from under the bath itself, it had been developed only ten years ago yet now, each home seemed to have one.

"Create a fire to sooth her pain, to start with this a ball of flame." She whispered, even as she spoke the words she questioned their true meaning ultimately no matter what she said, it would bring about her desire, she often questioned if they were truly needed. Daniel, as always, watched with awe as small as a spark hovered slightly above her hand, within seconds it seemed to expand to cover her palm almost as if it swelled and ignited within itself, finally the spherical ball was complete with the appearance of a miniature sun it hovered gently as it awaited her command, gently blowing on it she directed it towards the waiting firewood.

An hour or so had passed and Daniel had long since taken the horse and cart back to the village, finally Zo helped Acha into the steaming bath, a bath almost overflowing with bubbles and delicate scents, after showing Acha where the commodities were and placing her some clothes on the small hook behind the door she left. Although Acha stood at least two inches taller than her, she was sure the clothes would fit at least until her own clothes were clean, a task she got to straight away with her wooden bucket and scrubber in the back garden.

Acha emerged her short wet hair hanging just past her jaw line, it seemed somehow longer than before and now took on a rich oak colour opposed to the red muddy colour she was found with. Zo's shirt normally worn for odd jobs around the house looked almost as if it were made for her, it gripped all the right places, her trousers didn't look a miss either, again despite the height difference they finished just below her ankle, she was very lucky in the sense she had never gotten around to turning them up, Acha greeted her with a weary smile as she crossed the garden to her.

"Feeling better?" Zo asked pinning the last peg on her dripping leather trousers.

"Thanks." She nodded as she spoke before returning inside with Zo.

***

A week or so passed, Acha found herself at home with Zo and Daniel as their friendship bloomed. Meanwhile, Elly and her stalker were hot on her trail. Whoever was following her was an amateur, he made far too much noise, despite his flaws in tracking she had played along letting him believe that she was clueless. She sat by what would be her final camp until arriving at the town she believed Marise resided in. She felt no need to rest but her uninvited companion may, she smiled to herself as she rotated a small cooking bird above the fire, she could almost feel his hunger as his nostrils flared at the smell of the inviting food. Finally it was time.

"You must be hungry after your travels; your food ran out a few days ago. Come join me why don't you? There is more than enough." She smiled as she spoke awaiting his response, yet none came, she had waited this long, wearing him down, leading him in circles, hoping he would tire or lose interest, but the fact he remained close meant there was more to this than a simple game. Tonight being the last chance to find his motives, she hoped he would show himself, either that or she would have to kill him. She could not risk leading him to Mari without knowing his true intentions. The call of a night owl was her only reply "I know you've been following me, I aren't stupid, you didn't think you're travels would last this long or you'd have brought more supplies. You may as well come out and eat, there's no point pretending" a quiet rustle came from the nearby bushes.

"I… didn't think you knew…" His blond spiky hair, now not so neat as the journey's start filled with the leaves and debris of the forest, he sat on a log conveniently placed opposite Elly's sitting spot separating them by the fire she passed him some of the bird and watched smiling as he ate hungrily.

"You thought what I wanted you to." Her smile widened as their eyes met across the fire, he was on his second helping when he stopped suddenly in mid chew.

"Aren't you eating?" A sinking feeling spread from his stomach encapsulating his whole body as he realised she'd not so much as touched the food she had prepared.

"No… I'd be foolish to catch myself with my own poison now wouldn't I?"

"What?" Was all he managed to get out before he was interrupted

"Quite a nasty one it is too, you see I need to know why you're following me. I didn't think you'd volunteer the information so I thought it best to skip the pleasantries, you have two choices, we can wait about ten minutes while it seeps into your blood killing you painfully and slowly, by which point you'll talk anyway." She lingered on her words her voice strangely soothing despite the manner in which it spoke. "Or you can tell me now and I may have an antidote." Her lips spread into a triumphant grin as she looked across the fire at him, he was so young, unwise in the ways of the world, his eyes shone with terror, and power, yes there was power there, the kind she'd seen in one of his kind before, yet never one so young with such potential.

"I didn't want to." His voice breaking as he spoke interrupting the silence it had not taken as long as anticipated to break him. "He made me he said he'd kill my master."

"Who? Who made you?"

"You're Lord, Lord Blackwood."

"Your master? You're an Elementalist are you not?" He nodded as she spoke fear swelling within him, wondering how she knew so much about him. "I assume you're master set you free to learn from the elements." Again another nod. "Did he never tell you what becomes of a master once he has taught the student all he can?" Another nod answered her question. "And he released you from your training?"

"…Yes…" His voice now ringing with uncertainty. "But it's not what you're thinking I still had so much to learn.…"

"If he released you he obviously felt not, you see as you may or may not know Elementalists pass their power to the next generation, as he trained you and you master a skill, you actually took it from him, there can only ever be one master of any elemental skill at any one time, that's how these powers work, once you have learnt all his skills, his body returns to the elements that gave him life." Elly watched the painful realisation spread across his face; he knew his master was already dead.

"He… he was using me." He snapped all at once reminding Elly again of how young he was, panic registered in his face once more as he suddenly remembered. "The antidote." Elly smiled at him brightly.

"What antidote?"

"But you said…" He stopped realising that for at least the last few minutes of their conversation Elly had been helping herself to part of the poisoned bird, she smiled to herself as he realised this, she was wondering how long it would take.

"I lied… oh come on you've been following me for over a week, where could I have obtained it?" All at once he felt rather stupid, he had been following her and since day one she carried nothing but a sword which she never unsheathed and the knife she used to hunt her food.

"I notice you carry a sword." He said diverting the attention from his stupidity. "It doesn't suit you."

"It isn't mine; I'm just returning it to a friend." She turned the sheathed sword over in her hand effortlessly as she examined it. "So tell me, who did he tell you we were looking for?"

"He didn't, he said I would know when you found her" he volunteered the information despite feeling cheated by her previous ambush.

"I see, well I may as well tell you, since you're part of this as well now"

"What do you mean?" Elly shook her head slightly; he really had no idea of consequences.

"Well if you return to Lord Blackwood he will surely slay you for failing, you have no reason to follow his orders after his deception, either way you know too much and you are worth more to him dead now, than alive." She heard him gasp as though this thought hadn't occurred to him before hearing it from her. "Of course I will offer you protection if you help me."

"Help you with what?"

"Well you see this sword belongs to Mari, you may have heard of her, famous killer left his rule just over a year ago."

"Mari... Mari." He mulled the name over when his eyes widen she knew he had arrived at the correct conclusion. "You don't mean Marise Shi?"

"The one and only." She smiled bright tones shimmering in her voice. "Now before you get all preachy about how she's the ultimate evil hear me out." He gave a sigh, it was as if she had read his mind, but he knew he had little choice.

"I have little choice, if I go back I get killed, if I try to escape, I get killed, and I assume you'll kill me anyway if you don't like my answer." His voice full of the 'how do I get myself into these situations?' tone. "Anyway I heard she was destroyed." The thought of meeting the legendary larger than life killer pricked his interest yet screamed danger "why would you want to return her to him? She's lethal."

"You don't know the half." Elly smiled proudly which obviously came across as somewhat alarming as she met Eiji's questioning gaze. "Hear me out first, when she left, she was different no longer a killer."

"Now that I don't believe a leopard can't change its spots, you expect me to believe she woke up one day and thought hey I've had enough of killing now I'll go do something else?"

"Pretty much, anyway Lord Blackwood wants to reclaim her well with the release of Night, he wants someone who can protect him... Night also has a claim on her for various reasons. So I want to protect her."

"By taking her back?" His voice was outraged.

"No by stopping him from taking her back... before you leap to conclusions though... just meet her first and if you don't think she's worth protecting you can leave."

"And be killed anyway? Some choice." He rested his head on his hands as he leaned closer to the fire, where had it all gone wrong? He was meant to leave, learn more about the elements and return home, yet his master was dead and now whatever he did would ultimately wind up in his joining him.

"I think you'll be surprised, and like I say I will offer you my protection as long as you choose to travel besides me."

"Very well." He sighed. "Let's see what our legendary murderer has become, and then I shall choose my side." 'Death…or death.' He thought sceptically to himself, what choice exactly was there to make?

'If you live to make the choice.' Elly thought, considering his betrayal an option, but should he choose the place his loyalty lie poorly…

***

"Say Zo, what you reading?" Daniel appeared at the door, smiling at seeing his friend engrossed in a book a frown gripping her gentle features; she jumped a little turning to look at him.

"Just something the elder Robert gave me some time back, been promising I'd get reading it… but."

"But?"

"Well, he said I should protect it, that they would never think an outsider would have it but…" Daniel roused with curiosity approached her reading over her shoulder, he frowned with the distinct feeling he was missing something.

"It's blank?" He questioned looking from Zo to the book and back again.

"Not quite, I can make out the odd trace mark, maybe a notepad or something."

"Oh you know Robert, there's always history behind everything, even the fire wood he cut yesterday originally belonged to some ancient tree that offered him a piece for fighting off the wood eating snuggles of Tamson four." They both laughed, it was true, everything his hand touched had a mystical story behind it, it was one of the things Zo found so charming about this place. She grinned, she loved nothing more than spending an evening once a week listening to his tales.

"Still you never know, one day he may be telling the truth." She closed the book, wrapping it in ivory cloth before placing it inside her satchel.

"You really should stop putting things down that tear in the lining, you'll loose something." Daniel smiled. "Isn't it time you were off?"

"You're right, I'll be back soon, I need to pick up my supplies from Mr Rodgers." Mr Rodgers was the local green grocer who very kindly, after making his wife an excellent potion for her migraines, packed her order up every week for collection. He was an elderly gentleman Zo was very fond of; she always looked forwards to seeing him on Friday afternoons, catching up with the events of the village. Zo waved back to Daniel and Acha as she flung her bag over her shoulder before she called back. "Look after Acha for me."

"Sure." Daniel called out to no one in particular since she had long vanished from view.

***

As they waited for Zo's return, Acha continued to tell Daniel about her life before the talisman, of course leaving out the parts about her father and his betrayal. He noticed she now wore this around her neck secured on a woven piece of leather, made by three strips identical to those Zo used to tie her hair back, they were about a meter of so in length, being intertwined forming a strong loop to fit over her head like a chain, and wrapped artistically around until they spilt to hold the talisman securely, the twists the continued a little further until it was fastened off leaving a few tassels to dangle, no doubt made by Zo. Acha went on to explain it was the talisman itself that secured her life-force within a given host, if something were to happen and she would lose it, she would be sealed within once more until another living creature touched it, only then if she retrieved the it in time could she keep its body permanently. A dark shadow eclipsed the door Daniel turned to face it already speaking.

"That was…" But his eyes failed to rest upon Zo as he expected instead a colossal figure loomed blocking all but a fraction of the light from the door. From head to toe this giant was covered in body armour only his scowling face was absent from any form of protection, his matted beard fell to his chest plate as his eyes narrowed he raised his thick arm to point at Acha.

"I've come for her." His voice boomed, for a moment it seemed as if the very walls shook with his voice. Acha's eyes widened in sheer terror backing away as Daniel moved to form a barrier between her and her pursuer. His hands wrapped around one of the thick wooden sticks Zo had brought ready to fence the garden, holding it now it was more like a staff, which was not much of a comfort to Daniel, who, despite a vast amount of knowledge regarding the theory behind fighting and techniques, had never put any to practise, and to do so against such a gigantic creature frightened him all the more.

"Acha run!" He yelled. But before she could even move the giant's arm grabbed him by his neck flinging him through the open door, Acha winced at the sickening thud his body making contact with the floor made; he lay motionless, still gripping the pole in his hands. Acha looked for an escape but her exit had been blocked.

***

"Excuse me." Elly stepped out from nowhere in front of a person who was running towards the town. "I see you're in a hurry but I wondered…" She stopped as the girl turned to face her, shock registering on her face as she met the girl's electric blue eyes. The change was incredible, she looked so different, not just her hair which seemed to have lost its vibrant red colours for to take a lighter brown with lowlights of a colour once so vibrant it was like a fiery sunset, but her eyes too, they were calmer friendlier… and blue, she reminded Elly so much of that girl first brought to Blackwood's care. Elly found herself staring unable to continue her sentence; she had expected something, but this? Zo simply smiled at her politely waiting for her to continue.

"Are you alright?" She asked as the colour seemed to drain from Elly's face. "You look like you've seen a ghost." Elly seemed to say something yet neither Zo nor Eiji, could determine what had been spoken, they looked to her curiously trying to make out the words she spoke, waiting for her to speak again.

"We're looking for town, you'll have to forgive my friend, she's not been feeling too well." Eiji stepped in to avoid another long silence frowning at Elly as he did so, what had gotten into her? She didn't seem like the kind of person who just froze like that.

"Anything serious? I know a good doctor…"

"She'll be fine."

"Oh… good, well I'm heading town now if you want to…" A shooting pain through Zo's stomach made her double over as she gasped for breath before Eiji could ask if she was alright she whispered a name. "Acha." As she caught her breath she remembered a temporary side effect from the spell she used to waken her, for a short time, she would know when anything disturbed her greatly, from the feeling alone she knew she was in danger, which meant Daniel was too. "Excuse me." She called back sprinting in the direction she had come from, within seconds she had vanished from sight.

"What was that all about? Do you think we should follow her? Something seemed wrong." He questioned as Elly's vision fixed to where Zo had stood just moments ago until finally she spoke.

"Mari..." She uttered again this time a little louder than before, she couldn't believe it, she had stood face to face with her and still had been unable to utter a word, she couldn't explain why, but seeing her, she just froze, it was so uncharacteristic.

"You mean that... she was Marise Shi?" Surprise rang through his voice. "I expected her to be..." He paused thinking over his words carefully. "Taller, to say the least." He watched after the slender figure that was already disappearing into the forest.

"Not anymore, I made her forget... I can't believe how much she's..."

"Shouldn't we go after her? Something definitely wasn't right there." Elly nodded her expression still awed from this discovery, next time they met, she would tell her everything and take her away from this island, to take her to the place she belongs.

***

Driven by Acha's fear she made it home in record time, her vision fell on Daniel's motionless body lying in the grass a fair distance from the house, the world seemed to descend into an uneasy silence as she approached him.

"Daniel..." She whispered crouching over him checking his vital signs before glancing to her home as death like silence was replaced with the sound of terrified screams.

She charged into the house without a second thought grabbing a bottle from the side almost as second nature. She found Acha backed in a corner with no hope of escape; an enormous armoured giant approached her flinging the table, that she had used as a barrier between them effortlessly to the side. The creature turned as a shower of glass rained from his amour, its reaction seemed slow as it turned to study the new figure that appeared.

"You get away from her!" She yelled as anger began to burn deep within her as she added. "Now."

"What are you going to do little girl?" His voice boomed as Acha silently crawled along the floor as Zo tried to keep his attention from her escape. "She couldn't stop me what hope has a child like you got?" She gave a silent sigh of relief watching as Acha disappeared through the bathroom window. The giant lunged forwards, in what seemed like only a few steps he had covered the length of her room grabbing her quickly before she had a chance to even think about moving, he lifted her in the air, his giant hand clasped around her he gave a snort before launching her through the window, glass sprayed in all directions falling like tiny daggers impaling everything they rained on, she moved slightly to find herself only a matter of feet from where Daniel lay, pain exploded throughout her body, for a moment something else seemed to take over, scolding her for lying in pain, scolding her for being so weak, as she lay there in pain, an anger that would not allow her to surrender, she began to move despite the protests of her entire body, the pain somehow fuelling the raw energy she felt rising within her.

She reached Daniel touching his hand gently for but a second as she released his fingers from the garden post he still gripped; he stirred a little as she took it from his grasp. Using it for support she struggled to her feet, whispering in ancient tongue as she did so, the wind picked up slightly around her as a fiery tornado left her extended hand. The impact with the creature, although accurate, did little other than attract his attention from Acha's hiding place now under the supports of the house. The anger faded as the creature once more turned to face her, its eyes although barely visible through its helmet robbed her of her courage, she glanced around, wondering how best to lead it from her friends, it was large, it could cover space quicker than she could, especially since her body ached all over from the impact, but there had to be something, if she simply ran she would be leading it away from here, yet towards the town, if she made it that far, further people would be in danger, to reach any other place, she had to pass him, that left her with one choice, facing him, but what did she know about fighting? She didn't even have a weapon. Something told her, the second this post struck the creature would split it into a thousand tiny splinters.

As if answering her thoughts, something hit the ground before them, almost as if it was a gift from the Gods themselves, a sheathed sword lay close to her feet, she lifted it from the floor wrapping its belt around her with such speed it was almost as though she'd done it a thousand times before. She released the catch with her thumb, the sword was light, it wasn't until she looked down she realised why, having drawn the sword an inch from its hilt she saw the reason, the sword itself lacked a blade, she fastened the clip once again hoping it could be used as a deterrent, the sheath itself seemed to be made of some kind of metal, a metal she could not quite place from its structure, although apparently useless, maybe in its sheath it could prove useful as a weapon. She glanced around looking to whom she owed the thanks, yet no one seemed to be around, then again, she didn't have time to truly look.

Frustration, anger and fear rose within her as time after time she attacked the creature with the metal sheath and time after time he effortless countered her. She could not lose, there was too much at stake, Acha depended on her, she could not lose this fight, but what did she know about fighting? Her magic was ineffectual, his impenetrable armour somehow protecting him from all her magical attacks. Zo gasped as she felt her back collide with something solid the being now advanced towards her, little by little he had been driving her back until there was nowhere left for her to run, his giant hand propelling her head into the tree filling the air with a sickening splintering crack before the darkness took her as she felt herself sliding to the floor.

Acha's screams echoed through the darkness, yet she couldn't respond, she could hear Acha's futile attempts to dig her feet into the ground as she kicked and screamed against its grip as the creature began to carry her away, his voice boomed through the silent darkness.

"So you are the great power he wants? You are little more than a weak child not at all the challenge he made you out to be." The giant's voice shook the ground shaking the darkness from her vision.

"Remove... your... hands." A shower of armour exploded from his back, a strange glow radiated from the sword, held drawn the blade seemed to be formed of light itself, half shone with a light so white it seemed almost blue, where as the other half, a complete contrast shone black radiating a faint blood red aura. He turned throwing Acha to one side as he did so to facing his adversary, she scrambled to her feet running to Daniel as Zo stood to face the creature, the look in her eyes right then had scared Acha more than words could possibly have explained, she knew better than to intervene, that look, was the look of anger and hatred, she could only hope Zo knew what she was doing.

"I thought I'd dealt with you, this is becoming tiresome, I shall have to kill you." As his vision fell upon her, his eyes met with a strange recognition he was seeing the soul now which faced him, the soul of a warrior. "Why did I not see it before?" His heavy cestus struck out in a fearsome attack, but he was countered her sword slicing through his armour until his flesh erupted with bright red fluid, Zo stood awe struck holding the sword in her hand, now aware of standing before the being sword in hand, unsure how she arrived at this point, somehow it was like she had been summoned from the darkness, one second she was losing consciousness, the next she stood ready for battle a bladeless sword in her hand which by some form of magic had grown a blade of light and dark, everything happened so naturally from then it was almost as if it was fighting the battle for her, of course she knew this to be impossible, although the sword was clearly magic it did not possess the workings necessary for such a task, somehow... she knew. It was almost as if a forgotten part of her took over as she dodged the attacks and dealt her own it all felt so natural, until finally he fell, the blade of the sword vanished into a fine mist just as she placed it within its sheath.

"From this battle teach him shame; take him back from whence he came." She spoke now leaning upon the sheath to support her legs which threatened to give beneath her, her head still throbbing and clouding her vision from the earlier blow, everything she knew, told her she should not be conscious. His voice let out a howl just seconds before he vanished. As he vanished her knees gave and she was left kneeling on the floor where the monster lay only seconds before, noises and voices swam around her head as her senses began to dull, she was vaguely aware of a commotion happening around her.

"By the Gods Zo where did you learn to fight?" It was Daniel, his voice echoing around her head as he rushed to near her side, yet something stopped him reaching her, a figure's shadow in the woods had stopped him in his tracks, could it be that being was not alone? Zo felt the change in the air and looked to Daniel through the dark haze; his vision was fixed towards the woods, feeling his tension Zo spoke.

"Where's...Acha?" Her voice seemed almost alien as she spoke, she was aware of someone approaching now, she could hear their footsteps, her grip tightened on the sheathed sword.

"It's ok she's right here." A foggy blue haze passed in front of her, even through the haze she recognised her from the forest, it would be hard for anyone not to remember her, her vivid blue hair separated her from the crowd.

"Oh Elly… your sword." Zo looked from the sword that now lay besides her to the figure.

"That's ok it's yours." Elly smiled, crouching down to be level with the figure, her voice seemed so gentle.

"But it looks so…"

"No Mari, you misunderstand, it's yours." She whispered leaning towards her to ensure the words were only shared between the two of them.

"I think… you've mistaken… me for someone else… my… name's Zodiac…"

"Then how come you know my name when I never told you?" Zo opened her mouth as if to answer but was cut short by the overwhelming dizziness that encompassed her she felt someone's arms break her fall just as she fell into the darkness.

***

Voices swirled around the darkness of Zo's sleep, chanting, whispering from every direction

'Yesss.' Whispered one.

'She's the one.' Another voice echoed she turned through the darkness as if to face the voice, it was then she noticed the eyes, the darkness was littered with them, all watching, never blinking as they stared at her, their black pupils glaring at her following her every move

'Fun with this one.' Another voice from her side, then another behind her, each time she turned to face the voice, finding herself doing little more than turning in circles as they spoke in turn.

'She shall play.'

"Who are you?" The whispering stopped almost as if they didn't expect her to hear them. "What do you want?"

'Do you want to know the truth?' The shadow eyes spoke

'We could show you.' Another voice whispered tauntingly behind her.

"What truth?" Frustration rang in her voice, annoyance at her invisible visitors "What can you show me?"

'Yourself.' A voice from the left startled her.

'Will you play?'

'You do want to know, don't you?'

'We can feel it.'

'That's why we came.'

'Will you play?'

'Don't you want to know?' The voices chanted.

"Yes… tell me." Her voice pleaded the swirling voices she turned as if by her actions she would be able to locate one of those that watched from the shadows.

'We cannot.'

'He would not like it.'

'But if you would play.'

'We could show you.'

"How? How can you show me?"

'In a game.'
'An adventure.'
'Truths revealed.'
'Will you play?'
"Is it dangerous?" The voices laughed it wasn't until this point she was really sure it was more than one voice she heard.
'You fight well.'
'Wonder why?'
'Will you play?'
"Alright… I'll play your game…. what must I do?" She ask weakly sickness rising in her stomach as she accepted their challenge.
"Survive."

***

She awoke, the words fading, her breath sharp as the sick feeling rose within her, relief filled her as she realised she had been dreaming, she glanced around her room, with a sigh of relief, she was home.

"So you are the chosen?" She sat bolt upright, her vision swimming with the throbbing in her head. "You are our saviour." His tone etched with amusement as her vision found him, he stood besides her, for a moment she could only stare, but he too seemed surprised as his vision fell upon her, as if she had not been who he had expected to find. He was the most beautiful person she had ever seen, his autumn red hair tied into a long ponytail finishing near the centre of his back, he stood around six foot four, his slender muscular build silhouetted by the light flooding through the window, his white see through top and skin tight leather trouser accentuating his angelic figure, but that was not what prevented her words escaping, she was hypnotised by his gorgeous, vivid brown eyes, a brown unlike any other she had ever seen, he spoke again his voice filled with elemental rhythm. "So you think you can be our saviour?" His voice had lost the underlying tone of sarcasm, hearing him speak once more broke the spell, once more she found herself able to talk.

"Saviour?" Her voice shook slightly, where was everyone? How could a stranger just wander in her room unnoticed?

"You agreed to their game did you not?"

"Game?" A vague memory of a slipping dream fought to the surface of her mind, yet in that same second it had vanished.

"So they are playing with mortals again."

"And you are?"

"You may call me Seiken, they think you shall fail their challenges." He looked through the window. "There is little time left. It's a game, there are rules they must follow, although they will twist them to their needs, they do not know I am here… I have come to warn you." Once more he looked outside as he spoke quickly.

"Warn me?" She looked at him harder, she seemed to know this stranger from somewhere, he seemed so familiar to her, yet she could not place him.

"We shall help all we can." Again he glanced behind himself to look through Zo's window.

"What do mean your saviour?" Everything started to sink in, the words he was speaking now seemed to un-jumble where as before, they seemed to swim around her mind, she didn't dare look to where he was looking in fear that he would vanish back to the place he had appeared from.

"Their game, you've been selected to try to release our kind, with our imprisonment the barrier between our worlds is thinning... you are our last chance, after you there will be no more time..." This time she followed his gaze through the window outside, where she saw nothing out of the ordinary, as she turned to looked back, the door swung open.

"Zo, you're awake... who were you talking to?" Daniel glanced around the room as she did the same, looking to the place the stranger had stood.

"....Nobody." She questioned her own answer. "I had the strangest..."

"You're awake." The blue haired lady from before rushed to her side.

"Do I know you?" She looked at the stranger questioningly as she spoke.

"A lifetime ago." Elly smiled Zo looked around noticing the blond haired person, that had accompanied her before was now standing near the doorway a in the soon becoming crowded room. "I'm Elly and this is Eiji." He nodded politely at his introduction and shuffled further into the room.

"Say... you didn't have anything to do with..." Elly followed Zo's gaze outside to the battleground.

"Him... no, I think Night knows you're here."

"But he was after Acha" Zo protested.

"No." Elly moved closer perching herself on her bed to make room for Acha, who as if on queue, entered the room. "A simple case of mistaken identity, he was after the girl who lived here, Acha lives here, he saw her first, but you were his target." She explained.

"Elly.... Elly... I think I remember..." Zo questioned she had the same feeling of familiarity she had when she first met Daniel, as if she's seen her somewhere before, but unlike with Daniel, Zo managed to grasp something from the darkness "Didn't we use to live in the same house?"

"Something like that... yeah." She gave a strange smile, its meaning not quite readable.

"You said Night?" Zo suddenly realised, there were too many people all talking her head swam yet as she recalled this she suppressed a shudder. "Who are you referring to... and why would he be after us?" Elly stared with disbelief at her before she brought herself to answer.

"You mean you don't know?" Her voice radiated with the shock that registered on her face, as she looked around it seemed she was the only person who didn't know this name. "You know... Night." She stated as if believing her saying the name again would job her memory. "About yay big, evil?... No?" She gave a frustrated sigh motioning his height with her hand thinking perhaps she over did the potion just a little. "Well do you at least remember the Grimoire?" Elly shook her head already knowing the answer, looking around at the blank looks as she realised that only selective people knew of these texts, again Zo shook her head much to Elly's frustration, she gave a sigh, this was meant to have been so easy, the time had come to put phase two of the plan into operation, was it too much to ask for a little cooperation? "Very well, the Grimoire were used to seal away Night, by capturing his spirit and his power within seven books." Elly paused hearing slight guilt within her voice. "Then again all this was probably before you were born, and since no one speaks of it." She sighed. "Anyway, someone managed to obtain the books releasing him and his power. His power since has been growing and he has created a new army. I was sent to find you before he did… but it's too late, it's too dangerous for you to stay here any longer."

"Sent by who?" Daniel's eyes narrowed with suspicion, he gripped Zo's hand tightly watching Elly carefully from the opposite side of the bed giving Zo time to register exactly what was being said, after all she had only just come too from the blow it was bound to take time for things to register, especially this, all this time without so much as a whisper from her past and now facing all this she was finding it all a little overwhelming.

"By her Lord, Lord Blackwood, he wanted me to return her…" Elly stopped obviously changing her sentence before she continued. "Before *he* finds her, he doesn't want to lose her." Zo felt heat rising to her face.

"I don't want to go… I'm staying here." She stated quietly yet firmly, what was all this about her lord? That was ridiculous so what? Was she some kind of servant? A trophy of power? If so, if she was any of these, there would have been people looking for her, there was something not quite right about the entire situation.

"I'm not taking you back." Elly admitted earnestly. "But you can't stay here either. Especially, since now he knows you're whereabouts it's no longer safe."

"But this is my home." She protested. It had taken her mere weeks to feel a part of the community, as if she could truly believe this place was her home.

"So you're asking her to just up and leave the only place she's known as home, to leave behind all the people she loves?" Daniel's voice was more outraged than Zo's.

"She's in danger if she stays, he'll tear the village apart, killing everyone if that's what it takes to find her."

"All that effort for a witch?" Daniel forgot himself in a moment of disbelief

"You're a witch?" Acha's voice trembled, Zo hadn't realised she hadn't figured it out for herself "a good one right?" Her voice had underlying tones of panic Zo opened her mouth to answer but was interrupted abruptly.

"It's not the witch he's after." Eiji stated further explanations cut short by the weight of Elly's stare, it was a warning he didn't need twice.

"I don't want to leave." She repeated the noise of the room swimming through her head.

"Then you are signing this town's death certificate, one condemning all the people you claim to love."

"Why?" She shook her head tears spilling from her eyes as she did so, she was finding all of this a little overwhelming, who wouldn't? Everything seemed to have happened so quickly, her day had started out as normal, her life now being torn to shreds by the strangers who arrived here, Elly had never seen Mari on the verge of tears, it was a sight that made her heart ache. "Why go through all that?"

"Because you're unstoppable… that's why they both want you, you could tip the balance…"

"Zo this town can take anything thrown at it, how do you know you can trust her it could be a trick." Daniel put his arm around her pulling her close to him protectively.

"Don't be a fool next time it will be more than one weak hunter. He'll send an army. Nothing would survive can you really live with that? You have no choice; he has decided it is time."

"I have no choice… you're right." The voice seemed alien to her ears, although she knew it was herself who had spoken those words.

"Zo you can't leave, the people here need you." Daniel's voice was filled with desperation, he didn't want to lose her, she was his best friend.

"No they have your mum, she's a great doctor." Zo forced a smile but Daniel could not manage one in return, didn't she realise he wasn't talking about healers? "But where do we go from here?"

"I know a place you'll be safe."

"You're not taking her back to lord what's-his-name." Daniel snapped

"I have no intention of taking her back to Lord Blackwood… ever."

"I'll pack tonight." Zo's voice sounded distant, almost hollow

"We will leave tonight under nights cloak; *he* may have already watching now he knows for certain you're here."

Chapter two

A backpack and a satchel, this was all Zo needed to carry her life away, she had found it hard to believe that a life could be packed away so tidily, she looked back in the direction of her home for what was easily the tenth time since starting out, fears and concerns playing on her mind, was she really doing the right thing? How could she be so certain packing her life up and moving would keep them safe? Was she about to adopt the life of a traveller? Never staying in one place too long for fear of being discovered, if so, perhaps it would be better for her simply to return to her old life, regardless of who she was now, was she ultimately going to wind up returning to become the stranger she didn't remember? Pain and guilt knotted her stomach, in just under an hour Daniel and Acha would be arriving to her already deserted home to wish her farewell, only to find her gone.

Acha had begrudgingly left with Daniel to get her a parting gift, something to remember them by, they had barely stepped through the door when she hastened to pack, agreeing to meet the familiar stranger Elly, entrusting her life to the faint recognition she felt.

Leaving Daniel was the most difficult thing about the situation, but she desperately needed to avoid the long goodbye that would shatter her already aching heart, he had been her strength, he had taken her from a life of uncertainty and gave her a home and a future, she had lost everything with her memory, but he had given her more than he would ever realise, she would miss him more than everything else combined, Acha came second in her list, in their short time of knowing each other she had been like the sister she never had, she bit her lip forcing back the emotions, she couldn't believe she was never going to see either of them again, never again would she hear the epic tales of elder Robert, or help out around the village, never again would she find herself in Crowley, the place that had become her home.

Slowing her pace she made her way to the clearing where she and Daniel first met, her eyes finding the charred patch of ground in the centre of the clearing where she once built her fire, it was in this very place Daniel gave her his friendship and a home. For weeks, months, he had tried desperately to find someone who may have known her, searching the missing boards, asking of any news relating to missing people, but his search was futile. His parents had been so accommodating they had given consent for her to use their small hut as her home, in return once she had settled, she would assist Daniel's mother with the mixing of compounds. It had been a few weeks since their brief agreement before Daniel's mother, Angela, visited to see how she had settled in, it was then she really became part of the family, seeing the baron wasteland that was once her herb garden flourishing at the hands of the young girl brought a tear to her eye, as time passed they found they had much in common, Zo knew much about botany and alchemy, it was clear she had been well educated, her mannerisms were those found in a well raised family, that made the question of her disappearance all the more confusing. Angela had tried all sorts to retrieve her memory, she created various herbs and compound, none of which seemed to fill anymore of darkness that clouded her memory, Angela decided that something so horrific must have happened, that her bodies own defences had blocked it, protecting her from the painful recognition, perhaps this gap could offer some explanation as to why there was no reports of her disappearance.

A hand brought Zo back to reality, away from her fond memories of her life on this secluded island, Elly and Eiji had arrived, it was time to leave. Elly squeezed Zo's shoulder tightly feeling the heartache that spread within her, heartache along the lines of that she herself had felt when bringing her to this place. A small almost forgotten island, a place she would be safe...

...Elly sat in her room, the sun was already rising, it was nearly time for her to meet Marise, today would be a day to remember, they would stay in, eat and drink to their hearts content, enjoy themselves like there would be no tomorrow, because for Marise, there would not be, when the sun rose tomorrow everything would be different, Elly gave a sigh, did she really have to go through with this? Of course, she already knew the answer.

Their day went without a hitch, she had never seen Marise enjoy herself so much as they talked and reminisced indulging in the richest foods and finest wines, Elly had done well to keep her distraction from Marise's attention, especially considering how well they read one another.

As the sun set, she excused herself to her room, she had one final surprise for Marise, who retired to her room waiting in anticipation, it was hours later when Elly finally returned.

"Lee." Marise smiled as her door opened, in her hand Elly held two fine glasses and a dusty old bottle.

"This is older than you; it's worth a fair price on the market to collectors." She paused "sorry for the delay, it was quite a challenge retrieving it." She lied, it had been easy, it had been hidden in her room since she first came to work for Blackwood, but she had other things she had needed to attend to "what better way to toast the day" Elly smiled placing the glasses on the bedside table before popping the cork, she caught it in her other hand, handing it Marise as the bubbles spilled out of the bottle, she turned to fill the glasses, tipping the fluid, and the contents of a concealed phial into Marise's glass.

Marise didn't even hesitate in taking the first sip, a sight that made Elly's heartache, she trusted her so completely. Elly topped Marise's glass up, raising her own "Mari, you have possibly been the best thing in my life, whatever happens I will always love and cherish you as a friend, over the years you have become like family to me, like my sister" Marise moved to sit besides her, it was clear something was troubling Elly deeply.

"Lee... what's with the morbid look?" Marise questioned touching her hand as Elly took a drink from her glass.

"Now that you're twenty-one, you will leave all this behind and when you do, I shall miss you deeply."

"Lee." Marise smiled. "As long as you are here, there is no place I would rather be" Marise filled their empty glasses empting the bottle. "What makes you think such things?"

"You've become a fine young lady, whether you know it or not, you will leave all this behind."

"If that is true, then you shall be besides me." Marise stated softly. "Now cheer…" Marise paused, her breath frozen as she found herself unable to move, unable to breathe; an effect short lived by this potion, short lived but critical to its success.

"I'm so sorry Mari, this is the way it has to be." Elly stroked her face as she gazed back at her in shock. "I'll see you soon though." As Marise fell back, Elly caught her gently laying her on the bed kissing her on the forehead.

As was planned she removed her sword and hid it somewhere only she could find it, she took the backpack from her room changing Marise into the clothes that were inside, she sat her up tying her hair into a ponytail with the leather tie Marise had used to attach her sword to her wrist when she fought the shadow creature. Elly looked at her lying on the bed, it was difficult to believe how something as simple as changing her clothes into something more fashionable, yet still trousers, and fastening back her hair would make it so that even Elly herself, doubted she would recognise her if they passed each other in the street.

Finally she was ready, Elly opened the window lowering the rope to the ground, using the sheet from Marise's bed, she tied Marise to her back before descending the wall. At the bottom she carried her to the stables ensuring she remained hidden, returning the way she had came to return the sheet to the bed and hide the rope, before leaving through the front door.

She used an entrance to Collateral she had deliberately never revealed to anyone, it was well hidden and as such would provide a quick means of escape. Even when time was critical, like arriving at Drevera the night Zodiac went to see her mother, she used the entrance a day's travel away.

She passed quickly and silently through Collateral to the island of Crowley, an isolated island with just one town and a small unmanned port.

She secured the horse in the valley by the entrance of Collateral; there was no way the horse could make the steep climb up the mountains. She scanned the area, she needed somewhere sheltered, but not too far from a town, so when she woke, she could find her way to civilisation, or be found by it. When she awoke she would be alone, frightened, having no memories of her past, she had to ensure she could find a town. If it was Marise who would wake, there would be no difficulties but she knew it would not be Marise who found herself lost and alone, it would be Zodiac.

The final Grimoire had a special seal in place, it could only be taken by one sharing Night's blood that was pure of heart, or so the rumours said. If Marise had retained control much longer as warned by both Night and Fenris, Zodiac would have vanished completely along with any chance of seizing the final Grimoire, which location was still unknown. The only way to prevent this was to revive her by sealing Marise away and wait for the time the chosen would be united, this would see the realisation of their goals and the revealing of the final Grimoire.

She had thought of Crowley when deciding where her safe haven should be, she had found herself thinking back to Shemyaza port, where they met elder Robert, any place that did not need their elder's constant supervision was bound to be peaceful, it was perfect.

Her eyes caught sight of a forest the other end of the island, there was also another entrance to Collateral near there, the forest stretched for miles and was close to both the port and the town.

Her decision made, she took Marise into the clearing of the forest laying her carefully with the satchel Zodiac had brought with her when she first came to 'study' with Blackwood, it had been filled with herbs and potions, all of which had long since seen better days, Elly had carefully replaced each of the items with ones in good heath, ensuring the seeds Zodiac had collected would still be suitable for growing. She looked at the figure; she looked so young and innocent as she lay sleeping on the forest floor, as she slept her memories of her time as Marise Shi being sealed away in a place even the most skilled doctor couldn't find.

"I'm sorry Mari" she whispered "I will come and visit soon, when you are ready for the final task" with those words she returned to Collateral and Blackwood's mansion before anyone had even realised she was gone…

…But the feelings of her deeds lived on, the heartache, the guilt, feelings she would never wish upon anyone yet even so she saw their unmistakable tarnish within her friend's eyes, 'if only things could have been different' she thought watching her friends tearful gaze staring through the trees longingly towards home.

Zo's mind begged her to reconsider, she had only known this person a day and already she was taking her away from all she knew and loved. Although her unfounded trust for this person, strangely reassured her, but why now? Why after over a year had she come looking for her? And why was her arrival marked with the start of this trouble? And was it a coincidence the only hint of her past, a vague recollection of living in a place with this person came after her arrival? Part of her wanted to ignore the feelings of familiarity she had towards this stranger, to believe her stories lies, but she knew better than that, for some reason deep within her heart she knew this person spoke the truth and she couldn't ignore the proven danger, Elly's hand still on her shoulder turned her now to face the direction they would be heading, moving her body did little to stray her longing gaze from the direction of her home.

"Are you ready?" Elly's voice ached with concern towards her friend aware just how powerful the conflicting emotions she would be feeling were. "You're doing the right thing you know."

"They will be safe… won't they?" Her eyes swam with tears as she turned to look at Elly awaiting her response; she nodded gently as she took Zo's bag from her shoulder adjusting the straps slightly before placing it over her own. "Then… I guess… there is no point delaying further." She sighed taking her first determined step away from those she loved.

Elly, unsure what to say to her friend remained completely silent for the next half hour, feeling any words she could offer would do little to comfort her at this moment. Eiji however, chose not to speak for an entirely different reason, he walked side by side with Marise Shi, although *she* seemed oblivious to this fact *he* wasn't, the thought of walking side by side with that brutal murderer his master had so often told stories about around the campfire unnerved him, it was hard to believe this girl, and the legendary murderer were one and the same, he was unsure how he would feel when the time came to make his choice, but at least for the moment, there was little choice for him if he valued his life, he felt uneasy, as they walked he found himself glancing to her repeatedly worrying in case she would make a sudden move ending that which he was here to protect, his life, but looking at her now she seemed younger than he himself was and was, she was just like any other person in appearance, there was no signs of the marks of Hades it was claimed scarred her, nor could he see the image of his own death as he looked upon her, the rumours of this person, he knew were greatly exaggerated, but still he had not expected her to seem so normal she was not at all like the monster he had expected to face, unable to bare the uneasy atmosphere it was he who broke the silence

"So you're the le…" Elly shot him a warning stare stopping him in mid-sentence by the weight of the look alone, he had forgotten himself for a moment in the need to break the silence, saying the first thing that came to mind, something completely inappropriate, fortunately she stopped him in time, before any damage could be done, before they were presented with questions that could not yet be answered.

"I'm the what?" She questioned quietly, Elly had hoped she hadn't heard but such silence was unforgiving to a slip of the tongue.

"Legendary healer around these parts." Elly finished quickly; another look was shot to Eiji words exchanged that the darkness masked. "On our way here we were told there was a healer whose skill with herbs and potions was beyond all comprehension, I just knew it had to be you, that's why we came here." A quick, but not entirely satisfying save by Elly, looking at her, she could tell she was unconvinced, but her mind was elsewhere, too preoccupied to question further, for this she was glad, although she did seem to give an answer, something about someone called Angela, yet the name was the only thing clearly heard through her lowered tone.

They had not noticed the sound of their footsteps crunching on the grass below as they walked, until there was silence brought upon them by their sharp stop. Elly's arm outstretched in front of Zo ensuring she too stopped she seemed a little too preoccupied to noticed the events around her. The trees before them danced and shook with the shadows of firelight, blocking their view of those present before them it was clear someone had recently set up camp, the wood's air had yet to haze with the dense smoke from the fire that would be expected if the travellers had been their any length of time.

"The crossroads is just ahead, though a small island we get a few travellers who journey on a pilgrimage to follow the path of the priestess Sandra for example, many stop to rest here before visiting the temple, it's quite common. Nothing to worry about." Whispered Zo trying to convince herself that saying the figures at the firelight would pose no danger would make it so, but after recent events she was not so sure.

"Then why are you whispering?" Elly smiled passing Zo something, before she even realised what it was the sword was fasten around her waist in a flowing natural movement as though she had done it a million times before; her stomach sank seeing what she had done. "You forgot this." Elly added

'I had not forgotten it.' She thought to herself remembering the deliberate attempt to leave it behind despite the fact she nearly left with it in her possession twice. There was something about this strange item from her past that made her feel uneasy, it left her with a sick feeling deep in the pit of her stomach surpassing anything she had ever felt, growing as she looked intently at the sword, there was a feeling to it she didn't quite like, something about it seemed evil somehow. As she felt its weight against her hip she remembered the giant figure from earlier, the one that had started this nightmare, the being that came as a warning that she had overstayed her welcome. It was so difficult to prevent the sword delivering that final blow, it had been almost as if she had been fighting against its will, she had no choice but to remove him from her sight before she gave in to the will of the sword, to the temptation of power. She never wanted to feel that way again, so angry, so much hatred for what that thing was doing to her friends, raw emotion to the point it clouded her own judgement, for that one moment as she stood sword poised above the creature she was frightened of herself, frightened of what she may do, scared of the voice inside her mind whispering for her to finish him… she knew she could never mention to anyone how she felt back then, she feared their reactions, then again, now she was leaving her friends behind, the only people she could have told would have been Elly and Eiji, it was certainly not the kind of thing she would like to have heard from wither of them and so she chose the path of silence.

"We should go around to avoid any trouble." Eiji's statement seemed more like a question as he directed it to them, he seemed to be looking to Zo for an answer, or perhaps there was another thought behind that look, a thought she couldn't quite place.

"And let them get behind us choosing their time to strike? It's better to get them before they get us." Elly's words closed of this subject leaving no room for debate and with that, they began to wander towards firelight, by now, whoever sat at the crossroads would know they were approaching, they had attempted a silent approach destroyed by Eiji as he seemed to step on almost every twig his footsteps echoing with the breaking wood, if they had been oblivious to that, the cry he let out when his foot struck a rock would have given them away for certain.

"And you wondered how I knew you were following me." Elly whispered her head shaking in mild amusement. As they got closer they could make out the conversation clearly, one of the voices was a little too loud, almost as if they wanted to be overheard by those who approached.

"So anyway, I tried to tell her she couldn't sneak away, but still she had to try anyway." Daniel turned to look at the place Zo now stood, her mouth open slightly with the shock of finding her two friends awaiting her arrival, after a moment she smiled brightly her eyes twinkling in the firelight. Daniel had always been able to read her so well, his presence here served as a reminder of just how well, after they had left for home they must have taken the road from town heading straight here, shock, amusement and relief all displayed in her face as she looked upon them.

"Hey!" She finally spoke in a playfully whiny tone "what if I was waiting back at home for you to come and say goodbye?"

"But you aren't are you? You don't think we'd just let you leave with these people we don't know from Adam?"

"They *can not* come with us." Elly had silently watched until this point, her voice now firm and ruling. "They will get in the way, it will be hard enough to defend yourself if someone attacks, which I'm sure they will, let alone having to worry about these two as well." Her tone once more took the 'conversation is over' tone.

"We can take care of ourselves." Acha's voice timid but direct as it addressed her, they had no intention of letting this stranger tell them where they were and weren't welcome.

"Yeah? Like you did earlier?" Elly stated, reminding all of what had transpired hours ago with just those few words, they decided to ignore her comment, in fact they continued talking as if she wasn't even there.

"But what about school? And the garden?" Zo looked from Daniel to Acha in turn.

"School broke up yesterday." He tutted. "You never listen" he was joking of course, he knew her mind was all over the place at the moment, over the last day she had so much to take in, so much for her mind to sort, she was bound not to recall something as simple as the end of term.

"And Daniel's mum said she'd happily mind the garden while we went camping." Acha added.

"You really did think of everything, I'm glad you came but…"

"But this is not a game, it's not a camping trip either, her life is in danger." Elly snapped, unable to believe their deliberate attempt to ignore her, just who did they think she was anyway? As they had waited for Zo to regain consciousness in the house, they had clearly named her as Blackwood's daughter, how dare they try to argue, especially considering they knew her reputation well. It was a common known fact that Elly was the daughter of the one she had named as Zo's lord, but none knew that this was in fact nothing more than a story to cover her appearance there.

"We know it will be dangerous." Daniel once more choosing to ignore Elly. "Did you care about it being dangerous risking your life for me and Acha?" Daniel questioned rising to stand before her from his position by the fire, he stood between Zo and Elly, a deliberate move enforcing the fact, that to them, she was invisible, who were these strangers to dictate the choices of his friend? Surely, it was a choice only she herself should make.

"Elly…" Something changed in Zo's face, as she looked passed Daniel to her, "You said someone was after me… now they've already mistaken Acha for me once, and from my reaction know we're friends… they could just as easy go after them to get me, than come for me directly… if they took my friends…." Zo looked to Daniel and smiled softly as Daniel took the bait extending on what had just been said turning to acknowledge Elly for the first time since their arrival.

"I mean like you say it's not as if we can look after ourselves, and if you *do* know Zo you'll know she'd rather die than let anything happen to her friends so if…"

"Alright already." Elly sighed. "They can come, it seems I may have misjudged you." She shook her head her tone filled with annoyance, it seemed they were going to continue until she met their demands anyway, but as Zo turned to thank her she saw her smiling in the shadows.

"Besides." Eiji decided to add his opinion, already too late to aid the debate. "They won't be looking for a large group, just you and her, so it could work to our advantage." Elly glanced around the group again.

"Depends really… but for now it might."

***

"So what makes her any different than the others?" A voice echoed through a darkened room, a large room full of various life-forces even now, despite their obvious imprisonment, they were in heated debate.

"This one will die the others were lucky there were more of us free then." Another voice joined the conversation.

"Well they had to choose someone I suppose, they have us all now, this would be the last chance." Scoffed another

"Mew!" The room fell silent as a cat's cry filled the air, it had a strange authority to its tone.

"Their games will be the end of them you'll see, she's different, I see it in her eyes." Seiken argued to deaf ears, they had already decided the fate of this chosen party, it was annoying, he swore had it been anyone else they would have been a little more enthusiastic, but it hadn't been someone else, it had been her.

"You think a mortal can succeed where we ourselves failed? When those that came before her also met defeat. I don't think I need to remind you of this do I?"

"Meow! Mew raw!"

"I suppose we have little choice but to hope." The voice seemed to be answering the cat's voice.

"Having us all here like this means only one thing, he controls our world. I've seen it, the boundaries are already thinning." Seiken's voice desperately pleaded for them to listen but they seemed too intent on arguing, too intent on disagreeing, that was probably the reason they had all ended up here like this, so use to working alone that when the time came to cooperate they spent too much time arguing that when they finally decided on an action, there numbers had already been greatly reduced.

"It will be the end of us all."

"Why would they choose someone who could win?"

"No one ever wins… maybe she'll prove to be a challenge but little else you should know better than to get our hopes up child. It's been too long" Seiken glanced to the figure venom in his eyes as he heard his words, the figure cringed realising the disrespect he had spoken.

"No! You're not listening, they saw in her the weakness she has, the desire for a truth forgotten, they know the lengths she'll go to find it, they saw her weakness but in doing so overlooked her strength, they don't think she can win." Seiken pleaded with them to listen though despite their situation they were as stubborn as ever

"Seiken." An elder voice, the voice of his father, silenced the room there was a slight pessimism in his voice "You are young, angry, the others feel despite your power you are too optimistic, but if you say that she is the one, I don't doubt you. It is up to you to help her though, I shall watch the dreamers. You know the rules, they can't know you are helping her… you can't be gone too long if they notice, they will figure out about our powers and stop it, then she won't have a chance…"

"Mew roaw me?"

"Very well, Rowmeow shall cover for us should they return in our absence"

"But why me? I am not experienced in this field." The voice protested slightly though with nowhere near enough power to convince anyone this was something he didn't want.

"You approached her first did you not?"

"But I didn't mean to I was simply wondering who they got to play, after hearing them go on about them when they brought me here I couldn't help but wonder, the next thing I knew I was there." He felt now more than ever the need to justify how he came to cross the boundaries to stand before the chosen, especially considering the warnings he had received in the past.

"Seiken, you are young, but you are also stronger than me, you can stay away longer before needing to return. You are the only one who can succeed, you have created a bond with her already, after all, isn't she the one you have been watching? If you saw the boundary as you said, you know this game will be our last."

"It *will* be the last!" Determination in his voice as his voice rang through the darkness, yet his enthusiasm did little to convince the sceptical listeners.

***

They walked through the rest of that day until finally they stopped to set up camp the sun was hanging low on the horizon but as yet it had not began to tint the sky, it would be a few hours until the sun set completely set up camp, none of them complained about the continuous walking, or about the fact they were walking to the end of the island which led to absolutely nowhere, the figure was so confident in her steps, they simply followed unquestioningly. The time together had been beneficial for the newly found companions, after the initial hour of strained conversation they began to form a bond of friendship, looking at them now you would think you were gazing on a group of life long friends.

Elly sat close to the newly built fire, where the content of Zo's backpack was spread across the floor as she searched for supplies. Finally the smell of stew began to taint the air as the metal pot paced above the fire began to boil.

"So… anyone know any good ghost stories?" Eiji asked passing Elly the remaining ingredients for the meal. His question was met with silence. "No one? Come on you can't have a campfire without ghost stories." Another silence "oh very well, I'll go first" finally they gave him their attention. "It's not a ghost story as such, more like true survival or at least that's what my master called it when he told me." Elly glanced up from the stew, satisfied he had caught everyone's attention he continued. "It's a story of legend, although it happened just over seven years ago…" Eiji began his tale, there had been much speculation about what happened before his master saw her, but the information he gave, was the part of the story that never changed, it was the story of how Marise had obtained the Grimoire of light and life-force, none knew how the tale came to being since all but one were slaughtered on that day, it was a story however that Elly knew well, she had heard it from its creator, she found herself surprised at the tales accuracy…

…The Grimoire of light and life-force possessed the power of mind control, life affecting and healing magic, pretty much anything for physical or mental needs was stored within that book. It was for this reason the Idliod sent this particular book to Napier village. It was the only Grimoire Night had ever laid eyes on, when he first found it; it had been kept in a small bookcase in the town overlooked by all. It was this very place that Night discovered he could not, no matter how hard he tried, remove the book. The villagers, although they did not recognise him feared this stranger's interest, his stature alone gave away his power and his aura gave away his anger, fearing what may become there were to dispose of that he found of interest, yet instead of destroying it as had been planned it was relocated to the care of a wise old vicar. The vicar took the book in his hands and knew instantly its power, any fool should have felt its power, but not all of them would be able to resist the whispering commands that echoed in their mind, controlling their actions and thoughts, it was this alone that had seen the book relocated instead of destroyed. He wrapped the book in a silk cloth and carried it with him through thee village, using it to heal those in need by using its dormant powers. You see there is a power to the Grimoire even the Idliod did not expect, they had sealed the power of a God within its binding, but a God is a being so powerful with magic so unpredictable, that the Grimoire alone could not contain it, leaving the excess energies to leak out allowing the person who possessed the book to use some of the skills trapped within it. This book was a secret the vicar did not feel appropriate to share with his successor, as it stood at that time, his successor was too greedy, too selfish, the old vicar knew he would abuse its power, he believed until the day of his death, the young priest knew nothing of its powers, but this was not the case. The young priest was haunted by images of the book, it called to him in his dreams, ordering him to take control, whispering promises into his ear of how great they could become together, stories of the power they would share, the world could be his, but first he had to be given the book, or inherit it through the death of its owner. As the young priest realised the vicar would not share his secrets, he began to poison him, but the book forbad this action, for each time the vicar took the book within his hands, the poison was dissolved and the book would taunt the young priest more. Finally one day before supper he saw the vicar leave it in his room, he made light work of lifting the key from the vicars pocket ensuring he could not gain access to the book again. When the time came for them to dine he scattered a high concentration of poison over his master's food, he watched as the vicar tried to make it to the Grimoire only to find his door locked, his key missing from his pocket, he looked to the young priest, understanding all as he saw the key held within his hand, before Hermes came to collect him.

The young priest hid the murder from the town, it wasn't hard, the priest had been old and the book that possessed powers of suggestion was now his, as was the temple. Any who grew suspicion had their decision altered by the power of the book, but this was rarely needed most in the town were happy to offer their lives freely to the new vicar without 'persuasion' to the fateful day they all were murdered, all within the town obeyed his every command, even if it meant they would sacrifice the life of their only child. His power is absolute.

Marise stood on the dirt track just outside the town, it was a nice little village, very peaceful, everyone seemed to be in their homes eating tea ready for the night ahead, most of the workers had returned from a hard day in the towns and cities, it was easily home to around a hundred or more people.

The village itself had been built centuries ago, but the oldest part that remained standing was no older than a few decades, the town had visibly suffered many disasters and had been clearly rebuilt in several locations, it was rumoured the damage the town suffered was due to the town possessing a strong link to the Severaine, that and the fact it borders each lie on the edge of extreme elements, others say the disasters were caused by the immense power that was born there and that this young boy had been responsible for all the town's problems, but the true start of their problems began a long time before, so long ago that everyone, even those who remember the pilgrimages of old, have forgotten.

Marise stood on the dirt path for some time, the power of the Grimoire hung heavily in the air around her, just one person walked the streets, a young vicar, he hurried towards the church stopping in his tracks when he saw her watching from the other side of town, he stared at her for what seemed like an eternity, neither of them moving, until finally, Marise slowly walked towards him. Without previously laying eyes on her, from his posture alone it was clear he knew who she was, he knew she came for him. It seemed to her, that more and more people were recognising her at a glance, she didn't know whether to thank the wanted posters or her deeds, but he knew her and that is why he ran.

His hands firmly seized the Grimoire from the altar, he rushed to the window ordering the town to take up weapons to prevent this demon from reaching the church. The townsfolk scurried from their houses men, women and children all in someway armed be it with kitchen knifes, farming tools or swords, not a person remained who had not taken up arms against her. He clutched the book as the demon warrior took the lives of those that stood before her, cutting her way to the temple, cutting her way to him.

Marise smiled, the people of this town were too willing to give their life to someone else, so she took that which they freely offered, had they been stronger, had they even the slightest desire to think for themselves, to face up to reality instead of leaving everything in the hands of someone else, such weak mind control would not have worked. They were ready to die as long as they themselves weren't to blame.

Marise could have easily spared the town of bloodshed, at most killed two or three people on her journey to the temple, but such weakness annoyed her, she could have spared them, but she didn't. Not a living soul remained on the streets or in the houses except for one, the one she came for, the one that took residence in the temple.

As she approached, she felt another life-force enter the village, a powerful Elementalist, already giving training to a younger generation, she felt his basic skills had vanished leaving him only with those his student remained to learn. This was something Marise could never fully understand, it seemed at any one time there was only one Elementalist, who could at any one given time possess a skill. Elly had told her once that Elementalist would train to master the element they felt the strongest link to, they would learn to read it, like Hectarians learnt to read the environment. There were many variations on the elemental skills, but no two skills were ever the same. Elly had said a long time ago there had been a larger range of skills than those which were now available, Elementalists of past could draw on light and dark as well as various other things without being confined to earth, air, fire and water.

Elementalists were always trained, as they learnt the talent of their trainer, their trainer could no longer execute the skill, in effect, the student would take the master's skill. When a master had taught the student all they could learn, they would rejoin the elements that gave them life. There were many born that had the potential to become Elementalists, but the lack of trainers in this day and age, saw to it that few would know of their hidden potential.

He had not yet entered the village to gaze far enough to gaze upon the bloodbath she had created, she hesitated outside the temple, wondering if she should go back and see to it that word of the events here did not yet reach the public ear, but she was a day away from the nearest town, even should he leave now, she would be long gone before his return. She turned her attention back to the church, opening the wooden doors by the power of flame.

The vicar stood behind the altar watching in composed terror as a shadow stepped through the flames, like Hades through the gate to the underworld. He turned his eyes to the book clutched within his hands, trying to appear both calm and innocent as she approached, something he did rather poorly. Even now she could smell his fear, beads of sweat formed on his forehead as he focused the book's control onto her, he drew harder concentrating more and more on the power that enabled him to control those of the town, his pallor growing paler as the book's power failed to make her hesitate for even a second. Then she stood before him, only the altar between them.

"Mind games?" She smiled sadistically raising her eyebrow, it was a smile that seemed to freeze his blood, for a moment he was unable to speak, unable to move as he looked upon his own death, she ran her hand through her fiery red hair before speaking again. "Give me the book." She commanded a sudden thought entered the young vicar's mind, just as he could not take the book from his predecessor, she could not take it from him, if she were to kill him, it would once more belong to the church and the next holy man to cross the threshold and seize the book. He focused all his will summoning a greater strength from the book, this time she heard the faintest whisper in the back of her mind, a voice so faint, so weak it almost made her laugh aloud. "Very well... two can play at that, I will wait outside." She locked her sea green eyes on him for just a moment, there was so much she could do, so much fun she could have, she could simply whisper to his mind to give her the book, she could have him mutilate himself, kill himself even, but that was not her wish, she wanted to destroy him. "To kill a person is easy, but to completely destroy them is far more rewarding." She smiled sadistically seeing the fear her words brought.

As she reached the door she heard him cry in terror as his minds fears were realised, creatures like those he had never dared imagine crawled through the floorboards and the ceiling. There were creatures he had always feared, and things so frightening he could never imagine, he tried to ignore them, dismissing them as illusions, as mind games, but then he felt the breath of one behind him, the warm, damp, hungry breath that destroyed his logic. He turned to face it fearfully as it lashed out sinking its claws deep into his flesh, he was certain now, by the evidence of his own blood the creatures that stood before him were no illusion, their touch alone proved them to be as real as the blood he shed, he retreated from the creature clutching his shoulder tightly.

"I'll give you to the count of ten." She smiled, leaving the temple as the young vicar fought with him; she leaned against the wall her back towards the door and slowly began to count.

Marise was just about to reach ten when, as if on cue, the vicar skidded from the temple door falling to the floor, he quickly scrambled across the floor, a look of pure terror on his face as he fell to her feet he fell to her feet, his arms and front bloody and his clothing torn. Marise smiled, the young vicar would not even begin to believe each of his injuries were self inflicted, not from the illusions he even now, thought followed him, wishing to taste his blood. His shaking hand pushed the book towards her as she looked down upon him; she looked at him questioningly until he found the breath to speak.

"P...p...please... take it." His voice squeaked as he glanced nervously behind at the creatures that were now emerging from the church. "P...p...please, just send away your demons." She smiled taking the book from his grip, as soon as he released it the creatures vanished, yet the injuries remained, still bleeding and very real.

She turned slowly, there was no need to kill him, he was destroyed, a man pushed over the edge into insanity and now there was no life for him anywhere even though her magic had now been banished, he would be haunted by the images he saw, they would follow him in his mind until born of his own fears the images would return for him, looking at him now he was holding himself fairly well but she could see the cracks, he hid it well for the time being at least, but his sleep, his dreams would be his downfall. She would have let him live, she liked the idea of the torture and isolation his life would hold, she would have let him live, if not for the sentence he uttered "thank you... thank you God for sparing me." He cried into the air, no sooner had he finished his sentence then Marise turned sharply beheading him, the last words he heard, so plain, so clear.

"It was not God that would have spared you, it was me." She sheathed her sword and nodded at Hermes as he collected the vicar, she had seen a lot of him lately, today especially.

Just one person, excluding herself, stood with life in their body, the Elementalist who seemed to be rooted to the spot in fear as he gazed upon her, his already white hair now seemed dark against his pale complexion. She stopped mere feet away from him, for a moment they just looked at each other, she saw many things hidden in his eyes, recognition, fear and honour, as she looked at him and their eyes met something seemed to shift inside her, something convincing her to walk away, for that moment she lost control.

"Next life, you save me." Marise did not know she had spoken these words, neither did she remember leaving the village, by the time she realised he may have been left alive; it was too late to turn back...

..."He said it was hard to believe such a sweet voice and captivating smile came from such a person. He was said to be the only person to ever survive her gaze. Those she laid eyes on always died."

"He can't have been the only one... or no one would know who she was... like me, who are you talking about I never remember hearing such tales." Zo glanced around aware of the disbelief in everyone's eyes.

"You're kidding right?" Zo's expression told Daniel she was deadly serious. "You've never heard of Marise Shi!" His voice seemed to scream with disbelief, it was only a few days ago he had spoke of her to Acha, as he told her events of recent history, even she... or the person she inhabited more precisely before she died had knowledge of the tales of Marise Shi, thus Acha knew of her already, then again considering her amnesia, he wondered why it was not something he had thought about before, she was spared from the curse of knowing. "She was... well, still is, the most feared fighter of all time. A legendary warrior who slaughtered millions and burnt cities to the ground. She is feared as a God, but lacking in compassion is sometimes deemed to be much worse."

"So what happened to her?" Zo questioned curiously.

"Well some say when Night returns she will join him, if Elly's tales are true and he *has* returned then it goes to reason she would be besides him. Others say she met a stronger foe and met her end, where as me, I think she's laying low probably buying her time until she seizes the last Grimoire." Daniel continued to hold the attention of the others unaware of Elly slapping Eiji hard across the back of the head, Daniel was more familiar with the tale of the Grimoire than he had let on when Elly had questioned Zo about it, he wanted to hear just what this stranger had to say before giving away anything, by listening to her could ascertain if the words from her mouth were lies or truth, if they were lies he could have protected Zo, warning her about he deception, but it seemed she spoke nothing but the truth.

"You idiot!" She hissed. "What were you thinking?"

"I'm sorry... I wasn't... I forgot... I was just telling a story."

"Do you ever think before opening that mouth of yours?"

"I said I was sorry." He sulked.

"Ok... no harm done... this time." She whispered aware that the conversation of the others had already moved onto other things as she dished out the stew. Surprisingly, it seemed Zo had packed in the hope of her friends joining them; there were more than enough small wooden bowls to go around.

Zo found herself unintentionally withdrawn, her thoughts on that strange boy, Seiken, and his mysterious eyes that drew her right into his soul, right into his thoughts, making her forget her pain and worries, for that moment he was with her it seemed it was just him and her, everything else seemed to melt away into the distant background.

A rustling sound behind her snatched her from the depths of her mind, the others, oblivious to the sound continued eating and talking. Placing her dish slowly to the floor she glanced around locating the sound in a near by tree, two large black eyes peered out from the shadow, eyes she thought she should remember, eyes that brought with them danger, her hand fell to her sword, unnoticed by her until she felt its cool hilt held firm within her hand.

Everything went deadly quiet, the others had stopped in mid conversation and were now watching her with a mixture of expressions as she held her weapon ready to draw as she listened, more eyes appeared in the bushes and trees around them. A whispering that had been nothing but background noise for the last few minutes suddenly became noticeable to all.

'You are chosen.' Finally one voice stood out, it seemed to engulf the very air with its words, the others echoed his words, although only in whispers it sounded as though a tidal wave had crashed over their heads.

"There must be thousands of them." Acha whispered turning a full circle as she listened to the words; the same words spoke over and over.

"It's like they appeared from thin air, what can do that?" Questioned Eiji making a similar circular movement as though trying to determine the exact source of the many whispers.

"Demons?" Daniel gave one of several answers, the first one to enter his mind, an answer that was the closest they would get, they weren't demons, demons could only appear at night when their enchantment sealing them to the world beneath the surface was disrupted by the moonlight, this happened but once a year at the festival of Hades, Samhain.

"Chosen for what? Would probably be a better question." Elly joined the others who seemed to have formed an outwards facing circle, Zo however had not joined them still stood at the base of the tree looking up.

'Are you ready?' Again the words crashed over head

'What fun you'll be.' With those last words the dream returned as vivid as the creatures themselves, they promised her the truth, a truth that no one seemed to know, the truth that Elly would not mention. They had promised her answers, if she would play their game, not only that but their 'game' as they called it had something to do with the familiar stranger, Seiken, she remembered everything now, the dream, the subject of conversation between her and Seiken that her mind had lost leaving her with only his image, now she remembered she knew the answer to the question they spoke, his world was in danger, it was something to do with the eyes, something to do with their so called game, winning the game was their only hope, she was their hope and along the way she was promised the answers about herself.

"I'm ready." Her voice trembled a chorus of her name and questions filled the air almost drowning out the whispers, her friends shocked that she would answer such a question, shocked that she seemed to know to what they were referring and was ready for whatever it was, without so much as a word to them.

'She's ready.' The whispers again spoke in unison. *'Ever changing with the sun, your life shall be until you're done.'* A mocking echo of laughter resounded from around them before the world erupted in a flash of light, a light so bright no darkness remained. Her hand rose to her shoulder as a burning piercing flame danced across her skin, as the darkness returned she noticed hers was not the only hand that had found a wound, her friends now also stood their hands gripping their shoulders. An anger burned deep within her, the game or whatever it was had just started and already they cheated her, dragging her friends into something that didn't concern them.

"Cheats." She cried into the now silent air. "You said nothing about them. You asked me! Me!" She screamed her drawn sword hacking at the tree the creature had first appeared in, her voice filled with venom, a tone by the expressions of her friends they hadn't imagined existed and of all people it now exploded from her "Show yourself, I dare you!" The blade on her sword flashed wildly becoming even brighter, the others still hadn't moved, they simply watched her, taken aback by the venom and hatred in her voice as she screamed into the air. The leaves forced from the tree by her violent actions fluttered through the air in serenity despite the lack of it at that moment in time. Daniel's hand fell softly on her shoulder, she span raising her sword as if to strike until her eyes met his, he blinked, her eyes seemed to change before his stare, he blinked again dismissing it as a trick of the light

"What was all that about? What happened?" Daniel held contact with her piercing blue eyes.

"What does this symbol mean?" Acha asked rolling up her sleeve to reveal an upside down Y yet where the top of the down line should finish it continued down drawing level with the bottom of the symbol.

"It's a rune, a symbol used for those travelling between worlds. This one is known as 'boundaries' it means the setting of limits, but it's upside down, so I'm guessing it means just the opposite, maybe the opening of paths otherwise protected." As Daniel spoke his eyes never for a moment left Zo's 'you ok?' He mouthed at her concern showing in his eyes, never before had he seen her lose her temper, it was so out of character, Zo lowered her head shamefully before sitting on the floor as the wild energy left her.

"What's going on?" Elly's eyes fell to Zo as she took a seat, she turned away from Elly's words jabbing the ground gently with her sword.

"We're not playing games!" Eiji snapped before softening his tone. "If something's going to happen... we need all the information we can get." He examined the reversed boundaries symbol on his arm in a ploy to avoid looking at her mulling over his choices once more, death, or death, either way he may as well face it, for the moment he was stuck with them.

"I didn't know... I thought it was just me... I swear." Tears of frustration ran down her face as she spoke shaking her head slightly. She was angry at the situation, but angrier at herself for failing to comprehend the consequences of her actions. There was no way she was going to make things worse than they were by telling them the deal, telling them how *they* tempted her to play. "But the eyes... and I never agreed to this... never... I thought it would just be me."

"You're not making sense... what exactly is going on." Elly touched her hand gently.

"I... don't know. The eyes spoke of a game... and he... he needed my help... I said I would... I don't know... all I know is when I slept I was somewhere else, somewhere that needed my help." She tried to explain failing to find the words to do so.

"Who needs our help?" She questioned.

"He called himself Seiken he said I was to be the saviour... you weren't a part of it... they cheated!"

"Saviour?" Eiji almost scoffed at the thought of Marise being a saviour to anyone, then he remembered, she wasn't Marise anymore... she was completely different, apart from her looks, he hadn't even seen the resemblance until just, not really, in fact, he had begun to wonder if there had been a mistake somewhere, but now after seeing her little display, he knew, he had to be very careful around her, there was no doubt in his mind that she really was the murderer.

"He said something about worlds... thinning boundaries." Her voice had calmed a little as she spoke trying to make herself remember exactly what transpired "I don't know."

"Why didn't you say anything to us?" Acha joined the circle sitting in front of her.

"I couldn't remember... I thought it was a dream... I saw the eyes... then when I awoke after that Viking thing, *he* was in my room, when Daniel came in he just vanished... I thought... I thought it was a side effect from the knock on my head, you know a hallucination. That's all I know... I'm so sorry."

"Well I'm glad it happened." Zo looked straight at Daniel as he spoke taken back by his words. "If you're going exploring strange worlds, I want to be with you. You can't have all the fun, and it'll make one hell of a term paper." He wrapped his arm around Zo's shoulder holding her tightly.

"I agree, I mean at least we won't be where people are looking for you." Acha smiled as she became the recipient of Elly's questioning gaze.

"Yeah, I mean if they're going to cheat from the word 'go' it only makes sense to have someone watching your back." Zo was shocked, Eiji never seemed to feel comfortable around her, yet now when he had every right to hate her he was offering to watch her back, it was strange, from the time they met he seemed to have taken an instant dislike to her, but he seemed to be accommodating considering this. Zo turned her sights to Elly who had remained silent, she was smiling slightly as Zo's eyes met hers.

"What?" She shrugged. "I expected nothing less, you never turned down an adventure, always getting us into trouble… it'll be like old times."

Gradually as the night passed they settled down to sleep, Zo watched them sleeping for a while wondering what tomorrow held, wondering what they had been dragged into by her desire for truth, she could only imagine what dangers lay in wait, at the moment, very little made sense, she could only hope they would understand more of the situation before it was too late, but for now she was grateful to have such great friends, people that would stand besides her during this journey, with that thought she too settled down to sleep.

Chapter three

Zo awoke with a start, yet she couldn't remember sleeping, the fire's hot embers shone a dull yet piercing shade of red as they fought the losing battle to live, the world seemed somehow darker, despite the sun hanging fairly high in the sky it seemed to emit the shades expected if it were about to set from its position alone she estimated the time to be around three in the afternoon. As she glanced around the camp she realised the others had gone, their belongings still littered across the floor, slowly she began to pick them up wondering why they hadn't woke her, allowing her to sleep so late, despite being pressed for time, she also wondered how it could be she slept so late, normally she was a dawn riser, sleeping into the afternoon for her was unheard of. As she gathered the belongings together she couldn't help getting the overwhelming feeling something was wrong, the words she spoke to Elly just yesterday kept playing in her mind spurring her concerns.

'They could just as easy go after them to get me, than come for me directly... if they took my friends.'

What if *they* had taken them? Why else would she be left here alone?... Maybe they'd just gone looking for food... collecting supplies, she thought, as a more rational side emerged from her panic.

Finally the camp was clear, when they returned they could depart without delay... yet that nagging feeling that something wasn't quite right still played heavily on her mind. All the time she packed she had hoped at least one of them would return, but she was still alone and time was passing, perhaps they wanted to discuss last night's events away from her.

"Ah so you have... awoken, at last." A familiar voice emerged from the shadow of a near by tree. "I'm glad you came." Zo looked to Seiken finding herself captivated by him, once more the feeling of familiarity washing over her, she was almost certain she knew him from somewhere, now she stood face to face with him she knew it was no illusion. She had thoughts about where she may had seen him before, but they all seemed so unreal she knew even the idea of it was impossible, it was just a brief flash, but she was looking in a mirror, his image was what had looked back, the harder she tried to grasp the memory, the more she tried to make sense of the image she saw, the more it alluded her finally she surrendered and focused her attention back to their conversation.

"What do you mean came?... Came where?" Zo glanced around her ensuring she was still at their camp, satisfied she had not moved she looked back to Seiken.

"I have this for you... you would find one sooner or later." He emerged from the shadow, as he did, once again she was taken by his beauty he passed her a piece of tattered parchment, without thinking she tucked it deep within her pocket. "Just thought I'd give you a head start... the others are already here, I think you should get moving you are already late." With that he faded back into the shadows as if they themselves had taken him. 'Of course the others are here.' She thought to herself dismissively, whatever was he going on about? She shrugged dismissing his words as unimportant, she decided to locate her friends so they could depart, at least the stranger confirmed her friends were still in the area, she set to the task of locating them immediately.

She had barely taken a few steps into the forest when what stood before her brought her to an alarming halt, before her, stood a giant chasm, its depths immeasurable, almost like a hunters trap, come bottomless pit, she peered down it, wondering how someone could have made such a thing without disturbing their camp, her thoughts spiralled off wondering how it could appear there without anyone noticing, she stared deep into the hole, until her mind once more warned her that the others were still missing. It was that thought that made her shudder before stepping back holding onto a near by tree, as peering down the depths of the hole gave way to vertigo, from what she could tell, no one was down there then again, she couldn't actually see the bottom. Finally she moved around it, it was easily twenty meters in diameter, she used the trees for support unsure all the time why she hadn't just walked a little further along… maybe something worse was waiting elsewhere, she thought to herself.

Finally she reached the other side and continued on her way, having barely moved a few feet from the hole the trees came to an abrupt halt. Now she was more certain than ever something was a miss, before her lay the baron wasteland of a desert, nothing moved, and nothing grew but for a few scarcely littered cactuses, just mile upon mile of sand stretching out into the distance. She turned back to look at the trees, hoping it was some form of illusion, but even then she saw the slow curve of the trees. Instead of returning to camp she decided to follow them, it seemed almost as if someone had moved the area around their camp and placed it somewhere completely alien. Walking around she found something even more bizarre, with each major directional change, came a major change in climate. Dividing one from another was a simple line, the desert sands ended and taking their place to the West luscious green lands blossomed as heavy rain and thunder echoed. She blinked finding it hard to believe, a single line divided a desert from the rain, such a dramatic, impossible change, as she continued around she found the same occurrence, to the North mountains rose in the distance life bloomed, almost as if it was the very depiction of the earth itself, and finally, before returning to the desert in the South, came the East where mist and fog covered the landscape from her view yet again at the point the direction changed the fog and mists stopped not crossing the line… this vision of the land reminded her of something, she thought returning to the camp unaware of doing so. The desert, the rain, the mountains, the mist… they were all exaggerated images of the elements relating to their geographical representations

"Zo!" Acha's voice cried from the trees calling Zo back, Acha and Eiji now stood just inside the camp waiting for her, she was unaware exactly where they had come from but during their walk they seemed to have completely missed each other.

"Something is very wrong here." Zo said as she approached them, relief filling her to see at least the two of them, she glanced around looking for Daniel and Elly, but they were still missing.

"I know." Acha motioned in the direction of the hole, it seemed although they had been in the forest they hadn't ventured from it, so as they yet remained unaware of the sudden terrain change.

"Have you seen Daniel?" Elly questioned as she emerged from the woods behind Zo, it seemed as if they had all been looking for each other in these surroundings, missing each other by seconds, Elly had been drawn back by the sound of their conversation. "Oh and this… the answer to this is power." She threw a small stone tablet at Zo who caught it reading its inscription aloud.

"I am dangerous in the wrong hands; once you've tasted me you crave more. I can aid or destroy you depending on your strength and motivation." Elly took the rock back from her and placed it in her pocket.

"It's a riddle, the answer is power. It was by the camp when I woke up; no one was here so I thought I'd have a scout around."

"That's odd… No one was here when I woke up either." Muttered Eiji.

"Shouldn't we get moving? Daniel is out there somewhere, he could be in danger. Their game their rules." Muttered Elly, she wasn't really concerned about their missing group member, there was only one person in the group she was concerned about and another she was now responsible for, the other two were just excess baggage.

"Hey… did I hear my name?" They turned to see Daniel climbing down from a nearby tree until now he had been ignoring the conversation between his friends below, his attention has been completely stolen by the vision from the treetop "Something's not right here, I've just been looking around from up there you won't believe what I saw." His voice mingled with anxiety and awe.

"I know… we need to get moving." Zo pointed at the now visible hole it seemed to be growing rushing towards them, covering the ground erasing all that stood on it before "I think we've outstayed our welcome."

"But which way do we go?" Acha cringed as they broke into a run. The hole seemed to be chasing them from the forest until they broke free of the trees. They were but a little way out when they looked back, the hole had stopped after devouring the last tree, it sat now pulsing slightly as though breathing.

"I don't really fancy the desert." Zo was the first to answer "getting lost with no landmarks is the last thing we need."

"We'd do well to avoid the storms also." Added Elly she seemed to be cringing as she looked to the west.

"I reckon North. It's the least harsh of the environments; maybe we'll come across a town or something." Daniel gave an answer they all agreed on, their best bet was to find a town and maybe obtain some idea as to where they were.

"I guess it would help if we knew what we were after." Zo sighed remembering the stone Elly deciphered.

"Either way let's not stick around to see if that thing's still hungry." Eiji nodded towards the pulsing hole that had devoured the entire camp and stretched across the entirety of what was once the trees surrounding it.

***

The group traipsed across the land which harboured a few strange not quite right looking trees, although if asked *how* they didn't look quite right not one of them would be able to answer, they simply didn't.

"So where'd you think we are? I've never seen anywhere like this out of a book." Daniel questioned his voice filled with wonder; they had already been walking for what seemed like hours, the sun hanging low in the sky giving them just hours until sunset, he hoped they had found some shelter by then, who knows what dangers lay in wait after dark in this strange land?

"You know." A soft voice chimed gently, a voice Zo knew instantly from its elemental rhythm, it stopped her in her tracks as the words seem to flow gently through the very air landing softly, enriching the air around him. He once more made his appearance by a tree they had just past, the group turned to face him. He leaned casually against the nearby tree, it seemed to bloom within his presence, the tree itself seemed to emphasise his frame, his shape, his flawless beauty. "When sun sets here, the sun rises where you are… it's beautiful." He motioned to the already sinking sun as it hung low in the sky, yet his eyes never left Zo's gaze, she felt the heat rise to her face as she looked coyly to the floor avoid those brown eyes. A brown unique to only him, found nowhere but within the depths of himself. "When your people wake, Knights-errent becomes dangerous, when night falls the real danger arrives, you need to find somewhere safe before the last rays of light vanish from the horizon. Stay longer and… well, no one ever lasts the night. During the night here the real danger arrives." *What are these people doing here with her?'* Zo looked up at Seiken although he continued talking it was his voice she heard moments ago within her own mind. "Creatures and monsters born from the imagination of sleeping life-forces are released from the dreamer to this plain where they roam and live waiting for their next kill." *'I don't understand, shouldn't she have been with some other people, not this group? Is this part of their trickery?'* He walked closer to Zo, the smell of soft summer rain aired his presence, he smiled at her, his smile captivating, enticing, entrancing and like his name full of secrets.

"What do you mean safe?" Acha broke the silence that seemed to stretch for eternity, yet for Zo was over in a heartbeat. He took Zo's hand gently his touch was like fire on ice, burning and freezing where his fingers touched. His eyes remained gazing deep into her soul.

"I mean, just because *you* can't walk at night doesn't mean everything else isn't on the prowl while you cross over… true his minions can't capture you, it's against the rules." *'I can't believe it they all have the mark, what were they thinking?'* "Between twilight and sunrise you're safe from his minions… but after that is fair game… being of your upbringings." He tore his gaze from Zo to look straight at Daniel before dismissively glancing at the others. "I'm sure you can find somewhere, after all you've read enough books to know the rules." *'Well I guess it will work in our favour, but I just don't understand, first they choose her, then they involve these people, its almost as if they want us to win… which means… something bigger is going on than just this… I just can't see what it is; I'll have to ask Rowmeow.'* "Evil can't cross running water etc, but water is out for tonight. There's about an hour remaining until…"

"Can't you help us?" Acha's voice begged, Seiken stared at her heavily as she interrupted.

"You need something to keep evil in and keep evil out, that's all I can say… but I can warn you not everything here will be a trap." *'After all this is the realm of dreamers.'*

"There are what we call none-conscious dreamers, like you would be if you were just sleeping." He produced a small violet flower from the air passing it to Zo who turned an even deeper shade of red than when she believed she was somehow eavesdropping in on his thoughts. She looked to the flower holding it tightly to her chest smelling its sweet aroma, unaware of the others staring at her. When she looked up he had gone, she glanced around suddenly aware of the watching eyes.

"What?" She blushed.

"It talks! By the Gods it actually talks!" Zo turned to face Daniel before giving him a playful shove. "Now you've joined us I wonder if you could make sense of a few things."

"Like exactly what is this place?" Eiji finished the sentence. "That guy gave us the basic idea but…"

"From what I understand, it's the realm of dreamers." She smiled remembering how she got that information "kind of like a land of shadows, nightmares, dreams and imagination. Most things here, I think, were created by belief, collective consciousness or come from the minds of other life-forms. Yet at the same time, some of what we see comes from here, not from within the depths of our world's imagination… I think it's like our world in many respects, but here the sun follows the dreamer matching the turn of our world, when darkness comes here, the sun rises in its counterpart of our world. For the past few hours, what we've been seeing has come from our thoughts, memories or dreams as well as from other people." She stated, suddenly realising the vast amount of information she had actually gained about this place without being told it.

"Like that village." Whispered Acha with an underlying tone of wistfulness and fear. "We can't go there, no matter what, we can't… I… I once lived there… it's bound to be dangerous… considering." She trailed off into an inaudible mumble.

"Considering?" Questioned Elly realising in their time together there was only Zo and Acha who had not spoke of their past, Zo was understandable, she didn't remember hers, but Acha, she always seemed to change the subject so well that until this point no one had noticed.

"It's not important." She lowered her head slightly avoiding eye contact with anyone. "Just… I have bad memories of that place. Anyway." She continued without taking a breath. "Don't we need to find somewhere safe before nightfall?" It was not only true, but yet another way to change the topic without being questioned further.

"Well I've been thinking about that." Daniel ruffled his hair slightly as he spoke "I vaguely recall reading something along them lines, it's called a fairy ring… but I wouldn't know where to look."

"What is a fairy ring exactly?" Eiji asked seeming rather embarrassed at having to do so.

"It's a circle of mushrooms or was it flowers?… No it is mushrooms they happen because most forest mushrooms grow in circles, the old growth that lies in the middle are the first to die off, as it does so it leaves a toxic chemical behind inhibiting the growth of other plants."

"In legends it is said fairies dance in them, thus creating the circle, that's why they're called Fairy rings, or Fay rings." Elly added though with no real interest.

"I know what you mean." Acha's voice chimed with excitement. "I use to play in one in the forest by the village when I was little, the local shaman always use to chase me off and it's near where…" Her voice dropped as her mind clouded with thoughts of her father's betrayal. "Since the village is here I don't see why it should be in the forest there." Acha pointed to the small stretch of woods that ran alongside the village, Elly began to wonder if it had actually been there before Acha had mentioned it but could only draw the conclusion that it had.

***

By the time they arrived at the forest the sun was already sinking, the ring was there, just as Acha had described a circle of mushrooms more than big enough to comfortably fit them all.

"Careful not to step on any of them, I'm guessing it won't work if the circle is broken." Elly looked at Eiji, who got the hint straight away, making the extra effort to widen his step over them. He smiled at Elly once through the circle almost tripping over the backpack someone had been foolish enough to place right behind him

"So what happens now?" The last of the light fought for life on the horizon

"I'm not sure how it works… I guess we have to… go to sleep?" Zo volunteered.

"That being the case we'd better take one of these." Elly passed out a small red berry. "They induce sleep." Although no explanation had been needed only Zo and Elly had not taken them "I guess the thought of what they may see after dark is worse than whatever this berry may have done." She looked around at the fading images of the others, she smiled slightly before putting hers into her mouth she seemed to almost instantly fall asleep. Zo once more was the last to sleep; only she saw the darkness that circled them.

***

Screams echoed through the darkness, then everything was silent, a red glow surrounded her, fire burnt all around. The girl clutching something tightly to her chest left without looking back. Zo didn't want her to look back, for whatever reason she was afraid, afraid of this figure, afraid it would realise she was there, the figure stopped it seemed she had moved and the figure had just past her, she turned slowly to look at her, Zo felt hysteria rise within her as she saw the face that looked at her become visible through the darkness.

"Hey." Zo jumped as Elly's hand rested on her shoulder, she sat up nearly knocking her from her feet. "Are you alright?" Zo gasped for breath, beads of sweat hung on her forehead.

"Just a nightmare." She managed to state through her breathless gasps as the others exchanged curious looks, for the life of her she couldn't think what had scared her so much about the already fading dream, only vague segments lingered but the fear still tore at her soul. Suddenly she found herself looking around her the dream now nothing more that a fading memory as a new mystery rose from the darkness, she had absolutely no idea where they were. "Hey… where are we?" Her eyes fell on the vaguely familiar territory; the last remains of a gentle forest littered the surroundings, countryside fanned out at every angle, giving rise to the gentle slopes of the landscape.

"We've backtracked considerably." Elly replied not even attempting to answer the question, after all, she was meant to be unfamiliar with this island and the landscape they found themselves in. Daniel paced around a broken mushroom circle muttering to himself as he took in the area; finally he chose to share his thoughts with the group.

"Hey isn't this near where…" He began, glancing around once more. "It is! It's where my dad found you Acha."

"I know…" Her voice was little more than a whisper as she spoke. "My home use to be right there." She pointed to an area of dusty path and baron sands that seemed void of all life, despite this it did not seem to stand out from the surroundings until mentioned.

"That would mean somehow, when we slept in that place near your town we woke up in the circle we slept in on the boundaries of… here." Eiji deducted his voice expressing the confusion the others felt "So what… did we just pack up camp and walk here or something?"

"Doesn't anyone find it odd? That guy said the sun would be rising yet I make it at least two hours after sunrise"

"Does that mean we have to stay here all day?" Exclaimed Eiji, the whiney tone reminding Elly of that of a child.

"I shouldn't think so. Maybe it's just while we pass between worlds we need to be safe, remember how none of us were in that place when we awoke?" Zo paused taking the time to think over what she had just said. "When I arrived Seiken said you'd already arrived, yet none of you saw me at the camp if I was the last to wake… or sleep… whatever it is…" Zo paused glad for Elly's interruption

"Besides this circle is broken, it would offer little protection even if we were to stay within it and we need to get moving." Elly pointed to the clear break where the outer section of the mushrooms had died off.

"Is there any point going anywhere if we're just going to be moved around anyway?" Eiji sighed still not too convinced about leaving this circle, broken as it may be, anywhere they travel would just bring dawn to a new place after their journey through Knights-errent.

"Yes… besides…" Elly was watching Zo as she stared into the shrubs that grew near the boundaries of the circle.

"Who knows what we brought back with us…" Zo finished the others glanced at her strangely. "Keeps evil in keeps evil out." She reminded them; they followed her gaze to the bushes, for a moment they thought they saw a set of nightmarish teeth gleaming through the darkness.

"Ok but where are we heading? We won't get any further than last night and we walked for hours to find ourselves further back." Eiji again the first to complain.

"From here… I know a short cut… a few hours will see us to our destination." Elly hesitated before taking the first step out of the circle. Finally they were on the path heading for what looked like a small cluster of mountains ahead.

"So where are we heading?" Daniel asked remembering how when he was younger he took many a trip to the mountains; they always had a strange air about them, a mystery or perhaps secret hidden within them.

"You'll know when we get there." Elly answered closing the topic once and for all.

Chapter four

"By the Gods!" An echo of these words from all but Elly and Zo rang through the air from the mountain top as they looked down on the small village with a silver aura standing in the middle of the valley, it had come as a surprise to all, everyone here knew Crowley as an island with but one settlement and now they gazed upon a second, it came as a particular surprise to Daniel who had visited this area for years.

"How long has this been here?" Daniel gazed down into the valley at a small modest looking town. "I mean… I use to play around here all the time as a child and I never saw…"

"Forever." Elly stated bluntly cutting him off before he could continue; she began to walk down towards the simple town leaving no room for further questions, all in all approximately six or seven buildings made up its humble appearance.

"Then how come I've never seen it?" Daniel broke into a run to catch up with her as she scouted ahead, how could she, a stranger to these lands know about such a place? Something about her wasn't quite right, the place they were at now, was nowhere near the place they were heading before, wherever that was.

"It's a special village… only certain people can enter…" Zo spoke almost trance like as she stared at the village, aware she was answering but unable to place this newfound knowledge.

"You remember it?" Daniel questioned suddenly, surprised that such a thing could be remembered out of the blue, perhaps this could mean she was on the road to recovery, perhaps soon all her memories would return, since meeting with Elly, that was two things she had remembered, surely it was a good sign? At least there was one good thing about having her around.

"No… not this one… but at the same time yes…" She frowned hearing the impossible words she had just spoken, yet somehow they seemed to make sense, the longer she looked on the village, the more familiar it became, her frown grew more intense as she tried to remember, her concentration broken by Elly's words making her lose the fine string she was reaching for in that moment.

"What she means is, she has been there before but not from here." She stated adding more confusion to the matter.

"But how is that…" Eiji began soon to be cut off by Elly's begrudging explanation; she was beginning to feel like more like a guide than a traveller.

"It's simple. The village you see there before you is not a village, but a door way, there are possibly hundreds over this world. The village exists in an unmapped location, undetectable by beings or creatures of the world, this village was created to be a haven for magic users the world over, a place they could be safe, but in order for them to be able to get there with minimal delay, portals were set up to allow them to travel the distance in mere seconds." Elly gave a sigh as she led the group down the path with fewer hazards then she had hoped for, she had hoped at least one of them would have fallen taking an injury that would prevent their continuing.

A light mist seemed to radiate around the small village, the closer they stepped the thicker the mist seemed to be. The village itself, now seemed to have lost the silver outline, that before had traced around the edges of all they could see, Elly grabbed Zo's hand before she was able to enter, her earlier recollection leaving her curious as to whether or not, seeing this place would bring back further memories of her life, she was unsure if such things would make the task at hand simpler or harder, she had to believe it would be the latter, after all, if she was to learn the true objectives, could she cope with the task at hand? After all, it was Zo who had to complete this task, not Marise, that alone was the reason Elly was being careful about what information she was given, in fact, she was trying her best to give her nothing that would jog her memories, if she learnt too much of the truth, the entire plan would be ruined.

"You may want to cover up your weapon; we haven't come here for any trouble." She took Sword from Zo's belt without waiting for a response, once more finding herself surprised by its weight, although its master could carry it with little trouble, it was clear it did not like to be handled by any other than its creator, after a while of being carried by her, it had seemed to accept her as a temporary measure to allow it to reach its creator, this choice was clearly revoked on its reunion with its master. She turned the sword over once in her hand before untying the leather fasten that had moments ago restrained her friend's hair "I'll need this too." She stated watching as Zo shook her hair free, finding herself amazed how little she had really changed from past times. She smiled slightly lacing the sword's belt around Zo's midriff before securing it with the leather tie which had just enough length to circle her torso and secure the sword, finally after several knots, it seemed secure enough to hold position, at least until it was safe to remove. "That should do, here." She stated helping her into her own three quarter length coat, which seemed to conceal the hidden object better than had been expected, she took the jacket from Zo, however she did not wear it despite the chill in the air, she simply folded it up and placed it over her arm.

"What's the deal with this place anyway? I mean I've heard rumours of such a place existing but…" Elly gave a sigh wondering if the entire journey would be like this, if time after time she would more become source to the group's questions, she looked to Eiji having Daniel pestering her was bad enough, but if he were to start as well.

"A long time ago, this town housed the most respected magic users this world had seen, but foolishly, they *all* sacrificed their magic along with the others, to aid the Idliod in the creation of the Grimoire."

"Wait, so how come Zo can use magic? If it was all sacrificed surely…" Daniel took the question right from Zo's lips, it had been something both of them had wanted to ask since Elly had mentioned the sealing of Hectarian magic, after all it seemed if anyone knew the answer, she would, but neither of them at the time had thought to do so with so much going on.

"It's difficult to explain, the Elementalists refused to give their power, it was thought too dangerous to sacrifice their control, although it would have been of little use if they had. Night and Gaea go back a long way, yet still, her magic was intertwined with that of Hecate's to create the nine seals erected by the ancients, for every creature to sacrifice their magic would be to break the seals. Some Hectarians however, believed they had taken the power from the very life-force of the people who used it. It seems at least one Hectarian was able to somehow able to shield themselves from detection, thus the power was never taken from her." She looked to

Zo meaningfully. "The spell cast was so powerful, so complete, even the powers from unborn children and those that would be born in centuries to come who would have possessed the arts, would not know of their true destiny, nor would they taste the powers that could have been theirs. It was thought to be unnecessary, but the Idliod wanted to be certain, although unlikely, some in future generations may be born into this world with the fleeting remnants of what may have become great power, although their talents would never truly evolve. My only thought is she must have been shielded, made invisible so to speak, as would be the case if further Hectarians remain." Elly stated bluntly knowing that no such people exist, but it was better to be vague with this than to invite further questions, or even tell a truth none were ready to hear.

"So in other words you don't know?" Daniel questioned.

"The exact reason no, but if I were to explain the part I did know, it would go far above your level of comprehension." Elly snorted her reply as he made a mimicking motion behind her back, much to Zo's amusement. Elly oblivious to the others walked onto the dust road instantly vanishing from sight, they followed quickly, feeling the slight pull of resistance as they entered the silver light until finally their ears were greeted with the sounds of a busy city.

It was unmistakably different from the outside, an exact opposite in fact, the tiny deserted town had transformed into an enormous city bustling with life and buildings. The entrance had brought them in near the first of the local taverns, already jolly chanting and life flooded out onto the air of the near by street, people laughing, singing and generally being merry without a trouble in the world. The streets hummed with life, the small market stalls set on either the side of the paths spread their contents on brightly coloured blankets. Banter such as.

'You're robbing me…. I have a wife and three children to feed.' And

'You won't find a better deal anywhere.' Filled the air around them as they walked, occasionally the odd merchant would follow them goods in hand trying to convince them to buy, despite their persistence they never strayed too far from their stall, no doubt in fear of thieves. Eventually, as they exited the row of blankets, the merchants stopped following them, muttering to themselves quietly at having made the walk for nothing.

Elly remembered the first time she had brought Marise here all to clearly and wondered if seeing this place again would return such memories, later on, she would have to ensure she took a good look around.

It had everything, inns, floor level stores, tents, stores built into people's homes, everything you could imagine, anything you could ever want, all here and stretching as far as the eye could see.

"What is this place? It's amazing." Daniel questioned his voice filled with awe as he ventured from stall to stall, quickly glancing over everything with a keen eye, he had got the hint that they were not to dawdle, but still, he wished to look.

"It's kind of like a bazaar, but only certain people can enter, those who enter may bring guests you get the idea, once a person has entered they can return at any point." She answered while pulling him from a nearby stall, until now she had slowed her pace to allow a small amount of browsing, at least that is how it would have seemed to the others, but her unnoticed movements were almost predator like, almost like a hunter watching for any threat that may present itself, she was glad this place remained neutral to the conflicts of the outside world, but even so, not everyone that walked here lived here, it would take just one person and the entire plan would be ruined, but now the need to quicken their pace had presented itself, from the shadows, she had caught sight of a hunter.

"What kind of certain people?" Acha whispered timidly almost fearful of the answer to her question.

"Special people… it is kind of…" Elly stopped, as she had turned to look to Acha, the hunter had made his move, vanishing from sight. Despite the law immunity they had in this place, the law of a hunter was one of their own, she glanced quickly to Zo before scanning the area again, he had vanished completely. "Anyway, what we want is this way." She grabbed Daniel once more from the stores. "Anyone would think you were a child the way you carried on" She scolded leading them through the winding maze that was the city, looping around occasionally to throw off any watching from the shadows, she kept hearing words of awe and amazement, every now and then to her annoyance she would find herself having to back track a little way to find them, until eventually, when she stopped checking behind her, they stopped browsing knowing there was no choice but to follow, should they wish to see the outside world again. As she navigated the streets, Elly found herself recalling Marise's first visit to these walls…

…"Staying here should prove easier than anticipated." Elly smiled as they left the horses with the Collateral dealer for safe keeping, Elly's words broke Marise's gaze on the stable hand, he was a young boy no older than fourteen, she made a mental note of his appearance, from his short scruffy hair, to his cautious brown eyes, should anything happen to her horse he, would be personally responsible.

"Why's that?" She questioned glancing around, nothing seemed out of the ordinary, just everyday people going about their everyday business, the merchants sat either side of the wide dust track showing their goods to all that passed. Some of the small houses had shops built into them, their goods displayed on small ledges outside as well as inside, generally very little of great use or expense would be displayed outside, the real goods, that which would make a large profit, or be of interest to those with light fingers, always sat securely on the inside ledges, where the merchants could keep a close eye on their prized stock.

"Well, it doesn't seem like they know who you are." She smiled, as Marise had noticed, nothing was out of the ordinary, for their safety it would be better it stayed this way, if they were to draw unnecessary attention to themselves it could prove difficult to travel with ease. "The longer it stays this way, the easier it will be for us to travel, come on, let's get our room." Elly led the way through the winding paths of the town, it was much larger than Marise had first anticipated, it was little past noon and already the streets were filled with people, the roar of laughter from the near by taverns echoed through the air. Small tents and blankets lined the streets that they walked, merchants trying to push their goods towards all who passed by, telling them stories of how they need to feed their wife and children, saying anything they thought would seal them a sale, Elly and Marise passed through pretty much unnoticed.

Elly stopped at a small shop, it was different to all the others, it consisted of both a house and a tent, inside the tent, were some specialist goods that no thief would dare to steal, the tent itself led from the counter into the merchant's house, a blind man stood at the window as she examined the goods.

"Good day to you, I am Venrent, how can I be of service to you ladies today?" He extended his hand in warm greeting, Elly took his hand through the window shaking it gently "your hands are cold; perhaps you need some ginger to aid circulation?" He questioned.

"No thank you." Elly smiled withdrawing her hand. "My friend and I are about to start a great mission, I was hoping that I may buy some of your finest rope."

"What kind of rope are you looking for, I have many kinds, each threaded specifically for terrain, there's mountain rope, dungeon rope, training rope, climbing rope, trap rope..."

"Multipurpose." Elly interrupted, she didn't wish him to go through all twenty forms of rope she had already spotted behind the counter. "We are not really sure what we may face."

"Adventurer rope it is then." He vanished for a moment.

"What's the difference?" Marise questioned as the old man left the room, he seemed to pause in the doorway, Elly suddenly realised why.

"Strength and durability depending on how the sections are threaded, whether or not they have elastic properties and such, Mari, we could do with some more thread, would you go over there and fetch me some." Elly pointed to a small tent a good street from where they now stood; she had to get her away from this place quickly.

"What kind of thread?"

"For repairs." Elly smiled handing her some money. "Go, I will join you shortly." Marise left, she had barely reached the end of the street when the shop door opened and the elderly merchant reappeared at the window holding several lengths of rope.

"So where is it you ladies plan on journeying to?" Elly took them from him, sizing up the ones she wanted before handing the rest back to him, despite his blindness he navigated well.

"We're going on a pilgrimage, following the steps of the great priestess Sandra."

"I see, tell me, your companions name, is it Zodiac?" He questioned suddenly, he had to ask, he had been sure the voice he had heard was that of Kez's daughter.

"No I'm afraid not, is she too walking the path of the priestess, if we should meet her on our journey is there anything you wish me to tell her?" Elly questioned smiling slightly, he may be blind, but his senses were sharp, she would have to be more careful.

"Oh... no never mind, I could have sworn I heard her voice." He gave a sigh before smiling "not to worry, old age has an advantage over me, so that's four adventurer ropes at thirty-nine each, that's let's call it one-twenty shall we, for such a noble pilgrimage." Elly passed him several gold coins.

"Thank you." She smiled before leaving to find Marise that had been a little too close.

Marise waited patiently outside the small tent, watching each person as they walked the streets, she moved slightly as Elly approached passing her the ball of fine thread.

"What was that all about?" Marise had known she had wanted her to leave in silence, but her reason was unclear, it was something now they were free to talk, she felt the need to question.

"Venrent, the merchant back there is from Drevera, when you spoke earlier, there was recognition in his posture."

"But… I've never seen him before". Marise stated as she followed Elly as she led the way to the inn.

"True as that may be, I think he recognised you as your predecessor." Elly stated, all at once things became clear to her.

"But he's blind."

"But his senses are sharp, there are many things apart from looks that give away a person's identity, you know that." Elly stated as they finally reached the doors of the inn…

…Finally at the end of the winding paths, they reached a small inn, smaller by far than any of the others they had so far laid eyes on, it was possibly in one of the worst locations a small business could hope to stand, yet despite being hard to locate, its exterior showed no marks of its poor location.

"Elaineor!" The inn keeper greeted her with open arms as she set foot through the door. "I have reserved the three bedrooms just as you requested" His tubby arms spread wide as if to embrace her, his smile faded slightly as he met her cold gaze and his arms soon lowered, within seconds his mercenary smile had once more planted itself on his chubby face, as he waddled to the cash register, fidgeting underneath the desk before returning to them.

It was hard to look at him for too long, the explosion of colours painful to the eyes, his attire making him appear more like something you would find at a circus, rather than running an inn, his smile greeted the others until his eyes fell upon Zo, he stared at her sometime darkness wrinkled his brow. "I told you last time Elaineor" his voice although already low was silenced by a single wave of her hand.

"I see you are only a three bedroom inn, and as you see, along my path I seem to have acquired more companions maybe I should take my business elsewhere." She said flippantly.

"No, there's no need, no need at all I tell you, of course if there's any…" Another wave silenced him once more, Zo looked to Daniel, they both had wanted to hear the rest of that sentence.

"Very well, let us try this again, my companions and I wish to rest, we have much to discuss and in accordance with our prior arrangement. I am awaiting the handing over of the keys and the vacating of any other clients or help understand?"

"Of course, of course, whatever you wish my dear." He smiled rubbing his grimy little hands together. "But my silence does not come cheap." Elly nodded placing a tightly wrapped bundle of money on the counter in front of him he flicked through it listening to the hum of the notes knowing exactly how much had been placed before him by the flick of the last note, he frowned slightly. "You jest, do you not? My silence is not brought so cheaply, I have a wife and three children… imagine if people were to find out…" Before he could finish his face lit up as another bundle of rolled cash was placed before him, he took them in his hands that seemed to be covered in a strange pinkish goo.

"I could however, for this purchase my own inn." She sighed tapping the counter with her finger impatiently as he once more listened to the hum of the notes.

"Indeed, but you know very well you cannot guarantee your security in such a place,"

"Indeed." She sighed reluctantly, the old magic used to create this place had long since vanished, there was little choice but to pay what he asked well, there was one other option, but it was too messy, too much hassle, besides, as much as she hated the slimy innkeeper, this place was, as he said, secure, in fact, it was the safest place she knew, and she had been to many, she had spent much time in this inn with Marise, years in fact "they say there is not a more honest person than one who is paid highly for his services, especially since the rest of the money shall not be received until our departure. Although I am tempted to seek elsewhere they are not such con-merchants as you." She smiled leaning against the desk while the others just watched in awed horror.

"Ah, but should you do that, I have information now, that may cause more trouble than you wish to confront am I right? I mean I could let them know. True they may not see it at first but through hysteria, all things become clearer."

"Would the town, or more importantly *you*, survive if you did?" Elly turned to smile at Zo before returning to the conversation, she couldn't help feeling there was something in that look, she frowned trying to work out its code, trying to grasp the reason this place seemed familiar to her but was once more distracted by the innkeeper, she listened carefully hoping he would speak a further clue.

"Very well... my lips are sealed I shall take this half, then on my return, the other, should you be satisfied with the services I have provided... which of course I am sure you will be." His sticky fingers handed the set of keys to Elly, who didn't seem all too bothered that some of the gunk had been transferred to her own hands, in fact she seemed not to notice, for the second time since their arrival here, she was recalling her first trip here with Marise...

..."Elaineor!" No sooner had the bell above the door rang than this greeting filled the air, a stout man dressed in a bright yellow shirt rose to his feet from behind the counter, a mercenary smile on his face. "Could it be you have come to stay once more? It has been years. However did you convince your employer?"

"Blackwood?" She questioned sarcastically. "He is *not* my employer, I ask if you remember one thing, it is that."

"Well if you're here, does that mean this is...?" He looked at the figure that stood besides her, a frown forming on his face as he took in her child like appearance, she must have been no older than fifteen maybe sixteen, her vivid red hair framed her face giving her something of a wild appearance, although she wore black hakama trousers worn by all great warriors and assassins, she did not look like either, her black lace up top had splits in the shoulder leaving them uncovered in a possible attempt to reduce restriction of movement, the top itself was flattering and hugged her feminine figure tightly, yet there was still no escaping she was nothing more than a child and certainly not a warrior, Elly must be playing with him.

"Yes, this is Marise." Elaineor answered coldly seeing the shock on the innkeeper's face; she was clearly not what he had expected.

"This... she is Marise?" His tone taking on light humour, surely Elaineor was joking, the girl that stood before his was nothing more than a small child, her build alone was not that of a great warrior "I expected her to be..." He paused, something about the way the young assassin looked at him almost froze his blood, he swallowed hard before finding the courage to continue. "Taller, I expected her to be taller." His voice seemed to break, how could a child make him feel so weak? He had confronted grown men that did not hold that kind of power over him, Elly smiled admiring his courage to voice his criticism, but more than anything, she was grateful for Marise's reserve, she had cut many a man down for less than the words he had spoken.

"Another smart remark like that and it may be you remembering yourself taller." Marise whispered quietly leaning forwards onto the desk; he seemed to retreat a few steps.

"Sorry miss." He squeaked before turning his attention back to Elly as she moved Marise back behind her. "So, what brings you here this time?"

"A mission, that's all you need to know, now tell me, what do I owe you for the room?" She placed the small box on the desk.

"Normal conditions?" He asked rubbing his hands together at the joy of what was to come.

"No. it seems you already have guests, and as yet, the people of this town have not put the name to a face, so for now, just a room, besides, it would be difficult for you to explain to your guests why they all must leave" Elly glanced to the coat stand, it seemed the inn was almost at maximum capacity.

"For you Elaineor, I could justify anything."

"For me? Or my money?" She questioned dryly.

"How long do you plan on staying this time?" He questioned, deciding it better not to answer the proposed question, it was an answer she knew too well.

"Indefinitely." She answered, watching as the mercenary smile as it once more appeared on his face.

"Normal price." He smiled as a look of amusement crossed Elly's face.

"Normal price? For just a room?" She shook her head in mild amusement.

"One room or three, it's all the same."

"Please, humour me, explain your logic." She tapped her finger on the box resting on the counter.

"The way I see it, you're not only paying for a room, you're harbouring a criminal, my silence is a valuable asset."

"True as that may be, I could always ensure your silence." Marise warned, Elly silenced her with a raise of her hand, she become so aggressive lately, she always seemed to be hunting for blood, something Elly would have to address, she may be an assassin, but there was a healthy level of desire, watching everyone for something that would justify a kill was neither something she taught, nor something she could justify as healthy.

"For what you are asking, I could, of course, buy my own inn."

"True, but as you know, this inn is special." He answered smugly. "Not another one like it on the planet." Elly pushed the box towards him, he grabbed it quickly peering inside it, his eyes lighting up as he gazed upon its content before sliding a single key across the desk.

"Let me know when you require more… and *don't* think I won't be counting." She warned

"Exactly… how long is indefinitely?" His eyes flitted from Elly to the box several times.

"Now, if I knew that, it wouldn't be indefinitely now would it?" She questioned as she led Marise to their room. The room itself shared the same bad décor found throughout the rest of the house, the two beds rested at the far wall separated by some draws, at the base of the bed was a vanity table filled with strange ornaments.

Elly had barely placed her backpack down when Marise questioned her actions

"Why? Why pay him that much? I could have negotiated a much better offer." She fingered the hilt of her sword, an action Elly had seen too much of recently.

"Enough." Elly scolded. "I trust him, I've know his family for what seems like forever." She smiled thinking back over the years to her first stay in this inn.

"But he'd sell you out if the price was right!" She protested "it would be safer to…"

"I trust him." She repeated. "There is nothing as secure as greed. Besides, whatever the price, it could not compare to what I offer." She stated.

"But… where do you get such funding?" Marise questioned, wondering if perhaps Night paid for their expenses, but something told her she was wrong.

"For now, let's just say, money is not exactly an issue to someone like me." She stated finishing the conversation. Elly fingered each of the ornaments in turn, before searching the rest of the room, by the time she had finished she held several small pieces of ancient technology in her hand. "Come on; let's go get something to eat." Elly led Marise to the dining room, it was barely large enough to hold the enormous table that stood within it, she motioned for Marise to sit while she paid the innkeeper a visit.

"I trust everything is to your liking." The innkeeper smiled, Elly showed him the technology in her hand watching the horror on his face as she crushed them beneath her foot.

"It is now." She smiled. "How many times must I warn you? My conversations are not for your ears, and if you so much as even think of spying on us in your passage way, so help me I will have Marise deal with you, you are expendable as long as I have your keys, or do you forget I know the secrets of this place." She warned turning away. "And don't even think about putting them back tomorrow."

"I wouldn't dream of it." He whispered looking at the small pieces of broken technology, he should have known better by now, Elly always found his bugs. "I take it by your warning, you do not expect to be back tomorrow evening?" He questioned

"No." She stated. "I have made other arrangements."

"You know, I will still be charging you for your room, it is all the same to me whether you return or not." Elly nodded, she hadn't expected any different, before joining Marise at the table she hung her coat over the enormous portrait of the innkeeper, a portrait that disguised the entrance to one of the secret passages. She joined Marise at the table, taking her in a sandwich from the kitchen.

"So we won't be staying here tomorrow?" Marise questioned before taking a bite of the sandwich, she had been able to hear every word of Elly's conversation.

"No, we need to follow up on a lead I have."

"You mean a…" Elly raised her hand to silence Marise as two of the other lodgers passed them to go into the kitchen.

Elly glanced outside, it was already getting quite late, the torches lit the street corners, already the merchants were beginning to pack up their blankets.

"Tomorrow's going to be a busy day, so you're going to need plenty of rest, we'll start out at dawn"…

…"Aren't you forgetting something?" Elly asked sliding the keys over the loop slowly, he paused as he reached the door, she pulled herself away from the memory, it was a clever thing they had achieved here, the memories that Zo would have remembered that would be detrimental to their mission had been, by enchantment, transferred into Elly instead, that was one of Annabel's greatest skills, stopping the memories before they surfaced by transporting them into another being, but shortly, this would stop as Annabel was taken to the underworld, soon it would be time for the darkness to be filled, of course, before that could happen, certain events had to fall into place.

"I don't think so, blinds drawn, tea cooking, beds made, you have the keys… nope, nothing I can think of." He counted the points on his chubby fingers before turning to leave again.

"The passage keys maybe?" Elly dropped the last key over the ring the sound of it falling to meet the others seemed to slice through the silence, her gaze piecing through him.

"Passageways? Your suspicion offends…." He laughed nervously his gaze fell from hers before he dug deep into is pocket producing three small keys.

"Thank you." She smiled helping him through the door before locking it as he finally took his leave. The others followed her out of the foyer, still in silent horror over the amount of money she carelessly handed over without so much as a second thought, they knew she was of good upbringing, from a rich family, but still, what they had just witnessed surely bordered on insanity.

"Are you sure we can trust him?" Eiji was the first to speak, he alone aside from Elly that knew the threat that had left the innkeeper's lips, as they entered the bright red dining room barely big enough to hold the six place table already set with napkins cutlery, almost like a silver service restaurant, although from the bad décor it would barely pass for the children's playroom. A large portrait of the owner wearing the same pink and yellow striped trousers with and equally grotesque green and blue polka dot shirt hung on the wall opposite the drawn blinds, Elly took her coat from Zo who was busy warming herself by the log fire along with Daniel and Acha, they seemed to have been sharing a hushed conversation right up until the moment Elly had approached.

"He dare not betray us." She whispered as she passed him. "He would loose far too much money." Her tone returned to normal. "There is nothing as secure as greed. Besides I've used him a thousand times, each time we exchange the same playful banter although the price never varies." As she spoke she hung her coat over the giant portrait, despite its size the black leather coat just about covered it. "Anyway, once he's left the keys in the hands of another, he couldn't find his way back here with sextant readings. This place is like this town but to a lesser scale, once its keys are secured no one can enter without reservations and it cannot be located until expiry of said reservation, other than by who reside within of course." She checked under the table smiling slightly. "He's getting careless." She smiled unplugging the small microphone. "Now I'm certain there's no one listening there are a few things you need to know, after hearing them any of you are free to leave, with one obvious exception." She looked at Zo and gave her what she thought to be comforting smile that in fact sent shivers down her spine.

"What kind of things?" Daniel asked after a prompting nudge from Acha who now sat to one side of him at the dining table, Zo pulled a chair to his other side leaving Eiji and Elly sitting with a gap between them.

"Well, since you two invited yourselves along." She looked at Daniel and Acha. "And you had no choice but to accompany me." Her steady gaze resting on Eiji before turning away. "You should at least know what you're getting yourselves into." she sighed as she glanced around the table, this wasn't how it was meant to be, it was meant to be just her and Marise, she hadn't counted on being followed, nor on Marise's friends inviting themselves along, she gave another sigh "as you probably know the legends about Night, are true but he has been dormant, for over two decades, long enough for people to forget the true terror of his work, to doubt the sincerity of the tale, to even doubt his existence by referring to him as a legend, that along with the passing of time gives people time to tone down his stories making them less fearful, or twisting them to nothing more than fairytale, adopting the typical attitude of what does it matter now anyway? His powers *were* sealed away."

"But you said about the Grimoire before so who..." Daniel's interruption earned him a scolding look from across the table, he felt himself shrink away slightly as she continued.

"I'm getting to it... anyway, his powers were sealed away in some magical books called the Grimoire, they were a combined effort of all the Hectarians, who gave their power to the Idliod to aid their creation, the first four, sealed away his elemental magic, the fifth sealed his destructive or Black magic, the sixth, his light and life-force magic, you know mind control, healing, that kind of thing, but not even the Idliod knew what was contained within the seventh. Night was aware of the plan among them, and set out to face them. He had known ultimately it would come to this, before they could succeed with their plan would be he would try to stop them, but as the prophesies had told, he was overpowered, Blood magic of course, is by far the most potent magic, but these seven did something that far exceeded it, they gave not only their blood but life-force too, creating the most powerful seal of all." She looked up to see the blank expressions of those she spoke to, she wondered for a moment if they had been listening at all. "It is easier for me to show you." She removed a small crystal from her pocket, this seemed to grab their attention more than her story had.

"Is that..." Daniel gasped.

"A gossip crystal? Yes," She stated dismissively.

"Where did you get one? I heard rumours of such things, six are said to exist throughout the entire world, when you use it, you see facts as they were not as history dictates, each one is empowered with the memory of the earth Goddess herself... It is like watching the past play out before you uncorrupted by times translation." He gasped, all crystals in the right hands could do such things, but only gossip crystals would do so out of the hands of a God.

"Enough of the lesson, do you want to know or not?" Elly scolded as the four companions leaned in to look at the crystal...

..."Finally the last spell is complete, Hectarians the world over surrendered their power to us for this cause" the middle-aged man, now seeming much older leaned breathlessly against the table as he rose to his feet, watched by all, his black hair somehow seemed paler than the hours before, when the seven had sat to begin.

"Surely this method is reckless... if it were to fail." An elderly man rose to his feet, his shaking hand securing the cane that rested besides his chair, his cold grey eyes filled with doubt and worry.

"It is the only way, what other choice do we have, we are but mortal, he is a God"

"But... to use their magic, is to take it, Hectarian magic will be all but dead to the world." The other five sat in silence listening as the conversation volleyed between the two each stating convincing opinions on why their view was correct, the outcome would change the world forever one way or another.

"The only chance we have of overcoming him is to take his magic, don't you see? It is our *only* choice; it's our *only* chance to be free." The younger man banged his hand upon the solid oaken table as if to emphasise his point.

"But surely you must consider afterwards, not a single Hectarian will possess the power even to foil a simple attack, the magic that once powered our homes our cities will be lost forever as we return to the old ways, even should one emerge by some miracle, they could not develop their power, the lack of users ensures that, to nurse a spark so small alone into a flame would be impossible."

"There will be the Elementalists. True the price is high, but is it really? Is it too high a price to pay to ensure tomorrow for our children?"

"If we fail..." The old man lowered his head. "If we fail we have no hope to stand against him."

"If we do not try what hope is there then? You have seen yourself his history, if we leave him be, he will surely repeat his deeds." The younger man still as powerful as ever in his tones as the older man grew weary, he knew the young man's argument would win, but it was his place to stand against him, after all to not voice doubts is to weaken the power, each member must be completely committed to the decision, should the power of their magic not wish to be compromised.

He slowly glanced around the other members looking at each one in turn his eye contact piecing the souls of each as he did so. The younger man's eyes stayed focused on the old man opposite the table; at least a minute had passed before he spoke again.

"What would happen should he seize the books and his power once more be restored?" The younger man broke his gaze looking down to his battered sandals for but a second, this question had taken him by surprise, he was unsure why, but the possibility felt like cold icy finger down his spine, he suppressed a shudder.

"There will be none of such magical capabilities that could achieve that, no one with that power will remain, we have seen to that by the completion of the spell just done."

"But if there were."

"Should all the forces be penetrated? Should he find a Hectarian with enough of the now lost power to diminish the protective barriers? Impossible as that may be?" He smiled slightly finding the improbability of this final doubt amusing, the moment of doubt nothing more that a fading dream, the thoughts of such safeguards being defeated was impossible all this question had done was add to his already overconfident tone. "Are you forgetting even should they be obtained, the last book must be taken by his own kin of which he has none. It is impossible, for a being such as him, he could only create a child from love, something his long dead heart has no capacity for and besides, why would he interact with a race he finds so disgusting?"

"He could take it himself."

"Only should his heart be pure, then for what purpose would he need it?"

"Still, if it were the case would he not still have the other six, the six we were expecting and not the seventh which we know not its power?"

"True there is one more than expected." The young man touched the book that had formed before him, although this would lessen the final seal of the spell he was confident their plan would work what magic they possessed now would be enough to seal his powers and banish the books. "And within it we know not what secrets lay. Let us not focus on what is impossible, but what is possible, we can stop him now, but time grows short, so I ask you fellow members of the Idliod what be your choice?" The young man returned a respectful nod of the elder, he one who faced him in debate as he took his seat.

"Our soul's concerns were voiced and argued admirably by the former elder." The young red haired girl spoke up, her cat like ears twitching slightly as she became the recipient of stares from the other members.

"Indeed, I feel no matter how risky it is, it is less risky than him remaining unopposed." A gentlemen, was the next to speak, his voice been met with other mumbles of agreement before the young man commanded attention.

"Before you commit on this there are some other thoughts I wish to voice, firstly to thank my father for a well presented debate." He bowed his head to the elder man whose cane one more rested by his chair. "Secondly, as with all things, this too carries a cost, I believe you are all aware of the price that must be paid, still, no respect would be lost should any of you wish to leave and not continue, after all, we are the ones to pay the greater price for this freedom, if any of you have any doubts, speak now." Minutes of silence passed the young man were relieved to see none left "that said, we shall begin the final preparation." He joined them once more sitting at the table where in front of each of the seven members lay a book, each a different colour, each possessing a different symbol of the likes none of them had ever seen before. Inside, the pages remained blank, they linked hands around the table, making permanent their taking of Hectarian magic to fuel their spell, it would not be long now until he came.

The ground trembled as the room grew slightly darker, the Idliod exchanged a final glance before preparing themselves at what was to be their final resting place, each one in turn opened the book that had linked itself to their life force. They flicked through the pages as if to study what was on them, a huge light enveloped the room, their death was almost instant, but not in the slightest painless as their blood erupted from the bodies covering the books that lay before them. Night watched satisfied with his work, yet he knew something was not quite right, as he stood there he felt his energy leaving him, it was all happening as it had been written. He approached the one who had recently been inducted as the elder of the Idliod, he had carefully calculated breath still within his body, he was to suffer the most but not by actions, he was to know the truth, he was the one who betrayed him, the others like sheep had simply followed. He placed his hand on his head and smiled using his hair to raise him.

"What were you thinking? I see it all, your memories are no secret to me, you think you will find peace in knowing your books shall stop me." He watched as the young man smiled. "I knew your plan."

"Then... why..." He gasped still smiling.

"My own books here wall to wall at your disposal, do they not tell you of the rising of a maiden, or did you learn nothing from me? I shall wait, twelve years is a mere blink of an eye to one such as myself, I shall regain my powers, and claim yours by doing so when she arises."

"You... rely... too... much... on... hearsay." He smiled.

"That is where you are wrong." Night smiled leaning close to young man, he whispered quietly into his ear, the smile faded and his eyes grew wide with terror as he took his last breath. The bodies of the seven vanished, absorbed into the books, Night approached one of the books, watching it fade from the air as he smiled to himself "Patience has always been a strong point of mine"...

...As the image faded Elly placed the crystal back within her pocket and continued the tale where the images left off.

"Despite these words Night now was powerless but for his immortality and took this time to wandered the world in search of the seven books, when he felt their presence he made a note, yet without his powers he could never be certain if it was indeed a Grimoire or one of the nine seals contained on this world. Then one day, by sheer luck he came face to face with one, it was unguarded, hidden within a old bookcase overlooked by all who pass it, he ran his fingers along the books, finding they could go no further than the one it sat next to, even that sent searing pains up his arms and chest, although none knew who he was, they knew enough from his stature to fear him once he had left, the town feared he may return, and so handed the book that he had shown such an interest in into the care of the temple. His name had been watered down in the years that passed, only the elders of the villages who knew his wrath truly feared him, to others, even those whose homes he destroyed, he was becoming no more than a fairy tale, everything was going according to plan." She paused looking between them. "The first were located in temples it was thought no human would be able to survive, even if they were gifted with Hectarian magic, one appeared in a town hidden in an ordinary bookcase, looked over by until a stranger had showed an interest and it was relocated, another was sent to a place of myth and another to a place of darkness and rumour. As for the seventh, its whereabouts are a mystery, but once she seizes that last book, the last of his power will return."

"By her... you mean the one who already obtained the other six correct?" Eiji questioned frowning as he chose his words carefully, the last thing he wanted was another slap across the head, he was still recovering for the last one, although he didn't let on, it had hurt far more than he expected, he lowered his arm finding himself unconsciously rubbing the back of his head.

"Correct, if his final powers were to be released the world as we know it would be no more." Elly smiled slightly contemplating this thought for a moment.

"But Marise Shi disappeared ages ago." Daniel stated, Elly looked to him in surprise, before he had made out he knew nothing of the Grimoire, yet now he not only showed knowledge of them, but of the one who obtained them, Elly had believed none knew it was Marise who had collected them, she couldn't help wondering how he had come across the knowledge and if he knew, surely many others did also, his comment showed the need for extra caution, if they were to realise exactly what was happening, things would not run s smoothly.

"Indeed." Elly sighed not only did she not like the thought of him knowing things, he should not, she was growing tired of his interruptions. "But that doesn't mean she still can't get the final Grimoire, I repeat, the first three were hidden in impenetrable fortresses, do I really need to continue? The point is all seven of them were thought unobtainable and all but one has been retrieved, the seventh however, is meant to be the most secure as no one knows its whereabouts."

"Surely someone does… I mean it had to get there in the first place couldn't Marise just get the information from the person who hid it?"

"Impossible." Elly sighed wondering if they understood any of what she just spoke, or even the images they just watched, did he really think the books were sent to people to hide? That would have made things much easier.

"But the leader of the Idliod said…" Daniel began

"You would think so wouldn't you? Yet I'm certain there is a way for Marise to obtain that final book" Elly this time chose to interrupt Daniel. Unseen by anyone Acha sunk a little in her chair, the man she had seen in the crystal, although they did not actually *see* him as such, by name alone was her father, hidden under the black cape hiding his face from all; she knew it would be him, the man who used her to re-obtain his immortality. "You would be surprised what a little ambition and a lot of knowledge can do."

"You talk of her as if you know her." Acha spoke once she was certain Elly had finished, the thought of her knowing Marise unnerved her, especially if they were to discover her relations to the caped figure, all kinds of problems could arise.

"Yes, I do." Elly's answer as always was simple and to the point, also a catalyst for a million other questions, she smiled to herself as she ventured into the kitchen moments before the chief's timer sounded, even now it amused her she could make such simple mistakes.

"What!" Daniel exclaimed. "You've actually met her?" Elly left her answer until she had returned carrying the nicely browned chicken.

"Uh huh." She replied returning to the kitchen to carry in the bread and butter that had been carefully prepared for their arrival, well surely if she hadn't said something now, Eiji would have opened his mouth and put his foot right into it as normal. "I asked Mr Francis to prepare tea for us." She looked at the bread covered in the same gunk as his hands had previously, she looked at the others smiling at the thought of them eating it, but then she turned to Zo she gave a sigh returning to the kitchen quickly preparing some gunk free bread.

"So you've actually met her?… Face to face?… And lived?" Daniel avoided her attempt to change topics with ease.

"Uh huh… please help yourself, who knows when we'll get chance to eat like this again."

"But I thought none who met her survived" this time it was Acha who pressed the topic further.

"We were friends." Elly began to carve the giant chicken wondering if there would be anyway to safely store the leftovers for the trip; she was also waiting for the

69

reaction that would follow her comment.

"Friends!" Spat Daniel almost choking on the bread he had swallowed "with a blood thirsty murderer?"

"Yes." Elly passed Zo a plate with some meat and bread on, she was now the only person who wasn't eating, wherever she was, it wasn't in the room with the others, she seemed so far away, lost in her thoughts, Elly tried to place her location holding the plate a moment longer before placing it down, startling her as she did so. "Come see me after you have freshened up later, there is something I wish to… give you." The others all exchanged glances, all curious what this something could be, where as Zo simply nodded staring at the food before her.

***

"There are only three rooms; two of us will have to bunk together in the double rooms." Eiji stated emerging from the bathroom rubbing his hair vigorously with a towel, his clean clothes still warm from the furnace, they each in turn had used to wash and dry their clothes in, remarkable invention, more often than not the clothes were dry even before the wearer had finished pumping the water ready to shower.

"I shall stay with Elly then." Zo muttered, her hair still dripping, her shortest layer clinging to her face for a moment before she brushed it away, concern flickered through Daniel's eyes, of all people why had she chosen Elly? She could have chosen him, or if it was the female aspect, Acha, who she shared a room with for the past few months anyway, the others seemingly satisfied with this arrangement left to their rooms leaving Daniel and Zo alone in the hallway.

"Are you ok?" He asked touching her shoulder gently, she turned to him with an obviously forced smile, her eyes filled with an array of emotions.

"Yes." Her answer came out more like a question than the positive statement she had intended.

"What did Elaineor want?" He pulled his face as he spoke her name.

"Oh… she… erm, gave me some old clothes of mine…" She sighed. "For all I know they could be from the local store." She let out another sigh staring blankly towards the floor.

"Say… do you care for a walk before turning in?" He asked already knowing the answer, whenever things became a little too overwhelming for her, a walk had always seemed to calm her down, there had been many occasions as her memories came back when she grew frustrated or tired, she had tried so hard to retain the memories, to keep them coming, but the harder she tried the quicker they left leaving her more and more frustrated.

"Would you mind?" She looked at him gratefully tying her wet hair back into a ponytail, getting out of here, away from this inn, was something she desperately needed, she wanted for just a moment to leave Elly and everyone else behind. "And we could always go look at some of those stores while we're here." She smiled watching his face light up, she knew from the moment they arrived here he would be desperate to take a good look around, although most of the stores sold run of the mill items, there were the odd ones that seemed to have the odd rare and magical items. "I saw a few things you just have to get." Daniel couldn't help feeling this new found enthusiasm was a display for his benefit, he was right to a certain degree.

"That sounds wonderful." He linked her arm gently as they began towards the door.

"And where do you think you're going?" Just as they reached the door Elly's voice echoed from the staircase above stopping them in their tracks, for a moment everything fell silent as she walked towards them.

"For a walk... I need some air." Zo looked at Elly who now stood before them, her hardened expression seemed to soften a little, as she looked to her, for a second it seemed a strange sympathy crossed her features.

"Alright, but hurry back and don't draw any attention to yourselves... be back by sunset, here's a list of supplies we need, you know rope, food, that kind of thing, since you're going out, there's an excellent rope store not far from the tavern." She gave Daniel the list and some money, she leaned in close to him and whispered something he nodded and without wasting anymore time, they left.

"What did she say?" Zo asked linking Daniel once more as they entered the bustling town.

"She told me not to let you out of my sight." He watched her frown at his words.

"There's something she's not telling me."

"Everything?" He attempted to say it with little sarcasm but it came out wrong, well he could only be true to himself and that was what he truly believed she knew so much more than she would ever let on, he had to wonder why, she was planning to keep them safe, but other than that, they knew nothing more about the situation than when she first appeared.

"Well... yeah." Zo sighed leaning against the side of a pub, even from the outside she could feel the music as it vibrated through the walls along with eruptions of laughter. "It's just so... frustrating. I mean she knows everything about me... about what's happening... earlier I thought she was going to tell us something about what was going on, yet instead she told us a story, not related to me... or this situation, it's like she does it on purpose... she knows everything yet..." She gave a frustrated sigh wrapping her arms around herself.

"Treats you like a child? And answers one question with another?"

"Exactly, I mean I don't even know why I'm here, why was I in danger in the first place... it's not as if I have some great power" she stated, Daniel saw the concentration on her face as she probed the darkness, her memories, looking for anything that would offer a clue to what this was about.

"She seemed to think different." He stated finally after a few moments silence.

"Come on Daniel." She sighed as they started on their way again. "This." A small ball of flame erupted from the air above her hand. "This is the best I can do." She lied, there were other things she knew she could do, things so dark they chilled her to the bone, the conversation passer-bys them fell silent as people stopped to look, she quickly willed it to vanish, it was another few moments before conversation resumed at a hushed level.

"I've seen a lot of things, I've seen you create fire from air, I've seen you turn a baron waste land into a once more thriving herb garden, you use your magic to heal the sick. I've seen the effort and determination you put into every little thing you do, the love and hope you give to others... that's your real power Zo, not your magic, your heart." Daniel stated glancing over the sheer volume of ropes stored behind this particular store's counter.

"Zo did you say? Yes, yes, the resemblance is clear." The cashier extended the bag over the counter to Daniel before placing his coarse hands upon Zo's face.

"Excuse me?" Zo stepped back away from the unwelcome touch "who are you?"

"Forgive me our Zo, you must have forgotten, it's true, time has not been kind to me. I am Mr Venrent, from what I can gather you're just like your mother; tell me have you finished school then?"

"My mother?" Zo questioned in alarm, could it be this stranger knew her mother? His face did not seem familiar, yet at the same time there was something about the name, it was a name she had heard before somewhere.

"Yes, yes, come through, join me for a cup of tea and we shall talk, come, come." He hurried them through his tent into his home, showing them to the set of chairs within the small dimly lit room as he spoke his voice seemed mixed with tones of excitement and nerves. "Best not to be seen hey? Don't want to draw any attention to yourself in these parts, please sit, let me look at you." She sat where he motioned her before running his fingers over her face, she was about to protest when she realised the reasoning behind his actions, he was blind. "My, my, you have grown, I heard you talking out there, good job or I may never have known, anyway I thought to myself, is that our Kez? Of course I realised it couldn't be... I mean... your mother always smelled like rose petal, you your more of a plum blossom." Zo blushed finding his comment somewhat embarrassing. "Why you haven't been here for at least a decade if not longer... your poor mother, she was heartbroken when you left. That reminds me, I have something for you, she gave it me the day you left... never could figure out what the darned thing was, no matter, now you're back its only fitting you have it." He vanished into the other room, from where they sat it looked like he walked into darkness itself it seemed almost as if no light shone from the place he vanished, then again light was not really something he needed.

"Does this guy breathe through his ears?" Daniel whispered smiling, who ever this guy was he was grateful to him, he had returned a smile to her face, for to him there was no prettier sight, it warmed his heart to see her happy.

"So any how, she gives me this thing... well maybe I'm missing something here, but it seems to me it's a metal sphere with carvings and a few indents, I'm sure it use to do something mind..." No sooner had the cool metal touched Zo's fingers than it began playing a touching little melody. "Well, I'll be our Zo... what did you do? I've been playing with that thing for years, I just couldn't work it."

"I just..." Zo shrugged she hadn't the slightest idea "So how is my mum?" Venrent seemed to struggle for a few seconds to find the words to continue.

"You know, when you left I told her you'd return, it's been a long time though hasn't it?"

"I..." Zo smiled gently turning the musical ball over in her hands, she smiled thinking of her mother, she was thrilled to finally meet someone who knew her and ecstatic about the thought of returning home to see her at last, she had imagined the moment for so long, playing it out in her mind hundreds of times.

"Why did you never come home? Why did you wait so long?"

"I... I don't know where it is."

"You're kidding me child? You lost your way?"

"More like my memory... excluding this last year I have a nine year gap, I have no memory at all of the last nine years and even some time before that I can't recall, I don't know what happened if I was in an accident or something, I just... can't remember, I mean I awoke in an unfamiliar place, I knew somewhere I had to have a mum, a home, Daniel helped me search Crowley for information before we head to Mainland, but no one knew me, or heard of any missing people... I began to doubt whether my memories were even real, I mean I remembered so little, even my childhood... I think I remember leaving for school one day, that's the only really clear memory I really have aside from small pieces of my mum and Amelia."

"Crowley!" Mr Venrent exclaimed. "You did venture miles from home, as far as you could be for that matter, you're from Drevera, you can get there from here easy enough, just take the second exit on Boa Street, and there you are. How did you end up so far out?"

"I don't remember." She shook her head.

"I tell you, that memory of yours, it's worse than mine, tell you what I'll do for you, a few weeks back I did a favour for an alchemist, well you know the kind I mean, those who had the seed of magic, he does wonders with potions, anyway, I happened to mention I was getting a little forgetful and as a joke he made me something for amnesia, well he wanted to put something in the phial he gave me, so he thought what better than something we can both have a laugh at, I don't think I have been to him once without forgetting to take something with me, well since I don't need it you're welcome to it, wait there just one moment I shall fetch it." He left again quickly with what almost seemed to be a nervous spring to his step, he returned within seconds with the most breath taking little phial in his hand, within it clear syrup glistened. "Here drink this, but could I ask you to do it now, I couldn't bare to give this gift away, it has a lot of sentimental meaning you know, it's kind of my lucky charm, since I had it good things have happened, best of all running into you and being able to help you as you once did me. Of course it doesn't work straight away like everything it needs a little time." Zo smiled carefully removing the top from the phial drinking its contents without so much as a second thought, she didn't have the heart to tell him the sheer volume of potions and mixtures she had tried over the last year, it seemed none ever worked.

"It's like ice." She gasped as she felt its freezing liquid slide down her throat, Daniel, oblivious to her, was staring at her in paralysed horror.

"Anyway, an old man like me needs his rest, and I'm sure you have much to do am I right?" He felt her hand locating the phial before taking it from her.

"We do have the odd thing, but nothing that can't wait, please tell me of my mother." She paused.

"Alas our Zo, youth is on your side, an old man like me, failed vision and aching joints needs his rest, please, forgive me I really should rest, this has been far too much excitement for one day."

"If you have a moment I can make you a remedy for your pains."

"I already have one, such a sweet child." He smiled almost sadly. "Now hurry along, maybe you can visit tomorrow." He escorted them to the door. "I shall feel much better tomorrow." His wrinkled face stretched into a tired smile before he closed the shop door behind them, as he locked up his face grew solemn; he stood his hand resting on the door staring into the darkness with a heavy heart.

"You did well; your loyalty will be rewarded." A female's voice echoed from the darkest shadow, he knew it did not share a room with him, not like before, now it simply used the shadow as a means to communicate, he wasn't sure if it would cross through again… he didn't want to find out.

"You will keep your promise… you wont hurt her? Whatever does he want with such a sweet child?"

"He just wants her to remember… anything else is not your concern. A visitor shall call at the stroke of midnight to complete the contract." With that he felt its presence leave, he was alone once more.

***

"Are you sure you should have done that, I…" Daniel began to question worry still framing his brow from her earlier actions.

"You worry too much, he knew my mother, anyway Mr Venrent would never hurt me." She spoke almost as though she remembered him, a clever deception for his benefit; she didn't want him to worry unnecessarily.

"The world is more often than not very little like your ideals… it could have been poison or anything!"

"Then it's too late to worry now." She smiled. "Besides, he had this." She pulled out the sphere, at her touch it once more began to play. "It was my mum's she used it to lull me to sleep as a child, my father gave it to her before he…" She stopped suddenly frowning, for a second she nearly remembered something, something important, it danced on the edge of her mind teasing her until it vanished. "Mum said she would leave it in the hands of someone she trusted, so when I returned I could find my way home from a place that led to everywhere, I had forgotten until he gave it to me."

"So are you going?… Home that is?"

"I would like to… but… I mean I haven't seen my mum for the longest time, I wonder if she would still know me… I wonder if I'd know her." The tune switched become anxious, nervous and excitable as it played, it seemed as if the small ball reflected her moods turning them to music.

"Of course she'd know you, you're her daughter."

"Maybe, but… if I was to visit, would I put her in danger? I will think about it, as much as I want to go, for now I don't think I can." She smiled, there was another reason she didn't want to go, a reason she couldn't place but something in the back of her mind told her returning was not a good idea at all.

Elly was waiting at the stairway as they stepped into the hall, she stood leaning against the wall her arms crossed before her, she studied them a moment before speaking,

"You were longer than I expected." Although her tone was short it held an undertone of worry.

"I met someone I knew." Zo smiled walking past Elly towards the stairs unaware of the ghastly fear portrayed in Elly's eyes brought on by the words she spoke.

"Who? How do you know them?" Her voice sounded urgent. "You didn't tell them where we were staying did you?" She grabbed Zo's arm a little too hard preventing her taking another step forcing her to turn to look at her.

"No." Zo sighed. "He knows my mother."

"And you know this how? He could have been lying, you're a wanted person you know" Eiji joined the conversation emerging from the dining area with the remains of a sandwich in his hand.

"He gave me this." She pulled her arm free from Elly and thrust it into her pocket removing the music ball witch played an annoyed sounding tune, not in the slightest peaceful like it was before. "It belonged to my mother."

"...He could have got that anyway, don't you realise that? She didn't have to *give* it to him!" Elly snapped, although somewhat relieved, in the excitement she had failed to notice yet another of Eiji's slip of the tongue, had she heard, she would have questioned it by now.

"She did! I know she did!" The tune grew angrier as her temper rose. "This is all about you isn't it, you don't like it I remember them and not you! You're jealous!" She turned running up the stairs, Daniel went as if to follow but Elly stopped him short

"You, you're going to tell me everything." She stated, Eiji had disappeared after Zo up the stairs leaving just the two of them alone in the foyer.

"Everything?" He swallowed somehow keeping his voice from breaking, he knew she wouldn't like what he had to tell her. He didn't want to tell her anyway but he had a feeling he wasn't going to get the option to refuse.

"Everything." She stated staring deep into his eyes, he waited for the first question, a prompt or something but it never came, she just held his gaze for a while before directing it up the stairs and finally let go of his arm. "Ok you may go." She finally spoke, glancing up the stairs as she did so.

"But..." He paused, why was he going to pursue this? He didn't want to tell her anything, yet was he about to protest when she released him? He hurried up the stairs quickly.

"Go, I have more pressing matters to attend." She waited until he had left the room before speaking quietly to herself. "Eryx Venrent." She smiled.

***

After a single knock Eiji peered around the bedroom door, Zo was sitting on the bed she had claimed for her own, her knees hugged tightly into her chest., the room had two beds, between them both against the wall was a strange vanity table with assorts of ornaments placed upon them, the room, like every other in the house was brightly coloured with bad décor, she looked up at him briefly before turning away.

"Erm... may I come in?" He asked in what seemed to be a coy manner, of all the places he could have gone why had he found himself here? Why had he ventured to the room of the person behind the situation he found himself in? Into the room of a murderer.

"You've come to lecture me too?" She sighed trying the best she could to hide the emotions that lined her voice, she looked at him once again, a look warning him to stay away, yet swallowing hard he still entered finding himself sitting right besides her.

"No... I am sorry, I shouldn't have said anything before, I was out of line." He maintained eye contact with his feet as he spoke to her, never once removing them from their fixed position. "I was just… worried… like Elly, I didn't mean to upset you."

"It's not that, it's just everything happened so quickly, one day I was leading a normal life the next… I'm here, I don't even know why I'm in danger I have to trust these strangers… what's worse they know the bits of my past I don't and refuse to tell me, but hint that my past is why I suffer such danger now."

"To some extent, I know how it feels, one day your just minding your own business, the next… everything changes, no explanation as to why it happened to you."

"I'm sorry." She looked to Eiji. "It must have been hard leaving your master." Eiji looked up and nodded wondering if he had at some point mentioned this, or if she knew the path of an Elementalist herself.

"It was, but that's not what I was talking about." He smiled slightly. "I didn't always live with my master, I know what its like to be forced to leave everything behind, with little explanation… it's not easy, but you have something I didn't, friends, I often wonder the big 'what if', what if things had turned out different? But ultimately it comes down to one thing, you are who you are meant to be, fight it as you may, fate has a predestined path chosen for each of us, no matter how you fight it you can only be yourself, understand?" Zo nodded as Eiji took her hand in his and smiled, she really wasn't that bad, now more than ever he was finding it hard to believe this girl that sat besides him was the legendary murder he heard so much about.

"Sorry." A small voice came from the door. "I didn't mean to intrude." The door opened a crack more enough for them to make out Acha's silhouette against the hall light, Eiji rose to his feet making his way to the door, flicking Zo's wall mounted oil lamp on before he stepped aside for Acha to enter, it clicked a few times until it ignited.

"It's alright." He smiled. "I was just leaving."

"I only came to see how you were feeling." Acha walked across the brightly coloured room to Zo. "Hey are those new?" Acha looked at Zo, she now wore a pair of black hamoka trousers and a fitted back velvety top that laced up the front with a patch missing from either shoulder.

"Yeah." Zo stood up glancing down herself. "Apparently they use to be my favourite."

"Oh… Elly said we should start to think about leaving." There was a long silence finally broken by Zo quickly removing her clothes and ramming them into the bottom of her bag to wear her familiar ones.

"I'll just put these in here for now." She dressed quickly before carefully replacing the herbs.

Chapter five

Darkness momentarily bound their vision as they awoke in Knights-errent, after a few moments it cleared, yet the seriousness of the situation took a few more moments to be fully realised. Just as waking from a sleep, not everything became clear at once, it wasn't until they tried to move they found the problem, the cold force of rock pressed firmly on each of their backs as they found themselves secured in place by shackles gripping their wrists and feet to secure them in a fixed standing position against a huge rock. The question of how they came to be here not even crossing their minds as they focused on finding their escape. Daniel reached desperately for Zo's hand in an attempt to free her, yet no matter how hard he tried he could gain no more than an inch of ground, no where near the distance she stood from him. The shackles fit fairly loosely but not so much so they could hope to escape without aid, whoever had made these restraints knew exactly what they were doing, Elly tugged frantically at the chains yet found they would not work themselves free in the background a quiet name seemed to be chanted over and over but none were aware of it as they struggled not until all fell silent, their captors seemed to have left, they seemed to have vanished so quickly it was almost as if they had evaporated into the air.

"Anyone got any ideas on how to…" The ground shook around them underneath the weight of heavy footsteps, Eiji cringed deciding not to finish his question in favour of concentrating his efforts on his attempt to escape, but no matter how hard he struggled he did little more than redden his already hurting wrists as the hard metal scraped against them.

"Zo." Daniel whispered. "Magic?" His voice held hopeful reason as the steps grew closer, yet, at the same time he knew if it had been an option, they would not still be in this predicament, as he looked to her he could see she was deep in thought.

"I can't… I can't get the leverage, it would kill us all." She yanked at the chains as if to prove her point, if she was able to summon a fire hot enough to weaken the chains, she was certain they would suffer a critical injuries, she pulled against the chains, if she could twist enough, she may be able to summon a small enough flame to melt her own and then work on the others without worry, she only stopped struggling when the stench of the fowl creature was upon them. It was not a dragon, or at least not like any they had ever imagined existing, its large scaly body bore resemblance to one, yet the shape of its body was where all similarities ended, its enormous paws bore ridiculously long, painful looking, steel nails in place of its claws, rust starting at the place it first pierced the creatures flesh and extending to the very tip. Its skin was torn and twisted as it hung loose on the enormous creature some was gathered in folds by the enormous nails that penetrated various parts of its body as if they themselves held the creature's skin in place. The clear pain these caused was reflected in its eyes, the pain caused it anger, a deep anger that could only be soothed by the momentary joy of feasting on life's blood. Its overlarge tail seemed to be completely untouched by the rusted nails, in their place a huge mace dragged behind it, it was without question the most terrifying thing any of them had seen, it was horrific, but its mouth was, by all means, the scarcest feature, sneered into a wicked grin as it closed in on the sacrifices, its teeth shone brightly as the millions of stretched pins that filled its mouth shone in the sunlight, they still held the pierced amour of those it had previously feasted on, the paper thin teeth overstretched the creatures enormous bite and overfilled its mouth in another attempt to cause it agony, layer upon layer of these spread back so if its meal were to miss the first row it would be caught in one of the other hundred to guarantying the taste of blood, its only release from its eternal torture. Its putrid breath hung stale in the air enveloping all within in its decaying stench, it stood before them its nostrils twitching as it took in the scent of fresh food, Zo closed her eyes tightly as it approached, just then, as all seemed lost, a cry echoed through the air.

"Unhand those maidens you wretched fiend." A knight rode in upon a mighty white steed; his silver armour shining brightly, his voice was filled with heroism like a hero in the tacky plays. The knight turned looking towards them with a slimy wink. "Do not fear, for I Sir Earnest will protect you. Defender of righteousness, saviours of maidens, Hero, Knight… lover." He dismounted his steed smiling at the captives.

"I think I preferred the dragon." Zo whispered to Daniel as she still tried to work free the restraints, which despite the nature of their situation couldn't help sniggering, there was, after all, something highly amusing about watching the imitation knight prance around before them.

"Excuse me." Daniel interrupted Sir Earnest's fancy footwork as he danced around the dragon's feet; luckily as yet it had failed to notice his arrival. "How about you cut me down so I can free the others, while you do heroic battle with the beast… to save time."

"Do you jest?" He scoffed in mocking laughter. "A real knight would never let a commoner take the glory of the rescue." With those words he turned to face the dragon and their battle began.

"We're all going to die." Eiji stated quite bluntly, loud enough for all to hear, in the meantime Elly was still trying to work her arms free finally with a sigh she gave up, even she could not release these bonds, for the second time ever, she had been beaten by a restraint.

"He's getting pummelled." She stated, a strange smile crossing her lips as she watched the dragon swing the hero around before flinging him to the ground. "We need to do something before that idiot loses its attention." They all knew they had to do something, it was just none of them knew exactly *what* could be done.

"I wonder if he'll eat us whole." Acha's voice trailed off just as the dragons jaw began to descend upon the hero, she shuddered as she saw the teeth of the creature clearly stretching back to its throat, a sickening crack filled the air moments before the Knight seemed to vanish, a mere second away from his demise. The dragon sniffed the air around him looking for the prey that had somehow escaped his jaws.

"Hey." Eiji shouted, despite the hushing of the others he shouted again. "Can you help us with these chains?" Eiji saw Seiken standing at a distance from the dragon, although for some reason it failed to notice him despite the fact he stood clearly in its sight, Eiji continued to call, desperate to grab his attention.

The chains holding Daniel released sliding him to the floor, he smiled at Zo who stood behind the rock where she had melted the metal that passed through holding them in place, she was silently motioning for him to help release the others. Seiken began to slowly approach, to Eiji's dismay there was nothing rushed about his actions.

Then, his chains slipped, with movement in his arms again he unhooked the shackles from his wrists and ankles as Daniel hurried to help Zo with the final chain.

"How did you get out?" Eiji questioned as he gave a final tug to release the chains until finally they fell, but not as silently as those that were freed before him. The creature turned slowly giving a mighty roar seeing its dinner had escaped. Zo glanced to Elly who smiled watching her as she took her hand a splintering crack like the one before echoed as she snatched her thumb back into place, she was unsure exactly what made her think she could do that, but for a brief second she knew that she could and also that it would ultimately save them.

"Ok, I think you have succeeded in gathering your friend's attention, might I suggest... running?" Seiken questioned looking at the dragon as it brought its vision to face them, his tone as always, calm, clear and enticing.

The creature was studying them carefully, no doubt trying to decide if they too would vanish like his appetiser had.

"What the hell just happened?" Elly demanded as they broke into a run, the creature slowly turning to pursue them, confident that this time he would not be left so unsatisfied with his meal.

"Did I forget to mention?" Seiken stayed besides them as they ran, yet appeared to be making no effort whatsoever. "Not only can you interact with the dream walkers through your own choice, they too can interact with you, instead of *you* choosing to involve yourself in their dreams... you become part of it."

"You mean we were all just playing a role in that guy's fantasy?" Eiji gasped, the flat out running catching up to him, he glanced behind to gain his second wind, the creature was still in hot pursuit, and gaining and his rewording Seiken's explanation did little more than earn him a scornful look.

"What if..." Daniel panted, but knowing where this was heading Seiken had already began to answer... there was no time to waste.

"If he hadn't woke, you would all be dead." He looked at Zo smiling at her softly "or maybe not"

"If the village and everything was just part of his dream... then how come the creature still lingered with the chains that bound us?" Elly questioned.

"The chains are substance left over from that feeling of a dream... that moment between sleeping and waking, here we call it dream residue"

"And the creature?" Zo questioned again.

"The creature I'm afraid, is a native of this world." Although he ran with the others effortlessly, he never once looked where he ran, only at the one thing he found most intriguing, Zodiac. Silent words past between them as they ran, Zo found it hard to break his gaze but found it a necessity.

"I don't know if I understand." Acha panted gaining her motivation from the same place Eiji had previously, the creature was closing in, even now they could smell its hunger approaching rapidly.

"It's simple." Seiken stopped, the others for some reason also felt compelled to do so, more from necessity than any other reason, Seiken looked at them and sighed, Zo turned to face the monster, her hand already on her sword hilt and her mind already drawing on her magic, as he placed a hand on her shoulder her hand slowly slipped from the sword as a sphere of silver light enveloped them. The creature snorted pacing around the area its prey had stood just moments ago. "As I was saying, you can use things from people's dreams to help you in your quest, but it works the other way too. It's all a matter of chance, although you slept in a safe area this world changes and the areas within to a certain extent change also, thus it will be very rare for you to wake in the same location unless it's one of the seven fixed points and if you sleep in the same place you wake." The monster circled the area again, its roar shaking the ground violently. "Creatures such as this one dwell deep within the human mind, once something like this is born it generally resides here, yet most creatures that come from the thought of those from the world of the Goddess Gaea, existed here long before they terrorised your dreams."

"So… what if that guy hadn't woke… I mean." Daniel began, only to find himself cut off once more by Seiken.

"I told you, you'd be dead."

"No… I mean… why did he wake?" Daniel rephrased his somewhat vague question as he caught his breath.

"That's our job, ever had a dream where you're about to die but wake up that split second before you see it happen? That's us, our race is known as Spindles, just as you are humans…"

"Spindles?" He questioned.

"Yes." Seiken sighed. "You see… it's difficult to explain, many millennia ago we were discovered by your people, they found a way to monitor the sleeping mind… it turns out when we enter your dreams, or you enter our world as is truly the case, your brain waves change, they increase in activity until the point you jerk awake. These scientists called them Spindles believing they are what cause you to jerk awake… so when they discovered our kind later on near the end of their time, our kind were given that name. As you may gather our worlds have always coexisted one could not be without the other, although we did not come from your being, since the dawn of time we simply were. Yours is the world of material so to speak and ours the world of the mind, a world where anything can happen thus guardians, protectors are needed, to watch, ensuring things never get out of hand, we chose to accept this role, to watch and protect both worlds, you see, our two worlds are joined, more than anyone really cares to realise, one cannot survive without the other… the problem we have now, is since the Spindles have been captured, there are but two of us with the power to continue… even now, I must be careful, if he were to find we had this talent… he would find a way to inhibit it."

"Not everyone dreams of death… what do you do the rest of the time?" Eiji questioned cringing as he realised how his question must have sounded.

"We *do* have lives of our own." He stated bluntly. "Watching your people is not our only role, our true purpose is to guard the barrier between our two worlds, to ensure the nightmares don't filter over and become real again, if the barrier is weakened further, it's not only death our dreamers will have to fear, but every injury or ailment they obtain here, will pass over with them until there is nothing that distinguishes this world from yours." Seiken glanced around removing his hand from Zo's shoulder as he did so the silver sphere that circled them vanished, the others so focused on his words they had not, until this point, noticed the creature had gone. Seiken smiled at Zo who touched her shoulder where his hand had been.

"Seiken… what exactly are we after? I mean what are we doing here?" She questioned, her question did not receive an answer in the same tedious tone he had spoken to the others with.

"You mean you don't know?" His ageless brow wrinkled slightly. "I don't know if I should tell you… but I guess… since you do not know…" He paused thinking over this strange occurrence, with all those that came before them, before the lands were so dangerous, they always knew what they quested for, they always knew the purpose of their pilgrimage, why had the rules changed this time leaving them to wander aimlessly? Surely, that in itself was pointless and not within the boundaries of fair play?. Although the other 'games' as they were called were slightly different to this one "from my understanding, within our world there are five keys, sealed here from ages past, even my family could not tell you exactly when they arrived, looking back now it seems as if they have always been. It's rumoured that they are linked to the worlds by some kind of door, only once all the keys have been collected may it open, or something along those lines. We really don't know its true purpose, I only tell you what I was told when I was taken, the keys are said to dwell in five of the seven fixed locations of our world."

"These fixed locations, what are they exactly?" Daniel questioned once he had caught his breath.

"They are locations bound to your world for the purpose of this mythical door, a great mage, or perhaps even a God created these keys, so the secret of the door could never be revealed… but I overheard Night's creatures when they caught me speaking of how the door is our only chance of freedom, they mocked us, teased us, knowing our race could never pass through their bars… but they also spoke of the coming of another, one from the world of the Goddess Gaea, no more was spoken in my presence… the only thing I could give you was that map." Zo suddenly realised what he was spoke of and pulled the parchment from inside her jacket, Elly swiftly removed it from her hands studying it closely, as Daniel moved to look with difficulty over her shoulder, glancing around as he did so.

"I think this is the closest." He pointed to a small area on the map, glancing around again comparing the landmarks he had seen to those on the map, if there was one thing he could do really well, it was navigate, where he had pointed on the map words were written;

'I am hidden by trees yet once stood taller, my disguise hides my purpose and my purpose came from my disguise, I was built for hope, now bring despair. Once followed by many as a symbol of belief.'

"Well at least we know it's in the woods somewhere." Daniel stated looking at the vast forest that lay before them. "A religious statue perhaps that would explain the whole symbol of faith and followers thing."

"Yes because a statue would bring despair." Elly tutted shaking her head slightly.

"Well… maybe we could ask around… you did say the dreamers would be able to help right?" Acha looked to Seiken only to find he had already vanished.

"I don't fancy wandering around aimlessly; we know how this world is to adapting to people's thoughts." Elly stated, although Daniel may have seen several landmarks on the map, they were ones that she too had noticed, however, there was no guarantee they weren't just created from their mind, as they had discovered on their first visit, some of the scenery was taken straight from their memories. "Maybe our Elementalist can make things easier and locate the nearest town." Elly raised her eyebrow expectantly at Eiji who met her gaze with a blank expression; she gave a sigh wondering why she had expected anything different. "Did your master teach you anything?" She sighed. "Humans, villages, towns, all are alien in the natural environment, they destroy and pollute things around them, the natural world suffers as they bend it to their will... mankind destroy the natural world so they may live." Still no reaction. "You are in tune with the elements... with nature right?" She sighed wondering why she was even bothering; she should have known from his first blank stare that further explanations were pointless. "You should be able to locate areas nearby where the elements are dying... you know, a disruption in the natural aura."

"Oh" Eiji lowered his head "I have never..."

"I can help keep you grounded if you like, I use to... never mind." Acha moved as if to take Eiji's hand pulling away moments before they touched backing away as she did so "I..." She looked from him to Daniel, who as if on cue passed her a small pair of gloves he had been meaning to give her for some time now. She pulled them on smiling, although once in place on her hands they seemed to vanish as if they never were.

"Magic gloves... I picked them up from Collateral... I knew they'd come in handy, I meant to give them you earlier, but with everything that happened I kind of forgot." He watched as Acha examined her hands, he had wondered how exactly she would take this gesture and was now relieved she seemed to appreciate it.

"They're so... light, it's like I'm not even wearing them" she smiled taking Eiji's hand.

"Why would I need to be grounded?" His voice trembled slightly, as he looked between them nervously.

"The first time... it's difficult to remember where you are; it helps to be able to feel someone holding onto your physical body... to remind you where you are so you don't get lost."

"Or... we could just follow the sign." Daniel brushed some shrubs from a nearby post to reveal a name carved on a piece of wood, it appeared they were not too far from a town at all.

"Was that there before?" Zo moved to stand by him examining the mould ridden post, Eiji let out a sigh of relief as the others went to join them, this had been just what he had hoped for.

"I'm not sure... It just caught my eye while you were talking."

"I vote for following the sign" Eiji skilfully added to the end of Daniel's sentence without leaving chance for breath or objection.

***

Upon the distant horizon, a large forest loomed before them through a break in the trees they could see a small village. Daniel glanced up from the map parchment, then to Zo.

"I have been monitoring our progress and we are here... This town appears to be the town of Abaddon one of the seven fixed points Seiken spoke of." They stopped just short of the town, little sunlight could penetrate the trees canopies that stretched most of the way over the town, the town's centre was the only place where the branches of the trees did not shield the town from the light. It was a picturesque town, its small wooden houses built in a large circle, fresh, sweet smelling flowers brightened the gardens of the small houses, the appearance of the town alone, was enough to make anyone dismiss the rumours as hearsay. Nothing stirred within the town's boundaries, it gave the impression of a long deserted ghost town with one difference, the houses were still as new as the day they were built.

"I don't like this." Acha whispered as they entered the town their eyes scanning for any movement no matter how small.

"I'm sure I know this place." Zo whispered keeping to the low tone that seemed to be demanded by the silence of the area. "It looks so familiar." She looked to Elly hoping in hope to gain some form of confirmation that she did indeed know the place, as always she made no attempt to confirm or deny it.

"Its counterpart, that is to say 'Abaddon' in our World, was once home to one of the Grimoire I told you of" Elly stated surprising them all, none had heard of this town existing in their own world, the only reason Daniel had known it was the fact it was printed on the map.

"What happened to this place it's so quiet... deserted?" Daniel looked to Elly who once again seemed to possess all the answers.

"There are many rumours, as to what may have happened here many years ago, one of which is that the Grimoire sustained life here, on the day it was removed a terrible fate met the people of this town... that's what most who know of its existence choose to believe anyway, but the truth is always a little more sinister." Elly paused as if for dramatic effect "from what I understand ..."

"It was put under some form of spell." Zo walked slowly from house to house almost trance like as she spoke. "I know this story." Zo closed her eyes in concentration, her hand resting on a wooden gate post as she tried to pull the memory from the tip of her mind concern crossed Elly's brow unseen by anyone, news had reached her instantly of Annabel's death, that meant the memories could be reclaimed without screening hopefully she would not recall too much. "A curse was bestowed upon this village as punishment for an unforgivable act... death was too complicated for those who resided within, thus, they were sentenced to an eternal sleep, conscious of everything that transpires around them, awaiting a death never to come... punished for a crime they committed" she looked to Elly for confirmation, but again she gave nothing away, she did however seem a little relieved.

"They must have done something unspeakable to earn such a judgement." Acha placed her hand on Zo's shoulder startling her slightly.

"How come none of us have heard of this place? It has no place in history or legend." Daniel questioned looking form Zo to Elly wondering which one would answer it was Elly who finally spoke looking to Zo before beginning.

"The reason is, once the spell was completed, Mari summoned a monster to guard it and the surrounding area, its mere presence alone repels intruders, only people who know of this place can see it, that was part of the magic. When the spell was complete the town vanished off any map and thus was soon forgotten, rumours of the forest continue to this day, they call it now the forest of lost souls, any said to enter, will surely meet their death."

"What kind of monster?" Eiji questioned grabbing the most important word in the sentence, the one that affected them immediately, as he asked he glanced around he expected it to now be lurking behind them.

"It was remarkable, I have heard only the tales Mari told me, it not only guards the town, but feeds upon those resting in its induced sleep, it was truly a remarkable conjuring." She smiled remembering Marise's face when she had revelled in telling her of what had been accomplished.

"Not to tempt providence or anything… but, if such a creature exists within our world… It's only logical it exists here also." Daniel glanced around the quiet village as Eiji had just moments ago, watching carefully for any signs of movement.

"No… it can't enter the town. It was imprisoned within the church, as for the town people, it sustains their life-force by hunting those who wander too far into its territory, but there are only certain people it may hunt, and it is limited to the time it is permitted leave to find its prey, until its creator releases it, it will remain this way." Zo stated.

"Is this church… in the woods by chance?" A sudden realisation dawned upon him as he glanced around the village finding no church, only mile upon mile of trees greeting his vision. Eiji paused taking a breath as he approached a house, they all fell silent to watch him as he opened the door peering inside "if the town people are meant to be within the village… where are they?" Eiji walked around the house looking at the tidy kitchen giving the impression of having never been used, the never slept in bed and the shiny new bathroom everything gave the impression of having been barely used, he took everything in very quickly before he opened the window leaning through to look at the others. "Shouldn't they be sleeping? Shouldn't they be here?"

"Well the townsfolk may not be here… but we do have a lead as to where our clue takes us. Where's this church?" Zo shook her head as Daniel looked to her, then to Elly.

"How should I know? I wasn't the mastermind behind it, maybe you should ask Mari!" She snapped, why? Why hadn't she been told about the church? Mari told her everything why had chosen to keep something like that a secret?

"Since she is not here…" Daniel said his tone seeming somewhat relieved "the only other lead we have" he looked to Zo again.

"Why are you looking at me? I don't know anything." Her voice trembled defensively as the others turned to look at her, the town on the whole made her feel that way that mingled with her own questions of how she knows about the town only added to her building anxiety.

"But… you did mention it in the first place." Acha volunteered almost timidly.

"I don't know anything." Zo snapped. "Maybe you can find something in the town to help us… Just don't ask me!" She turned her back to the others before running deeper into the town Daniel went to pursue stopped by Elly raising her arm in front of him.

"I'll go." She stated in a tone that could not be argued with, before she vanished after her.

"That was... strange." Daniel commented staring in the direction both Elly and Zo had vanished in "I guess she's..."

"Think about it." Eiji came out of the house holding a piece of parchment in his hand. "You two chose to involve yourself in this matter, she didn't have a choice, one day she was taken from everything she knew, her life turned upside down."

"It's not easy for Acha either, but she doesn't make such a fuss." Daniel suddenly gasped surprised at his own words, it was almost as if they weren't his own, he never begrudged Zo's actions, if anything he understood.

"That's because there is no reason to make one, since I was sealed away I knew all along my fate... I know who I am; I couldn't imagine how it must feel not to." Acha smiled, all the time from the moment she first slept she dreamt of this world, this destiny as she lay within the ground it whispered to her through her dreams of what changes occurred, she was more prepared for this world than the others first realised, but slowly they were beginning to understand, all along, this was the time she was born for. Breaking away from her thoughts she looked to the others a wave of dizziness passed over her before she spoke. "Shouldn't we be looking for clues?"

"No need... I got this from inside..." Eiji lifted the piece of parchment to their attention he unfolded it to show them a small map.

"Why didn't you..."

"I guess... I thought it might be wise to let them to talk a while, there seem to be some things they need to discuss; besides it's no different than the one we were given earlier." Daniel opened the map Seiken had given Zo and compared them.

"They're identical." Daniel sighed looking at them. "Even down to the writing."

"Almost but not quite." Eiji turned the map over revealing a small amount of barely legible scrawls. "It says." Eiji cleared his throat and began to read as Acha moved to sit herself on a small mound under a tree looking somewhat flushed "Congratulations, it seems you have found your destination, the game is now underway. Playing is simple, you need only survive, winning is somewhat more of a challenge, you must collect the five keys from various locations on this world, obtaining them moves you closer to the release of the Spindles. Of course the clock ticks on, the longer they are away from home, the more dangerous this world is to you and your world... there are only a few rules. The first, between sunrise and sunset of this world you are hunted by us.... should you stay after this point you need not worry for I doubt you will live to see the rising sun, the second, after sunset my hunters may not take you. But once my hunters *do* take you, you are mine to do as I please." Eiji and Daniel suddenly grew very tired and joined Acha by the autumn tree, he look at it realising just moments before, it had thrived with life.

"This place is odd; I swear this tree was in full life just moments ago." Daniel stated, as if reading Eiji's mind before giving a yawn. "I wonder where Zo and Elly have got to" he leaned back against a tree awaiting their return.

While they were studying the map, Elly wandered the village looking for Zo her thoughts on their last visit here, last time she had been here, she had nearly lost Marise to the dark forces within the village, they had schemed and planned hard to get everything to fall into place and unknowingly, Elly had left her in great danger, thankfully, she returned in time to save her, but the effects this place had had on her had followed her for some time afterwards. Marise had been amazing that night, surrounded by the nightmarish creatures she did not fight, she summoned a being to feed on them as they had tried to on her, but she had never mentioned the sealing of this creature into a church, forbidding it from preying on those it wished, it was an action that did not seem like her at all, but Marise had not spoken of it, leaving her to wonder if perhaps the other persona, Zodiac, had been responsible for this feat.

Elly stood for a moment her hands on her hips looking at Daniel, Eiji and Acha all asleep against a tree, Zo was following at some distance behind feeling somewhat ashamed of her earlier outburst, she had been unable to control her outburst, with the more patches of things she remembered, the more frustrated she grew trying to grab more of the fragment her mind had offered, yet the harder she tried, the more difficult it became, it didn't help when they had pushed her to recall more, something she would have loved to have obliged with if she could have, then suddenly the emotions took over.

"Come on you three we don't have time to mess around, we need to get moving." She stood above them her shadow casting over them yet not one of them moved, a strange feeling descended on Elly.

"They're not messing Lee, My Abi, Aburamushi, that is, did this." Elly turned in shock to look at Zo who simply smiled back as if nothing had just transpired. She approached them at the tree leaving Elly bewildered, had those words just came form her lips?

"I'm sorry about earlier; I shouldn't have snapped... did you manage to find anything?" Still no response or movement Zo looked to Elly who seemed to have something on her mind, only when she noticed her looking did she approach.

"I think we need to get them out of here... now." She lifted Eiji up placing him in a fireman's lift over her shoulder heading to the town border.

"Zo..." Acha whispered weakly as she was pulled to her feet.

"Acha?" The relief in her voice to hear her friend rang clearly through the concern. "What happened?"

"I don't know..." Zo hooked her arm under her shoulder supporting her weight as she tried to move, she glanced back at Daniel not comfortable with the thought of leaving him alone, just then Elly returned taking him in the same manner she had Eiji moments before. "I felt a little off so sat down while Eiji read his discovery, then we started to get tired... the next thing I knew they were asleep... then you came and got us." Zo steadied Acha as they made their way towards the edge of town.

"Maybe it has something to do with the magic in this place, after all, its inhabitants were forced into eternal slumber, maybe those who enter are also subjected to its power?... There was no one in the town but from what Seiken told us of this place, every dreamer has a home... they must be somewhere on this world" finally they caught up with Elly who was trying to rouse Eiji but to no avail, even the forest in which they stood was filled with a deadly silence, the only sound, came from the gentle wind teasing the trees at it passed.

"It's no use." Elly sighed moving away from Eiji. "It seems the creature's sleep enchantment even embraces this area... what we need is a good piece of counter magic." She looked straight at Zo watching her intently as she helped Acha to the floor "like, oh I don't know, a magical ward?"

"I got it the first time… you don't have to keep on." Zo touched Acha's face gently checking her temperature and healthy, she seemed fine all in all just a little tired and anaemic perhaps, she never did eat that much, it seemed it was beginning to catch up with her. "I wonder why we weren't affected." Zo wondered aloud not expecting an answer yet receiving one all the same.

"I guess…" Elly paused a moment, she had almost volunteered the truth, she knew full well why neither of them had been affected by the creatures sleep, but to explain would compromise the situation… but she had already begun to answer "maybe we were just lucky?" She cringed ever so slightly as she answered, was that really the best she could come up with? Well, she always thought it was better to be vague than weave a complicated web of lies, all the more difficult to be freed from.

"Yeah… maybe" Zo sighed, it was clear that Elly knew more than she was letting on, 'just once' she wondered 'would it be too much to get a straight answer?' Finally, she was ready, she had read the surrounding environment and knew just what to ask, she took a deep breath before she began. "Awaken and alert we wish to keep, I set up a ward to counter this sleep." A silver light momentarily surrounded them before fading to transparent.

"Do you always do that?" Try as she did Elly could not hide the amusement within her voice.

"What?" Zo glanced up from Daniel's side.

"Rhyme… you never use to."

"So… how did I use to…"

"Never mind." She smiled thinking back to the appearance of those eyes, even then, she had thought their rhymes pointless, but now it was clear, they had been mocking her. Well what had she expected? Mari no longer asked for magic, but since her memories are incomplete, it only went to reason she may still feel them necessary, yet still, they sounded so stupid, they would have to talk, she couldn't stand it if she was to continue this through their journey.

She watched Eiji for a moment his fingers twitched as the sleep began to ware off. Daniel awoke with a start gasping for breath as he found himself sitting in the middle of a strange forest, Elly, Zo and Acha all staring at him, seconds later Eiji awoke clutching his chest. Although neither Daniel nor Eiji had spoken, they seemed to be out of danger, yet Acha still sat as pale as ever breathing shallowly.

"Acha… are you ok?" Zo took her hand from Eiji's forehead happy that both he and Daniel were fine.

"I think she…" Elly began but stopped as the area around them grew darker, almost as if summer was turning to autumn but only within the area touched by Zo's ward, the flowers withered and died leaving brown stems in place of what once were fully blooming roses. The trees shifted and changed dropping their leaves as if autumn had descended, the grass drooped turning the pale autumn shades, in less than thirty seconds the entire area within the spell was withered as it spread they could only watch the earthly sleep spread.

"Oh no." Zo whispered sadly seeing what she had done. "But I read them right… I swear." Acha pulled herself to her feet like the others it seemed she was now recovering and the colour was once more returning to her face. She joined the others just as the shifting autumn had finished encapsulating all within the ward, not a single flower was left in bloom and not a single green leaf hung on the trees, Zo quickly localised the magic to follow each person instead of walking within a life destroying field. She looked to Acha. "I guess this place doesn't like my magic much" she placed her hand upon the bark of a nearby tree and shuddered, it was almost as if her magic had torn the life from it.

"What happened back there… one minute you were fine the next we couldn't wake you?" Zo offered Daniel a hand to his feet.

"I'm not really sure, it was the strangest thing, one minute I was listening to Eiji read something, the next everything grew darker, I felt so tired, I would go as far as to say I had fallen asleep, but I heard everything that happened in the world around me, although try as I might I couldn't move, or talk…Eiji?" Daniel questioned seeing the look of terror on Eiji's face.

"Didn't you see it?" Eiji whispered "the creature from the darkness… it saw us… it pulled some kind of silver cord from us attaching it to itself… then there came the screams, the tortured cries of those souls it feeds off, each begging for mercy over and over again…"

"I don't think we need to worry about it just yet…" Elly began, knowing that in due time they would indeed have to face the creature as the journeys destination seemed to lead to its home. "A ward has been set up to counter its effects; you should be alright for now… what else can you tell us of it?"

"Nothing…. just that it seemed really excited about something… and a name kept repeating over and over in my mind, Aburamushi" Eiji shuddered at the mere sound of the name "But what I don't understand… It saw me and Daniel… but somehow you evaded its vision. Why?"

"Lucky I guess… Maybe it targeted a certain area" Elly answered again

"Maybe, but then how come Acha was unaffected?"

"Maybe it prefers males" Elly felt her foot firmly on the shovel digging deeper and deeper.

"But surely this wasn't an all male town?" Daniel intervened, a feeling deep within his stomach similar to the one Zo has had previously, the sinking feeling that told you someone knew more than they were willing to let on.

"Well I know its creator so I guess I got immunity."

"What about Zo and Acha?" He questioned stubbornly

"Well that's easy, Acha has a different kind of life force to most people and Zo… well… she has the power of magic."

"But so does Eiji." Daniel was about to press the issue further when he heard Zo gasp, in that split second of silence it seemed to cut through the air like a knife. Elly rushed to her, looking at her cautiously trying to make out the point her vision focused on as she stood trance like, whatever was going on Elly knew exactly how to break it, a loud crack rang through the air as she slapped her, hard, startling the silent birds from their homes in the trees, without even time to blink Zo had retaliated, her fist clenched stopping barely an inch from Elly's face, the others let out a breath, for split second there she had them quite concerned, unseen by the others, Elly smiled.

"Lee." Zo spoke quietly lowering her hand to touch her on the side of her face smiling as she did so. "You see the problem here." She subtly glanced in the direction where the others stood.

"What problem?" Daniel although unable to hear anything sharply picked up one word 'problem' Zo turned to look at Daniel, for a second he could have sworn that there was remnants of something hidden within her eyes, something he couldn't quite place.

"A problem?" Zo questioned aware that she had spoken but unsure exactly where she was going with it. "Oh yes… I remember, we still need to find the church and it's getting late." Elly gave her a puzzled look before a flicker of understanding crossed her mind.

'Don't worry Mari' she thought to herself.

***

"So my daughter has awoke." The cool voice stated, although quiet, it commanded total attention. Night paced around the cauldron his dark hooded robe trailed behind him on the floor, within his hand he held a small crystal he smiled at it, watching the figures as they went about their business.

"Yes my lord… only, as yet the outcome is somewhat uncertain… It may take longer than anticipated to bring her around." It was impossible to tell who the voice could belong to, the form of communication distorted it beyond any possible recognition, Night and Night alone knew whose the voice that beckoned was.

"And what of the old man, did he keep to his side of the bargain?" Night asked just for courtesy sake, he knew the trouble they had gone to, to ensure all had gone to plan.

"Yes, I watched myself."

"And the machine?" He lowered the crystal placing it deep within his pocket, the answer to this question he could not predict, what they touched upon was ancient technology long forgotten, it was difficult to say how it would function now. To be recreated after such a vast time phase, who knew what the outcome would be? There were many things that could go wrong, over the last years he had encountered a lot of them and rectified them.

"There are no problems." The voice from the cauldron responded with very little delay. "As for your daughter, I imagine that once Knights-errent takes its tole… although sire, what if they should fail?" A sharp sound of realisation echoed through the voice, when this was been planned failure was never an option… but now, things had taken unexpected twists, unpredictable influences such as the presence of those not expected had not been taken into account.

"Then they will remain there forever, the boundaries of the worlds will vanish and havoc shall be freed upon the earth" Night smiled at the thought, yet, at the same time, this unique form of peril was not exactly what he had in mind, although would work all the same to his needs.

"A lot is at stake my lord should they meet with misfortune."

"Then see to it they don't. The mind is a tricky thing things forgotten can seem second nature, I think they will be safe considering. The Spindles can only be released by my victory, there is no other way, I am not worried, or, do you forget exactly who it is we are dealing with? My daughter will be fine, the company she keeps will only add to the entertainment."

"Entertainment? My lord, I feel they are the ones that hinder our progress, I could have them destroyed."

"As I said before, I am not worried, I would not be surprised if they do not have their uses, tell me have you gained further information on the location of the final Grimoire?"

"No sire, but I promise it shall be delivered to you personally... although I do believe the location you initially believed is the better lead, although as yet, we remain without conformation."

"Very well, I guess this is a good time for me to use the patience I developed in all my years of waiting."

"Or you could go out there and cast judgement, remind people your true power; they seem to have grown insolent and forgotten."

"All in good time, besides, I do believe it is time to make good my deal with that old man"

"You're going in person?"

"But of course... you know my minions cannot approach, the blind have senses that do not allow them to draw near... it will be interesting to see how they react when they have faded... all those years of teasing them, shall not go unpunished... I cannot stand a man whose favour can be brought... at least I can gain enjoyment watching as my army draw closer when he is no longer protected by the unseeing eye... besides... I may have use for him yet... who knows, let my minions have their fun."

Chapter six

"This is it?" Eiji's voice was filled with disillusion as he stopped at the foot of a mossy mound upon which stood the crumbled ruins of what once would have been a spectacular monument. "I expected something a little less desolate." He gave a disappointed sigh as they walked slowly to the door, it was a magnificent piece of carving, or rather it would have been in its day, it was about four inches thick, carvings embedded deep within the wood, some warn and faded but for the most part covered by a moss like substance.

Elly pushed at the door expecting it to crack, fall away, or even open, yet nothing went as planned, the door, despite its unstable appearance, stood as firm as ever.

"It's sealed by some kind of magic." Zo touched the door. "If we could get inside it could be opened easily, it seems only the creature… can open this side… which would make sense… I guess it keeps people from wandering in while it's out hunting?"

"So we need to look for another way in." Eiji sighed.

"No need, over here." Daniel called, motioning for them to follow, they hurried to were he stood, a mound of stones slanted towards the church where a hole no bigger than a person had crumbled from its walls, from the plants and debris it was a safe assumption that it had been in this state of disrepair for sometime.

Hesitantly they made their way up to the crumbled entrance, inside was dark, no, black, would be a more accurate description, as not even a ray of outside light seemed to shine within its walls, it was like peering into the void itself, until now, they had avoided mention of the creature, yet it seemed they were about to enter its domain, it was impossible to miss the uneasy air that spread amongst them.

"Well, I guess we go in?" Zo swallowed as she stepped closer to the hole in the crumbled wall, she leaned forwards slowly trying to peer deeper inside, trying to get an idea of what they would face, but the uniform darkness remained, Eiji suddenly grabbed her startling her slightly

"You could fall forever…" He looked down into the eternal pit of darkness unconsciously turning a small pebble over and over in his hand. "There may not even be a floor." He took his hand from her shoulder questioning silently what the next move would be, running over possible options in his mind, none of which seemed plausible, Zo placed her hand on his stilling the rock, she smiled slightly taking it from him.

"I didn't plan on jumping in." She stated turning the rock over once in her hand "the suns rays are full of might, bestow on this the gift of light." She whispered hearing the wind rise slowly all around whispering her bidding, she saw from the corner of her vision Elly rolling her eyes moments before a small ball of light appeared. It was no bigger in size than a small plum, it shone brightly illuminating the air around it as it hovered suspended before her, she glanced down to the rock in her hands and sighed, Daniel, although watching as always in awe, had a slight frown crossing his brow, mirroring that on the face of his friend. She glanced down to the rock in her hand and back to the ball of light once more, "that's not what I meant to…" Zo's words were spoken with such soft confusion they were barely audible. She stepped closer to the edge until there was no ground left, reaching for the ball of light as she approached she found her fingers passed smoothly through it leaving it in the place it had first appeared, she tried a few more times before giving up, painfully aware of the stares from the others, the weight of the stares alone made her feel the need to excuse her mistake. "I guess I'm feeling a little off" that was the only justification she could think of for the strange occurrence, when it came to magic she normally had no problem commanding its total obedience, yet for some reason, this time, it chose to ignore her will for it to enter the stone taking a firm residence in front of her.

Supporting herself against the wall, she leaned in, the light shining bright enough to make out the wooden floor below, although uneven, it appeared sound enough.

"There's a floor... it looks solid enough." She pulled herself back out of the gaping hole turning to face them. "Then again I guess we were always going in." Eiji passed Zo the rope as if reading her mind. She lowered it into the hole giving Eiji the signal when it reached the bottom, he used the remaining slack to fasten it to a nearby tree not only around the trunk but around a few of the branches just to be sure. He gave it a few tugs checking it was sturdy, before making his way back to the others, who had already started their decent into the unknown territory of Aburamushi.

Zo was the first to touch the floor, being the barer of light, she thought it only right she should descend first, so those who followed could see what they were entering, she leaned against the damp wall, a strange pain radiating across her body, during that fleeting moment she thought herself subjected to a curse of some sort, perhaps an ancient magic sealed within the place to ward off intruders, her entire body felt as if it was being torn apart from the inside, but then, as quickly as it came within seconds it had faded almost as if it never been, the others seemed to suffer no such side effect, perhaps it was a warning meant only for her.

"I bet an old place like this has a back up generator, many of the old buildings like this do." Daniel positioned himself to stand by Zo which was not difficult since she was the only source of light around, although the hovering ball shone brightly it barely made a difference to the darkness, it was almost like a small candle, it only lit things in its close proximity making everything else all the more darker.

"I don't know... with all this water... do you think it would still work?" Ache joined the others in their tight circle wiping the drops of cold water off her skin that fell from above.

"Only one way to be sure..." Elly turned to look at Zo expectantly.

"Huh?" She shook her head suddenly aware that someone had been speaking to her, why was she suddenly feeling so tired? Could it be the creature was penetrating her magical ward?

"We were saying if we could see a little more maybe we could find the starter for the generator." She repeated watching her carefully, she could read her well enough by now to know something wasn't quite right, she seemed pale, confused, Elly looked to her a moment longer waiting for her words to sink in.

"Oh... yeah." Daniel looked at her questioningly as she answered, she was clearly distracted, but by what he was unsure, he glanced around wondering if perhaps her senses had told her something they had missed, then again, from her reactions he had to wonder if she was even really in the same room as them. "A tiny flame can burn so bright, enhance us now this power of light." A blinding flash encased the entire room, a light so bright it hid things almost as well as the darkness had, as it slowly began to fade as Zo fell to her knees gasping for breath watching as her friends vanished into the darkness. It had only lasted seconds but in that time Elly had vanished into the darkness and the others had become merely silhouettes and vanished as they too searched for the starter, it gradually grew darker until no light at all remained.

Suddenly from the darkness came a mighty racket seconds before lights began to flicker and spring into life, the smell of gas being forced through its pipes and ignited hung heavily in the air, although the light was only faint, due to the sheer lack of torches, it served its purpose, besides the several torches ensured they saw more than they wanted to. All too clearly they saw the answer to the questions they had been asking themselves over and over, everyone but Zo, who was bent over on her hands and knees puling herself from the floor, there before their very eyes, the riddle of the missing town people was answered.

"By the Gods it's some kind of..." Daniel stopped unsure exactly how to finish the sentence, Acha stared in open mouth horror as another red water droplet fell from above her, it seemed to fall in slow motion as the realisation of the situation dawned upon them, it exploded in tiny fragments as the droplet was forced to compress on impact with her skin, the torches light acting as a amplifier to the horror they saw, the lighting just right to create the most horrific scene they had ever set eyes upon, compared to this, the dragon seemed normal, flesh torn to breaking point, stretched beyond the realms of possibility as at least a hundred suspended bodies each hung in grotesque positions, their flesh twisted to prevent break, yet not one of the bodies seemed to be decaying, they hung like fresh corpses, still with blood dripping from their wounds, each of their dark ringed bloodshot eyes seemed to stare at them accusingly, boring into their soul, it seemed almost as if these barely clothed figures watched their every move from their twisted disfigured positions, , blood stained the walls and floor like a carpet of red paint, each space being filled by more and more drops as they seemed to be more frequent, almost as if their company had excited them, got the blood pumping through their lifeless corpses, it fell now like a gentle rain, at first they convinced themselves this increase was due to the heat in the room provided by the maps, it was common knowledge heat increased the circulation, but all rational thought was destroyed the instant they heard the first chain move, it was a slow sound, it rattled through the church like the toll of a bell, another one joined in short at first, perhaps a trick of the wind they reasoned ignoring the rational side of their mind telling them there was none, then all fell silent once more, everything grew calm silence once more returning, they walked the room carefully looking for whatever it could be that brought them here, looking for a key, a symbol anything that they could collect, they had to find it, they knew time was growing short, soon, the creature that had left the bloody trail to the door would return and not one of them wanted to join the ceiling artwork. A hand reached down suddenly, swiping at the air as the room spring into life, the chains above then began to shake as those held in place suspended, began to fight and struggle, their death like moans and screams of torment echoing through the small church as they fought, they fought with quick unnatural movements, stretching their skin further and further as they fought. Acha became aware of a strange noise that echoed through her, a noise that did not belong in the place, a noise that was neither chains, the dead or the generator, a noise she should know but couldn't place. A loud crack echoed through the air as Elly struck her, it was only then when the strange noise stopped she had realised it was coming from her a few sparks seemed to hang in the air as the silence descended, with that one noise, everything had once more descended into the uneasy silence.

"Do you want to join them?" Elly hissed nodding towards the ceiling; Acha's eyes were wide in terror as she shook her head slowly. "Keep that up and you will be, or are you forgetting, there's a monster not too far from here." Elly looked towards the bloody footprints leading to the door casually as if to prove a point. "It probably already knows we're here; forget that, the whole island probably knows were here. Lets just get what we came for and go before it decides to add us to its collection."

"Surely we can't just leave them here... right?" Eiji looked to the others for support, there was nothing more horrific than the thought of leaving those bodies hanging from the ceiling, his senses alone told him they weren't dead, not really, perhaps they were to look that way, but there was no room in the realm of dreamers for beings who belonged with Hades, they were simply displayed that way, they were the town people of Abaddon, those caught under the curse of Marise Shi, surely this was their only chance to free them, to return them to their normal life. "Right?" He questioned again a little more power behind his voice as Daniel and Acha turned to look at Elly, after all she seemed to be the one with all the answers, besides, they doubt it would be as easy as simply finding a way to unhook the victims, not that scaling a church walls wouldn't prove a challenge, but if this was truly Marise's doing, things would be far more complicated.

"Do you think Mari would just let anyone waltz in and free her prisoners?" Elly looked straight at him, ignoring the urges to look again at the people above her, it reminded her of a famous piece of art work she had seen as a child, but that had been destroyed like most things when the time of the ancients came to a halt, if she was to make a reference to it, things would get far more complicated.

"But she's not here she wouldn't know." He protested looking again at the mothers, children and families suspended above in their gruesome positions, he was certain now after their little performance they really were watching him.

"Although *she* may not be here, her magic is, nothing would ever be left as simple as just releasing them, her work is always encrypted. It's the way she works, she likes to be sure... besides, this place is just a limbo, if you truly wanted to help them you couldn't do it here it would have to be attempted at the spells origin... right?" Elly turned to look at Zo realising she had been very quiet since their descent and then she saw why. Acha was at her side instantly touching her shoulder as she knelt on the floor, it seemed she had been their some time, the blood from the rain covered her hair and back, looking at her she seemed so tired.

"Zo" she gasped, "are you ok?"

"I think... I over did it." She whispered as Acha helped her to her feet, it was a helping hand she desperately needed, despite her efforts previously, she had lacked the strength to stand, the small orb glowing dimly as it followed her every move.

Daniel was busy examining a figure that had caught his eye, she appeared so life like, yet unlike the others she clearly was not, she made no attempt to move or struggle like those above them had previously, this figure had stayed motionless the entire time. The girl looked somehow familiar, her long golden brown curls fell just short of her chest, her eyes although filled with blood, still had within them the slightest hints of baby blue, he knew without a doubt she wasn't a native of Abaddon. In the few seconds of laying eyes on her, the image robbed him of all those years he had thought about how peaceful it would be to die in your sleep, although he had not come to realise that which Eiji had previously, had he, he may have executed a little more caution, this girl was proof it was far from it. Suddenly, without reason her name left his lips, plucked from the air as he concentrated on her image, he knew it was her name and now he knew her.

"Liza." As he heard himself say it he realised why she looked so familiar, she had been on the missing poster board for about two weeks now, a place he regularly checked in case one day it bore a picture of his friend, she was the daughter of a well known family, it was thought possible kidnapping, although there had been rumours she had run away to escape her world and live with the one she wished to marry, a marriage condemned by her family due to the boys upbringing, sadly, he had been an orphan, his land and home taken from him by law when no will was found, he was but a young boy then and was sent to a temple to be raised, where he worked hard to bring money to them, despite it not being a requirement. As a child, he picked apples and tended the garden, as he grew he ran errands around town, he was a lovely boy with a heart of gold, but Liza's parents could never see past his penniless past. They found the boy beaten to an inch of his life near the town of Abaddon, he fingered those that pursued them, yet they claim never to have touched the girl, although it had been their plan to hold her for ransom, but the boy had blocked their path, never surrendering until she had put some distance between them, the last time they saw her she was seen running into the forest of lost souls.

Her body was suspended like the others from above by rusted fishing hooks, strategically placed to present her in a crucifix position, although the horror of the painful demise did not stop there, moments before her death her stomach had been split across forcing all that rested within to fall with gravity, although the mass of organs were still suspended from her body, it was clear she had died from shock, although had she not, she would have slowly bled to death. It was from the pool of blood below her the footprints leading to the door had first appeared, the blood was fresh, Daniel was wiling to wager her flesh was barely cold but lacked the stomach and the courage to test his theory.

"I think... maybe that's what we're after." Daniel pointed into what use to be the girl's stomach within it a small circular object awaited a small piece of blood stained paper attached to it, even from a few feet away Daniel could make out the words "Zodiac Marise Shi." Daniel looked to Zo. "It has your name on it."

"Do you think Marise is after these too?" Acha questioned looking at Zo as she stared into the stomach of the girl with a sick horror.

"Maybe it's more like a calling card, you know to Zodiac Love Mari." Elly answered without a second for thought. "I mean this *is* her monster and she *will* know who's coming for it."

"So his whole Knights-errent thing... do you think it's her doing?" Daniel stepped back to give Zo some room.

"No… I don't… think so." Zo said in a quiet whisper as she got within reaching distance of the corpse, everything fell silent except for the pounding of her heart within her head as she got closer and closer before extending her arm, the light before her lit up more than she cared to see, she closed her eyes tightly, her fingers gripped tightly around the object, she opened her eyes quickly swearing she felt something by the object move, just as she was about to pull away the girl's head shifted, turning sharply, unnaturally to look at her, try as she might she could not remove her hand from the girl, it was not that it had become embedded or trapped she simply could not move or take a single step away. Eiji grabbed her shoulder puling her back sharply as at least ten of the fish hooks suspending the bodies shot from somewhere to one side of them, thanks to Eiji's quick reactions brought on by his understanding of this place only one had actually grabbed her, they looked to its source hearing the sound of chains, they barley missed a glimpse of the shadow moving from where they had been fired from, the girl's arms swiped violently at her but thanks to the hooks holding her lacked the leverage needed to strike, her hand stopping just inches away from Zo's horrified face.

"Stay still." Eiji whispered looking at the blood running from Zo's arm, he bent slowly unfastening the knife from his boot, watching the area around for any tell tale signs of movement, quickly he sliced the invisible string that seemed to be trying to pull away, the wire made a sharp pang as it recoiled. "It has got to come out." He squeezed the flesh around the hook hard.

"Erm…guys?" Daniel almost whispered as everyone's attention was on Eiji watching him and the surroundings intently as the corpses jumped to life once more

"It will have to go right through" he saw the serrated edge knowing there was no other choice, just like all the times he had caught himself on a fishing hook, he would now do for her what his master did for him so many times.

"Guys?" Daniel repeated a little louder,

"Ready?" Zo nodded closing her eyes tightly as Eiji began to push and turn the hook, she bit her lip as the pain exploded up her arm, then in a second, it was over, Eiji threw the bloody hook to the floor, which Elly quickly picked up sliding it into her pocket without notice, she was no so foolish as to leave something that could be used for magic in a place belonging to a beast, especially considering that if the beasts summoner was to die, it would be granted immortality, who knows what such a thing born from Hades would be capable of.

"Guys!" Daniel's voice echoed around the church bouncing off the walls several times, by the time it had faded the others were looking at him. "The footsteps… never left the church." He whispered in the same manner a child would in fear of getting caught, not that it really mattered, all of them had made so much noise it was impossible to believe they had been unheard. Daniel pointed to a small detail within the blood stained hellhole they had failed to notice… the faded footsteps leading to the door taking a new route easy to miss on the blood stained walls, but there sure enough was blood smeared up the wall where the creature had ventured. A single drop of blood fell from above landing on Acha's flawless skin, knowing the area they stood to be corpse free all but Acha looked up to see its source, although masked by the shadows, all to be seen was a pair of eyes looking down at them from the ceiling above. It was then they ran. First to the door banging on it hoping that it would give, yet just like before it stood firm, Elly tried the handle, after all hadn't Zo said it could be opened from the inside? Meanwhile seeing that path blocked Zo and Acha ran to the hole, finding their rope kindly wrapped into a neat circle at their feet, Elly grabbed it having followed them, hurrying them back towards the door, there wasn't one of them who could climb that wall, all the time the creature watched above not moving much, just watching as they ran.

"Sword... now." Elly commanded shoving Zo ahead of them with a force that nearly made her lose her balance, despite stumbling a few steps the sword was drawn on command, a strange light filled the air momentarily as its blade of dark and light formed, the glowing orb before her faded slightly as the blade was called. The door seemed to shatter even before the sword had touched it, although she was sure this was just a figment of her imagination, something about it just didn't sit right, as the strike followed through the sword faded into a fine wisp leaving her holding the drawn hilt. "I'd keep it out just in case." Elly stated as she hurried them out of the building.

"It's not like I had a choice." Zo gasped trying to keep up with the others, Daniel grabbed her hand as she started to fall behind, he glanced at her wondering if this was really the same girl who could run for miles with little effort, to see her so out of breath, looking so tired, was unnatural, he could not remember ever seeing her this way, almost as if every step was an effort, he seemed to be literally dragging her, forcing her steps. He didn't need to glance behind to confirm his fears, yet for some reason he still did, the creature was following, a fair distance separating them, but closing quickly, its movements were as unnatural as its tangled mass of bones and muscle that constructed it, despite its awkward build somehow it began to gain. It was not a creature of their world, but they already knew that, they knew it was a creature pulled from the very centre of the underworld, a summoning, even so knowing this did not provide them comfort, knowing that the thing that chased them should never be, that the very principal behind it impossible, did not comfort them at all, and why would it? The impossible creature that was neither human nor beast, that had the appearance of a thing that's skin had been pealed away followed them, no matter how much logic, how unreal the creature was, it did not change the fact it pursued them. As it pursued, its organs moved with it, trembling with its every step, there was something playful in its movements, it was gaining, yet then for a moment it seemed to slow allowing them to gain distance again. For the most part it looked almost human, maybe once, long ago it had been, it ran on all fours almost dog like, but somehow it seemed more twisted, as it ran it almost seemed as if its hind legs were going to overtake its almost human looking hands, yet fell back at the last second, the only other feature that gave it away instantly as none human, except its hind legs, was its not quite human shaped skull filled with razor sharp canine teeth, the same size as a large dogs would be, yet filed into triangles to give a fine point capable of tearing through flesh and maybe even bone, but testing that theory was something none of them wished to do.

"How come it left the church? I thought it was restrained." Eiji gasped putting in that little extra effort to stop from falling behind, besides, it seemed last place belonged to Zo as Daniel pulled her along desperately.

"It seems its creator released it." Elly cringed avoiding the urge to glance back, she had failed to judge her actions, by having Zodiac break the door, any restraints binding the creature into place had been broken… "I warned you Mari encrypted things… or maybe… it's hunting, after all it is free to hunt remember." She added for the benefit of the others, Eiji knowing what he did, already, knew more than he wanted to, he turned his vision forwards suddenly noticing there seemed to be a sixth member to their party, a figure that seemed to be leading the way through the forest barely a few paces ahead of them.

The creature remained in hot pursuit as they ran through the forest, although when they entered, they had only seemed to have walked for minutes, yet now it seemed to stretch before them forever, then again, something told them they were not running towards the town of Abaddon and this was a good thing.

Given the creature's unnatural build it seemed to have no trouble keeping pace with them, yet at the same time the gap between them never closed. It seemed to remain the same distance away whether they ran faster or slower, it adjusted its pace to keep this gap, it was clear to them now, not only were they lost somewhere deep within the forest, but the creature was toying with them, letting them think they had a chance when clearly they had none. It knew that eventually it would have them, the same thought raced through each of their minds as the gap began to close, how could you fight such a creation? It should be dead yet it lived, as a being summoned from the underworld, it would live until it's creator passed or failing that, until it found a way to become immortal and break the binds of the spell that summoned it, the gap between them grew smaller and smaller, a gap this time they were finding difficult to widen it drew closer by the second. It had stopped playing.

***

Night appeared before Eryx Venrent who immediately rose from his old beaten chair that stood before the recently lit log fire, he had been wondering how long it would take for one of his minions to pay him a visit, but for the man himself to arrive, that was something he had not expected. He ran his hand around the back of the chair willing his old bones to move to face the place he felt radiated the unmistakable power; a tired smile crossed his wrinkled brow as he faced the direction he knew the God stood.

"You truly are a man of your word, I thought maybe you would have had your minions descend upon me after all, they have been watching me for some time now… ever since I…" The elderly man paused deciding it was better not to proceed with the direction of that conversation. "Yet… you come to me smelling of promise." The old man gave a slight respectful bow towards the area which Night stood, although Night did not speak, he simply watched for a moment, he and Eryx had once been great friends, until the day he betrayed him, an act he would never forgive him for, but he had paid a heavy price, Night had taken his vision vowing to complete his revenge when the time suited him. "Although I have to wonder, what a mighty power such of yourself could want with a child like our Zo." Eryx asked the question, he knew but part of the answer, he knew part of the reason Night would seek her, but even without his sight, it was clear there was something more to this than what he knew.

"All in good time old friend, first I have a deal to uphold, to deliver that which I promised in exchange for your service." Night was in front of him before he had even felt him move, he felt the draft of air pass before him as Night waved his hand before his sightless eyes, something changed, he felt it start deep within him, then all at once the darkness became a little lighter although he still could not see, he knew it would only be a matter of time. "Do not strain yourself, to see after such a long time is a shock to the system." The old man felt his way back around to sit in his chair, he could barely make out the flickering light of the fire before him, but this was more than he had seen for over twenty years, anticipation filled the air around him as the flickering flames came into blurred view, now he could make out colours, shapes, everything was coming back quicker than he first expected.

"Tell me, what are your plans for Zodiac?"

"I'm sure all will become clear in time, first a drink." He touched the old man's hand guiding his fingers around the tall glass. "Your promised youth will be found only at the bottom of this, although it needs to enter your system, this may take an hour or so, maybe less. As for sweet Kez's child, she was born for one true purpose, and that was to serve me, see for yourself." Night smiled passing a picture to the old man, he squinted at it finding a slight amount of focus on the parchment, he stared open mouthed, she was the spitting image of her mother, her long brown held the same warm red glow that reflected the very warmth of her heart it was tied back loosely the shorter layers falling from it framing her face gently, her eyes however unlike Kez's were a stunning blue, no doubt her eyes came from her father's side of the family. She was kneeling by a small hut, a trowel in her hand smiling brightly as she tended the garden, she had her mothers smile. "I was surprised at how much she matured, I never thought a year's training would have been adequate but something happened while she was in training that proved me wrong." The old man passed the picture back to him and smiled, maybe a girl of such pure heart and soul could bring a softness to his eye, it was clear how much he cared for her, maybe, she could ease his temper and calm his rage, she was so pure she just may be able to do it.

"Gods rest my heart, she looks just like her mother at that age, how Kez would smile to see." He took another mouthful of the sweet tasting liquid tasted somewhat like a fine mead he had once drunk in his younger days.

"The resemblance *is* remarkable; this was taken six months ago when we were looking for her. You see, she somehow vanished from Blackwood's care and ended up in Crowley, no memory of her reign."

"Reign? What a strange word you choose to use."

"Indeed, anyway I must depart I have many things to attend old sir."

"Forgive me for asking, but for this favour, are we… even now?" The old man shuddered as he heard Night laugh; it was a deep haunting laugh that could suck the soul from his very being if that was his desire.

"Even? I have paid you for your favours, this is no more than an exchange of goods for a service, surely a trader such as yourself should recognise this. My minions have watched you for some time plotting how to carry out my revenge, of course… they could not approach after all could you sense them… you'll find with your sight restored that sixth sense of yours will quickly vanish… then we will be even." With those final words Night vanished leaving the old man with a sinking feeling in the pit of the stomach, he knew one day he would have to answer to Night's judgement and was just fooling himself believing this single act would atone for what he did, fooling himself to believe that their friendship of old may offer some form of redemption.

The old man sat back on his chair thinking back over the day, before he knew what was happening voices were running through his mind, with no control whatsoever, he had no choice but to listen.

'*I have a nine year gap… I awoke in an unfamiliar place.*' Her voice echoed in his mind as images of the past began to race through it as he travelled back to eleven years it was Zo's twelfth birthday, she wasn't to have a party no one wanted to be acquainted with her kind, instead, she left for the Blackwood academy how her mother shone with pride…

'*She somehow vanished from Blackwood's care and ended up in Crowley.*'
'*No memory of her reign.*'
'*No memory at all of the last nine years.*'
'*I never thought a years training would have been adequate.*'

Eight years ago Marise Shi appeared it was rumoured she worked for a lord by the name of Blackwood, although those who uttered the accusation only spoke it once…

'*I did not feel a year to be adequate.*' The man awoke in a cold sweat unaware of when his consciousness had left him, he lay on the floor in front of the extinguished embers of the fire, his entire body shaking, he was unsure where those dreams had come from but a deep terror resided within him as he realised what he had been too foolish to see before, Night didn't care about Zo for the reasons he had first thought, he cared about her because of her power, he could use her to obtain the Grimoire, he could use her to train his armies as a commander to his reign, was that the truth behind why he sought her?

"By the Gods what have I done?" He raised his once wrinkled hand to cover his face feeling that it now possessed the texture of youth. "Why didn't I see it before?" He questioned. "The dates were there, but this old fool couldn't join the dots, too blind to see the awful truth that had lay before me so clearly, what curse have I bestowed upon Zo?… Upon our world?" In his hand he still held Night's elixir, he stood quickly smashing the glass into the fire as he cursed, had he known this before, he would never have agreed to the deal, he now knew the true terrors that he had helped to release, he had but one choice and that was to try to stop her before anything happened, he wondered if perhaps she would listen to reason, Zo he knew would, if it wasn't already too late, he had to tell her everything.

From the distance he felt them, Night's Minions were still watching, he had to make this right before the sense that repelled them faded, mere hours had passed and already it his senses become so much weaker, then again, knowing Night as he did, he doubt his revenge would be instantiations.

***

"There's no way we can out run it!" Daniel gasped the extra effort of keeping Zo up with him was really beginning to take its toll, suddenly her hand jerked from his followed by the sound of her hitting the ground. He skidded to a stop as did the others as if on cue she turned quickly sitting to face the creature. "Zo!" He panted turning back before he could even move the creature was upon her, she felt its sickening breath upon her face as it sniffed the air around her, its hands rested on her shoulders its hind legs straddling her, it glanced up towards them it's teeth snarling at them, warning them away.

"What should we do?" An unfamiliar voice whispered, they turned to look at him, his short brown hair loose and ragged, his questioning eyes so dark against his pale completion, he stood amongst them almost as if he had been there all along. "We… have to kill it… before it gets her." Eiji stepped forward to the challenge a light breeze began to rise around them.

"No!" Elly commanded grabbing his arm breaking the concentration. "Wait." As much as she feared what this could mean, she had to trust in the creature, trust it would know its creator, hope that it would not action what it seemed to be threatening as it stood on top of her. They knew for certain Zo lacked the energy to fight it off, her poor attempt at running had proven that, she lay now, eyes wide in terror as she struggled for breath, yet at the same time, there was certain calmness to her. Obeying Elly was their only option, she always seemed to know best and could only hope that this would not prove to be the one time she was wrong, the creature snarled and growled as it sniffed the air a little more, Eiji shifted uncomfortably waiting for the signal, waiting for a command that would mean he could do something, anything to get that horrible creature away from them, away from her, despite who she was, he felt the need to protect her at this moment. The creature looked at Zo, tilting its head to one side as it studied her carefully, its red eyes taking in every single detail her copper low-lighted hair, her fearful blue eyes, everything to the small spec of blood on her right cheek from her kneeling in the blood rain, without warning its tongue stretched licking her cheek leaving behind a trail of saliva and blood, but Zo did not move, she did not make a sound, her eyes gazed up in awestruck horror, her body trembling, it quickly dismounted nudging her arm slightly as it stood besides her, she lay for a moment longer simply staring up into the green foliage, long after the creatures weight had moved, long after it had nudged her prompting a response. Finally she found the strength to move, her eyes staring blankly ahead, it watched over her as she pulled herself to her knees, there was something almost protective about the way it was behaving, it seemed eager for her to stand and refused to stray from her side while still looking to the others growling with murderous intent, it stood for just a moment besides as she gained her balance, her vision now fixed on the blood stained grass as she rested against a tree, it glanced to her quickly her before taking off after the others, who for whatever reason, remained fixed to the spot as the creature came for her, for a second Zo could only stare at the place the creature had been but then, all of a sudden, like coming out of a trance something inside her snapped.

"Enough!" She screamed angrily as the echo of her voice ricocheted around the deserted forest, the creature stopped dead, just staring at the place the others stood. The stranger's eyes locked coldly with Zo's cold heartless gaze, her hand rested on her hilt as the stranger glanced to the creature and back to her again. The creature padded the ground uncertainly and like the stranger looked between her and him as she swayed slightly even with the trees support, the ball of light before her chest illuminating her ghastly pallor, enhanced by the dark streaks of blood left by the creature, seizing the confusion Eiji completed what he had started from nowhere the air grew denser, darker as a pale ash descended around them thickening the air until they could not even see each other. Zo felt an arm grab her from the blindness she tried to fight it at first, but it wouldn't release her and she was too weak to argue, the hand began to lead her away as Eiji led them the ash parting around him as they walked until they emerged from the forest by a crystal clear stream.

"Who are you?" Acha was the first to ask what the others had been desperate to know since the stranger's appearance.

"My name in Abi." He looked around the group almost as if he expected some form of recognition, giving a boyish smile when he received none.

"Abi that's an unusual name for a boy." Acha commented before she could stop herself, there was a moment of silence before he answered.

"It's short for Gabriel, I never liked it much." He ruffled his hair uncomfortably as he flashed her charming smile. "I really aught to thank you for what you did back there, your saved me from that creature."

"How?" Elly questioned suspiciously.

"You didn't see me?... I.... I was hiding. You see I got trapped in that church, the creature on the prowl and all, I thought I could save some of the people, but I couldn't get back out, it knew I was there but, it couldn't find me." He looked to Zo before the others; he squinted at the light that shone before her. "He was so close to finding me when you appeared, if not for you I never would have escaped." He joined Acha as she knelt by the riverbank watching for a moment as she washed the stains from her arms, as Zo approached he shifted uncomfortably. "I'm sorry to ask... but cant you do something about that light... being in the dark so long, it hurts my eyes" he rubbed them slightly as if to enforce his words, she turned her back to him shaking her head gently Daniel looked to her, she wasn't quite seeming like her self.

"We need to cross the river, who knows how long it will take for that creature to track us down again." They followed Elly down the stream they had been walking a while until they finally reached an old bridge, it was the kind of bridge seen in children's drawings, the perfect arch from one side straight across to the other, Elly was the first to cross the bridge followed by Daniel, then Zo the stranger looked at it hesitantly frowning slightly

"I can't cross this." He stated sadly looking back at Acha.

"What do you mean, is there something you need to do?"

"No, nothing like that... it's just... I know I'm asleep and this is all within my dream... but unlike you, I don't possess the mark that allows me to walk into the boundaries of others dreams... yet I fear that if you leave me... it will find me again, it would never let me escape from that place." He wrapped his arms around himself at the thought of the creature's return.

"The mark?" Acha tilted her head to one side before realising what he spoke of "How... well what would you need to do to be able to come along with us?"

"Only one baring the mark may pass it on to others so they can aid them in their adventure... I can be useful, won't you taken me with you?"

"What do I need to do?" Acha asked suspiciously, remembering a story she was told when she was younger about a troll in a cave, the only way for it to escape was for another to take its place.

"That's simple." He smiled handing her a small knife. "You just need to give me the symbol, then we can cross the bridge, together." He said as if reading her fears,

Acha smiled at his answer, the blood had already began to drip from the boy's arm into the stream as Zo spoke.

"No." She stated softly her voice seemed so distant, despite her words she was unsure the reasoning behind them, her reaction had been that of tired fear as she still tried to understand the events involving the strange creature. "I mean do you think it's such a..." By the time she had spoken it was already too late, they were crossing the bridge.

"I don't know how to thank you!" He exclaimed reaching the other side he ruffled his hair again and looked at Zo "I know..." He stepped towards her, as he did so she stepped back, she didn't know why, but she felt threatened by this stranger. "I know a few tricks, I'm sure I can put that light of your out... that is if you wish." He took another step again a step she once more matched in the opposite direction. "It won't hurt, it's just magic reversal, please it's the least I can do after all you've done for me, his hands reached out to be either side of the glowing orb, Zo frowned, for some unknown reason, the idea did not appeal to her, regardless how ill this particular magic was making her feel, she didn't trust him.

"Umemi." Seiken appeared from nowhere as always, she stepped back just before Abi's hands closed around the orb. "Magic here is very different to that in your world, it is connected to you, as the barer of the sacrifice rune, every piece of magic you do effects you from the moment you entered this world even although you did not possess the rune at the time, your light, for example is projected from your soul, if it were to be extinguished... you in turn would die. To destroy your magic, is to destroy you. Another thing, it takes a lot more effort to sustain magic here, to use it for any length of time is potentially deadly." Zo stepped further back still her hands coming up to protectively cover the light.

"But Abi knew that." She whispered before looking accusingly at the figure finally making sense of her confusion. "You!" She snarled looking up at him as he laughed, "I knew there was something odd, I just couldn't finger it. Aburamushi, that creature wasn't after us, it was after you that was the guardian, summoned to protect the innocent people, to keep you in order"

"Pity it can't cross boundaries isn't it? I guess the great summoner never thought that I would be released." He took a swipe at the orb once more, missing thanks only to Seiken's quick reflexes in sweeping his legs from under him as he struck; he got up quickly, looking at each of them in turn smiling as he did so. "Again I thank you for your help." He laughed, dusting himself down. "In return, I shall spare you... this time." With those words he vanished like a dreamer waking from their dream, they knew by this alone, this part of his life-force was being reunited with its ties to their world, Acha still clutched within her hand the bloody knife she used to free the creature, she dropped it quickly realising what she had done.

"I don't understand, what just happened?" Acha question turning to look at Zo, her face seemed to show the reminiscence of a smile, but she knew it was just a trick of the light.

"That creature before it wasn't after us, it was after Abi, Aburamushi is a shape shifter, it can assume the form of most life forms, although Marise was cruel there was also another side to her, to ensure it posed only a threat to a certain area a guardian was created, one that would scare even the bravest men, ensuring only the ignorant and foolish, ventured into the lair of Aburamushi." Zo stated suddenly to the confusion of all, Eiji and Elly both turned to look at her sharply.

"Why didn't you say anything before? When we were at the church, fleeing from it? Or before I gave him passage through the boundaries?" Acha demanded

"I didn't know, the guardian told me its story, it tried to warn me, but I couldn't make out what it was saying, it spoken in an ancient tongue, it has taken me this long to translate." Zo lied slightly as she glanced across to Elly, she had understood all too well every word it had spoken and why wouldn't she have considering the circumstances? "Maybe Elly should have told you about it." They all turned to look at her.

"Hey, don't look at me. I… I didn't know." She lowered her vision slightly to look at the ground "s*he* never told me!" She snapped making her way back to the central point on the bridge, if what Zo had just said about the guardian, was true, it was unlike the Marise she knew, it left her wondering what secrets the guardian could have whispered, could the other side to Marise, Zo had spoken about, been her? Did that means she now knew? Elly glanced towards the sky it was growing late; staying on the bridge would be the safest option considering the area.

"But why was it sealed away in the first place?" Acha questioned

"You saw for yourself how manipulative it is, free it could do all kinds of danger and it feeds on people's life force… although, I don't think it has to. To have something like that running around without boundaries… would not be a good thing. That thing needs to be banished, or at least the original spell reversed." Elly looked at Zo who was sitting on the edge of the bridge looking very tired as she turned the small rune over in her hands for a while staring at it unseeingly.

"I think maybe we have done enough damage. It's getting late" Zo spoke wearily placing the rune into a small pouch.

"My thoughts exactly, we should stop here tonight, and when we get home we head for Abaddon."

"And besides." Added Daniel moving to sit besides Zo. "If what Seiken said about magic is right the sooner we get back the better." He smiled at Zo as they made themselves comfortable.

Chapter seven

"How dare you? What the hell were you thinking?" Zo screamed the second Elly appeared, she sat up squinting against the light at the bottom of her bed, as her eyes adjusted she could make out the silhouette of the angry figure, Zo fingered a small ornament on the dressing table, easing Elly's vision as the light faded leaving the object glowing for a short moment, she stood arms crossed looking down to her waiting to hear what she had to say, Elly rubbed her eyes as she swung her legs out of bed. "Don't you release how dangerous it was? Do you think if I would have known...?" Zo stopped as Eiji, Daniel and Acha sneaked past the door, they were on the way to meet them but hearing Zo's angry screams they knew better than to disturb them.

"What are you talking about?" Elly stretched glancing around the room as she spoke.

"I should have known." Zo continued as if not hearing Elly's question, ignoring the look of complete bewilderment on her face as she lowered her tone, harshly yet quietly she continued "the first day we met... you called me Mari!" She tuned her back on Elly hiding the tears that welled in her eyes, Elly stared at her a moment wondering if she had really said what she thought she had heard. "Did you really think you could keep something like that from me? Did you think I wouldn't find out?"

"Mari... I... how did you find out?" Elly stood now awe struck; it was, as she feared, the secrets the guardian spoke of were those she was never going to mention.

"The guardian told me, you know the one *I* created although it spoke in ancient tongue, I heard its every word, over and over it called me master, it was then I released, the places I knew, the information I recalled without knowing its source... I'm a fool for not realizing sooner, then again, who would want to add the facts to find out they are... now, how did Daniel put it?... Oh yes, a blood thirsty murderer!" Although her words were only quiet the anger behind them made even Elly flinch. "Why was it you came to me really? I was never in any danger you came to take me back didn't you? To hand me over to your Lord?" Zo couldn't understand anything her mind raced with doubts and fears, how could she, the person who cared for every living thing, become the sought after Marise Shi, the blood thirty killer without morals, just what had happened over those years of darkness? What had she become? Now she knew the truth, she feared more than anything she would she become the very thing she despised most.

"Not you..." Elly stopped covering her mouth as Zo turned to leave. "No wait, you don't understand." She called after her, cursing under her breath, she hadn't been prepared for this.

"I understand perfectly" she stood at the door and answered without even looking back

"I wasn't..." Elly paused, her hand falling to her gossip crystal, there was something she had to do before she could pursue this further, before she could smooth over this mess before it was too late, but she had to be quick, who knew what she would do in this frame of mind.

Zo stormed down the stairs, a strange hollow feeling rising in the pit of her stomach, she felt physically sick, she just wanted to get away, to leave it all behind… back then, during the time she had forgotten, she was deadly, as she thought hard about the dark void that was her past, she could not think of anything that could have made her that way, she still recalled no more than before, yet now she knew the truth. But how could it have happened? She had a wonderful home, a loving mother, she was even accepted into a renowned school of the arts, although, as she could remember, she w*as* the only student there… she frowned willing herself to remember more, how could she possibly be that bloodthirsty murderer? No it was wrong, that creature had to be lying, but Elly's expression had told her otherwise, just what was going on?

"Zo are you ok? What's happened? You're shaking." Daniel stepped in front of her; suddenly she became aware that she was pacing back and forth along side the dining room table as a million new thoughts stampeded through her mind, thoughts that made her verge on illness as she realized the true meaning behind this revolution, just how many people had she killed? She looked up to Daniel then to Acha, a new thought in her mind filling up the already overcrowded jumble, if they were to stay, they would be in danger, not just from the journey, but from her.

"I want you both to go back home… I'm leaving now, and you *don't* want to follow me." Her voice was cold, expressionless as her gaze fell towards the door, she had to get out right now, she needed some air.

"But Zo." He looked at her, the anger in her eyes sent a shiver down his spine, never had he seen her so worked up about something, just what had gone on between her and Elly? Well he was sure going to find out, everything recently had just been so confusing, he could understand her confusion, but not so much this anger, a cold, seething anger that radiated from her person

"What's going on?" Eiji walked in from the kitchen seeing Zo and Daniel standing in an eye lock, they both looked away, he put some toast on the table along with a jug of water his stomach sank, from the look on her face it was painfully clear what was happening, somehow, she had found out the truth.

"Maybe you should ask your partner in crime… or better yet, Split Company before she betrays you too." She slung her satchel over her shoulder, her backpack already resting on the other as she stamped towards the door

"You can't just leave. What about Knights-errent?" That wasn't exactly what Acha had wanted to say, she wanted to ask why? What had happened? Anything to prevent her walking through the door, yet it still closed behind her. Daniel went to go after her, but was stopped once more by Elly, why was it she always seemed to get in the way?

***

A hand grabbed her as she walked towards the exit she had chosen, pulling her gently into a side street, something about her had clearly changed since she left the inn, her hair shone red reflecting the anger of her soul, her eyes bore menacingly into the stranger.

"Plum blossom." The young man whispered, knowing immediately that she was not the person to whom he was speaking, she was different from the photo he had seen, he knew this was not his Zo, she looked down at his hand which gripped her arm tightly, before looking at the brown haired youth, he was older than her, yet now, in appearance by just a few years, possessing a build suitable for a solider within Blackwood's army. His eyes were an old grey, within them much knowledge was held, the eyes never lied and right now they showed this man was afraid, she could see it clearly. She smiled at him feeling his hand tremble upon her arm, near by the cheers from the pub could be heard, it seemed something was happening there that gripped the attention of all those passing by. "I know who you are." He whispered looking towards the ground then back towards the main street where now, not a soul passed, he suddenly realised his actions had been those of a fool, what had he truly hoped to achieve by confronting her?

"Then might I suggest you remove that hand before I take the liberty myself?" His hand moved with lightening speed, there was no resemblance to the girl he had spoken to before in his home, nor to the picture Night had shown him, this girls hair shone a brilliant red, brown lowlights clearly evident, her eyes were not blue as the picture had told, but a deep sea green and like the sea, under its surface lay many horrors just waiting to tear him apart… at the same time, they had that luring, 'come on in the water's fine' look to them, beautiful but deadly. "Now old man, tell me, how do I find Night?"

"What makes you think…?" Before he could finish his question, her sword was drawn and at his throat pinning him against the wall with lightening fast speed, a speed that even the Gods would be challenged to meet.

"You reek of his magic old man, just as your house did when Zodiac stopped by… now tell me where to find him or you shall not have time to enjoy your bargained youth." He felt the sword press harder against his throat as a warm trickle of blood ran down his neck.

"I don't know… I swear, he came from and vanished into the shadows, he contacted me, I swear, I do not know." She looked up seeing a person in brightly dressed attire standing at the edge of the side street watching, she knew him and thus knew exactly where his next point of call would be, he would go to see Lee, someone she did not care to face at this moment.

"You're lucky this time." She glanced to the street where the figure had once stood "You breathe a word of this to anyone and you will wish I *had* killed you. Besides, I'm sure Night has his own plan for you… can't you feel them?" She taunted. "His minions are watching you old man." She stated coldly removing her sword throwing him to the floor smiling as her scrabbled in the dirt to get away. She turned her back on him leaving him lying in the street, the man that saw her posed no threat to her, neither of them did, but she did not want to confront Elly, not until she had put a few things straight, she had to decide how exactly they would meet, as friends, or as enemies.

***

"I thought you said there would be no trouble!" The inn door flew open Elly greeted the inn keeper with a smile as the door slammed shut behind him, his bright clothes drenched with sweat as he gasped for breath, his podgy face almost as bright as his top

"Whatever do you mean?" Elly asked in a tone implying she had more of an idea than she wished to let on, again a strange smile crossed her lips. She looked to the dining room, the door was tightly closed, yet she knew just on the other side sat two people oblivious to the identity of their friend; she couldn't help wondering when they too would put the pieces together like she had this morning.

"I just saw her outside, sword to some poor youth's throat! We agreed this place was out of her influence." He spat, Daniel knew something was going on he stood causally by the door listening to the hushed tones of conversations, he glanced across at Acha and Eiji, who seemed unaware the event was even transpiring as they began to eat the toast Eiji had prepared, as he listened he grew more and more concerned, surely they weren't talking about Zo? The event he had just described did not sound like his friend at all, she was always so calm, so nice, she never lost her temper even when things were at their worst, although recently there was no denying there had been a change, she had been quick to anger, but even so, threatening another's life was definitely not something she would do, not unless it was in her own defence, even then, he doubt she would have the ability to make true her threat.

"Is he dead?" Elly finally asked after the innkeeper had finished his ranting, that question alone made Daniel's stomach churn, why would she ask something like that so calmly? As if that wasn't disturbing enough, what she said next really disturbed him.

"No but…"

"Then count your blessings." Daniel had heard enough he opened the door, the conversation falling silent as he did so, he walked right up to Elly, determination in his eyes, if this was his friend they were talking about, it was time he was told what this was all about.

"*What* is going on?" He demanded, he knew they were talking about his best friend and he of all people needed to know if there was something wrong, he always worried about her so much, although his words had been perfectly clear they ignored him completely.

"I can't believe I let you bring her here."

"Which way did she go?" Elly handed him the rest of the money as she did so all concern left his face and was replaced instantly by the mercenary smile he was known for.

"It looked like she was heading Tran-gin Street." He flicked the money past his ear before breathing in its scent, all signs of his distress vanished in an instant as he found comfort in his money.

"Thanks." Elly stopped her hand on the front door, Acha and Eiji now stood at the dining room entrance with the distinct feeling that they had missed the crucial points of an important conversation, having arrived only in time to see Elly complete payment. "Daniel, Acha, don't you have some place to be?"

"Exactly what did you two fight about?" Daniel walked a little closer to Elly positioning himself carefully between her and the door sealing her escape, this was not a subject he was about to drop at her say so.

"I believe she told you to go home that's all *you* need to know." She glanced at Eiji. "I can meet up with you later." She passed him a piece of paper containing a street name and directions; he looked at it and nodded. "I will meet you there"

"But say they do go home, there's still Knights-errent to contend with..." They looked at Elly hopefully as Eiji fought for them.

"No. They need to go home; it's far too dangerous for them to come any further." Elly opened the door glancing back at them, leaving Daniel to wonder how she had passed him without his notice.

"Then I suppose I shall accompany them, and we will meet up later?" He questioned looking again at the paper; she nodded as she left closing the door gently to, Eiji was already painfully aware of the looks from Daniel and Acha he became recipient to.

"So where exactly is Tran Gin Street?" Acha questioned crossing her arms in front of her standing between Eiji and the door.

"All you need to know is your not going that way, anything else is not your concern."

"Is Zo in some kind of danger?" Daniel questioned from behind as Eiji turned to face him Acha subtly removed her invisible gloves.

"You could put it that way." He sighed, he wanted to tell them everything to explain what was going on, it was clear these people cared so much for her, but it was not something his honour would permit.

"And you're taking us home?" Daniel nodded to Acha.

"I never said that." Eiji turned quickly grabbing Acha's sleeved arm, she looked to him in shock as he gave her a warning look before releasing her. "I said you're not going that way... I know a short cut, remember?" He waved the piece of paper at them before placing the keys on the inn keeper's counter watching as he counted them one by one to ensure they were all still there.

***

"So what exactly is going on? Elly clearly knows more than she lets on... what's this danger that is responsible for this?" Daniel asked as they walked the streets of Collateral out of Elly and Eiji, Eiji had seemed to be the one not deliberately hiding things and next to Elly, he held the answers they needed.

"It's really not my place to say." Eiji glanced at the street names before matching one up with his paper, he had been successfully sidestepping this conversation for some time now, but they were persistent, despite his many obvious attempts to avoid the topic, they refused to let it drop.

"Is it something to do with what they were fighting about earlier?" Daniel persistent as ever refused to drop the topic, his best friend was in some kind of trouble and he was determined to find out what it was.

"Possibly, but I know as much as you about what happened this morning, but it was bound to happen sometime. Think about it, Elly knows everything that Zo has forgotten, but she won't let on even the slightest clue, there's bound to be tension between them, especially when Zo finds out something she feels it was her right to know all along"

"And what is that?" Daniel prompted before they felt the slight resistance as they passed though the silver barrier, when they emerged they were in a place seemingly untouched by people, mile upon mile on fields and forest spread as far and the eye could see.

"Careful around here it is the home to many wild beast, my master told me great tales of the creatures he encountered here."

"You know as well don't you?" Acha ignored Eiji's attempt to change the topic of conversation and with a Daniel like persistence pushed it further.

"Please don't ask me anymore, I won't betray her trust."

"You're referring to Elly?" Daniel scoffed although he admired that Eiji was an honest and trustworthy person, he wished for once he would be given a straight answer all the time they spent asking he knew they would get no further information from him, not deliberately anyway, but he may slip up and so they had to try, they needed to understand more about the situation and with each passing minute the thought grew that it was something more dangerous than they first expected. But Eiji remained true to his word, that was just one of the many things that made him so honourable, yet right now it was an annoying virtue.

"That's all I'm saying, just because I know what is happening does not give me the right to speak it, the story belongs solely to the person who writes it, it's no one else's place to tell."

"Yet you found out about it from Elly?" Daniel couldn't help feeling somewhat infuriated, why should a complete stranger be allowed to know more about his best friend than he, or she herself knew?

"I did not ask for the story, I was told it, then I was given a choice, to live or to die." He gave a sigh quickly glancing around the area, something was close.

"And yet you refuse to tell us even though she threatened your life? You still protect her?"

"It's not her I am protecting." He snapped his words brought realization to both Daniel and Acha's face, whatever this matter was, it was clearly important, perhaps it had some political relevance with it involving Blackwood's daughter Elly, could it be Zo unknowingly held some information crucial or detrimental to him without her even knowing? Something so secret that even the uttering of it would jeopardize her safety? If so, then perhaps that would explain why there had been no advertisement of her disappearance, in fear for her safety, it certainly would take a long time to locate someone without the communities' watchful eye, perhaps they feared if they were to know she had vanished, then whatever information she held would fall into enemy hands.

***

"I knew you would come Lee." Elly heard her voice before she could even see her, as she walked a little further through the woods she saw the clearing, the red haired girl sat there on a large fallen tree, her back to the approaching figure.

"Mari." Elly smiled hastening her pace to join her, the figure turned to look at her sharply, her green eyes boring into Elly for a moment before they softened.

"Has much changed since I was banished?" She leaned back against one of the branches, bitterness in her voice as she cast her vision skywards.

"Very little." She replied moving to join her on the branch.

"Of all the people to betray me I did not think it would be you, I would cut you down here, if I thought I could win… it is always a bit of a chance with you." Marise fingered the hilt of her sword gently as if contemplating something,

"Why do you say that?" Elly touched her pocket as if confirming something was still within her possession, Mari knew this move too well, she was ensuring that should she choose to fight, she had a weapon to defend herself with.

"Zodiac. You helped her return did you not? It took so long for me to seal her away before, and you brought her back, over a year has passed since then, I have had time to think about why you would have done it, I believe you had the best intentions… you did, didn't you?"

"Mari, you have to understand, there are so many reasons I did what I did, I saw her shadow within your eyes, occasionally she would cause your hesitation, because of her, that boy lived, because of her, the Elementalist walked, Aburamushi, who you created, was sealed by a guardian to protect the innocent. Lord Blackwood noticed these things too, I had to do something, you practically begged me, you went on about how things could have been different."

"And the real reason?"

"You have me there." Elly smiled giving a shrug. "The initial order came from much higher, I think it was part of his plan, to seize the final Grimoire, remember only one pure of heart and such… but what I said before, I was concerned for you, I didn't know what the potion would do, he simply told me it would help you to gain the final book and that once you had taken it, I was to choose a peaceful island where no one would bother you. A place you had never been, he mentioned nothing about the method, when I saw the outcome I was shocked, I never thought that was the plan, I don't know what I thought it would do, but it wasn't what I expected. In honesty I didn't even know how it had affected you until I met her, after you had taken the potion you just collapsed, so I did all I could and carried out his orders. After I gave it you I was committed to follow through so, I followed Night's instructions. While you were unconscious from the potion, I found a small island, not much use to anyone really and I left you there knowing that somehow things would work out, that I could come and get you when Night decided the time was right." She spoke softly yet without remorse.

"Don't worry; I would never challenge you…" She paused as if to consider her words. "But, maybe it would have been wise for us to discuss it first." She leaned up from the branch turning herself to sit by her.

"What did you mean about having time to think about it? Are you somehow aware of all that transpires?"

"In some respects… Zo still uses me, to repress her sadness, in her heart she knows something terrible has happened." Marise gave a wicked grin "her sleep is full of nightmares, sometimes she will see something reminding her of events from the past, although before she can recall them, her self defence mechanisms kick in… I see a lot of things through a window as such… But Daniel, that boy to me is a complete mystery, it's as if he makes her forget, I know his name, but he is what makes my return so difficult, her friendship with him is strong, I feel her within me now, thinking of the harsh words she spoke, unaware even that I am here… I am not truly sure what happens to me when I'm not in control, but during my reign it was as if she was never there, I could not feel her as I can now."

"That will be rectified when we find the final book, it seems Night has set us a little challenge, ultimately I think it will serve some purpose in his quest else he would not have gone to so much effort… do you know, she released Aburamushi?"

"*I* let him leave… I also felt him grow in power, tell me are you going there now to undo what I did?"

"It would break one of the seals; I feel that is his plan… to weaken that which our ancestors constructed"

"Speaking of troublesome obstacles." Marise smiled. "I'm thinking it would be better to remove three annoying ones."

"That is a little rash, besides, besides Eiji is under my protection." Elly glanced over the hills; no doubt they had started out now. "I am sure they will have their uses, if only to ensure things stay on course."

"When this is over…"

"You have my word you may do whatever you wish to them, it is a fitting reward for the sacrifices you have made."

***

Acha's scream filled the air as a giant beast collapsed before them, it was a strange looking creature with the mane of a lion, the beak of an eagle, in size it was very similar to a horse, yet bore the stocky build of a lion and razor sharp claws.

"Daniel, are you alright?" Acha called scrambling to her feet from the place just he had forced her as he forced her from the creature's path as it had pounced. It seemed to have come from nowhere, they had heard Eiji's warning, but not in time to save them from the creature's strike as it pounced from the undergrowth to where they stood, she rushed to his side shaking him gently as he lay on the floor, they both felt the vibrations through the earth as the falling creature hit the floor. Daniel gasped in pain clutching his chest where his torn white t-shirt began to stain with blood. The wind died as Eiji finished his spell watching to ensure the creature would not move again before joining Acha at his side.

"We need a doctor and fast." Eiji looked at the three giant gaping wounds across Daniel's chest; the wounds seemed to have a pulse of their own as the blood forced its way through, if they didn't stop the bleeding soon…

"Daniel, you idiot." Acha scolded concern ringing through her voice. "I could have just found another…" She pulled him tightly into a hug before encouraging him to lye back flat on the floor, although the wound was bad, the shock seemed to be somehow slowing the blood flow, Daniel's pallor was ghastly. Secretly, they all knew that the chances of them reaching help in time was virtually impossible, he reached out grabbing Acha's hand tightly.

"Please, find Zo; make sure she is… alright." He whispered, his words sticking in his throat.

"Of course, Zo… if we can find her she can help." Acha looked from Eiji to Daniel.

"I was to meet Elly somewhere over this hill." He glanced towards the rise on the horizon, you stay here and watch him the creature's scent should ward off any curiosity, so no matter what, just stay put until I get back." He ordered as he took off in the direction he had motioned stopping after a few feet, before taking his knife from his boots, he looked back to them before throwing it, it landed upright in the ground within a foot of Acha, before he took to running again.

"Eiji please hurry… there isn't much time." She whispered looking out over the fields to the hill he had vanished over just seconds ago.

***

Marise gasped, her hand shooting to her chest, she blinked. Her eyes changed before Elly's concerned vision.

"Daniel." Zo gasped in shock, glancing around like a startled animal trying to take in her surroundings, having no memory of how she arrived where she was. "Where's Daniel?" She almost shouted, her hand gripping Elly's arm tightly any concerns about her whereabouts slipping from her mind as if they had never even arose.

"What…" Elly began to question Zo, finding herself a little confused by what had transpired, she was in mid conversation with Marise then suddenly out of nowhere, *she* appeared. Elly didn't have time to finish her sentence before Eiji came tearing over the hill screaming her name

"Elly, thank the Gods." He gasped barely able to speak between breaths. "It's Daniel… he's hurt, bad." He leaned over placing his hands on his knees as he gasped for breath Elly looked to Zo

"How did you…" Elly stopped she thought I better not to question further, Marise was right, the group were trouble, they challenged her control.

"Eiji, tell me, what happened?" Zo demanded, her voice filled with fear as he stood gasping for breath, when he didn't answer she pressed further not realizing his gasps for breath were hindering his ability to speak. "Where is he? Where's Daniel?" He took a few more big breaths before forcing the words.

"Over the brow, need a doctor, there isn't much time." Eiji gasped before he had even finished his sentence Zo had took off at lightening fast speed in the direction Eiji had appeared from.

"How odd." Elly stated watching her vanishing figure.

"What?"

"Never mind, we should go after her." Elly began to walk with no hurry about her pace began to follow Zo.

"We need to get a doctor!" Eiji protested finally able to talk without having to pause for breath.

"There's no point." Elly stated coldly watching Eiji as he looked from her to the distance wondering if he could make it, estimating the distance to Collateral, if they ran flat out, surely they could just about make it.

"If we hurry… we could make it back before…"

***

"Zo, over here!" She heard Acha's cries before she could even see them, a small figure just off the horizon waved frantically. She skidded across the damp grass until she finally stopped dropping to Daniel's side, she didn't need to look twice to see he was in immediate danger, her hand rested on his forehead probing his mind and body for the initial diagnosis, her heart racing as she scanned the environment simultaneously looking for a way to heal him quickly, the woodland was the answer, trees that could heal themselves over great periods of time, she just needed to accelerate the process through her, if they would permit her to call upon them, she turned her attention away from them focusing fully on Daniel, although clear what he suffered externally who knew what poisons or inhibitors may have been introduced through the creatures claws.

"What happened?" Although she had run a fair distance, it seemed to as if she had been mere steps away, showing nearly no signs of fatigue, and only slightly short of breath.

"The beast, it came from nowhere… Daniel saved me." She sobbed guilt for her friends injury taking over her emotions as she looked to the beast, Zo glanced at it quickly before turning her attention back to him.

"His pulse is faint, Acha watch for the others…" Acha nodded turning her back on them watching the horizon for the small figures to appear like she had when she was waiting for Zo. *'Now listen to me'* Zo whispered not with her voice but with her mind, she spoke to him mind to mind, the manner in which she did so was not as calm as she had intended, she only hoped that through her, he wouldn't feel how hopeless the situation was, even if the forces leant her their power, there was no certainty she would be able to perform the rites required, it had been so long since she had attempted healing on such a great scale, it was a complex process, so much could go wrong and her relationship with him would further complicate things. Hectarians, should never attempt magic on those they are close to, the results of doing so were uncertain, but there was no choice. She had to act quickly, she could already feel Hades' messenger hovering around the area awaiting the outcome, it was really going to be that close, if she was to heal him, she needed to keep him focused, if he was to slip much further, she would have to battle Hermes for his life, but for now, he simply watched. *'Concentrate on my voice, focus.'* She commanded as she felt his mind weakening further, she touched her finger from his head to hers sealing the bond between their minds to free up her hands to start the healing process, she tore the remaining shirt tatters from around the wound, it looked bad through the shirt, but that was nothing compared to the mess that lay beneath it, seeing this alone made her all the more aware of the ever approaching footsteps of death, already he was closer than expected. *'How do you get into these messes?'* She thought suddenly after a moment of drawn out silence, realizing she had been quiet for too long as she focused on the first part of the enchantment, if the silence remained unbroken, she may lose his attention and then it would be over, her hand pressed tightly down on the first wound, she hesitated once more, a strange feeling creeping over her, almost like de-javu, a feeling that she had done something very similar to someone before, someone she cared deeply for, she shrugged it off, there was not the time to be distracted.

The claw marks were twice the size of her hand in length stretching across almost the entirety of his chest

'First that Viking guy, now this, you would think I would know better by now than to leave you on your own.' She gasped feeling the force of nature flowing into her body, feeling the millions of silver threads from all life around connecting to her. *'I'm so sorry.'* She

gritted her teeth feeling the flesh beneath her hand become coated in a fine sap before it began to close, but Hermes still crept ever closer, she had hoped by now, at the very least, his pace would have slowed, that was normally the case, yet he remained steady, constant, what was she missing? Was there something else or did things really hand so close in the balance. The gentle wind becoming stronger as her needs became more demanding, once the first was completely covered she placed her hand on the next, allowing the coating sap to continue its job alone as it bound the wound together, she concentrated seeing with her mind the plants and trees offering her a little of their eternal life, and in the way they would in nature, went about healing his wounds, creating through her magic a protective sap that encapsulated the wound while it closed. *Just one more... Daniel.*' She found her mind almost screaming at him as his pulse grew weaker, she was finding it difficult to keep his mind attentive, worse still, she could almost feel Hermes breath upon her, she knew if she was to turn, he would be as visible as Acha, for this reason alone she did not look, hoping if she failed to acknowledge him, he would halt his approach, he did not. It was impossible now to concentrate on keeping his wandering attention while the same time concentrate on healing him physically, normally she would have to chose one or the other, but this time there was no choice, to keep him here she needed his mind, but she also needed to heal the wounds and now she and Hermes both competed for his attention, it was a battle she could not afford to lose, a battle she would not lose, no matter what. No matter how hard she tried as she tried to keep him focused on her, the wound would not seal, it was impossible to do both with a wound such as this one, but if she couldn't, she would lose him. She hesitated a moment, there was but one option, she needed to keep his attention, she needed him to focus on something other than the pain and tiredness, but with there being only one way to do this, she would risk losing him forever, but at least he would live, she had no choice but to use a method that filled her with fear and dread, but his life meant more than anything to her, she had vowed to protect him and so, in fear for his life she did the only thing she could, and offered a bit of herself to him her childhood, her thoughts, her memories, as she opened her mind the crisp steps of Hermes stopped, feeling it grab Daniel, he knew now, this moment was not yet the time for this person he had lost all holds on the wounded person. Her memories held his attention fully where she herself had failed, she released him into her mind, into her memories knowing this was the only way she could now focus on healing, finally the final wound began to close. Echoing in her mind Zo could hear Acha shouting her name over and over, but it seemed so far away, she had to ignore it, she had to concentrate. Whatever was happening would have to wait, if she broke concentration now all her work would be undone. Finally the last cut was sealed, her eyes shot open, although she was never actually aware of closing them it was always the case, once the initial diagnosis was complete her mind took over, everything she saw from that point was not through the eyes of her body, but through her mind's eye, Amelia had always called it healing lore.

"Zo!" Acha cried again pointing to her top, Zo looked down seeing a quickly vanishing blood stain it was not that she had been wounded, nor was it an occurrence she could explain and so, no matter how disturbing she found the faded bloodstains, she pushed them from her mind. She glanced up at a nearby tree, watching as it shed a single leaf in autumn colours, she caught it gently within her hand thanking the tree silently, she looked to Daniel, his life signs were becoming stronger, she touched her forehead before she placed her other hand on Daniel's, she kept it there for a moment until she was satisfied he would be safe.

"That was amazing!" Eiji exclaimed moving to sit besides her, she was unsure exactly how long they had been there, she had to wonder if perhaps the steps she heard had been theirs, but she knew otherwise, but the thought it had been so close, had scared her beyond belief.

"He's still very weak." She gasped, not all too surprised to find herself trembling uncontrollably. "He has lost a fair bit of blood but he should be alright." She sighed, for a moment her eyes locked on a figure on the horizon, as she looked it seemed to make a polite gesture before vanishing into mist, she glanced to Daniel in relief ensuring he was still breathing and hadn't changed his mind about his recovery. When she finally caught her breath she asked something that had been bothering her for some time. "How did I end up here anyway? Isn't this close to that village we are heading to? I don't even remember leaving."

"You mean you can't remember?" Elly questioned. "It must be the shock after you stormed out I went after you, you were already on your way before I managed to catch up, I was barely with you seconds when Eiji appeared." She smiled to herself she was beginning to understand more and more about the situation she was facing.

'I'm glad that figures gone.' Zo looked to Daniel sharply hearing his thoughts before words even left his mouth, she looked away quickly.

"How... come... we woke in Collateral?" Daniel questioned quietly raising himself up steadily to rest on his elbows, he glanced down to his chest where only three pale fading lines remained of his injury, he opened his mouth to say something, yet for a second words escaped him, when he finally found the right ones, Zo placed her finger to her lips hushing him and smiled.

"Rest." She whispered, she placed the autumn leaf within his hand.

'I just wanted to thank you.' Zo was looking at Daniel the entire time, she knew the words never left his mouth yet she heard them all the same, she bit her lip, concern crossing her brown, the realization of what happened hitting her, increasing the burden she already bore. Now she had to protect her mind from him as well as hide her true emotions, everything was becoming so complicated.

'I was afraid something like this might happen.' She silently scolded herself for being so careless feeling the heat rise to her cheeks

"Like what?" Daniel asked seemingly out of nowhere earning him strange looks from everyone except Zo who turned a deeper red, Daniel had spoken before he had had chance to realize the words she had spoken were silent.

"Collateral," Elly finally broke the silence, deciding to share a piece of her knowledge with them. "Well, it *is* a place beyond all common laws, it exists everywhere yet nowhere. Within it there is a path to everywhere, since we slept in a place of no boundaries, there was nowhere on the planet it could place us which we wouldn't already be."

"So how come I was heading to Abaddon?" Zo questioned as the colour in her cheeks finally faded, her vision fixed timidly on Daniel watching him as he tried to make sense of the most recent occurrence.

"You said something about releasing the magic and checking the town to see if anything had altered since releasing the creature."

"Oh." Her answer was short, she couldn't remember anything like Elly had said, the last thing she remembered before the feeling of fear for Daniel's life, was telling them all to go home, everything after that was blank, but she never remembered feeling so angry, maybe Elly was right, maybe she had been blinded by some form of emotion, that was the only explanation, at least she hoped it was.

"If... the magic from the town was uncast... would the creature we released... vanish?" Acha joined the conversation already knowing the answer she would receive would not be the one she hoped for.

"Doubtful." Elly replied flatly seeing the drop in Acha's face "it might be worth a try though" Elly smiled reassuringly at her, knowing it would not make the slightest bit of difference to Aburamushi, but releasing the bond between the worlds already partly destroyed once when Marise took the Grimoire, would prove to be useful in the larger scale of things. As for the summoned creature it would do little more than release it from its feeding habits, a creature like that doesn't *have* to feed off others to live that was simply part of the magic.

"But wouldn't Marise need to release the spell herself, after all it is her magic?" For a second Acha's hopes had been raised until she realized the obvious.

"True, but we have a magic user of our own here that I don't doubt could equal, if not surpass her talents, that rule only applies to weaker magic users, they never possess the power to release another's spell..." Elly placed her arm round Zo's shoulder hugging her slightly before releasing her, she knew in theory Zo should be equal to Marise in magic, but to say so flippantly may invoke yet another questioning session and right now, for peace of mind this was the last thing they needed, who knew what Zo's answer would be? Especially after recent events.

"I..."

"Nonsense, it's worth a try" Eiji interrupted before she had chance to protest. "I mean after all, don't you want to help all those innocent people Marise Shi imprisoned Zo?" Eiji added her name to the end for impact, oblivious to all but Zo and Elly before he began walking away followed by Elly and Acha, he knew in his heart that they would follow, after all, she, in a manner of speaking was not Marise, he had faith that she would do what her former self would not, the right thing.

Zo extended her hand to Daniel helping to pull him to his feet; in his hand he still clutched the leaf she had given him. He shivered against the wind looking at the tattered remains of his shirt, before he knew what was happening, Zo held her arm out presenting him with the shirt she had only moments ago been wearing, Daniel smiled taking it from her, seeing that she had only been using it to cover the top she had been wearing, a top that extenuated her slender figure, it laced up the front, sleeve wise, they were full length fitting tightly around her arms, although where the shoulders were had no material, the sleeves were only attached underneath, he wondered why she had never worn that top before, it was stunning.

As he pulled the shirt over his head, his nostrils flared with her scent, the smell of plum blossom, he inhaled deeply pulling his jacket back on and around him, she smiled looking at him, all in all he was none too worse for wear, but she couldn't help wondering when the unexpected side effect would wear off, she heard his voice in her mind seconds before he spoke.

"Zo there's something…" He stopped hearing her thoughts as clear as if they were his own, despite that he continued. "Zo… when you… well, you know, went into my mind." He stopped seeing her blush he took a breath before continuing again. "Well."

"Come on you two, we're falling behind." Acha called she had waited for them as Elly and Eiji carried on ahead, she waved at them before quickening her pace to catch up, wondering if they would do the same.

'You can read my mind… I know… I don't know how… it just…' she stopped hearing his words,

'No, not that.' He sounded almost timid as if he didn't want to be a burden but felt as if there was something she must know, she looked to him curiously her heart pounded as he looked away in a deliberate attempt to avoid her gaze.

"Then what?" She asked aloud as the others vanished over the hill making no attempt to slow their pace just as she and Daniel made no attempt to quicken theirs.

"I don't know, they think just because my cuts have faded…" He chuntered to himself before looking at her, a serious look on his normally carefree face. "About that, thanks, I had no idea you could…" He shivered again wrapping his jacket closer around him. She stopped rummaging in her bag, he followed her lead waiting with his back to her as he continued to speak, perhaps not looking at her would make this easier, he took a breath yet despite the opportunity he continued with his previous sentence. "I mean it was incredible." He sighed wrapping his arms around himself against the cold…

…He thought back to the small voice quiet at first, drawing him towards it, pulling him from the darkness into a small speck of light pulling him away from another voice, a far stronger voice that despite his best efforts to concentrate on her, began to stifle her tiny cries to him. But as the light enveloped him, her words grew louder, although the spaces between them grew, he saw her kneeling before him, silver light connecting her to the nature around twisting through her body down her hands to his wounds, he felt the concentration it took to keep the flickering light between their minds active, he saw a figure in the distance, a figure he knew owned the other voice that called him, the figure beckoned him, luring him closer, he had almost felt as if while lying there he was somehow moving towards the figure, but still he fought, he fought to hang on to the tired words of his friend that so desperately tried to save him, yet still, against his best efforts he moved towards the stranger, he was close enough to see his features now, close enough to reach out and take the extended hand, which despite his strongest effort he reached for, he could smell the underworld on this figure, their hands barely a moment apart, if their skin touched, it would be the end. Electricity filled the air as a bright light snatched him back, once more he lay before Zo, the figure once more in the distance, but the light was not satisfied with merely pulling him away it continued its battle to keep him to the point he was drawn into her mind. The silver light pulled him into her thoughts into her mind, warming him as he heard the sound of ancient songs sang as a lullaby, the whisper of childhood dreams passed before his eyes, her first spell, the light took him deeper into her mind, past the light and into the darkness…

…"Daniel." She repeated again passing him some green coloured liquid and fastening his fingers around a piece of root. "You're in shock, drink this, it's a blend of herbs, although your body has recovered your mind hasn't, this will help." Normally she wouldn't dream of giving a person in shock a drink, but this was entirely different to the shock from an injury, this was the aftermath of his body realizing something that was wrong had now vanished. It was the moments of confusion that after being healed that could be quiet deadly if not treated with this special concoction, he drank the bitter tasting liquid quickly pulling a repulsed face, wondering as he did so if perhaps the taste of the liquid was revenge for intruding on her private thoughts, no matter how vile the medicine she had given to him, not once had the taste made them want to vomit like this did now, Zo pushed the root towards him taking the hint he began to chew on it as Zo began placing things carefully back within her bag. "I'm sorry for the taste I have no Candicious, that's what I use to sweeten the flavour." She smiled lightly. "Of course it's not my way of punishing you." He blushed realizing just as her thoughts were clear to him; his were also as clear to her. "Besides, it tastes so bad, you forgot about your symptoms." She stated, it was only now Daniel realized he had stopped shaking.

"So how long does this mind thing last then?" He asked in a very Eiji like manner directing attention away from his embarrassment, he moved to stand near her as she made another batch of the bitter liquid tipping it into her water bottle.

"I don't know… it… has never happened before." She shook the bottle gently avoiding looking at him as she did so.

"What about with Acha, I mean you knew she was in danger…"

"That was different, I was on the tip of her consciousness, I was aware of her, and any powerful emotions she had, it was nothing like this." She placed the satchel back over her shoulder.

"Oh." He smiled slightly

"I also think its better if no one else finds out."

"Is this the reason you've never used your powers on me?" Daniel thought back to all the times he had cut or hurt himself, she had always seemed to want to do something for him, but he was never sure what, until now.

"Kind of… It's dangerous for a magic user to be emotionally involved with the people she uses it on, it has side effects, that's why they tend to keep to themselves… if they get too involved they let their emotions rule their magic and things like this happen." Zo stared out over the horizon her mind weighed down with worry, all of a sudden Daniel felt her spirit lift. "Not to worry hey?" She smiled. "It's not like I can't tell what you're thinking anyway… It's easy enough to block, I mean I don't really want to know what I'm getting for my birthday, so I'll tell you how." Daniel suddenly got the impression she wasn't quite a cheerful as she was trying to imply, but just now he lack the skill to read her inner most emotions, then again, she had become quite skilled at shielding them recently anyway.

"Hey, who says you're getting anything?" He shoved her playfully as they approached the others, who had decided it was better to wait.

"Daniel, are you alright to continue?" Elly questioned noticing the change in his pallor; Daniel took a mouthful of water from the bottle Eiji passed him,

"Thanks." He smiled relieved to be washing the vile taste from him mouth with something more than another mouthful of the evil tasting fluid. As he passed it back to him he looked to Elly, only to discover she hadn't waited for his response and was already pushing on. Eiji offered the water to the others who politely refused. "Come on." Daniel sighed. "We're falling behind again." He placed his hand on his chest his breathing becoming slightly laboured.

"Are you sure you're ok?" Eiji questioned concern flickering through his eyes.

"Just stings a little" He replied taking a sip from the bottle he held within his hand that Zo was encouraging him to drink from as she lifted it to his mouth as he drank she released her grip turning to look at the others.

"You two go on ahead, we'll catch up." Zo smiled at Eiji and Acha who both had an air of concern about them.

"We don't mind… really." Acha smiled.

"It's ok, really, go." She seemed quite insistent so they surrendered to her wishes; Daniel was looking at her questioningly but waited for the others to leave before asking.

"The perfect time for what?" In answer to his question Zo simply smiled once more rummaging through her satchel.

"I should have given it you before…" She moved some things finding it to be quite difficult to locate. "But I wanted to save it for your birthday… but I think you may need it now." She looked up smiling before pulling six folded sticks, from her bag each one exactly the same length secured together by a piece of string, each one was about a foot in length, each section contained unique symbols and carving etched into the wood. As she undid the string Daniel saw a faint ray of light passing from the end of each stick into the next.

"What is it?" He took the mahogany coloured wood from her, expecting it to be fairly heavy yet finding himself surprised at its lack of weight he passed it between his hands

"It's a weapon… here." She took it from him. "Let me show you." She flicked in into a solid staff spinning it skilfully before it detached itself, again she span it like a professional, different parts attaching and releasing to provide a varied combination of weapons. "I made it myself, when I younger I saw one just like it in a dream, I thought how nice it was." She smiled remembering, handing it back over to Daniel. "I think you will find its perfect for you, it's joined together by magic, the links between them will grow and shrink as you wish to create a weapon for any situation. It has an excellent defence against magic; maybe later I can show you." She smiled watching Daniel as he flicked the stick into several forms; he had never been able to control a weapon, despite his father trying to teach him on many occasions, but this weapon as different, this weapon worked from the mind.

"It's incredible! It's almost like it knows exactly what I want it to do, then do it." He smiled looping it over his belt to hang in three equal sections

"It does it's magic. I made it just for you." She smiled he glanced down at it again

"It has even got symbols… but I don't recognize any of them." He fingered them stopping again noticing his name was carved on one of the sections in the ancient language "it must have taken you ages, the carvings alone are so detailed."

"Three months, while you were at college." She smiled answering his question with minimal delay. "I'm not sure why I packed it; I intended to leave it for your discovery, lucky huh? Just don't tell anyone where you got it... Ok?"

"Especially Elly right?" Daniel said catching a slight glimpse of a buried thought.

"Yes, you see, this weapon... may be the only thing that will protect you from..." Zo paused lowering her head, the darkened mood that descended upon her had been impossible to hide.

"Yourself?" Daniel questioned softly taking her hand in his; she looked away from him, blinking away the tears quickly before he could see.

"How did you..." She whispered her vision fixed anywhere but on him.

"I saw all the clues, but I wasn't certain until..."

"I healed you..." She whispered remembering how she opened her mind to him, she knew there would be a danger of him venturing beyond what she offered, beyond the memories of childhood, but it was either that or lose him forever, besides, it was not like she was going to keep it a secret, not from Daniel, was it? It was a question even she was not sure of the answer to, she feared what his knowing would mean. "I didn't know I swear." Her tone suddenly becoming defensive. "I only just found out myself... that's why I sent you away before I didn't want to put you in any danger."

"Don't worry." He smiled at her reassuringly as they approached the others, his smile alone comforted her more than he would know, the reaction she had expected when he learnt the truth had been far different from the one she received, yet, at the same time, there was something he was keeping from her.

"Are you ready?" Elly walked up to meet Zo and Daniel as they got closer, Eiji and Elly sat on the outskirts of Abaddon, in this world it was found hidden deep within the forest waiting their arrival, despite the dense forest they had entered, they had located them with ease.

"What is it exactly I am meant to be doing?" She questioned uncertainty gripping her now as she stood before the town, What if she couldn't do it? She glanced to Daniel, there was so much to discuss but now situations dictated their conversation to end prematurely.

"Just release the spell, it's fairly simple... but while I'm in these parts I have an errand to run, so if you will excuse me, I should be not be too long." Elly stated

"You mean, you're not... coming in with me? But this was your idea." Zo asked questioning the sudden change in Elly, less than an hour ago she was all for being here, yet now she didn't intend to stay.

"We don't have time to waste, it is quicker if I do this now than take you all with me later, you will be fine." Without anymore room for argument Elly walked away.

Hesitantly Zo entered the town followed by the others who matched her slow pace, looking through the windows of the houses, they found each bed had within it a person, where beds were not enough they had been laid on the sofa, their fires extinguished and their windows shut, the curtains of each house were closed tightly creating an artificial night within the houses.

"I guess I work my way from end to start then." She spoke to herself feeling the complicated webs that weaved into the spell, each thread looping and crossing another, she had to be careful not to damage the makeup if she wished everyone to get out of this alive. A faint sea green aura began to shine around her illuminating the air around her fading slowly to become an electric blue.

She felt the pull of the earth as she seized the first thread of magic within her mind crossing and curving it under and around those that came before it, as she did so ancient poetry gently falling from her lips, the flowers in the nearby gardens aged and died, bringing life to new seeds once again as the force she felt from the earth pulled her to her knees, she knew now she had started she could not finish, to stop now would be more dangerous.

Daniel watched her fall, running to be besides her stopped by Eiji.

"You can't interfere, what she's doing is delicate, if a none magic person was to interfere, they could damage the threads she unwinds… it may kill her."

"What do you mean May? Barely an hour ago she exhausted herself bringing me back from the brink of death, now she needs to unwind a spell equal to her full power when she isn't in possession of it?… If we don't do something, it will kill her slowly, by substituting her life force for magic when she has no power left." Eiji agreed with what Daniel had said, perhaps it wasn't one of the greatest ideas in the world to face her with such a challenge before she was given chance to recover, but if what Elly had said earlier was correct, once Aburamushi was released within Knights-errent, there was only a limited time to release this spell before the people would be granted eternal sleep, each one of them adding to the power of Aburamushi, yet by releasing the spell they would release the final ties of his imprisonment.

"Daniel…" Eiji sighed watching as Zo grew tired, by his calculations, the spell was halfway unravelled, there was no way she alone would possess the power to release it, even now he feared for her, although Elly had assured him everything would be fine and knowing what he knew, he trusted her word, when it came to the life of this person anyway, but why did everything have to be so close? A figure appeared before her, it was almost as if he had simply turned to face her passing from unseen to visible in a single step, reaching down he took her hand in his, pulling her gently to her feet. His long black hair fastened neatly back into a long ponytail, his electric blue eyes meeting with hers as she turned her tired gaze upwards, she smiled gently, the figure shared the same glow connecting them to the earth, although tired she remained standing with the aid of the stranger until the final ray of blue light had faded. She opened her mouth as if to say something but before the words would come she could found herself falling forwards to be caught in his embrace. He held her close for just a moment before picking her up in his arms walking her from the town's boundaries. When they were clear of the woods he lowered her gently to the floor, touching her pale skin while the others just watched in shock unsure exactly what to say to the mysterious stranger.

"You should know by now." He whispered. "I've never let anything harm you…" He looked to her friends raising his voice so they could hear. "It was careless of you to have her take on such a task given the circumstances, you *must* be more careful." He brushed a stray piece of hair from her face with a tenderness and concern that made Daniel uneasy.

"Will she be alright?" Daniel stepped forward the first to address him taking his attention away from his friend, putting an end to that gentle caress.

"I believe so." He looked back to her waving one hand over the other, within it appeared five amulets. "I believe these will aid you on your travels." He passed them to Daniel before lifting Zo slightly, a small phial appearing from thin air, he placed it at her lips ensuring she swallowed its contents. "This will help speed up the recovery." He answered the question although no one yet had asked, they hadn't needed to, Daniel had looked ready to interrupt, he couldn't say he blamed him, how was he to know he meant this girl no harm?

"Why are you helping us?" Acha stepped forwards; the man looked her up and down before answering her question.

"Knights-errent is a place filled with unimaginable danger, to fail would be to sign the death warrant of the planet... yet." He glanced down at Zo as she stirred from her sleep. "There is something, even more valuable at stake." There was a momentary silence while people exchanged questioning glances before Zo's eyes opened. She studied the stranger intently as he looked to her friends, she was convinced she recognised him from somewhere, his raven black hair captured the spectrum as the light danced across it, he turned to look at her and smiled, the smile reaching all the way to his electric blue eyes. "One thing that does bother me, am I correct in understanding you have help from a force of their world? I mean, as I was lead to understand the entirety of the Spindle race are captive, is it not your mission to free them?" The stranger looked between them, wondering if any would be so kind as to answer.

"Seiken?" Eiji questioned without stopping for thought, for a second he cringed remembering how often Elly scolded him for opening his mouth, but surely it couldn't do any harm, after all he had just saved Zo's life and aided in releasing of a powerful spell.

"Ah is see, a Spindle *has* come to your aid, interesting." He slowly began to walk away satisfied that his work was somehow completed.

"Wait." Zo called after him, as if on her command he stopped and turned to face her, her voice though barely a whisper had not gone unnoticed. "Who are you?"

"Who am I?" He smiled sadly as if he expected her to know. "My name is not important, maybe we shall have time for introductions next time we meet." Before their very eyes he vanished once more as if turning into nothing. Daniel's hands tightened on the amulets within his grasp, wondering not only how the stranger could possibly have aided his friend in the release of a Hectarian spell when magic was rumoured dead, but how he could have known there was another member to their group, his eyes bore into the place the figure had stood, more than anything else he wondered exactly what his relationship with Zo had been, he had looked wounded when she asked who he was, there was clearly more to this meeting than a stranger's concerns, how had he known she was in danger? Was he an employee of her lord? One sent to watch him and keep her safe? Or was there perhaps more to it then that? The way he touched her alone sung of a deep bond, just who was he?

Chapter eight

"How is it possible?" Night paced back and forth across the enormous room, across the length of the table and up to the full-length window that filtered a gentle light into the room. He climbed the seven stairs towards the door before pacing back down to the cauldron. "We have all the Spindles." He glanced across the room flicking the gossip crystal idly between his fingers.

"Yes sire." A dark figure stood within the shadows, watching him pace.

"Yet one is helping them, has there been any fluctuations in the magical barriers? Have the guards noticed anything out of the ordinary?" He raised his glass from the table holding it to the light as if to examine the ruby red liquid within a sudden thought entering his troubled mind. "Then again, this may just work to our advantage." He smiled a sudden idea dawning on him, although this was an unexpected twist but even so, it had the potential to work to his favour. He placed the glass back on the table glancing towards his visitor as they spoke.

"That one may have escaped you?" The shadow questioned uncertainly.

"That one within our possession has found a way to help them." Seiken's image flashed within the cauldron. "Go, bring me the one we call Seiken." He phrased the sentence carefully, he knew much of the Spindle race and their development although after this world's last cycle had not spent as much time in their world as previously, but he knew one thing that would never change, each Spindle, like all living things, possess two names, a social name, the name given to them by their parents or a name they are recognised by and their real name, a name kept secret from all those within their lives, a name that reflected the true power of their being, a name so powerful it should never be uttered by a creature from either world, a name only discovered by those who could look deep into the souls of a person not those that created them. He knew Seiken's name just from looking at him through the depths of the cauldron, he was, after all, once a God, a God that aided with creation itself, but fortunately, he was also familiar with their world and its secrets. Knowing a Spindle's true name was dangerous, he would never utter it, in or away from his presence, the repercussions, even to one such as him, would be great.

"And security?" The figure lingered awaiting his command, Night hesitated for but a moment before his answer.

"I see no concerns, bring me that Spindle... and while you're at it, find Aburamushi." Night smiled the plan now already developed within his mind; this was going to turn out better than he had hoped. When Marise had summoned that creature from Hades all those years ago, he never imagined he would find a use for him, the guardian was no longer a concern, since Aburamushi had been released, it had returned home once more. Night knew Aburamushi would be difficult to locate, especially since it was now free from the restrictions of boundaries, it would no doubt, now, be after the one thing he wanted more than anything, life, life not based around the survival of both Marise and Zodiac, something that would eventual fail, while Marise created Aburamushi, she had used Zodiac's power to summon it, even had she not realised it herself, once one gained full control, either the summoner or the caster's spell would be broken and Aburamushi would return to Hades, there were only two ways to prevent his ultimate demise, by his own hand kill those that created him taking their life-force and sealing it within him, or find a way to break his ties to them and obtain a life of his own. Aburamushi was not stupid, quite the opposite in fact, he knew should either of his creators vanish he would become nothing more than a memory and Night knew this beings desire well enough to know it would not sit back and idly await that fate.

"Yes sire, consider it done." The figure melted backwards into the shadow, before it faded completely it moved slightly as if to give a bow.

Moments later Seiken was thrown from the darkness to Night's feet, his hands now securely fastened before him by a strange cord that shifted through all the colours of the spectrum as it held him, these were the only restraints that seemed to have purpose although he wore one on each ankle and another one around his neck like a collar.

"My Lord, the Spindle known as Seiken." The voice from the shadow introduced the figure it had deposited, although it knew there was no need, Night knew all too well who lay before him.

"Very good." Night walked around him taking in his appearance carefully, looking over his fiery red hair and his gentle features, Night crouched to meet his eyes, there was fear within the delicate brown, yet there was something else too, even now Night knew he was not a Spindle of the last cycle, his eyes were different. Although Spindles were immortal there were those who chose to become mortal, to cross over into 'the world of the Goddess Gaea' as they called it. When this occurred a new Spindle was born, a Spindle that would possess the same wisdom and knowledge as the one who had came before him, the knowledge of Knights-errent would be removed, left with their successor as they made that final step through the boundaries. A smile crossed Night's lips but only for a second. "You're Eryx's successor, why am I not surprised?" He stated watching Seiken's eyes widen in shock as he was left to wonder how he could have known his predecessor. Night shook his head in mild amusement before looking back into the shadows, Eryx too had a fascination with people he couldn't have, but one person in particular had sealed his fate. He had even crossed into the mortal world to obtain her, yet somehow he retained some of his knowledge of Knights-errent. It was the first time he and Night competed for anything, although the word competition would imply that there was a challenge in the actions where truly, there was none. Even so Eryx couldn't stand the thought of Night having her, he wanted her to himself and ironically his successor had the same infatuation with this family. "And Aburamushi?" He questioned to the shadow figure.

"With his new found freedom he is proving very difficult to locate, although he should be located within the hour."

"Very good, then you are excused." There was hesitation from the shadow, almost as if they were expecting a different reaction.

"But Sire." It began cut short by Night's words.

"These restraints were created by the best to be the best is that correct?"

"That is true my lord, they link themselves to the creatures genetic makeup ensuring they cannot pose any threat."

"Escape from such a wonderful creation is impossible, correct?"

"Sire as you know, I myself made them, they were tried on many creatures before I presented them to you."

"Then I see no reason why you should remain, if the restraints will hold him, there is nothing to fear, and if there were, I am sure I could handle him on my own."

"Oh yes Sire, I did not mean to imply…" Night raised his hand to silence the shadow

"Had I thought you did, I would not be standing by so idly. Now if you will excuse us, I have a proposition for my friend and you have work to do." Night waved a hand dismissively and the shadow vanished.

"I am no friend of yours!" Seiken spat the very words themselves hanging bitterly in his mouth. He struggled against the strange bonds but with every movement found himself growing weaker, to pull himself to his knees was an effort he swore had almost killed him, but there had to be a way to escape, there just had to.

"It's no use struggling, those bonds are a high developed genetic seal, they adapt to its host feeding from their power, the more you struggle, the more powerful they become, draining your energy until you have nothing left to fight with. Here" Night pulled a chair from the nearby table turning it to face the struggling Spindle, without the energy to protest, Night placed him in it.

"I know who you are, I have already chosen my side, anything you have to say is pointless." Sprays of his auburn hair had pulled loose from the struggle making him look somewhat wild and dangerous, he sat breathing heavily, catching, his breath from his previous struggle. He knew what Night said to be true, at this second there was very little he could do but wait, if he didn't struggle now, perhaps he would regain enough energy to break the bonds in a quick, unexpected desperate attempt.

"Well if nothing else, it spares me the introductions." He walked away a little to take in Seiken's appearance it seemed he was no older than his daughter in appearance, although his uniquely brown eyes held more knowledge than any one person could expect to learn in the entirety of their life. Night's knowledge of Eryx placed him as a Spindle for only twenty-four years, yet the knowledge he possessed dated far before his appearance on Knights-errent, but had he been there previously he would have known, the power and knowledge he saw, was clearly that passed from his predecessor. Then again, there was something different about him, an age about his presence that no passed wisdom could create, but surely had he been around before, when he was close with the Spindles, he would have known of his existence, not only that, but this boy had a very Eryx air about him, from his reaction alone it was clear he stepped into his place. Night studied him harder for a moment, he was certain this child was older than he first thought, considering his heritage, he had to be, but how could they have kept a being like him so secret?

Seiken, was an unusual Spindle, his appearance, although similar to those of this world was different to any other of his race Night had encountered, true there were those who looked mortal, human, but something about his appearance, about the look in his eyes proved his was different, yet even he couldn't place how. Each Spindle had a never changing form unique only to them and this was his, human, yet slightly different. Build wise he was slender; it would be easy to fall into the deception that he would possess no strength, any foolish enough to believe this would soon learn the error of their thinking, his build disguised his strength well. "As for you choosing sides, it does not really matter; the outcome will always be my victory." Night smiled.

"Clearly to contain such arrogance you do not know your challenger." Seiken glared at Night trying once more to release the bonds; if he could just escape he would only need to dodge the guards, navigate the castle, find an exit and free his people without any of them being seen. He gave a frustrated sigh leaning back into the chair, even if he were to break free of the chains, there was little chance he could do much else, he had no choice but to listen to what Night had to say, the reality of the situation hitting him then, their only hope *really was* the success of this 'game'.

"On the contrary." Night smiled to himself as Seiken stopped fighting against the bonds. "I know her very well."

"Tell me what do you wish to gain from destroying both our worlds?" He snapped, ultimately this would happen if things continued on the course they were heading, should his kind not return to defend the barrier, there was a very real chance both words would be forced into havoc and a mode of self-destruction as it tried to right the wrongs that occurred, maybe if he could discover his ultimate goal he could warn his Umemi and armed with knowledge perhaps they could stop his plan before it was set into motion.

"Destroy them?" Night questioned an imitation shock held in his voice. "You have me all wrong, I don't want to destroy the world, I want to save it." He walked across to the enormous window stretching from floor to ceiling and with a wave of his hands the drapes opened.

As the heavy drapes parted Seiken squinted against the light his vision adjusting after so long spent in the dark confines of the prison, even the light of this room had, at first, been too bright to bear, he blinked several times. "Tell me, what do you see out there?" When finally his eyes adjusted Seiken realized he could see for miles, small towns littered across the land. Despite the vision if what lay before him, Seiken did not answer, he merely looked out on a world nothing like his own, a world man had destroyed to create life for themselves, unlike his world, the damage caused down there was permanent. "Can't you see it? The deceit, the treachery, the greed. That is the way of the world now, not like before, never would you expect a knife through your back, in my day your killer looked you straight in the eyes. It's not just the corruption; the people on this planet take it for granted, raping it of its energy and resources, always taking, yet never giving a thought to returning. They need to learn their place, they have become too arrogant, everything is not theirs to take as they wish." Night's voice was calm yet undertones of outrage and disgust lined his words.

"So… you want to… destroy them?" Seiken wasn't sure he was quite following the conversation, if he wanted to destroy them he clearly had the power so why this? What was there to gain by all this?

"Not all of them, a majority, yes. But once my plan is complete, the world will not tremble to man, but man to the world as it was millennia ago, the world's magic has all but been extinguished. Although we can thank the Idliod for that, but even they cannot take all the blame it is down to them, out there." He started through the window with disgust, a burning hatred reflected in his eyes. "Things need to change, those people exploiting the poor to line their pockets with gold, those who take yet never return, the lazy class, who do nothing but wait for others to feed and clothe them, the leaches on society that are of no use to anyone, they all need to be destroyed. Those few remaining, will serve me, although I shall not be the ruler, it will be the Gaea that is their mistress, I shall simply take back what was taken from me so long ago, I shall become the God they all feared once more. The Goddess Gaea has waited long enough, for the final sign of the prophecy and now it is upon us, I *shall* fulfil it."

"But then, are you not showing them the same persecution you just spoke of." Seiken was unsure truly how much he could say, but for the moment he knew there was something Night wanted of him, some reason why he was summoned to his presence, although he trod on thin ice, he somehow knew that true to his word, Night would not harm him, or his people.

"When the world was born, like animals, humans too would hunt and were hunted, survival of the fittest the scripts call it, a word where to survive is to live and failure costs the ultimate price. Magic ran wild across the earth none could tame it, it moulded things in the way they should have stayed, eventually man discovered a way to seal it. Since then, they have grown arrogant, self-absorbed. They have forgotten their place, but they will soon relearn it when everything reverts to the way it was."

"You're talking about unleashing the Severaine! To do such a thing, to unleash such a power... it's reckless, you know it can't be controlled now." Seiken could barely believe what he was hearing, in millennias past it took hundreds of generations to finally devise a way to seal its power, the seals have been in tact ever since, this world has forgotten its ancestors and their old knowledge long since buried by the sands of time, if the Severaine was released there was little chance of anyone finding a path to seal it, most of them didn't even acknowledge there was life before them, they lived in a bubble of ignorance and those who acknowledged the existence of others before them couldn't even begin to comprehend the kind of knowledge and power they held, despite the ancient technology that littered the world, the people of it had no comprehension what the time they called, the time of the ancients was really capable of. Although he knew the world was prone to complete full cycles, this cycle was far from over, since the last civilization of this planet was buried at the start of the New Gods Era, mere centuries had passed, they were not ready to face that challenge that would seal the Severaine, they were not developed and thus, now was the perfect time for Night to act, once released, they would never be permitted to develop enough to seal its power.

"Perhaps, but any further details on this matter do not concern you. Now down to business, the reason I brought you here." Night released he may have gotten a little carried away in trying to win the young Spindle over, it would be much easier to have him join him willingly, than to resort to other means, he would have his full cooperation, it was just a matter of knowing if they would be doing it the easy way, or the hard way.

"I'm not interested!" Seiken stated simply, he had been wondering the reason he had been summoned and was relieved to find they were about to discuss it, the sooner it was proposed, the sooner he could refuse and be returned to his people, there was nothing Night could say, nothing he could offer that would make him betray his people, his planet, there was only one hope for freedom and he would trust her to keep her word.

"We shall see, it seems you have little option other than to hear me out." Seiken was still gazing out of the window when Night decided to once again draw the heavy drapes, what he was going to say was important, the young Spindles distraction was not an option, it was vital he absorbed his every word.

"How is it that I am in your world?" This question had been bothering Seiken for sometime and although eager to leave, the answer may provide him with insight on how to get his people home. "Is this place...?"

"This place, neither exists here, nor in any other reality, although is accessible from any like most Gods' homes. Now as I was saying, I know you are helping our travellers." Seiken felt himself turn pale at his words, his stomach churned under his stare as he sat wondering how it was possible for him to know such things. "You may find my proposition, difficult to refuse."

***

"Are you sure you're alright?" Daniel placed his hand on Zo's shoulder worry crossing his wrinkled brow, she glanced up at him and smiled nodding, yet this did little to convince him, he glanced down at a book he had brought along for the trip, not really looking at it, he knew exactly which page the relevant information was on, after all this was his favourite book, the edges of the pages so warn they had began to curl, but still, he flicked through its pages slowly as he tried to make out what she was thinking. Since the stranger had left she had been trying to place him, she was convinced she knew him somehow, perhaps if she was to find the answer, it may solve some riddles concerning her past, she looked to him pushing the thoughts from her mind to focus on him. "Well." He finally broke the silence placing his book on the ground for all to see. "These amulets, seem to be of ancient origin used by those possessing the gift of astral travel, I guess what he said, was correct"

"It is my father use to possess an identical charm." Acha sighed almost as if she was reluctant to have revealed so much.

"Your father used magic?" Eiji questioned, although Acha had spoken much of her life, she spoke only of the time she lived in, when it came to more personal things, she barely uttered a word. She never mentioned her family, avoiding the topic whenever possible, she spoke only of the flowing fields the way of life now destroyed, pretty much everything as if it was pulled straight from a text book. From what they understood of her tales and descriptions her time was somewhere after the time that legends say the great battle of the Gods had ended and Prometheus gave the gift of fire to man moving them from the caves to their small modest dwellings. But this was the first time she had ever mentioned anything regarding her family that would give any insight into her past.

"In a manner of speaking, yes. My father use to use an identical charm for just that purpose, but things were different back then, those with immense power were Gods, with the power Zo and Eiji possess, back in my time they would have been worshiped, the magic we had was very limited and only those of certain families developed the gift, healing, blessings, astral travel... It was rumoured in the past angels came down from above and created a human highbred, ones that could use magic like the Gods could and shared their knowledge among the people, of course we all believed this to be nothing more than a fairy tale, the laws on the tablets made it clear, it was forbidden for any angel to be involved with a human, although they existed they were not to talk to humans, it was forbidden, should any be found to have defied the rules all touched by them would die. Even so ancient stories told of one, Shemyaza, who allegedly did this and was punished by the greater forces, it was rumoured there were others, ones who were never caught that followed his example, hiding away their children and families from those who would harm them. Humans too joined the hunt believing that aiding the angels would secure them a nice place in the underworld as they carried out the will of the Gods, they hunted and killed each other, accusing innocent people of being hybrids, it was a time known as the great witch hunt, any possessing the powers of magic or accused of doing so were hunted and tortured into confession. The dark angels spurred them on allow them to commit murder under the flag of justice after all they were temptation and for each soul they condemned their power would grow. Looking at how magic had developed I can only assume the legends were true, although, now it seems only scarce few and Elementalists can use it. I do not pretend to understand the difference between them. The new Gods came into possession of the tablets of prophesies they laughed at the tablet, banishing it so no one could get ideas from that which was written upon it and seek to fulfil the prophesies carved within its stone, one night it was taken from the monument and never seen again the Gods must have believed if no one was able to read it, then the concepts of that written upon it could never be. It seemed they had forgotten that even their fates had been written and acted out as Zeus rose up and dethroned his father Chronos, before knowledge of this tablet even reached them. Once this tablet had vanished the Gods once more took people back on Olympus, people like shamans and other holy people used astral projection to visit the Gods to learn from them, many of the Gods were harsh, and their lessons long so they provided us with amulets that meant as one left the physical being of this world they would not wander and always would return to the place they had been, before these were developed the Gods would lose a lot of their loyal servants who reappeared around the volcanoes that posed as a doorway to their kingdom, no man could ever walk there and hope to return, but always they seemed to appear there when they crossed back into the world, thus the Gods bestowed upon a few these gifts so they can return in safety to the place they originated." They all listened with great interest, that was the kind of tale was never told in any texts, Acha had so many interesting stories to tell that she could write an accurate book for a study, although most would say her word was inaccurate as unlike history, her knowledge of that time had not been altered by word of mouth, it was simply told as it was remembered by someone familiar with that time.

There was a long period of silence before Eiji broke the illusion by taking one of the amulets from the floor before Zo who had been busy threading leather ties through the hole to form a secure necklace similar to the one she had made for Acha but without the design and effort put into making it, this was just a tie fastened through the provided hole with knots either side for added security.

"I wonder how he knew there were five of us." He questioned, flicking the charm over before passing it back to Zo. "And our names." He turned the others over finding the one with his name carved on the back against the name was also a symbol, the symbol on Zo's was identical to the that of the rune key they had obtained from the church, each charm differed only by one symbol, were they to assume these symbols represented the keys meant for them?

"Well, he knew about Knights-errent and the Spindles, I guess it only goes to reason he knows who we are and how many of us there are." Daniel had been asking himself the same question over and over and this was the only answer he could conjure. "Of course I'm more concerned about how he knew where to find us, who he is, why he possesses Hectarian arts and more importantly whose side he is on." Daniel took a breath after reeling out the questions that had been circling his mind.

"Surely ours." Eiji answered. "I mean he helped Zo, and he gave us these charms to help us on our way." Eiji placed the charm over his neck tucking it securely under his shirt.

"True, but why us? Why did he choose to help us? And what brought him here in the first place?" Daniel closed his book placing it back into the rucksack Zo had brought, he had brought a bag of his own, yet it had been insisted he placed all items within her rucksack, which now seemed to take permanent residence in Elly's possession.

"Maybe it's just like he said, there's something more valuable at stake." Eiji wasn't sure who this guy was, but he was sure that he was genuine in his attempts to help.

"Like what?" Daniel glanced at Zo thinking how if she could just place him, just remember a little more of her long forgotten past, how much easier it would be to trust the stranger, especially considering what her recent explorations into her past had divulged. He hadn't realised he was staring at her until she looked up to him and smiled as she finished threading the last tie she leaned forward passing him and Acha theirs. Acha looked at the amulet already around her neck knowing that if she wished to keep this body the charm had to stay on, Zo motioned for her to approach, as she did so she took the amulet from her pulling her sleeve up she shrank the cord to form a secure bracelet, with the excess she crossed it up her arm tying it again when the cord ran out. "Another thing, why did he leave so quickly?" Zo finished tying the bracelet pulling Acha's sleeve down, over it.

"The people in Abaddon are different to you and me… I just can't remember how." Zo silently scolded herself, unsure if when the people began to wake if they would truly be in the danger she felt, but for now there was little they could do, they had to wait for Elly's return. "Besides, it is not like we can leave until Elly returns anyway; I bet she could tell us what they are." The fact she had just used the word 'what' unnerved her almost as much as Elly's sudden appearance.

"They're children of Hades." Elly seemed to appear from nowhere as if she had been waiting for her name to crop up before making her appearance. "Abaddon, you know the devil, Hades, the town wasn't called that without reason. All those that reside, are those cursed by the Gods, destined to live forever as the creatures your parents frightened you with when you were young. Sure they look human now, and they'll even try to convince you they are, but when the sun sets you have to be sure you're nowhere near, they undergo a transformation."

"Into what?" Acha questioned aware that sunset, although a good few hours away, was drawing closer, she glanced nervously towards the forest.

"You name it, Banshee, wolf, demon, anything capable of killing really, first they trick people into spending the night, feeding them, making them welcome, those who stay never see the light of another sun, of course if no one stays they hunt, why do you think we have so many missing people?" Elly smiled, she loved nothing more than a good scare story to set the mood, of course, things were different the first time she visited here over five years ago, Marise thrived on fear.

"There's not been many in the last five years." Daniel felt he had to add his part to the conversation, when he was younger his parents told him all the time of groups of missing children and adults that stayed out after dark, of course, you didn't hear that kind of thing anymore.

"Well don't you think that's about right? They have been trapped until now, and I warn you, tonight they *will* hunt." She smiled knowing not only would they hunt but they would also find a new ally, when the sunset tonight the world would make a powerful enemy in them. "I suggest we try to put as much distance as possible between us and them." This place was dangerous, the town held many memories for Elly, it was the second time Marise had almost lost her life. This place was not somewhere to be taken lightly, although, Elly blamed her own carelessness for what had happened here that night.

"Agreed." Daniel went to offer Zo a hand up to find she was already standing. "Are you sure you're up to it?" He looked at Zo who still looked a little pale,

"Shouldn't I be the one asking you that? You're the one who was at death's door." She smiled touched by his concern.

'And you came unbelievably close yourself' He whispered to her mind.

"So where have you been anyway?" Eiji questioned as Elly grabbed the backpack

"Well, it would not have been fitting to leave Liza in the town, especially tonight, then she truly would be dead, I took her home."

"Liza is alive?" Daniel questioned suddenly.

"Of course, she was in Knights-errent, dead people don't dream in the realms of Knights-errent, she was simply subjected to Aburamushi's form of suspended animation."

They began to walk, the sun barely a few hours from setting and getting away seemed more urgent than they first believed, they stayed to the track unsure really where they were heading just that it was in the right direction, away from Abaddon.

"Hey where you Kids heading?" An elderly farmer slowed his wagon to trot pulling on the horses reigns gently, he had gentle features, although tired, his dusty coloured eyes sparkled, he offered them a warm smile as they turned to look at Elly, after all it was her idea to head down this track and she had given none of them the slightest clue where they were heading.

"We're heading to the ring of fire." Elly smiled at the elderly gentleman.

"My word, I haven't heard that name since I was a boy, it's a good hike though, I'm heading to a town close by if you want to hop on."

"We couldn't just accept a lift, can we not be of some assistance to you in return?" Eiji asked seeing the wagon filled with fruit and vegetables, perhaps they could help him with unloading or something.

"All I ask is for the pleasant conversation of your companion." He looked to Elly and smiled. "It is, after all, a long and lonely road, besides I am heading your way, a few extra heads only proves to liven up the journey." Elly nodded, the others climbed aboard the back of the wagon to sit amongst the home-grown fruit and vegetables.

"So where about are you heading?" Elly asked joining the driver at the front of the cart. When he was satisfied everyone was safe he picked up the reigns and commanded the horse into motion.

"Heading? Oh yes, there's a new master at the castle on Ishitar Island, I have come baring gifts as is customary, that's my offering back their with your friends." He turned to look at them "I wouldn't miss some if you are hungry. The ship will leave tonight and you? What takes you to the ring of fire?"

"My companions and I are on a quest, we seek a safe place to sleep." She answered simply, still eyeing the traveller suspiciously as he gave a wry smile.

"Ah I understand." He glanced back at Zo and smiled. "The young witch is in trouble." Zo frowned slightly how could he tell she was Hectarian just by looking at her? True, Elementalist had a certain 'look' about them, but Hectarians didn't, did they?

"What exactly is this ring of fire?" Zo questioned feeling slightly embarrassed

"It's an circle of ancient volcanoes dating back to the world of the ancients or so it is told, they are found on the very end of the island, well there is more land but neither man nor beast could ever reach it and say even if they did they would never survive, there's no water past that point, from the second the volcanoes start nothing but desert stretches to lands end... the rings of fire." He smiled. "It hasn't been called that for years, the volcanoes have been dormant for about a year now, even before they only sparked and erupted flame, nothing more they never seemed to do any real damage, sure camps were burnt, but no one really got hurt, well there was one time when several people got killed, but considering the force we are dealing with it is nothing compares to what it would have been should they unleash their true powers." Elly smiled glancing at Zo who had the distinct feeling she was missing a personal joke as Elly thought back to the first time the volcanoes had erupted.

Marise had stood at the very top of the highest peak of the rings of fire. That village had annoyed her that day and she wanted to see them squirm. The villagers had thought themselves Gods, refusing to aid a local of the village this side of the rings. Of course the villages still didn't know of a settlement behind the unfathomable heights, it was thought that the terrain there was fit for no person, especially since it seemed there was no way around or over from the inland point of view. Their foolishness that day had cost the life of the local, who had been out to collect some imported food for the Blackwood mansion, seeing his goods they descended on him, caring more for the goods than the life of the traveller.

Marise had been the one to punish them, standing above them all she raised her arms, the illusions so real that even the strongest willed could not fight it, the ground shook and the skies darkened in their world as lava began to spew from the mountain tops, all their homes had gone up in smoke as Marise hurled flaming hot fireballs at the town, the casualties that day were high, the fatalities three, the three youths that had stolen the life of her traveller.

They rebuilt their town by the roadside, thinking themselves far enough away from the volcanoes while still close enough to enjoy the richness it provided, but sure enough they would slowly begin to sneak back, only to have their homes destroyed again. Elly couldn't help but appreciate Marise's twisted humour.

"Anyway." The old man continued picking up the tale where Elly left off. "It's rumoured, there is no safer place for travellers, because of the volcanoes, any searching magic or old technology spies are rendered useless in that area, if someone were looking for you, especially someone who still had the gift." He paused. "I am not such an old fool to think it was extinguished completely, your friend here proves that. Anyway, to stay in such a place is the safest haven in the world, no man or God could ever find you there, you could disappear, so to speak. Of course because of this, there are a few bounty hunters that roam the area and many unsavoury characters as you would imagine, in fact last I heard Razieal, the bandit commander had set up base in those parts, but they tend to work at night so there should be no concerns as long as you have left by the time they return at daybreak." He turned back to Elly. "Your friend looks awfully familiar, is she from around these parts?" He asked quietly, Zo leaned in hear Elly's reply, yet found herself disappointed.

"She's from everywhere, she never stayed in one place for too long, chances are you have seen her, at some point." Elly smiled again, the volcanoes now on the horizon. "Anyway, I believe this is where we get off." She smiled turning to the old man, he nodded as he pulled the cart aside. "Oh sir, our quest is of a secret nature, I trust you will tell no one of what you saw and heard." She smiled placing some money on his seat.

"I was young once too, quests are fun, but also secret, it would not do to have groups of people after the same goal." He smiled pushing the money back. "Since I never had travellers, I don't know what this is for." He smiled at Elly, who looked down to the money. "I do not require payment for a service I have not provided." Elly smiled at the old man.

"I know, but you have saved us a great deal of time and effort, for that we are most grateful and insist you take it."

"I have a better idea." He smiled stepping down from the cart, before grabbing a small bag placing in some fruit and vegetables and handing them to her "If you wish to pay me, then you shall do it for my food, not my favours, although you could not carry what this would buy." He smiled he was young and proud once too, Elly smiled taking the bag from him, as long as he accepted the money, there was no issue.

"That's fine, I don't require change, it would weigh too heavy in our pockets, I guess your wife would wish to know where the funds came from." She extended her hand, he shook it before remounting his wagon, they waved him goodbye thanking him again for his troubles. "Besides you're lucky to have any left with those four in the back" She added bringing a lighter mood to the air as she removed a small piece of apple pulp from Zo's chin.

It was another hour until they reached the forest before the volcanoes, it was thick green woodland covered with shrubs and bushes, it was easy to see why the bandits would find this so appealing, even should they be followed back, the surrounding would make their escape a certainty.

"We'll stay here tonight." Elly dropped her bag to the ground and disappeared into the surrounding forest, it seemed she was checking the area. Zo busied herself getting a few twigs and nearby sticks to create a small fire, but it was clear they would need more than the immediate area could provide, she glanced around, she disliked the feeling of numbness this place gave her, her senses normally so tuned with the surrounded area now dead to the world around her, after all, her senses were in reality, nothing more than a location spell to keep her aware of all that was around her, allowing her to search and read the elements.

"I shall get the fire wood." Acha volunteered almost as if reading Zo's mind. As she walked past Eiji she grabbed his arm. "It will be quicker with the two of us." She looked at him encouragingly he nodded, following her into the woods, they walked for about ten minutes before stopping to collect wood, finally Eiji broke the silence.

"What's going on?" He asked his voice nothing more than a whisper, he glanced around the area, only now did he realise how far from camp they were, given the old man's stories it was better if they kept their tones low so not to attract unwanted attention.

"That's what I wanted to ask you." She paused feeling herself blush slightly. "First Elly vanished then that stranger appears, we have barely been here five seconds and she vanishes again." She picked another piece of wood from the floor to avoid looking at him, hoping he wouldn't see the redness in her face that confronting him brought.

"Wait you think I…" Eiji seemed baffled, although in fairness understood, after all from day one he arrived with Elly, it made sense that she would think he knew her motives, and to a certain extent it was true.

"That you know? Don't you?" Eiji shook his head. "Then… exactly what is this deal you have with her?" A suddenly realisation dawned on him.

"No, you have it all wrong." He stopped so they could talk, it was clear she was just looking out for her friends, since he had first met her, she had become so much more confident, to the point now she would challenge someone to protect those she cared for, he didn't want to see this confidence destroyed, he needed to give her some form of answer, but if he could avoid doing so politely he would.

"Do I?" She questioned rather cynically

"Yes… Elly, that is to say she…" How could he get out of this one? He couldn't really explain the truth of the situation, how could he tell Zo's friend that Elly wanted to reawaken Marise Shi and enlist her into the aid of Night? That he was helping her in fear of his own life? How could he tell her that Zo, the person who saved Acha's life, was really a wanted murderer? He could not betray her trust that way, when Zo was ready to tell her, she would and only she had the right to do so, but at the same time lying was not in his nature.

"She is trying to find Marise right? And you're helping her, what will happen when you find her? What were you promised?" Acha prompted, after a long drawn out silence.

"No, you have it wrong, the only reason I am with Elly, is because I know too much, I told you before, to leave is to die, until she releases me that is." Eiji sighed thinking back to how this all started with the best of intentions, then somehow he ended up mixed up in this whole thing, not that he minded, he enjoyed the company of the people he was with, he was just too careless.

"What do you know that is so valuable?" She questioned sitting on a log, this seemed like it would be a long conversation, he joined her, although never looked at her, just at his hands and the pile of wood he placed at his feet.

"Marise Shi's whereabouts… and her weakness." He answered truthfully,

"So she does live" Acha glanced across at Eiji, he had just confirmed what she believed all the time, that Marise Shi was still alive, waiting, but she had to wonder, if Eiji knew a thing such as her location, had he shared it with Elly? "And what about Zo? What part does she have to play in all this? Why does Elly want her? I know something big is happening and I know Zo has a part to play whether or not she wishes it. If we are in danger, don't we have a right to know what that danger is?"

"I swear, I don't know what she has planned, or even if there is a plan, the only thing I know is that Elly wants to protect Zo, as much as you may doubt that, it's what I know to be the truth. Elly cares deeply for her."

"For her? Or for the role she has to play?" She questioned coldly knowing that this was another question that he couldn't answer, if he spoke the truth he had no idea of what her plans may be.

"Only Elly can answer that." Eiji sighed picking the firewood up.

"You said you know Marise's whereabouts, are you leading her to her?" Acha questioned realising as she asked Eiji had made no attempt to lead them anywhere, he like them was being lead by her.

"I don't need to." He stated, a silence descended upon them stretching on for some time as they collected more sticks and branches, as they did so both of them wondered why they would need so much only to build a fire for food, yet still they collected, it was Acha who once more broke the silence.

"If it makes any difference I believe you." She said after some thought, she really believed that he was worthy of her trust. "And I believe in you… Eiji, there's something I want to tell you, but it can go no further…" Acha sighed, she had to tell someone, it had been eating away at her since Collateral now, yet at the same time she feared what speaking the truth would mean, but time after time Eiji had proved to be honest and defend his word, she knew she could trust him with this, even if he did know Marise Shi's whereabouts the news would not reach her from him, she took a breath readying herself to continue but before she spoke she was interrupted.

"Good job I'm not the enemy or you would both be dead" Elly appeared from the darkness to stand besides them. "Sorry I was so long, I had some business to attend"

"What kind of business?" Acha enquired shifting the firewood uncomfortably as she lifted it from the floor.

"None of yours." She smiled sarcastically.

"Well we really should get this back to the others." Eiji glanced down at the wood in his arms and began to walk away knowing he would not get very far, he had the feeling that Elly had been around longer than she implied with her sudden appearance.

"Before you do." The pure chill in her voice froze him to the spot. "I do not appreciate being the topic of other people's conversations." She looked at both of them meaningfully, all at once Acha was glad her confession got no further.

"You know what they say, listeners never hear the best of themselves" Eiji smiled but his attempt to lighten the mood had failed miserably.

"Eiji, a word." Elly commanded, she looked up at Acha who taking the hint continued back towards the camp. "We need to be on our guard." Her voice had now lost the chill from before. "My sources tell me there's a bounty on our friend's head and that there are at least a few hoping to cash in on it."

"You mean Marise right?" Eiji questioned, Marise had always had a price on her head, why had Elly brought this up now? Perhaps it was due to the old man's warning of hunters in these parts. He moved, shifting the wood, it wasn't so much that it was heavy, just awkward, a little like their conversation, Elly didn't seem to trust any of them, he couldn't help wondering why she was so willing to divulge information to him, he could only reason, it was because he was the only one who knew the truth and he knew exactly where he stood with her, his betrayal would mean his death.

"No I mean Zodiac" Eiji couldn't help feeling shocked wondering what justification they had, Zo had done nothing wrong, she had barely even left Crowley before they uprooted her.

"Ah." Was all he managed to say, no matter how hard he tried he could not think of any words to follow up.

"Ah is right, you know what this means…" She questioned, her voice dropping slightly.

"Wait a minute, what has Zo done that could possibly warrant a bounty?" He decided to ask, after all, any with a bounty on their head have committed some form of crime, but what could she have done? Elly answered his question with a smile.

"Since when does that matter with bounty hunters? You write a request, go to a guild and offer a price, job done, no questions asked." She wondered if he had believed it had worked some other way, the truth of the matter was, if you had money, you could do anything, money was the only law bounty hunters respected, it was not about right and wrong, they were simply hired assassins parading under the cloak of justice.

"I think we best hurry back." He began to run suddenly realising what danger could await them on their return, images of death and slaughter crossing his mind, but whose the blood would be that filled his mind was unknown, either way, facing Zo with such confrontation would not be a good thing, not considering her past, not considering what she had just learnt. "We need to warn…" Before Eiji could finish the sentence he heard Acha scream.

"Looks like we're too late."

***

"Look it *is* her." Two men hid deep within the undergrowth of the trees watching a figure as she piled the existing fire wood into a circle. "The one from the poster, just like we were told." He passed a small poster to the other man, who examined it quickly, within the undergrowth they did a quick round of rock paper scissors, the tall dark man winning, with scissors, he took the poster back from his brother who was of a smaller frame and build, he disappeared around the side listening for his cue, this was the way they had always done it, it was fool proof.

"Zodiac Althea I believe?" The tall man emerged from the bushes, he stood at about six foot, he smiled at the girl a twinkle crossing his hazel eyes, her hand was already resting on her sword, her partner, unknown by name to the hunters stopped unpacking what appeared to be food rations to look at the stranger questioningly,

"Yes, and you are?" Her hand relaxed from her sword, had she been aware of his brother hiding nearby things would not be quite so simple, watching this, the other man smiled from the bushes, it was clear this child did not know she was hunted yet, nor would have time to share that information with anyone else. He looked her up and down she was so frail, he wondered what a child like this could do to warrant such a bounty, but his was not the place to ask, that was the beauty of being a hunter.

"I'm Ben." He smiled, clearly a well practiced smile, it seemed friendly, comforting, she returned the gesture but it soon faded when she heard his next words. "We don't want any trouble, so I think you should come with us." He cursed silently as her posture straightened without moving she glanced around, she glanced to her partner questioningly a silent message seemed to pass between them as her partner stopped momentarily before continuing to unpack, it was clear they felt no danger from him, her mind was clearly on other things, something that would work to their advantage.

"Why would I want to do that?" She watched as he placed his hand in his long brown battered coat, her hand shooting to her hilt once more, something inside her commanding her to draw, a wild force calling to her, she had only felt it once before, back when she fought with the Viking monster, it was something she feared, something that scared her more than anything, the power was crying to her soul.

"It's like I said, you're Zodiac Althea." Out of his coat he pulled a small parchment, he flicked it open to reveal a sketch of her. That was the signal his brother moved with grace and speed placing the jagged edge of the razor sharp knife at her partner's throat. Daniel heard the anger in her mind as she scolded herself for being so careless, scolded herself for dropping her guard and not picking up the lurking life force, then again, searching magic was useless in this place, she was reminded what that actually meant when Ben had emerged from the undergrowth without prior warning. Anger sparkled in her fragile eyes, memories dancing on the surface of her mind trying to remind her, trying to warn her, Ben smiled at her introducing his brother Simon, although his words never met her ears, they were drowned out by someone, a female screaming her name over and over telling her to run, it was a voice that seemed so familiar and then, there was silence, broken only by Ben's mocking tones.

"I know what you're thinking." He sneered as his brother tightened the ropes around his prisoner. "A child like you could not know the first principle of fighting."

'Zo.' She heard Daniel's voice filled with desperation and question, it seemed he too could hear the cries that echoed through her mind, as he fought against the ropes now binding him to the tree, he heard a strange voice filling her thoughts, it cried her name over and over begging for her to leave while she could, a voice he couldn't place, a memory he knew she couldn't find, then there was another voice. He watched as she drew her sword, an understanding of what was to happen slowly forming before him.

"I know a few tricks." She tried to sound threatening, only it sounded more fearful than she had hoped, her best friend lay at the mercy of bounty hunters, the only way to save him was to fight... She couldn't fail, his life, his safety, depended on her. A silver flame formed at her fingertips, Simon finished the final knots and smiled joining his brother, already satisfied that they would earn their money today. The ground seemed to absorb the flame as it fell from her hand, the men snorted as if it was a failed attempt, before they could make their comments a huge circle of flames encompassed them shooting from the ground, yet burning nothing

'*Daniel, get the others out of here*' A simple spark flew from the fire perishing the ropes that bound him to the tree, although Daniel could not make out if this was a deliberate action, he knew one thing for certain, what she had just instructed him and what she had actually thought were two different things, her initial thought wasn't for the others safety, but for the safety of him and of the bounty hunters who advanced upon her, something frightened her, so much she felt that the only way to be safe was to distance herself from him. That was the last thing he got from her before she closed herself off, he tried to reach her, but this level of blocking far surpassed anything she had done before, then he heard Acha scream.

The sword tilted in her hand as she looked to those who opposed her, she had known from the beginning this moment would come, the moment that fear and need took over and all rationality was lost, that was the time *she* thrived and she feared this moment with all her heart, the moment she would lose control.

"A barrier, very clever." Ben snorted moving to stand besides his brother both trapped within the fiery wall.

"I suppose that is what common sense would seem like to those who have none." She sneered, she could still feel her on the edge of her mind, but that would soon be over, nothing was going to interfere. She didn't wait for the first strike, instead she chose to make it, her sword barley dodged by Simon as his brother pulled him away, half a second later and the sword would have been stained with his blood.

"I see you *do* know a few moves." Ben smiled giving his brother some kind of hand gesture, she smiled, they claimed the title bounty hunters, but she doubted they had made a single catch, such amateurs.

"Oh, I know a lot more than that." The bone chilling tones in her voice made even them struggle to repress a shudder, her posture was different now, confident, alert, a ball of flames formed in her left hand, her sword poised and ready to strike in the other. "I hope you prove to be more than an easy kill, I may have grown rusty." The two men made their move their short swords drawn, a clearly predictable move, one attacked high, the other low, the ball of flames engulfed Simon leaving Ben with a poor hearted excuse for a charge attack while his brother rolled on the ground trying to extinguish the flames. "I guess not." She sighed as a spray of blood erupted from Ben's back as the blade followed through. "What a disappointment." Ben fought against the blade finding himself unable to break its grasp and unable, despite his closeness, to lay a single blow on her, using her foot she pushed him from her sword, Simon screamed as he rushed to his brother's side, crying as blood trickled from his mouth.

He looked up to her eyes filled with venom and pain, a wicked sneer crossed her lips as she raised her eyebrow as if in challenge, a challenge he foolishly accepted, yet never had the chance to see through, he got within a foot of her, she had made no effort to move, she was unprepared, he was going to do it, he drew his second blade, but both blows were blocked one by the hilt, the other blade as she moved with lightening fast speed, she grabbed his right sword by the hilt, turning it sharply before forcing it into his throat. She smiled as he gasped for breath a strange gargling sound coming from his throat until he finally fell, looking at them, both as they lay before her, a look of satisfaction crossed her face.

"Zo." Daniel gasped staring in disbelief through the flames, despite her telling him to leave, he had been unable to do anything but watch, rooted to the spot in awed horror, as he spoke the flames vanished instantly taking the corpses of the dead with them into the unknown leaving only the charred remains at the tip of the grass, she flicked the blood from her sword looking at him.

"Daniel." Marise smiled.

Chapter nine

"I see they found her." Night smiled watching the gossip crystal as it followed the progress of the battle. "It is just as I had expected, the darkness lies dormant within her even now. Yet now it is awakening again, we must get things in motion before she revives completely and becomes beyond our control." He glanced across to a small sealed door, it would not be long now before the change had to be made, too much of the emptiness had filtered through and with things how they were, there was no room for the cold-heartedness she was beginning to display now the chamber lay empty. They had to trust her, as it stood now, she could care little for their safety and such was reflected through her actions. Although there were fleeting moments when the concern for the job shone through, he felt the wrong approach was being taken, if things continued on the path they were, the mission forced upon them would end in loss and he did not like to lose. It was time for a change, the previous watcher had passed on leaving bitterness and resentment in the empty chamber, although mostly she remained her own person, it was an unexplainable flaw that she picked up some of *their* characteristics, luckily, he knew just who the replacement would be.

***

"Acha!" Eiji ran to her side she looked strangely pale against the dark wood of the dying tree. "What's wrong?"

"I didn't mean to." She whispered, shrinking herself down against the tree to hug her knees tightly.

"Didn't mean to what?" Eiji squatted to her level, watching as she gave her answer in the form of a sideward glance, he followed her line of vision, but from where he squat nothing was visible over the giant log that blocked his vision. He stood slowly approaching slowly until his eyes rested upon the crumpled clothes that lay just to its other side.

"It was an accident, he came out of nowhere." Acha whispered desperately as glanced down to the rough looking bandit that motionless on the floor, he no more than a child, but from his appearance alone, it was clear he had been living this life for some time, he must have been taken in by a gang of bandits, it was not an uncommon act, children rarely attracted suspicion. He couldn't help feeling the twang of sympathy for him; the boy he looked at now could have easily been him, had his master not saved him.

Swinging his legs over the log he crouched before him checking his vital signs unconsciously glancing towards Acha as he did so, he was barely alive how could she have done such a thing in the short time that transpired? And how was such a result achieved so cleanly, the only abrasions on him seemed to be that from a fall. Despite the clear danger to the boys life, his senses told him given time to rest he would make a full recovery, Eiji suppressed a shudder, whatever Acha had done, had shortened his life span, he could feel it through the figure, the best thing they could do for all their sakes was to leave him resting where he lay, they could not risk taking him to camp, where one bandit is, others are never too far behind.

"What happened?" Acha glanced away from his questioning eyes as he approached her once more.

"I killed him, like before." She sighed her stomach still churning from the shock as she forced the pictures of the boy from her mind. "I was heading back, then next thing I knew he grabbed me, I went to scream but he placed his hand over my mouth... and I... killed him."

"You didn't kill him." Eiji stated once more crouching to her level; he saw a sad relief fill her eyes. "Besides, I'm sure whatever you did to him was justified."

"He's alive?" Eiji nodded in response, the look in her eyes reinforcing his concern, it truly seemed as if she hadn't mean to hurt him, almost as if she was unaware of what exactly had happened, but how was it possible to nearly kill someone by accident? Surely she knew what she was doing, she had to. Elly appeared besides them, glancing dismissively over the figure behind the log.

"Why did you scream?" She questioned rolling the boy onto his back with her foot, it was clear he had not had the chance to lay more than a hand on her, so why panic?

"I thought I'd killed him..."

"But you feel better now right? Now you have some energy?" Acha looked up at Elly her mouth wide in shock, although she had revealed many things to them that was not something she discussed, it was her shameful secret, a secret she worked so hard to conceal from all.

"How..."

"Oh come on it was obvious, especially in Knights-errent, we made them think the creature didn't see you because you're a displaced life force, you told us that yourself, but the true reason was you used your surroundings to revitalise your body, for that split second, you become part of them, then in the ward, everything within it died almost instantly, they all believed it was her magic, but it was you, your life-force is anaemic and must take life from other sources to keep you alive and that's why Daniel gave you those gloves, so you could touch people and things without destroying them..." Acha gasped as Elly made this revelation, surprised at just how much she had learnt just by watching subtle actions, she couldn't help being amazed how accurately she had pieced it together.

"They... don't know... at least not all of it." She whispered dusting herself off as she stood. "Not about... well, you know." She glanced towards the body; Eiji opened his mouth as if to say something, quickly cut short by Elly's interruption.

"Now is not the time for the questions, we should head back." She stated while Eiji collected the scattered wood before leading the way back to the camp, although he knew it was only a short distance away, he glanced back to ensure Acha was still following, for the last five minutes she had been uneasily quiet. He walked still looking at her; she seemed quite shook up by the whole experience.

His senses warned him to turn, warning him about something solid that stood in his path, he turned sharply, his senses warning of imminent danger, yet nothing stood before him, just the trodden path through the trees, he smiled slightly, reminding himself of how much he still had to learn not realising that what he felt was not nature around him, after all in this place those senses had been blocked, what he actually felt was the aura of magic, he had barely taken another step when something knocked him from his feet, he looked up just in time to see some blue sparks flying across the air revealing some form of large dome, from its curve, it was clear it would cover their entire camp.

"Mari." Elly whispered placing her hand to the invisible field, where she touched sparked for but a second before allowing her hand to pass through.

"Mari?" Acha questioned fearfully glancing between Elly to Eiji. "But Zo and Daniel are in there, we need to warn them!" Elly stepped through the field not looking back as she calmly walked towards the camp, much to Acha's distress, there was nothing rushed about her actions, she went to follow only to find herself greeted only by the solid field that had moments before struck Eiji. "How'd she…" Acha began but decided not to continue with a question neither of them could answer.

***

Daniel backed away slowly, in the last few minutes, everything had changed, his arm already bleeding from where her blade had struck. Her movement, so quick, he did not have time to dodge, although had he tried, he would now be dead instead of only wounded. *She* had expected him to at least try to avoid her strike, yet looking now; it seemed she had clearly overestimated his abilities. Had he dodged, the sword would not merely have cut his arm, the battle would be over, it was a tactic she had used many times before, only idiots, or the most skilled fighters would not dodge, and he was definitely not the latter.

"You have stood in my way too long, with you out of the picture…" She advanced towards him finding no need to finish her sentence, should she have been herself she could have cut him down in a second, but she knew she had to be careful, even now, *she* was fighting for control, this fight had to be addressed carefully should she wish the end result to be her victory, doing too much too soon, would steal her upper hand making it more difficult to retain control, but no worries, it was not as if someone like this would ever really taste the full force of her powers. Even so, Zodiac was a limitation she had to be constantly aware of, a reason why she could not perform at her peak. Each step she took he matched in the opposite direction, but he was running quickly out of space, he moved his hand from his wound to take his weapon.

"I don't want to fight you." His voice trembled as she grew ever closer; even now he knew he could be no match for her. Only fear rooting him to the spot before as she had struck had meant he still breathed, all his senses screamed for him to jump away from the blade, yet for his very life he could not move.

"Funny." She smiled. "I want to kill you." Daniel flicked together the staff crossing it in front of himself defensively. "I've cut through the finest armour, with this sword; do you really think your stick can stop me?" She sneered pulling the hair tie from her hair fastening it around her wrist and the hilt of the sword. Then she came at him, instead of moving he just stood rooted to the spot with fear, he once more found himself paralysed, unable to do anything but watch, what was it about this person that inflicted this paralysis upon him? He could only watch as the sword gleamed shining brightly as it swept towards him cutting through the air with the sound of his death, behind the blade, he could see she was smiling, just before the blow landed he tuned slightly raising the staff, the sword ricocheting from it as he gave a sigh of relief, she stepped back from her landing position turning to look at him, an ecstatic glimmer in her eyes as the swords light intensified. Blue fire formed in her left hand as she moved to face him, he found room to take one more single step backwards, he felt the solid pressure of the tree behind him, his legs trembling as they threatened to give beneath him.

"Mari, No!" Elly commanded appearing from nowhere to position herself slightly in front him, her left arm stretched out protectively, her hand opened dropping what appeared to be dice to the floor, as they vanished from the earth, just seconds before a sword appeared in her hand, the flame made contact with the sword, for a moment Daniel thought the flames were a mere after effect until he realised the truth, the sword she held was made from wood and was burning rapidly, she dropped it to the floor as it erupted in flames, the dice reappearing back in her hands. "You will not harm him." She ordered her eyes fixed calmly on Marise.

"And you would oppose me? You would fight me? For him?" Marise tilted her head to one side questioningly as her best friend stood protecting the enemy.

"I shall," she whispered lowering the extended arm as her and Marise locked vision.

"Your weapon has always been one of chance my friend, what would happen should you obtain another like the one you just did? Do you think then, you could pose any threat?" Elly placed the dice in her pocket stepping away from Daniel.

"If you wanted him dead, I could not stop you... Nor would I have made it in time." She added, although strictly speaking, what she had said was not true, after all, it was she herself who had trained Marise in the art of combat, it would have been foolish to fight at full strength, but as long as Marise was under the misconception her words were true, there was nothing to worry about. She broke eye contact with her for but a moment to glance at Daniel, all in all, he seemed to have faired quite well, a single slash on his upper arm gripped tightly by his hand and some form of carved staff still clutched in the injured arm, it appeared to be collapsible into a few pieces, no doubt held together by some form of chain, she reminded herself of the job at hand, removing her attention from Daniel's strange weapon, there was something about it that seemed... familiar, but it couldn't have been what she was thinking of.

"That is where you are wrong." As Marise spoke another flame appeared in her hand. "Let us pretend you did not make it, give me a while before you return." From the corner of her eye Elly saw Daniel stiffen slightly, she knew he did not trust her, but did he really think she would step aside and let him be killed? Then again, she hadn't known the choice herself until now so perhaps his fear was justified, this time she had chose to protect him, next time, he may not be so lucky.

"I cannot do that." Elly changed her stance ready for battle. "If you insist on fighting for this, I will meet your challenge, but if I win, you must swear not to harm him while he is involved in this situation." Elly placed her hand in her pocket waiting for the verdict, Marise was not stupid, if she took this battle and lost, she knew she would never have the chance to attempt it again being bound to her word by defeat, yet, if she were to win...

"You would truly oppose me..." She questioned again, her voice seemed to waver slightly with the tones of betrayal. "For him?" She sheathed her sword before blowing on the flame as it extinguished a small strand of smoke rose from her hand. She looked straight at Daniel her green eyes locking with his, the promise of threat hung within them. "You know, Lee won't always be around to protect you." A sadistic smile crossed her lips as she turned away. "You have company." She warned and with those words, she vanished into the trees.

Her counterpart would soon regain control, she had done well to even scratch him, let alone engage in battle as Zodiac fought to regain control, she had fought with an unbelievable power that threatened her control and even now, she was unsure if it was herself, or Zodiac that carried them deep within the forest.

Seconds after she had vanished Acha and Eiji appeared, Daniel gave a big sigh sliding down the tree as his legs kept their earlier promise to give beneath him,

"By the Gods Daniel! Are you alright" Acha rushed to his side noticing his ghastly pallor before anything else? "What happened?" Acha lifted his sleeve to reveal the slice across his arm, she looked to him questioning, her eyes almost tearful.

"Where's Zo?" Eiji interrupted Acha's fussing, his tone etched with concern, he moved to take her satchel from the floor so Acha could dress Daniel's wound. As he did so he noticed a splash of blood across the bag and around the floor where it lay. It was only when he had it in his hands he saw the area fully, unsure why he had failed to notice it before. Pools of blood spread across the area, two people lay dead within it, he looked to the others questioningly as they seemed unaware of the corpses or even the stained grass, as he looked back, it had vanished, he glanced to the satchel, again finding no evidence of what he knew he had seen. He shook his head slowly, remembering something his master had told him about, a strange phenomena called echoes, echoes were traces left behind of those who had suffered before death, echoes of life only seen by the living, it was something Elementalists were aware of, something the world allowed them to see, there were some Elementalists who would dedicate their lives to travelling the world, helping to disperse the more troublesome echoes, those that were so powerful it was not only their kind who could see them. Some echoes were violent and dangerous to people, threatening the lives of those who saw them. He felt a lump rise in his throat as he swallowed hard, this had been the first he had seen, it had left him with a sick feeling deep in the pit of his stomach, and a horrible realisation of what had transpired before their arrival, Zo had drawn first blood, he had really hoped he would not see this day, he had recently came to acknowledge her as an ally and a friend, she was a strong person, he thought if anyone's will could triumph it would be hers, but alone, it could truly be, she did not possess the strength needed, the killer had now surfaced a battle of time and wills would soon begin.

"I'm sure she's safe." Elly answered without leaving time for anyone else to talk, Elly took the bag from him passing it to Acha. "You treat Daniel's wounds, no doubt there is some puree ready made, I shall start the fire." Acha took the bag from her surprised at the weight a collection of herbs could become.

"But you can't just leave her! What about the bounty hunters?" She protested still holding the bag as she was struck by Elly's cruelty, how could she want to just leave her out there, alone? Elly glanced at Eiji who simply shrugged in reply to her warning look.

"I don't think..." Daniel paused steadying both his hands and his breath before continuing. "They'll be bothering us again too soon." He flinched against the sting of the puree as Acha rubbed it into his flesh, it always hurt, but it seemed to hurt a lot more now his best friend wasn't the one applying it.

"They were here? Are they the ones that..." She looked down to Daniel's arm before bandaging it, she offered him a gentle smile although it never quite reached her eyes, they were too full of questions, questions she knew he wouldn't answer, she glanced across to Eiji and Elly who were deep in hushed conversation, their voices little more than an inaudible mumble. She decided to press the issues that were bothering her "So what happened?... I mean this clearly isn't the cut of a normal sword." Although he didn't answer, his silence had said more than any words could have, it was just as she had suspected, she turned to lean against the tree besides him giving a sigh as she did so. Zo must have grown careless, after all, she couldn't fight really, maybe she caught him trying to save him from an attacker, the sheer guilt driving her to leave, couldn't she see it had just been an accident? If she hadn't have tried to protect him, what would they have come back to then? Had she just left out of guilt? Or had she pursued the attackers to ensure their safety, after all, she knew they were all out there wandering somewhere within the trees, if they could attack Zo, they could just as easily have attacked them, that had to be it, but still, she found herself surprised she had left him with just Elly. "Daniel... I'm sorry; I shouldn't have taken Eiji with me... if he had been here..."

"You shouldn't blame yourself, it was just a matter of time... maybe if you hadn't have taken him, he would have been hurt too, or maybe worse, they would have got you instead." Daniel seemed to be going through the motions of talking and although, she didn't doubt, he meant every word with the sincerity it was intended, she wondered if he actually knew anything that had been said, right at this moment he seemed so distant.

"Do you think she'll come back?" Acha asked watching as Daniel started deep into the trees, no doubt at the place he had last seen her, maybe she felt responsible for not being able to protect him, maybe she blamed herself for him being injured, whatever was wrong, she knew out there was not a safe place for her, especially since now there was a bounty on her head and if she had pursued the bandits, then surely she was putting herself in worse danger, maybe once she had had time to forgive herself for Daniel's injury, she would return, but hopefully, it would not be too long, it was nearly time to leave.

"I don't know, I just don't know." He sighed sadly in response to Acha's question, she gasped, this had not been the response she had expected, not from him.

"Ok, we have decided to proceed to Knights-errent without her." Although Eiji had approached them, he never looked at them just at the ground stabbing it with his foot in an attempt to avoid the looks they gave him.

"You mean Elaineor decided." Daniel spat, despite her good intentions earlier, he couldn't help feeling this entire mess was her fault, without her they were fine, none of this would ever have happened if only she'd have stayed away. He resented her and what she represented; she had appeared from nowhere turning their lives upside down just as they were happy, she had not been around for over a year, why couldn't she have just stayed away? Well in truth he knew the answer, he knew what she wanted now and it made him hate her all the more.

"Wait a minute." Acha stood up slowly dusting herself own. "This doesn't make sense. You travel the world looking for her, insist she leaves her home, her friends, then leave her out here where she's in more danger... Why bother finding her in the first place?" Acha glanced from Eiji to Elly demanding an explanation as Daniel looked to her in surprise, she really had changed, she was no longer the timid girl they had first met.

"Knights-errent is different from here, chances are, we won't be near any woods at all according to what I can make out from the map." Eiji pulled the map from his pocket that he had obtained in Abaddon. "It will be easier to find her there, than in this undergrowth and if we hurry, we may just find her before she vanishes from sight." He paused lowering his tone a little. "I don't like it any more than you..." There seemed to be something more to that sentence but Acha couldn't quite determine what.

***

"Ah so you have returned." Seiken walked into view behind Zo's reflection in the stream, she sat about a mile or so from the place she had arrived, and now sat staring resentfully at the figure that looked back, she glanced at his reflection in the water before turning to look at him, something about him seemed different, then again, at the moment a lot of thing seemed different. "Where are your companions?" He glanced around slowly as if to check they hadn't suddenly appeared in the vicinity.

"I... left them..." She sighed turning back towards the stream. "It's for the best... I tried to kill my best friend." She wrapped her arms around herself protectively as the wind whipped around the stream and shook the nearby trees before dying down to a soft whisper once more. Why of all things had she remembered that? Of course she knew the answer, Marise. Marise had somehow ensured that during her control she wouldn't miss the slightest detail.

"I see." He glanced around again. "They know your secret, yet they venture here to find you all the same." He smiled to himself looking in the direction she had moments ago walked to reach this stream, when he turned back to face her it was gone, just concern crossed his brow.

"Is everything ok... has something happened?" She asked following Seiken's vision the distance, he seemed to be focusing on the top of a small incline.

"Why do you ask?"

"You seem... different... troubled?" She glanced at him, although she spoke to him he never looked to her, there was clearly something wrong, something weighing heavily on his mind, at this very moment in time it was as if they were strangers.

"I'm sorry, I'm aware how little time there is, it's not your concern, tell me now you are here, what are your plans?" He looked at her briefly before glancing once more to the same place on the horizon.

"If you mean, am I going to find them?... I cannot." She sighed. "I shall continue alone, I doubt they can get too far without this." She pulled a piece of parchment from her trouser pocket showing it to Seiken.

"What's that?" He questioned

"It's the map you gave us... remember?" Zo frowned slightly before scolding herself, there he was trying to help her, trying to save his race, and all she was worried about was he seemed a little distracted, she smiled slightly scolding herself again for pursuing this feeling, surely she too would feel as he did now, situations reversed.

"Ah... yes, so much has happened since then, I forgot. Anyway, to what brings me here, your next target. Some, on your travels will say you should pass only through the mine fields, these are those under *his* influence, do not listen, although most know the true dangers of that place and will no doubt instruct you accordingly, so to avoid confusion, I feel it best I tell you, you must head straight through the contour plains, it is the safest and quickest way to balance, the next rune. Once you get through speak to the villagers, they will know where you need to go from there." He began to walk away towards the rise his attention had been focused on. "Since your friends have arrived, I shall warn them also." Zo glanced away for a moment, she had wondered if they would follow and it seemed that, as she had both expected and feared, they had.

"Seiken." She called after him, although he didn't stop, she knew he had heard her. "I would be grateful if you didn't mention our meeting." He turned to look at her and smiled.

"Head North." He called back pointing before continuing on his way. She frowned slightly realising the sheer volume of information he had just provided her with, was time really so short he needed to push them? She glanced back one more time to see him on the top of the rise before she headed the direction he had pointed.

***

"Seiken." Acha waved frantically as he appeared on the horizon before them, as he joined the group she spoke again. "Seiken have you seen Zo? We got separated."

"She is..." He gave a sigh. "I cannot lie, she wished me not to tell you, she is in great danger, even now, she makes her way to the courts, true it is the location of the next rune, but it is not her hands that must remove it, the court is not a friendly place, all that pass through its doors are judged by the most terrifying adjudicator, themselves. Few survive the punishment they bestow on themselves... she told me what happened, I tried to warn her, but..."

"She went anyway." Daniel sighed finishing his sentence, why did she have to be so stubborn? "Well she has a head start, we better push on." Daniel looked at him surprised to see him still standing among them, normally he said his piece and vanished, yet now he seemed to hover uncertainly. "Which way is it?" He asked not expecting an answer.

"North, although I must warn you, there are two routes which you might take many will say you should head through the contour plains, the people around those parts always send people that way, it is by far the most dangerous route, I suggest you follow the route your friend will be taking, by crossing the mine field, if they tell you any different ignore them, there are many of Night's spies in this world now, remember, they wish only to kill you. The mines are mainly inactive, if you tread careful there should be no problems. North." He pointed again in the direction before walking off.

"Well I never expected a straight answer he never normally gives us any information at all." Daniel watched for a second as he walked away before turning his attention to the others.

"He never normally walks either." Acha pointed out. "Maybe he has a dream to stop nearby, who knows, we know so little of him." She added noticing now he had vanished completely from view. Without another word they set off, Eiji pulled the map from his pocket thinking how lucky it was that Zo had retained possession of the other one, come to think of it, he could not remember even showing her this one. He shrugged to himself studying it and the landscape before them carefully.

"There's no court on here to the North." Eiji glanced over the map once more just to be certain.

"Well it won't be, it's a fixed point with a riddle we now don't need to solve." Acha pointed to the cross north of their location it was one of the seven fixed points and the only one to the North, she looked up at him and smiled before following Elly, who had already began walking in the direction Seiken pointed.

"The longer you study that thing the larger her lead gets." Eiji took the map from Daniel who nodded, it was true if they hoped to catch up with her in time, they had to hurry, he knew first hand how difficult she was to keep up with, let alone catch up to.

***

Zo glanced at the road ahead, true enough all those she encountered warned her to avoid the mine fields, they hurried her in the direction of the contour plains, even as she stood not far from the fork they warned her from the dangerous ground, she felt Daniel, somewhere in the back of her mind she heard his thoughts, they were gaining, with every second she stood there they grew closer, the thought of facing them again after what had happened became more and more difficult with each step she took, she couldn't face them she was ashamed, ashamed and frightened. She knew what Marise had done, she couldn't stand to have Daniel look at her that way... she had to keep moving, but which way? She stood at a large fork in the road, both routes covered by trees.

"Either way I'm heading North." She muttered to herself, her heart lifting when she caught sight of a young peddler heading in the opposite direction.

"Excuse me I am looking for the contour plains."

"You're heading that way? And I thought you were crazy when you were just talking to yourself." The peddler began to continue on his way stopped only by the desperation in her voice.

"No please, I need something from just past there; lives depend on my getting there, please." The peddler turned to look at her, glancing her over suspiciously.

"The only place past there till the ends of the earth is a small mining village, there is nothing of great worth there." He gestured down the left fork.

"A mining village?" Zo questioned wondering how balance could fit into that scenario.

"Are you not familiar with the lay of the land? I myself am on a quest of great importance but even the most stu... brave adventurers, will not venture that way, it is far too dangerous, although it may be safer for you to head through those mine fields." The peddler glanced behind her taking in the lay of the land. "But there's a port three days walk from here you could take a boat and sail around that would be the wiser choice." He smiled turning to point Zo in the direction of the mentioned port.

"My instructions are clear, I must head through the plains, I don't have time to…"

"Fine, but it would be safer if you travelled in numbers, when you find some willing to travel besides you into death, take the North East path, that shall lead you to the mine field, of course, if you wish to live, the port is South East from here." He paused scratching his head. "I have said enough, my time is also short." He began to walk away

"Thank you, I hope your quest goes well." She smiled turning to continue up the road.

"I have to rely on more than hope; I have wasted enough time already." He chuntered as he walked away. It took a further five minutes to move from the fork in the road, both paths were marked by trees, for this she was grateful, she knew the others were already catching up and this may just conceal her from them, maybe if they didn't see her they would turn back. She took the opposite path to that she had been advised knowing it would lead to her destination.

***

"Excuse me; sorry to bother you I can see you are in a hurry." Daniel stopped a young peddler heading towards them. "Have you seen a young lady on this path, brown hair?" Daniel waited in anticipation for the answer.

"I've just seen one person on my travel, heading north she was, I told her to head to the port this way, but she was insistent she had to cross some field or other, I told her if she had to go that way the North-East route to the mine field was the safest of the two if travelling in numbers, but I wish she would have taken the port route."

"Many thanks." Acha smiled. "If we can ever return the favour." The peddler nodded

"I doubt we shall meet again my lady, but the sentiment is appreciated, I would hurry if you hope to catch up, we crossed paths about fifteen minutes ago." With these words the peddler continued on his way.

"Right you heard him, he said she took the mine field's path, we must hurry if we wish to catch up to her." They paused at the path taking the route opposite from the one their friend had just moments before.

***

Daniel jumped over the warning fence bringing himself to stand on the edge of the fields, the fields were covered by a light mist that seemed growing heavier by the second, as it swooped across the land, even if she was only five minutes ahead, it would be almost impossible to see her. Acha gave a disheartened sigh leaning against a dying tree, wondering if they would ever catch up.

"Are you sure it's safe… I mean there's no way of knowing where the explosives are." Eiji hesitated before stepping over the fence he stepped backwards his mind warning him not to continue over until the problem was solved, this however was something Daniel had already considered, he stood by a log about four foot in length already facing the direction they were heading, it was almost as if it had been left for them, sitting on the grass just over the fence. Daniel smiled, although Zo was trying to get away from them, she didn't wish them any harm, this action here proved it, it seemed the rest of the party thought so too.

"Mines are triggered by pressure... It's our only chance of catching her we must hurry; we can use this as a trigger." Eiji hopped over the fence, he knew there was never any choice to this matter, if what Seiken had said about the court was true, there wasn't time to waste.

The log rolled a few feet at a time before them, each time they waited for it to settle before giving it another shove, standing motionless, braced and ready to hit the ground should needs dictate only relaxing when its movement stopped. They had been doing this for about twenty minutes now and estimated they were at least half way across the field, they stopped for but a moment to search for shadows through the mist, anything that would indicate Zo had been there, but there was nothing, Daniel gave a sigh as they began to walk again, Eiji turned suddenly, they had not been moving long, but Acha no longer followed.

"Where's Acha?" The others stopped turning to face him, a deadly silence descended upon them as they scanned the misty fields for signs of their friend.

***

'What happened?' Acha thought rising steadily to her feet. *'One second I was... and now?'* Her vision met with nothing but darkness, she felt around in a complete circle damp mud and stone sticking to her hands before she glanced up to a bright light, for a second she thought it may have been *the* light, the one her mother told her collected the dead, had she stepped on a mine? A panic rose within her, to get his far only to die, surely that was wrong, as she stood within the darkness she took a breath calming herself, had this been *the* light, then surely the place she found herself in now, the tunnel, would not be surrounded by mud and stones, it was only once the initial confusion had died she saw clearly what had happened, she had somehow fell into a giant hole.

Digging her fingers in the dirt she tried to climb its heights, but each time she did, she just slipped against the damp walls,

"Are you alright?" *you alright?* Daniel's voice echoed around the small hole as a silhouette appeared in the light above much to her relief, for a moment she had feared they hadn't noticed, feared that when they did they would be unable to find her, and a small part of her feared, even should they notice, they wouldn't try to turn back at all.

"I think so," *think so,* she called back. "I'm in a hole," *a hole,* she called up wondering why she had stated the obvious, surely everyone knew exactly where she was.

"The ground seems to have just given." *Just given,* Daniel called back. "Elly has head back to get some vines." *Some vines,* she listened to Daniel's voice echoing unable to describe the relief she felt that they had noticed her missing; she felt around the edges again beginning to feel a little claustrophobic, a sick nagging sensation tugging at her stomach. She was still afraid, yet now, as the silence seemed to stretch forever, it seemed somehow worse than just being stuck, the silence made her nervous, it played tricks on her mind making her believe the sound of her breath echoing quietly, was not in fact a sound that belong to her, the small pebbles that fell from the edge occasionally sounded like a clawed creatures steps, the silence quickened her heart as every sound she heard became twisted by her fears making her believe she was not alone, finally, she had to speak.

"Has she gone alone?" *Alone?* She called up to Daniel who still leaned over the hole. Daniel leaned up as if looking for something before answering.

"No Eiji went with her." *With her.* "But I can't see them now." *Them now* his voice echoed before he spoke again. "Did you hurt yourself? Are you alright?" *You alright?*

"Don't worry, I'll be alright." *Won't be alright* the conversation fell dead as they both heard the final echo.

***

Zo stopped at the fork, where the mine field joined the contour plains becoming one road again, something was wrong, she felt fear and desperation on the edge of Daniel's mind, she heard his thoughts clearly now, begging for Eiji and Elly to hurry, she tried her best to ignore it and even managed to take another step away.

"Damn it." She cursed. "Who am I kidding?" She turned running in the direction of Daniel's thoughts, they got louder and louder, it seems they weren't too far behind. Now and again she felt soft earth tremble beneath her feet, cringing expecting any second to go up in flames as she questioned over and over why they had taken such a dangerous path, was it her fault? After all, it was the quicker route, had they gone this way to ensure they caught up with her? Had she put them in danger again?

***

"Daniel!" Acha screamed, fear transforming the words to an inaudible whisper she called his name over and over yet there was no reply and his silhouette had vanished. She stood gasping for breath in the darkness, the walls feeling as if they were caving in around her, from nowhere she heard a small clawing sound from the wall close to her, she reassured herself, she had touched each wall in turn, they were solid. She could just about hear Daniel above her shouting for Eiji and Elly to hurry, knowing there was no way he could reach her, knowing there was no way, they could reach him either, but feeling the need to try, he wondered if they could even hear his cries.

Something crawled across her shoulder; she let out a scream before realising it was a rope descending from above. She grabbed it tightly clutching with all her might as she scrabbled trying to climb the slimy walls but despite their best efforts it wasn't quick enough. There was a piecing howl followed by Acha's agonised screams, something pulled on the rope an extra weight pulling them towards the hole, as Acha kicked her legs frantically trying to shake off the giant claw the creature embedded in her leg as it tried to pull her back, refusing to release its prey.

Finally they heard it fall pulling the rope harder, faster, until she appeared at the top her hands clutching the rope and the solid ground around her as they pulled her from the hole.

"Zo!" Daniel gasped finally able to think, when she appeared he had no chance to say anything, there were more pressing issues, yet now, he could finally express how glad he was to see her, relief filling his voice as he spoke. "You came back." He pulled her satchel from his shoulder, throughout the entire ordeal it never moved away from him, he went to hand it to her lowering his arm slowly when she didn't take it, Acha felt the uneasiness pass through the air.

"Thank the Gods Zo, if it wasn't for you I would have been…" Acha stopped looking at the expression on Zo's face, she was so clearly uncomfortable, she had the expression of that you may find on a stranger suddenly mixed in with a group of people that all knew each other, uneasy and desperate to get away.

"It was foolish of me to take the rope, I apologise." She stated quietly, unsure exactly *when* she had obtained possession of it, her arm extended holding the wrapped rope to him, for a moment it hung loosely in her hand before he took it from her unsure what else he could do. He looked from the rope to her, trying to find the words that would make her stay, trying to find any words in fact, but he failed, standing there in silence.

"How did you find us… this mist is… like soup." Acha gasped clutching the tear in her leg, it didn't seem to be bleeding too badly yet it stung and throbbed as if it was ten times its size and depth.

"I heard you screaming… I couldn't leave you in danger… But you're safe now." She smiled gently despite the monotone of her voice. She glanced down to Acha's bleeding leg, it was not as bad as she had expected, it would be simple to treat, she turned slowly to walk away.

'You are more than skilled enough to treat this wound.' She projected the words into Daniel's mind as she glanced back, a sadness crossing her face, Daniel couldn't hide the shock from her words, that was not what he had expected, for a moment he stood staring at her, her bag held loosely in one hand the rope in his other, was this it? Was she really going to just walk away?

'You're not staying?' He questioned as she turned away, the hurt in his eyes was something she didn't wish anyone to suffer, it was easier if she left.

'How can I?' She questioned him silently, Acha sat on the floor looking between the two of them with a feeling she was missing something, something important.

'We're your friends, nothing will change that.' Daniel answered knowing this conversation was not one for Acha to be included in, it was something personal between him and Zo, something they needed to resolve.

'I tried to kill you.' She felt the shock in Daniel's mind it was almost as if he hadn't expected her to remember, or at least to be so blunt about what she knew. *'She let me remember.'* She lowered her gaze to the floor crossing her right arm across her body protectively even thinking the words hurt, she knew this probably wasn't the best way to go about things, she was not self piteous by nature, but she felt so alien, so alone, and it would be safer for all if she were to stay that way.

'But it wasn't you.' He protested knowing that she had every intention to leave them there, he couldn't blame her, it was the shock, but it was a shock for him too, a shock he had dealt with and was ready to move past, why couldn't she see that? Why did she have to be like this?

'It was, that's what you don't understand… What if next time…'

'What ifs spoil everything, whether you are here or not she will find me, I cannot turn my back on you for things out of your control... I just don't understand... Why me?' Daniel shifted glancing away from Zo to Acha who seemed to be feeling uncomfortable as the silence stretched on, as she sat unaware of their secret conversation, she was glancing between them, waiting for either of them to talk, for one of them to say something, anything.

'She feels you are a threat... She knows nothing about you, about us the last year, you're something I kept from her... You're dangerous, that's why I can't stay.' Daniel took a determined step towards her.

'I can fight my own battles, even against you, I don't need you to protect me.' He had to convince her, he needed her to stay, she was in more danger than she cared to realise, especially now she knew the truth, it gave Marise more power.

'Would you be prepared to kill me? Would you?' She pushed him already knowing the answer, she knew she couldn't stay she had to make him except that too,

'I...'

'She wouldn't hesitate'

"Please somebody say something." Acha pleaded still sitting on the floor the tense silence becoming too much for her to take, Zo looked back at Acha and smiled.

"Goodbye." She had only walked a few more steps when Daniel stopped her again.

"Zo... if you go to that court alone... How do you expect to survive if you can't even forgive yourself for a silly accident?" He added the last part for Acha's benefit, unsure exactly what she thought of this situation, but he knew enough from her questions when she treated him, to know there was no doubt in her mind that his injury had been somehow caused by Zo.

"Court?" Zo stopped turning back to face him.

"Didn't Seiken tell you?... He said he warned you?" Daniel questioned surprise registering in his eyes.

"Tell me what?" She questioned Acha seemed relieved that once more the silence had been filled with conversation, Zo didn't actually look him in the eyes, she couldn't bring herself to do it, but she knew there was something in what he was trying to tell her.

"The court of divine judgement... it's where the next rune lies, please don't go alone." He begged lowering his head to hide the pain in his eyes

'Daniel I can't risk...' Her silent protest was interrupted

'I will just follow you. I mean it!' He threatened she nodded slowly knowing that he sincerely meant it. 'I will follow no matter the danger because... I could not bare to lose another friend.' Zo had already surrendered and had began treating Acha's wound with the pre-mixed paste, it was clear it had already been used once leaving enough for one more application, she knew without having to think that the rest had gone to treat the wound inflicted on Daniel by her sword.

'Another?' Zo thought to herself knowing this was a thought she was not meant to have heard, she had already began wrapping the bandage gently around Acha's leg. The bleeding although light, had already began to ease off, with the paste applied it would soon stop and become less inflamed.

"Thank goodness you found us." Acha again broke the strained silence. "Eiji and Elly have yet to return… If you hadn't have come, I would be… dead."

"Acha you do realise I can't heal this like I did Daniel?" Acha nodded this was something she was fully aware of.

"Why's that?" Daniel asked curiosity taking over once more, it made Zo smile, he was being just like his old self, always questioning everything, even if it was a little forced.

"It's hard to explain." Zo stated not really wanting to answer, but wanting to make the effort. "This body, although it was transformed to take on her original appearance, isn't her body. If I used nature to try to heal this, it would not aid me, as far as it is concerned the life force occupier has already departed, her body needs to heal naturally. It's not, in a manner of speaking, her body." She repeated for emphasis.

"I thought as much." Acha smiled. "But, if it involves you tapping into my thoughts and conscious they belong to me so you can right?" She remembered feeling Zo on the tip of her mind before she woke in Daniel's house, she had provided her with the strength she needed to take charge, it was something she would never forget, without her help she would never have woke, she had tried so hard to re-establish control on the body after her initial entrance, but her efforts had been in vain, the energy she had taken had not been enough. The energy she had and took from around her did nothing more than go towards maintaining basic functions.

"That's right, that's how I roused you the first time we met, all done." Zo smiled finishing up, aware that she was beginning to run low on bandages as she placed the herbs back into her satchel, she never remembered leaving it with Daniel before she left, it had never crossed her mind during her travels either, but she was glad he remembered to bring it along.

"Zo!" Eiji exclaimed his figure appearing through the mist. "You found her!" As he came into view they saw the enormous vines gripped in his hands

"Well she found us." Acha smiled. "Good job too a moment longer and I would have been dinner." She pointed to her leg as Zo helped her to her feet, at first she cringed applying a little weight onto the sore area, already easing as she took energy from the life around her to speed up the body's natural process of healing, Elly took the vine from Eiji wrapping it around her waist and passing it on, it was a wise thought, at least they could be sure no one fell down the disused mines.

"As soon as we are out of here I'll make you something for the pain." Zo smiled she knew it was about a five minute walk to the exit of this place, Acha should be alright for that time, and besides, it wasn't wise to hang around in a place that had creatures such as the one they encountered.

"You're… staying with us… right?" Eiji questioned the silence seemed to stretch forever until finally she answered

"For now" She glanced across at Daniel "Yes."

Chapter ten

A huge dirty city intruded on the picturesque landscape, until it had became visible, it seemed only mountains stretched on through the uninhabited area, yet now it was clear the initial conception was wrong. The town instead of being on the same level, zigzagged up the mountain side, the buildings of the city were built on enormous wooden supports each section propped up by wooden pillars both vertical and diagonal, although there was no question that it was sound, it was an eye sore on the otherwise beautiful landscape.

The platforms continued to rise right up until the mouth of an enormous cave, through the centre of the village to the mouth of this cave, stood an enormous free standing conveyer belt system, powered by a small turn wheel at its base, it seemed items were placed within and four people worked together to move them in a circle, which in turn would rotate the conveyer.

"I do not think these people will know anything of what we seek." Acha walked behind Daniel and Zo glancing around for anything resembling a court, yet seeing nothing but the humble houses and work stations.

"Even so… I think it best not to tell them the entire story." Elly whispered a small argument seemed to be occurring not far from where they stood. The miners turned to look at the strangers, all sounds instantly hushing. A young man stepped forward, his short blond-brown hair stained with the colour of soot not unlike the rest of him, he wiped his sooty hands down his stained white t-shirt.

"Excuse me." Daniel stepped forward, surprised that Elly had not jumped at the chance of leading. "My friends and I are travellers, we are seeking an ancient court, we were told perhaps you would know of its location." There was a long stretch of silence before the young village chief finally spoke.

"What interest do you have in such a place?" He glanced to an elderly man that stood besides him, clearly his father in this world, if not in their own.

"A friend of ours spoke of it once; I am after a key that was left inside."

"Must be a mighty important key for you to come all this way?" The old man stepped forwards rubbing his arms looking at them curiously.

"Then you know of it?" Daniel question recognising something within the old man's eyes, he nodded looking to his son. "I believe these may be the ones who can help us." His son frowned but agreed.

"We know of it." He admitted. "It blocks our path, we seek something just past it, I have lost about a dozen men to that place, we even tried to tunnel around but the ground will not allow it, the only way past is through it… I shall grant you passage through my caves, although you must go alone without a guide, and it will cost you one ruebluebyal crystal." Daniel sighed he knew this had seemed too easy.

"I'm afraid we carry no such item." He glanced at Elly hopefully who slowly shook her head, the village chief laughed, although the villagers around him did not join in on his amusement.

"Of course not, it can only be found deep within the centre of the mine." Daniel glanced across to Zo, defeat showing in his eyes, a short silence past before the chief began to walk away. "If you care to hear my proposition…" He glanced back to them who, quickly taking the hint, followed him into a small cabin, when they all were inside he closed the door, they sat at a small table looking at the chief and his father waiting to hear what they had to say.

It was a simple hut and as the one that belong to the chief no doubt the grandest, it comprised of five first floor rooms, two bedrooms, a kitchen, a bathroom and the place they sat now, the windows were simply holes carved into the wood split into four small sections.

"As I said the ruebluebyal stone is located just past the court which you seek, it is an ancient building from many millennia ago, or so it is thought, I heard a rumour when I was a boy, that this is one of the buildings left standing from those that came before us. I stood near it myself once, anyway, while you are looking for your key, as payment for the use of our mines, we request you bring this back for us, agreed?" Daniel glanced to the other group members, there seemed to be no objections amongst them, besides, it was their only chance if they were to refuse, they could never find what they sought.

"Agreed." Daniel answered, really there was no choice, and they either took this request, or failed their quest, the chief smiled, although it lacked sincerity.

"Excellent, then please, follow me." The young man stood gesturing his guests outside, leading them up the twisting supports to the foot of the cave. A giant metal grid hung above it secured by rope, the chief motioned then in, no sooner had they stepped inside, than the gate came crashing down sealing their exit.

"Hey! We already agreed to help you!" Daniel protested his hands gripping around the metal bars; the young chief went as if to speak but was cut off by his father.

"Please, this is not as it seems, it's for your own safety, when you return you may raise the barrier with the crank inside." He paused, as if considering something, a few moments passed until he spoke again. "You really should know the truth about this situation."

"Father no!" Protested the young chief although he knew his words alone were not enough to stop him, nor would they hide his shame. "This concern belongs to our people."

"And they are aiding us, they have a right to know, this gate will offer some protection, should anything happen outside, you will know the instant this gate is destroyed, it will send a slight tremor to all parts of the mine, but fear not, they are sturdy and will not collapse." The old man smiled gently.

"But why would anything happen?" Acha questioned stepping towards the gate curiously.

"Although time is short, I feel it best to tell you." He gave a sigh before starting the story. "Thirteen days ago a lord arrived, he rode a creature the size of a large horse yet its head was that of a snake and its horse like body was covered in black feathers, yet, where a horses hoof would finish it bore claws, never in my life have I seen such a creature, it was clear he was from a far off land. Anyway, he approached us, a strange device clutched within his gold coated fingers, he looked to the strange creature he had rode on and nodded as if it were to understand him. "It's here." He stated. Despite his clear interest in something here, he made no attempt to talk with us, the village was distressed by his appearance, and there was something… unnerving about him and his interest. We gathered the men at the gate where you now stand, protecting the livelihood of our town, before heading up we had decided it was best to send our families away, it was a quick decision and although none of us could explain it, there was something threatening about him, even though he had yet to address us. Finally, after walking around the village he called for the elder, my son, it was his first day as village chief, I had retired the title the set of the last sun. We both met with him in our dwellings, he spoke of a rare stone, a ruebluebyal crystal, he required it for the offering to the new king, he had to bring the rarest of stones, of course, we had already sent our offering as is written, but he had his to gather and sought this stone within our mines, he demanded the crystal and gave us the means to track it, this device." He passed it through the bars to Acha who examined it closely before looking back at him waiting for him to continue.

"Why couldn't he get it himself?" Daniel questioned

"Well he could, he explained it to us very clearly, for him to obtain it, he would do it the only way he knew how, it would mean the destruction of our home and the levelling of our mines... he wanted to use explosives at the centre of the mines which ultimately would collapse our home and the area around it. Therefore, he said since we have the tools he would give us fourteen days before he would return, had we not obtained the stone by then, he would use his method. We have sent teams of men in, the first team informed us the giant building that blocked the path was impossible to pass; we have dug many tunnels around yet never seem to get on its other side. Three days ago we sent someone through, they never returned since then two more of our villagers have vanished we can only assume they went the same way... Since you are heading for the court, maybe you know something of its secrets, thus while you are there, if you could bring us back this stone... you are our last hope, we cannot send anymore of our men in... but you are different." He smiled hopefully.

"We shall return before sunset." Acha smiled touching the elders hand with her gloved one. "Although maybe to be safe, you should evacuate." She looked at him meaningfully knowing that the faith he claimed to have in them was genuine.

"We shall wait for your return." A gentle smile crossed his wrinkled brow. "Until the last second." He added.

"I understand." She knew in her heart this would be the response, those who would leave were already be gone, a sinking feeling hit the pit of her stomach, they had to succeed, the town was wagering everything on their success, she could not disappoint them. "We shall be back before sunset, with the stone."

"There are many other paths you can take, in that device is a map of our tunnels, I programmed it in myself, if anything were to happen here, there is always another way." With those words they began to head deep into the tunnel.

"They won't come back, you know that." The village chief placed his hand on his father's shoulder motioning for him to lead the way down, his father however, refused to be led.

"I shall wait here for signs of their return." The chief glanced back at his father who was now sitting by the closed gate, he watched the travellers until they faded from view.

They had been walking for about an hour through the strangely lit cave, unable to discover why this cave was not pitch black, they were miles from any exit and no holes of light shone through, yet it was almost like walking on a rainy day. There was light coming from somewhere, yet the source could not be seen.

When the tunnel opened they stood for a moment mouths open as they gazed upon it, although they had been told it was here, it was impossible to believe until they looked upon it with their own eyes.

It was enormous. It towered right to the top of the opening, it appeared to have been built by carving it into the stone and removing the mountain from around it, it was made of purely of this stone, not a single brick or break was visible in the entire structure. All in all it was about ten stories high, higher by far than anything this world now saw. At either side of it were enormous walls making it impossible for anyone to walk past, as the miners said the only way past, was through. At the very top of the building, still in the same stone stood what Daniel recognised as the figure of justice, although it was difficult to make out and slightly different to the interpretations he had previously seen, it none the less was meant to be her, a blindfolded lady holding in her hands a golden set of scales.

"This building must be old." Eiji gasped trying to take in the sheer height of it. A tall door stood clearly as the entrance, although tall it was narrow, to the point where they could only enter single file. Daniel strained against it until it began to move opening inwards; one after another they stepped inside.

***

"Daniel wake up. This isn't funny, wake up!" Through the darkness he felt two hands on his shoulders shaking him gently, he opened his eyes an odd feeling descending upon him, a boy, no older than seventeen with short messy black hair leaned over him, his blue eyes registering relief as Daniel looked at him he went through the motions. "How many fingers am I holding up?" He waved his hand quickly in front of Daniel, far too quickly for him to see, let alone count the fingers, before vanishing bringing back a glass of water, Daniel sat confused for a second, wasn't he just moments ago somewhere else? He sipped the water his memory flooding back to him.

"Stephen! You're alright!" Although as he expressed this relief, he was unsure why he felt the need to.

"Of course I am, it is you who is on the floor." He smiled offering his hand to Daniel before pulling him to his feet

"What happened?" Daniel glanced around; they were in Stephen's mum's kitchen, a place he had spent most of his days planning his adventures and travels. He watched as Stephen walked across to the pantry, removing what could only be a pitcher of his mum's lemonade, never had anyone tasted anything like this, she always made extra when Daniel came around.

"Stress maybe, you were going on about the college you wanted to attend the courses you would take then next thing I knew, boom, you sprawled out over the floor, maybe what happened last year plays a part in it, I mean you have been…" His voice trailed off into silence before he grabbed two glasses and filled them to the top with the liquid; he placed one in front of Daniel who had only just finished the water. "Are you sure you don't want to go see your mum?"

"Nah, I'm fine, really." He caught a glimpse of himself in the mirror a strange sensation washing over him that something was different, but he couldn't quite finger it, his brown hair hung as always just short of the bottom of his ears, his fringe neatly parted down the middle, his dark eyes shone brightly back at him, he knew then nothing was different, the mirror didn't lie, but for a few moments he thought he looked younger, he shrugged it off, it was probably due to his pale competition.

"If you're sure." Stephen glanced over his friend again with uncertainty, but knew better than to argue. "Come on... I have something to show you." A hidden tone of excitement filled his friend's voice as he led Daniel to the stairs, Daniel stopped at the bottom of then carrying with him the strangest feeling of deja-vu, he watched as his friend hurried up the stairs, not waiting to see if he followed.

"A star fragment?" Stephen turned to face him, amazement on his face.

"It's true! You really can read my mind just like mum says." He laughed before continuing up the stairs, when Daniel had caught up Stephen already held a small black box in his hand, Daniel could feel his friend's excitement as he stood waiting to show him.

He opened the box slowly for effect glancing in first to ensure it was still where he had left it, Daniel heard himself gasp as he saw the small rock shining brightly in the box, almost as if it was a star plucked from the sky, it seemed to twinkle as he gazed upon it. Daniel had always envisioned the stars as something out of his reach, something no man would ever gaze upon but from afar, they had never seen a single star fall to Earth, meteors yes, but never a star, he wondered if this was the first, as he gazed upon it he felt the strangest awe, he wondered what events it had seen in its life, he hadn't realised he had been daydreaming until Stephen spoke again.

"Dad thinks it's only part of it, he watched it fall and fetched it for me, he said once it entered it split into three sections, they didn't land too far from here... I thought maybe that could be today's adventure." He grinned lifting it from the box.

"No!" For some unknown reason, panic filled Daniel's thoughts at the idea of going today, Stephen looked at him curiously as he placed the star fragment around his neck, Daniel saw he had threaded some cord through a small hole at one of the ends, he tucked it in his shirt, waiting for an explanation for the uncharacteristic outburst. "Not today, I have a bad feeling..." It was true, something about the idea of going on an adventure today sat uneasy with him.

"In the morning then? Stay over tonight, we can plan our path... Besides, it is raining a little." Stephen looked out of the window at the gentle spots of rain that fell. "Maybe the rain will unearth them." Although he didn't sound convinced, there was clearly something wrong, maybe it had not been such a good idea suggesting it, so soon after the incident downstairs.

Daniel and Stephen unfolded their map, they had been studying it for hours now, marking little places where based on the first fragments location the other two may have landed. A huge clap of thunder echoed around the small island as the rain began to hammer down, not thirty minutes later Stephen's father rushed in soaked to the bone.

"Sure glad you two lads are here." He gave a heart felt sigh of relief. "I thought you were heading down to the river, I looked everywhere for you while helping set the barriers, the river burst it banks, when I couldn't see you I thought the worst! After all, you planned to go down today, Daniel, I'll let your father know you're here, you should stay tonight, I'm heading back down to finish the barricades." Daniel and

Stephen exchanged meaningful glances as his father spoke, Daniel watched him leave a strange nagging sensation tugged at the back of his mind, something dancing on the tip of his consciousness that he couldn't quite reach, he shrugged the feeling away, the relief he felt now that he and Stephen had stayed home was far more greater than the troubles of a fading dream.

***

Acha paused looking at the others, she noticed instantly Zo was missing and turned to face the door they had entered to wait for her, only, it had long since vanished.

She glanced around the miles of fields a strange joy filling her heart as she listened to the bird song.

"Who would have thought that door would lead to somewhere like this and not a building at all?" She smiled she turned a full circle enjoying the beautiful green surroundings all the time watching for Zo, certain she would appear at some point. The pure blue sky, grew darker although not a cloud crossed it, the singing animals fell silent.

Then without warning, everything became silent, it was as though, in that second, she had gone deaf, not a creature bayed nor sound crossed the earth but for her footsteps, it was only when she listened to them, to the crunching of the ground beneath her feet, she realised the others were not walking. For some reason, as she turned she looked to the floor, a grey circle starting from her feet grew around her, everything in its vicinity began to lose its energy and die, the grass near her turned yellow before withering into dirt as the trees leaves faded to the colours of autumn before falling.

"Acha." Elly's voice whispered from behind her, she turned to face them to see her Eiji and Daniel lying on the floor, a ghastly pallor to their faces. They seemed unable to move, unable to speak yet somehow, Elly had managed to grab her attention, she looked around unsure what to do, panic echoing around her head in the form of a deafening heartbeat. "Stop…" Elly gasped extending her arm towards her before collapsing fully to the floor. She rushed to Daniel checking his pulse, he hung on by a mere thread beating so slightly at first she thought she had missed it, then to Eiji, again, the results were not much different. As she approached Elly she heard a voice through the silence, although quiet, in the complete silence it seemed to demand total attention.

"Acha, I understand how you survived, my spell was imperfect." Acha stood to look at the stranger, she recognised him instantly. Although saw nothing more of him than a shadow, his dark image stood proud against the beacon of death that surrounded him, a death that stretched as far as the eye could see.

"What did you do to my friends?" She demanded an answer, finding inside her a bravery she never knew existed, as she faced Night, a former God before he became mortal to father her, now a rising God again, although she feared him, her friends were in danger.

"I am afraid; I cannot take credit for what transpired here, although your little act has saved me much time."

"You… you're behind Knights-errent, your behind the abduction of the Spindles… this… it's another trick, undo your magic!" She demanded desperately taking a single step forward before glancing down at her friends, although she could not see the darkened figure she knew he was smiling.

"I cannot undo the curse that you create; I can only take it from you."

"What do you mean?... This is not my doing... I am in control of my powers; this is one of your tricks!" Although filled with power, Acha couldn't help doubting the words she spoke, she had only lived with her curse a few months, she knew she could not master it in such a short period of time... but this?.... There was no way she could destroy an entire area... was there?

"Have you forgotten already? Let me refresh your memory. Tell me; are these actions of someone in control?" He waved his arm the scenery around her shifted and changed, although she knew it to be an illusion, a memory from her mind, she watched, not fighting his magic.

She watched as she was born again, an attacker grabbing her tightly to prevent her escape, yet it was he who could not escape, she watched his face twist with agony as his life-force was ripped from him, at the very last second she saw tears in his eyes before he fell to the floor, never to rise again. She watched again as Daniel withdrew quickly from her touch, she watched as Zo carried her from Abaddon, a trail of subtle death following, she was mistaken when she thought Zo's ward had killed the nature, all along it was her, she watched as the bandit jumped out to grab her, she barely managed to force him away before he died, even here, in Knights-errent, she had leaned against a tree before the mine fields, it soon withered and died at her touch. Acha gasped falling to her knees in tears as the dying world around her came back into view. It was true, she wasn't in control, she didn't control her powers, they controller her, they took what they needed when they needed it without her even being aware of it for most part until it was too late.

"Did you not wonder why the area your town once stood never grew with grass even after all this time? Did you not wonder why everything around it thrived and grew while the area you were sealed within remained dead? You took the life of everything there to keep your own, to preserve your life force. That is how your power works; you take life so the body you are in holds true to your image, holds true to the nature of those who live around you." He circled her slowly looking down to her as she knelt before him sobbing. "Everything the normal persons body does without thinking, digestion, chemical balance, homeostasis, you need to take life from other places to keep it running, that's why you become anaemic when your body needs more than you have provided that's when your power becomes even wilder."

"Does... magic not work on that same principle?" Acha questioned wiping the tears from her eyes she couldn't let him get to her, her friends lives were at stake.

"You refer to your... friend? Believe me it's very different, nature offers to her its strength, your magic is a force which rapes it, stripping it against its will to maintain your life. Your magic takes life, your friend's does not, the power I gave you is far too dirty to be called magic, it little more than a curse." Acha still knelt at his feet, although he was so close, the darkness still enveloped him she looked at her hands through blurred eyes thinking of the truth he had just spoken.

"A curse... there is so much I don't..." She looked up at him realisation in her tearful eyes.

"I could take it from you, I created it, I alone can remove it." His voice seemed filled with compassion although Acha knew he stood to gain from this. Her curse was after all his mistake and Gods didn't make mistakes.

"Would my friends..." She paused, finding it hard to believe she was even considering taking his offer; she glanced from her hands to her friends aware that although there may be another way, at the present she couldn't see it and time was running out.

"They would recover... Tell me, don't you long to be free, it's been so long..." He extended his hand down to Acha. "Take my hand; I can end your suffering." Acha looked from him to her friends and slowly reached for him.

***

Day light broke through the day sky as the sun rose Daniel and Stephen were already up, although they had barely slept, neither felt tried nor remembered seeing the night sky, yet the sun rose now, so clearly night *had* passed. They packed a small bag of food and water, along with the map before heading out towards where they guessed the stones would be the river.

'Please stop!' A female voice seemed to echo around Daniel's mind stopping him in his tracks; Stephen stopped short, a questioning expression on his face.

"Are you..." He began but was cut off by Daniel hushing him, a few moments passed before Daniel spoke, yet his tone remained low.

"Did you hear that?" There was another extended moment of silence as the two friends stood listening, finally Daniel shrugged heading towards the sounds of the river.

'Please...' The voice cried Daniel outstretched his arm in front of Stephen stopping once more.

"Didn't you hear that?" He questioned again finding it difficult to believe that Stephen had missed it twice now, all the time he stood there thinking how familiar the voice felt, like fading dream recognition played on the tip of his mind.

"You're day dreaming." Stephen smiled beginning to walk once more Daniel ran slightly to catch up, the nagging feeling still playing on his mind.

'Daniel!' The voice cried. *'Please.'* They were the last audible words he heard until a scream echoed around his mind he fell to his knees unable to do anything but wait for the pain to vanish.

"Zo." He whispered finally remembering, Stephen glanced at his friend in horror as the forgotten resurfaced, Daniel could only watch as the past played before him...

..."Hey look I see one!" Stephen climbed down the edge of a cliff near the river, below them, on a small ledge a piece of star called out twinkling brightly daring them to seize it.

"It's too dangerous." Daniel complained as his friends tried to edge closer. *"Lets come back when the rivers calmer."* Daniel went to grab his friend but found himself holding his back pack instead as he passed it over, he glanced from the pack to Stephen before throwing it to one side, reaching for him again.

"No good, at this rate it will be washed away, we'll lose it forever!" Stephen protested watching the raging water below, before he scrambled a little further down the rocks leaving

Daniel no choice but to follow. Somewhere overhead lightning flashed, followed immediately by the roar of thunder as the rain grew heavier, Daniel grabbed Stephen's wrist as he got closer,

"It's too dangerous, we have to go back." Daniel tried to pull his friend back yet found Stephen's will stronger than his strength, he had no choice but to stay, it was clear he was not giving up on this.

"I just need… just a little further…" Stephen gave out a yell as the ledge he stood on crumbled collapsing into the water below, Daniel grabbed tighter, although the rain made it difficult to get a good grip, he pulled as hard as he could as his friend begged him not to let go, but even now he felt him slipping. He swore over and over he wouldn't let go, just then without warning the tree which Daniel's other hand so desperately clung pulled from the earth uprooting the tree, both of them fell crashing into the river below. Daniel felt the burning pain of his lungs as he was forced underwater still holding tightly onto his friend. But the tree had also fell, falling where Daniel had, robbing him of consciousness, as the world around him faded into darkness, he felt his grip on Stephen slip, for a split second before the darkness took him, he swore he saw a light encircle him pulling him towards the surface…

…"I woke on the river bank, the rising water lapping at my face, to this day I don't know how I got there… I remember the area I woke in was unfamiliar, I ran for miles looking for you, hoping you had somehow fought your way to shore, maybe the same thing that had somehow saved me saved you… I looked for hours but was no closer to where we parted, I thought, maybe if I got back I would find you there… but I couldn't walk any further… my legs gave beneath me leaving me sitting just looking over the river… It was your father that found me, he had seen us fall and tried his best to help us, he set patrols across the length of the island… when he found me, he wrapped me in a blanket glancing around hopefully, I could see the questions in his eyes, why me and not you? The same question I asked myself over and over." Daniel glanced to Stephen not sure what he expected, Stephen just smiled as if to humour him.

"Don't be silly, you must have dreamt it, we haven't even been to the river yet… look if you are that worried, let's head back." He placed his hand on Daniel's shoulder as he slowly got to his feet. "Maybe you hit your head when you fell yesterday, let's get you back"

"You're right." He whispered, the lump still hurting his throat from the painful memory "I have to go back… This isn't real, as much as I want it to be… you died six years ago, I don't know how, maybe it's the magic of this world, but for a moment, I forgot that… but it was good to see you again." Daniel slowly turned his back on Stephen, unsure exactly where it was he was heading.

"Stay." His friend's voice begged as he ran to catch up with him. "Please."

"This isn't real…" Daniel silently scolded himself sadly for being so foolish.

"It can be, you don't have to remember this, it can go back, to like before, I am your best friend, doesn't that mean anything to you?" He pleaded. "I am offering you everything that we lost. Please don't choose her over me."

"Stephen, not a day goes by that I do not regret what happened that day, I filled the past six years with what ifs. I blamed myself for what happened completely, I withdrew from everything, I thought life a meaningless sham that laughed in my face taking those I cared for most away from me. But… when I met her, I finally began to forgive myself, she saved me Stephen… and although I could not save you, she needs me now, and maybe, I can succeed with her, where I failed with you… I wish things could have been different, but, if I don't leave now… I don't want to fill the rest of my life with more what ifs." Daniel looked meaningfully at Stephen, glad that for some reason he had been given this chance to see him once more.

"It could be different this time."

"After I lost you I stopped fighting, only since I met her, did the battle start again, please I have to go, surely you understand." Daniel went to place his hand on Stephen's shoulder then pulled away,

"You would forget me?" He questioned sadly moments before Daniel wrapped his arms around him.

"No, I could never, you are one of the reasons I am who I am, one of the reasons I fight on against all odds… she is the other." Stephen hugged him back patting him on the back as he did so; the scenery around them began to change.

"You will not change your mind?" Daniel pulled away finding himself standing in a rather large, empty room his friend still standing before him.

"I cannot." Stephen grabbed his hand placing a small object in it closing Daniel's fingers around the glowing light. "That makes two." He smiled; he hesitated as he stood before the door. "I am glad to see you do not blame yourself any longer, or this would have turned out much different, this place is only as unforgiving as you are to yourself. There is more at stake in this world than you care to realise… I am sorry." Stephen whispered his image now fading.

"Sorry why?" Daniel questioned stepping forwards towards his friend who seemed to be fading into the air around him.

"Because this will be the third time…" But before he could finish he had faded, Daniel stood for a moment staring in disbelief at where his friend had stood, he opened his hand slowly finding a star fragment shining brightly at him, he smiled sadly placing it around his neck with the amulet. His hand rested on the door, yet he did not expect it to open so easily, once he had stepped out he began to shout Zo's name.

***

"What will happen… to me I mean?" Acha pulled her hand back hesitantly, in her heart she knew the answer, but she felt like it was a question she needed to ask. The shadow glanced down at her; he glanced over the barley living bodies as they lay on the grass fighting for their lives before looking back to her.

"Isn't the question, what will become of them if you don't, more appropriate?" He questioned stopping to stand before her.

"How… do I know this isn't a trick like before?"

"My dear daughter, the only person that died before… should have been you. There is a lot more than just your life on the line, they took you in cared for you. They are your friends, is there really a choice? Do you know how painful it is, to have you life-force ripped from your body whilst you live?" Acha glanced from her friends and back up at him again her hand almost touching his when she heard it.

"Zo!" Even in the middle of nowhere Acha heard that cry and it only took seconds to realise who it came from.

"Daniel?" She whispered questioningly looking at his motionless body on the ground near her feet; she heard the voice again before snatching her hand from the shadow. "Daniel!" She shouted she looked at the shadow. "This *is* a trick!" She snarled, to her relief, the scenery around her faded leaving her and a strange dog like creature, with the body of a man and the head of a dog, yet its human body was covered with fur, Acha knew that although this was not her father, had she surrendered her powers, the outcome would have been the same, the Jackal man approached her.

"It is no trick the images you saw could easily becomes real." He snarled, he had been so close...

"Zo?" Daniel shouted by what seemed to be right next to her.

"You know, your friend really should not be shouting, who knows what may hear him." The creature lunged for her hand but she moved swiftly away

"You want to feel my power so badly." She snarled grabbing the creatures arm, she felt its life begin to absorb into her, the creature fell to the floor, although something about it felt different than all the other times, Acha raised her hands to her ears as they started to itch, only to find it changing into a small pointy almost like an elf ear, she touched it curiously, it was clear what had happened, it was like Seiken had said, magic in this world was different, she brushed her hair over them and stepped from the dark room through a door that had appeared from nowhere, she gasped, surprised to find the world around her void of colour, it was then she released the ears were not the only side effect of using her powers in this world, she rushed through the door and collided with Daniel she gave a small scream.

"Acha?" He questioned surprised to see her, she grabbed his arms gently looking him up and down as if ensuring he was real.

"Daniel... Thank the Gods. I thought I'd killed you... back there." She glanced back towards the closed door she had just left. "You... are real... aren't you?" Daniel looked Acha in the eyes, aware there was something different about her, but not wishing to bring it up he answered.

"Of course I'm real... We need to find Zo, she's in real danger" He pulled out of her grip and continued down the corridor trusting she would follow.

"How do you know?" She questioned following him before moving to walk besides him.

"I just feel it." Acha grabbed him pulling him to the floor, a look of bewilderment crossed his face, it was then he saw the huge window he nearly stepped right in front of, curious as always he couldn't help peering over the ledge before Acha pulled him down shaking her head, but the images he had seen were already burning into his conscious, row upon row of strange man like creature each with the head of a dog, row upon row of humans tied awaiting their trial, blood ran like a river through the room he leaned against the wall gasping in sheer terror as his wide eyes fixed unseeingly onto the wall before them, it was some time before he moved, pushing the images of death from his mind an action encouraged by the sound of his friend's screams.

"We should work our way up." Acha said catching the scent of something in the air, although unable to place it, even so, she knew it meant danger. "There are no more doors on this level leading anywhere but the judgement room." Daniel nodded crawling slowly under the window aware Acha followed closely behind, he jumped as judges hammer pounded and a voice cried for mercy. Finally they ducked around the corner to a flight of stairs giving them two choices, a small draft rose from below them, they already knew which direction they would head, the basement seemed more of an escape route, the draft alone indicated there was some form of exit down there, Daniel glanced at the sign pointing towards court rooms '10-100' a strange blue and purple tiled flag hung on the wall blowing slightly in the breeze.

"Daniel." Acha whispered a sickly scent hanging in the air, she turned to look to him completely shocked when he grabbed her arm pulling her into a small nook covered by a strange unknown flag, footsteps echoed around them, they seemed to slow as they passed the area, even stop for a moment outside the place they hid, before proceeding, then once more everything was silent. "How did you know… about the nook?" She questioned although she had the feeling something was coming she had no clue as to where they could have hid unnoticed.

"There was one at the bottom of the stairs covered by a flag, it shook in the draft, I just hoped I was right, old places like these are full of nooks and crannies… wait here" Daniel crept forward to where the staircase turned at a right angle, his hand on his folded weapon as he peered around the corner, he signalled Acha to join him, they must have walked three flights of stairs without so much as an exit to be seen, occasionally finding the need to duck behind old armour displayed as small gremlin like creature hurried past chuntering to themselves in a foreign language.

***

Elly pressed her back to the wall taking a breath, someone was coming, they were trying to be quiet, someone knew she was there and wanted to get the drop on her, she stood close to the opening a stone battle axe in her hands poised and ready to strike. She didn't have time for games, she needed to find the others, who it seemed, had decided to head off before waiting for her to arrive, or worse, something else might have taken them, either way, she needed information and where better to obtain it from those who tried to hunt her. She heard them draw closer, there was more than one approaching, she could slay the first, then the other, fearfully, would tell her all, it was a technique that had worked so often. Finally, there was movement, she swung her axe accurately before she even saw who it was she was striking, she paused in horror as she saw who stood before her, the axe stopped under the command of an expert barely a centimetre from Daniel's head, Elly dropped the axe, moving quickly to cover Acha's scream. The axe vanished into the air as sparks flew around Elly's hand now clamped on Acha's mouth. Finally Elly let go, her arm stinging from contact with Acha for even that short time, she opened her hand closing it again around some dice, before slipping them into her pocket, Daniel realised now this was the second time her weapon had vanished into the air but incorrectly assumed the force behind such an occurrence was magic.

"Where have you been?" She scolded in whispers once they had collected themselves, it was clear she was angry at them. "I've searched everywhere from the foyer to here!" She glanced around the corner expecting to see Zo and Eiji yet found herself disappointed.

"We... wait a minute... you mean you walked straight in?... Right into this building?" Acha questioned glancing around feeling somewhat exposed as they stood in the middle of a hallway.

"Yes, didn't you?" She raised her eyebrow at them curiously, she watched Daniel his hand still rubbing his forehead, for a moment she second guessed if she had stopped in time, he rubbed his temple lightly as a shooting pain tore through it.

"We need to get moving." Daniel stated. "We still don't know where to find Zo... or Eiji."

"Well they aren't beneath us." Elly stated in a matter of fact tone. "There were two locked doors, the others led to the chamber of judgement."

"Two doors?" Acha whispered a thought blooming in her mind, a conclusion that Elly had already put together moments before. "Then we just need to find the next lock door." Her voice trailed off remembering what that creature had said about shouting. "Quietly." She added.

***

Zo glanced around finding herself standing in a place so familiar to her dreams, but how had she ended up here? Wasn't she about to join the others in the court? Maybe they were already here, yet, only Daniel had stepped in before her... She glanced around the darkened area hoping to catch sight of anything but that which lay before her. She turned slowly to grab the door, thinking the idea of journeying through here was not so wise after all, her hand fumbled through the air a few times at the place the door should have been, she turned slowly only to see what she already knew, it had vanished.

"What is this place?" She asked herself, knowing the answer, the tall tombstones and statues being a clear indication that she stood in a cemetery.

She knew the outside world was bathed in daylight, yet for some reason, the place she found herself was in midnight hours with a moonless sky. The only light seemed to come from the cloudless sky and a small light flickering near the edge of the cemetery. She shuddered wrapping her arms around herself comfortingly, hoping with all her heart the others would arrive, but she knew it was not to be, this was *her* nightmare, a nightmare no one else would share.

Small flame torches seemed to ignite lighting a small winding dirt track through the centre of the graves, she seemed to know this place, it was the start of a nightmare she had suffered with since she first woke in Crowley. Always started the same way, the torches would lead right down the centre of the grave yard allowing herself to be led she would walk guided by them, they lit before her yet extinguished behind her escorting her in a bubble of light as she made her way. Even now the flames waited for her to begin the first step of her uncertain journey, with no other choice she began to walk, the flames were waiting for her. They flickered excitedly when they saw she was to follow, the flames danced, playing tricks with her mind, twisting the black trees into horrific shapes, giving the impression of movement, where she hoped there was none. She held her breath as she turned down the path, she knew what came next, the small cabin with a single candle sitting expectantly in its window, its tiny flame dancing against the wind, if she could make it to the cabin she would be safe, she didn't know how she knew, for she never made it, she always seemed to wake just past the next torch, it was something she was hoping for now, the last place she wanted to be was here.

She passed it, hoping she would wake as usual, sweat beaded on her forehead gasping for breath, she never knew what was so frightening about that dream, she had seen far more horrific images in the dark pits of her dreams, but for some reason, this place had always truly scarred her, she closed her eyes taking the next step begging to wake. But she didn't wake up, as the deep rooted fear in her mind had told her she wouldn't. She quickened her pace a fifteen minute run would see her safely inside, for some reason now, a panic began to rise within her, for an unknown reason, she felt as if she needed to scream, to run as quick as her legs would carry her and prey that she made it to the cabin, it was then she saw movement on the ground before her, she glanced to the small light, although from her location she couldn't make out its source, as the flame flickered on the window, everything seemed so far away, so completely hopeless, she knew at that point as she looked on, she would not make it.

A shadow stepped before her, she stepped back in shock her hands crossing onto her chest with a deep intake of breath, it was only seconds before that breath was released as the light of the torches bathed the figure never had she been so happy to see anyone.

"Daniel." She smiled relief pulsing through her body as she stepped forward to embrace him; he stepped away from her touch. She looked at him questioningly, it was then she saw it, the hate, the anger in his eyes. "Daniel… I…" She didn't know what to say he moved forwards grabbing her wrapping his hand around her arm holding it tightly, a little too tightly before he even spoke, when he did it was a cold heartless tone… the way she had expected when first he found out her secret. It seemed her initial thoughts were correct, maybe all prior concern were for the safety of Acha and the ease of travel, although she had hoped there was more to it than that, looking now she was clearly wrong. In his eyes he held betrayal and anger, looking at him now she wondered how he could have hidden such a powerful emotion from her, she stood rooted to the spot, unable to move or say anymore, the sheer force of his emotions robbing her of the words.

"Come with me." He ordered pulling her in the direction he moved. "There is something I must show you." Even had she wanted to, with the strength of his grip she could not object, she had no choice but to follow, further and further away from the place she knew she would be safe, the light from the cabin becoming nothing more than a minuet speck on the horizon, finally they stopped, they stood at the highest point of the cemetery looking out as far as the eye could see in every direction lay the graves of thousands of people. "Every tomb, every grave within here has its own story." He began; he didn't look at her, just over the vast see of marble and stone that lay before them.

"Daniel why are…" He grabbed her harder warning her to listen, with that single movement he had almost forced her to her knees, she never remembered him being so strong, he had always seemed so gentle, yet now, because of her actions he had transformed into a being filled with anger and resentment, all the traits she associated with him, gone.

"Each life so different, yet they share one thing in common, do you care to guess what that is?" Zo shook her head, tears welling in her eyes as she looked to him his grip increased as he snarled at her. "Think harder, you know this one, you know what each one of these have in common?" His grip sent splinters of pain shooting up her arm, this time forcing her to her knees before him; he maintained the pressure, keeping her where she knelt.

"Daniel please… stop, you're hurting me." She tried to pull free of his grasp, normally it would be no effort, yet he stood firm, unmovable almost unaware that she even fought against him.

"I'll tell you shall I?… It's you! Each grave before you is a person you killed, or a life you destroyed, I never released just how many until I saw it for myself, or I never would have been so quick forgiving you. You drove your sword through their flesh and watched as they begged for their lives, it didn't matter how much they begged, the outcome was always the same. You never stopped to consider that there were consequences to your actions, you thought you were untouchable… you made your last mistake when you turned on me." A gravel echoed through the night sky as he flung her from the mound to the floor below, hands pushed through the soil to grab her, scratching at her skin to hold her in place and although she fought, she lacked the power to break their hold, there were too many, they were too strong. Daniel stood looking down at her, never moving from the place he stood as this transpired before him. "I would like to introduce you to your judge," he bowed, "your jury," he waved his hand around the graves "and the executioner." He pulled a short sword from somewhere on his person, his face shining sinisterly in the midnight light she felt herself shaking as she saw the demonic flames sparkling in his eyes.

"Please… no!" She screamed fighting against the clawing hands as Daniel walked down into the crowd of the dead.

She caught a glimpse of him as they dragged her towards the graves; he was watching smiling as they dug their rotting fingers into her flesh each one demanding their pound. Their hungry vengeful cries silenced as he appeared promising to give them what they craved, promising to deliver a justice that was long over due he tapped the short sword, that would become the very tool of justice, against his hand as he began to speak.

"They want you to suffer… They want you to feel the same despair they did, the hopelessness, the fear, they want to watch you bleed, dying slowly aware of the pain of each breath, preying it will be your last only to find another one follows, they want to watch the life slowly fade, they want to see it extinguished, at that point when your body can take no more and you are too weak to fight… when you lie unable to move, the darkness wrapping around you like a stifling blanket, only then shall you know their pain, only this way can you repent." He stood almost upon her smiling as he listened to her beg.

"Daniel… please." She begged forcing back the tears, for that second their eyes met she ceased to fight, for a second, she thought maybe something had changed, again, she was wrong, she saw it in his eyes, she fought once more pulling against the arms of the dead.

"Did you think I would ever truly forgive you? You tried to kill me, it's not only in the magic of this place, I see what I must do, I must do what is right. You tried to kill me, now I shall succeed with you, where you failed with me." He stepped closer to her again, with all her strength she pulled away screaming as she felt her skin tear and bleed where the dead had grabbed, yet somehow she failed to break their grasp, she called on everything within her and screamed as flames erupted from around her body, flames that forced the hand to release her while she felt it burning herself, she scrabbled to her feet. Even this final attempt was to no avail, more hands replaced those that had released her, the dead threw themselves on her once more forcing her back to the floor, there were too many of them. Escape… was impossible.

***

Daniel gasped, the pain of her screams echoing around his mind as he leaned against the wall catching his breath, it seemed as if moving was an effort, the screams drove him to the brink of madness, exploding in his mind without a second of silence, he had been doing well to hide the discomfort he was feeling and trying his best to settle the morbid dread that rose within him, he had after all promised to discuss this skill with no one, it was a promise he would keep, but right now, it was becoming so difficult.

"Daniel are you alright?" Acha turned to look at him as he gasped for breath, he looked up at her and concern crossing his brow, they were running out of time, since he had first heard her, it seemed an age had passed, her final words begging him to stop, he could only imagine what she was facing, since she found out her true identity, she held so much guilt, a guilt this place would thrive on.

"I… yes… it's… this headache." He shifted uncomfortably massaging his temple, then the screams went silent. He glanced around aware of the sudden relief the silence had created, but the relief did not last long, for the longest time he had heard her terrified screams, and now, there was nothing.

"I'm sure Zo can whip something up for that she has everything in that bag of hers." She pointed to Zo's satchel which he still carried.

"We have to find her first." Elly stated beginning to walk away, wishing she knew exactly where to start.

***

"Since the day he was born, this town has met with nothing but disaster." Eiji heard a voice his mind somehow knew belonged to his biological father; it drifted through the bedroom door, a voice the sleeping child would not have heard. Eiji stood looking over himself as a child, he had no regrets in his life, well he did, but he learned to live with them, there was nothing this place could show him that would drive him to surrender to their desire.

"Maybe there is some other explanation?" His mother whispered following the tall man into the boy's room, he picked the sleeping infant up in his arms despite the pleading of his wife as she tried to stop him from taking the child.

"It is the only way, you know that." He stated carrying the child to the air outside.

"What's going on daddy?" The child whispered sleepily as he was roused from his slumber by the cool night air.

"We must evacuate the town, Night is planning a great attack, we need to get you to safety while we stay and fight." His father smiled.

"I can help daddy. I can help protect you both." He whispered, as his mother erupted in quiet sobs.

"You can barely lift a knife... we need you to stay here... so we don't have to worry about you getting hurt, do you understand?" His father stated finally after a long drawn out silence.

They were quite a distance from the town when they finally stopped, they had taken him into the mountains that watched over their village and now they were there, his father wasted no time placing him in a cave a few miles from the town his mother gave him a hug placing in his hand a knife, a knife he could barely hold in his tiny hands.

"Isn't there some other way?" She whispered hugging the child tightly, she felt her husbands encouraging hand forcing her to release him. "The priest, he is surely lying."

"The priest speaks only the will of God." He snapped pulling her from the cave, leaving her powerless to do anything but watch as her husband rolled the bolder before the cave as he had been instructed. He found it quite light but there was no chance a small child could move it, there he would stay away from the world, unable to inflict harm on others.

"I'm sorry." His mother whispered placing her hand on the stone that separated her from her son, how was it possible that her husband had convinced her to do this, how could they abandon their first child under the instructions of the priest's apprentice? How could he have convinced her husband he truly was a pawn of Hades?

"May God forgive us?" His father whispered taking his tearful wife in his arms as they head back to the village.

This isn't right!' Eiji thought to himself following his parents. *They were evacuating ...the town was destroyed.*' Just outside the town boundaries his mother stopped again looking back over the path they had just walked, the vision of the place her son was imprisoned blocked by the dense forest.

"Are you sure we did the right thing? He's just a baby." She sobbed as felt her husband's arms tighten around her once more as he pulled her close, why did everyone have to listen to that man? Why couldn't they have just moved as she had planned, found a life elsewhere, there had been so many options, how could they be sure this was the right one, it felt so wrong.

"Since the day of his birth, this town has been plagued with disaster... our son... no that thing was possessed, you heard the vicar, the devil himself had taken our child... he was no longer our son"

"You're wrong; he's just a child... our child." She protested as he hurried her back to town, worried the longer they stood talking the more likely she was to change her mind and do something they all would regret.

"It is better you don't think of him that way... he was the cause of it all."

"He was always so gentle... he never hurt a fly." She sobbed wishing she could go back and take him in her arms once more, go back and undo what they had just done, leave the town for good, pretending the whole thing never happened, but her husband, was just so controlling, he controlled her every thought, her every movement to the point she had began to doubt if even her thoughts were her own. Him, or that man somehow controlled every aspect of her life.

"No, not a fly, he destroyed our village, it's as the vicar said it all began with his birth."

"Is it done?" A young vicar waited on the edge of town for their return questioning them the second they returned; he watched as Lisa erupted in tears, he had his answer. "It's ok my child, God understands your pain, he sends these things to try us and by God they do. Today you passed his test, for this he shall surely bless your next child." Lisa placed her hand on the small lump on her stomach Jed's hand took her hand in his.

"Blessed." He repeated after the vicar watching as he walked away back into the shelter of his church. "See Lisa… all is as it should be." He smiled.

A strange distortion filled the air surrounding Eiji, he watched the moon in the sky as it entered its next cycle, a week had passed since he watched that scene. He watched as Lisa crept to the place her son had been abandoned, she had finally decided to break free of their control, to run and never look back, as she had thought about that night, she realised, if they could force her to abandon one child, they could force her to abandon the second, she scolded herself for being so weak, for bending to their will, it was almost as if it had not been her thinking, after days of protesting for a reason unknown to her she gave up to her husband's command, at the time she was thinking, at least if she went with him, she would be able to find him and not just wake one morning to find him gone, he had come that day holding a holy book in his hand, demanding for the good of the town she did as he requested, for some reason, she had agreed, agreed to a decision that repulsed her so much. The vicar had come around that night, congratulating her on her actions, promising things would be different with the next child, it was then she packed, that man would never see her baby.

As Eiji watched her hurry away, in his heart, he knew she was going to look for him, but it was too late, his new father, his master had already found him taking him home to raise him as his own.

A large shadow descended on the town, the sky grew dark and black, though he could not see Eiji knew it was Night, he ran to the village knowing he could be no help, he could neither be seen or touched by anyone of this world. The vicar grabbed Jed in his arms, for a moment Eiji truly believed it was to save him, until he swung him around to absorb the magic and weapons thrown towards him, at the town's boundaries he dropped him leaving him barely alive to watch as the man who respected him most left for dead.

"Why are you showing me this?" Eiji asked the scenery around him faded to darkness.

"I thought it made a good introduction, I do so like to know about the people I meet, to get a feel for them, your parents believed you a child of Hades, they were not too far from the truth, you did cause all the elemental disasters to your town, it was a wake in your powers, it cost so many lives… but it is the same power that lets you do this." Eiji watched as he saw his training with his master, the learning of his skills all the time the image played the darkness spoke. "But it is not without its curse, the laws of nature mean it also does this." Again the image of the village as Night attacked. "He came for your power, so rare in one so young… and then there was your adopted mother." Eiji watched again as the image of a beautiful lady angelic blond hair fanned across the pillow on her bed, the young Eiji grabbed her hand, in a few moments, she would die. The image changed to that of his master, Eiji remembered how quickly he had grown old in the last few hours of their time together. "You see, Elementalists are born to live in solitude to live only among the elements, why do you think your master travelled alone so often? It is the fate of your kind, your destiny to walk alone with only the elements besides you. Those who reject that truth have it forced upon them. Despite how you hide it your feelings have developed for your companions... The same tragedy will befall all others whose life you have touched... Everyone you get close to will die."

"That's a lie!" Eiji screamed amazed at the force behind his own words, although it was true that most Elementalists did live alone, they chose to live that way it was their choice not one forced upon them. He held that thought in his mind repeating it over and over again reassuring himself.

"Really?" The darkness spoke reading his thoughts. "Lets se shall we... Zodiac, whether she knows it or not, is half dead already... Then there's Daniel, you led him to that creature if it wasn't for Zo's healing he would be dead... Acha by all rights died centuries ago, as for Elaineor..."

"What do you mean about Acha being dead?" He demanded though Eiji knew part of the truth about her power and her living since early times, he was never sure how she got from there to here.

"All in good time, you need to realise what I speak is the truth, but you will come to see that in time, then maybe we will talk again... you know where the exit is, you knew since you arrived yet you stayed to listen, what does that say? It tells me you want to hear the truth; you want to know before it is too late."

"It says I am a fool!" He spat. "True my master's books spoke of such... folklore that is all this hearsay is. Or have you, in your infinite wisdom, forgotten my master was married!" Eiji couldn't believe how angry this was making him, although he did not know why, he knew everything the darkness spoke was lies, twisted lies, it had to be.

"It seems it is you who has forgotten." The voice replied firmly. "The time they spent together was minimal; he did it to save her, why do you think he had a separate house? He did it to save her, he brought you home to her unaware you shared the same talents, but your mother, a fine woman knew from the moment she held you, she gave up her life to be with you, you became the child she could never have, and ultimately the cause of her death." Eiji glanced around the darkness unable to argue anymore, he had run out of energy for this conversation, he turned taking hold of the door handle that he was aware of all along, he would not stay and listen to such outrageous lies, he would not, he turned the handle sharply before looking back into the darkness.

"Running away from the truth?" The voice mocked.

"No, I will not abandon those who depend on me, especially on the words of a creature who won't even appear before me." He flung the door outwards, aware that its path it had collided with something possibly the wall, or if he was really unlucky, a guard of the court, he stepped through closing it quickly behind him to find Daniel and Elly standing behind it, he glanced down seeing Acha sitting on the floor her hand clutched to her face.

"Eiji." Relief filled Daniel's voice as he gazed upon him; it almost seemed as if they were expecting something else to emerge from the closed door.

"By the Gods Acha, I'm sorry, are you alright?" He closed the door quietly bending down to her level she nodded moving her hands her nose twitching slightly.

"Serves me right for not looking where I was going." She smiled rubbing the sides of her nose.

"This place is so odd; it's like the hall of forgotten memories." He glanced around as if waiting for something else to appear before him.

"You too?" Daniel questioned as Eiji pulled Acha to her feet.

"Yeah… I knew where the exit was all along… yet I had to watch, I had to follow my parents." He turned to Acha "You sure you're ok?" She nodded wiping the tears from her eyes.

"Your parents?" She questioned wondering what each person had seen in their temporary prison.

"After they left…" Eiji glanced around frowning slightly. "Aren't we one short?" He smoothly changed the conversation to one he felt more comfortable with, he liked his friends, trusted them even, but there were certain things, private things, he was not ready to reveal.

"Well at least it will be easier now." Elly smiled looking expectantly at Eiji before continuing. "You can pinpoint her life-force." It wasn't a question but a statement; she crossed her arms looking at him expectantly.

"Sorry?" He questioned feeling that maybe Elly was the one with the powers since she always seemed to know exactly how to use them, in ways he had never even considered.

"Alright." She sighed many thoughts crossing her mind as she realised the small extent of his knowledge, the main one being what theory his master taught exactly she begrudgingly began to explain. "She is a magic user, as such she uses nature's energy to create, nature is her power, have you not noticed that strange feeling you get around her?" Elly crossed her arms.

"I… thought it was nerves… her being…" He paused looking at Acha then to Daniel. "A stranger and all." Elly smiled amazed he had managed to take his foot so smoothly from the shovel.

"Nerves… right." She rolled her eyes. "What you feel is the life of another magic user a person like yourself tuned to nature… you should feel that quality in her." Eiji looked at her his expression blank then he smiled to himself.

"Well… now that you mention it…" He paused as if for dramatic effect, "No! You are mistaking me for a master; I have only just been released to learn all this… I have not had time to get a feel for the spirits, nor communicate with them." He sighed, why did everyone expect so much? As far as his powers were concerned he was still a novice, although he held the powers of his master he had not learned to utilise them fully, nor had he learnt to define the different forces and feelings each element provided depending on situations, that was, after all, what the journey after leaving his master was about, that is what he travelled to discover.

"I see, Acha?" Elly turned away from Eiji to look at her.

"I cannot do anything of that level, I am simply… displaced." She sighed wishing she could help, she knew what powers her body held, this was not one of them.

"Then I guess we keep looking." Elly sighed she was always fully of such great ideas, but never with the people to carry them through… only once had she travelled with one deserving of her ideas, and that was over a year ago.

Chapter eleven

Night glanced around the chamber, it had been empty over a week now, ever since her last observer passed away, it was clear she was missing the company, missing what having someone besides her meant, but the issue of the emptiness would soon be resolved. A young girl knocked gently on the door, her mouse brown hair tied sensibly back into a neat ponytail, Night turned offering her a warm smile as she lingered at the door, this would be the first time in twelve years he had taken someone to see her, with the exception of Marise of course.

"You requested my presence my lord?" She bowed slightly before entering the chambers as beckoned, she walked slowly, fearfully, to stand besides him, she was loyal to him and only him, but this did not mean she did not fear him. Quite the opposite, her fear however, was not why she served him so loyally.

"Elisha, I am glad you came." He moved to stand beside her so the girl could clearly see that which his body had obstructed previously. She heard herself gasp amazed at what stood before her, through the second doorway stood a room filled with books, more books and manuscripts than she had ever seen, more books than there than in the enormous library, a place she spent all her waking hours. They stretched back as far as her eye could see, she stood awestruck, she had never imagined such a place existed within this building, but it led her to wonder why she was being shown it now, as if reading her thoughts, Night addressed her in lowered tones. "I would like to introduce you to someone." She followed her master through the winding cases of books to a small area clear of everything, here there lay a large case, around six foot in length, small lights twinkled on and off around it as if communicating to each other in code, it seemed to be created from the old technology she had read so much about, she found herself curious to learn more. She wanted to approach it, she wanted to feel the cool metal against her skin as she looked upon that she thought she would never see, but her fear suppressed by her thirst for knowledge she advanced, she felt exposed in the large space, her reflection looking back at her from the surroundings of the vessel where it seemed mirrors had been placed. "This is Elaineor." He motioned towards the case.

Approaching slowly, almost fearfully she heard herself once more gasp as she beheld what lay within, she hadn't been sure what to expect, many different ideas had run through her mind as she drew close, yet what she saw, was not even within the boundaries of what had been expected, within the case lay a delicate form, a young lady in her late twenties, her hip length hair a unique shade of blue, a colour she had never seen on any living form before, she lay there as if in rest, a strange suit covering her head to toe outlining the slender curves of her body, from the suit ran wires connecting her to the case she slept within.

"Is she ill?" Elisha questioned remembering having read something about regeneration chambers back in the time of the ancients, used to heal those who are ill, other than that one thought she was unsure what to make of the strange thing she saw before her. She had read so much, that after all was her job as Night's researcher, although she accepted this role, Night had never called upon her until now, she studied for hours only to find information Night already knew, she couldn't help feeling she was in some sort of training, for what she was not sure, she was loyal to him and only him, she studied hard day and night, in hope to please him, in hope to show her gratitude for all he had done for her, yet she never came across a description of anything like that which she saw now, her assumption was based on several texts but the chamber itself was lacking several of the key ingredients to be what she had thought.

"No." Night stated motioning towards a chair; she sat obediently wondering what his plan for her would be. Night smiled at her, she was possibly his loyalist ally, that is why he had taken her from her broken home when her parents had passed away, normally he would never dream of taking in a child, perhaps it was his parental instincts, but for whatever reason, he had taken her in that day and not once had he regret it, she was barely twelve at the time and alone.

He had sat with her many days since he found her, watching over her, teaching her, he had been the one who taught her to read, something she had always been grateful for. He raised her as if she were his own daughter, someone once said, he was trying to replace that which he knew he could never have, although there was some truth to these words never should they have been spoken and for his disrespect, that person suffered.

He gave her everything she could ask for, she loved to learn, so he gave her the library, when she questioned him he simply informed her he needed a well read researcher, he paid her well for her work, although what he truly needed her for, she was not ready, but when she grew, she would be perfect and now, she had grown to suit his needs perfectly.

To many, it seemed as if she was his favourite, but he did the same for all those that chose to stand besides him, he showed each one of them respect they earned, he was fair and just, until it came to the world outside and the people who lived in their bubble of ignorance within it.

"I shall tell you her story." He waved his hand before a mirror, colours swirled around the mirror settling to display the images of the tale her told.

"This is Elaineor, Lain or Elly, whichever you may wish to call her. Her story began a long time ago, she was born before the new Gods claimed power and the Severaine destroyed that world, in the time before Zeus. As you know that was many lifetimes ago now. She worked as a servant for what, back then, was a wealthy family who were trying to right a terrible wrong, that had opened a chain of events that lead to her being taken into their home. You see, Lain came from what was know then, as a broken family, her mother worked for a multinational cooperation working all the hours to make money to put food on the table, luckily all this was done away with at the releasing of the Severaine, anyway, one day the boss 'by accident' it was claimed, killed her mother, knowing she had a young child he took her into her home promising to raise her as their own. But Lain would have no such thing, she cooked and cleaned, in return, she was fed, clothed and given shelter. Every waking moment she knew there was something more to life, something she was missing, something she needed to seize, but she lacked the power to do so. She loved her job, the family she worked for treated her not as a servant, but as a friend, she sat at the same table to eat with them, she was even permitted to address them by their first names. Despite this great blessing, she longed for much more, she longed to be free, yet at the same time she found herself bound to these people with an unseen bond, perhaps the bond is better named fear of the unknown. She was a talented girl; she was one of few who could read in that time. You see although they were far more advanced than we ourselves were, it becoming increasingly more expensive to be educated, only the rich could afford to learn and thus got the better jobs and became richer still, the lower class as they called them, were once educated, but with rising costs soon education became a luxury most could not afford. Many children would tend house and head to work in any manual labour they could get. The reason Lain could read was not because she attended school, but the master of the house had taught her this skill when he took her in as a child knowing that one day, she would pass it on to their children in return before they were sent to school. Of course, this was all a facade this couple had both being declared sterile meaning they could never hope to bare a child. But one day miracle of miracles they bore a child, Lain was requested to spend hour upon hour reading him stories of great heroes and of times past. The master many night would stand just outside the door listening as she told the stories with such enthusiasm you would have thought it was her facing the Cyclopes, she brought the stories to life, but this was not something she did for the amusement of the child, her enthusiasm came from the heart felt desire that it *was* her out there enjoying the freedom of the adventures, she saw herself fighting her way past the Gods and challenging the great beasts." Night paused to look at the figure lying in the case before him, smiling gently to himself, if she hadn't realised then the treachery of this couple, she knew as soon as she met this fate exactly what had transpired. Night continued this introduction knowing Elisha could introduce herself to Lain perfectly well by herself, the same could not be said for the figure before them, Lain would not have chance while she travelled with the chosen. "Then one day, a new book appeared one she had never read before, it was the story of a great traveller who gazed upon the knowledge of the Gods, it detailed his journeys and great adventures. She read it to the child. As the words danced around her breathing life into the stories within she knew this was a sign, in her hand had fallen a map, a map to that which she longed for. As she read the stories they seemed so familiar, almost as if she *had* been there, as if it called to her soul. It was that very night that she left. She gathered enough food for a short travel, but only that she was due from her services and left, having no idea that she was playing into their hands, walking into the trap *they* had laid for her, this had been *their* plan all along. She travelled for years, sharing many great adventures, writing them in her journal, you may have read it." Elisha shook her head as she glanced to the figure, although she had never come across her journal, she had however, read some of her exploits. "She went by the name of Lain, so no one could track her to her life before. Finally, after three years she finally reached the land she quested for, although she had travelled it many times, she failed to see that which she had sought. But now she was ready, the markings stood clear for her to see. The Gods knew this day would come, it was written and they had prepared for it, well Zeus had, for it was he who ensured the child would be in that families care, it was he who requested the scrolls to be placed only when the time was right, for he knew once she found this, she would leave and it would take further years of travelling and mastery of many different skills before she could see what was before her eyes. Zeus spent this time collecting allies. The Gods rejoiced the time would soon come. Upon Olympus they started a mighty war, a war so powerful, so all consuming that, as was planned, they failed to notice a young lady walking into their kingdom until it was too late. The knowledge of the Gods, at this time, was stored within a great mountain, she stood for a few moments in disbelief, never before had she seen such a sight, the entire mountain was hollow, in its centre a light rain fell into a giant silver pool that seemed to bubble from the ground below it, a staircase rose either side of it, she stood there gazing upon her dream, unsure what to do now her quest had met with victory, although she was unsure of her actions, the Gods knew she would never dream of missing the chance and, as they had predicted, she walked slowly to the pool, a smile on her face and a gleam in her eyes, happy that all her years of work had finally paid off, finally she had reached her goal. She hesitated a moment, unsure of her next step, it was all too tempting. And then, she followed the actions expected, she jumped into the pool, yet as she did so, she found herself not rushing towards the silver water, but floating above it, as the water touched her, her awareness spread, she felt all the tiny lines of the water's source stretching across the planet's surface, sharing its secrets, its powers, and the knowledge of the world's inhabitants. Had Coronus not returned when he did, she would have become one of them, a Goddess, containing the knowledge of all the Earth, Zeus felt him weaken as the girl took their knowledge and with a pre-planned precision, he took this opportunity to overthrow his father, taking his throne and banishing him from the kingdom of Olympus forever. Quickly, while the power of the Gods still remained within him, he chose his final task wisely and that was to deal with Lain. He pulled her from the pool of knowledge shaking her like a rag doll, he no longer possessed the strength for torture and so, did the only thing within his power. He placed her in eternal sleep, suspended animation if you will, for her to wait until the time he regained his throne and possessed the strength to make her pay. Although it was never to be, Zeus had learnt from his father's weakness and saw it fit to bestow the knowledge of the pool to the Gods themselves, so never again could a mortal approach it. Myself, Gaea and Selene were the only old ones to survive that did not side with Zeus, after all, we took no side, although when I became mortal I did fear that I would never return."

"Did the other Gods perish?" Elisha questioned, although she had read many a tale, none stated what happened to those that opposed their new ruler, never had she found the answer to what became of a God that had lost their powers, surely something became of them, but she had always been led to understand that Gods were immortal and so, could not die, but that teaching in itself raised questions such as, what became of the Gods now vanished?

"Not as such, Zeus allowed them to serve under him should they wish… As for those who chose to reject his offer…" He paused as if in contemplation. "A God is a strange being, people's belief is what gives them power, those that were forgotten lost their powers and became, mortal."

"So what of you… Gaea and Selene, were you punished for remaining neutral?" She questioned, her eyes staring at him thirsty for more knowledge.

"Myself, as always I chose no side, myself, Gaea, Selene and of course, Chaos are the oldest of our kind, due to this they began to fear us, they made people forget me, erased me from their histories until I too became mortal. As for Gaea, most do not remember her name, but there is no denying she is there, that is what keeps her alive. Selene however has always been a loner and possesses the power to create a key the future may require, so she was permitted to continue as normal." He waited for her next question, knowing there would be many, he did not need to speak of chaos, chaos through history had always been found beside the one who would be named victor, in this battle, he had sided with Zeus.

"But you are a God once more, how?"

"I restored myself, it took years of training and a bold deal with Hades… But back to the reason you are here." He smiled, the time for questions about him had passed, this was all he cared to reveal for the moment. "Your job will be to sustain her knowledge, around her you will find every book ever written, just ask a question and the most accurate answer will find you… watch… who is Lain?" He questioned a single book floated to his hand he grabbed it as he demonstrated the ease to Elisha, he smiled slightly releasing it once more as he did so it vanished into the air. "Of course, there is certain information I do not allow her to have, these texts will not be located within this room, and references to it erased. Her last observer 'passed away' not long ago, the feeling of emptiness within this chamber does not suit her personality, thus she grows colder to those we need alive." He smiled. "Your job is to do what you love the most, read… read and watch." He waved his hand before the mirrors, images of a strange court room flickered on them before becoming steady images. "There is but one catch to this job, you must never, under any circumstances, leave this room once this job begins, at least not without talking to me first, it is dangerous, not to her but to yourself, you will become linked with her and must remain in this room, anything you require, should be located within these walls, there is a kitchen stocked daily from an outside source you can request anything you need or want, if there is something you lack… or require at any time, either call myself, or leave a message for Matilda in the kitchen cupboards. Matilda, will see to all your needs without stepping foot near the place, she will place what you request in a box which is placed in a portal leading to the kitchen, are there any questions?"

"No my lord, it will be a great honour to serve you." She paused briefly. "Well, there is one, how did she come to be here?" It was a question Night had expected to be asked far earlier than this and an answer Elisha needed to hear.

"I found her not long after I had regained my powers, I knew she would be useful, she wanted so much to live and so we made a deal, I would create for her a vessel in which she could live. A marionette, if you will, linked to her conscious by the case you see before you. In exchange for the chance to live, she would train to help me when the time came. It was a challenge, but finally I recreated enough of the old world's technology to achieve this, the marionette, however I could not get it to look human, but as soon as Elly's conscience entered it, it seemed to grow and develop, and as I had hoped, it took on the form of a human, but underneath it all the body out there is still nothing more that a machine, her body here is now more like a link into her mind, after all her consciousness is within the machine. The first thing she did was smile, it took her about three months to master the basic controls, once she had we parted ways and she went on to have many great adventures. More recently, within your lifetime that is, I found another purpose for her, to protect and train someone for me. I had spent a long time improving the vessel ensuring she would return at least once a century, the first was, after all, a prototype, there were many things I could do to improve it, but for this task at hand now, she needed the best, even then there were limitations on the marionette I created, nothing that would make the common mind suspicious, especially given considering their ignorance to the world around them, yet now you would not even know she was not human she has complete emotions, not capped by the marionettes limitations and there is only one problem we cannot overcome, thunderstorms, they can temporarily damage her, but just in the last three years, we overcome the problem with water, well, she'd still find it a struggle to stay afloat." He laughed. "But it wouldn't damage the vessel… now if there are no further questions." Elisha shook her head eager to begin her new role she thanked Night once more before he left.

***

"Wait." Daniel gasped as an overwhelming feeling engulfed him for just a few seconds he heard Zo scream. It erupted through the unnerving silence in a short burst just seconds before all her thoughts became surrounded by a barrier like the one she had taught him to guard his mind with. "She's in here." He placed his hand to the door; it had barely been there seconds, when he felt an electric current race up his arm before propelling him backwards with a loud crack.

"Whatever gives you that idea?" Eiji smiled helping him to his feet. "I guess we just break the door down?" Eiji questioned. "I can short out the field with water." He started to gather his energy but Acha stepped between him and the door, he looked at her questioningly.

"That barrier… It's not from this building." She went to touch the barrier but changed her mind at the last second. "She uses magic, it's similar to the field back at our camp, Zo must have used it to keep people out before when you were attacked, she probably didn't even realise she was doing it, it's something people with magic use to drive people away from dangerous situations, it's part of her, she probably isn't even aware that it's here…" She glanced to the others, she couldn't explain how she knew what it was, she had only seen something like it twice before, once at the camp, the other time was a long time ago used by the village shaman to keep his conjuring within a set area, and to keep others from around it from feeling its effects.

"Then I guess we just wait, I will keep a look out." Elly stated disappearing around the corner, she was glad for this chance to leave, in the last few moments something had changed, the empty feeling following her for the two weeks had suddenly been replaced by something different, she glanced back at the others, her hand sealing around the gossip crystal as she turned the corner.

'Zo?' Daniel called with his mind, trying desperately to reach her on some level, he could still hear broken lines of her thoughts hopefully it worked both ways, he moved to lean against the wall just short of the field's reach. *'It's Daniel are you listening?'* He sat down his back to the wall watching the others pace trying to find a way to break through without hurting her or themselves in the process.

***

"It's not my fault… please." She begged as he stood over her, his sword at her throat as he smiled down at her tearful face triumphantly, she had stopped fighting now, he seriously doubted she would fight even if the creatures were not holding her so tightly, he could see it in her eyes, she was broken, she had surrendered.

"Tears?" He snorted. "Monsters do not cry, save your trickery."

"Daniel… whatever this place has done to you… fight it… I'm not saying I don't deserve whatever…" Her words were broken by her gasps for breath as he placed his left hand on the top of the sword applying a little more pressure, not enough to break the skin but enough to silence her.

"You really don't get it at all do you? Not everything is about you, just as this isn't about me, it's about the needs of many." He moved his hand from the top of his sword to motion to the rotting corpses that watched in anticipation, there was silence among them as each one watched each head turned to look at them, in their eyes she could see a hunger.

'Zo….listen to me.'

"I am listening, I'm sorry, I'm so sorry." She sobbed Daniel's as gaze of hatred fell upon her.

"Do you think the moment of fleeting regret before your death is enough? Do you think that will satisfy *their* needs? Do you think that will save you? Just as they suffer for the desire of revenge, you shall suffer in the realms of Hades." He looked away over his sea of followers as they stood waiting impatiently, seeing her chance as the pressure on her throat lifted slightly, she slid from under the blade, but not quick enough, he felt her movement across the blade stabbing it down to impale her shoulder, she screamed in agony as it pierced her flesh pinning her to the floor. "You can't escape your punishment." He warned as his hand twisted the blade in her shoulder as she screamed in agony, her own hand finding the hilt of her sword, she pulled it free quickly from its sheath the creatures cowered against its light, with a flick of the wrist, she spun the blade in a complete circle barley inches above herself crossing over her shoulder to slice through the sword imprisoning her, a movement she hadn't even realised until she was free, a movement that seemed to be spurred by instinct, an action she hadn't even realised had occurred until the pressure lifted. The shard itself, however, remained firmly implanted within in her shoulder, but there was no pressure now holding her to the spot. From behind him, Daniel seized another sword "Now are you fighting me as Zodiac… or Marise? Not that it matters, since you're both the same." He sneered, his sword poised in an offensive stance, he watched her challengingly, the trial had begun.

'Fight it Zo.'

"I don't want to fight you." She took her sword from her left hand into her right feeling the warmth of blood running down her arm from her injury, but that wasn't the only thing she felt, deep in the forgotten regions of her mind, something stirred, she knew exactly what it meant, she wasn't just fighting against Daniel anymore, she fought against her darkness, a battle she feared to fight, a battle she did not have the strength to win.

"That's funny I want to kill you." Daniel stated smiling ironically. "Wasn't that what you said to me? Seems the tables have tuned now, you have no choice."

'Zo... we're all waiting for you outside... not in there out here, whatever you see in there, it's not real we are all outside the door.' The voice came again, this was the first time she realised it was not Daniel who was speaking to her, but a voice speaking to her mind, she touched her hand to her shoulder, how could this be not real? A million thoughts ran through her mind in that second, the truth now nothing but a blur, she knew there was only one thing to do, only one way to discover the truth.

"I will fight you." She whispered defeated, before she even finished the sentence Daniel had attacked, carrying out an almost perfect impaling move, almost because somehow she had managed to lift her sword in time to ricochet it, she knew why of course, it was the same reason as before, when she had faced that colossal figure back home, Marise had improved on her initial training, if it came second nature to Marise, it would to her as well, yet even so Marise would always make the better opponent, after all, she had only a shadow of her skills and instincts, she sidestepped another blow, ducking in time to miss the sweep of the sword, he was skilled, yet still failed to land a blow. She had her answer.

"Daniel can't handle a weapon... not even a sword." She looked at him as he came at her again.

"Wrong." Their swords crossed. "I wanted you to think that, you know it's me, you're just finding a reason now to kill me, giving yourself an excuse, justification, just like Marise was your excuse for everything you did. I *am* Daniel; can you really stain your sword with my blood?" Zo glanced around relieved that his army of the dead stayed a radius of about four feet away from them; it seemed they really hated the swords light, they acted almost as if it burned them, for this small thing she was grateful.

"I can stain this with Daniel's blood, no more than you can now, stain yours with mine." Zo cringed, that strange feeling clawing to the surface, those words were almost not hers. "Daniel cannot hold a sword, let alone use one!" She repeated as their swords crossed again she felt Marise's strength begin to surface, she knew if she didn't concentrate she would lose more than the battle... she released a fireball as their swords stuck once more, burning her hand as it did his, with another strike his sword flew from his hands landing on the ground behind her. The fight was over.

She stood with her sword pressed to his throat as he backed up against a tree, it trembled in her hands as her heart and mind gave conflicting signals. It was just like before, it was everything she could manage not to force it through his throat, she fought against the driving force that willed the blade forward, but lacked the strength to pull away.

"Why do you hesitate murderer...? Why fight your nature?" Daniel questioned his eyes locking on hers; within them he saw the fear, not only in his own eyes, but in hers. The sword pushed a little harder against his throat no matter how hard she tried she couldn't seem to lower it.

Time seemed to stretch for an eternity, a million thoughts and fears racing through her mind as they stood in deadlock, thoughts that weren't entirely her own. Finally, the force she fought surrender, it released her so suddenly she stumbled backwards a few steps, it dropped as she released a relieved breath in that moment, she had doubted her strength to walk away.

"You owe me…" Her voice could manage nothing more than a whisper a bile rising in her throat, it had been close, a paper thin line in fact, she didn't look back to the figure as she spoke, her vision focused only on the small cabin surrounded by the dead who wanted her blood. "Now go!" She whispered hoarsely as her gaze washed over the sea of the dead, each still waiting for their pound of flesh. Daniel looked at her, still stood with his back to the tree, his hand on his throat where her sword had pressed, a realisation reflected in his eyes.

"The inability to land that final blow… that is what separates you from her." She turned back to look at him but he had vanished. His words just then had given her a new found strength, strength from deep within her.

"I am not a killer." She whispered. "I have never taken a life. "I am not Marise, I am not a killer." She repeated the words over and over in a soft whisper a whisper that brought with it strength, Marise had killed countless people, but she, Zodiac, had never taken the life of another being, the creature had given her hope, a line of comfort she could use to distinguish herself from Marise and as long as that line remained in tact, she would remember who she was, she was Zodiac Althea, a healer, a person who valued life and could never take it. "I am not a killer." She whispered again surprised such words could give her so much power.

Although the dead kept their distance she didn't wish to be there a second longer, what just happened had scared her more than the creatures that lay in wait, try as she did to lower that sword she could not, she was sure she would have killed him, she remembered the sheer strength it had taken to stop the blade from taking his life, almost as if she was playing tug a war against a stronger foe, should she have not found the strength from somewhere inside, the situation now, would be very different… It was close, and worse, she knew as long as she drew that sword, it was always going to be.

She ran towards the small flickering of light of the cabin, her sword still drawn keeping the un-dead at bay only when her shaking hand has gripped and turned the door handle did she sheath it.

Daniel stood from his position against the wall moving to the door nervously for the last fifteen minutes he had not heard a single thought from her mind he had barely reached the door when it flung open Zo falling into his open arms.

"Zo… thank the Gods." He whispered in her ears as she threw her arms around him despite the pain it caused, he held her tightly feeling the fear and desperation that forced the tears from her eyes as she held onto him for dear life, they both stood never moving for what seemed like an age, not a word passing between them as they held each other, neither wishing to let go.

"Daniel… I." She pulled herself away from him finally, the pain from her movements sending sparks through her body. "Thank you." She wiped her eyes in a quick embarrassed movement before she took her bag from his shoulder placing it on the ground. Acha and Eiji had remained silent, watching with concern and curiosity as she had simply stood their crying in Daniel's firm embrace looking far worse for ware than any of they had when they emerged from their door, only Eiji an Daniel held some understanding of why, a place of judgement was harsh on a person like her, a person who had taken the lives of many, she watched their eyes as they followed the blood from her arm to her wound, they did nothing but stare in horror, not one of them spoke, she untied the top of her top pulling it from her shoulder, she saw Daniel grow pale as he moved to kneel besides her in an attempt to help, but he wasn't sure exactly what he could do. She placed her hands to the back of her shoulder before realising she could not reach the remaining fragments of the blade still embedded within her wound. Just as she gave up she felt a cool hand on her shoulder sending shooting pain through her body, she leaned forward cowering from the touch. Elly looked to her and smiled.

"Rough time?" She questioned smiling gently, as Zo met her eyes she saw within them a new determination, whatever had happened in there had given her some hope and from the looks of her wounds, she had paid a high price to find it, or perhaps, the cost had been equal to what she had gained. Without warning she squeezed the wound so the metal tip protruded from the back, she pushed it gently forwards watching as Zo managed to grab the piece now extending from the front of her shoulder, after all, it would be foolish for Elly to remove it, it would create a far bigger wound.

Zo seemed to freeze as her fingers found the jagged edge of the severed blade; it wasn't until Elly leaned forwards to take her hand she pulled. Fire exploded around her shoulder as she gasped for breath, Elly already had began wrapping a bandage around the lower part of the wound as Zo leant forwards gasping for breath, Daniel passed some herbs to Zo as Elly covered the injury he kept hearing a phase repeated over and over in her mind, the very phrase that gave a small shimmer of hope to her otherwise saddened eyes, he smiled gently to himself, relieved she found some comfort in what she thought, it was true it was something he had wanted to say, but simply hearing him saying the words she now thought, would have been meaningless, it was something she had to discover for herself, something that gave her hope and a new determination not to become what history dictated she had.

"It's ok." Zo smiled looking at him, hearing the concern and questions of his thoughts as he looked from her, to the bloody section of sword she held in her hand, he opened his mouth to object. "We don't have time." Elly stood up having completed the bandaging she stepped to one side.

"But your arm… and…" He stopped looking at the scratches across her back shuddering to think what she had gone through in there.

"It's ok." She said again in a tone of calmness she did not feel, she touched Daniel's shoulder with her good arm, before placing her hand over the wound pressing on it lightly, Daniel simply sighed watching as she did so.

"I have located where we need to go." Elly stepped forward offering to take the satchel from Zo she shook her head placing it across herself so it rested on her good shoulder hanging the same side as her sword. "It's heavily guarded so we are going to need a distraction." Elly whispered moving to walk besides Zo, Zo nodded her hand still gripping the bandaged area.

"I'll take care of that." She added for the benefit of the others earning herself injured looks as they wondered what she could possibly do without giving their position away.

Elly motioned for silence as they reached the top of the stairs, already they could hear the growls and pacing of the creatures that resided on the floor they were about to enter. The next floor up would be the roof, and consequently had an entirely different staircase to the one they had just climbed; it would have been so much easier should they have been able to continue all the way to the top.

"What's your plan?" Eiji whispered touching her shoulder moving his hand quickly as he felt her shy away, a look of pain on her face, he could tell just from touching her the pain she suffered, he also knew as a Hectarian, if the wound had been inflicted anywhere but here, she would have had no trouble healing herself, sure the smaller scratches she could heal when she got home, but whatever made that injury knew exactly what it was doing, it was something no magic could heal, they both knew that, yet he still felt her try, he felt the sprits offering their help, the power entering her body, yet for some reason the wound would not heal… he only wished there was something he could do.

She looked to Eiji and took a deep breath, she felt as if a thousand eyes were watching, seconds later there was the sound of footsteps echoed very faintly down the hall and the breaking of glass, all but Elly and Zo retreated a few steps as the guards jumped to attention most running to investigate the cause of the disturbance.

"What was that?" Acha whispered fearfully

"An illusion?" Eiji questioned suddenly realising why neither Zo nor Elly had reacted at the sounds. Zo smiled and nodded, leaving him wondering what else she was capable of, yet a small part deep in the back of his mind warned him that he never wanted to find out.

"There's still a few guards, lets hurry before the others return." Elly clutched a marble staff tightly in her hands ready to battle, she moved to step into view Eiji stopping her

"Let me." Eiji stepped out to where the guards could see him, a faint aura of silver shimmered around him, the guards already charged towards him weapons draw, Daniel and Acha began to worry when they reached striking distance, only before they could land their weapon an enormous eruption of water somehow appeared from the wall turning to make impact with the enemy sending them to the end of the corridor. Seizing their chance they ran to the stair well located a few doors down from where they stood, Eiji found himself somehow amazed that Elly had know exactly which door lead to the desired route having not had the opportunity to fully investigate.

Finally they reached the roof, the door already open as if they had been expected. Elly lowered the large wooden lock down over the door.

"Why are there no guards up here?" Daniel questioned suspiciously glancing around the roof, with the exception of the stature in the centre of the building there nothing about.

"That's why." Acha glanced over the waist height wall to look down, seeing the guards and creatures alike fleeing the building in masses. "I don't understand." She commented as all but Daniel came to look. He was busy pacing around the central statue.

"The rune we are after is balance right?" He questioned examining the base of the statue carefully.

"I believe so… why?" Eiji joined him trying to locate what it was that had caught his friend's attention, he glanced to Daniel asking for an explanation with but a single look at the statue, he had his answer.

"This statue is made of the same thing this court is... I'm willing to bet, it runs all through the centre of the building but we couldn't see it because we never walked around that area just the side rooms." He stopped pacing looking at the scales held within justices hands; he thought hard wondering if when he gazed into the court room filled with those dog creatures if he had seen a central pillar, he finally decided he had.

"What do you mean?" Zo questioned a distinct feeling that she was missing something as she came to join them.

"This statue is... a balancing rod, like the kind used in large buildings millions of years ago to stop the tall buildings falling over, it is perfectly balanced, so if we were to say, remove the balance rune from the left hand part of the scale... the building would collapse." He paused staring at the statue before walking around it once more.

"So if we take it... we die?" Acha's question did not need an answer; it was clear what was being said. "Can't we just replace the rune straight away with something of equal weight?"

"The laws are different here... I'm guessing from how those creatures ran, the second it's removed the building will fall from under our feet... not like in our world where they would have swayed and then toppled. There was a long moment of silence while they weighed their options; they knew they had to take the rune Zo and Eiji whispered to each other as if trying to concoct a secret plan.

"I'm not sure it would work that way..." She paused considering the success of the plan for a moment... "I'll try my best." She smiled linking Daniel's and Acha's arms. Eiji linked Elly's and Elly Acha's, after ensuring her sleeves covered any flesh she would make contact with, she had a good idea of what they were to try, and was less than fifty percent convinced of the success rate, but again as Daniel had pointed out, the rules here were different.

"Daniel... when I say go.... grab the rune." Eiji moved to stand near Daniel meaning they stood in a broken circle, Daniel nodded his hand resting barely a centimetre from his grasp, Eiji nodded at Zo who began to chant, a silver ball forming over them, before it got to Daniel he heard Eiji shout. "Go!" He grabbed the rune feeling Eiji grab him arms, as the circle completed, the ground below them began to shake and the building crumble Daniel and Acha closed their eyes as a light green mist enveloped Eiji. They braced themselves to fall as the ground disappeared from beneath their feet as the building collapsed in a heap. They opened their eyes in time to see a tornado whip around them, the winds pushing up on the silver ward, Zo had created to contain them, they slowly drifted down its centre, beads of sweat forming on both Eiji and Zo's brow as they concentrated they were barely ten foot from the floor when the ward vanished leaving both Zo and Eiji sitting on the floor taking heavy breaths. Elly released Eiji and Acha and disappeared into the cloud of dust caused by the rubble.

When she returned some time later they were ready to leave. Elly placed a small purple stone in Acha's hand.

"Time to head back." She stated smiling triumphantly.

"Easier said than done." Daniel commented looking at the eight tunnels in the area they stood in. "Which way did we come in?" Elly began to walk away.

"That's easy." She answered barely giving Daniel time to finish the sentence. "It's this one." They ran to catch up with her as she began to head down the tunnel, they followed not out of a sense of trust, but because she always seemed to know exactly where they needed to go.

Chapter twelve

"I don't believe it!" The village chief exclaimed rubbing his sooty hands down his stained white t-shirt; he paused for a moment looking at his father. "Are you sure?" The old man nodded glancing up to the sealed cave at the top of their village.

"It crumbled just over thirty minutes ago, that was the tremor that you felt." The miners all grouped around listening intently to their conversation could it be true? Could that monstrosity that threatened their very homes now be gone?

"Shall I raise the gate? We all know that internal lever doesn't work." The chief glanced over to the gates and shook his head slowly.

"No I will go and meet them." He began back up the slopes his father had only moments ago descended with such speed, wondering how it was possible that they succeeded where his own men had failed, he simply stood for a moment in disbelief as he discovered not only had they succeeded in their task, but they now waited at the gate having already tried the leaver.

"I was surprised to hear you had succeeded." His eyes locked on the stone clutched in Acha's hand, it truly was the item they sought, Elly smiled at him with hidden meaning, it was a smile that sent shivers down his spine and drove fear into his heart. "May I?" He held his hand out on his side of the gate for the stone, Acha stepped forwards stopped quickly by Elly's arm.

"Raise the gate." She ordered, the village chief stepped back a pace making way for his father who approached.

"Please forgive us." His voice seemed older than before, shaking slightly with the tones of betrayal.

"Forgive you? For what? You need only raise the barrier to make this admirable" Elly's hand still stretched before Acha preventing her from advancing further.

"It would be more dangerous to raise it, than it would for you to navigate to another exit... you see." The old man glanced around before continuing in lowered tones. "*He* has returned, he will be here within minutes, true he will spare the villagers... but yourselves." He looked away from them towards the commotion already starting at the foot of the town. "He is powerful, even if you stood a chance of defeating him before; you are tired from your ordeal." He looked to Zo who was clutching her shoulder tightly, then to the others wondering what possibly could have faced then, then again, it wasn't surprising one of them got hurt, the courts were guarding by those creatures, and true they never hurt his men, but... "He will know we did not mine the rock ourselves, legends told of the coming of someone who could make the great building crumble... he will know you are here. It is said you carry great treasure... He will surely wish to present you to the new heir... That device I gave you, it will lead you to the nearest exit, forgive us, we did not know it would end this way." He bowed slightly to them.

"So, what you are saying is, you let us venture into certain death and now you refuse to..." Acha stepped around Elly stopping her short.

"I understand." She smiled placing her hand through the gate to offer him the stone, the old mans cool grey eyes met with hers for a moment before he smiled taking it from her. "Can you give us an idea of which tunnel to take first?" He nodded, it was the least he could do, especially since things had played out as they had.

"From where you emerge take the third tunnel to the left, follow it through to the end… However, the creatures from the court shall be regrouping; you must be quick with your escape." Behind him a small commotion started at the foot of the village, on the horizon they saw the mighty creature which had landed just moments ago. "Go… we shall stall him all we can… Please…" He glanced back to them with desperation the village chief already on the way down.

Again, they found themselves at the tunnel mouth looking at the crumbled remains of the court, the creatures that once dwelled within, now regrouping just as the old man had said, yet somehow, they looked different now, more like an army, an explosion of snarls and foreign words argued across the air finally one voice silenced them all.

"We should…" Elly began but was soon cut short,

"Shh." Acha lifted her hand silencing them. "Listen." She leaned forwards slightly, wondering why they weren't paying attention and why she had became the recipient of such strange looks.

"I can't hear anything but growling." Eiji whispered Acha glanced around back at them she raised a hand subtly to her ear, suddenly realising why it was she heard and understood them.

"They said, the chosen have taken the key… Time now is that of the hunt, they are close." She whispered pausing again to listen, aware she had missed some of the words as she translated for the benefit of the others. "They are separating into seven teams, one for each tunnel." Acha glanced the room but counted eight including the one they were in, the snarls of many filled the air again as they began to choose their leaders and comrades.

"You can understand them… how?" Eiji questioned.

"I… touched one of them… in my trial, it was Night at first… but as I left… it became one of those… it seems in this world, I take on some attributes of those I touch." She shifted her hair to briefly reveal her pointy ears before quickly covering them once more. "I can understand them… I have their sight and smell too… I don't know how long… wait." She stopped catching words. "They're going to get weapons… from the far chamber." They watched and waited as the demon dog like creatures began to move further away, then they made their move.

They had scarcely reached the entrance of the desired tunnel when the first group emerged weapons in hands, they stood staring at each other for what seemed like an eternity but was, in fact, only a matter of seconds, other creatures joined them, joining in the chant they had started, quickly they turned and ran.

"What are they saying?" Daniel questioned as he ran down the tunnel.

"You don't want to know." She whispered. "Just run." Just ahead of them they saw the tunnel split into two.

"Which way?" Daniel questioned Elly who had been looking at the device the old man gave then when first they left on the mission.

"I don't know this thing is useless, it doesn't work." They stopped measuring their choices, both waiting for a decision and trying to make one. It seemed that despite the creatures' appearance they either ran slower than them, or were waiting for the remainder of their pack before pursuing, as yet it seemed they had not followed. Zo quickly removed her bandage from her still bleeding shoulder looking at it quickly, her feet begging her to move to choose a tunnel, but somehow, she knew she must wait, but she couldn't think why. The chants began to grow louder until finally Elly made a choice.

"Left." She stated positively, with her instruction they began running, all but Eiji and Zo moved from that spot.

"What are you doing?" He snarled suspiciously as he watched her drop the blood covered bandage at the start of the passage they chosen.

"Throwing them off." She answered her hand now clutched over the open wound, she only hoped since the wound itself was bleeding only very lightly the scent of the wound be lost by that of the bandage.

"Shouldn't it be on the one we are *not* using then?" He demanded wondering what the she was playing at.

"Exactly... They'll expect it to mislead them... Not to be true in the way we head." Eiji nodded now understanding this choice, as they ran to catch up with the others who were only a little way ahead of them, even so the darkness of the tunnel made it impossible to make out their silhouettes.

Acha stopped as snarls erupted around the tunnel in echoes.

"They found the bandage?" She seemed unsure of what this meant until she saw Zo and Eiji, who had finally caught up. "They think it's a trick and are heading the other way." Zo looked at Eiji meaningfully. "But a small search team, about four maybe five are coming this way just to make sure. They could let them know we are here before we even have chance to run. Their footsteps were already echoing at the cavern entrance.

Eiji touched Acha on her shoulder lightly before pointing to a small hole, in the brickwork; it was about a foot high by four foot in width, it was impossible to see in the darkened area, a perfect hiding place. Despite not knowing what lay within Eiji pushed himself through, water quietly splashed around, it seemed this tunnel led to something, there was a slight undercurrent in the water towards the way they were heading. The others followed as he silently indicted there was plenty of room. The inside was quite unusual, it was not by any means a man made tunnel, it seemed the waters current had eaten away at the stone work forming a passage about four foot across that seemed to stretch into the distance. The overhead wall was made by the same watermarks, although this unnerved Eiji, as it meant that at some point the water had risen above any air gap now, he reassured himself that with the hole they had just entered it would surely be impossible for the water to raise that high again. His friends entered slowly. as he had just moments ago, moving themselves to grip the water made grooves on outside walls, Elly seemed to hesitate a moment just outside, when she entered the water, it seemed she gripped the walls as if her very life depended on it, just as Acha had, even through the darkness, Eiji could see the panic on both of their faces, could it be they couldn't swim? The footsteps approached, they all seemed to hold their breath as they heard the sniffing of the creatures.

Outside, being slightly lighter, they could just make out the giant boots of some of the dog creatures as they stopped outside. Acha cringed feeling the creatures within the water, swam around their legs, aware now of a slight colour to her vision as she looked under the waters surface, she could see creatures move beneath it, she gripped the wall harder as something the size of a large water snake brushed past, she knew in this world, there was no chance of it being something so harmless, her heart pounded in her chest so loud she feared the creatures would hear, if her grip was to slip from the wall there was no way she could suppress her panic, she would drown.

The boots stood outside for some time before exchanging snarling noises, the sound of their departed footsteps echoed around the small corridor fading into the distance once more. They looked at Acha as if to check it was safe.

"He was right." She whispered in response to the looks barely visible through the darkness, it was all she could do to keep her voice steady, although she couldn't see it, she knew her knuckles had turned white from gripping the wall so hard, all she could focus on was getting out of the watery grave. "Nothing lies ahead but the furnace, no one has passed this way, the door remains unopened... we must head back, quickly and report." Acha spoke slowly realising her vision was not the only thing now fading, her ability to understand was strained, she only hoped she had it right. They waited a while longer before moving from the water, making certain their movement would not be heard. The small pools left as they emerged soon evaporated in the heat of the stone tunnel, despite the heat, Eiji shivered rubbing his arms and legs.

"Is everyone ok?" He whispered still rubbing his legs, they all nodded as they began towards what the creatures referred to as the furnace, unsure if there was any way out, but knowing it was the only choice they had. Throughout the caves a tremor hit shaking the ground slightly, a few small rocks began to fall from overhead but the stone corridor was stable, they had no worries that it would fall, they knew this tremor meant one thing; the tunnel gate had been breached.

The temperature grew hotter by the second as they continued towards the end of the passage, any moisture remaining on them by this point had evaporated into the air, leaving them gasping for breath as the hot air began to burn their face and lungs.

They finally came to a halt outside an enormous metal door, it stretched from the floor to the very tip of the ceiling, it was clearly a door, yet with no handles there seemed to be no way to open it. Elly smiled triumphantly looking between the worried faces as they realised all their trekking had been for nothing, as they thought their journey was worthless as they stood before the metal barricade, her hand rested on a torch to the left hand side of the door, as she pulled it down a small wheel appeared behind it, the torch becoming the handle needed to drive the system, taking the hint Zo did the same on the other side, although she found the wheel almost impossible to turn as her shoulder complained against the pressure. Eiji took over from her, they managed to get the door open a crack big enough for them to pass, Elly turned her side a little further just to be sure. Hot stagnant air raced from the room taking their breath away as it passed them turning the once clear air into a sticky haze. Fighting against the sickly heat of the air they stepped through quickly, the doors closing behind them as the pulley unwound.

The inhabitants knew the enormous room as the furnace and once they had entered it, it was clear why, although not entirely practical in its design in their world, in this world's rules were different and it seemed this 'furnace' as they called it would provide heating to anywhere the metal pipes led. Just below the crumbled path they stood bubbled the deadly hot molten lava it stretched from wall to wall throughout the entire room ignoring all the principal they knew about it, the bubbles hissed and spat as air pockets forced their way up it's splashed uncomfortably close to where they stood. Throughout the room huge metal pipes ran across and were suspended from the tall ceiling, most of the pipes starting just above path level around the room. The path was crumbled, across the distance of the room, the other side of the path could just be made out against the hazy horizon, but they knew without looking there was no way to get to it.

"What do we do now? There's no way we can turn back the tunnels are filled with those demons... and they know the door has opened." Acha paced the floor noticing the lack of mechanism needed to open the door from this side, it seemed once in this room, it was assumed you would be passing over the collapsed walkway... or perhaps, the beings here did not fear such things, perhaps they could leap the distance in a single bound whatever the reason, they were trapped.

"This is a furnace... that means the heat has to be going somewhere." Daniel stated, knowing that this obvious information didn't help the situation much; he looked briefly to Elly who stood examining one of the two pipes running just off the side to the path.

"These two pipes lead out of here... fairly close to the surface." She stated after a moment's silence, the knowledge seemed to come from nowhere, but that seemed to be one of the many mysterious aspects to her personality, she seemed to know everything. "We can edge across the maintenance ledge... it's fairly steep to start but it levels out further up."

"Well what's our other option, go back out and get eaten alive?" Zo stated not really liking either option, she was working on the assumption that somehow there would be a way to open the giant doors from this side, although no such device had yet been located, but still, the only real choice was the one she mentioned, unless of course they wanted to sit here and wait for death. Choice one could have them plummeting to a quick yet fiery death, choice two had them facing an army of creatures, both were dangerous, but surely this choice would have to be the safer, she griped her shoulder tightly as the wound once more reminded her of its presence with a spasm of intense pain, if they were to fight, there was no way she could protect both Acha and Daniel, not with the sheer amount of numbers they would be facing, nor could she use magic to destroy the creatures quickly should she wish to live. She joined Acha at the edge of the path, she seemed to be watching something, a look of horror on her face, as she got closer she heard the strange popping sound matched with a scuttling noise coming from one of the pipes, every now and then something would drop from the pipe exploding as it hit the lava.

"What are they?" Acha questioned rubbing her arms as the hairs rose sending tiny prickling sensations all over her body,

"Baby spiders... just hatched from the look of them." Daniel moved to stand by Zo, placing his hand on her good shoulder momentarily before wiping his sweating brow, they had to get moving soon, it was just too hot.

"Babies? They're the size of my hand." Eiji joined the conversation, when they had first entered the room, he was hoping to relieve the heat with a light mist created from the water vapour in the air, however he was soon reminded that if he was to create such a thing, he would be doing nothing more than intensifying the heat as the water would act like magnifying glasses and begin to boil on their skin.

"True, but you can see part of the substance they hatch from." Daniel pointed as another one fell into the bubbling lava a strange silvery thread attached to them, shimmering in the heat as they fell.

"I would hate to meet their parents." He shivered at the thought of it. "All in favour of the left pipe." He raised his hand hurrying to Elly, she had begun to wonder when a decision would be made, she could wait far longer in this heat than them, but then, would she have to see them all to safety?

"Do you really need to ask?" Elly joined the conversation lacking the heat fatigue in her voice that the others unknowingly held. "I doubt we would fit up there with them as well... then again, you might move quicker." She paused, a smile crossing her face. "...Besides, the left one is more structurally sound." As they looked at the pipes the right one did seem to bend out slightly almost as if it could fall from the wall at any second, but the other sat flush against the wall, nor did it climb so high either, it stopped halfway up the wall and exited, it would be a difficult climb, but definitely better than the other option.

"I'll go first." Eiji gently moved Zo away from the side so he could get a clear view of what needed to be done.

"My thoughts exactly." Elly smiled, although Eiji offered out of chivalry, he would always be the first choice after all, his elemental nature should sense approaching obstacles and his powers meant he could use distance attacks before any danger got too close, at least that was her train of thought, although with his past efforts of such tasks, she hoped her theory would not be tested. She also feared his clumsy nature would land them in trouble, but it was him or Mari... after all, she had no real connection to him, she watched him gripped the wall tightly as he began to edge across the small ledge, he pressed himself tightly against the wall, afraid to look down as he felt the heat rising from the lava the heat burning his legs as he edged across. Finally as he reached the pipe, he hesitated for a moment not daring to look back at the others in fear of seeing what lay below him.

"There seems to be... holes... it should help with climbing." His voice trembled, as he ducked into the pipe, Elly sent Daniel across, he couldn't help wondering if this had been planned more than she was letting on, she seemed to know exactly which order she wished people to advance in. Elly motioned for Acha to go next, she looked at Zo almost fearfully, but knew there was no other choice the creatures were advancing, in greater numbers, ten minutes and they would be outside, there really was no time to waste and with the skills of their kind faded, it was getting more difficult to mark their location by sound. Acha glanced back, before entering the tunnel, Elly motioned for Zo to proceed.

"After you." Zo smiled politely, although her tone seemed lacking in such courtesy as she motioned for Elly to take the lead, although she had never given her reason to doubt her, something just didn't seem right about the concept of having her bring up the rear.

"I wouldn't run out on you know." She responded, waiting for her reply, it was one she had suspected it seemed she and Marise had more in common than she first realised, either that, or Marise's dormant persona was filtering through more than she anticipated.

"But still." She motioned again her voice holding a little more insistence than before, despite not liking the idea much, Elly, made her way across the narrow ledge, by now the footsteps of the guards echoed down the corridor for all to hear, it would only be moments before they entered the chamber. Elly stopped just outside the pipe turning back to look at her.

"Just like you… never trusting anyone to watch your back." Elly stated before entered the pipe, as she did, she felt the sickening heat rising from the lava pools below, the metal pipe was not as hot to touch as she or the others had expected, in fact, it was barely warm, whatever this strange metal was, it seemed not to be a good heat conductor, despite this the air that flowed through it took their breath away. Eiji scrabbled as the footholds began to fade as he reached the top of the pipe.

"It levels off here." He whispered, his voice echoed through the pipe. "I bet you could…" A large clang resonated through the pipe sending vibrations down. "No… It's big enough to crawl through." He stated rubbing his head waiting for the others to catch up.

"Is there any light up there?" Elly asked aware of the scraping from below them, the creatures were trying to operate the door, she thought maybe she should have replaced the torches, creatures with their mentality usually have very little brain, it would take them a while to realise where the release mechanism was, then again, if they had explored these tunnels before, her actions would have done little more than slow their escape. She felt the curve in the pipe approaching, it would be better if all of them had made it to the level platform before they entered the room, although it was clear there was only one real way they could escape, if they were familiar with dreamers they may forget their identities for a while and believe them to have woken, even so, there was a lot left to chance.

"None… It's pitch… We could get lost in here forever, going around in circles, lost." He called back anxiously, moments before the doors below opened, snarling and growling echoed from all around they froze quietly not daring to move, or even breathe, they paced the ground below them.

It seemed like an age had passed until they finally left, yet they stayed frozen longer still until the snarls were inaudible to Acha's ears, it was only then they continued.

"We need to get out of here as soon as we can." Acha whispered finally. "They were not too concerned about the chance that we had escaped, in fact, they found it quite amusing. They said something about a creature called Catspidres living within the tunnels of the furnace, they were certain we would not escape."

"Catspidres?" Elly questioned, her movements pausing for a moment. "Then I suggest we pick up the pace, I doubt very much any of you would want to encounter one of those."

"What are they?" Eiji called back, now more than ever feeling the pressure of leading them to safety.

"Well, they are creatures very much like baby spiders only much larger, like the ones you saw back in the furnace room, once they bite a victim, the victim is cursed to become one, they twist and deform the human body, splitting the flesh as new limbs and features form, very painful I must admit. The whole process takes about six hours to complete, by which point the victim has been driven completely insane by the pain, they then become a creature of this world, hunting and killing those who stumble into its territory, they are a deadly predator. When their race is low in numbers the body will die and from it will crawl hundreds of the little things, almost like the body itself was a giant egg sac and in many respects it is, you see this adult creature, not only devours the body of the human for energy, it devours its life-force too, each life force this creature has captured is stored within it, transformed into a small Catspidres waiting just under the skin to be hatched. Unfortunately for their race, only ten percent of any born actually survive then out of that only three percent will find a human suitable to become an egg sac to continue their race. A strange race really, humans are the only way they can continue to breed. You see the life-force Catspidres only live for three moon changes before they die, they only have this time to find a host for their next generation, these baby Catspidres if you will, never can evolve to become a creature capable of birth… it's a rather strange cycle really." Elly smiled aware that her tale had motivated a sharp increase in pace.

"The passage takes a sharp left." Eiji whispered nervously as the others caught up. "Only left." He added as if to answer silent questions, he had just mastered the art of feel crawling when he saw a dim spot of light on the horizon, his heart leapt; he was sure now more than ever they were not alone in this tunnel something was heading their way… He glanced up uncertainly seeing the vague outlines of the pipe and cautiously rose to his feet before moving into the light, above him was some form of circular vent, although he couldn't see where it led, he knew it was empty, no life stirred above them, at least, not as he could tell. "I need a foot up… I'm sure this will come loose…" Daniel knelt on the floor below him offering him a large enough rise to reach the vent, with Elly's hand he steadied himself finding he could just wrap his fingers around the holes, he looked at the grooves before turning the vent quarter a turn, to line the hole and the prong together, he gave it a hard push the vent lifted easily from its place, grabbing the edges and with the help of Daniel he pulled himself into the room above, bellows of steam flowed down the tunnel as he turned to help Daniel up, once up they took a hand each and pulled the others into the room.

"A sauna?" Daniel questioned as he glanced around the room there were tiled seats and a pile of rocks resting on top of the rid in the centre of the room, he glanced around tying to locate the exit.

"Ancient baths." Elly added walking to the wall, she touched a small circle, it gave a faint glow before opening, for a second Daniel just stood in disbelief as the cool air rushed around him, she had located the door so easily, yet it had been well concealed, invisible to the eye unless you knew where to look, after all, he himself had been looking all this time without luck.

"My Gods." Acha gasped as she rushed out into the cool air, her and the others clothes now covered with a strange green substance, no doubt from the pipes. "It's fit for a king." She looked out over the huge tiled area, everywhere was so clean and white, an enormous bath took centre stage, the water in it however not as appealing as the thought of the bath, it was covered in the same green foam they found over themselves.

"Emperor, Acha." Elly corrected softly as she glanced around. "These are ancient roman baths… well almost they're not quite accurate…" She added glancing around.

"My Gods, I did not believe any culture from that age still existed… I mean their world crumbled millennia ago; I have read only myths… How can a place like this exist it's…" Daniel was cut short on his awed rant when Seiken appeared.

"Disused, located just below the surface, contained within a secret tunnel." Seiken approached the slimy green foamed bath pulling some form of lever; the bath drained washing itself with water until all trace of previous grime had been removed. "And safe." He added, before looking into the giant bath, which now stood empty and clean of all alien products, he flicked the lever up once, as he did so, water came gushing down from the edges of the bath filling the air with strange and wonderful fragrances until it was full again. He flicked another switch and the darkened room filled with power, the lights lit and a generator somewhere buzzed. "Not a creature of this world knows of it but us. With nightfall closing in it would be the safest place for you, you can rest, shower, bathe, freshen up… you look like you need it. You will find this place will cater to your every need." He quickly showed them around pointing out the showers, the dry rooms, the saunas, this place had everything. When he had finished the tour he stopped by an amazing wooden carved door, he looked at Elly. "There are two or so hours until sunset." He looked to the others. "Kick back, relax and wash away the grime, it's not like you could achieve anything in that time anyway." He turned slowly and left through the door.

"I guess we could do with freshening up a little." Despite the new found heat of the room Zo shivered thinking back to all those dirty creatures clawing at her, she walked to Eiji who was sitting on one of the heated benched, she placed her hand on her shoulder, moving it quickly as she felt a shooting pain rise up her leg, Eiji turned quickly knowing she had felt it.

"Oh, it's nothing; I caught myself in the tunnel." He answered before Zo even had chance to ask, he couldn't tell her the truth, not after what Elly had said earlier, nor could he explain how he knew what she had felt, it seemed he was somehow getting use to the feel of her magic, possibly because she had used it so much around him, it seemed every person she touched was subjected to an assessment of heath and injuries, that was the curse and blessing of being a healer. A sympathetic touch, his master had called it, a touch alerting those with healing magic of all physical ails of the people they come in contact with.

"I can make you something for it." She whispered aware that he had been talking in low tones, no doubt trying to keep his injury from the others, a wish that she respected.

"When we get back, sure." He smiled nervously heading to the showers. They were amazing, there were about ten different cubicles spread around the edges of the room, he entered the first, the shower room itself was enormous, it was easily the size of his bedroom back when he had just been taken in by his master, it was full of different scents, shampoos and gels, placed expertly in alphabetical order of fragrance spread across two shelves. There was a full length mirror standing just next to a cupboard equal in height to that of the mirror, he opened it slowly as if not wanting to be caught. Within it hung a luxurious dressing gown, enormous towels and several assortments of swimming gear, no doubt for use in the bath. He slipped the lock on the door sitting on he small bench just outside of the shower itself wrapping a towel around himself he examined his leg carefully, before placing his clothes in a large almost bath sized area, as he did so it filled with water, he could see the grime lifting off moments later huge powerful sprays of water began beating at his clothes working any remaining dirt from them all the time filling the air with the scents Eiji liked the best. Picking the items he wanted from the shelf he got into the shower and pulling the wooden door separating the shower from the changing area.

After the shower he slipped the gown on before finding the first aid kit he used to bandage his leg, it was high enough to be covered by the gown without inviting questions, his stomach sank, a feeling of foreboding washing over him. When he emerged Elly took his wet clothes from him and placed them with a pile of others, he looked to see that they had all found the joys of the small shower cupboard and now sat together wearing the swimwear provided as they sat talking in the large bath, it wasn't until he saw them in it he realised its true size, it could easily sit about twenty people in without them having to sit within touching distance of anyone else, Elly however did not join them, she was pacing forward and back gathering up the wet clothes that they had spread on the heated tiles.

"Come on Elly, you could do with a rest." Zo invited her to join them.

"No thank you, a shower is quite enough... I will put the clothes in the dry room." Eiji stopped close to the bath, his head felt light and fuzzy from the heat, deciding a bath would not be such a good idea he made his way to the heated tiles, he needed time to think, besides, joining them would invite questions about his injury, they were already looking at the strange scrape marks on Zo's skin it would not be long before they asked. He lay down on one of the many heated platforms, feeling the heat warm and relax his tired muscles.

"Zo." Daniel's voice became serious the smile fading from his lips, he couldn't put it off any longer. "What happened?" He saw her shift uncomfortably for a second.

"What do you mean?" She asked rubbing water up her arms, she knew he would have to ask at some point, but him actually doing so made her feel all the more self-conscious, both him and Acha had noticed the strange scratches up her arms and legs as she entered the bath, and now they were staring, she was only glad the room had a first aid kit so she could redress her shoulder and restock her satchel with supplies, if they were alarmed by the fading scratches, surely they would be more so with the hole through her shoulder, it still bled, but as yet, had not penetrated the bandages, when they got back home, she knew she would need some help in stitching it, but this wound, these marks were the physical proof of the lesson she learnt, whenever she was unsure of her self, she knew she could take strength from the wound reminding herself of that line between her and Marise. *'I m not a killer.'* .She thought to herself touching her dressing.

"In that room... what happened?" He asked gently, knowing she knew what he was talking about and at the same time felt her desire for him to drop the subject, yet she knew now he had mentioned it there was little choice.

"It's... not important." She whispered turning away as she saw flashes of the rotting corpses grabbing at her, she rubbed more water up her arms, although she had said it wasn't important, it was what happened in there was more important than she could explain, her experience had given her a new strength, strength to fight on.

"Ok... you'll tell me when you're ready." He touched her arm gently. "Since we have some time to kill now, you could always heal them." He smiled

"I can't." She whispered pathetically.

"Why? Surely that hole in your shoulder isn't doing you any favours."

"No Daniel, I mean I can't." She raised her voice slightly. "It's something about this place, I can heal others, but not myself... when I get home maybe I can do something about the scratches... but this." She motioned to her shoulder. "They have already told me there is nothing they can do." *'And even if there was, I need it as a reminder.'* She thought to herself. She knew why she could not heal it hers was the rune of sacrifice, she could heal those of this world with the cost of taking their injury for her own, an injury she knew she would not be able to heal, or there would be no point in this world setting such limitations, just as she knew she could not heal her own wounds nor would she heal those she took from another, but the wound, although painful was good, with it came an understanding of herself and in years to come, she could look upon the scar and remind herself the truth. Daniel went to speak but was cut sort by Elly.

"Come on you three, get dressed." They looked up to find Elly and Eiji already clothes in their now clean clothes. "If Seiken was right, two hours is nearly up." Zo and Acha sighed, the bath had been pleasant, but as always Elly was right, they took their now dry clothes from her arms and disappeared into the shower cubicles.

Zo smiled looking at her top, there was a fine almost invisible thread sewing up the hole the sword had made in her sleeve, so fine, it was difficult to see against the normal weave of the material unless you knew exactly where to look, Elly had always repaired her clothes with such expertise. Once dressed, they joined Eiji to lie on some of the hot tiles finding it the most inviting place to settle for the night.

"Well Seiken did say it was safe." Zo smiled comfortably wondering why every safe place couldn't be this relaxing. With that, they each in turn took a berry from Elly and closed their eyes.

***

Zo awoke in the predawn light aware of being alone, it took her a few moments to realise why, she rose to her feet to head back towards where the others had made came, even now the gentle scents of the baths' hung lightly in her hair, she looked at her arms, the scent was not the only thing to follow her back. As Seiken had warned at journeys start, her injuries had too, her shoulder throbbed with pain, she decided now was as good a time as any to repair some of the damage. She went to grab her satchel only to realise it had been left with Daniel, she closed her eyes and concentrated, the cuts and scrapes up her arms began to fade, but the shoulder wound remained as prominent as ever, for this the spirits could do little than help remove but a small amount of the pain temporarily, but for this momentary relief she was grateful.

"Zo there you are!" Acha rushed to her side as she appeared at their camp. "Have you seen Eiji?" Zo glanced around the camp quickly as if to confirm he wasn't there.

"No... why?" She questioned knowing the reason, obviously he was missing.

"Well… we don't think… he woke, we were hoping he'd gone to find you, but Elly was the first back and she said she never saw him."

"What?" Zo questioned glancing around again a sick feeling rising in her stomach, she couldn't feel his presence.

"Have you noticed something else?" Daniel questioned looking towards the sun that had only moments ago began to rise, his stomach sank and churned as he brought himself to say the next words. "It's dawn"

"And…" Zo questioned not quite following where he was going with this, Daniel opened a small note book.

"Well, every time we have crossed back it has taken at least two hours for completion of crossing back, it has always been two hours after sunrise when we woke, meaning we should never see dawn… Zo, Seiken lied it wasn't two hours to sunset, it must have been at least four." Zo looked again at the rising sun, the amber light spilled over the horizon as if the sky itself was on fire.

"But why?" She questioned suddenly becoming aware of the pain in her shoulder again. "Why would he lie to us about something like that? He's never led us wrong before, has he?" She questioned unsure now of the truth herself, moments ago she trusted Seiken with her life, now she was not sure he was worthy of that trust.

Chapter thirteen

"Ah Eiji I see you have yet to wake." Seiken appeared at the carved wooden door through which he had previously made his exit. "The Snarson's bite will do that, it's highly toxic."

"You knew about..." Eiji began, looking down to his wound as he spoke a wave of relief passing through him; Seiken had called the creature a Snarson not a Catspidre.

"The fish? Of course, this is my world, you are simply visiting." He glanced around the empty baths. "The others have, woken?" He questioned glancing around again and to the door as if to confirm they were the only people around, this single action unnerved Eiji a little, why hadn't Seiken said something before? If he had maybe Zo could have made some antidote to the creature's poison, Eiji sighed, it was his own fault, he should have just told them what had happened, but after what Elly had said in the pipes how could he? After all, following that tale, he himself had begun to believe he would transform into some horrific creature, if he were to have told the others, panic would have ensued.

"Yes... about ten minutes ago they completely vanished, is it dark out? Am I safe?" He sighed, it had been just over an hour since they settled for sleep, he had watched his comrades' bodies as they had faded into nothing, yet as tired as he grew he could not join them. He wondered how he was going to keep himself entertained until they returned, hoping the poison was slow spreading enough, to give him chance to explain to Zo, on her return, what had happened, as long as he didn't move much, the poison's path would be slower. Eiji felt his head swim, he had been growing more tired as the time passed, he had thought this an effect of the berry, but only now did he realised why, it was the toxin from the bite.

"Like I said, no creature of this world knows of this place... of course Night's minions not being not of this world would, but after dusk you are safe from them." Seiken smiled as Eiji moved to sit once more on the heated tiles.

"Then I am lucky it is after dusk... The rules said they can't touch us after... Can they?" A cold shiver ran down Eiji's spine, he suddenly got the strangest feeling he wasn't alone, he glanced around nothing but shadows met his gaze, although he could have sworn moments ago it had been much lighter than it was now.

"No... Funny thing about that though." Seiken walked to the wooden door pulling it open, he stepped back as a mass of shadows spilled through the doors surrounding the room. "It's still an hour to sunset."

"But you said..." Eiji gasped as the shadows descended on him fighting against them was exhausting as he tried to avoid their icy fingers. Although doing so only quickened the poison's path through his body, but he would fight until he had to surrender, to it or them.

"I say a lot of things, like the mine fields are the safest way, I didn't think you all would make it that was some luck..." Seiken smiled watching as he fought.

"You lied!" Eiji spat trying to launch himself towards Seiken as the creatures held him back. "You knew about the bite, you knew I couldn't wake! You planned this all along, why?" Eiji gave up struggling it made his head spin.

"I was made a proposition I could not refuse." He motioned for the creatures to follow. "As you may have discovered, it's no use fighting, the poison is already effecting your nervous system, in about five minutes, I wont have to worry about you trying to escape, you'll be as good as paralysed until the antidote is administered… Or you die" Eiji felt himself forced to surrender as he was dragged into the shadows, in the last few moments the poison had become so potent he could barely move his feet, it was almost as if his acknowledging it, combined with his struggle had quickened the effects of its attack. Darkness surrounded his vision, as his eyes closed he heard Seiken's voice echo through the shadows. "What do you know? Still thirty minutes to sunset." He could hear the triumph in his voice as the world around him began to sway, he once more found himself thinking that which he thought so often.

'Why me?'

***

"You have returned." Night rose from his seat, placing down the text he had been reading, as he rose to greet his company. "And I see you brought the boy." Eiji was barely conscious, through the darkness he tried to move his limbs, he put so much effort into the simplest movement, his mind willing his body to respond, yet through the darkness and the numbness, he was no longer sure he even had a body to move, he felt like just a mind, a consciousness alone, a consciousness that had just awoke from a thrilling dream to return to the nothingness of the large empty void, he tried to call out for help, finding he had no voice, for a moment, he felt as though he was descending through the void but as soon as it started it had stopped once more, through the darkness he heard something, very faint, very muffled, but it seemed something shared this space with him.

"As you said my Liege"

"Good, now be sure they hear of the antidote." Seiken stopped as if to question the words he had heard.

"As you wish, what should I do with the boy?" He glanced down at Eiji who seemed now to be almost under the full effects of the poison, soon he would slip into a lapse of consciousness, a sleep that existed in this realm as well as their own, but this was unlike an ordinary sleep, it did not mean you would wake in another world, but stay in the one you reside in. But outside of Knights-errent, it was called a coma.

"Proceed as planned, take him to the new heir and have him do as he see fit, I believe there is a bounty on their head in that area, I am sure there is much they wish to extract, and if they should happen on some knowledge that proves useful… I'm sure you understand." Night smiled to himself, so far all had proceeded as planned, but the next steps were the most important ones, they were the ones that would have the most effect on this situation.

"Yes my Liege, is it safe to leave him there while no one sleeps?" He questioned unsurely wondering if there was some fluke chance he may escape or be placed in life threatening danger.

"Of course, my minions will take good care of him until that area's dreamers awake, do not fear, they shall fill them in on the details when they arrive, of course, you could always stay if you wish." With those final words Seiken vanished taking Eiji into the shadows with him.

***

"We have to go back!" Acha pleaded pacing back and forth across the clearing, where the charred remains of the fire blew across the surroundings in the gentle breeze. "He could be in danger." She stopped pacing briefly to look at the others asking for their support of her decision, wondering why it was taking so long for them to make such an obvious choice, something had happened between them sleeping in Knight-errent and waking here, something that had prevented Eiji from returning, something they needed to go back and face before it was too late.

"But… Seiken said it was safe…" Zo lowered her head slightly wondering if she could trust the validity of his words.

"Seiken also said the sun was set but that does not make it so." Acha snapped before resuming her pacing.

"He wouldn't betray us." It seemed to be more of a question than a statement, she looked to the others hoping they would agree, yet each one had the same sceptical look upon their faces. Even she herself had to admit, something had changed, the last time they had met Seiken hadn't seemed like himself he seemed colder, less like the person she thought she remembered.

"Zo… What do you really know about this guy?" Daniel questioned softly carefully choosing his words, it was clear Zo had some kind of link to this person for whatever reason, she believed him to be very important in her life, each time she saw him, Daniel received the same feeling of familiarity, feelings so strong that even he had began to believe that he had played some important role in her past, and would play it again in the future, but just like Zo, he could not place what this connection was or where it had originated from.

"I know he saved us from that dragon, from Aburamushi and he gave us a head start with the map."

"Did he really?" Elly questioned joining the conversation. "He ran with us from the dragon, tapped into your magic to fend it off with his own, he merely warned you of Aburamushi's intention, and although he did give us a map, it proved no use until we found the first location where one waited for us anyway." She tapped on her finger with each point that she had made as if to enforce them.

"How did you know about the map?" Zo questioned realising Elly had not been in the village when the others found it, she had been with her, after all, she herself had only just found out about it as she and Daniel both pulled a map out ready for inspection, Elly couldn't have known about it, she had been with her.

"I was there." She paused sighing.

"No you weren't you were with me when the others found it."

"Then someone must have told me or I saw it, what difference does it make? We used it to navigate to the minefields anyway, what is important now is the location of our…" She paused a moment rethinking her sentence. "Eiji"

"We should head back." Acha repeated her previous suggestion stopping to stand with the others, why weren't they listening to her; he could be in serious danger?

"We can't." Elly stated aware that that information would not be sufficient to keep any of them happy. "It's nightfall there it's too dangerous."

"Who's there?" Zo turned to face the undergrowth Daniel moved swiftly to step besides her, placing his hand on her arm, which had already seized the hilt of her sword.

Questions crossed his wrinkled brow as Daniel saw himself emerge from the bushes in front of him, it was like looking into a mirror, the figure had the same ear length brown hair, the same dark eyes, Daniel found himself moving slightly to see if the reflection would do the same, it did not.

"Oh it's you." Zo sighed releasing her sword to find herself wondering at which point she had grabbed it.

"Forgive the intrusion." Daniel moved again feeling slightly unnerved as his mirror image spoke yet at the same time wondering if he truly sounded like that. "Your friend is in danger, please miss forgive my intrusion." Zo glanced at him; he seemed more timid than when they first met.

"Eiji? You know where he is?" Acha stepped forward catching only the end of the sentence, interested to hear what this strange living reflection had to say about the danger their friend found himself in.

"Yes, he was detained, the one you know as Seiken planned it to be so." Daniel shot a meaningful glance at Zo who in an attempt to ignore it by focused her vision on the new arrival, although this did little to block his thoughts which came through as clear as day.

"Detained how?" Elly questioned trying to keep her tone simply enquiring although failing as hints concern filtered through, she had to this point been silent, watching the others reactions, watching the creature, analysing it, it was clear it was some form of shape shifter, although very limited in what forms it could actually take, the faint smell of blood around it made her believe it had followed them, or had been sent from the court.

"Before you reached the furnace, you took shelter from some of my race, although, unlike me now, they show their true appearance, I use magic to seem less disturbing to your view." Daniel looked at the creature and smiled in amusement wondering how disturbed that creature would feel should *it* come face to face with *its* living reflection. "Anyway, the Snarson's, they are the creatures in the water, be sure to tell you that.... They are deadly to dreamers... People in your world bit by them, their minds seem to be trapped in our reality unable to return... a coma, that's what you call it yes? They are left to wander our world until they stumble on the antidote, or the ones they love give up... It's different for you, since you completely cross over not just your mind you lose but your body too, since it is his physical form that took the bite, he would not wander our world, like the body would in your world, he would lose most of his consciousness, like those in this world, but remain mostly aware of what transpired. It's just like any poison, after so long, the person dies, it can be hours, even days, but eventually..." He paused looking at them ensuring they understood the words he had spoken.

"Are you saying he was bit?" Acha screeched. "Why didn't he say anything?"

"Yes, although I am afraid I cannot answer your second question, I do not know your friend as you do, I must leave now before your gateway seals."

"Wait!" Zo commanded the creature stopped in mid turn. "You mentioned an antidote, what does it look like? Where do we find it?" The creature turned back slightly and nodded.

"Of course, the Narca berry originates from pirates isle, the next land from there your friend will wait in the presence of the new heir, we are even now? Yes?" He questioned Zo smiled at him.

"Yes, thank you." The Daniel creature then vanished as he turned away from them.

"There's a town just through the rings of fire, we should rest, we have had little time to do so over the last few days." Elly did not wait for them to agree she simply set out, Daniel was about to protest remembering what the old man had said about the area being uninhabited, but thought better of it, after all, Elly was always right. Acha heard her stomach rumble she placed her hand to it gently.

"Well, I am kind of hungry." She admitted,

"And we will get a chance to think about how we locate Eiji." Zo added following Elly's lead.

***

"You Elementalists are more resilient than I thought." A strange voice oozed through Eiji's darkened mind, small bubbles of light rose momentarily lighting the darkness before they popped, through these brief moments he tried to make out what lay past the veil of darkness he had grown accustomed to. "I guess your key skill must lie within water, no mater, although you still hold your consciousness, you are of no threat, your magical base will do little than dilute the effect." The voice seemed to grow more distant as if the figure were leaving, a few moments later a darkness surrounded him, he found himself able to make out his surroundings, he was lying on a cold dirty floor in a dank musty smelling prison of some description, slowly he moved slightly, he knew he was not alone, all the time he had the feeling someone had been trying to reach him, to take him from the darkness, and now he lay within the strange cell, he felt the presence of that person.

He could see dim colours of all shades pulsing across the dimly lit cell, he moved again into a kneel feeling his vision swim and reality bend around him. A bright light appeared all around, the hum of many voices interrupted his thoughts and visions of the darkened room until his vision found reality again, it seemed the bite also caused hallucinations, how else could he explain the drastic change between the rooms? He felt the floor give beneath him, the pockets of reality distorting as his arms gave, he felt as if he would fall forever into the darkened void that opened before him.

He suddenly began to hear strange beeping noises, the darkness once more faded into the bright room; it was a strange noise, unlike anything he had ever heard before, a noise so quiet it was almost drowned out by a conversation between two people when a voice pulled him back.

"Try not to move." It whispered weakly, it seemed even the whispered took so much effort from its source, as the shadow spoke the light pulsing from its source grew brighter.

"Who are you? Why are you helping me?" Eiji felt himself whispered he vaguely remembered the same voice pulling him back from the light a few times since his arrival, it comforted him calling him back to reality, there came no reply, just laboured breathing from the corner of the tiny six by twelve cell. Eiji fought to kneel, he felt almost as if his body was defying him; an age seemed to pass as he once more fought slowly to his knees. Occasionally the light and chatter would beckon him, but he focused, he had to fight the illusion, finally, he was on his knees again finding support against the damp, mossy, brick wall, he turned slowly to find the source of the glowing light, a boy sat breathing heavily, as if every breath an effort, as the light flared up Eiji could make out the red shimmer of his long hair when the light next pulsed, Eiji suddenly realised who it was that he shared his prison with. "You!" He snarled trying to find the strength to strike out at the figure, he raised his hand though fell against the wall his strength void of all the angry energy he felt. "Traitor!" He hissed leaning against the wall, to support his kneeling body, Seiken opened his eyes, the light shone brighter.

"I am… many things…" He barely whispered, had there been any form of noise, even a light breeze, it would have drowned out his words completely. "But a traitor I am not." Eiji felt a twinge of sympathy, but only for moment, it was clearly a painful effort for him to talk, he could feel the bonds that bound him pulling at his life-force, but then again, he deserved it, he had only himself to blame for the situation he now found himself in, he had betrayed them.

"You led them right to me!…" Eiji tried to raise his voice but found an exhausted whisper was all he could manage. "We trusted you… it seems… your arrangement made you… no better off than… me." Eiji gasped finishing his sentence with difficulty, his body exploded in pain, as it did so he could hear the chatter from the other place in the back of his mind.

"I… do not know what you talk of, I am not for sale." He answered after a short period had passed, long enough for Eiji to catch his breath.

"You sold yourself to Night! I hope he paid well, you betrayed me, and you betrayed Zo." Eiji spat feeling a little of his strength return.

"What?" Seiken's voice rang through the prison as it did so the light from the chains that bound him exploded, Eiji saw the shock and questions in his face, seconds later the light died Seiken cried in pain moments before he slumped against the wall. The lights from his bonds exploded again as Eiji felt him grab his arm, his grip was weak, his hands shaking as he held on to him his mouth moved as he tried to forced the words, finally they came. "I… could… never… betray my… Umemi."

"But I saw you." Eiji whispered not as certain as he had been moments before, Seiken gasped his hand falling from Eiji's arm those were the last words Seiken heard for a while, his eyes closed and his breathing became shallow.

Eiji sat listening to him breathing, his conversation with Seiken had exhausted him, but clearly Seiken more so, he comforted himself the best way he could, there were answers he needed, answers he could only get from Seiken, but he was certain, there was more going on than met the eye. Seiken had been genuinely shocked, a shock not possible for even a performer to display, but a stomach churning, heartfelt shock, it made even Eiji question the validity of what he had seen, but that was the problem, he *had* seen him, Seiken had come for him, like death to the aged.

Eiji's lungs began to hurt each breath seemed to burn with intense pain Seiken had only been unconscious for five minutes and already the hallucinations had taken him as many times, sometimes he just heard the low murmur of voices, others he would see a blinding light and hazy things shuffling around him. He sat alone forcing himself back to reality, back to Seiken, thoughts racing through his minds, questions and fears rising to the surface, he knew, whatever his captors had planned, he was in no state to fight them off. He rested himself against the cold wall, listening for the change in Seiken's breathing that would mean he was awake, when that change came, he would have some explaining to do.

***

"Is it just me, or does this place give you the creeps?" Daniel walked besides Zo down the path leading into the village, children clearly around, yet they didn't play, nor did they make a sound.

"What do you mean?" Whispered Acha, slowing her pace to join the hushed conversation.

"A town like this should be filled with noise, the sound of life, even the children are quiet, my home town is half this size and twice as loud with the noise of life... it's like walking in a ghost town." Daniel found himself also whispered adhering to the town's atmosphere.

The town itself was amazing to look at. It stood proudly just outside the ring of volcanoes, a cliff face rose behind it, past the cliff face another rise was visible but beyond the first could not be seen. The area itself seemed to display an aura of power, although its source could not be located. The city itself had a ground floor Inn possibly holding about seven separate rooms, well a town like this away from the eyes of travellers would never need to worry about crowding, even should people know of it, the tunnels that they ventured through to arrive here were treacherous, a person could be trapped in there for the rest of their lives never again to see the light of day.

The bar of this town doubled as a café, a door separating the two dividing it in half, it had a few nice wooden tables outside, and huge front windows, the smell of exotic foods filled the air making all that pass by realise the extent of their hunger.

Several agricultural barns and storage sheds were scattered throughout the town, it seemed almost everyone here would be lending hand to cultivate the miles of fields around; it seemed they grew all their own food, making journeys past the rings of fire unnecessary. From the amount of houses they estimated about sixty people lived in this small community, yet it was so quiet.

"Elly..." Daniel turned to ask her a question only to find she had vanished from view, he glanced around the town unable to locate her anywhere, he wondered at what point she had vanished, then again, his attention had been elsewhere since their arrival, namely taking in the strange wonders of this hidden village, no doubt known to none but those who ventured from it, it was strange how the ground bore vegetation, yet seemed sand like in appearance.

"She was here a moment ago." Acha also glanced around the only person who was not taking in the town was Zo, who stood almost paralysed as she gazed forwards...

"You're travellers aren't you? We don't get many in these parts on account of the labyrinth under the rings of fire, how did you..." The voice of a young man behind Zo started her, she turned to look at him as he went on about the Labyrinth, she took in his appearance, a feeling of familiarity washing over her, his hair was short, scruffy hair swept back with small debris from his field labour clinging in it, his hands covered in dirt from the fields his skin tone considerably darker than her own, yet there was a look in his eyes, a recognition, she wondered for a moment how it could be she would be recognised in a hidden village, it was then he confirmed her fears. "Ah Miss Shi, that explains it, welcome back, I see you have brought some companions, I saw Lady Elly a moment go, she was heading to the Inn to book your normal room." He looked away from her to glance her companions over critically, as if making a mental note of everything about their person. "As Miss Shi's guests I doubt I need to warn you, but still… as new comers to this town, it is my duty to inform you. This town is under the control of the twilight empire, no form of rough housing or disrespectable behaviour is tolerated to either people or property. Should at any time, you disrespect our laws, you shall find yourself facing the judgement of the high court." He glanced across towards the rise on the horizon giving the impression beyond it was where the court would be found; he looked back to Zo and smiled. "Please enjoy your peaceful stay and sample our fine fruits." He smiled passing both Daniel and Acha a strange peach coloured, apple like fruit. He turned steadily and walked away back towards the fields. Zo felt her stomach sink repeating to herself over and over the words that brought her comfort, she knew Daniel must be sick of hearing them, if, it was part of her mind he could reach, but in that small truth, she found some strength, she was panicking slightly, after all, they knew her here, she waited for Acha's reaction wondering what her thoughts on what had just transpired were, she hadn't wanted her to find out this way, but she wasn't ready to tell her not yet, it was too late now, it seemed the farmer had introduced her to Acha without even realising.

"I've never had a greeting like that before." Acha smiled looking at the strange apple like fruit she held in her hand, she was just about to take a bite when Elly appeared taking it from her and placing it in quickly within her own pocket. Acha stared in disbelief for moment before wrapping her arm around Zo's shoulder. "So… it seems you've been here before missy." Acha smiled wondering how it was they knew Elly by name but referred to her as something so unusual, then again, she did not pretend to understand the customs of others, maybe it was an endearing term, like sweetheart or darling, either way, it seemed her friend had been here at least a few times, especially to have acquired 'a regular room' at the Inn.

"Huh?" A gentle smile crossed Zo's face, lifting some of the worries from her brow, because of the accent here Acha hadn't really caught what he had said, for this she was grateful, it was one less thing to worry about, she would tell her, but at a point when the time was right, at the moment everything just seemed so wrong, if she were to tell Acha this now, her very reaction might foil their attempts at rescuing Eiji, although she could not guarantee how she would react, after all, she had been so wrong about Daniel, yet still, she could not chance her reaction being the one she expected. "Oh… yes, I am well travelled… I think." She smiled again. Daniel gave a sigh of relief before he looked away from her. He knew that smile, it was heartbreaking, a smile she used to cover her worries and fears, a smile she used to cover her pain so others were clueless to it, he was not as easy fooled, as those who accepted it unquestioningly, he saw the torment that lay just under the surface, he couldn't help wondering why no one else did, he also heard her repeating the same phrase over and over since they arrived here, as if she needed to remind herself time and time again, she was not, who the people here thought.

"I have booked the lodgings for tonight; shall we go to the cafe? I have saved the table." Without waiting for their answer she hurried off towards in its direction, they followed her; she was already sat at the table making herself comfortable when they finally caught up.

Daniel grabbed a menu from the table and began to study it, amazed that he had never even heard of most of what they served.

"I took the liberty." Elly plucked the menu from Daniel's hand placing it to one side, ignoring his looks of annoyance as she did so; she placed it back on the small wooden table just as the waitress approached.

"I can't wait to try the foreign cuisine I've never been to…" His words were cut short by the incredibly fast service, what he didn't know, was that Elly had ordered before she left to book the room, meaning it had simply been nicely timed.

"I thought you would be missing mum's home cooking, all the products are specially imported… overseas." She added smiling as Daniel looked to his food. "I thought it best to leave the culture to a point when there is not a rescue mission to plan, we don't want you to get ill." Elly smiled amusement crossing her face as Daniel looked from her to the plate a number of times, before sighing, he looked at the apple in his hand, well at least he had something to try, he had barely finished the thought when Elly's cool fingers had touched his hand removing the apple from his grasp, he stared at her in disbelief.

"I suppose you're right." He sighed unable to hide the disappointment in his voice as he looked back down at the plate of steamed vegetables and meat, he couldn't help thinking what was served on the other tables looked, and smelled, more inviting. The waitress hurried back placing the same meal before Acha; she brushed her blond hair from her face with the back of her hand, smiling as she poured some water into the empty glasses on the table. Elly was presented with some meat mixed with vegetables in a small bowl, the same as that had moments before been placed before Zo.

"Lobby, just like mum use to make, isn't that right miss?" Her ruby red lips forming a gentle smile as she filled Zo's glass with water. "Would you care to sample some of our local wine, on the house of course, for such special guests?" She looked at Daniel and winked, he moved to take the menu once more.

"That would be…" Again Daniel found himself cut off by Elly's interruption.

"No thank you, it does not agree with our metabolism, besides you know we don't accept this kind of compliment, we would not want to be portrayed as thugs, but could bring us some of your imported Machica?" Daniel looked to her in surprise at her choice of words, 'we would not want to be portrayed as thugs'.

"Yes Miss Elly, although I must warn you the price has risen considerably since your last visit, import is becoming increasingly more difficult to get."

"Shipping trouble is it?" Elly questioned, she remembered how hard it had been to negotiate the first shipping contract for this place, normal export was out of the question, they had to find someone who would keep their town a secret, someone whose silence could be easily brought.

"No miss, it has just become more difficult to get since the pirates upped their rates, of course we always keep some just in case you should stop by, although our wine is selling well, they have gotten greedy demanding more of the shares, so there isn't much..."

"Sara kitchen!" A voice commanded, she gave a small bow before hurrying away, as she left she passed the bottle of selected to wine to another waitress who brought it to their table, Elly examined the bottle curiously as she poured the glass, she preferred it when wines had labels, but in this town it was uncommon.

"They aren't aloud external produce? Not even to try it?" Acha questioned in disbelief.

"You have to understand, this town has a very delicate ecosystem, the food here is funded by the exports, they eat what they sow, their local wine sells for a small fortune outside, it's brewed near the centre of one of the volcanoes. The food they grow is for them, the fruit is mainly for the wine. The people here, because of the lack of rain and fertile soil, have a completely different genetic makeup, one that lets them survive in these conditions, some of our food, would be like poison to them." She spoke with a lowered voice so no one outside their table could overhear. She glanced around, the café had become quite empty, out of the ten or so tables inside, only the furthest four still had people sat at them. The others seemed to have left through the back door which led to the bar.

"Still if the wine is expensive, the funds should be pumped back into the town... this town does not look wealthy." Daniel added glancing around, from the outside it had looked neat and presentable, but inside you could make out small cracks in the ceiling, splits in the wooden walls and doors, although all in all it was a charming little café.

"Well I'm sure you know the saying, the rich get richer? All profits are pumped into the court and into scientific research, its all funding for the prison court."

"Prison court?" Acha questioned unsure if she had heard correctly, she pushed her plate to one side having eaten more than her fill; she had to admit the food had been cooked to perfection, just the way she liked it, glancing around it seemed everyone else was just as satisfied.

"Yes, it's a court that doubles as a prison, once caught by the twilight soldiers... although, most people think them a myth, criminals are tried and sentenced there." She rolled her eyes thinking, prison court, how more of a concise description could she have given. "And hospital, and come to think of it I think the research labs are there too, everything owned by the twilight empires." She added Acha stood stretching slightly as she listened.

"I think I shall go for a walk while you finish up here." She smiled stretching again, she glanced around once more before heading to the door, Daniel rushed after her, leaving Elly to examine the open wine that Zo had just poured.

"Are you alright?" He touched her arm gently as she reached the door.

"Uh-huh." She nodded. "It's been a long time since I've seen a working harvest; it kind of reminds me of home."

"Do you want some company?" Daniel questioned already knowing what her answer would be, her hand already resting on the wooden door.

"No that's alright, but thanks." She smiled, Daniel nodded returned to the table where Zo was nursing a glass of wine, she had been deciding whether or not drinking would be a good idea, but met by Elly's stare she placed it back on the table, it didn't smell like what they ordered anyway, she wasn't sure how she knew that exactly, but something about it just didn't seem right. It had been on table second less than a second when the table jerked sending it and the bottle crashing to the floor.

***

"So what you're saying is even though you have no water the food you grow is never treated?" Acha leaned forward on her knees as she sat on a slight bank watching as farmer worked the area near her, he had proven to be good conversation, they did everything here, a lot like they did when she was a girl.

"That's right young miss, we just plant them, after that they take care of themselves." He mopped his brow with the back of his hand before continuing with his work,

"Forgive the questions, but your soil is like sand, and from the climate it's clear you don't get much rainfall"

"True young Miss, but beneath that soil life thrives." A scream erupted from the café although it wasn't very loud with the town being as quiet as it was it was clearly audible throughout. "Oh dear." The farmer sighed and lowered his head to concentrate on work.

Without a thought Acha jumped to her feet running towards the café, she stopped around the back near the kitchen exit when she hear voices.

"I'm sorry it was an accident." Acha recognised the girl's voice instantly it was the one who had served them moments ago; her voice trembled as it filled with fear. Acha paused by the corner of the café, her back pressed to the wall as she listened, the streets had emptied quickly, only she now stood in the open, even the farmers seemed to have vanished from their crop.

"Don't you realise who she is, what were you thinking?" The voice that had summoned her to the kitchen before scolded her quietly. "You could have done some serious harm if they hadn't realised…"

"I know, I'm sorry, I didn't know it was the wrong bottle, truly I didn't." She cried. Acha heard the sound of footsteps pacing back and forth as if in rushed contemplation, a short silence passed until the chief spoke once more.

"Run, with any luck you can make it before they arrive, don't ask me how, but they will know and will be on the way, go I shall stall them." The girl nodded turning the corner at such speed she could not stop before colliding with Acha, she fell from her feet trembling, her eyes filled with fear.

"Are you in some kind of trouble?" Acha helped her to her feet, even though she wore gloves she could feel the dormant life sleeping within her.

"Please I meant no harm; please don't let them take me." She begged her brown eyes welling with tears as she glanced around fearfully.

"Who?" Acha questioned unsure who this girl was so terrified of, so desperate to escape from.

"The twilight empire." She whispered almost afraid to speak their name. "I meant no harm to your friends, honest I didn't."

"Quickly, I know where you can hide." Acha smile reassuringly placing her coat over the girls trembling body leading her towards the Inn, she left her by the window to one of the rooms, knowing she could always get her attention whichever room they would be in.

The Inn itself was quite large considering the lack of guests to this area, it was a lot like all the other buildings, built mainly of wood, except this one building, as Acha had noted previously, had windows that had somehow been made to be sliding, although there wasn't a full seal around the edge of the window, as they had no rain, there was no cause to be concerned about leaks filtering through. Taking a breath she entered the foyer, it was a small area with a semi circular wooden built counter, there was only one route she could take to get to any of the four bedrooms, the other seemed to lead to a sitting room and a dining room. She approached the desk aware that time was short, the elderly lady sat at the desk without looking at her.

"Elaineor has booked our room I believe." As she spoke the lady placed a key on the desk, again without looking up, Acha slid it off trying to walk casually to the room, quickly, but not so quick it would cause suspicion, as she entered the room, before anything, she switched the shower on to drown out any talking or noise they may cause. It was times like this she was glad that, unlike normal houses, Inns had automatic pumping showers, if it hadn't pumping the water pressure up ready for the shower would have taken much more time than they had. She slid the window open signalling for Sara before helping her through into the room.

"They're here." She whispered just before a knock came on the door, Acha glanced around the room quickly, her eyes falling on the bed, she tiptoed around lifting the sheets, material had been sewn over the wooden frame, the beds themselves were hollow, she signalled for Sara to help her slide the mattress off, once off, she tilted the bed making a slit with Eiji's knife in the bottom of it. Another knock came at the door making both her and Sara jump.

"Just a minute." She called motioning for Sara to move under she lowered the bed frame over her sliding the mattress back in place, quickly she removed her clothes standing in the shower, taking the showerhead off hosing herself down and soaking her hair, quickly as she grabbed the towel, she heard another knock, she was just at the door when the it came again, she opened the door a crack to peer through, two burley men stood at her door, she opened it further feeling the heat rise to her face as the two men looked her up and down before they pushed the door open inviting themselves in.

"Is there something I can help you with?" Acha tried her best annoyed voice, after all they *had* just dragged her from the shower, they had to believe that anyway and it wasn't exactly comfortable standing before two men in nothing more than a towel.

"You took your time." Acha looked to the man who spoke, his short black hair was gelled back without a single hair misplaced she looked to the other man, if not for a few subtle differences they could have been mistaken as twins, they both wore a deep purple uniform, although the one who had just spoke was slightly taller than the one who seemed to be snooping around the room.

"Well, I *was* in the shower." She responded, both men stopped to look at her and then to the set of wet footprints leading from the bathroom, the taller man nodded and his partner vanished into the bathroom.

"Do you always shower with the window open?" The taller man asked as Acha went to follow his partner; she stopped turning to look at him.

"It stops the glass from steaming, keeps the room dryer too." She answered trying to see what the other man was doing without luck.

"Checks out sir, the timer says five minutes thirty-two seconds." The shorter man came to stand by his partner.

"Is there a problem? Who exactly are you?" She questioned feeling her patience slipping as she began to grow quiet cold, although the climate itself was warm; the open window caused a big draft chilling her.

"Sorry ma'am, we're from twilight enterprises, a dangerous criminal has escaped." The tall one answered.

"We're doing the rounds." Added the shorter one.

"Please excuse me if I sound rude, but it's quite chilly, is there anything else I can…" She trailed off glancing down at the towel she was wearing aware that they were doing the same.

"Forgive us, with you being new in town, we thought she may try something… it's not very often we get visitors, in fact, I would say it was somewhat of a rarity." The smaller man began to walk around the room again as if looking for something. "She's fairly new too you see, you never know with her type."

"Although I am new, I *am* with Elaineor and…"

"Lady Elly?" The smaller man interrupted and stopped looking around the room. "Forgive us, we did not realise you were together. Please forgive the intrusion." He made his way towards the door. "Oh, by the way, have you tried our fruit?" He questioned his hand holding the door handle tightly looking back to her slyly.

"Not yet, but I do have two pieces for after the shower, everyone here is so generous." She smiled, hoping now someone would not get scolded for their generosity, this seemed a very highly strung town. "Well of course, one belongs to my friend, they're not both mine." She added nervously.

"Ah that explains it." She heard one of them whisper.

"Sorry?" She questioned.

"We'll leave you to it; let us know if you see her." They exchanged glances and walked out of the door, stopping only when she called them back.

"Wait a minute, see who?" She questioned knowing this was one of the things they would 'mark' her on; she knew this game very well, possibly better than they did.

"Ah, did we not say?" The two men smiled and turned back to face her.

"No." She answered flatly, although they had been searching the room, they never seemed to actually move anything; the only thing they really checked was the cupboards.

"Oh never mind, I'm sure she wont bother you, she would be a fool to approach Lady Elly's guests, but if you see her, she's about your age short blond hair brown eyes, pretty looking, worked at the café, I think her name was Sarah, Sara, something like that." He scratched his head as if trying to remember the name; Acha knew this was still part of their game.

"Sara?" She pretended to mull the name over. "Oh yes… I think she was the one that served us… What did she do?"

"That does not concern you. Please go back to your business." The guards turned and began to walk away; Acha closed the door knowing they now stood in listening range, they were checking on her, as she flicked the lock muttering to herself for their benefit.

"Damn, I hope there's still water, Zo will kill me." She walked back into the bathroom, sensing their presence outside, she stepped back into the shower, she washed her hair, knowing they were still listening she began to hum, a further ten minutes had passed before she quickly got out of the shower she dried her hair on the towel moving various objects in the bathroom before starting to dress, finally they left. She let out a sigh closing the window. "Sorry about that, they were listening in." Acha whispered pulling the mattress from the bed before tilting it so Sara could climb back out through the split at the bottom.

"Thanks… how did you know about the fruit?" She whispered rising to her feet, you don't have any do you?"

"Something a farmer said, besides, it was clear they were counting life forces, the fruit has its own, since they were here so quickly I assumed they tracked the unusual number of life forces." Acha smiled.

"But why did you say two? How did you know?" Sara dusted herself down before helping Acha pull the mattress back onto the bed.

"Well, you're pregnant right? I can feel a life inside you." Acha blushed the look on Sara's face told her she was wrong, but there was no mistaking what she felt.

"Ah… No, I will explain later, but not here… You will give me chance to explain?… Did you say this was Elly's room?" Sara asked a thought dawning on her

"Yes why?"

"Perfect, there's an exit here to the courts, it's where I'm heading, she and Marise used it all the time to avoid the climb."

"How do you know that?" Acha questioned amazed at this girls local knowledge, from her accent it was clear she was not from these parts.

"When I was younger, I heard rumours Marise Shi the beautiful swords warrior was staying, I wanted to see, after all she and I are the same age, yet she has… done so much. The men always spoke of her; it's true she is beautiful. Anyway I watched them through the very window you let me in through; I watched as they vanished into the bathroom floor, there's clearly a trapdoor or something." She felt along the floor, he fingers tracing over the wooden floor before pulling one of the beams up, as she did so a whole section lifted with it.

"I shall join you until you are safe." Acha smiled following the girl down the darkened tunnel.

"No need, I am heading to the courts, I doubt I'll ever be safe." She turned to face Acha who was already lowering the trapdoor above them. "Please, you have helped enough."

"The courts?" Acha questions wondering why she would head to the very place she was trying to avoid. She glanced around the cold stone passage, it reminded Acha of the stories her mother told her when she was a child, an adventurer would always end up in a large stone walled tunnel, searching for one object that could save the world, although the tunnels in her mother's stories were always lit by some form of torch, these were not, instead it seemed there were strange stones every few feet that emitted a strange orange glow keeping the cave's lightening just above complete darkness, it seemed to be a straight path, and luckily, Sara seemed to know exactly which way they needed to go.

"I believe they are responsible for my brother's disappearance." She sighed quietly walking on.

"Then I shall help you, we can find him together, I am sure of it." Sara turned to Acha smiling with relief.

"I never would have thought." She shook her head gently in disbelief.

"What's that?"

"Oh, nothing." She smiled at Acha, there was a long silence until Acha finally spoke.

"What were you saying, about the life-force earlier?" She questioned unable to hide her curiosity any longer.

"Ah yes." Sara placed a hand on her stomach. "This land has always been baron, there is no water but for that we take from the sea, but it is only suitable for bathing, it's kind of hard to explain, the food here is grown with thanks to parasites that live beneath our ground, they feed on the rich chemicals from the volcanoes, as it lives, it excretes a chemical that somehow hydrates the area meaning it is are not effected by the harsh climate. For about a century now, when a child is born, they are taken to the courts and a young parasite is implanted into the baby, here it sleeps, feeding of the electric impulses of the nerves, the nutrients from the food grown here keeps both it and the host healthy, that's why our people can only eat food grown from this soil. But lately... something strange happened, the laws have been tightened, people are being taken to the court for nothing and never returning. Three days ago, I received a letter from my brother, he was frightened, it went on about an amazing discovery that they had stumbled on a way to wake the parasite, they found while it was awake, the host became like a puppet unable to control their actions as they fell under control of the parasite, but strangely enough, the parasite listened to other hosts, doing as they wished, it's all a bit confusing really, he went on to write about how only three of his team remained, the bodies of the other three had turned up brutally killed, I knew I had to come home, when I got here, all I could find was his diary. I found out his other team members had also vanished not long before he did, each one of them turning up hacked to pieces... I only hope... we're not too late." Her eyes filed with tears which she quickly rubbed away with the back of her hand.

"You think the twilight empire took him?" Acha placed her hand comfortingly on the girl's shoulder as they stopped for a moment in the darkened tunnel.

"I think so... I fear what they may do, they are always more violent when she's around... that's the reason I left in the first place." Sara rubbed her hands up and down her arms, despite the heat outside it was cool in the depths of the strange tunnel.

"Who?" Acha had a good idea, but she needed o hear it for herself.

"Your friend."

"Elaineor." Acha sighed confirming her fears, also leading her to believe their being here seems to be some how initiated the event that had transpired, she was sure of it, even though they didn't arrive until today, she was certain now it was something to do with Elaineor. "Why is it, wherever she arrives, there's always trouble?" Acha sighed again, could this have been somehow linked to her disappearance outside Abaddon?

"Maybe it's because she travels with Marise Shi." Sara covered her mouth as soon as the words had escaped, her eyes shone in fear as she looked to Acha.

"What?" Acha questioned shock in her voice, true she knew Elly had known her, but travelled with her? This was new information, it suddenly made her a lot more dangerous than when she was simply looking for her.

"I'm sorry I meant no harm, she's always been nice to us, she even got my brother the job at the court, please I beg you, please don't say anything… what was I thinking? She's your friend… I'm sorry please." She begged bowing before Acha as she paused for a second confusion crossing her brow.

"I don't travel with her, just Elly, although I guess what you say is true, she use to, but as you saw she's not with us…" Acha trailed off, another thought crossing her mind, it was something she has not even thought of until Sara had mentioned it, it was a simple case of mistaken identity. "You mean Zo?" She smiled. "No you have it all wrong, Marise is much taller, her hair is red and her eyes are green, although thinking now, I can see why you were worried, but…" Acha smiled to herself, the thought of Zo being that murderer was just too unreal.

"Sure as the sky is blue you travel with none other." Sara enforced, unsure what her game was.

"I see the resemblance now you have said it, but believe me; Zo is as gentle as they come." She answered a mild tone of amusement in her voice.

"Zodiac Shi?" Sara questioned Acha stopped a moment, all this time she never knew what her surname was.

"I'm not sure of her surname." She admitted shamefully, the amusement had now faded, Sara was pushing this topic more and more, it was beginning to make her uncomfortable.

"Look, this town… Just before the second rise is the Blackwood mansion, it's not common knowledge, I understand that, but they are one and the same, years ago Zodiac arrived at Blackwood's mansion, she was about twelve I think, Marie Shi is her alias, a name she uses to cover the guilt, to blame it on someone else so she doesn't have to face up to what she's done!"

"If that were true, how come you know this and no one else does?" 'Blackwood.' She thought to herself. 'Wasn't that the name of the lord Elly said Zo served under, the one who wanted her returned, could it really just be coincidence he lives here?'

"Aside from Elaineor and… Zo, as you call her? Well, its quite simple really, when Zo first arrived my brother was at that age where he sought adventure, as a dare he decided to sneak into Blackwood's mansion, I thought I would never see him again, after the climbed that wall, but when he returned, I expected to hear all about his adventure, but alien to his character he said nothing, I heard him sneaking from the house at night, about a month of this occurred before I followed him, I watched as he climbed the balcony and crept through the open window, I followed him watching him through the window as he talked and laughed to possibly the most beautiful girl my age I had ever seen, clearly an outsider, you don't get any with such fair skin tones in these parts, besides Elaineor that is, but she too is an outsider, she's been here so long though people seem to forget that. I couldn't understand what she was doing there, it was said only his warriors and Elaineor could gain access to the property, from her build it was clear she was neither, and besides Elaineor, there were no other women permitted in the building, all the food was prepared in a separate section. Yet, sure enough I saw her, it seemed she and my brother had become friends, I saw the panic in her face as she saw me at the window, but as you said, she was so gentle, my brother introduced us, she seemed happy to have another friend, she seemed so kind and gentle. One day we went to meet her as planned but found not her, but Elaineor, she warned us away, after that, I was scared for him especially after what Elaineor had said. Six month later we saw her again, something had changed in her gentle eyes, she seemed so sad and alone, she walked straight to Michael vowing to protect him and the village, no matter what, she left for while, but every night Michael would still sneak out to the high place where they use to count the stars together, I saw her return one evening, knowing where she could find Michael, I rushed to her, as I touched her arm she drew he sword as if to strike me, her green eyes met me coldly, I knew then it was not the same person that had left, that now stood before me, I put the rumour about Marise together with this information and discovered the truth. I tried to warn Michael, but he had already fallen too deep, but strangely I found them a few days later on the high place, chatting as if nothing had happened, I confronted her about Marise, it was clear her denial was nothing but lies, my brother only met with her a few times, after that night, she warned him away, I heard her, she told him it was getting too dangerous, she couldn't trust herself, she was scared, but as long as he was safe she knew she could find the strength, he promised to stay away, but I heard him cry out at night for her, after mother died she had been his only friend, the only one other than myself that did not avoid him, mother was very sick before she died, a mind sickness the doctors said, those that knew her, feared her family may have contracted it also, it was hard on him when she left… but it was for the best… then, the day she returns, he goes missing, not only that, she never even asked of him…"

They walked in silence for a while Acha still trying to swallow the vast amount of information she had heard, the small coincidences leaping to Acha's mind, if this were true, then it explained more than she cared to imagine.

"This is where we will part." Sara broke the silence as they approached a flight of stairs dimly lit in the cave stretching upwards into more darkness, it was clear this was the very base of the courts, what lay above she could only imagine.

"Part?" Acha questioned taken back by this sudden decision. "I said I would help you did I not?" Acha heard her own voice as she spoke it sounded somewhat shaken, quieter than normal, she kept thinking about how all this time she had been so concerned about them finding out who she was she never even thought that the real threat had been stood besides her all the time. She had to warn Daniel, but first she had a promise to keep… 'The last Grimoire.' Acha thought to herself. 'That's what this is about, all this time she must have known I was his daughter, she planned it from the start to get that final book, Elly said she was cunning… all this time I didn't even realise, I trusted her without question, I had no reason to doubt her.' Acha scolded herself silently as she grew angry about the truth she just discovered; angry she had been so blind not to see it from the start.

"I appreciate it." Sara smiled sitting on the steps.

"It's the least I can do; you just helped me more than you could know." She sat on the steps besides Sara as she worried now, not only about what lay ahead, but what she had left behind too, Daniel, he was alone with her, clueless, she could only prey he would be safe.

***

"I don't know about you but I feel really at home here" Zo sighed helping Daniel up to the top of the cliff, a huge tree grew at the top looking strangely alien as it stood proudly on the grass, she glanced back over the town, she could see everything so clearly from where she stood, she lay next to Daniel

'Shall we count the stars?' A voice whispered in her mind, for a second she thought it was Daniel, but realised almost immediately it wasn't. The voice was so familiar, it called from her memories, yet she couldn't place it, the harder she tried to seize it, to remember, the more she lost of what she had caught, in that second the voice whispered to her, she swore she remembered something, yet now, it was gone.

"Lying here, now in the shade of this tree, I feel like I could have done this a thousand times before." Zo sighed contently, for the first time since their travel had began, she felt comfortable, she felt guilty for it, especially considering one of their friends was in such great danger. Daniel sat up slowly glancing over the cliff face.

"Zo... what was the name of that guy Elly mentioned when you first met? Blackwood?" He questioned without giving her chance to answer, she gave a contented sigh, as she watched the clouds passing slowly overhead, had she not been so relaxed, she would have picked up the strange tones held within his voice. As he posed the question, he felt the walls surround her mind as once more she reminded herself what he already knew.

"Yeah, something like that, why?" She answered with a calmness the voice of her mind did not share, she turned her head taking her gaze from them to look at Daniel, seeing his face she sat up to look where he was staring.

"It seems he lives just there." He pointed to a huge area surrounded by tall walls, within the area was several small buildings surrounding one giant one, the main building itself was about three stories high and made of stone, it almost seemed to be a relic from the old world, parts of it had clearly been rebuilt, with nowhere near the skill used to construct it, the materials too didn't match the area's that had been rebuilt. He had overheard someone speaking of him earlier as they made their way to this place, thankfully, Zo had not heard and he had questioned himself, whether or not he would tell her. "Odd that Elly didn't happen to mention it." He added as Zo slowly stood making her way down the cliff face overlooking the mansion. "Hey wait up." He called after her suddenly finding himself shocked at the distance she had covered in a matter of seconds, he didn't need to ask where she was heading her thoughts were open to him, but even if they weren't he knew exactly where she was going and what she wanted, she wanted answers.

***

It had been a long time since Marise had come to live in the walls of Blackwood's mansion, as he was faced with Elly; he was now filled with the same excitement he had been when Elly brought him news of the mission's success…

…"So?" Lord Blackwood rushed to Elly's side after she returned from putting the young girl to bed, they walked through the empty halls in silence, he glanced to

Elaineor, even now he still found her vibrant blue hair shocking, he was sure she would be the only mortal with hair of that colour, then again, considering where she came from, he doubted she was mortal at all. It was a fact he continually reminded himself of whenever he got too comfortable in her presence, she carried out his every wish with accuracy, she had been in his service for over a decade now and still her strange beauty had not altered. He used her for all the tasks he did not find it fitting, or within his skill to undertake, being his 'daughter' in the public eye made the resistance she met minimal. Even without this safeguard in place, she had an air of natural talent about her and could be very persuasive if it meant getting something she wanted.

There had been many questions asked when he had introduced her to the council, they wondered why he had not mentioned his family before, of course, one in his position couldn't reveal too much about his family, he had to keep them safe. But with the recent death of Elaineor's mother, he had decided it was best for her to now live with him in the public eye. Many, to his relief, said he was too young to have a daughter her age, after all, in appearance she seemed to be easily in her late twenties and Blackwood himself was no older than mid forties, Blackwood would always thank them, advising his daughter looked old beyond her years.

Under normal circumstances he would not have dreamt of taking a stranger into his life, he would have felt put out by even the thought of it, but there were three reasons he could not refuse, the first and most important being the person who had sent Elaineor to him, the second, he could not fault her work, as for the third, he was promised something he had always strived for, power.

Elly waited until she had reached the kitchen to talk, placing a pot of water over the open fire.

"All went as planned, her darkness was unleashed, now it has awoken we can start the real training." Elly, should have been pleased that their goal had been achieved, but it was clear something was bothering her about the events that occurred, everything had not gone to plan, there was one more casualty than expected, one more causality than what was wanted. She and Night had reached Drevera at the same time, both alarmed to find those that they had sent to carry out the mission, had not arrived, alarmed to discover the town was still in peril. They rushed on towards the town finding a barrier surrounding the entire area, an invisible form of protectional magic that refused them entry, try as they did neither of them could pass. Finally, Elly had managed to break through, but by then, it was already too late.

"What will happen to Zodiac?" He questioned flippantly, it was not something that bothered him, he just needed to guard against any inconvenience this adjustment may create, as long as he got what he had been promised, he could care little for the consequences.

"For now, she will be sealed away when the darkness awakens; we just need to ensure it stays that way." She stated pulling some leaves from a plant that stood on the stone work surface. Blackwood's house was unlike anything that existed anymore except for the courts of twilight and the two castles of the world, they were relics completely undamaged by the release of the Severaine, they were all that remained of a time long since past, a time people now called, the time of the ancients. A lot of the rich and powerful had their mansions constructed on the ruins of another, using the parts that remained intact as their own, proud to own such houses and not ashamed to draw attention to their riches. But this mansion, the courts, and the small pieces of technology still found today were all that proved the existence of people before them.

It had been a time of great achievement, but also great damage, as civilisation grew and developed, the world withered and died. The Severaine was released as Zeus rose up to fight Chronos in his mission to be God of the universe and take his place on the eternal throne, the Severaine along with the battle of the Gods, destroyed life and collapsed the entire structure of the world and civilisation as it was then. To start with, the people who survived this great disaster, were forced back into the caves as they learnt to survive all over again and now, after centuries, they had finally constructed small houses made from materials in abundance near where they lived, some, the richer people, had mansions now some even extended to three layers, but only the rich could afford such things. Sometimes Elly missed the old power, she missed being able to cook things by placing them in a heating device for a few seconds, she missed the easy way of life, yet, she enjoyed this life much more, everything was simple, uncomplicated, there were a few schools, medicine consisted of botany and a few 'new science' techniques, but people were also forgetting now with their leaps and bounds, how to live with nature, they were getting greedy and power hungry.

"How? How do plan to keep her sealed away so the darkness does not need the time to manifest itself?" Blackwood asked as Elly stood staring into the night sky, she took the bubbling pot from the fire tipping the water into the ceramic cup she had been adding the leaves to; she stirred it gently as she answered.

"Simple, I will administer this potion, this will see that the darkness remains awake, it was incredible, you should have seen her fight, such grace, such power, with more training she may even be able to beat me, on a bad day." Elly smiled tipping the potion into the camomile tea, she left smiling to herself as she heard Blackwood's words.

"So my Marise Shi has awoken"...

..."So she *is* here." Blackwood climbed up the stairs from his cellar to meet his guest; he had been expecting her visit for some time now and was relieved to find the wait was finally over.

"Yes." Elly replied her tone short and to the point as always, there was clearly no love lost between these two, she started at him awaiting his next question.

"Well, where is she?" He prompted after a short pause, trying to look behind her already knowing that she wasn't there.

"That is none of your concern." Elly stated entering the cellar chamber almost forcing Blackwood back down the stairs as she closed the door behind her. "It is unfortunate we had to travel this way, an unavoidable detour, you know how it is." She smiled feeling his anger bubbling under the surface of his cool exterior, he paced back and forth across the length of his table for moment before losing the calm exterior, he slammed his hands on it yelling as he did so.

"What! What are you talking about? Your job was to return her to me!" He screamed the anger he had held so composed just moments ago, now released in force. "Are you forgetting who you work for?" He snarled, if he had the strength she did not doubt, he would tip the table up, she watched him smiling.

"No, but maybe you are." She watched realisation fall on his face, it had been so long since she joined his 'team', the details of where she came from had almost been forgotten. Night had always been too good to him, giving him this mansion, control over the twilight empire, all this, he got as thanks for the tasks he accomplished, yet had it not been for her, none of it would have been possible, she wasn't jealous, she didn't need thanks for her work, and the thanks she *was* given far surpassed that of material gain, yet still, she could not understand why he employed such a weak dirty little rodent like Blackwood. "Do not go looking for her, this is the only warning you will get, and the reason I am here. Now if you will excuse me, I have business to attend." She slowly walked up the stairs aware of the defeated looks he gave her as he watched her leave, once the door had closed he smiled to himself, he had no intention of looking for her, she would be rushing to him any minute and due to his knowing Elly would return here without her, as she made her way here, their paths would not cross, as he received news of their arrival, he knew they would come through this way and had spent many hours preparing for his audience with Elly, but he held the cards now, or more specifically the only card. Now all he had to do was wait.

***

"Are you sure you know what you are doing?" Daniel rushed after her although they were on level ground he still was finding it hard to keep up; the giant wall loomed before them now. "What do you plan on doing? What answers can he give you?" Zo stopped turning to look at Daniel, the heartbreaking smile on her face, he touched her arm as finally he caught up, the mansion wall now towering above them.

"I don't know." She whispered, the smile fading a little, he felt her fear even through the walls she had constructed, she was frightened for so many reasons, the main one being this would prove once and for all the truth behind her identity, even though she knew it, this was the first time she would truly be faced with it.

"Then why? Why put yourself through all this?" Daniel already knew the answer, she wasn't doing this for her, but for him, she needed answers, answers to questions she hadn't even thought of yet, she wanted to know the how's and whys of happened, of how Marise was created, only by understanding this could she try to find a way to stop her, a way to protect her friends from the murderer within, to stop her being so afraid of being alone with him, with anyone, in case she tried to hurt them, she tried to push the incident away from her mind. "I understand… but what are you going to do?" His voice so gentle it was almost a whisper, she turned to sit against the mansion wall, it was easily four times their height, it would be nearly impossible to scale its heights without some form of help.

"I don't know." She sighed, she had got this far, so close to answers, yet now she was here she hesitated, afraid of what she may find just past the walls, it was so easy to get here, but getting through the gates inside, that would be the hardest step, not physically, but mentally.

"Did you hear?" An excited voice called out from what seemed like far away though it grew louder as its owner hurried forwards, no doubt to join the few guards on the gate as they stood watch.

"No, what?" Another voice questioned, clearly belonging to one of the guards on the patrol of the gate, Zo and Daniel sat in silence listening exchanging curious glances.

"Well, I was just outside, I heard it from Ben, he just escorted Lady Elaineor into Lord Blackwood's chamber. It seems Miss Marise is in the village even as we speak, but Lady Elaineor refuses to bring her home."

"That's hardly surprising." Spoke the same cool voice that had enquired it seemed knew more on this topic than he first let on. "Nothing gets past her, he's a fool for even trying, she properly knows he imprisoned that friend of hers and wishes to avoid unnecessary bloodshed, you know Lady Elly has always watched out for us." There were a few mummers of agreement, Daniel and Zo exchanged silent concerns.

'When did you last see Acha?' Zo questioned a sickening feeling rising to her throat as she heard their conversations; she did not like what was being implied.

"Tell you what I wouldn't like to be on duty when she finds out... I wouldn't even like to be on the island." One of the guards stated.

'Not since she left at breakfast... three hours ago.' He answered thinking to himself how it wasn't really breakfast, but still she knew what he meant.

Daniel cringed as he watched Zo rise to her feet, he knew what she was planning even now, she dusted herself down and head towards where the voices came from, Daniel heard their conversation die as no doubt she stood before them, he began to follow staying away from view so he could move quickly to intervene if needed.

"Where is my friend what has he done with her?" She demanded, even from around the corner the anger in her voice made him shudder, her voice was cold, heartless, there was no way they would dare not answer, the voice in her mind grew weaker and more desperate as she was faced with the truth. *'I am not a killer, I am not a murderer'*

"A... at the court house... M...Miss, that's all we know, he was taken there today... when he heard you may be passing... please that's all we know." The guard fell to her feet, she felt herself blush slightly, she paused unsure what to say, or even how to react, she tried to push the panic away, over and over she repeated her magic words, the words that eased the nausea that the truth of her past had brought.

"I think it is best no one knows you are here." Daniel turned the corner to stand besides Zo, who at this moment in time, seemed a little lost about what to do as she stood in silence, a look of surprise across her face staring at the figure that cowered before her, shocked at the fearful reaction portrayed by all the guards, they were really afraid of her. "I am sure the guards understand." Daniel gave the guards a meaningful look who looked up at him nodding frantically, catching his meaning, Zo nodded gratefully at Daniel.

"You are right as always..." She sighed giving a disheartened tut, since she stood before them, she may as well play the role. "They are just lucky you turned up when you did." She turned slowly and walked away, leaning against the wall when she had turned the corner out of view, the guards were still shaking his hand thanking him. The question of who he was did not even come into the equation, who he was, was not important, the fact he had just saved their lives was the only important detail in any of this.

"You're lucky she listened this time, but if Blackwood were to discover..."

"No sir, I understand, she, nor you, were ever here, thank you." They repeated their thanks and promised not to breathe a word several more times before he left.

"Good." Daniel walked away after Zo, he turned the corner to find her leaning tearfully against the wall, what just happened had made the reality she discovered, all the more real, all the more frightening, the guards had been terrified of her.

"I don't know what his plan is, but we need to save Acha." She looked up to him who nodded, just then Elly appeared.

"I thought I may find you here, it was only a matter of time until you discovered this place."

"Elly!" Zo's voice filled with relief as she emerged from some nearby trees, she never thought she would have been so glad to see her; it was everything she could do not to embrace her.

"Planning on finding answers?" She questioned as if she was the one who could see her thoughts instead of Daniel.

"She already found one." Daniel interrupted coldly. "It seems Blackwood has taken Acha."

"That sneak… I knew there was something phoney about that tantrum of his… he must have planned it this way knowing I had no intention of returning you, he took out his own insurance, did you find out where she is?" Elly sighed she was very tired of Blackwood's games.

"The guards informed us they took her to the court." Zo joined the conversation, although at that moment, she felt as if she was watching it all from somewhere very far away, somehow none of what was happening seemed very real.

"He planned to use her as a bargaining chip to get you back, we must hurry, it's about time I told you the truth about this place." She knew from the silence of the Guards they would remain true to their word, they wouldn't dare even whisper what had just transpired.

Chapter fourteen

"So anyway, what's your name?" Sara leaned forwards from her place on the steps to get a good look at Acha, her short dark hair now framing her now pale completion, she looked up to her smiling softly.

"Acha, sorry I didn't realise I hadn't introduced myself." She hesitated as she decided whether or not to offer her hand, she decided against it.

"Acha?" Sara smiled repeating the name gently as if committing it to memory. "That's an old name, from about 100 NGE if I'm not mistaken." Sara stated glancing up the stairs again.

"Close, 150. That's when I was born." Acha smiled, her vision following Sara's timid gaze up the mountain of stairs, not even realising the truth her words implied.

"Your name you mean? That's when your name was born." She covered her mouth as she giggled, Acha nodded realising how odd her statement would sound to someone not knowing the circumstances, she was so use to talking freely around the others, she hadn't even considered the need for caution around a stranger, honesty just seemed so natural, of course with recent events, it was clear it was not the same for *everyone* she travelled with.

"Something like that, so what's the plan?" She questioned aware of Sara's impatience, from her constant glances up into the darkness and back again, Sara stopped giggling her face growing serious.

"Plan?" She questioned, clearly she had been so wrapped up in getting here she hadn't even thought to do once she arrived.

"Well, we can't just walk in and expect them to take us to your brother." Acha touched Sara's hand gently as she sighed.

"I see..." Her face seemed to drop as the glimmer of hope in her eyes began to fade. "I... guess I didn't really think it through, maybe I should have told..."

"Nonsense, we don't need anyone's help, just a plan." Acha cut her off short knowing where that particular sentence was heading, she smiled seeing the hope rekindle in Sara's eyes.

"Well... we need to find out where he was taken." Sara volunteered, it was something Acha had already thought of, if this place was anywhere near as large as the court in Knights-errent, they could wander around lost for hours, it was time, from her understanding of Sara's tale, they did not have to waste.

"How about we walk around until we find him... We have to start somewhere." A sudden thought dawned on Acha, it was an unusual one but it just may work. "If we don't come across too many people I can make sure they don't see us." She saw Sara's face light with joy.

"You possess the power of invisibility?" Awe filled her voice as she gazed upon her getting to her feet a new excitement filling her.

"Well... No." Acha smiled gently squeezing her hand. "But I can influence people so they don't remember seeing us... I think... but for the most part let us hope they are too wrapped up in other things to notice." Sara nodded

"Right then." Without another word they stood having stared up into the darkness long enough, they exchanged looks nodding to each other as slowly they began the ascent into the unknown darkness.

***

"You need to do this alone" Elly stopped without warning on the hill they had been descending, the huge court now in view from where they stood at the peak of a steep cliff face, the climb to the court would be every bit as steep as the one they had just made, they gazed upon it now taking the time to catch their breath, it was every inch the double of the one they had seen crumble in Knights-errent, but this one was above the surface and did not seem to be carved from a mountain, instead it was made from brick, Zo stood in awe for a moment wondering how such a thing could stand, things like this were all said to collapse millennia ago even before the world was born again after the fight between Zeus and Chronos. She wondered how many times she had stood here before looking at this very sight, and wondered if every time she had, she had been filled with such awe. "If am not mistaken, the guards will now be approaching the village, he has sent an escort for you, he wants to tell you in person, to bargain with you, to assess your current worth, if we do not return, he will grow suspicious. I will keep him busy, whereas you, Daniel." She turned to look at him. "You must give them the run around, make them truly believe she is somewhere in town. Now will be the best chance for you to go, security will be light." Elly placed her hand on Zo's shoulder seeing the look of doubt and fear in her eyes. "Remember who you are, if you doubt for just one second you will put us all in great danger… Acha's life depends on your ability to convince them, as does ours, you need to be in and out no questions asked, before Blackwood grows suspicious." Elly gave her a look of warmth and encouragement before releasing her, a lot was counting on her ability to act like a person she so desperately wanted to escape from.

"Zo, I will not fail you." Daniel stated squeezing her good shoulder gently before he turned and began to walk towards the town.

"Nor I you." She smiled sadly, a feeling of sick and dread nestling in her stomach as she thought about what lay ahead, she stood a moment longer looking at the great building that stood before her, she had to focus, she had to remove all doubt and fear from her mind, a task easier said than done, this was something she knew she would never be ready for, but with so much at stake she found putting one foot before the other to face the truth not quite as hard as she expected.

As she approached its door, the court house seemed to grow above her every part of her wanted to stop to take it in, it towered so tall above her casting its great shadow across the uneven landscape, it was a view to behold, it was unlike anything she had seen in this world, but she could not stop, she scolded herself silently lowering her head to stare straight ahead, if she *had* been here so many times, surely, she would not pause to look at such a thing, her head held high with not so much as a word to the doorman she stepped inside, he straightened slightly, seeming to hold his breath as she passed, she heard him sigh as the door close behind her.

The door had taken her into a magnificent foyer, it consisted of four possible routes, the centre room was filled by a large reception, randomly placed around were small wooden tables and chairs. She walked straight into this area, taking in her surroundings quickly hoping nothing would be determined from the quick glance around. Reminding herself she had been here many times she quickly chose a random door hoping her choice alone would not see her in some form of storage cupboard blowing her cover all together, could she really talk her way out of that situation should it arise? Surely she would not need to, Marise was feared and regardless of how silly, surely none would dare to question her choice. The choice of door and commitment to the result was all decided within seconds, she didn't even stop before walking straight towards double doors, situated just past the reception area, hoping silently that she had made the right choice, she knew time was of the essence, she could not afford to get lost in a building of this size, she needed to be straight in straight out. The receptionist glanced up with a smile, it soon faded when she saw who had entered and was amazed, to find how busy she had become with imaginary work. Not that it mattered Zo had ignored her completely, walking across the floor to the double doors trying to determine if they were push or pull before she approached.

The hall was practically empty, everything about the hall she found herself in seemed sterile, from the clean tiled floors to the clean white walls, there was a slight chill to the corridor, a chill she hoped was responsible for the hairs on the back of her neck moving to stand on end, she repressed a shudder.

She was completely lost, without even a clue as to where she should be heading for, the beating of her heart grew louder and louder, racing in time with the footsteps that approached, she knew already the best course of action to gain the information she so desperately needed, it was the only option she could think of, and as much as she despised it, no matter how hard she thought about it, there was no alternative. It was either this, or wander round aimlessly hoping no one would grow suspicious to her, although there was that silent part of her answering her fears, whispering to her a comforting, yet unnerving, thought. 'If they do catch on, I would just have to kill them.' Even now she couldn't distinguish if it was her own mind that thought that, or a thought from Marise, she knew whose thoughts she hoped it was, but in effect, she was Marise, just one thing distinguished them according to the being in Knights-errent, that thought, no matter how small brought her a small about of comfort, if she could be distinguished from the killer, then surely they were not the same, it was a lie, she knew it, but it was a lie that brought her comfort, her mind repeating the comment to herself as she walked towards the footsteps.

'I am not a killer'. The thought brought her more comfort the more she repeated it, never had she stained her hands with another's blood, the day that happened would be the day Marise won, the day Zo lost all she believed in, it was a small line between life and death, but this paper thin line, no matter how small the meaning was something so enormous it kept her sane, it reduced her fears, no matter how much she was like that murderer, they were not the same. *'I am not a killer'*

She steadied her breath as she psyched herself up approaching one of the men dressed in white lab coats, grabbed him on the way past as he pretended he couldn't see her, the papers he had been shuffling in an attempt to avoid her now scatted across the floor, his colleagues watching in horror as she grabbed him, before continuing on their way after the warning glance she gave them.

"Where has Blackwood put my prisoner?" Her voice was low, filled with anger and annoyance, this is how she imaged *she* would be from the glimpse she had caught of her.

"P...P...Prisoner?" The man stammered all colour draining from his face as she pulled him to one side, away from his path into the room he had been about to enter, he was clearly petrified, in the deep recess of her mind, she couldn't help feeling some sympathy for him and once more, as she held the man pinned to the wall, her thoughts of comfort allowed her to continue without fear, because even thought they thought she was Marise, this was the line that divided them, a line Zo treasured with all of her heart.

"Yes. I have been informed she was brought here this morning!" She snapped in an authoritarian tone, she could see now the man had began to tremble slightly, he raced his hand through his once neat black hair nervously shifting positions under the weight of her stare. His back was now pressed firmly against the wall, panic forbidding him to speak until finally he forced the words free.

"Erm... I..." He swallowed tying hard to regain his posture but failing. "The only person they brought in today... well the details are confidential." He shrank slightly as he met the intensity of her cold stare; he pulled at his collar swallowing hard. "Not to you of course." He laughed nervously. "I was just saying..." She grabbed his lapel pulling him closer to her, aware that although she was shorter than him it had the desired effect. "Hospital ward... recovering from surgery." He almost fell to the floor when she released him; she looked him over once more before she began to walk away.

"Erm... Miss." His voice broke. "We have a new pass system... and erm... well... please take mine." His hand was shaking so badly the small plastic pass vibrated in his hands, she waited for him to bring it to her before snatching it, he cowered back making himself small against the white wall as he pressed himself against it, not moving until he was sure she had gone.

The last door stood before her now, the pass had proved useful, she stood now on the hospital ward of course, it was not only the pass that made her task easier, the manned lift had been very helpful indeed, ordering to go to the hospital ward she found the trip took her near the very top of the building and the operator had disabled all other floor collection signals permitting a quick, stop-free trip, she had saved so much time with this approach, as long as she kept sight of the truth, she now did not fear people mistaking her for the cold blooded murderer, nor did she fear she would lose herself in their belief. All around her, she could feel the pain of others; she had long since lost count of the sleeping casualties she had passed all in such a short space of time.

Elly had explained how this place was used for human experiments, but she also knew, if she did so much as looked in their direction, it would create suspicion, she now stood before the final door on the ward, a door a young nurse had almost broke her neck trying to get the key for her when she had demanded that she see her prisoner immediately. She turned the key in the lock stepping without hesitation in to the dark room, although everything about her screamed for her to look before entering she knew Marise would not, so nor could she.

She could hear the monitor beeping at the back of the room, the small dimly lit room, housed a single bed with a wooden guard like that found on a child's crib, the entire room was filled with what seemed to be ancient technology, all the time she stood leaning on the closed door Elly's voice echoing around her head.

They use the ward for many kinds of human research experiments, who knows truly what goes on within those walls and for what purpose.' There had been a cruel smile on her face as she had told her, again she obviously knew more than she was willing to say, and that Marise can walk around so freely, clearly showed that she too, saw more of this place than she would like to have believed. She felt the wall around the door trying to find the lights without luck.

"Acha?" She whispered almost afraid of being overheard even though she knew this was impossible, after all, the nurse said not a sound could be heard through those walls, she approached the bed slowly lowering the bar on its side.

"Angel? I'd know that voice anywhere... I knew you would come back." The voice whispered, she knew immediately this was not Acha, for starters, although weak the voice that spoke to her in whispers, was male, it was a discovery that filled her with confusion and doubt, if this wasn't Acha, then who was it? "If only it had been earlier, we could have run together from your watcher." Zo approached the bed as the figure within began to cough, she leaned over him, gasping, she knew his face, she knew his sea green eyes and his light brown hair, he looked a lot like Daniel, in some ways anyway, maybe he was the reason she felt so comfortable with Daniel from the time they first met.

"By the Gods." She whispered she could think of little else to say as she moved to sit besides him.

"Zoe, I don't have long... I have fought all I can; I can't tell you how happy I am the last face I see, shall be that of my angel, my best friend." A weak smile crossed his lips, a small drop of dried blood rested in the corner of his smile. "I tried to keep it secret... I have done a terrible thing, will you hear my confession?" He whispered, a name came to her as he stretched his hand to touch hers, he sat on the side of the bed hesitantly, he smiled as she spoke his name.

"Michael..." She whispered squeezing his hand gently, as she did so, a rush of memories came flooding back to her, to start with just pieces, fragments, flowers, running together, hiding from guards, laughing, but the more she saw the more she remember of this boy, of her first friend.

"I always liked you better this way." He gasped in pain as he spoke. "Like the day we first met. Will you listen?" She nodded he moved to rest his head closer to her arm, she touched his face gently removing the tear from the outside corner of his eye, she wondered how she could ever have left him, he had always been so alone but for his father and younger brother, why hadn't she taken him with her when she left? But in her heart she knew the answer, it was the same reason that she would not take Daniel when the time came for the quest to end and that reason was a prophesy she heard around the time she first arrived in this small village.

"Forgive me Zoe, I have failed, you trusted me in his job, a job to protect them and my colleagues, we accidentally stumbled on a way to wake the parasite... it seems there are two breeds, the normal parasite found in most our people... but there is another the Hikoriti, which we discovered slept within me and within other younger hosts... we swore not to reveal our findings... but one by one they killed us all, until they discovered the truth... I can control them as can those possessing it after my death. I fought as long as I could my friend, forgive me." Michael began to cough, more drops of blood smudged on his pale completion.

"Hikoriti?" Zo moved closer to him, he turned his head now resting on her lap as she stroked his hair gently.

"Yes... a special parasite... they stole my diary... for some reason... my parasite was different, my actions will cost the town... already they have placed it in its new host... but when I die..." He began to cough once more, moments passed until he could speak again. "You have to save them." He gave a cry of pain, the white sheets on his bed growing darker with blood from his stomach, even now she knew there was nothing she could do to heal him, the people here lived in harmony with the parasite in their body, once removed, the host always died, no matter how skilled she was in healing, she knew that none from this village would respond to her healing touch. "How beautiful you were that day, you looked so sad and alone, brushing your hair before the mirror, I knew you were different then." He raised his shaking arm to touch her cheek; she placed her hand over his to hold it there tears welling in her eyes. "You grew more beautiful with each passing hour, heaven should I see it will pale against your beauty. The light shone so gently across the floor, your hair so warm I wanted to reach out and touch it, to take you in my arms and runaway where we could both be free, that day, it day was so warm, despite being so late, I remember you turned and smiled at me, seeing me at your window in the mirror, I was so scared, but you smiled so brightly, pushing me to the cupboard as your watcher Elly prowled around, you weren't allowed friends, whatever would she think? All the times we ran from my little brother to the high place, come he's not looking, let us escape and count the stars together one last time my Zoe." His hand grew heavy in hers, she remembered him so vividly now, he had been the one who brought her escape from the four walls she had been imprisoned in, he had been her first friend, her best friend, the one who had done so much for her and asked for nothing in return but a smile...

...Releasing her grip on Michael, Zo dismounted the horse before he walked her to the peer it was just before dawn, she was certain her trainer would have noticed her gone by now, there was no time for a long goodbye, once on the boat it would take until dusk to arrive back at her home, her heart leapt with the anticipation of seeing her mother again.

"I can't thank you enough." She whispered her electric blue eyes filled with tears as she hugged him tightly, over the last few months he had been the best friend she had ever had, the only friend she had ever had, and now, he had provided her with the means to return home to see her mother. She couldn't thank him enough for the freedom from her training her had given her everyday. Before she left, she had ensured he would know the level of her gratitude, by giving him a chance, where normally there would be none. "Lord Blackwood spoke of needing a scholar in the courts today, a science researcher, he was too busy so gave me the profiles, I recommended you for the position, it's what you've always dreamed of."

"There's something else?" Michael knew her well enough by now to know there was something more to this story, his green eyes searched her for the answer he sought, she wasn't quite telling the whole truth, he saw it in her eyes.

"Yes..." She sighed. "Remember I told you of the darkness I felt within me? I'm scared Michael, scared I will lose control... I can't see you again, for both you and your family's safety. You have been the greatest friend I could ever ask for... but if I don't do this..." Zo paused, thinking back to the words she heard outside her door just last night before she left to meet with Michael.

Elaineor had stood outside her door, as always she lay in bed pretending to sleep, waiting for her to leave so she could meet with Michael. Lord Blackwood had approached, she knew his footsteps anywhere, they had a determined sound to them as he rushed to the door, their voices were nothing more than low whispers, but being awake she heard them all too clearly. They spoke of her friendship with a person from outside the walls, she knew at once they referred to Michael, if the guards were to see him again, they would shoot to kill. When Elaineor had entered her room to find Zo awake, she admitted everything, she admitted they knew of her secret meetings with the boy and asked what it would take to stop her from seeing him. Thinking only of Michael she asked for the one thing he wanted more than anything, to be a scholar at the court researching into the new science, he had dreamt of a chance like this his whole life, he studied alone in the walls of him home, it was exactly this reason, he thought it nothing more than a dream, Blackwood would never employ anyone without some form of formal education, he longed to work hard in hope that someday he would have his own lab and team. Elaineor agreed but starting tomorrow, should she see him again, Michael and his family would pay the price. But tonight was all Zo had needed, tonight was the night she would visit her home, but even now she had no intention of returning.

"I understand." Michael sighed, understand? How could he understand? He thought to himself hearing his own words. "Why?" He questioned, whatever the reason, he needed to hear it.

"Because, aside from my mother and Amelia, you are the person I hold dearest in this world, I promise I will protect you no matter what." She touched him lightly; a silver field surrounded him for but a second as she smiled. "Also, I have no intention off returning and becoming what they wish of me." He watched as she vanished into the shadows knowing there was nothing he could say or do to change her mind, and realising, perhaps her leaving was for the best, especially for her...

...A lump rose to her throat as she lowered his hand wiping the blood from his face and the tears from his eyes, she leaned forwards kissing him gently on the forehead

"I'm sorry." She whispered pulling away.

"Michael!" Sara screamed pushing Zo to one side holding his lifeless hand tightly. "Michael hold on, please." She turned to Zo accusation in her eyes. "You!" She snarled "You murderer, you promised to protect him... why didn't you save him! Why?" She screamed Acha grabbed Sara tightly pulling her into a hug as she glared at Zo.

"Acha, you're safe." Zo almost swallowed her words when she saw the look in her friend's eyes as she held the sobbing waitress. "I heard you were captured."

"Oh yes, heaven forbid something should happen to me." She spat bitterly even speaking to her made her feel sick, the very words seemed dirty, after all the things Sara had told her, all the truth making holes in Zo's lies. How could she stand there now with such a convincing act of concern? "Careful Marise it almost sounds as if you care." She watched as the colour drained from Zo's face, so she *had* discovered the truth after all.

"I... I can explain." Zo's voice was nothing more than a whisper as the shock took her breath from her, even her thoughts that brought so much comfort before did little to calm her emotions now.

"It *is* true?" She seemed more shocked by the immediate confirmation, she didn't event try to deny it. "I had my doubts but you don't even bother to deny it! Well I don't need your explanations, I understand all too well, what was it Elly said about a little ambition? How did you find out? Did *he* tell you?" She snarled tightening her grip on Sara, who beneath her heavy sobs, invisible to the others smiled.

"What?" Zo's voice was full of questions, so much so Acha almost believed she had no idea what she spoke of, she had to admit, with acting skills like that, it was no wonder she had her fooled, she had everyone fooled.

"My father, did he tell you who I was, that *was* your plan wasn't it? To use me to get the other book, only a blood relative and so forth." She hissed, Zo looked to Sara who was still sobbing against Acha's chest, this clearly wasn't the time for this, she did not have the strength for this discussion and this was certainly not the time or place for it.

Acha fell silent as if remembering herself, she glanced to Michael's body lying on the bed.

"When you come to leave no one will question you, it is all I can do." Zo whispered forcing herself to hide the despair and sadness fighting its way to the surface, she could not afford to show emotion, especially if the people around here were to take her next command, she placed the pass on the bed, before touching Sara on the shoulder, a strange shudder passing through her as she did so, Acha pulled her away from her touch protectively, with nothing left to say she opened the door to leave.

"You really are heartless, you killed her brother and that's all you have to say for yourself?" Zo paused a moment as if she wished to say something, but changing her mind, she walked away in silence; it took all her effort to keep the posture expected by those around. Sara pulled herself away once Zo had left wiping her reddened eyes.

"I had hoped it wouldn't end this way, it's all her fault, she did this to us, he was all I had left." She cried placing the stained sheet over his face. "I want her to suffer, she deserves to... I know she's your friend... but..." Sara erupted in tears once more.

"*Was* my friend, at least I thought so, using people like that she deserves everything she gets." Acha pulled Sara close again. "But what can I do? I would help if I could, but..." Sara once more pulled away from Acha's embrace wiping fresh tears from her face.

"You really mean that? I know someone who can help you." She whispered. "I can't use her myself, there's no way ... But you are already in her group... Maybe we can do something... I just want her to pay for destroying my life; I want to avenge my brother..." She sniffled before breaking into tears again.

***

Daniel backed away down one of the streets, it seemed the people here were less than happy to have them return, their weapons cocked and their scythes poised as they advanced, he turned quickly to find Elly just a matter of feet away from him in the same predicament, it seemed all the town, for some reason, during their short absence, had decided they were no longer welcome and there was no sign of the guards that Elly had warned off, perhaps seeing the people's reactions here, they had concluded their job as complete. Night watched through the mirror holding the gossip crystal, a smile of amusement crossing his face.

"Are you sure this boy understands?" Night questioned, the mirror splitting into half to show Blackwood holding a small crystal.

"Yes sir, as you can see, although temporary, the operation was a success, meaning every living person containing the lesser parasite is now under our control."

"You do realise what the outcome will be of this, I trust you have taken the necessary precautions." Night swilled the ruby fluid around his glass before placing it down once more.

"Yes my Lord, the Hikoriti will be dead within the hour, as soon as its host has grown cold."

"Then what of the town people, it would be a shame to have to start again." Night sighed knowing that Blackwood would have thought of something, in fact he didn't only know he had, he knew what he had thought of also. After all it would be foolish to leave something so important to just one man, but Blackwood still had information he had yet to share with him and Night needed to be certain he could trust him completely, if he passed his test on this little project, there was no reason why he couldn't be moved to bigger and better things.

"The control is fairly easy, it's a mixture of different pitched notes only audible to parasites, we have recordings of both the awaken and the sleep cries, so once this trial has passed, we should be able to control them without the Hikoriti, we have tested this on several small groups and found it most effective. Although it seemed somehow more effective over blood relations, that boy didn't know what hit him when we brought his little brother in, he as good as handed over the research to save him, it is a shame he has no more family, maybe we could have made the host do it instead of this substitute, that I believe, would have had a greater impact than what we are doing now." Night ran his finger around the glass as it did so it sang in different pitched tones. "Oh I nearly forgot, it turns out there is more than one of these parasites, but only one at any time can be the alpha parasite so to speak, I have already located the next host, so if things turn nasty, we can always use the child." Night smiled at Blackwood's words, it seemed since that event nearly ten years ago he had decided it was better to keep everything on the level with him, after all, although he hadn't realised it at the time, his final action in the creation of Marise came at a very dear personal cost to Night, since that time he tried so hard to make amends for his misjudgement, Night had placed it down to experience, how could he have known what no one had told him?

"Very well, let's begin, I believe she has arrived… Let us place cracks in that barrier of hers and tear it to the ground, then we both will get what we desire, Marise will soon stand besides me." Despite the commitment of his words, something about the tone in his voice seemed almost sad.

"And what of your daughter?" He questioned, an undertone of concern ringing through his voice.

"I do not think there is a way to save both, I need Marise to release the final seals, I need her power... but." Night paused wondering why he spoke of such things to Blackwood.

"I understand your predicament my lord, she is so much like the woman you loved, it's a shame there must be a sacrifice."

"All things worth while have a sacrifice, some sacrifices are greater than others, these are the things that are truly worth obtaining." He answered simply.

***

Zo gave a big sigh as she left the building, the doorman suddenly found the need for his presence inside leaving her alone at the foot of the building, she felt the barriers around her mind slowly begin to fall away, tears already forming in her eyes and as she grew further away small sobs could be heard leaving her, since parting with Daniel she had built the barriers so high to avoid distraction, now they were fading she instantly knew there was something wrong, her sobs subsided as the severity of what she felt hit her, she scrambled the cliff face as fast as she could, stopping only when the village was in sight, she could clearly make Daniel out, after all, both he and Elly were surrounded by the villagers as they shoved and poked them with all manner of weapons as if herding them somewhere. They stood with their backs to each other and although from this distance she just make out their silhouettes, even so, she knew Daniel was frightened, posture alone dictated this. Elly however, seemed well composed given the circumstances, almost confident that should things take a turn for the worst, it would be her who came out on top, somehow Zo also knew she could handle herself, even against such a large crowd, a voice stopped her advance towards the town, although she was unsure what she could do once she had arrived there.

"I knew you would come." She turned quickly to find its source. A sickly looking blond man stepped from behind the tree, he leaned on it a moment for support, clutching the bloody bandages that wrapped around his abdomen, the first thing he did when he moved again was lock eyes with her, never again to glance away.

Zo, at first, thought she could help him, but the realisation of the situation grew clearer, she glanced down to Daniel and Elly again, memories of Michael's words, pieced together with the stranger's wounds left only one, horrible conclusion.

"You... your using the Hikoriti, you're making them do this." She gasped

"You're better than I gave you credit for... funny thing though." The man let out a painful gasp his hazel eyes filling with immeasurable pain as he fell to his knees, despite this his large hazel eyes, filled with such pain and fear, remained locked on hers, he breathed deeply speaking through clenched teeth. "This thing inside me, it will only live until all electrical impulses have stopped in its host... If that happens before I die, I lose control... funny thing about that." He gave a strained chuckle. "When I loose control... they will kill everything, even themselves, you'll have a massacre on your hands young Miss." He kneeled forwards a little smiling to himself, he had his reasons for accepting this suicide mission, reasons, none but he and the voices truly could understand.

"I don't understand." She tried to buy time, while she kept him talking the townsfolk seemed less violent towards her friends, maybe they could see their chance and make a run for it, while he was distracted while talking to her he could focus less on them, maybe they could escape. She glanced away once more from his stare to look at her friends, turning back their eyes locked again, she couldn't escape the weight of his gaze despite how hard she tried she couldn't not look at him, and what was worse, she knew where this scenario was heading.

"When the Hikoriti realises the impulses on its host have stopped, you will all die, you see they have both a physical and a psychic link with their host it seems, it will grow angry, especially since it will realise that wherever it is now still lives. It will seek to destroy all those under its influence, any creature locked under its control will be destroyed. Even now the Hikoriti is counting down to its host shut down, three minutes." His voice seemed to challenge her insecurities, he knew she was afraid of what was to follow it was almost as if he knew the words of comfort she used and wished to strip them away from her.

"Why? Why are you doing this?" She begged. "What do you hope to gain?" She heard a shot echo through the air, glancing down she saw Daniel gripping his arm.

"A scratch, I never miss twice." He threatened. "Now you know I'm serious..."

"What do you want from me?" She demanded already knowing what the answer would be, his eyes smiled slightly through the pain.

"It's simple really... either you kill me... or them, it's an easy choice. You are Marise Shi, you have the power of life and death within your hand, yet you hesitate to use it to save those you care for most. Frightened?" He sneered continuing his count down Lord Blackwood had explained the situation fully, the only thing he would regret is that he would not live to see the fruits of his labour, but at least the voices would leave him too, horrible little voices screaming in his mind, the dirty thoughts of humanity forever screaming, what he wouldn't pay for a little silence.

Zo stared at him in horror, frightened couldn't come close to what she felt, she knew each time she used that sword, her alter ego grew stronger, the more she used it, the more danger her friends would be in, not from those who wished them harm, but from herself, if she was to kill him, she would lose herself, she would destroy that paper thin line dividing her and Marise, a line that gave her strength. She feared what would happened should she surrender to this stranger's will, yet, she was left with no choice she looked down at the others the countdown echoing through her mind as she drew her sword. She called on Marise, on her strength, she had no desire to see this through, but Marise liked to kill, she lived for this, she begged for her to take control as the timer hit one minute.

The sword trembled at his throat, all the time his eyes remained fastened on hers, he reminded her now of a dear caught in a hunters trap, alone, terrified and knowing what was to follow, yet he was not a dear, he was a person, and he had every right to live, as he spoke the number twenty she knew what she preyed for was never to be, yet all the same she felt Marise at the back of her mind, watching relishing in the torture she was going through, enjoying the event that was about to come, the line she so recently found would be gone forever and then, there was little that could stand in her way. Closing her eyes she swung her sword, she felt the resistance as it struck his flesh, she felt the nausea hit her as she followed through, although her eyes remained closed she seemed to see everything so clearly, his eyes somehow still seemed to be locked with hers, as if she never closed them at all, she couldn't escape his stare making what she did all the more difficult, a light rain began to fall, it was then the countdown stopped.

Time seemed to freeze as she stood there in the rain, she feared to open her eyes, as the images of his death faded, she heard the body slump to the floor, all too aware what had fallen moments ago was not rain, this place never had rain.

She stood shaking, as nausea rose within her as an empty feeling filled her chest, stepping away from the body, she opened her eyes to see Acha now standing over the dead figure, she was unsure when they had arrived but both she and Sara were covered in the same blood rain that covered her and the ground around them, as she stood staring at them in horror it took all her self control, all her strength not to be sick, she took a step backwards away from them.

"Finally shown your true colours." Acha snorted turning her back on her and walking away, she took another step back stifling a cry as nausea passed over her, she felt gentle arms of darkness embrace her, she felt almost as if she were flying, but then something changed, she was falling deeper and deeper into the darkness, hands grabbing at her as she fell, somewhere from far, far away she heard Daniel screaming her name, but there was another voice too, a whisper that simply said. 'Two more'.

Chapter fifteen

Zo opened her eyes, in the brief moment before she did so she almost had a feeling of serenity, then, as the images of what transpired raced through her mind, it vanished as if it had never existed, she sat up placing her hands to her face as the bloody rain began to fall time and time again, she heard the door open and close quietly.

"You're awake, that was quite a fall we were worried." Zo turned to look at him slowly, she knew how carefully he had chosen his words, aware of the eggshells he seemed to be steeping on. He was trying to pretend nothing had happened, but it was something she could not do, she had crossed the line, she had destroyed the only boundary that separated her from Marise, she had taken another's life.

"Daniel… I…" She whispered swallowing hard; she wondered if he knew exactly what had transpired up there, if he was aware of the outcome, if he knew what she had done. She looked at her shaking hands sadly, although clean now, due to the fact they had cleaned her up before she came too, they seemed so dirty, as if still soaked in the blood rain. "Just now… before… I…" She knew what she wanted to say but couldn't find the words, no matter how hard she tried, she couldn't put together that sentence, she couldn't bring herself to say it. Daniel squeezed her hand gently lowering it to rest on the bed as he stood.

"I won't be a minute, I just realised… I need to get something." He offered her a short comforting smile and hurried out of the room, he closed the door quickly, leaning against it, tears running down his face as he listened to her heartfelt sobs through the wooden door. He didn't know what he had expected, what he thought he would face, but sitting there in the room with her was ten times worse than he imagined, she was heartbroken to the point it hurt him, he couldn't let her see him like this, she wouldn't understand. From inside the room he heard her crying, how he wanted to comfort her, to take her in his arms and tell her everything would be alright, but he knew it wouldn't be, he knew the impact this had on her, about the feelings she had about herself, what she had done back then she had done for the right reasons, but as far as Zo was concerned, there was no right reason to take another's life and now the one thing that had given her hope, the one phase he had heard her same time and time again, to give her comfort, now bore no meaning, now she had stained her hands with blood, she could no longer see a line dividing her from Marise.

He felt a hand on his shoulder; it startled him slightly to see Elly standing next to him.

"How is she?" She whispered knowing she could not be over heard, Daniel wiped the dampness from his own face, as he met Elly's eyes, there were a lot of things phoney about her, things he didn't trust, but she seemed to genuinely care.

"She's been crying for hours." He whispered matching her tone, suddenly aware of how much time had passed since he had left her, he really wanted to help, but he himself felt so helpless, he had no idea what it felt like to do what she had, he knew the grief of loss, that was a heavy burden to carry alone, but this was different, this was something he couldn't relate to, he didn't know where to start. More than anything he just wanted to take her in his arms telling her everything would be alright, to take away the pain she felt, for this he would give anything.

"It's just like when…" Elly stopped deciding not to continue with that train of conversation. "Shall I talk to her?" Daniel was surprised that Elly has even asked, normally she just went ahead and did what she felt like no questions asked, she seemed to have changed a little since they were in Knights-errent last, he was surprised, she had not only asked, but stood now waiting for a reply.

"No… I should… I just don't know what to say." He admitted shamefully. He worried if he went in there, he would say the wrong thing, make her feel worse, but he also knew this stupid act of saying nothing that he was doing now, must be a thousand times worse than him being there with her, trying to share her pain.

"Why waste your time? You'll think differently when I tell you who she really is, right Elaineor?" Acha appeared through the door, the inn had been deserted since they had returned with her, until this point everything had been silent, conversation had been carried out in low inaudible tones only to be heard by those involved. Acha however, was unconcerned who heard what she had to say. Elly simply stared her right in the eyes, and it was Acha who looked away.

"I will begin preparations for tonight; we still have much to do." She turned and walked away glancing back at Daniel, not having to wonder what truths would be told, she did however, choose to stay in earshot, although she knew what this was about, she had to determine how this would effect the mission, maybe it would be just the two of them as it was meant to be, maybe three when Eiji was safe.

"What do you mean?" Daniel questioned his voice no longer a whisper.

"That… that thing in there, the one pretending to be our friend, I wouldn't waste your concern on her, she wouldn't on you." Acha spat, Daniel could see the anger and disgust in her face as she looked towards the door. She had always seemed so calm, so delicate, seeing her like this was completely out of character, it made him question what had turned her this way, the person he saw now barely resembled his friend at all.

"What are you…" Daniel had a feeling he didn't need to ask what had ignited the vicious tones and dangerous attitude, he feared the truth had found her, before Zo had chance to inform her herself.

"She killed someone up there, but that's not all, she's a good actress, I'll give her that. I never would have guessed she knew all along." Acha spat pacing back and forth in front of the door trying to find a way to tell him, why was she hesitating? It was only the truth, but even so, she had to find the right words, after all, Daniel cared deeply for that monster, despite the hate she had for that creature, she had to consider Daniel's feelings in all this too.

"Knew what?" Daniel was getting tired of this, she knew something, although he was not sure if it was what he knew, he needed to find out, maybe try to diffuse this situation somehow.

"That I'm Night's daughter." Daniel gasped, his breath holding in it some relief, this had not been what he expected, Acha was Night's daughter? "She knew all this time, I'm his blood, don't you see, she planned it from the start. Pretending to care and befriend us, but really all she really wanted is that book. The final Grimoire." Acha let out a breath as she stopped pacing.

"That's insane. Firstly you don't share his blood, not now anyway, you could take that book no more than I could, or are you forgetting, that body is not yours, it's not your blood in there, nor his either!" Daniel snapped, suddenly, everything seemed to have become more complicated. "Secondly, it was me that fetched Zo to bring her to your aid, she never even knew of your existence before she saved your life." He gave a frustrated sigh.

"That's what she wants you to believe, don't you know who she is? Are you too blind to see it? The person in there claiming to be your friend is Marise Shi!" Acha spat the words at him, Daniel's anger for some reason seemed to die he lowered his head finding support against the wooden panels of the door, so she had learnt the truth, and worse, her reaction had been the one Zo had feared most.

"I know." He muttered quietly.

"Even if... you know?" She gasped suddenly realising what he had said, it hadn't been an answer she had imagined in *any* of the imaginary scenarios she ran through before finally approaching him. He watched Acha's face fill with betrayal and questions, how could he know? How could he know and not tell her?

"Yes." He admitted, glancing towards the door.

"You know and yet you still..." All the energy had died from Acha's voice now and had been replaced with confusion. "I don't understand... didn't you see her true nature before, when you were fighting for your lives? She killed someone; she sliced his head clean off his body. That's all she's ever done, all she ever does is kill people, she's a murderer! A murderer who will do whatever it takes to get what she wants!"

"True nature you say?" Daniel asked quietly his voice filled with dormant anger. "If Zo had not done what she did, there would be more dead than just one you can, add me and Elly to that list and every person here that possesses a parasite. Someone has shown their true colours today, but it wasn't her." He turned away from her placing is hand on the door. He was so angry at this whole mess, he was angry at Acha for acting in the very way Zo had feared, he was angry at Elly for bringing them to this town in the first place, it was clearly out of their way and as far as he could see there was no real reason for them to be here, surely any other town would have been just as a suitable for planning a rescue mission. He was angry that once again Zo had been put in a position where she had to protect him, to sacrifice her beliefs in order to keep him safe, but more than anything he was angry at himself, angry at not being there for her when she needed him the most.

"What do you mean more dead?"

"That man she killed had some kind of alpha parasite planted in him; he was using it to control the actions of the town people by controlling the parasites, but..." Daniel stopped to look at her, it was clear she knew this story.

"The Hikoriti... I knew it had been separated from its host... and its host's death would cause the death of others if it lived but..." Acha remembered the information given to her by Sara, poor Sara who now had nowhere left to turn, who as soon as they arrived back, had vanished without a trace except for the note she had left with the time and place to meet her friend. How could Daniel even try to justify what she had done? One life or many it's still murder all the same, is she meant to understand because, perhaps this time, Marise Shi killed for the right reason? What about all those that came before that? "But that doesn't change a thing, she's a heartless murderer!"

"Really, do you think so?" Daniel's voice still oozed with his dormant anger. "Then why have I been standing outside here for Gods know how long listening to her cry? Listening to her torture herself over what happened back there."

"It's a trick." Acha hissed, why wasn't he listening? She was trying to save him.

"If you really think so, maybe it is better for you to leave, find some friends as fair weathered as you… then again, you're no shining angel, if I remember correctly you killed someone before my father found you, funny I don't remember you shedding a single tear." He turned the handle on the door, he had stood listening to her too long now, there was a place he was meant to be and looking back over the last few hours he was disappointed he had not been there.

"That was different." She protested.

"Oh yes, that's right, unlike Zo, you did it to save your own life." He pushed the door open, closing and locking it behind him, clearly finishing the conversation as he left her standing in the hall. "Hey." He sat on the bed besides her she looked so pale, so fragile. "How are you feeling? I'm sorry I was so long." He smiled gently looking into her reddened eyes as more tears fell from them.

"She's right." Zo cried she never looked at Daniel she just sat in the bed looking down at her hands. "I am a murderer." She looked away out of her window to the high place still feeling the rain falling on her skin, burning her with its touch.

"You heard that?" Daniel pulled her towards him; she didn't protest she just stared over the arms that surrounded her, her vision still fixed on the high place, the place of her nightmares. What that creature said in Knights-errent about the difference between her and Marise being the ability to kill was meaningless now, how she wished it had been true, but if it had been, then would her actions not have killed those possessing the parasite? There was only one result to whichever path she took and that was the path of a murderer.

"How could I not? But… I didn't know." Zo whispered Daniel tightened his grip on her protectively, he had never seen her like this before, she had always taken everything in her stride, even leaving. Sure she had her moments, her tears and upsets, but given the situation who wouldn't, but she was always strong enough to overcome her feelings, to do what needed to be done, but right now, despite his company she seemed so isolated, so lost, it was almost as if she was nothing more than an empty shell, barely a shadow of her old self remaining.

"Know what?" He whispered pulling her closer, holding her now so tightly he feared he would crush her, if only he could make the hurting stop, erase the last few weeks of her life, he would have done things so differently, first of all, she would not have been there when Elly visited, they would have been far away.

"What she said before, I didn't know she was Night's daughter, even if I had it wouldn't matter? It wouldn't have made any difference."

"I know." He shushed her gently rocking her slightly as he kissed the top of her head.

"I killed him Daniel..." She said emptily. "With my own hands, I killed him." She covered her face with her hands again, pulling away from his embrace as she did so, what right did she have to be comforted for her unforgivable act?

"Shh, but if you hadn't I, nor most of this town would be here now, that one life saved so many."

"But... his life was not mine to take... I am a healer, I use magic to give life, not take it... I am no better than... her... no, I am her..." Daniel grabbed her again pulling her back to hold her tightly.

"Hear anything good?" Elly's voice startled Acha, she turned quickly to look at her unsure of how long she had been watching, unlike most people Elly was different, she could never tell when she was near. "You know, listeners never here the best of themselves." With that she walked away, Acha watched her for a moment before rushing after her.

"Wait, Elly, I need to ask you something." Elly slowed her pace smiling to herself as she waited.

***

When Daniel and Zo finally emerged they found Elly and Acha waiting outside her room, she looked down to the floor, she couldn't stand the way they were looking at her, Elly's looks of sympathy and concern, versus Acha's looks of hate and betrayal.

"I'm sorry we have things to do... I should not have been so selfish, what plans do we have for Eiji's rescue?" Elly stepped in front of her touching her chin with her cold hand lifting her face to look her in the eyes, Zo looked away, although Elly did not move her hand.

"You needed time, are you feeling better now?" Elly moved her hand as Zo's eyes filled with tears as she moved from quickly away from her touch. Better, how could she be feeling better? She had become that which she detested more than anything in the world.

"We don't have much time." She turned her back to both Elly and Acha wrapping her arms across herself protectively.

"Very well, come, I will discuss my ideas, although there is little we can really do until we see where he is being held, but we can still start looking for the antidote. Daniel, you still have the map right?" Daniel nodded passing Elly the map before he and Zo followed her into the dining room. "Right what did that thing say about the Narca berries?" Elly glanced around; she remembered all too well what he had said but wondered if anyone else would care to volunteer the information.

"The berry is on pirates' isle, the land next to there with a new king is where Eiji will be." Elly smiled as Acha's appeared in the doorway before moving to join them.

"Pirates isle it is then." Elly unrolled the map.

"These fixed locations, each have a counter part in our world right?" Daniel crossed the church and the court locations off the map, well this one here, this is my home, it would be little more than a village, so that's out of the question. But in our world, there is a castle that's just had a new king right?"

"Yes, that old guy that gave us a lift to the rings of fire said something about it, Ishitar Island wasn't it?" Zo suddenly joined the conversation, she had to make an effort, her own self pity could not jeopardise Eiji's life, or she would be more of a monster than she already believed herself to be.

"He said something about a new heir to the throne." Elly smiled, this was more like it, although she had already formulated her own ideas about how this journey would plan out, if they were to get through this, friends or not, they needed to act like a team.

"Yes, he was taking his finest stock as an offering, he said the ship left last night meaning…"

"We can cross off all the fixed points on this island as well that leaves these two." Daniel pointed to two small locations on the map. "But this is the only one with an island near it…"

"It's also the only one with a castle." Elly smiled. "But we were after the antidote remember." Daniel glanced to Elly, again knowing she had arrived at this conclusion a long time before they had even began this discussion, but he also knew exactly what she was trying to do, and for this single act, he was grateful, perhaps, she wasn't quite as cold as she liked them to think, in fact, she had really changed since their first meeting.

"Well, we could always ask about legends of pirates." Acha stepped a little closer to the map. "Don't you think the shape of those islands is a little odd?" Daniel turned the map a little as if to study it.

"You're right it looks like the constellation of Tredious the legendary pirate." Daniel added, glancing across to Zo, he remembered how back in Crowley she use to tell him the stories behind the names of the stars, the more common ones he knew himself, but there were so many he had never heard, so many adventures he had not imagined, every word she spoke was like magic bringing the stories to life before his very eyes, now her empty gaze was fixed steadily on the map, although he doubted she was truly seeing it.

"Right then, I suggest make a move, after getting there, finding this place is down to us, that means pulling every resource, asking every traveller, we cant afford to take a wrong turn." Elly folded the map up passing it back to Daniel.

"But it's still hours to sunset." He commented as he took the map from her folding it up placing it in his pocket.

"True, but by the time you have finished faffing about it will be about time…" She winked at Zo who forced a smile. "Besides, it's a good chance to gather supplies, who knows what we'll be up against."

"You're the most organised we'll leave that to you." Daniel smiled knowing instantly what she meant, again he appreciated the effort she was making, she nodded at him as if to acknowledge his request, but they both knew there was more to that single gesture than the others would think. "Acha and I have things we need to discuss."

"Me?" Acha's voice shrieked with surprise.

"Yes, you, me and Zo." He answered

"I think I'll pass." She looked to Zo wrinkling her nose slightly as if looking at something that disgusted her. "I have nothing to say to the likes of her." Acha turned and began to walk away.

"But…" Daniel was stopped by Zo's interruption.

"It's ok." She sighed. "I don't blame her." Daniel watched as Acha left the room, as he watched her he couldn't help wondering what happened to the promise of truce that occurred earlier.

"Zo, can I meet you in Knights-errent? I have a few things I need to do before I can come."

"Sure." She smiled sadly. "Take all the time you need." She watched with a sinking feeling in her stomach as he hurried after Acha.

***

"I thought I would find you here." Daniel stood in the doorway of the main lounge, Acha never looked away from her fixed gaze outside the enormous bay window, the farms and mountains stretched as far as the eye could seen, no matter where you stood, you would always be facing the mountains, right now, Acha gazed out over the ring of volcanoes they had travelled through to arrive here.

"Daniel, I don't understand." She sighed finally turning to look at him. "You know who she is, what she is. She is the very personification of evil, yet you defend her, why?" Daniel pulled up a small wooden chair.

"Acha, I, more than anyone in this group, has a right to hate her, to agree with you, but…" He gave a sigh, how could he possibly explain this to someone who was so content with hating her?

"You? Hate her?" She spat venomously. "The way you feel about her is clear, how can you even begin to state such a claim?"

"Acha, I trust you, and I know that you would not betray my trust. What I am about to tell you must never… and I mean never, leave this room, once said, it must never be mentioned again, understand?"

"I…" Acha paused for a moment and nodded, after all, as angry as she was, it wasn't Daniel she was angry with, she and Daniel were still friends and as such she would be true to her word, just as no doubt he had been true to his by not telling her the true identity of the monster they travelled with.

"Just before my seventeenth birthday I received a letter from my brother, it came to my school, mail from him always did, my parents never forgave him for joining the mercenaries, after all, my mother has seen what happens to those on both side of war and could not understand why her own child would wish to cause such harm, and as you know, my father is a like minded pacifist. Anyway as I said, I received a letter, my brother was writing to tell me he had leave coming and to invite me over for the duration of the fortnight on mainland. With the help of my lecturer, who knew my brother well, we convinced my parents it was a field trip during the term holiday to study the festival of Mainland, every year a group of students would travel across to see it; it wasn't hard to convince them. They agreed I could go and even gave me a bit towards the trip, I worked every afternoon after school for a month, earning money however I could, until finally, it was time to go, my brother met me at the harbour." Daniel gazed out of the window seeing the past as it played before him. "I remember the impatience as I was waiting for the boat to stop; it had been three years since I had last seen him, many thoughts raced through my mind, would he know me? Would he still want me around? At last I saw him; he had grown so much, barely had the boat hit the dock than I was off the ship embracing him, right in the middle of the port. I was meant to stay for the entirety of his leave, although I had barely been there a few days when my visit was cut short. I lay in the small mercenary camp building, my brother was now quite a high rank so he got his own small house, they all did on account of them never leaving the base except for duty or leave, I use the term base loosely it was really just a small village created and built by them. Anyway, I'm getting off track... I lay in bed one night looking at the stars through my window, the village was lit only by candles you see, it was one of those villages that don't really exist, secret in every sense of the word, to light it up would invite travellers. The skies were clear that night and there was comforting warmth to the air, I remember looking out at them thinking about when I was back home, wondering if they were the same stars he would see." He paused, now beginning to wonder if he was doing the right thing in telling her this, with the exception of Stephen, he had spoke of these events to no one, but he had to make her see things the way he did, it was the only way to put an end to this uncomfortable situation, he decided to continue. "It was around midnight, I was so filled with excitement after all, there I was with my big brother, he had always been somewhat of a hero to me, a quiet knock came at the door, hearing the low tones of hushed conversation between my brother and a stranger, I crept out of bed listening at the door, I couldn't catch much of the conversation, just bits where the stranger's voice broke, something about a girl who, later I discovered to be Marise Shi, had arrived at the neighbouring village. I heard my brother's footsteps pacing across the floor as if in silent contemplation. I watched through the keyhole unable to see the stranger but aware that my brother kept glancing this way, then I heard his words all to clearly, words that shattered my very being"...

..."My little brother sleeps in the room next door, should I not return, please see he gets home safely."

"Sir in all due respect you are on leave, I only inform you so you may watch the village in my absence, I should not even ask, all law dictates you are not here"

"I know..." Daniel watched through the keyhole as his brother fastened his sword around his waist pulling his coat on. "Your wife is with child, it would be foolish for you to attend and deprive your child of a father" although the tones of their conversation were urgent they never rose above a whisper.

"Sir." The stranger moved to stop my brother but backed down.

"I order you to stay here, protect this village, if you disobey me so help me I will have you disciplined, get the troops to follow once they are adequately prepared." His brother, Adam, left the room, Daniel watched him hurry out through the window, before forcing it open, aware of the door behind him opening as he jumped from the window in pursuit of his brother, he ran as fast as his legs would carry him pursuing his brother towards the red glow of the skyline. The town itself was one they had passed through, not too far from the port. Daniel stood in the cloak of the forest the smell of death hung heavily in the air, corpses of the townsfolk littered the floor like grass across a meadow. Despite this as Daniel watched in frozen horror, his brother did not hesitate, he rushed onward into the town, all the time Daniel stood watching in paralysed fear he wondered how so much damage could be caused by one person, it was then he first saw her, she was not a person but a demon, her hair was crimson red, flying wildly in the breeze created by her swift movements, Daniel's heart leapt with both fear and amazement, with just one swing of her sword she struck down three men with seemingly little effort, she was of his age, if not younger, yet she showed such mastery in the art of murder. She stood for but a second placing something in her bag that until this point she had held within her hand as she fought. It was then Adam stepped forward, before his attack had even landed she was clear from the striking path, her sword stabbed through his back as she flipped over him. Daniel screamed running from the bushes somehow finding within his hands a sword the adrenaline rushing as he charged to protect his brother, hoping, begging that it was not too late to save him. With all his being he wanted to kill her, he wanted to drive the sword through her blackened heart and watch her die, the gap between them was closing the heavy sword lifted under the flag of protection and poised with the strength of his anger, from nowhere he heard a voice around him, within that brief second he felt someone pulling him back, with such force he lost his breath and the sword in one swift movement, he fought and fought for freedom as the figure wrapped itself over him protectively refusing to comply to his demands, as he screamed after his brother, Marise walked closer and closer, as she did so the figures grip grew stronger, the wild energy and thoughts of vengeance now being replaced with the fear of death, a death that stood before him, she flicked her sword clean of blood as she stared at the figure that held him.

"So he's the one you choose?" Those were the words she spoke although to him they made no sense, she turned her cold gaze him. "It's pointless to continue I have what I came for." Suddenly Daniel realised the figure that had stopped him had now not only released him, but seemed to have vanished into the air, leaving him to wonder if ever a figure had truly grabbed him or if it was just his mind compensating for his sudden fear paralysis, a paralysis that even now he felt gripping him as he sat looking up to her, she looked him straight in the eyes, he found himself unable to move no matter how hard he tried, although if he could move he wasn't sure if he would flight or flee, but it was a choice no longer his to decide, his body had chose not to obey any commands from its master. He flinched as she thrust the hilt of a sword towards him, as he looked at it, he realised it was his brother's, he took it in his hand once more aware of the weight of a weapon used to take another's life, aware of the weight of the burden his brother had carried since he chose to become a mercenary. She sheathed her sword as she turned away, she paused for a moment, something about her stance changed, then she spoke, her voice somehow different from before, almost trapped.

"The blood you stain your hands with will never clean, just be covered by more blood, if you want to, take your revenge take it now I welcome it." She continued walking. Words could not explain how much he wanted to ram the sword through her, to accept and win her challenge, but for all his anger and hatred he could not move and she just got further and further away. A cold hand touched his shoulder breaking his gaze on the place she had vanished.

"Do not be in such a hurry to die." A voice whispered in his ears, his touch was the same as the one who had held him, the one who had protected him from that murderer. The hand was still on his shoulder when he heard someone call his name.

"Daniel." The voice screamed grabbing him as the sword fell from his trembling hands "Daniel are you alright?" He felt the cold hand recede...

…"I wondered after, how it was that my brother's friend did not see the figure that had saved me, I tried so hard to answer but the words seemed to stick in my throat as I knelt staring at the place I had last seen her. I don't remember how I got home, I just woke in my bed one night, mum said a doctor had brought me back from the field trip and that I had been very sick. For a minute, on waking, I thought it was all a dream, no, I wished it was all a dream… But the truth is, Marise Shi killed my brother." He stopped, amazed that now, after all this time he had managed to once again tell the story from start to finish, his throat still hurting from the pain back then.

"Daniel, I had no idea, I'm so sorry." Acha could think of nothing to say for a moment, but that moment quickly past. "Then surely, you of all people should understand."

"You still don't get it do you? Zo is not that person, if she was…"

"No, I think it is you who doesn't understand, there is no Zo and Marise, Marise is just a name she was given, a name she used, an excuse to pass the blame to someone else. They aren't two separate people; Zo just chose to use that to her advantage just as she chooses not to remember."

"How can you state such a claim?"

"Zo use to live here, in this very village, she came here when she was twelve, her childhood friend just died, she sat in the same room with another friend, Sara, from the café, but she claims not to remember her, yet when Zo first met her, there was no Marise which means if this whole façade is true, then she should remember being 'Zo' thus remember her friends of old. So how come she doesn't?" Acha gave a frustrated sigh he just wasn't listening? Couldn't he see that she was right?

"That would be my fault." Elly entered the room; neither Acha nor Daniel could guess how long she had been there. "Sorry to intrude I could hear your screams from down the hall."

"What do you mean your fault?" Daniel questioned suspiciously.

"It's true what you said, they are one and the same, but that phase only lasted through the first months of her training, we pushed her harder knowing a line would develop where Zo would stop and Marise would start. That had been the plan all along, after all, all Hectarians possess this darkness, and the darkness in this case, was made to take on its own identity through a serious of pla… unfortunate events, that was how he had wanted it. Eventually, Zo vanished entirely, she no longer regained control. After weeks of training with Marise, we ensured she had been fully sealed away. Then one day, the seal seemed to weaken, little moments would filter through where Marise was no longer in control. Blackwood, saw a few of these, but luckily, I had noticed it first. The night Marise vanished, I went to her room, using ancient lore I created a potion to seal Marise away, leaving Zo with no memories of what had transpired, after all, she had been Blackwood's assassin too long at that point, to the day she remains unaware of anything that transpired after she left home to go to college at the start of her twelfth year, to start with I would imagine that she would have been unable to recall events even before that. I wanted her to be happy, and I knew that could never be with Blackwood pulling the strings, as time passed I thought I had waited too long to bring her back, when Zo had vanished completely, I thought the chance had passed forever, but thankfully, I was wrong."

"Why are you telling us this?" Daniel questioned as Acha sat looking rather sick.

"I do not claim to know Zo, my kinship and loyalty *is* with Marise, and I serve her, that is my sole purpose at this time, but one thing is blatantly clear, even if you are too blind to see it. Zo holds you both very dear, dearer than anything in this world, every time she is forced to draw that sword, she loses a part of herself to Marise, thus was the symbolism behind the blade she forged, to bind dark and light, but each forever will fight for control, but in equal measures, the darkness will always win and that blade will eventual turn to a blade of darkness. Sometimes, you won't notice Marise just under her consciousness when she fights, but sometimes, Marise awakens. Either way, each summoning of the blade takes more away from Zo, this she understands all too well. One day when she draws that sword, there will be no return, her time is measured, yet each time you are threatened, she fights on, concerns for herself not even flickering in the back of her mind, she is willing to sacrifice herself for you, that is true friendship. It's a shame only one of you sees that."

"But before, she killed someone…. I saw her." Acha protested pathetically, she could not deny Elly had explained more than needed, but as she said; her mission was to serve Marise.

"I believe, if you were listening, that Daniel has already explained that. If I were you, I would be looking at the big picture; did it come easy to her? Did she just draw her sword and have done with? Or did she try everything else in her power first? Now I suggest that we get ready to leave. Acha, the rune on your arm will only pass through boundaries if the rune symbol says it can do so. Do you understand?" Elly placed some ink and a quill on the table and walked away followed by Daniel.

Chapter sixteen

Zo arrived in Knights-errent long before the others, departing straight after Daniel and Acha had left, much Elly's disapproval, she had gone to great measures to warn her it may not be safe travelling to such a place before the sun had set. Despite this warning, she had agreed to help by detaining the others while she did what she needed to. Zo had lied about why she wished to start out so early and was certain Elly had picked up on this, yet all the same she had agreed to help, right now more than anything she wanted to be alone, the events of the high place had left her questioning many things, she had believed to be the truth. It left her with many questions, the first of which was why Elly had decided they should travel to the secret town, instead of any of the nearby towns or villages, was it truly just so they could rest undisturbed? If that had been the case, there was surely an error of judgement there. But more than anything, as she sat, she wondered what else she could have done, the answer nothing, now seemed to provide some comfort, she had done the only thing she could have in the situation she had been presented with, she had taken the only possible action. For this reason, could she consider forgiving herself for taking the life of another? After all, by doing so she saved the lives of so many people. There was another voice to her reason, although it took some time for her to realise it was not a thought of her own.

'Why worry? He would have been dead now anyway.' It dismissed her decision as irrelevant trying to sway her to accept its belief that human life was unimportant, she pushed the voice aside, that had been another reason she had wanted to come here, she just wanted time to think, as the potion from Collateral began to take effect, the small whispers she had heard telling her how to think, what to say, how to act, had become stronger, she was doing things she would not normally consider by second nature. What were once just fragments of memories, now becoming small scenes acting out before her, scenes that made her stomach turn, could she truly be this person? A person who hated and destroyed so much without a second thought?

She stared at her sword, taking in the details of the finally carved hilt; it seemed to weigh nothing in her hands, although to her mind its weight had become immeasurable. Each life taken pulled on the sword increasing its weight and the more she remembered, the heavier it grew, a life was indeed a heavy burden. She clicked the hilt up and down unaware she was doing so while she thought, several paths racing through her mind as she tried to find solutions to that which would lie before her. She felt now, more than ever, that her time was limited, growing shorter by each passing second, but before she could surrender, she had to see Daniel and Acha to safety, her sword and her future, no matter how short, would not be weighed down further by her failure to keep them safe.

She liked her life better this way, for the first time ever she had friends, when she was younger she dreamt of a life like this, but her retention of Hectarian powers saw to it no one would accept her, after all, she was different to them, and people feared that which was different, that was why even today there were villages where both Demi-humans and humans would not be accepted. With all her heart she wished things could be different, she wished that she did not have to return to the purpose she was trained for, she wished Marise would be the one to vanish, but she felt it more often that she cared to think, that dark desire to destroy those who opposed her, those who so much as looked at her the wrong way. But she was not Marise, but she *was* growing stronger to the point she, now, nearly always, felt her on the tip of her mind, projecting her feelings towards her, even she herself was beginning to doubt they were not one, especially, since there was no longer a definable line between her and Marise, what was to say she was not truly her in a sleeping state now waking?

There was at least one part of Marise she envied, and that was the complete unconcern for peoples opinions, Marise, from what she understood, would have felt nothing for the betrayal of Acha, more than likely, she would simply have killed her, she had heard the whispers to her mind when she challenged her in the court and again when she saw her at the high place, the whispers that told her how much better she would feel if she took her sword to the traitor, so far, she had managed to ignore them, yet now, they were becoming more powerful, she just hoped they were not stronger than her. The inability to be hurt and pushed around by others was another thing she envied. When she took the potion from Collateral, she knew there would be consequences but she had never imagined the extent of them, never had she imagined such clarity, then again, nor had she accepted to discover she would have harboured such a violent past. The blood rain had brought back visions of more terror than she had imagined in her darkest nightmare, more so because the images she beheld were fact, not illusions created by the demons of sleep reminding you of the horrors that could befall the world, but visions that were in fact memories of events that had not only, occurred it had been she herself who had created them.

"Penny for your thoughts." Zo jumped slightly as Daniel moved to sit beside her, she had been so far away at that moment, she had not even noticed his appearance until it was too late.

"You build your walls so high Daniel Starfire." She glanced at him wondering if the walls he built, were to hide his feelings about her act, she pushed that thought to one side as they fell, granting her access to the concern and worry he was feeling towards her, the flood of emotions made her falter slightly. "I didn't even sense your presence."

"I think you're just distracted." He smiled warmly. "Acha said something just now that got me thinking... how much do you remember? I don't mean how much you want to know, how much do you know? You have been very quiet since Collateral, I began thinking surely that potion had some effect, but I'm guessing you don't really want to talk about it."

"I have never deceived you about anything. But... lately, since Collateral, I remember fragments... It's because she's getting stronger again, her memories filter through... But I never lied to you."

"I never said you did, I just don't think it's something you should have to deal with on your own." The more he had spoken to Acha after leaving her, the more he realised how little Zo had really said recently, she had been quiet, the conversations between them almost strained as she maintained her front with that heartbreaking smile.

"Initially... there was a slow join between us, it seemed to develop as I was trained, she was my darkness, you see every Hectarian is born neutral, made up of equal parts good and bad, that's why in major wars they never really picked sides just fought for those who they stayed with, but if a Hectarian chose to fight for good, the darkness gets stored away, so while they fight the world's darkness, they also fight their own. When a Hectarian goes to darkness, their good is suppressed, it was once said that darkness is stronger, but the light has more numbers, those embracing darkness do not struggle against the light, as those who choose light do against the darkness. Marise was my darkness nurtured by my trainers she became her own being. Near the beginning I started to suffer blackouts, I'm not sure what triggered them really, but I began to wonder why no one noticed my absence, as time passed the blackouts stretched into longer phases, I began to think that surely they would notice I was not around, I mean, I wouldn't be in lectures or at the meal table, surely someone would notice my absence after all, I was the only student there, I couldn't exactly get lost in the crowd." She gave a sad, half-hearted laugh. "The day I realised why they hadn't missed me, was that day that the darkness won. The next thing I knew I woke in this strange land with nothing behind me but darkness, not even knowing that which I spoke of just."

"And now?" He questioned moving closer, he extended his hand to comfort her as she looked away, pulling back as she began to speak.

"Now it's sunset and the final darkness is approaching, this time it will be eternal." She sighed, she knew she was fighting a losing battle to outrun the setting sun, to outrun the wave of darkness that crept ever closer.

"I guess that makes it somewhat ironic to be trapped in perpetual light, never seeing darkness of either world." Daniel paused, he was not really sure what words of comfort he could offer and in a very Eiji fashion, he had said the first thing that came to mind in order to avoid a drawn out silence. "Zo, you'll get through this, you've said it yourself, something's different now, you have friends, friends that will sacrifice themselves for you. We will protect you with every bit as much determination and commitment as you protect us, we will not let you lose yourself." He smiled as she looked up at him. "I promise." She looked to him meaningfully as he offered a warm smile.

Elly appeared on the tile bed she had chosen as her own sitting up as Zo and Daniel moved across to join her.

"It seems at the moment the only real choice we have is to follow rumour and head to the coast, we are certain to encounter a town or something before arriving there." Elly stated unaware of any of the conversation that had occurred prior to her sudden arrival, she walked to the door stopped only by Zo's quiet protesting.

"Aren't we waiting for Acha?" She asked gently.

"I do not think that necessary, do you really think it's wise having someone so fickle watching your back?" Elly didn't turn to look at Zo, she only paused in the doorway.

"But what if something..." She protested the rest of her words lost in Elly's harsh words.

"Did she concern herself over you? I think not." She spat.

"She had every right to be disappointed in me, I should have told her the truth when I first learned it, I should have trusted her." Although she spoke the words, Zo couldn't help wondering if she had told Acha, if her reaction would have been any different to the one she received now.

"Like she does you, you mean?"

"Why should she? True I have never lied to her but I haven't been truthful with her either, that is just as bad."

"But nor was she truthful with you." Elly sighed still not turning back. "Tell me did you know she is Night's daughter? Did you know she is related to the person behind this? Related to the person that drove you from your home? Her deception is the same as yours all but for small detail, hers was deliberate."

"What does it matter? A persons past and bloodline do not dictate who they are; such things are meaningless, so what if Night is her father? What does that mean exactly? Nothing." She snapped feeling her temper rising, Daniel placed a hand on her shoulder calming her; he saw Acha standing behind her in the shadows.

"You clearly differ in opinions there." Elly stated coldly she too was aware of Acha's appearance despite the fact she had not turned to see it.

"It means you can use her to get the last book... or at least that's what she thinks...right?" Daniel looked right at her as he spoke, Zo turned slowly to see her standing in the shadows.

"Well, why else would she take me in, look after me, protect me with her life?" Acha's voice seemed vicious, she honestly couldn't see why someone would do that for her, for anyone in fact, it's like Sophie said, there is always a motive for every act of kindness, discovering it is the hard part.

"Is that what you think?" She whispered turning away, Daniel was the only one to see the extent of the pain, the depth of the blow she had struck, her heavy lashes lowered to the floor, despite this, she tried to keep her head high, not turning back to look at the one whose word had struck her a deadly blow. "We should go, Eiji is in trouble, or have you forgotten." Those were her only words, they were low and empty ringing of a pain she tried to conceal, she winced against the pain as she pulled the satchel over her shoulder, it was a pain, just hours ago that would have brought her comfort, but now it was a pain that was nothing more than a reminder of a broken boundary. "Let's go, there is a lot of ground to cover." She glanced at Elly quickly as she moved to permit her to pass, she followed quickly not looking back to see if they followed.

"Mari, it's always been like this, allies they just cause you pain, they are a weakness you are better off without."

"And you? Are you not an ally?" She questioned in monotone.

"That is different." She stated truthfully, Marise was the only one to truly understand the reason behind her being, she knew they were more than allies and Elly was no weakness.

"True, how else could it be you do not age, I suppose if you are lucky on the draw. You could match... if not surpass her skill, so how come she was sent as the assassin? How come she gathered the Grimoire with such a clear superior, there is so much I still don't understand."

"As the darkness comes, you will understand more than, I daresay, you want to." That single comment made Zo question how long Elly had been present before making her presence known.

"But..." She sighed, resisting the temptation to look back and see if they were alright. "The more I remember, the stronger she becomes, back there, I felt her watching, I felt the desire to eliminate the weakness rising up within me, what if... what if I can't stop her and one of my friends get hurt?"

"I will not lie to you, it is my job to protect Mari, but she is the darkness you created, so it is just as important I protect you from anything that might harm you... understand?" Elly glanced back to see Acha and Daniel following behind just out of hearing range, no doubt a subtle gesture enforced by Daniel, she sighed to herself 'besides, he said they have a role to play in this.' Elly thought to herself, a subtle smile crossed her face. 'I wonder if they would be so quick to try to protect her if they knew what she will do.'

***

Eiji's eyes were blinded with light as they opened, he was no longer in the dark place with Seiken, but now lay surrounded in some sort of light barrier, it arched over his head as if a solid field, almost like the ward Zo had used in Abaddon, yet this one was not quite as stable, it was created by several mirrors bouncing and fanning the light from some sort of tunnel above him, across the entire field, different colours danced. Footsteps echoed around the room drawing closer, he closed his eyes quickly hoping to learn something of his captors.

"But that's what I am saying, there was some strange activity." A soft voice protested with a gentle annoyance, almost as though she had said it time and time again without it reaching the ears of the person she addressed.

"As I said before, it's impossible, this field, prevents all external contact, being an Elementalist, his water based nature will be diluting the poison as we speak so he will come too soon..." Eiji opened his eyes again, involuntarily letting out a heartfelt groan as pain exploded through his stomach, the two figures rushed to the outside of the field.

"Where... am I?" He whispered surprised at hearing the weakness in his own voice.

"This is castle Iris; you were brought here after you collapsed." A girl not much older than him crouched in front of the field, her pale blond hair falling forwards as she moved closer, as his eyes regained focused, he saw she wore an outfit that resembled that of a doctor's aid.

"Who... are you?"

"Me? I'm Julie; I have been monitoring you all night."

"Julie enough, do not associate yourself with criminals." Eiji glanced up slowly to see a dark haired common-place man standing besides her now placing his hand on her shoulder.

"That does not mean he is any less entitled to my care." She snapped as she did so she covered her mouth.

"Do as you are bid, now he is conscious you are no longer needed, don't waste our medicine on someone who will soon be dead. Anyway I want you away from here, word has it there is a rescue party on its way, they are fools to think they can overpower the defence of these walls to save this murderer." He spat.

"Murderer?" Eiji slowly pushed himself into a sitting position feeling his head spin as he did so,

"You think we are so uneducated as not to recognise one of the marked bandits? Lord Seiken told us of you, once we have destroyed your rescuers you are to be drawn and quartered at sunrise." Julie opened her mouth to protest at the man's words. "Silence, I will have no more of your 'objections' Lord Seiken spoke the truth, how dare you question him?"

"But…"

"To your room, I will tolerate no more of your insubordination, you do gooders are all the same, that's how you end up dead."

"Yes sir." She lowered her head walking away he listened until her footsteps had completely faded.

"The other marked bandits should be arriving soon, even in the unlikely event that they do make it here, your whole cell is a trap, the second the light is broken, boom! No more bandits"

"Marked bandits?" Eiji questioned as the arms he was resting on grew weak shaking under his weight.

"Is the poison affecting your brain, or is this one of your tricks?" The man scolded pointing to a large wanted poster on the sterile white walls. "This fortress is the best place to end your days; Lord Benjamin has become unstoppable since Lord Seiken passed down the rune of power." Eiji felt himself begin to sway as the rest of the words became an incoherent jumble of sounds, his vision twisted the figure in the room until finally a swirling darkness took him once more, he was aware of falling, it seemed as if he fell forever until he hit the cold floor, although really it was less than a second.

***

"Eiji pay attention!" His master's scolding voice echoed through the air, at the sound of it a few nearby birds took to flight, he looked up to see his master standing above him as he sat in the small rocky stream.

"Sorry master I…"

"It's alright, go on, be off with you, you're no use to me like this." Eiji nodded as his master smiled gently, he had barely been back a week and already his student has lost his focus.

Eiji jumped to his feet and disappeared into the woods where only moments ago, he had seen the figure. A boy no older than eight sat on a fallen tree in the woods waiting for him to catch up; he swung his legs back and forth his heals making a small thud each time they hit the bark.

"I have the information on that town you wanted, mind you, it wasn't easy. Marise Shi burnt it to the ground not too long ago; those who survived are thinly spread across the continent, if at all they do exist at all. It seems that it never endured much fortune."

"Tell me what did you discover?" Eiji's voice trembled with excitement, this town, the one that had been destroyed he knew to be his home and now for the first time ever, he was to hear news of his home, perhaps if he knew where he came from, he could understand more about his future, more about the person he was and why his parents had felt the need to do what they did.

"Historically it has been the centre for all major disasters, earthquakes, floods, fires, droughts, rumour has it the area of land it was built on has a strong elemental link to Severaine." The young boy swung his legs smiling, the Severaine was a myth barely spoke of these days, only those who spent their time in the company of books could even have chance of discovering its existence, even so, for most it was a forbidden topic, the boy had come to understand it was not that people didn't know about it, but feared what remembering and discussing it could do.

"Meaning?"

"Meaning its location, although a beneficial to the people living there, stands on the border of all natural environments, water, forest, mountains and such, meaning it creates a problem as to which one will dominate the area of land deemed neutral, the elements fight over the right to the border, this has subjected the area to high rate natural disasters." The boy shook his head. "Anyway years ago now, it's said Night himself rose to attack the small village, rumour had it, something of great importance was hidden there but for some reason he left empty handed, yet even so, most of the town folks survived, then just two weeks ago, Night sent a warrior demanding some form of literature, operating a different policy to Night, the entire village was destroyed, a rain of death and terror of the likes none has seen, this wave continued until the target was handed over, when the priest handed the book over and begged for the lives of the town people, you see he swore to this warrior he would get it, when he returned he found the town, but for a few people, had all but been wiped out, he surrendered the book, begging for the remaining lives of the small town, the warrior laughed smiled viciously before continuing the killing spree."

"Well what was this book? Why is it so important?"

"Well it seems that when the Idliod sealed Night's power, because of the area's link to Severaine, it was a location selected to hide one of the Grimoire."

"Grimoire?" Eiji questioned rubbing the back of his head, he knew this story but wanted to be completely sure about the implications of the tale told,

"You know, the seven books used to seal Night's power. It's rumoured that this was what Night was after, all those years ago, only... they hadn't even been created then, people today seem to forget this, that means there was something else." The young boy sighed, a few moments of silence passed between them. "I'm sorry but I have to ask, is it true, you were born there?"

"Erm... well, sure that's what I'm told... Did anyone survive?"

"I'm not sure." The boy sighed. "The story itself came from a traveller who was passing through at the time, an Elementalist like yourself. Gods know how he made it out alive, that's why we know so much of the final events. Although in fairness, the only person who *really* knows what happened that day is that traveller, and no one can even remember what he looked like and even I can tell it has been fabricated and twisted as it passed from one to another…" The boy paused as if in thought. "Is there anyone you wish us to try to locate?"

"Sorry?" Eiji suddenly realised the young boy was waiting for a response to a question he hadn't even heard as he stared unseeingly to the rich forest before him.

"Is there anyone you wish us to locate?" The boy repeated again looking questioningly at Eiji.

"No… No thanks." He smiled passing the young boy a parcel that until now he had kept hidden deep within his shirt.

"Very well, if there is anything, you know where to find me right?" The young boy jumped from the tree and began to run.

"I sure do PI, thanks… I hope it helps your mum." Eiji called after him as he entered deeper into the forest.

Eiji had been all to happy to give the boy as much medicine as he needed, but after PI saw how much the first dose helped his mother, he insisted he worked to pay off the debt, there was nothing Eiji could think of that he wanted, but PI had always been this way, once a week he would come to Eiji to place his order and refuse to take it unless he could give something back, at first he asked little things, stories from the outside world, he wasn't interested in anything in particular, just helping the boy's mother, but PI began to ask for harder tasks saying that those he was presented with were not to the value of the medicine that was saving the life of his mother, so Eiji gave him one last task on the condition that he takes the medicine as long as it takes to research and then until he knows of something else he wishes to know, blinded by the challenge PI agreed. It had only taken two weeks to obtain all the information he needed, a young boy of that age, so amazing with gathering of information, he had to wonder how he did it.

Eiji now had other things on his mind; something that PI had said opened an entirely new possibility to him, one he had to follow through, just as the boy had taken off deep into the forest, Eiji too now raced towards his master's tree top home.

"Master" He opened the door to his master's home standing in the gentle light, the leaves shook and whispered in the breeze drowning out the sounds of his breathless gasps as he leaned against the doorframe, his master sprung to his feet seeing the urgency in his student's eyes.

"Where's the fire?" He started towards the door, but stopped at Eiji's next words.

"At Napier Village it seems…" Eiji entered closing the door gently behind him, his movements were slow his vision simply staring ahead.

"Ah…" His master moved to the table and motioned for him to join him.

"So… it *was* you!" Eiji knew this just from the look in his master's eyes, that, and the fact he had sat ready to discuss this topic further. "Why? Why didn't you tell me?"

"I am sorry, what can I say? I know it was your birth place… Maybe even your parents lived there…but I saw the place, if they had been there…" He shook his head.

"I have no ties to that place or those people… but… but you still should have told me. It *was* my home or so you say, you have always been honest, why has that changed since you have returned?" His master shook his head once more before lowering his gaze to the table surface.

"Eiji." He sighed gently. "I would have told you, I was not ready, it's true, it was me. Back then, at that village, death herself looked me in the eyes and smiled." Eiji saw his master's hands tremble slightly before he moved them from view, seeing this, all his anger died leaving him wondering what possibly could have happened that was so terrible the mere thought of it turned his master pale, the story from PI was bound to be an embellishment.

"I heard Night sent a warrior to the village, what was he like?"

"*She* was only a child, about fifteen or so, yet she had the power of the devil, the scenes of death she created so horrific, that even the mind fails to comprehend their true horror, the town lay dead before me, I stood at the edge of the village, no doubt the last person, but herself, alive, she walked slowly to me, try as I may I couldn't seem to move, she looked me right in the eyes, they were so old for one so young, but something changed, they grew almost gentle. 'Next life, you save me.' That was what she said, she turned and slowly walked away never looking back, she didn't need to, if I had so much as moved, she would have known, she was just so aware of everything…"

"What did she mean?" Eiji questioned intrigued by this new story.

"It means, Eiji, we have to train harder, something is on the horizon, the elements grow restless."

"But… you didn't answer my question." His master smiled.

***

"Say mum?" Eiji followed a beautiful lady around, he must have been no older than six as he mirrored her steps, he stretched up on his tiptoes placing a plate on the side where his adoptive mother had placed the ones she carried.

"What's matter?" She turned and smiled crouching to his level.

"Where's dad?" He questioned hugging the women tightly, gripping her blond curls gently in his hands.

"He's training why?" She questioned pulling away to look at him.

"No reason. Mum, what's this Severaine you keep talking about?"

"You'll find out when you're older."

"What's that mean?"

"You ask too many questions." She laughed gently tapping him gently on the nose, it was a sound even in his age he had never forgotten, it was the most beautiful sound he had ever heard, like a thousand angels singing in beautiful harmony, but she soon stopped laughing when she saw Eiji's eyes welling with tears as he looked up at her.

"Mum… you won't leave me too… like before… like those strangers?"

"Eiji." She smiled gently picking him up in her arms, they had always been honest about what had happened to him, about how they found him, it was the only way to keep his trust, it was the right thing to do. "No matter what, I'll never leave you; I'll always be right besides you."

***

"How odd." Another scientist dressed in appropriate attire watched the monitors, his dark black hair ruffled after a hard night. "Are you sure he's one of them?"

"Certain why?" The common place, dark haired man from before walked up to the rather frail looking scientist; power oozed from him to the extent the scientist retreated as he approached.

"All his memories, his life, none of it resembles anything they are accused of, look, he grew up on Mainland, a place not of this world, he was abandoned by his family and taken in by another, he was adopted, trained and finally a few weeks ago made a deal with a Lord Blackwood which led him to meet the others… who also seem…"

"What trickery is this?" He roared. "Our Lord said they were cunning, but to overpower modern science! That is all the proof you need." He pointed to Eiji who lay unconscious on the floor. "That mark, that is all the proof you need." He repeated pointing out the symbol.

"We did however learn something of interest sir." The scientist was almost afraid to speak to him, it was clear his anger rested on the surface, waiting to see if this development would release it.

"And what, may I ask, is that?" He questioned through clenched teeth.

"The others seem to possess some runes themselves, sacrifice and balance."

"To each their purpose shall be revealed." He muttered to himself. "Since their runes dictate their fate, and it has attached its symbol to their destiny… maybe we could claim their power without suffering its consequences… with the added power of their runes, we could be invincible." He paced eagerly back and forth, pleased at the thought of this new concept. "We could request all enemies slay themselves, the rune of power combined with that of sacrifice would mean the world could be ours. I must tell Lord Benjamin, I must brief him immediately of this new development."

***

Since appearing in Knights-errent they had done nothing but walk, walk through the forest lands and the open fields, all had been silent, not a dreamer or town to be seen as they head towards the bay that would lead them towards the town they could access what they hoped to be pirates isle from. As they trekked through the field the uneasy silence was replaced by small whimpers of animals' echoed from all around.

"Sounds like a cat?" Daniel questioned stopping as he glanced around. "By the Gods." He whispered as they entered the field the noises were generating from, before them stretched a large field in which hundreds of kittens were buried to their necks in the ground. Zo rushed over about to dig one out when a farmer approached.

"Admiring my crop are yer?" He questioned, his shadow absorbing all the light from Zo. "Been a good year this time"

"What are you doing?" Daniel asked horrified watching as the little kitten heads followed him sceptically as he approached,

"Farming cats… who else do you think keeps the rodent problem down?" The farmer stooped to one of the kittens that tried to bite him, he smiled petting it on the head as it continued to snap. "This ones ripe." He smiled grabbing the scruff of its neck pulling it from the ground; it gave out a small mew sound before it was completely free from the soil.

"Cat farming?" Daniel questioned in disbelief.

"Well sure, you see, every town you go to has cats, more than likely its me who farm the little critters, its a fine business, I pluck the crop and pass them on to the towns to control the rat problem, don't tell me you never heard of me." They shook their head much to the farmer's disappointment. "Well where else do you think cats come from?" He smiled, pulling another from the ground and placed it in a box with several others; they sat with their heads on the edge of it looking curiously out.

"That one's got no tail what happened?" Zo questioned still trying to come to terms with the strange situation.

"That's a very special one my dear." He stroked the head of the small black and white cat; it raised its head accepting the fuss gratefully. "This one's a Manx, he'll have a very special home, somewhat of a rarity, or more accurately a crop mutation. Now is there anything I can help you folks with or were you just passing to admire this year's crop… perhaps I can interest you in one?"

"No thanks." Zo smiled. "Maybe when our adventure is over." The farmer placed another kitten in the box smiling. "But… maybe you can help us. We are after something called pirates isle, it's where we can obtain narca berries I believe?"

"Couldn't say much about the island, but I know where your berries are, well kind of, in fact, I'm on my way there now with this shipment, a great home for my young friends is a fishing town." He smiled fussing each of the heads of the eleven kittens. "Could do with someone riding in the back, you know, keep an eye on them, they get quite curious after they been unearthed, I lost may a kitten as they go off to explore the territory, all seem to find homes mind you, so it doesn't hurt… there's a lovely old lady just down the way, they all seem to flock to her, perhaps it's the saucers of milk and fresh fish she leaves for the little ones." He smiled to himself attaching the last reins to the horse. "Besides there's plenty of room in the back."

Although a short journey, it would have taken much longer on foot, throughout the journey the little kittens scrabbled and climbed from the boxes, Daniel sat watching Zo as she scooped them up in her hands smiling fussing them before placing them back in the box, no sooner had one been put back, another tried its daring escape. Sure enough, the journey passed quickly and Daniel swore to himself the first thing he would do when this was over would be to get her a kitten.

They hopped out on the edge of town outside an old house where the first of the kittens were to be delivered thanking the driver as they went on their way.

Splitting up when they reached the small port town, they began to search for information on this pirates isle, the town was large considering it had been classed a fishing town, normally that gave the impression of a few small houses dotted around, but this town was of no such appearance. The shops and sea front restaurants were built from brick and mortar, the small residential homes of wood from the nearby forest, after a good hour trekking through the landscape they finally surrendered meeting up none the wiser than when they first arrived.

"It's no use." Acha sighed. "No one has even heard of these pirates, let alone knows where they are based; I really thought we were onto something with this island thing". She joined the others sitting by the dock, positioning herself as far as possible from Zo yet still within the group, Daniel was glancing over the menu, she glanced over his shoulder curiously, looking at the seafood delicacies that filled the page.

"Narca berry pudding!" They stated in synchronisation, before Daniel carried on. "Maybe we have been asking the wrong questions, after all it was said on the isle near our destination the berries grow... maybe they can point is in the right direction, besides, didn't the farmer say he knew about the berries but nothing on the pirates, I don't know why we didn't think of it before." As Daniel and Acha vanished into the café, Zo moved from the table to sit by on the concrete wall that lined the water's edge by this dock, her legs hanging over the side barely missing the water's surface, she leaned forwards through the first of bars leaning on it as she watched her own reflection with what could only be described as unfamiliarity Elly moved to sit besides her, mirroring her posture.

"Are you alright, you've been unusually quiet." A long silence stretched out as she watched Zo staring deep into the water below, all of a sudden the spoken words registered.

"I'm surprised... I know I don't have long left, yet I still sit here now." She muttered a gentle breeze whipping around them teasing its misty fingers through their hair, Zo closed her eyes feeling the winds gentle embrace; it seemed to almost call out to her.

"Sorry?" Elly questioned not quite following the conversation.

"Well, Marise." Zo almost whispered her name as if fear of saying it too loud would disturb her. "She's not been active since before, I could almost believe this whole thing wasn't real... it doesn't feel it." She sighed her vision now following a following the rise and fall of a small bird as it flew across the waters surface.

"You need to keep things in perspective, why would she want to? What is there here to entertain her? Think about it." Elly knew the real reason Marise had been quiet, her last visit had take a lot out of her, she had been surprised she had even managed scratch Daniel, especially since that quick change between Zo and Marise, last time he was in danger on the way to Abaddon. However, she would not dream of telling Zo this, the more she doubted her own strength, doubted herself, the more power she gave Marise.

"Yeah I suppose." She whispered bringing her knees in to her chest as she sat on the wall. "I'm scared." Zo whispered barely able to believe she had spoken these words aloud. "I am afraid of death, afraid of vanishing... but saying I don't want it, will not change things. No matter how hard I fight, I cannot change the course of my own destiny." Elly looked to her in surprise, a twang of sympathy in her chest, she hid it well, locking her emotions under the surface where they would not burden anyone, but looking now, she could tell she was really scared, no matter how hard she tried to hide it. In that one moment, Elly felt as close to Zo as she did to Marise, it was a feeling that surprised even her.

"At the end of the day she is part of you, I think to a certain extent you misunderstand what she is... she..."

"We found it! A small island to the east, it's where the berries originates!" Acha ran from the small café followed by Daniel who was buried in his map. For once, Elly was glad for the interruption, maybe it had been the desperate look in her eyes, the sadness, but for some unknown reason, after her previous thought about how her doubts increased Marise's strength, she had nearly followed through with something she was never to revel to anyone, something Zo could use to her advantage, she turned to listen to what Daniel had to say.

"It seems that would put us due south of one of the fixed locations… On those islands that look like the constellation as we originally thought. There are no rumours of pirates but there *is* a castle with a small town secured inside its walls, it's said it was built to withstand a pirate attack… other than that…" Daniel stopped looking at Zo's face, as she spoke he began folding the map, in the instant that she looked to him, she had seemed truly afraid, yet within seconds she had replaced her mask, a mask that shielded her emotions from those around her, almost flawless as she gave that smile that didn't quite reach her eyes, but this time it was different than before, even the smile itself seemed filled with heartbreak. He knew her well enough to read her eyes, she maintained this front for their benefit and should he address it, he feared that she would recall her decision to leave them and so, as much as he disliked the idea, he left it unmentioned, he could only offer her support and again, it was her choice if she chose to accept.

"There hasn't been a single boat departure since we got here though." She looked to him sadly, he had tried so hard to get the information, yet even so they found themselves unable to proceed, in the same situation they were in just moments ago.

"True, they don't sail until tomorrow, but, the owner of the café said they were due a collection of berries and would run us over, as for getting the rest of the way, it seems there isn't a boat built that could sail the treacherous current of the sea across there. Even so, I say we get the berries first, then maybe we will find someone who is willing to lend a helping hand, there's always someone with the stu… courage to try." As he spoke he led them towards a small rickety looking collection boat, he paused climbing aboard, the boat. "Besides…" Daniel paused looking back to the café but chose never to continue his sentence.

***

"What were you thinking?" A voice erupted from the café just after the small boat had set sail; it was clearly aimed towards the elderly woman who, with a smile of triumph was watching the ship set sail.

"Did you not know who they were?" She hissed back into the café. "They are that gang… you know the ones with the marks, I figure they're best out of our way, leave them there to rot." She replied as her well built son emerged from the café, his shadow almost blocking out any light that would have shone through the doorway, a white apron hung around his neck.

"But that's Narca berry isle, how will we make our pudding now?" His mother's hand slapped him across the back of his head, although she needed to stand on her tiptoes to do it.

"And what do you think those are? Narca berry isle may have been the place they originated from, but it's not the only place you can get the damn things, look around you they're everywhere, soon as the first seed hit shore they spread like wildfire."

"Oh… you don't need a shipment at all then… you're just going to strand them there… But what if they get off and want our heads… They were a member missing…"

"Well, they'd have to escape first and it's a long way to swim... Funny thing though, they didn't seem much like the rumours, actually that young boy was quite nice, like the son I never had." She smiled watching the boat fade into the distance.

"Aw mum." He stated looking down to his mother sorrowfully.

***

They had arrived quite quickly on the island, it was comprised of mainly evergreen trees making up a solid forest, the trees had started right on the edge of the island from the point the small rowing boat had stopped allowing them to scramble the muddy banks with the aid of tree roots. Once to the top they thanked the rowers who were already on their way back to grab their collection crew from the main boat. Underneath the trees, almost invisible at first glance were small brown red bushes, each containing berries of the same colour making them almost impossible to see. The island itself seemed to be deserted, not a single animal track marked the soil.

"You sure this will be enough?" Daniel sighed dropping some more berries into Zo's bag; he seemed to be a little distracted. "Well let's take just a few more to be on the safe side." He stated pulling another twig from a nearby bush and placing it in the bag. "Then again, if it's not enough we can get some more if we get back to the dock."

"What do you mean?" Acha stopped collecting and turned to face him.

"Well, look at them." He sighed "They're identical to the ones in the town, the ones that grew by the road, they're everywhere we have been, they're not exactly a rarity." He stated.

"So why offer to take us here? Are they more potent?" Acha sighed as she noticed the boat had now vanished from their view.

"No one has been on this island for years, if at all anyone ever has, they just wanted us out of the way, surely you realised that." Elly stated pulling something once more out of her pocket as she continued. "I would have thought it was clear when they sailed off shortly after we entered this area."

"But why?" Acha questioned, there was a crack of paper being flipped open. "Marked bandits?" She read questioningly as she gazed upon the wanted poster in Elly's grasp. "But..."

"Well think about it." Elly sighed. "We violated a sacred church, collapsed a court and no doubt have committed crimes without even realising it along the way. It's only logical this world would take action against such behaviour, and besides."

"You mean it won't simply be part of someone's dream?" Zo questioned already knowing the answer, unaware that Daniel had slipped off into the trees as the topic had turned to the marked bandits.

"Afraid not, it's very much like our own world, some kind of law enforcement to keep the peace isn't too unreasonable of an idea, after all this world has its own inhabitants, not to mention those creatures that brought us here. Since keeping the peace seems to be the Spindles' role, in their absence I wouldn't be surprised if this was their doing." Elly took the poster back from Acha and folded it up, it was only then she noticed what had been missing for some time. "Say where's Daniel?"

"He was here a second ago, he can't have gone far." Zo glanced around frantically, he was doing this too often, didn't he realise how dangerous it was, sure he had been lucky until now, but how long could he truly do this for and expect to be safe? "I hope." She added, who knew what they would find on the island, since their arrival there Zo had felt a pulling sensation, the whispers on the wind that previously embraced her at the port had been growing louder, almost as if it had not been the wind at all, but just a calling being carried by it.

"Well we better look for him." Elly began to walk into the undergrowth while Zo lingered back drawing an arrow facing the way they were heading in the ground.

The island although small was quite sheltered, the tall trees blocked any view of anything you may approach, as well as trapping the light to the extent they only walked in the equivalent of a well lit night.

A small shout echoed around them, the voice was one they knew at instant, although it contained no urgency there was something hidden in its depths, lost as it echoed as bounced around the forest, did he really expect them to be able to locate him by a call alone. Against the odds, they found him quickly as they entered a large clearing Daniel ran to greet them.

"Look it's an ancient shrine of some sort, I have never seen these markings before, it's incredible!" His voice clearly filled with awe as he glanced to each of them in turn, both Zo and Elly smiled.

"It's also our ticket out." Elly approached the sealed shrine placing her hand on the door. "Ma..." She looked to Zo and stopping a second before continuing. "Would you do the honours?" Zo approached the door instincts whispering in her mind as she repeated the ancient words that called to her, the voice seemed to be that she had heard calling previously on the wind, she placed her hands upon two small engravings on the door as she did so the paper thing carvings began to glow a strange brown as the roots of nearby trees began to intertwine in the indents of the carvings, as the last hole was filled the piercing shade of brown dazzled them for but a moment before the doors pulled apart. Zo stood still staring at the door, that brown had seemed so familiar, as she stood staring she heard the quiet whispers in the back of her mind, unaware that Elly looked on with interest, Zo was unaware the doors now stood open before them, all she could hear around her were these whispers, they were calling to her.

'What?' She questioned silently. *'What do you want me to do?'* The voices whispered again, she knew what it was asking her was wrong. *'If I release it then what?'* She questioned already knowing the answer, knowing that no matter what, she could not do as the whispers asked, yet at the same time she felt the magic rise within her, she seemed powerless to control her words, the whispers circled her, she felt the force of their movements as they swirled around her, somewhere, far beneath the world it was waiting, waiting for its freedom, it had been waiting for centuries, sealed there by a strange force, a strange seal, she gasped as she felt the second of the three break, the silent words still leaving her, as her magic began to attempt the third.

"Zo?" Daniel questioned as she stood before the open door she seemed to snap from whatever trance she was in Daniel smiled she turned to look at him, her vision now broken from the dark roots. "What is this place?"

"I thought you studied mythology... then again." Elly smirked. "The Ampotanians were famous for their architecture, you may have heard brief tales, but they are long forgotten now but for a few words of rumour, but one thing no one remembers is they were also famous for their mines, amongst other things." She looked at Zo and smiled. "In early history, before boats were even a concept they once dug straight under a lake, it was soon after this they began to notice the change in earth finding rich minerals underneath the waters bed, some say it was skill that they knew when to surface, although in reality, it was the land composition that became woody and less rich. They linked the lands building tunnels and shrines to their deities, telling none their secrets of travel. They were a very quiet race and did not approach those of foreign lands despite the fact they travelled to them. They still erected shines for the believers of their deities." Elly looked at the strange carvings on the door, this shine had been erected to Geburah, a demon of destruction, the carvings told the story of how he turned on mankind trying to destroy them all, and how he was sealed within the shrine they had used to honour him, three seals had been placed, hope, strength and survival, the demon would have infinite chance to find a host to release the seals, within their life, events would remove them, long ago, the demon had chosen Marise in hope that she could break the bonds by destroying hope in others, exploiting their weakness and sacrificing her victims, for only when the seals had been broken by their opposite, could the demon be free. Geburah's thoughts had failed, for it was within the host the bonds that sealed him must be destroyed, but only since hope was lost did he realise this was the key, on the high place Zo had lost her hope and the first seal had been broken, just now, she lost her strength as she failed to fight the whispers that took control of her powers. Another few moments and the third would have been released, but there was not hurry now, he knew it was just a matter of time until he was free. Elly was impressed Zo had found the strength to fight the hypnotic whispers at first, yet she also felt her surrender to their will, releasing the second seal, had not been for Daniel, perhaps things would have turned out differently, she was lucky really, this time there was something to distract her from the traps, perhaps it would be safer if she led the way through the dark labyrinth that would await, she could not risk the demon's whispers hurrying along her plan.

"I've never heard of them." Daniel looked to Elly for more insight on this forgotten culture.

"It doesn't surprise me, few have, their existence was all but erased by the Mesagen in late 725 OGE"

"You mean before the war of the Gods? Before NGE? But how... how could you know this?" Daniel questioned.

"It's not important how I know it, just that I do. Now hush, let's see where this leads... the people of the island said the water was un-sailable, yet..." Not another word was spoken as they descended into darkness, Elly took the lead knowing what would lie ahead, never letting Zo fall from her side, if the whispers were to come again down here, everything would be for nothing the demon would take their lives and she could not complete this mission alone and so, she watched her like a hawk.

Chapter seventeen

"They found the tunnel? Then all proceeds as plan." Night smiled to himself as voice from the shadows of walls answered softly. There was nothing particularly unusual about the shadow, it was a long shapeless form, it was only when examining the room closely, pairing up the shadows with their sources that it became apparent, that unlike the other, this one had no source.

"Indeed, a nice touch of mythology makes things all the more believable even in a dream world."

"Have things been prepared at the castle?" He asked, it was, like in Blackwood's case, nothing more than a formality.

"Yes sir, I must say, using that girl to upset the balance was genius, none but you could compose such a cunning plan, I swear in that split second I saw her heart shatter, her defences are weakening, she feels it."

"Yes… She does." Night looked deep into the gossip crystal once more before walking away.

***

"Gaea, oldest and wisest of the deities, I will revive you from your slavery, soon you shall be the master once more." Night stood before a stunning women, her long earth brown hair fanned across the floor from where she sat, although rich in colour over the last millennia it had paled considerably as she had been destroyed by those on the surface, she looked up to Night as he bowed his head, she stood to greet him placing her delicate hand on his shoulder.

"Night we have long been friends, what is with this formality, tell me what ails you?" The softness in her voice surprised him even now, it was filled with all the gentleness of nature, but he also knew there was a darker, savage side to her, one that he had only ever witnessed when she was free, the untameable power of the earth itself.

"Nothing, the cause is far greater than the sacrifices, how lives the Severaine?" Gaea turned leading him to a large mirror like looking glass, as she touched it, a window to wherever she wished appeared before them.

"There has been a change, something is happening that is awaking the sleeping power, when they sealed your magic away it's sleep grew deeper and its manifestation became nothing more than a spark, as if the Grimoire they created aided the barriers that were erected, now you are once more reclaiming your power, the barrier weakens and the Severaine thrives once more, soon it shall be awake and the power it has stored during its slumber shall be released as it roams the surface world. The seven barriers are weakening, it seems two have been destroyed, is this your plan?" She smiled gently, looking from Night to the Severaine, she knew this was his plan, he had spoke of it many times but now something played on the tip of his conscience, if the prophesies had been correct, he would rise again, but there was something distracting him, something he hadn't been prepared for… his daughter, he had distanced himself from her for so long, yet as he saw how she had grown, how much like her mother she was, the doubt within him rose. This situation was messy, unpredictable, first he suffered at the hands of another, but this time, it would be he himself that would bring about the pain. She viewed this development in two ways, it was good for him to hold something dear to him, something other than a grudge, but by doing so he became conflicted, to fulfil the prophecy, she must seize the final Grimoire and sacrifice herself before him so that the dark maiden Marise Shi could rise and free the final barriers that would, at that point, be the only force that imprisoned the Severaine, once Marise rose this final time, there would be nothing left to interfere with her desires, with the final darkness the Severaine would be free, but at the same time he would have to sacrifice the one, he wished more than anything to protect. Night knew what she was thinking and smiled softly, they had always been able to read each other like an open book. "Perhaps when I was not so tired, I could have controlled my pet, but now, now I fear the power we will unleash will be too great, people have stolen much of my energy, tell me, what do we do if I fail to create dominance? As Gods we cannot interfere with the destiny of man." She looked to him meaningfully as if to link the words to an unspoken conversation.

"If that is what comes to pass, we shall do what we always do, inspire a quest among man to retrieve the Spiritwest." Night paused. "I understand, this is the way it has always been for us Gods. Once my daughter returns with the final Grimoire, everything will proceed as planned, the Severaine will soon be free, prepare yourself, the day draws near." Even as he spoke Night was wishing there was another way, a way he could both fulfil the prophesy and spare his daughter so he may get to know her, but he could not let his feelings interfere, this was by far too important.

***

"See what did I tell you? A straight route through." Elly smiled as she offered Zo a hand out of the steep slope that had become the tunnels mouth, Daniel brought up the rear still amazed how Elly had navigated through the black tunnels, to a dark dead-end only to find a door that once more opened at the command of magic, it was almost as if she had walked it a million times before. Zo offered Acha a hand up the steep bank, but the notion was dismissed entirely making it clear that she would rather struggle alone than take her hand, Daniel was the last to emerge and accepted Zo's hand not because he needed to, but because he wanted to, it was more a symbolic gesture than anything else.

"A castle?" Daniel questioned as his eyes adjusted to the pale light of the overcast island, out of all the places he had expected to emerge, within walking distance to an enormous castle was not one of them. It was the mirror image of a castle he had seen drawn, a castle that resided on Ishitar Island which placed them at the location they were aiming for. It was surrounded by an enormous wall, a wall so high that only the very tips of the castle were visible, its entrance was barricaded by a huge wooden gate, even from this distance it was clear it was operated by an intricate pulley system, thick chains entered the castle walls near the top of the hinging gate. The fort itself stood in a strategically sound location, behind it, rose steep faced mountains that descended right into the sea, making a sea attack impossible, in front of it stretched a large open area of marshland, nowhere in sight where a single soldier could be concealed.

"Of course... power, the riddle from before." Zo looked to Elly she had the kind of expression found on someone waiting for everyone else to get up to speed, she smiled at her thankfully making Zo think she had been waiting for this realisation some time, it also made her wonder why she had not thought to say anything herself.

"Let's hurry." Acha started towards the castle but stopped short at Daniel's question.

"Fair play, we all want to get in there and rescue Eiji, but how do we plan to get inside? We're wanted; it's not so simple as just walking in, not now anyway." He sighed; Acha rejoined the group, an action she clearly wasn't too thrilled with.

"True..." Elly started, the same expression on her face, it was clear she had it planned out, waiting only for the others to draw the same conclusion as she, she paused a while for effect. "But I believe Acha can move between life-forms... Maybe control a guard, cause a diversion while we sneak in, we can take her body with us, so all she will need to do is track the amulet once we're inside."

"Well... I..." Acha blushed slightly at the sudden attention, she had barely used her powers, but a sudden thought gave her new confidence, something that had been discussed earlier, she had, after all, found a tutor who was teaching her to use her powers. "Ok... I can create a diversion, just something to distract the guards while you sneak in right?"

"You got it." Elly glanced at Zo and Daniel, she hadn't expected this to be so easy, she had expected far more resistance, she was glad this was not the case, the traveller she had seen recently was growing ever closer to the castle, he was the perfect target, if not him, then who knows how long they would have to wait for another to approach. "We'll wait for you to send a signal."

"Okay." Acha rushed off to a young merchant, his dark hair, although short, had grown messy during his travels. "Excuse me." She called waving to him as she made her way over, he stopped waiting for her to catch up, she smiled gratefully. "I'm really sorry, I'm new to the area and I'm a little lost." She panted after the run pulling one of the invisible gloves from her hands, as she did so it took on leather appearance once more. "Can you tell me, the name of this castle? Maybe then, I can find my way." She asked glancing towards it meaningfully, she had become quite the actor recently, true she was reserved, but with the help of her tutor she was really finding herself.

"Sure milady, this is the castle of Iris." He scratched his head thinking how she must truly be a stranger to the lands not to know the castle or its location.

"Iris? Well thank you." She smiled extending her hand to the traveller, no sooner had they touched than Acha's body fell to the floor, she flexed the fingers of the traveller amazed at how much control she had gained since speaking and training with Sofie. She watched through the merchant's eyes as Elly scooped up her body, she felt no different than before, except there was a small awareness of a sleeping form in the back of her mind.

"I shall not be long; you shall know when it is safe to enter." The merchant's voice spoke, already she knew his every thought, although he slept, while she possessed the host, his memories were hers to share, she watched until the others had taken shelter around from the door hiding away from sight, sheltering her body from the elements.

"Stop, who goes there." A voice boomed from the sealed gates.

"Its I, Sir Catgar, I come baring gifts for the new lord as is customary." Acha was unsure how much information she had really needed to divulge, the stranger who asked this of her, seemed somewhat familiar, although she knew she herself had never set eyes upon him she wondered if the same would be true for her host.

"Hey Catgar, been a while." A hand slapped the merchant on the back once through the fort's gates. The switch was almost instant. "Best you hurry along, our lord is waiting." The merchant rubbed the back of his head questions appearing in his eyes, he stood for a few moments in a dazed confusion until he finally spoke.

"Y...yes of course." He nodded at the guard before hurrying on his way.

'I can't believe it.' Acha thought to herself, now exploring the depths of her new hosts mind. *'Even here in this world, the worries and fears of the dreamers hide within the shadows, it was just as I hoped, just as Sofie had implied.'*

"Knight Robin, what ever is the matter." A stout man approached, clearly their captain by his dress and decoration his commander motioned for him to approach.

"I wish not to alarm anyone sir..." Acha whispered in Robin's voice. "But... I believe... I just laid sights on a manslayer."

"I beg you pardon?" The captain questioned removing his gloves; he had clearly noticed the ghastly pallor of his knight and was now concerned for his well-being, after all Robin had only recently recovered from a serious illness which had brought him close to his deathbed, plaguing him with illusions.

"No, no, I am certain, gather the men we are under attack..."

"Explain yourself; I feel no threats are you feeling alright?" He touched Robin's forehead as she jumped she saw Robin shudder.

"My word!" The commander's voice boomed, at the outburst the guards all rushed forwards. "It's true, Knight Robin, gather your troops for attack, alert the perimeter, they are all to report here, immediately." It was not long before his wishes were met, as the troops gathered they huddled together permitting him to speak in lowered tones to spare the public any panic which the news may spur. "Listen closely, we have an advantage, the enemy is unaware we are onto them, ready your weapons and follow me." Acha saw this comment was pointless the men had come armed and ready for battle; all that was left was for her, or more accurately, the commander to lead them. "We have to be sure, attack while we still have the upper hand, our target." He marched the guards from the base, despite their number their movements were silent but for the hushed tones of their commander. "Is no less than..." There was a dramatic pause as they turned the corner, his eyes resting on the group of travellers. "Marise Shi." He drew his sword pointing it at the travellers; some of the army faltered yet all stood their ground as they looked upon the figures.

"By the God's look that poor girl's already dead..." A soldier cried his vision falling on Acha's body cradled in Elly's arms, Zo stood before them, but it was not her they saw, it was the manslayer that slept within her soul, they saw her now, as Acha did.

"Men attack." The captain screamed. "Buy some time for the innocent to flee to safety!" With a loud roar they charged, Daniel grabbed Zo's arm pulling her gently as she moved to meet their accusation, she stood before her friends her hand gripping the hilt of her sword, but she lacked the will to draw immediately, she stood almost paralysed by the sea of men that washed towards her, Acha's eyes shot open.

"Go." She commanded inexpressively. "Do what we came for." Elly pulled Acha to her feet, for the first time ever she seemed almost surprised by what had occurred, unable to understand how such a simple request had turned out this way.

"Acha, what did you do?" She questioned, realising she could not hold her own weight, for some unknown reason, she supported her all the same, pulling her away from where Zo stood protecting them. Acha smiled watching as the army descended only moments away from the attack.

"Go." Zo commanded again. "I will hold them off… with them here the castle will be…" She pulled her arm free from Daniel.

"Zo… what will you do?" He went to touch her arm again but receded at the last second, she never turned back to answer him, her vision stayed fixed as the soldiers were nearly upon her, she would have to draw soon, the sinking in her stomach warned her that much, Elly was already helping Acha away, she just needed to ensure Daniel too reached safety.

"The only thing I can… they came here for Marise, they will get me."

"It's dangerous to use her like that." Daniel protested knowing it was already too late; the sword was now drawn, although he could not remember seeing the movement that drew it.

"You still here?" Her voice was harsh filled with threat, a warning he chose to ignore.

"I'll go, but understand this; I'm coming back for her." She turned to face him smiling as she did so, it was a cold bone chilling smile filled with sadistic pleasure.

"I'm counting on it." As the first guard attacked he reluctantly left catching up with Elly, it was an easy thing to do, after all she half carried Acha away from harms way, he hated leaving her, he hated the thought of turning his back and running, but if he didn't… if he didn't Zo would never forgive him, she had once more sacrificed control to buy them time, it was an act he could not waste.

***

Marise watched the army approach, she remembered the lay of this land so well from when she and Elly had visited its true source in their world, although this was years ago, it seemed like only yesterday, Elly had revealed many secrets about this place to her, the most surprising of all being that a temple of Gaea was sealed beneath it…

"Many centuries ago, near the place Castlefort stands, there was a temple erected for Gaea, the earth goddess. Before the Severaine was completely sealed there was an enormous shift in the earth's tectonic plates changing the very look of the earth as it was then and sealing the temples entrance, the temple had been constructed underground, and remained unharmed, as did this castle. This temple is the place that the Grimoire of earth resides, but it is also said that many changes were made on its arrival to ensure its protection should a mortal stumble across the entrance to the temple." Elly knocked on the traveller's entrance gate to Castlefort. "And one more thing, I feel we will be coming here often, so it would be in our best interest not to attract unnecessary attention, besides, I have a job to do that will grant us access for now."

"For Blackwood?" Marise questioned.

"Well it is better to keep him happy." She answered before the eye slot shot back at the top of the gate.

"Who goes there?" Commanded the voice of the two eyes that had now appeared at the slot, his eyes flicked back and forth looking over the two figures carefully

"I am Lady Elaineor, and this is my attendant Ilinda, I have come from Mainland from Knightsbridge with a gift from my father, Lord Blackwood, to thank the king for his on going support." The eye slots closed as the guard vanished for a moment, only for him to return seconds later.

"I'm sorry miss, but we have no record of your audience."

"Oh." Elly sighed looking to the floor timidly. "Then I shall travel back to inform my father his messenger did not arrive, he was so sure... I mean he sent me without an escort." Another guard moved to the eye slot and glanced at the two women, neither were built as warriors, and one was but a child.

"I see your maid carries a sword." Said the new guard, the authority in his voice showed him to be of high rank. Elly leaned across Marise pulling the sheath from her belt before removing the hilt, the blade, which was formed by light and dark magic, did not appear.

"You mean this?" Elly questioned. "My father had her carry it as a deterrent, it's quite useless." The gate opened slightly as the captain of the guards emerged to examine the sword and sheath; he took them from her examining them closely.

"It's heavy too." The captain nodded at his men who opened the gate. "Look, this area is no place for two lady travellers, not with assassins on the loose; I can't understand why your father would send you without escort." The captain glanced around motioning for them to enter the walls.

"My father is a strange man, he was concerned that if I came with guards, I would not only be viewed as a target, but you may worry about our intentions." Elly passed a box to the captain for examination; he glanced through the jewels and treasures that were for the king carefully before passing them back.

"Right, well the king is in conference out of the area until late this evening, but you may see him tomorrow, I will have the maids make you up a room, your servant can stay in the servant quarters." The captain smiled.

"Thank you... only, would it be a great inconvenience to have her with me?" Elly moved closer to the captain to speak in lowered tones. "It's just, she's only a child. Since her mother passed away she hardly speaks a word, my father looked after her mother, helping with the expenses for medicine as her ill heath increased, when finally she passed, father took her into his home as a daughter, but she insisted on working off her debt... I just want to protect her... perhaps, I worry more than I need to... but she *is* just a child."

"I did think her a little young to be a servant, but who am I to judge." The captain whispered smiling at the young girl. "Very well, I shall see to it, in the meantime, feel free to explore the castle and the town, when you grow tired just ask a maid where your room is." The captain took the bags from them, except the backpack, which Elly had insisted she kept. He led them through the grand streets of Castlefort, each house within its walls was uniformly tidy, made of the same grey stone, with the same doors and windows, even the stone streets seemed uniformly coloured. Elly and Marise made an attempt to take in the surroundings until finally they stood at the stone arch entrance to the castle.

It was more magnificent than Marise had expected, it stood at least six times the height of a normal house and was still concealed from view by the surrounding wall, the four towers that were just visible over the protecting wall around the city, were easily twice the height of the castle, at the top of each one was stationed a guard. The captain excused himself leaving them to take in the castle.

"Attendant?" Marise questioned once he was far from view.

"Sorry." Elly smiled the amusement in her tones indicating that she wasn't in the least bit sorry. "Come on, the passage we want is this way, from here, we just need to get below." Elly led her through the stone passages of the enormous castle, the entire building was made of stone, both inside and out, the only thing not of this material as yet, seemed to be the huge wooden doors that sealed the rooms. Elly led Marise around with ease, almost as if she had been there many times before. She glanced around before opening a secret passage, what they were looking for, would be found near the passages end. They descended the stone staircase in silence, before following the maze of corridors beneath the castles surface, a maze so complex, any venturing down here would be lucky to ever see the light of day again....

***

Daniel breathed heavily as they entered the cold stone walls of the castle, the town itself was quiet, not a soul walked the streets, although this was hardly surprising given that the guards had just been sent to battle they were no doubt hiding, barricading themselves in their homes, Elly walked slowly supporting Acha so not to let her fall behind, although as she did so she wondered why she bothered, why it had seemed so important to bring her with them? Daniel leaned on the wall waiting.

"What the hell were you thinking?" Although he never raised his voice the words struck Acha as if he had.

"I'm thinking..." She stated slowly through grit teeth avoiding Daniel's gaze. "We get Eiji and hightail out of here, leave her to clean up her own mess."

"You just don't get it do you?" Daniel spoke through grit teeth, every part of him screamed out to shake some sense into her, to shout and scream, but despite this he stood firm, exercising a self-control he was surprised to find given the situation.

"Daniel, there's no time for this now." Elly interrupted. "We have to get Eiji and get out of here as soon as possible, we have to go back for her while there is still time."

"Elly that's not Zo fighting them." Daniel stated blandly.

"By now, I'd say not..." Elly looked meaningfully between him and Acha.

"No, you misunderstand; back then... she knew... she wanted more than anything to protect us... she summoned Marise herself before the sword was even drawn."

"Idiot." Elly hissed looking straight at Acha, although it *had* proved a fantastic diversion, it was not what she had in mind, she also feared that this one act of stupidity could jeopardise the entire mission, the whole reason behind their appearance here would be destroyed, if they lost her this early on, everything was for nothing, she looked to Daniel. "Doesn't she realise how serious that is? She's pushing her luck, she knows the consequences." She glanced back to Acha releasing her from her support to stand on her own. "You stupid child! Do you know what you've done?" Elly knew full well she couldn't even begin to comprehend the result of her actions.

"I brought judgement." Acha said defiantly. "You're just under her spell, you'll see."

"No, you may just have destroyed the only person who ever really gave a damn. Why the hell do you think she stayed?" Elly could feel the rage building up, were they truly about to lose everything? Lose what the last twenty-three years had been working towards all because of one moment? All because of one unpredictable action from someone who shouldn't have even been with them, if Marise was to be reborn now, it was over.

"She wants to fight! That's her nature." She snapped

"Again you're wrong as always. She stayed because her place has always been between her friends and those who wish them harm." She thought back to Michael, it had been a part of the young girl she had respected, especially when she faced her for his safety. "She stayed because if she were to run they would see us fully, if even one had strayed their vision who do you think they would have seen, us… or the branded ones, with a bounty on their head that could keep a small family rich for a lifetime, but let's for a moment say she did take the chance and ran hoping we made the gates, who would have brought up the rear? Who did I carry here?" Elly questioned venomously Acha gasped her eyes widening at the thought of a new possibility. "And what's more, for you, she became something she detests with all her soul, but she didn't even think about it, the skills, the awareness, the reflexes, all of the things that made Marise great, can only come with Marise, she is the only one who knows the full potential, any skills she possess are weak compared to Marise's true power. If she couldn't be sure where each one of the army you brought was, we would all be in real trouble now. You say it's in her nature to fight, maybe it's in Marise's to some extent and maybe she shares some of these skills, but is it in her nature? No it's in her nature to protect those she cares for, she's a healer, a nature's child or haven't you noticed? As I said her place was and always will be between you and those who wish to hurt you, it's a shame you are too stupid to see that!"

"I didn't ask her to fight for me." Acha's riotousness faded from her voice.

"You didn't have to. I don't know Zodiac as well as Marise, but she wants to protect you, *that* was clear from the first time I met her, when she was risking her life for you, yet again."

"But that was her fault they wanted her not me." She protested weakly

"Regardless, she fought for you; she never thought for one second she would best him, she just wanted to buy *you* time to escape. She protects those she loves, that's the kind of person she is, I hope you are truly satisfied with what you destroyed. I hope that look of betrayal she gave you before standing to fight haunts you forever. Which, if you're lucky, won't be too long with the irreparable damage you just did!" Elly took a breath to continue but was interrupted.

"Hey I know you." A small voice sounded from a nearby bedroom followed almost immediately by a young girl dressed as a doctor's aid stepping from a nearby door, her pale blond hair falling just below her elbows. "You're friends of Eiji." Elly, in a very Zo like reaction, took a defensive position between Daniel, Acha and the stranger. "I saw you in his dreams. Please, come this way, I can take you close to the chamber of his imprisonment." She whispered almost fearful that the castle walls listened.

"How do we know we can trust you?" Daniel questioned

"The same way I know 'the marked bandits' will not kill me, please quickly, my father called the knights to battle, now is your best chance… if they return." Julie glanced around quickly before leading the way.

***

"Now you're fighting armies." Marise looked up to the source of the voice and smiled, blood from her victims smeared across her arms and face

"Indeed." She turned her back to him slicing the final standing soldier through his chest with little effort, as she glanced around for movement she noticed most of those which she fought had somehow vanished, but she had known this previously, some that she had fought vanished before her blade had struck or before the final blow had landed, no matter they would return in no hurry. "Now if you will excuse me." Marise began to walk away.

"Mari, you know it is not time yet." The voice stopped her movement; she turned slowly to look at the concealed figure, a figure that addressed her with such familiarity.

"True, but if she is stupid enough to summon me, then she must suffer the consequences of her actions." She turned to look at the figure very little of him could be seen, he wore a huge cloak the hood shadowing any of his features, even so Marise knew that should it start, this would be one battle she would not walk away from, the being that stood before her was as a God and for that matter, one she was familiar with.

"You're time will come shortly, for now, there is a bigger picture you must step back to see." The figure waved his arm a door appeared in thin air, Marise stood looking at it, even her magic could not produce such a thing, a simple door complete with handle, Marise knew too well it would be an portal to somewhere.

"My time is now!" Marise spoke while examining the door trying to unlock its mysteries. "I refuse to be locked away this time, there is at least one person's whose blood I must taste."

"About that." The figure sighed. "For now, just get along, Zodiac will return when you grow tired, after all, this is *her* body, and with *her* friends is her environment, as it stands she possesses the upper hand, oh and one more thing." He looked up to Marise as she twisted her sword in one of the soldiers heads, a soldier that dared to move while she still stood before him, the figure offered his hand to her. "The boy, Daniel, he is mine, you have no claim on him understand?"

"So… I can't have any fun?" She took his hand, suppressing a shudder as their hands met, the being that took her hand was one of such tremendous power a mere click of his fingers could have ended her life in a second, although despite this awesome power, he was not complete, there was something missing in his aura, something perhaps he shielded from her, she had never really paid him much attention when last they met.

"Not yet. Now if you have quite finished." He glanced around the field littered with corpses. "Your friends are through that door." He opened it guiding her through by the hand leaving no room for protest; after she had entered he closed the door behind her.

"Z..." Daniel stopped realising the person that stood before them was not his dearest friend, Acha and Elly now stopped searching for something around Eiji's light barrier and looked up.

"Lee." She smiled enticingly, looking at Elly as she made her way down towards them, her walk was like that of a hunter. "Been a while. And you..." She looked to Acha who despite her best efforts stepped back letting out a slight whimper when their eyes met, Acha looked at her fearfully, the person that stood before her now was so different than the one they had left behind, everything about her was different, her stance, her aura, her whole presence seemed to breathe danger. "Acha yes?" She didn't wait for an answer. "I couldn't have done it better myself, how about just for now, I don't kill you." Marise winked at her as Acha grew increasingly more pale. "So what have I missed?" She turned as Elly approached her.

"Mari, no trouble ok?" She looked from Marise to Daniel as if to emphasis her point.

"Seems like some form of Pandora's box." She smiled deliberately avoiding the question. "Do you really want to let out what's inside?" She approached the field touching it lightly. "Why don't they produce real challenges any more?" She questioned walking a complete circle around the holding cell like a cat stalking its prey.

"It's unstable the slightest imbalance in the light the components will collapse causing a big enough explosion to wipe out this entire room and spread at speed to destroy the corridor. We were going to reflect the mirrors, but again the imbalance would be too great, the safest way would be to disconnect the sun beacon at the top but it would take longer than we have." Elly explained as Marise drew her sword.

"Sun beacon?" Marise questioned knowing she would never be too old for Elly's enlightenment.

"Yes, it's the device they use to gather the light energy from the sun, it's a large crystal which transports and stores the light's energy, in this case, half the energy travels down a beam to this room, where it is split and made to create a solid field of light, but due to the energy conversion, it becomes highly instable so the slightest imbalance causes an explosion. The power it stores throughout the day keeps it running at the same capacity overnight, it is quite a remarkable creation, yet at the same time..." Elly stopped aware of the others looking at her.

"And you are certain you want him alive?" Marise spun her sword in a few circular movements with a flick of her wrist, her piecing gaze passing over Eiji who lay unconscious on the floor.

"Mari, he is under my protection." That was the only answer Marise had needed.

"Lucky him." She smiled flipping her sword to the light side she walked around the barrier once more as if looking for something, Elly was already making her way to the door, yet the others stood and watched in awe, she gently inserted her sword into the barrier, the light part of her sword began to shine a brilliant white, a white so bright it seemed blue, a small section opened briefly she retracted her sword without entering, Elly now stood at the door knowing that not only had she solved the riddle of the retention cell, the solution she had found would not be the one she used, then came the words she had expected. "I suggest you run." She looked to Elly and smiled, the smile was returned as she swung her sword shattering the first side of the field, before it had even began to collapse she had passed through grabbing the scruff of Eiji's shirt and shattering the other side in one smooth movement. The others had made it to the door by the time the explosion began Elly rushed the others through into the smoke filled the corridor, it seemed like an age before the smoke settled, but when it did Marise was approaching dragging Eiji behind her. "Here's your toy." She flicked him at Elly who caught his limp body, Daniel and Acha simply stood open mouthed staring in disbelief at what they had just witnessed. Daniel swallowed as Marise approached caressing his face with her sword she eyed him before retracting the blade, Daniel gasped as he felt the warmth of blood as it ran down his face.

"Must you destroy everything?" Elly questioned shaking her head in mild amusement, in answer Marise simply smiled.

"Power is it?" She turned to Elly to look at the smouldering remains of the room and corridor they had barley escaped in time.

"Well if nothing else the guards know we are here." Daniel whispered not expecting her to hear, a deep shiver passed through his spine as he heard her laugh.

"Guards? Do you think I would let even one live? The only power to worry about here is me, let's press on. Surely this castle has more entertainment to offer." Marise clicked her fingers, the door before them vanishing into flames, the others found it impossible to keep up, so followed the path of destruction she left. The only thing that concerned Elly at this point was how over destructive she was being, although she was ruthless she was normally quite sensible about it, something had annoyed her, there was more than just a, 'I'm glad to be back' feel about what she was doing, it was almost as if she was trying to prove a point, but to who?

***

Marise finally entered the chamber of the Lord; she scanned him over with little interest before addressing him.

"Give me your rune now." She commanded, although her voice was gentle something about the way she spoke oozed with threat.

"W…Why? Why would I give it to you, this rune gave me my army." He pulled a cord by his chair ringing a giant bell.

"Look out your window child and see what has become of your *great* warriors." The young lord rose to his feet to meet her challenge, he turned back slowly to face her.

"Your friends have done a good job, but I am more than a match for any girl, if you want my rune you must take it from my cold dead body." Something about the way she smiled made him shudder, as he drew his sword.

"Fine by me." She matched his stance waiting for his first attack.

Acha and Daniel stopped to catch their breath seeing that they had finally caught up with her, yet at the same time, they were not relieved at having done so, as their gaze met with battle.

"I guess she's not as skilled as rumours say." Acha whispered, Elly took the satchel from Daniel and began pawing through it.

"No… she's just playing with him, cat to mouse." Elly looked at Acha her eyes piercing right into her soul. "She could kill him at any time, but that would be foolish without first taking the time to size up the guardian."

"Guardian?" Daniel questioned as Elly returned to making the narca berry puree.

"There are two challenges to a rune, let's say the rune already belongs to someone, once that rune holder is destroyed the one who wishes to claim it must prove their worth by wagering their lives in battle to the protector of the rune, the guardian links itself to the one whom it is destined to be with, runes that are not in the possession of someone still contain the guardians but they will only link to the one who is meant to retrieve them, think about it, each time we have taken a rune, there was something to overcome, each time we may have died in the process." Elly glanced to the battle "It's over." Despite her warning, when the final blow was struck Acha screamed as blood sprayed from the body and painted the walls. She breathed a sigh of relief to find he still breathed, his weak voice pleading Marise for mercy.

"From your cold, dead, body was it?" She smiled down at the young lord as he begged for his life. "It would be dishonourable not to stick to our agreement." She lifted him up to his knees by his hair stabbing her sword through his throat. He grabbed the blade as it protruded through as he coughed and choked she snatched the rune from its cord around his neck pushing him from her sword with her foot. She placed the pendent in the centre of the room as a dark cloud began to rise from it, as it did Marise pointed her open hand towards the doorway in which the others sat creating a small impenetrable field much like the one near the circle of fire separating them from her.

Finally the smoke took on a solid form, it was every bit the demon she had expected, its razor sharp fangs stained red with blood, its jagged claws, capable of doing irreparable damage to anything they would strike, and its greatest weapon, an enormous barbed tail that grew thinner to a razor sharp point, capable of impaling its prey with little effort. Its four red eyes focused on her for but a moment before it turned slowly to look towards Elly, distracted only by the blow Marise struck as she flipped over its side, as the creature turned she summoned an enormous ball of flame to her launching it at the creature, although a direct hit it seemed not to penetrate the demons thick hide yet, at the same time small blisters appeared on her arm where the same heat thrown at the demon had somehow been reflected to her. She looked to Elly.

"Lee, don't tell me, my rune was sacrifice." She sighed, shifting the sword in her hand. Daniel and Acha watched in shock, it was clear why she had a place in legend as the most dangerous warrior of all time, such speed, grace and accuracy was behind each movement, the creature due to its size should have been fairly slow, yet its attacks fell at a speed impossible to its body. Despite this it was unable as yet to lay a single blow, it was so unnatural watching her fight, it was a skill they imagined only a God could possess. Then something happened, for a split second Marise looked away, something had caught her attention, something that made even her stop for that brief second, but that second was all that was needed, the creature turned, dealing what would have been a deadly blow with its spear like tail if she hadn't moved, its razor sharp tail pieced her already injured shoulder, although she didn't let out a single sound, she simply drew back as far as the barbed tail would allow before slicing the end of it clean off, she forced the remaining part through her shoulder before dogging its next blow. She moved quickly, in a blink of an eye she was on the creatures back slicing her sword through its head with the aid of gravity as she jumped down decapitating it. Yet the creature continued to move to fight. The others could do nothing but watch in morbid fascination as the headless creature fought back, it seemed almost as if she took flight as she attacked, putting as much force behind each blow as she could, but she was injured now, it was starting to slow her somewhat, she stood for a moment, the blood from her own wound began to run down her arm spiralling around her blade. Having now completed administering the potion to Eiji and seeing the start of his recovery Elly too began to watch. The battle grew more intense, as the being simply refused to die.

"That thing is an immortal, how can she win?" Acha whispered

"It's not immortal as such, that creature is one of the most powerful of this time, it's caused by fear, fear and power run hand in hand, when a ruler possesses this rune the fear of those he controls makes the rune stronger, thus the guardian grows and the power the rune provides does also, it's a never ending cycle." Elly gave a sigh as Marise once more slowed to catch her breath, it was only a second, unnoticeable to the others that watched, but Elly was all too familiar with her fighting patterns. "She's using up more energy than she has." Daniel glanced to Elly with concern, her vision fixed firmly inside the room. "Even so she will not be defeated." It seemed Elly was not talking to either of them, he followed her vision, he swore for a second he saw a dark figure in the shadow of the room, near the exact place Marise had looked before being struck, when Daniel blinked the figure had gone. Marise raised her sword and with a final scream tore the creature's chest apart ripping its heart from its body as it fell to the floor to lie at her feet. The heart still beat slightly until she sliced it apart to remove the pendent, as she took it in her hand, the creature itself and all the blood shed by it, turned to mist entering the pendent once more.

Elly stepped through the field; Daniel went as if to follow finding his way still blocked for a second until the field vanished.

"Lee." Marise smiled taking her hand she turned it over before placing the power rune in her hand.

"Did you have to drag it out so? We have a deadline." Elly smiled playfully.

"True, but where's the fun in that… It's been a while since I have been able to let loose." Elly smiled and Marise and shook her head.

"You never change, but you do grow careless." Elly touched the open wound on Marise's shoulder.

"Blame my stupid half, I guess that's the trouble with this world, not to mention my rune, I can't heal, but it proves to make things interesting." Marise looked at the body of the young Heir. "This is one mess we won't have time to clean… shall we" Marise motioned towards an exit in the back of the room that until that point none of them had noticed.

"There they are… assassins! They murdered our lord, our Heir!" Marise's hand fell to the hilt of her sword about five guards approached followed by demons in guard like amour, Elly placed her hand on Marise's shoulder shaking her head.

"Now is not the time." Elly walked away, supporting Eiji's weight, although he was not yet fully conscious, he had the awareness to be able to put one foot in front of the other as he was guided, waiting at the door she saw the others through as the guards hesitated by the entrance. Once they had all passed through Marise turned and slowly walked away, their will to live let her, she smiled to herself walking away; she hadn't had this much fun assassinating someone since Max Radillion…

The mansion was enormous, although compared to Blackwood's, which was an undamaged monument from eras past, it was small, but even at half the size it was a magnificent example of the skills from times past, a side wall and the roof were the only visible places where repairs had been made. Below their concealed location on the steep mountain side, they could just make out the small town of Napier village below, a small town that sat on the borders of desert, marsh, mountain and a healthy looking grassy terrain.

"Ok, remember, we do not know who else in there knows of Max's discovery, primary target is Max Radillion, you know him, tall skinny man, been to Blackwood's meetings in Knightsbridge a few times." She nodded as Elly explained, she knew him well, a slimy little weasel, she knew, one day would be her target, she was grateful for having this opportunity, she always wondered who would get him first, his own men, or her. "Contact…" Elly paused a second before continuing. "Ishatar Valantie, the contact must get out alive, understand?" Marise's face seemed to glow with anticipation.

"No boundaries?" She questioned, her eyes scanning over the mansions security.

"Just that one."

"The contact, how will I know her?"

"He gave no details, but you know his type." Marise nodded before making her way to the wooden gates, it was little after noon, security at this time was always light, after all, no one was stupid enough to make an attack in broad daylight. Still, she knew she had to be careful, on the North and South of the perimeter stood two large watchtowers, each housing two guards, if either of them were to sound the bell positioned at the top of the tower, the game was over and her target would no doubt escape.

Walking through the gate was not an option either, she had already counted at least four of her wanted posters on the inside perimeter, she watched as the guards patrolled, a group of four, with two rookies, then three groups of two. That made fourteen guards, fairly high numbers considering the time of day.

She hid in a tree near the Northern tower, covered by the protection of the tree's leaves as she lay on the branch timing the laps the ground force made, she noticed that this tower's watch area, slightly overlapped the watch area of the Southern tower, even with this fact, the guards could only see clothing and silhouettes of the adjacent guards, something that could work to her advantage.

Finally she was ready, she jumped to the wall using its cracks and bricks to allow her to climb, thirty seconds until the guards checked this way, then one minute until her path was clear.

Five seconds left, she saw the support beams of the tower, she judged their distance carefully before launching herself onto it, three seconds to the floor guards' appearance, she pulled herself below the base of the platform resting on top of the highest support.

The guards passed, not so much as glancing in her directions, the next passers would not be so flippant, but if she were to move too much now, the other watchtower would see her entrance. She slid slowly to the side of the enormous support using the one running parallel to keep her in location before she realised this a bad idea swapping to the other beam she angled herself so her vision could not see the courtyard, hence their vision would not find her.

After what seemed like an eternity, the large gap between patrols was upon her, making her way to the back view of the tower she pulled herself over the edge landing silently behind the East and South facing guards as they scanned the court yard while the South watch tower looked out over the nearby forest area. Her hand gripped the mouth of the first guard as her sword drove through his body, his legs gave beneath him as his body became lifeless, Marise moved him silently as possible to impale his figure against the nearby roof support with his own short sword, an action that could not be done without attracting his partners attention, he turned to face her, not a word escaped him before he was struck down his neck snapped as she grabbed him....five seconds remaining until view change, she glanced around, there wasn't enough time to secure him. She leaned his limp body against her his large build covering any trace of her presence.

She stood for some time, moving the figure's head occasionally by using her hand on the back of his neck; finally, the watch had stopped. She took the rope attached to the bell, severing it to tie him into location. It was then she saw them, two guards on the roof of the building, they were paying little attention to their job, but still, they could pose a threat should they notice the Southern watch towers bodies missing, she had to execute similar cautions on that tower as well when she reached it.

Grabbing two spears from the rack they had stored in the corner, she jumped from the edge of the tower landing outside the walls perimeters, quickly she made her way to the southern tower, scaling it the same way she had previously, all the time counting. She leapt to the tower driving the first spear through the head of the closest guard, his partner turned, losing his hand as he turned to sound the alarm, without a second thought she followed through severing his head from his body, His lifeless body fell to the floor, the roof guards now looked straight at her, they seemed to hesitate for a second, it was this hesitation that cost their lives. She took the hand fitting preloaded crossbow from her recent kill using it to send two of the five preloaded arrows into their hearts, killing them instantly before strapping the weapon to her wrist.

She descended inside the gates, slicing the ladder from half way up ensuring no one could climb it, she raced to the other tower, caring little if any should see her, now, there was no way to raise an alarm, the mission was as good as completed. Despite this she rolled under the tower behind its main support as they turned the corner, she waited for them to get closer before she emerged slicing the ladder of the watch tower, the guards saw her, fear filled their eyes as they ran quickly to engage in combat, they never had chance to draw their sword as the smell of burnt flesh filled the air, the others followed, hearing the commotion, they were disappointingly easy to slay, she took cover at the edge of the building waiting for the next party to set eyes on their dead comrades only to be silenced.

None remained standing. She was surprised, not one of the guards had thought to try to reach the Southern tower to raise the alarm, but compared to Blackwood's guards, these were little more than rookies, although it seemed they had been training for some time they had never really had chance to test their skills, and now only when the opportunity presented itself, they saw how unprepared they were.

The mansion entrance was clear of guards, room by room she searched, killing silently any she would cross. She grabbed a lady from the kitchen meeting her fearful brown eyes as her sword was forced to her throat

"Name?" She commanded glancing her over, she was fairly pretty, blond

"G...Grace." She stammered

"You're demi-human?" The young lady removed her hat to reveal her cat like ears she trembled nervously as Marise lowered her sword. "I suggest you leave." Marise released the lady before exiting the room grabbing the three small tubs of lighter oil leaving a trail as she walked.

The second floor was nearly empty, it seemed this area was set aside for residence and special servants, but there were still a few people alive here, one was hiding in this very room. She opened the cupboard pulling the young woman to her feet, another blond

"Ishatar Valantie I presume?" The figure nodded. "You're not on my list today." Marise eyed her up and down carefully, her senses warned her of approaching figures, two of them, feeling them enter the room she spoke without the need to turn and confirm their presence. "Max I presume, how about you hand over the documentation now?" She released her grip on the 'contact' and turned to face Max, who seemed to have employed a rather sturdy looking bounty hunter.

"So it's true, you do work for Blackwood." Marise raised her eyebrow at his words in mild amusement. "I just needed proof, which I thank you for providing, I had my sister leak the information to him, he has always been sweet on her." Marise smiled coldly, none of them saw the strike that killed her, but his sister collapsed to the floor as Marise seemed to sheath her sword.

"That was rather stupid, she was not on my list today, but you had to gloat, do you really think I didn't know?"

"What?" Max questioned outraged.

"Your sister, Valantie wasn't our contact, she wasn't on my list because Blackwood is an old pervert and wants her to himself you idiot. I mean come on, he let it slip to her in the first place, in turn she told you so you could gain support of the council and have Blackwood disgraced, even despite her treachery, he is a sucker when it comes to women."

"Is that why he keeps you?" Max smiled

"No he was too busy with your sister." Marise smiled sarcastically. "So what's with the muscle, I give him about thirty seconds until I come through him for you, I wont even draw my sword... how about we up the odds... do you bet your life on this bounty hunter skill?"

"He could finish you in the time it takes for me to finish one cigar." He smiled pulling a cigar from his pocket and lighting it as if to prove a point.

"That's a bet then, dangerous habit smoking, it'll kill you." She smiled looking back to the bounty hunter as Max spoke again.

"This isn't just any bounty hunter, assassin. This is assassin hunter Victor."

"So what's his speciality?" She questioned dryly, a moments silence passed as they eyed each other up for battle. "Surely Maxy, an assassin *hunter* should do some actual hunting... the way I see it, he's just a guy with a title to remind himself of what he is meant to be doing." She dodged his strike without the need to draw her sword. "That and to cover his own inadequacy, what your money brought you is a worthless sack of overconfidence."

"You have a sharp tongue for a child; let's see if your skills are as quick as your mouth." Max sneered as he began to exit the room. "What my money brought me is your bounty and failing all else, time to escape." He laughed, Marise rolled avoiding another swipe of the sword letting off the remaining three arrows in the preloaded crossbow she had taken from the tower, Max screamed as they pieced his flesh rooting him to his spot against the wall.

"Tut tut Maxy, I thought you wanted to watch." She rolled again grabbing the assassin hunter's arm as he tried to land a blow; she spun quickly under the outstretched limb taking it with her behind him dislocating it as she forced his own sword through his stomach, his sword still clutched in his own hand. He screamed in pain trying to remove it, but found it impossible before he collapsed. Marise turned to Max who was trying to wiggle his way out of the three quarter size arrows, blood from his arms and leg now staining his tailor-made suit. "Now for you." She pulled a fresh cigar from his pocket before extinguishing the old one on the wall by his head, lighting it she placed it in his mouth, pouring the remaining lighter oil over and around him. "Dangerous habit this, didn't I tell you it would kill you?" She smiled. "Oh don't worry, I wouldn't leave you like this... where would the fun in that be?... I want to make sure there isn't the slightest hope for escape, as you lose consciousness from blood loss, the last thing you will feel is your flesh melting as you burn alive. I give you the time it takes you, to finish one cigar." She smiled slicing her sword across his leg before turning and walking away...

***

Marise awoke to the sweet scents of home, the exotic fruits, the clean air, she found it hard to believe they had already travelled this far. Climbing from her bed she took a quick shower taking the time to examine her wound before heading to the dining room, spread on the table was a map, it seemed Elly had been examining this since returning, the pale liquid in the small glass on the table was unmistakable her favourite drink, it seemed she had stepped out for a second. Marise smiled running her fingers through her quickly drying hair before taking the quill from the table she was about to write on it when something caught her attention.

"Lee." Elly had barley approached the door when she heard her name not needing to wait for confirmation of her presence Marise continued, knowing she was there without the need to turn back. "This place Knights-errent it's like a documented form of history."

"Explain." Elly approached the table looking over the map a needle and thread already in her hand to stitch the wound, Elly knew from past experience this was one of the toughest wounds to stitch alone.

"Ok, well Abaddon, the Grimoire of darkness, Napier village, the Grimoire of light and life force, the perpetual forest, the Grimoire of air, Castlefort, the place we have just came from was in the vicinity of the Grimoire of earth, the courts of twilight, the Grimoire of fire, the mountain of the spirits the Grimoire of water each of the seven locations must be a place a Grimoire was sealed." Marise traced her finger along the seven fixed points on the map of Knights-errent she stopped at the final location, the only one from which she had not retrieved a book. "That means… the final Grimoire lies here." She pointed to a small almost deserted island. "Crowley."

"Well, you were there for some time… surely if it was there you would have known." Elly knew this wasn't strictly true, she was just stalling for time while the others left the house, luckily, Marise was never wise to her deception. Elly moved to sit her facing away from the window as she began to stitch her shoulder as they spoke, shortly she would have to meet Eiji on the trail or he would never get back here in time for them to leave.

"Maybe not, these seven locations are key magical points, each one before baring a home to the Grimoire, it was thought to be one of the seals created to restrain the Severaine, hence why they are fixed points in the ever changing world of Knights-errent, as the worlds are linked their magic residue flows over sealing these points from this world's change for protection, meaning the points can only be released if both worlds are accessible, but once we took the first book, the barriers only weakened for a spilt second long enough for you to locate the next, but each time it grew more difficult because the remaining barriers strengthened. If we were to destroy the barriers, the seventh book's location would without a doubt be revealed to us."

"How do you plan on doing that?" Elly questioned watching Daniel as he walked from the building; it seemed as if he was looking for something.

"Well, first we take out the first five Severaine barriers that can only be released in Knights-errent, they happen to be part of the magic composition that makes up the protection beacon for the Grimoire, then we destroy the barriers we know of in our world if still standing once they are done, that means reversing any sealing spells I may have cast along the way, once this is done the seventh barrier will be weak enough to pinpoint its location and then we can get the final Grimoire and rule besides Night."

"True as that may be, you know as well as I, it cannot be your current self that seizes the book." She finished the final knot on the stitches, although even stitched, it was still one nasty wound, the stitches did little than hold the wound together, but until this was over, she knew neither Marise or Zodiac would be able to use healing powers for their own aid.

"Then what do you suggest?" Marise questioned waiting for the response.

***

"Are you sure?" Acha asked timidly. "I did as you instructed before but…" She sat at the edge of her bed swinging her legs gently looking towards the floor as oppose to her visitor.

"You doubt me?" A gentle voice questioned, a young lady stood before her, her long blond hair fell in gentle curves to her waist, she tipped Acha's head to look into her beautiful blue eyes, she pulled away slowly, still after all this time found it hard to believe the one that stood before her was an angel, she was everything she had imagined, the innocent eyes, the soft voice, the large flowing white wings, yet still she doubted somewhat she was being told.

"I... no... it's just." Acha sighed, she found this conversation their most strained yet, all the other times Sofie had visited it had been like the return of an old friend, everything she had spoken made so much sense, it all seemed so right, but even now, that haunting look of betrayal played on her mind, not only that and the clear change between her and Marise had left her doubtful.

"Acha I understand." She smiled gently locking eyes with her. "I feel your confusion. The pretence from before is bound to leave you somewhat confused about where her loyalties lie, but I assure you, everything she did that day was for her own selfish desires."

"I... I really thought, back then, she was my friend." Tears welled in Acha's eyes, things had become much more complicated since meeting Sofie, but, in the same way, everything was also clearer, especially since she explained what actions were taken and why, even the simplest gesture had a million schemes behind it, it was all so clear, yet still she didn't want to believe it.

"You know that was her intention, to gain your trust, to win your friendship, if it hadn't been for me you would still be being fooled by her, you're so innocent, so trusting, how could she not take advantage of the situation, her only thought, her only desire from this, was not your friendship, it was the book. You are her easiest ticket to it, can't you see? She used you, and as painful as it is, it is better you discover this now, from a true friend like me, than someone who would mislead you from when first you met. You were her shortcut, her easiest option, is it not better to win your trust and have you go willingly than force you and draw attention to herself in the process?"

"But... true I am his daughter, when I was sealed away all those years ago I became no longer his flesh and blood, I am whoever's flesh I take, so not his by anything but life-force, there is no way I could take that book." The angel paused after Acha had finished, almost as if in silent contemplation, she was indeed a bright young girl, but too innocent and trusting.

"Maybe this is a mere oversight on her part, she is not the most rational of people, but one thing is painfully clear, if you don't act, everyone you care for, all those too involved to see through her spells, those I cannot reach, they will all be destroyed and everything you have fought to live for, to protect, will go up in smoke, this is your destiny, you are the only one who can end this. Only you can save your friends from certain doom." Acha looked to the angel a new confidence filling her eyes.

"Tell me, what must I do?" The angel placed a gentle hand on her shoulder before perching herself on the edge of the bed.

***

"Zo!" Daniel's voice echoed through the forest he had just emerged from, he had been searching for her for the best part of an hour without luck. Finally, he found her in the clearing just before the rise to the high place practicing her sword skills. Already he knew it was not the person he had been seeking, he had hoped the switch back had somehow sealed away her monster, but was devastated to find he had been very much mistaken. "Zo." He said again, a little shakier than last time, Marise was ignoring him completely. "You and Acha, you really need some time to sort this out." As pathetic as they were, the words he chose were what his thoughts provided, he had thought of so many things to say, but none of them would leave him, as he stood facing her, his mind went blank spilling out the first sentence that came to mind. Marise turned to look at him, again as their eyes met he felt himself falter, yet continued forwards regardless of what his better judgement warned.

"Is that, the best you can do?" Marise's hand gripped her sword as she mocked him, it was clear from her posture she was still in an incredible amount of pain with her wound, yet she wasn't the kind of person to let something like that hold her back. "I had expected so much more from you after your previous challenge, just making it all the more clear that again, I have overestimated you, I find you a disappointment, I don't know what she sees in you, you're are about as much use as a rusty blade, well," She scoffed. "Less I would have to say, if I were being completely honest." Daniel clenched his fists at her mocking words, something about her infuriated him more than he could possibly imagine, maybe it was the sheer anger at her controlling his friend, maybe it was the complete lack of respect she had for anything and everyone, but more realistic than any of those reasons, was he hated her because she kept taking away the people he loved, first his brother and now the one he loved more than life itself, he did not want to lose her, not to her not to anyone, he would do anything to protect her, anything.

"I don't care if you are the world renowned Marise Shi." Daniel was surprised at the force and venom behind his own voice. "You release my friend now!"

"And if I don't?" She questioned a challenging smile crossing on her lips before she continued. "Tell you what, I am not completely heartless, how about a proposition, we fight, if you defeat me, I shall give you her back, for now that is." Her smiled chilled Daniel to the bone. "However, if I win, you and your life belong to me." Daniel stood staring at her for a moment in disbelief, he knew there was no way he could win, but if he didn't try he would loose her forever… Daniel felt the sinking feeling hit his stomach as he nodded accepting her challenge. There was never really any choice; his best friend was being sucked into a void dominated by Marise Shi. He snapped his staff into solid form, with this simple movement their battle began.

Before he had even blinked Marise had vanished from before his eyes and was about to deliver the first blow, even before he had located her the staff pulled up to block her overhead attack, Marise smiled somersaulting back to land before him.

"I see you are not completely without skill." She smiled. "Or maybe it has something to do with the carvings on that magic staff of yours, I do wonder how someone like you could get his hands on such so rare and valuable weapon, no worries, I will take it from your lifeless body soon enough. A huge ball of flame hovered above her hand. "There's only one way to beat a staff like yours." She threw the ball, it travelled at an incredible speed, Daniel lined himself up hoping he could somehow knock it back or dodge from its path, but were he to dodge he would leave himself open. Moments before impact the ball split into about ten smaller balls, he knew there was no way to counter them all, he closed his eyes for impact yet as they approached a magnificent blue field covered the length of his body absorbing the balls he heaved a sigh of relief as the first one hit, although he was quickly reduced to his knees, his small victory somewhat hollow as Marise sliced his open back. "You're staff may be magic, but you don't have the fighting skill necessary to use it to your advantage." She laughed. "Come on get up, I'm not finished with you yet." Daniel rose steadily to his feet as if by her command, she tossed another fireball towards it, Daniel sidestepped just in time for it to sail past so he could block another attack, she launched attack after attack, Daniel suffered only small scrapes from those he did not quite block, he knew all too well had she been completely serious, the battle would have finished long ago. She nodded slightly before attacking again; it was painfully clear how much she was holding back. No sooner had her blow struck his staff a seething pain of fire spread across his back. "Did you really think *I* would miss?" She taunted, striking his leg as the fire distracted him, Daniel fell to the floor once more, there wasn't a part of him that wasn't somehow scratched by her weapon, even the tiniest of cuts now seemed more severe as he gasped for air, he knelt a few feet before her, try as he did he could not summon the strength to stand, she spun her sword in a few circles impatiently before poising it for battle, waiting to see if he could muster the will, the strength to once more stand before her. "I guess the victor is clear, time to claim my spoils." She walked towards him stopped by a figure appearing from the air to stand between them.

"Marise enough!" The figure commanded, Daniel looked to the dark haired figure recognition in his eyes before the arms that supported him to kneel collapsed sending him to the floor.

"But..." She protested, her hand rising protectively to her shoulder, which was once more bleeding through its cover, Daniel was aware of the distant conversation as darkness rocked him to sleep.

"I believe I made myself perfectly clear about hurting my daughter's friends." He snapped.

"But even so rules apply." As Marise spoke the figure was glancing down at Daniel, he was in serious need of medical aid, there was no time to stand and argue, he snapped his fingers, the protests silenced as Marise fell to the floor, caught only by the figures swift movements, Daniel forced himself from the darkness just long enough to see the figure the stranger held was no longer Marise, he lowered her to the floor with such tenderness, almost as if he was afraid she may break, this was the last thing Daniel saw before the darkness took him completely.

***

"Daniel?" Zo whispered opening her eyes to the strangest feeling of deja-vu, as she gazed upon the stranger from Abaddon, the stranger smiled reassuringly. She let out a cry as she became suddenly aware of the pain from her shoulder, it seemed the wound had been reopened, estimating its size she knew she was wrong, something must have happened, something to injure her further, but she couldn't even begin to imagine what.

"He'll be alright, well, after you have seen to him that is, as for your shoulder." He passed his hand over it, she felt the pain instantly relieve. "Although circumstances dictate this cannot be healed by magic, this should help relieve the pain for a few hours at least." She lay not moving for a second a strange feeling drifting over her.

"I remember you from before, from the village but also..." She stayed in his arms a moment longer while she fought for the memory, within his arms she felt safe, protected, but she had no time for such feelings, she pulled herself into a sitting position so she could see Daniel, she almost cried with horror when she saw the blood and burns that covered his body. "By the Gods what did I do?" She whispered raising her hand to her mouth. "Daniel?" She moved around placing her hand on his chest, he opened his eyes slightly for some unknown reason, he smiled at her. She closed her eyes, not for concentration, but because she couldn't bare to look at what she had done, she whispered inaudibly to the winds that rose around her, Daniel watched through her mind as the tiny orbs of nature enter her body before connecting to her in fine silver threads. The threads joined and connected inside her to form a larger thread leaving her hands her fingers her chest joining her to him as he drifted away he felt himself being pulled into her once more, she felt his presence in her mind, sharing the images the flashed before her, the blood, the violence, everything she hated about herself on display for him to see, without even a thought, psychic walls erected to keep him out, but he had already seen too much, she was losing her focus, this was the reason why Hectarians never formed bond of friendship. She continued to heal feeling dirty and sick to the stomach of the images she had just seen. Daniel stood at the edge of her mind now blocked by the walls she had summoned, she wanted to keep him from her mind, keep him from the truth, although she knew he had already witnessed it first hand, she continued building the walls, yet as she did a single image from him entered her mind an image she held on to.

'Is this how he sees me?' She moved her hands across his body as their conscience linked, she watched his memories, through his eyes, she watched as a beautiful girl smiled brightly her electric blue eyes enchanting, making the beauty of nature pale in her presence, her brown copper hair shimmered gently as she ran before him. Finally, they stopped, setting down the picnic in their favourite place, she had never realised it then, but that night he had watched the sunset through her eyes. The moon had risen slowly, it had been such a perfect night, the image had soothed her, comforted her more than he could know, but then the violence started, she was alone again, stood in a dark void with nothing around her but the bodies of the dead, the floor was lined as far as she could see, corpses littered the field like grass, each of them grabbing her pointing at her accusing her, behind her flames lit the horizon. She tried to run yet as she did the dead grabbed at her pulling her down. She held on knowing if she was to stop now, she would not be able to try to heal him again for some time, she tried to block the images but despite her efforts, they grew stronger more horrific until finally, she removed her hand pushing the images deep within the recess of her mind, although the sick haunting feeling they left followed her. She wiped the tears from her eyes as Daniel gasped, almost as if he himself was waking from a nightmare, the images of death and violence still floating before his eyes, were these the images that haunted her so? The reason she called out in the night?

"Daniel I..." She looked away so he couldn't see the fresh tears that had formed in her eyes, yet in the attempt to avert her eyes from Daniel she met eyes with the stranger from Abaddon.

"Zodiac, your friend understands, he chose to fight that battle and face the consequences that came with it, if he hadn't taken that risk I doubt you would be sitting here now." The figure smiled gently crouching to wipe the tears from her eyes, his touch was so gentle, so tender, she closed her eyes as he wiped them away, before standing once more, he smiled at her gently, then, in the blink of an eye he was gone.

"Daniel." Zo sighed still averting her gaze, she felt his hand rest on hers, turning to look at him she saw he was smiling.

"I like these eyes best." He whispered pulling her into him, he held her tightly fearing to let her go, he breathed deep the aroma of plum blossom he had come to adore. "For a moment there..." His voice trembled slightly. "I thought I had lost you." Zo opened her mouth as if to reply but changed her mind, although she would never know if he heard the words she was to speak.

'You almost had.' She had felt it then, the touch of death upon her shoulder as she stood on the edge of obscurity, if not for the stranger's intervention, if not for him calling her back, she would have vanished forever.

"Ah there you are." Eiji emerged from a nearby tree, blushing as he saw their embrace. "Sorry I..." He turned to walk away unsure exactly what to say, he was already so tired, if it hadn't been for Elly meeting him along the track with a horse, he would be nowhere near the area yet, he had barely had chance to eat when she had requested him find the remainder of the group while she gathered supplies.

"No, it's ok." Zo pulled away rising to her feet followed by Daniel, Eiji watched as she tried to subtly wipe the tears from her eyes unable to miss the spreading patch of blood from her shoulder, Daniel too was covered in blood and scrapes, although the source of these he could not locate. "What's wrong?" She asked, Eiji somehow got the feeling that it should have been himself that asked that question.

"Elly's looking for you, she's ready to leave."

"Leave?" Questioned Daniel unable to hide the surprise in his tones.

"For Collateral, it seems it is the quickest route to our next destination."

"I see." Zo and Daniel dusted themselves down. "Eiji, I'm glad you're feeling better." She smiled, aware that he filched slightly as she linked him. "It wasn't the same without you." He looked down to her, slight bewilderment crossing his eyes.

"Erm... thanks." He blushed slightly, unsure what to say exactly, he noticed she also linked Daniel.

"Eiji, there's something I've been meaning to ask you... How did you end up here, with us I mean?"

"It's a long story." Eiji sighed, he knew at one point someone would have to ask, but hadn't decided how much he was willing to tell.

"You really are quite the mystery." She smiled once more looking towards the forest, which they were now heading towards.

"Not really, fate's path just led me here I guess."

"Maybe when this is all over, you can tell me everything." Eiji looked across to Zo, Daniel cringed expecting Eiji to state what all feared to be the truth, instead, to his surprise he simply smiled back.

"Sure, why not."

Chapter eighteen

"Zo listen... about before." Acha slowed her pace to walk besides her, respectfully, Elly took Daniel and Eiji to one side with the pretence of browsing, yet never really leaving hearing range, it was clear they had things to talk about, and if things were to go smoothly, it was better they did this as soon as possible, she could not afford their arguments to jeopardise the mission, at the same time, they felt uneasy, a delicate bond of trust had been shattered and so, they remained close, there was no telling what may happen. "I feel awful." Acha sighed stopping in the centre of the dirt track, much to the annoyance of those who had to walk around her. "I want to work this out; things can't go on as they are... I need to talk to you about this, until I understand why you did what you did, until I have heard your side of what happened... we can't move on from this... I don't want to feel this way, you're one of my only friends, I am just so consumed by this. It's hard to focus on anything else... I was hoping, you would give me the chance to talk this through, to explain." She lowered her vision to the floor. "That is... if you want to." Daniel and Elly exchanged cautious glances leaving Eiji to question what had happened, while Elly began to explain the events after his imprisonment, Zo had began to answer the request.

"I think..." She paused a sickening feeling rising to her throat, she swallowed hard, a million concerns and doubts crossing her mind before she finally answered. "I think that would be a wonderful idea." She never looked to Acha when she answered, she simply stared at the dirt track before them leading into the town's centre, Zo looked up aware the others still hovered close, Acha was aware of it too.

"Somewhere outside Collateral, while we do these can pick up much needed supplies." Acha smiled reassuringly at Zo. "A random road so no one can interrupt or eavesdrop?" She continued very much in the hinting style of Elly.

"We get the idea." Elly interrupted the continuous hints, although she had to wonder why Acha seemed so eager to take this conversation outside the walls of Collateral, especially when there were so many places within the city that would be just as private. "If you're that worried why not hire a couple of horses, you would be sure to out run us then." Elly smirked, before moving to examine the contents of a nearby store; Acha disappeared down one of the side streets quickly, her sudden disappearance surprising all.

"Are you sure you know what you're doing?" Eiji was the first to approach Zo. "Elly told me what happened." He added as she looked up to Elly.

"I know... but I have to take the chance and..." Before she could continue Acha returned with two impressive looking steeds, she had barely been gone a minute before her return, it did raise a few questioned about whether they had been waiting, but they were questioned left unasked.

"I was only joking." Elly whispered just loud enough for everyone to hear.

"True but it wasn't a bad idea, the less time we find looking for somewhere quiet, the sooner we can get to what's important, right Zo?" Zo looked at Daniel questioningly.

'I have to trust her.' She thought freely so he could hear, she wondered if he had also heard all the doubts echoing in her mind, since she last healed him, their connection had grown stronger, it was something she had to be constantly aware of, or else he may discover the truth, a truth she fought so hard to keep from everyone.

'But she's already betrayed you twice, yet now you will go riding with her to Gods know where and we can't even check if you're alright?' Daniel protested unsure if Acha's turning on her would, in Zo's eyes, be classed as a betrayal, in his it certainly was, she had betrayed Zo's friendship, then, after that, she endangered her life.

'If I don't, then what?' Daniel knew from the feelings behind this thought she was already resigned to going regardless of the outcome of this conversation, regardless of her instincts warning her not to go, regardless of what anyone or anything had to say, she was going.

'But if you do and…'

'I can handle myself… besides I'll send a sign as soon as we hit danger.' Zo shifted uncomfortably, aware the others were staring at her she still had yet to answer Acha's question, her shoulder began to twinge again, it seemed whatever suppressant magic the familiar stranger had used was beginning to wear off.

'As soon as?' Daniel questioned immediately as she had finished her last thought.

'I meant if, if we hit danger'

'It's not the we I'm worried about are you sure…' Zo looked away form him

'I have no choice, things cant progress as they are, better we settle this alone, one way or another this has to end.'

'But…' Zo couldn't help feeling the concern in his mind. *'Fine, but you better come back.'* Zo smiled at him

"Right." She said finally. "Sorry, I was miles away." She stated suddenly aware of how long had passed in silence during her conversation with Daniel.

"Your shoulder?" Eiji questioned, noticing that although it seemed to have stopped bleeding for the moment, the pain she was suffering slowly returned, she hid it well, it showed as merely a shadow in the back of her eyes, he wouldn't have noticed if it hadn't been for his mother displaying the same traits as she suffered with the illness that eventually killed her.

"Yes, the suppressant magic is wearing off." She gave a half hearted smiled and mounted the horse.

"Suppressant magic, you can do that?" Eiji questioned as she shifted uncomfortably on the horse, she didn't care much for saddles, she had always ridden bare back, or at least, this is what she thought, she seemed so comfortable on a horse, and she was sure she could almost remember galloping around, the wind blowing through her hair as she sought new adventure, just her and her best friend. She shifted again finally settling into the saddle, before pulling a small metal sphere from her pocket, she looked at it uncertainly.

"I can, but not on myself since I came across this rune, it doesn't really work, just like I can't heal myself."

"Then who…" Eiji questioned, Zo felt herself blush unsure if she should tell them of the strange encounter.

"We really should be off." Acha interrupted at Zo's relief, she threw the small silver ball to Daniel, it took him less than a second to realise it was the small ball given to her from the merchant in this very place, as Daniel held it in his hands, no music left its sphere.

"Look after this for me will you." She smiled before turning the horse to follow Acha; she looked at the street name as they began down towards the faint glow that was the portal. *'Commerce Avenue.'* She thought to herself, unsure if Daniel also had picked up on the clue, she sent it, more than anything, to put his mind at ease, even now, she could feel his concern.

Finally they passed through the portal emerging on a small island where there were no settlements just mile after mile of forest and the small grassland before it started which they now stood on. The entire island seemed miles above the waters the water's surface, it was almost as if this entire island was located on the top of a flattened sea mountain. Through the silence, they could just about make out the sound of the waves crashing on the cliff face below

On the way Acha had gone to great lengths to say she had heard of this place from the young man she had borrowed the horses from.

Zo had barely caught up when her horse began to shift she pulled gently on the reins trying to settle it with little luck, as she glanced around trying to locate the cause of this unease. With an all mighty buck the horse gave out a cry nearly throwing her from the saddle before taking off towards the forest, Zo heard Acha scream her name and begin to take off after her, what she never realised as she heard the cries go softer, Acha was no longer pursuing, she had barely entered a few feet into the forest before someone stopped her.

The horse ignored its master's orders to stop, the forest was as black as night, she turned quickly feeling the weight of someone behind her; she gave out a sigh of relief to see it was Seiken, but then a new fear filled her.

"Umemi wake up." The voice filled with elemental rhythm danced around her ears, all around her things seemed to grow a little darker, then the eyes all around came into view, they surrounded her completely, watching from the shadows of the trees, hiding in the branches watching as the horse ran on, deeper into the forest. Zo closed her eyes tightly as she shook her head in disbelief, willing them away; as she opened them once more the eyes had vanished along with Seiken. She glanced around just to make sure, even though they had vanished, she still felt as if she was being watched, nothing but the canopies of trees met her vision above her, canopies so well formed they protected the thorny undergrowth from the sun's rays. She tightened her grip on the reigns, something about this place, about this forest unnerved her, perhaps it was because, like the forest outside the rings of fire, she felt a complete numbness of all her senses.

***

Acha watched as Zo's horse flew deeper and deeper into the forest, the angel holding the reigns of her own horse helped her down.

"Acha Night." She whispered helping her down from the horse as she was gently stroking it to calm it. Acha looked up to her, still breathless from the shock of nearly being lost to the forest. "You did as promised." She smiled watching as the forest floor came to life with moving roots. "The forest will take it from here, you need not worry, your part is over." Acha moved slightly feeling something on her leg, as she looked down she saw the roots of the trees slithering across the floor, moving to wrap around her, fixing her to the spot before pulling back, forcing her to the floor, she screamed for Sofie's aid but she did nothing only watch as the roots work their way up her legs to her thighs, Sofie smiled gently her body shifting to take a new form, a form Acha knew instantly as that of Aburamushi.

"You!" She hissed looking at him as she tried to fight her way free from the roots holding her to the floor. "You tricked me!" She clawed at the ground trying to get free without luck finding the vines now wrapped around her wrists holding her firmly to the spot, so Aburamushi could examine her properly, he leaned forward, taking in everything about her, her looks, her clothes, he leaned closer still, touching her hair, touching her face before, breathing in her scent, she was helpless now to do anything, no matter how hard she fought, the vines fought harder, stealing her breath as they coiled around her like an enormous snake forcing the life from its prey.

"I never tricked you." He spoke again, this time in a softer voice, a voice she knew well, the creature changed before her to take on the form of Sara, the waitress she helped gain entry to the courts of twilight. The figure changed again to Seiken "It's just you chose to believe me over someone who has only tried to help you, to protect you." He changed to one final form, tears welling in Acha's eyes as she saw herself mounting the horse. "And what's more, you just signed the death warrant of all your friends, as I said, only you *could have* saved your friends from certain doom, it's just a shame you chose the wrong path." She turned the horse around as Acha screamed. "I should think by the time this was over…" Aburamushi laughed watching as Acha was dragged deeper and deeper into the forest. With all her will she called her powers to drain the life from these trees, without luck, all she could do was scream until the trees stopped her by coiling their roots tightly around her mouth, she felt them grow tighter and tighter around her ribs, forcing the breath from her body until finally she could no longer fight, she let out a final whimper as she lost consciousness.

***

The horse finally slowed to a stop, leaning forwards Zo stroked its nose gently, she lifted the saddle from it leaving it on the forest floor, it was then she saw the cause of its distress, a large rock had been placed under the saddle, but that was not the only thing that had caused it to panic, there was a darkness, something she felt so clearly herself from outside the forest, but now she had entered, she had lost all feeling of it ever being here, all feeling of everything for that matter. She remounted the horse searching it deeper for answers, but it was more difficult to get a reading from animals their thought pattern and understandings were completely different to the human and demi-humans of the planet. She glanced around convinced the horse was now calm, as it started once more listening to its master's voice. There was no sign of Acha anywhere although she could have sworn Acha had followed her into the forest, an attempt to help maybe? Or was it just an elaborate deception? Then a scream pierced the air, it seemed to come from all around, pinpointing its main direction Zo turned the horse heading in that direction hoping her tracking skill were still as good as they use to be, but soon she found they weren't. Her senses were inhibited by a strange magic and the place itself. Seemed impossible to navigate, the horse had only paced a few steps when it halted refusing to take a further step. Zo glanced around cautiously, nothing but trees met her vision, normally, this would be the kind of place where she would go to seek comfort, but there was nothing comforting about the place she was in now.

"Umemi." Seiken's voice whispered. "Wake up." Zo turned to look at him, he stood as clear as day on the ground feet away from the horse, it was different than last time they met, her eyes locked on his, already she could feel the heat rising to her face as she stared fixated on him.

"I am awake aren't I?" She questioned turning away to speak, in fear she would forever be lost in the depths of his eyes, she couldn't get distracted, not now, she had to find Acha.

"If you are, how can I be standing here?" She felt herself jump slightly before turning to look at him only to find he had vanished once more.

Acha's screams still echoed through the air as Zo tried to push the horse onwards, without warning it bucked flinging her from its back, she heard herself scream, yet instead of the ground she found herself embraced by Seiken's arms, she was powerless to do anything but to watch as the horse sped away into the darkness of the forest, she felt herself fall hitting the floor hit her as Seiken, once more, vanished.

"How far... have we come into the forest?" Zo questioned, fearing after asking such a thing aloud, that something may answer, to her relief nothing did, she brushed herself down as she began to walk.

"Umemi." He stood before her at a nearby tree. "You are in great danger, this is no ordinary forest." Acha screamed once more the sound of her voice seemed to dissolve Seiken into the air; she was growing sick of this place and its illusions. She glanced around, watching for any nasty surprises before breaking into a run, she dodged and jumped the sleeping trees and roots that lay in her way, misjudging them sometimes and falling hard to the ground, as she scrabbled to get up, her mind made her believe the roots themselves were trying to ensnare her, as they grabbed her ankle and seemed to coiled around her as she ran, she shook free quickly, sickness rising to her stomach as an air of silence fell upon her, Acha's screams had stopped. All around was nothing but the sound of deadly silence, she walked on.

***

"Commerce Avenue? Are you sure, that street has been inactive for... years at least." Elly couldn't hide the concern in her voice as they stood on the edge of the abandoned dirt track at the very edge of Collateral. It seemed no one had lived in this area from some time, the modest houses boarded up, unused and forgotten, much like this part of the town.

"Positive, I saw her and Acha take down it not long after they left." Daniel answered strictly speaking it was a lie, but he knew without a doubt, it was the way they had gone.

"But that gateway has been out of service for what seems like forever, it's none operational, Miss Elly see for yourself." An elderly man, a powerful Hectarian in his time, offered Elly the chance to test his theory. There had been many concerns raised since Daniel first mentioned this over an hour ago asking curiously where it led, Elly had gone straight to the village elder when she had discovered the truth, an old man about ninety but with the youth and dexterity of one half his age, he too had seemed concerned about the notion he had presented, alarmed that anyone could have gone down this particular street. Elly paced the avenue finding a road end but nothing more, she walked back sighing.

"What's in Commerce Avenue?" Eiji questioned looking at the grave expression on everyone's faces.

"It was condemned centuries ago now, it was rumoured it led to the island that was home to none other than the perpetual forest." The old man sighed. "But to pass through now is…" Daniel looked to Elly, her timescale had been far shorter than that the elder had just claimed, could it be Elly was wrong? Or perhaps, more likely, she was hiding something from them again.

"You mean the forest of silence? The forest of sleep?" Daniel interrupted, beating Eiji by seconds to the question. He stopped pacing the dirt track awaiting the much feared answer, if they had gone there, that would explain why Daniel felt nothing of Zo's presence, that and sheer distance.

"All of those yes." Elly answered. "Rumour has it, the Gods feared Night afraid he would rebel against them while they worked on turning him mortal, to protect themselves they created a small haven, on it they erected an enormous forest full of traps and lore, that forest was called the perpetual forest. Within this forest the Gods gave the trees life, not only that, but all those that entered found they could no longer use magic, it was stolen to feed to trees around them thus blocking any magic attempt within it, the other feature to this forest was travellers began to lose the ability to define reality from dream, when anyone but its creator Gods, their guests, summons or guardians would enter, the forest would sense their presence and…"

"Eat them!" The old man interrupted, unlike when Daniel interrupted, Elly did not give him a scornful look. "You see, the forest causes sleep unlike anything known to these worlds, the trees lore their victim to its centre, feeding images into their mind, then as they reached it they would never awake again, the trees are said to absorb them into their bark feeding on their life-force for centuries, until nothing remained of the ones it had captured, but as I said, the door has been sealed for…" There was no time to finish his sentence before, from nowhere, Acha appeared on horse back, a panic stricken look on her face, she rode so hard that on seeing them she nearly fell straight off the horse.

"Come quick." She panted urgency ringing in her voice. "Something terrible has happened." She gasped for breath pausing for a moment before continuing. Daniel rushed to her side, knowing that Zo was not also going to miraculously appear down a sealed street. "I was riding with Zo and we appeared on this island, her horse went galloping into the forest of perpetual night! You have to hurry." Daniel offered Acha his hand helping her down from the horse as Elly watched an odd expression on her face, despite a strange doubt at the back of his mind he went to leave until Elly pulled him back.

"What are you doing?" He snapped, trying to break free of her grip.

"I do not think it is wise to rush in, let's go to the tavern, have a drink and Miss Night can tell us exactly what happened."

"But Zo… she's in trouble." Daniel protested aware Acha was doing so also. Elly slapped the horse sending it on its way back to its owner.

"True." Elly said calmly. "But it would be pointless to rush in and be trapped ourselves, besides we need as much information as possible regarding the forest of perpetual night, I thought it was merely a legend." Elly led Acha through the town, her hand pressed firmly on the small of her back as she encouraged the movement; she only released her when they entered the small tavern that sat just outside the boundaries of the disused town.

"But you just said…" Elly shot a silencing look at Daniel; this was the only warning he would need.

"Acha, how did you escape? Maybe you can give us some insight as to how to get her out." Elly questioned thanking the waiter, that without so much as a word, had brought and left a few drinks.

"I never went in." She answered a tone of urgency in her voice as she glanced through the window in the general direction of the street.

"But your horse was covered in leaves and forest debris."

"Was it?"

"Most definitely." Elly kept the same calm tones she had since Daniel had helped her from the horse.

"Oh. Well I can assure you I most definitely did not, I could only watch as she vanished." Elly looked to Eiji, who in turn, turned his sight to Daniel.

"We're wasting time, surely she can tell us all this on the way." He sighed impatiently a sick nauseating feeling swimming around him.

"I have to agree, in that place, who knows what dangers lurk, time is of the essence." Acha stood followed by Daniel.

"Daniel, be patent." Elly scolded. "To head into the forest of perpetual night is just what they want. We need to plan this carefully, or else we will end up trapped for eternity." Daniel sighed following Acha, Elly rolled her eyes, they were always so impatient, if they had just waited a few more moments, she gave a sigh with no choice she left they had already covered a lot of ground, but even should they get there before her, they would be unable to go any further.

***

"Umemi, you need to get out of here!" Zo stopped looking to Seiken

"Why are you here?" She snapped, not so much at him, more at the situation she found herself in. She grew more and more lost and with this realisation came frustration, despite Acha's screams having stopped, she felt she was no closer to finding her than she was ten minutes ago.

"You're asleep again." His gentle voice didn't rise to her short tone.

"Sure just like to you said the mine fields were safe!" She spat suddenly, remembering now why she was to be careful of him, reminding herself why she shouldn't find herself forgetting everything as she looked upon him.

"What?" Seiken questioned, the utter bewilderment on his face made her doubt the words she had spoken.

"After last time, how can I trust you?" She turned away continuing walking hoping somehow to come across Acha, it was more difficult to pinpoint her without her screams for guidance, in this place, none of her magic seemed to work either.

"Umemi, you have to believe me, think back, was that really me that stood before you and endangered your life?" He sighed, his voice although maintaining its soft questions had an underlying sadness to it, he wasn't really sure what had happened, but from his conversation with Eiji it seemed serious, he met her eyes before continuing. "Night discovered I was helping you, he imprisoned me; ask Eiji if you doubt my words, it could not have been me!" He stressed this time his voice rose to meet her accusation.

"You're here now, did you, by some miracle, escape?" Zo wasn't sure what had come over her, this wasn't like her at all.

"This place is different, last time you think we met, it was Aburamushi, the one Acha released. Ume you have to wake up they know you are here." He glanced around nervously. "Please."

"Even if I am asleep as you say, it's day. They cannot touch me by their own rules, right?" Zo felt the unexplainable anger begin to fade. "Don't I only have to contend with the monsters after your nightfall?"

"You don't understand, in Knights-errent, this is the forest of perpetual night, or in your world you call it the perpetual forest, the sleeping forest, the forest of silence, whichever you choose, it is *always* night here, the time phase you have to contend with is the one you enter from, normal rules do not apply this is their territory, their ground, those who step inside are fair game regardless of what rules are set. Acha knew this, she knew this…"

"I know." Zo sighed reluctantly, she had felt it even before they had set out to this place, and again as they arrived here, it felt almost as if she knew the place, she had just been so desperate to believe she was wrong.

"Then why argue so?" His voice seemed to plead for her to listen he took her hand gently in his and sighed.

"This, this is the third time she has betrayed me, I was hoping things would play different, but as soon as I saw this place I knew, she really hates me this much, enough to sell me to the enemy." Zo sighed.

"It must be hard." Zo pulled her hand away from Seiken

"Excuse me?" She questioned unsure exactly what he meant by his words Seiken grabbed her shaking her gently

"I said wake up, they're coming!" He release his grip. "In this place both your sword and magic are useless, please wake up." He clapped his hands, for a second the scenery changed, but all too soon she was back facing Seiken a wave of panic rising in her as she felt the darkness. "Run then!" He exclaimed pointing her in the direction of the exit, his voice seemed desperate, alien to its normal calm exterior. "Whichever way your mind tells you to go, follow the other, you must leave this place." He called as she ran.

Zo stopped she felt a slight tingling of her powers slumbering within her, before her there seemed to be nothing but trees, yet when she blinked again she saw the exit, as she saw the place they had first arrived, she paused, now she knew the secret of this place.

"Not without Acha." She stopped dropping her bag where she stood and running towards what her mind convinced her were the thinner trees.

"But she betrayed you!" Seiken shouted after her, eight more steps, eight more steps and she would have been free from the forest, she knew how close she was to the exit, Seiken was sure of it, yet she turned back.

"I know." She continued without looking back only to find Seiken had appeared in front of her.

"Three times she deliberately turned on you, endangering your life... Why must you risk yours to save her?" He could have understood this actions if maybe it was Daniel, or a good friend, but to risk her life for someone that wants more than anything to destroy her, it didn't make sense at all, he appeared again before her.

"If I don't... all her thoughts of me become true, and despite that, she only acted on what her heart believes, she's pure that way."

"She will do it again you know." Seiken called after her growing tired, although this place was different and the bonds that bound him back in Knights-errent didn't affect his passage here, travelling here still made him weary.

"I'll be ready, I need to address this one thing at a time, I must find her, to the centre first." She called back

"No, wake up first!" He shouted with all his power to ensure it reached her, he could only hope for the next few moments, while he recovered, she would be safe.

***

"That's funny." Acha said to herself as she looked around the gentle forest lit by the warm glow of dawn light, it danced across the pale forest as the trees swayed gently in the soft breeze. "I could have sworn..." Her words trailed off as an elderly lady approached, she was fairly small, her old clothes now worn and tattered hanging on her frail body, but her smile was so warm, so friendly, she stopped to stand just before her.

"Tell me child, what brings you to these woods?" Her voice was filled with age and hidden weakness, her voice seemed somehow and distant, although she stood right besides her for the power behind her voice had she stood any further away her words may have been lost.

"Who are you?" Acha questioned startled by her sudden appearance from nowhere.

"Just a stranger with little time." She sighed looking at the young girl there was something about her that reminded her of herself at that age something pure. "You?" She questioned.

"My names Acha." She smiled unable to hide the bewilderment in her face.

"Acha?" She smiled as Acha nodded. "That's quite an old fashioned name; tell me Acha, what brought you to this accursed place?" Acha lowered her head feeling ashamed of her story, yet she felt compelled to tell it anyway.

"I met an angel, she told me to do things, horrible things to a friend of mine... but... she was an angel, I thought she had to be right, only... I betrayed that friend by the words I had thought were so pure, even now, her life is in danger, if she survives, she will hate me. I became the very monster I accused her of being, but justified it under the flag of righteousness. Just like those in my own time, led astray by the angels and being condemned for the sins they committed under the flag of justice, I never thought I would see myself repeat that mistake."

"And while you did this, how did it make you feel, what did your heart tell you?" The old lady took Acha's hand in her old trembling one, looking deep into Acha's eyes, for a moment there was silence as Acha thought back to all the things she had said and done.

"I felt betrayed, I think that is the main reason I was so ready to believe what I was told. My friend had kept a secret from me, I hated that she felt she couldn't trust me, but all the time I was doing it, I kept asking myself over and over why, looking back on how I behaved, I see why she didn't tell me, she was afraid of the very behaviour I displayed. Yet this being of purity with her sweet words turned me against her, I truly thought at the time it was for the greater good."

"And now?" The old lady drew closer, eagerly awaiting the words she thought would follow.

"Now?" She shook her head, despair shining clearly in her earth brown eyes as she looked at the figure standing before her. "Now I know I should have stood by my friend no matter what…" Acha sighed.

"You know my dear, innocence is a gift almost lost these days, those that possess it are taken for a fool and lose it quickly through the ways of the world, but it still remains a charming trait." The old lady smiled as she ran her hand over her tatter clothes as if she was searching for something.

"There is no one to blame but myself, I say it was the angel's words that caused this, but that's nothing but an excuse. It is my own fault for listening, Zo never gave me a single reason to doubt her, yet time and time again I betrayed her, each time she offered me another chance no matter how hard it was, or how simple the gesture she made." Acha though back to how Zo had offered her a hand as they climbed from the underground tunnel to show her willingness to overlook everything to offer a hand of friendship, she even agreed to come to this place, although she clearly feared what would happen if she did, she still took the chance. "Everything seems clearer now, as we left, she passed to Daniel her mother's keepsake, it seemed so meaningless at the time, but now I see, she didn't expect to return… but she came anyway, all the time she knew, so why? Why did she come?" Acha began to cry as the old lady pulled her into a hug.

"Because that's what a true friend does." The elderly lady whispered gently in her ear before pulling away. "A true friend never stops believing no matter what." The lady placed a small box in Acha's hand. "Accept this gift for the elaborate lesson you have learnt, although innocence is a rarity, a true friend who holds that much faith is rarer still, if you get the chance, you need to tell her, to make things right." The old lady seemed to grow transparent for a second,

"I can't accept this." Acha turned the small wooden box over in her hand.

"My time here is at an end, two centuries have passed within this forest, I have no children to pass on my lessons, I prey you will get the chance I never had." With those final words the lady vanished into the air with a gentle breeze.

***

Roots wrapped around Zo's legs as she kicked and fought her way to the centre. Finally as she approached, she saw a small cottage, at its front the prettiest flower bed she had ever seen, she shook her head, the world around her twisting back to its true form of towering trees. In the very centre stood an enormous tree, there just under the skin of the bark she saw Acha, she was deadly still under the transparent bark, not a breath left her body, Zo rushed to the tree, falling several times as her feet tangled in the roots of near by trees, she touched the surface of the tree just under where Acha rested before drawing the sword as the blade failed to appear she remembered Seiken's warning about this place. She clipped the hilt into the sheath before using it to chip away at the bark on the tree shouting Acha's name over and over.

A sickening thud followed by an explosion of lights behind her eyes forced her to her knees, she screamed as she felt something crawling up her leg tightly wrapping so it took all her effort to move, it crawled with such haste fastening around her forcing the hilted sword from her hand as it did so, she felt it wrap tightly round her waist still climbing, she let out a scream, unable to escape its lethal embrace.

Zo pulled away from the gentle arms that embraced her, a beautiful lady stood before her, her hands still touching Zo's shoulders. Her gentle brown hair swaying in the wind as she took that one step back to look at her, Zo felt the shock tremble through her body, she didn't even utter a word before she stepped forward embracing the figure clinging tightly to her clothes as if her very life depended on it.

"Shh… it's alright, I'm here now." The figure held her gently whispering words of comfort softly into her ear they seemed to embrace forever until finally Zo let go, as she did the figure stepped back once more to take in her appearance as Zo mirrored her movement in disbelief. "My what a fine young lady you've become." The figure smiled softly at Zo bringing another stream of tears to her eyes.

"Mum… before, back then… I…" Zo shook her head unable to continue, but unsure what she would have said had she continued, her mum smiled leading the way into the picturesque cabin.

"Umemi, you can't block me out." Zo glanced back seeing the image of Seiken standing at the doorstep. "Do you even know…" His image vanished by the sheer power of her will, she pushed the door to, smiling brightly as she moved to join her mother by the fire, resting her head on her chest listening to the soothing sound of her heartbeat.

Chapter nineteen

"It's like I said." The village elder followed Elly as she emerged from the pub, he had been waiting outside since she had hurried her companions in, Elly arrived first at the street end despite Daniel and Acha leaving before her, she had, after all, spent much time within this city and knew all its shortcuts, she stopped at the edge of the street seeing the protection barrier shining softly. The town despite being accessible from many locations could never be exited though anything but one of the paths, it was said this city had stood before the great disasters long before this cycle of the world; many people however dismissed this rumour, stating that they were built in order to create a safe haven from Night. Elly however, was not so easily convinced, the land outside this city was unknown to anyone, Marise had once said the barrier that surround this city was an atmosphere stabiliser that created an artificial atmosphere by drawing on the presence of the people within it, this alone left Elly wondering where this strange town could be, but she was certain it was not of this planet. She looked again at the barrier before speaking. "It's sealed." She smiled at the elder dismissingly in quiet contemplation, knowing that he, as well as they themselves, had only moments ago seen someone enter through it on horse back, she placed two small circular metal objects on the ground without a word she glanced at Eiji, as they moved to join her, they wondered how it was she had managed to get her first.

"Water?" He questioned, for once, to her surprise it seemed he was following her train of thought he outstretched his hand his face glowing with concentration, slowly between the two metal objects an almost invisible layer of water began to rise. Once it had reached what they could only estimate as door height, Eiji let out a sigh of relief lowering his hands.

Elly hesitated a second, a million thoughts and fears running through her mind, she didn't like water at the best of times, she hated it with a passion and the thought of willingly stepping into a portal made from it was all the more unnerving, she actually had to reminded herself what was at stake to force her feet to move. Daniel watched in amazement, instead of her appearing at the other side, she had vanished completely from view, he followed her cautiously into the unknown followed closely by Eiji and Acha, the elder who had been with them however, did not follow, it was not his place he simply stared in bewilderment, before returning to his business about the town seconds after he was sure the portal had vanished.

"How..." Daniel began to question somewhat amazed at what had just transpired, he was unsure what exactly to expect when he stepped into the fine film of water, he felt as though he had been pushed at great speed to this location, leaving him a little disorientated when he stepped from it. He glanced around the small island, other than the small area of open ground they stood on, everything before them was covered with forest, it was incredible, looking at the forest for a second he almost believed the trees themselves created a wall that could not be passed, a impenetrable barricade that made entrance seem impossible as a bark fence protected the outer forest, but as he took another few steps he saw this was just an illusion, there was a clear opening.

"Basic science, light travels in a straight line and this is said to be the quickest way between two points, but what if light was made to curve thus reducing the distance? You see water bends light and as distance is measured in such creating a container in which to bend light, combined with the correct elements can become a portal. As you cross through it, it bends the light between you and the point of exit meaning instead of hours the travel takes only seconds, you studied magic I thought you would have heard of it." Eiji smiled, surprised at having remembered so much of what his master taught him, it was the kind of explanation they would have expected from Elly, not him and this was clearly reflected in their faces.

"No… but logically it makes sense, I suppose." He rubbed his head taking in a mental note of the information he had been told to write up in his journal.

"Luckily this was used as a portal previously, so the foundation magic remained, otherwise it would have taken much longer to map its path, we just needed to create a path through." Eiji smiled at Daniel before glancing around for Acha, he had seen her emerge from the shield just seconds before it had closed.

"But how do we get back?" Daniel questioned as any trace of the portal completely vanished.

"We'll discuss that later, did you get everything?" Elly turned to Eiji, also noticing Acha was not among them, she glanced around for a moment trying to pinpoint her location.

"Yes… I don't…."

"You came?" Seiken seemed almost surprised by their appearance he glanced over them quickly before continuing. "Thank the stars; Acha and Umemi have been trapped." Only seconds after he spoke did Acha appear before them.

"You can talk; you led us astray before, besides as you can clearly see Acha is here." Daniel pointed to her as she stood a little way back from them now much to everyone's relief, it seemed somehow, before, she had escaped their gaze.

"As you wish." He sighed and turned to walk away, if not for the situation, he would have. "But tell me, where is her necklace?" He questioned his back still to them, they turned to look at her, Seiken knew if there was one thing Aburamushi could not do, it was duplicate items of magical potential, just like he could not have predicted that straight after emerging from the portal, that Seiken would summon them to Knights-errent, hence Acha's figure had only just appeared as he realised what must have happened and followed them.

"I lost it… back in the forest". She stated flippantly as she shifted uncomfortably under the weight of their stares, she quickly shifted her vision to Seiken, who turned now to face them, he could not walk away from this, no matter how much he wanted to, what was at stake was far too important.

"But I thought you said you never went in." Elly stated almost smugly.

"Does it matter? What's important is that Zo is trapped in there and yet again, the son of Crystenia is causing problems, he did this before remember, when he nearly got me killed." She snapped.

"Wait a minute." Eiji interrupted looking from Acha to Seiken. "Back then, in Knights-errent, it wasn't Seiken, he's imprisoned in Night's tower… I remember seeing him there while I was captive, he came to help… there was something glowing around him, restraints of some kind." Eiji couldn't think why he had failed to mention this before, but so much had happened, it had slipped his mind, but until this point, he wasn't even sure the images he had seen during his imprisonment were real, he had seen so many strange things, why believe it to be anything more than another illusion?

"Magic inhibitors." Seiken stated bluntly looking almost ashamed as the details of his capture were revealed.

"So how come you're here now?" Acha questioned sceptically.

"You know more than anyone, this place is exempt from rules, even ours."

"The son of Crystenia?" Daniel questioned the rushed conversation finally entering his troubled mind.

"Crystenia is my home, the capitol of our world, but no one here would know that, it is not information I have divulged correct?"

"You told me, before." Acha protested already aware she was losing the battle.

"Very well, then tell me, what is my name?" Acha paused, Seiken knew the creature posing as Acha had already blown its cover, just as he knew, even if it's very existence depended on it, he could never speak his name. That was one of the wonderful things about summoned creatures, why any brought to life in their world did not last long, a summon had the ability to look deep into the minds of others, but when talking to a Spindle, they never seem to pick up on the alias all of their race use, and speaking their true name brings disastrous consequences. Although in the world of Gaea knowing the true name of a being gives a person power over it, in his world, for his people at least, speaking their true name gives them power over the being, he waited. The reason this particular creature had survived in their world was because he, along with its creator, had sealed it within one of the seven sealed locations, as long as it was sealed, it could do no real harm, this creature had been different to the others, it seemed to have been split into two parts, one part resided in their world, the other in Knights-errent, as such, they were unable to destroy it, but now it had been released from its seal and united with the half in the physical world, it was on borrowed time, its immorality came from the fact it was split between a world of eternity and the world of Gaea, but now it was free, its life would slowly trickle away unless it found a way to overcome its new found mortality and one of the methods of gaining such, was to bring the one who summoned him to sleep forever within the forest of perpetual night, as long as its host survived, it was immortal and those trapped within the forests sleep were all but such themselves until the day the forest devoured their life-force completely, but two centuries would be more than enough time for him to combat his problem.

"I thought your life-force was contained within that pendent?" Daniel added, suddenly fitting into place that strange gnawing feeling at the back of his mind since her arrival. Acha shifted into the first form of Aburamushi, smiling at them as he summoned a portal, in that second, none of them seemed to be able to move to stop him until he had passed through completely. Daniel went as if to pursue but hit only air where the portal had been.

"He will have completely sealed the portal now." Seiken stated glancing towards the area Aburamushi had made its exit, knowing that when the time came for them to leave, they would have to set up the foundations, yet as long as their destination was the same as that they had come through, it would not take as long as they could follow the magic residue.

"Then how will we get back?" Daniel questioned once more.

"Let's concentrate on getting them out first." Elly motioned towards the forest aware of how much time had already been wasted since their arrival, had this been Aburamushi's plan? Would they now arrive those few seconds too late? After all, this being was intelligent, he was trying to kill his creator in a way that would not harm its existence so any chance of banishment was destroyed, but not only that, he knew each of them and their actions, surely he would have known she would not accept the imperfect copy he had created and to stay to challenge him, all the time in doing so, Marise fought for her life, if they were too late, if her body and life-force had become separate accepting the reality the forest presented, it would be too late. "Seiken, how are they doing?" She questioned, what if questions running through her mind, what if she had just followed Aburamushi? Would that have been so bad? What if now they don't make it in time to save them?

"Well..." He thought of saying something sarcastic he had little time for people like them, but before he continued, he changed his mind. "Acha's still fighting, that is quite a good sign I'd say, especially since the time that has passed since her arrival... Umemi... Zodiac..." He said sadly. "She gave up long ago; even I can't reach her now." He sighed feeling as if somehow he had failed her by not being stronger, there had been times before, when she travelled with Elly, that he had succeeded in pulling her from the darkness that held her, drawing her away from Marise's seals and captor, he had always been able to reach her, but now, now, for the first time ever, it truly seemed that she had ventured past his reach.

"That brings me to my next question, why are we here?" Elly crossed her arms looking straight at Seiken accusingly.

"Apologies, I had little choice, if I were to speak with you, I needed to induce this sleep on your arrival... Although Night's chains bind me in your world and mine, the power of this place sits in neither, that is how I come to be before you now, but my time here is still limited." He looked towards the forest meaningfully, there wasn't time to explain this, he had to try to get back to her.

"You mean we're asleep?" Eiji questioned in disbelief.

"Yes, but you can wake up now." Seiken appeared to vanish into thin air as they switched between the worlds, but it was not he that vanished; only they who had awoke.

"So how do we get them out, without loosing the way ourselves?" Daniel looked towards the deadly silent forest a sinking feeling in his stomach, somewhere among those trees, Zo had surrendered, something he never thought she would do, it made him fear that which lay within the forest.

"Well if you hadn't been in such a hurry to leave I was hoping for a few hints or slips us from the impostor Acha." Elly sighed, although this was true, it may also have been the one thing that means that they would be too late, why hadn't she just killed the impostor on the spot?

"You mean you knew?" Daniel questioned sharply.

"Of course only inhabitants of Knights-errent call this place the forest of perpetual night, we call it the perpetual forest, but think about it, that's the same name that appeared on the map of the fixed locations." As Elly spoke, she was knocking a large peg into the ground fastening around it some form of shiny yarn, she gripped a large ball of it within her hands tugging it a few times as she ensured it was secure around the peg. "We'll find our way out the same way treasure hunters do as they navigate the caves. Without a further word the three of them head into the forest, they had barley walked a few steps when Eiji stooped picking Zo's satchel from the floor.

"She was nearly out, by here she surely could feel her magic, she could see the truth as we can now, the forest magic is weaker here, but was it weak enough? Is this the power of the forest?" Eiji questioned passing the satchel to Daniel who slung it over his shoulder holding it tightly against himself before glancing around cautiously, just up ahead the forest was submerged in complete darkness, minimal light filtered through, as he looked to the floor he saw the answer to why she had almost made it out, almost but not completely, she had turned back for one reason and one reason only, and it wasn't the power of the forest.

"There's only one set of tracks… she went back, for Acha." Daniel sighed, even though she had known this was bound to happen, she still had ventured back into the forest for her, unable to leave her behind to face her judgement, this did not sound like the action of someone who was ready to surrender, yet, inside he knew the words Seiken spoke were the truth, he saw reflected in his eyes.

They pressed on, barely a space between any of them as they trekked through the forest, the trees blocking the light creating an artificial night; they blindly navigated deeper and deeper through the trees. Everything was deadly silent, the only sound was that of the trees moving in the breeze and they were too occupied to notice there wasn't one.

Elly stopped quickly, stretching her arm out before the others, for a brief second she had seen the eyes watching whispering, but then as quickly as they appeared, they had vanished back into the darkness.

"Be careful." She whispered as she lowered her arm. "They know we're here." she glanced around as she spoke scanning the darkness.

"Who?" Eiji questioned neither he nor Daniel had seen the eyes for that fleeting moment, then again neither of them were close to her calibre.

"Our esteemed hosts, it seems we are under the spell of the forest, we're asleep." She whispered.

"You are." Seiken however did not whisper his voice startled them a voice, so loud against the silence. "Not to give the game away but those who enter these woods after the first few steps find themselves looking for the exit, may I suggest you do the same?" A branch swiped at Seiken from nowhere as it touched him he vanished, it was by this alone they gathered they were now awake.

"Why the exit?" Eiji questioned reducing his tone to a whisper to fit the silence of the surrounding environment. He looked to Elly following backwards the string she held, as he did so, noticing it seemed to lead deeper into the woods, where as at this precise moment they seemed to be heading for a lighter area, then it dawned on him, something the others had only just realised. "The elder said something about it leading travellers seeking its exit deeper towards its centre." Eiji was the first to continue walking; heading them towards the light area that always remained up ahead.

"I'm not going to keep wasting my energy warning you when I could be trying to reach her." Seiken stood at a nearby tree. "Wake up." He commanded before giving a sigh. "If you don't you'll die." He turned his back to them. "I can't believe I have to trust Umemi's life to such amateurs." In the instant that he vanished Elly had already thrown her dice, a huge battle axe appeared in her hands, the blade shone for a moment its blade forming of a strange black metal, a metal Elly knew instantly it was a similar to that making up the composition to that of Marise's hilt, they were close.

"Who you calling an amateur?" She whispered ducking as the scenery before them shifted to reveal a giant monster blocking the path, its scaled body was partly covered in spikes, the scales themselves seemed like tiny fragments of armour in both composition and strength, a few more steps and they all would have been dead without even knowing what hit them. It gave out a roar, shooting mouthfuls of splinters towards them, watching them with its hateful leaf green eyes as they dived from the path of death. Eiji rolled from the spikes path cursing as he failed to find his combat knife tucked in his boot, it was only now he remember passing it to Acha all that time ago when they first set out on the journey, it seemed so long ago now. He glanced at the spikes quickly before something heavy stuck in the ground before him, Elly smiled, it was almost as if she had read his mind, there in the ground before him was a knife, of course he didn't know what good it would do, but better to be armed than not, just as he bent to grab it another fountain of spikes passed over his head warning him to concentrate more on the battle, than thoughts of the past, Daniel snapped open his staff.

"Just stay back Daniel, your stick is useless here." Elly called to him.

"I can fight too." He protested readying himself for battle.

"True, but it would be more useful if you could find some other way to help us." Eiji intervened. "You have a great skill with knowledge, you think fast on your feet… There's no way we can defeat or outrun this thing in simple battle." Daniel nodded flicking his staff together, he scaled the heights of a nearby tree, he swore, as he climbed, it was almost as if the tree was trying to throw him off, once at the top it made no more such efforts leaving Daniel wondering how he had become so clumsy.

"There's a slight decline in trees about half a mile to the right." He shouted to them as he looked out over the sea of green and the gentle curve of the trees in the distance. As he spoke Elly took a swing at the creature with her axe, it howled in pain at the wound she had caused, yet, at the same time, it was almost as if she had failed to injure it at all as it continued to move and fight unhindered by the bloodless wound, if not for the howl, she would have believed herself to miss the strike entirely, it was clear she would need more than strength to beat this thing, or even escape it.

"And?" Eiji called back throwing the knife at the creature, realising he could never get close enough to safely strike, the knife embedded itself in the creature, although again it was as if it didn't even notice.

"My guess from the angle, and the lack of trees over that area would be a sixty foot drop steep sides, about thirty feet across." This time Elly caught what he offered.

"Brilliant." She exclaimed, it was just the break they needed, perhaps this forest wasn't as harsh as she remembered. "Okay, Eiji listen up." She dodged its swiping tale and appeared at his side. Daniel rushed down the tree but found he was unable to catch a single word, before he had even reached the floor; they took off running leaving him behind. The giant creature, as expected, followed them.

Daniel raced after them aware he was more to the side then them and somehow had managed to pass the creature, Eiji and Elly. He could only thank all the time he spent racing with Zo, he hid behind a small tree waiting for their approach, looking for an opening where he could aid them, all at once they came to view without a pause for thought Elly grabbed Eiji tightly and leaped over the side of the canyon much to his surprise. The creature however, did not behave as planned, it was not as stupid as they had hoped, a common misconception with large beasts as Daniel had discovered in his mythological studies class, the beasts that had more contact with humans did little for the intelligence rating of those who stayed away and were not known to hunt humans, he had often wondered if anyone had considered the possibility they did hunt, but were too intelligent to ever be caught. The creature slid to a slow halt at the canyons edge scraping and snorting in the dirt.

Daniel could just make out a spray of Elly's blue hair looking closer; he saw her hand gripping tightly onto a root of a tree that tried so desperately to grow on the edge of the step cliff face. Occasionally the creature would rear up onto its back paws landing heavily above the area Elly and Eiji clung for life, sending small tremors through the already unstable ground. They hung just under the root, ensuring the creature was unable to see them, although in a few moments it wouldn't matter, the tree was already fighting its way loose from the soil in a desperate attempt to free itself and take those who trespassed within the forest with it, a second set back that had not been predicted, the trees here seemed to be alive, this one at least was surely trying to send them plummeting to an early grave.

Daniel in the meantime, was rummaging through the bag, luckily being down wind he remained unnoticed by the creature, who had once more resorted to sniffing the cliff edge. He rolled under the massive beast aware that just one wrong move from the creature would end his life, he wrapped the rope loosely around the creatures legs, relieved that through its thick scale like skin it could not feel him do so, once secured he rolled through and to the other side of the forest, aware now the creature would detect his scent, he quickly threw the rope over a tree branch climbing it again to the trees disapproval and wrapping it around several other branches. He saw Elly gripping Eiji tightly around his waist as the final root tried to force its way free of the bank, tightening the rope he jumped from the tree holding the rope tightly, the rope slid around the branches tightening the rope around the creatures legs pulling them towards to its centre until it had no choice but to obey gravity, as the creature fell, he released the remaining rope to lower himself to the floor and secure it around the base of the tree. Taking a large step around the creature, he warily approached the side of the chasm. Seeing him Elly swung Eiji enough so he could grab Daniel's hand, after pulling him to safety the tree shook derooting itself but not before both Daniel and Eiji had managed to grab Elly. As they pulled her to safety they swore they saw the tree walk a little before settling its roots into the ground.

Elly dusted her clothes free of the dirt from the chasm wall before examining the creature who lay strangely still for something that should still have been conscious, dismissing her thought she smiled at Daniel taking the string from on top of the satchel, Daniel hadn't even realised he had taken it with him when he had followed them. Eiji and Elly started on ahead and Daniel collected Zo's bag from the side, although they were walking, their pace was slow as they waiting for him to catch up.

"See, I told you would think of something, all you need is a little…" Elly was interrupted when a hand thrust against her back stopping her in mid sentence knocking both her and Eiji to the floor as Daniel threw himself upon them forcing them to the floor as a rainbow of darts showered overhead falling just inches away from where they now lay, Eiji gasped looking wide eyed at the rows of darts landing less than an inch from his face. Elly moved quickly rising to her feet to see the creature although still floor bound lining up its next shot.

"Daniel!" She gasped seeing several of the spikes protruding from his back as he rose to his feet, she barely had time to pull him to the side away from the line of fire to behind a nearby tree, she summoned forth a weapon, this time, a large metal two handed sword appeared in her possession, in the blink of an eye she was besides the creature removing its head in a similar movement to that Marise had, when she removed the head of the demon, however unlike the demon, no fluid left its body on its decapitation, the enormous body simply slumped to the floor, Elly watched for a moment longer, ensuring this time it really wouldn't bother them, the lack of blood disturbed her a little, things always bled, yet it seemed almost as if the creature lying before them now was never really alive… She approached them again in their new found shelter which was in reality nothing more than a small area of clearing just to the right of the first row of trees, now understanding the will of this place a little more she commended their decision, it was no wonder people got lost when the trees seemed to move, silent words passed between her and Eiji as she approached, he was already removing the spikes from Daniel's back, in a subtle movement Elly brushed a few from her own leg, unnoticed by anyone.

"Eiji… how is he?" She questioned looking over Eiji's shoulder to see the damage closely.

"*He* is fine." Daniel answered through grit teeth as Eiji continued to remove the spikes.

"I've already removed seven." He sighed looking at Daniel's back; it seemed he had taken a huge amount of the fired darts in order to protect them. "About three quarter depth." He added knowing immediately from Elly's expression they were not to breathe a word of this to Daniel until absolutely necessary.

"We must hurry." She sighed looking to him once more, if he had just left it, they would have got her and this would not be an issue now, yet at the same time she was flattered that he seemed to care enough to put himself in the firing line without a thought to the consequences. "We've come too far to turn back, pushing on is our best bet."

"I said I am fine, they were barely scratches, they don't even hurt." He lied, well sure they hurt, but no more than any other scratch or large splinter, in fact the pain was beginning to subside now since the last of the darts had been removed. Daniel got to his feet aware of Elly and Eiji exchanging strange glances before walking on.

They walked in silence for some time, somehow knowing they were awake without the need for confirmation, the roots seemed to twist beneath their feet attempting to trip them as they walked carefully past. Daniel's pace had slowed slightly, meaning when he tripped, both Eiji and Elly extended their arms to grab him, his head swam for a moment while he regained his footing, the scenery around him now seemed duller, darker than before, he wondered if perhaps it was his mind playing tricks, it had been so dark since they entered, it seemed almost impossible it could grow any darker. They pulled him to his feet, holding onto him while he steadied himself before starting out again, they had barely taken ten steps when he tripped again this time landing on his knees as his vision began to blur before him a strange wave of nausea passed over him, as Eiji and Elly once more pulled him to his feet.

"Ok." He sighed defeated. "Tell me about the poison." He had known since the creature had first spat the darts that they were laced with poison, although he had hoped ignoring this would help them push on quicker. He had hoped they didn't know, but it seemed they did despite his attempts to ignore it, what *did* surprise him, however, was the surprise now registering on their faces when they realised he knew.

"Those spikes, as you say, were laced with a fast acting poison, if you don't get medical attention soon, you'll die." Elly stated bluntly, they stopped letting him rest, all the time she didn't speak mulling over the chances of success, the poison although fast acting should give them enough time to reach Zo and make an antidote before it became critical, however, she was also very aware, that things did not always proceed as desired within the boundaries of this forest, she estimated the maximum time they had after darts first impact was three hours, only two of which remained and already the poison was already excelling beyond the normal time phase. "Eiji, follow the cord back, take him to the medic at collateral, the poison is excelling at a rate I hadn't anticipated." She stated finally, she was confident she could make this journey alone.

"No." Daniel pulled himself away stumbling onwards, he felt as if he had had a few too many drinks, without the merriness that went with it. "We must… find Zo." He gasped feeling worse now for having his thoughts about the poison confirmed, it had been easier to ignore all the aches, pains and sickness when he was pretending nothing was wrong, the fact that his companions weren't fussing over him had made it easier, yet now the air around them had changed, now they knew and there was no reason for pretence, he felt a hundred times worse than if he had remained quiet.

"Daniel." Elly smiled, she would have been lying if she had said she was not impressed at his commitment to his friend regardless of the personal cost, it was something she herself understood completely, something she understood, and respected. "You're right… It would be quicker." They let him walk ahead a little, subtly allowing him to set the pace.

"Look, Acha!" He gasped falling to his knees, as he did so, his hand falling on the cold metal of Zo's sword, Elly picked him up in a fireman's lift. "Weren't you hit too?" He questioned quietly thinking back to the incident, Elly shook her head

"No Daniel… you saved us both." She answered; Eiji was already examining the tree where he could see Acha's suspended body under its transparent bark. "It seemed Zo tried to get her out." Eiji ran his fingers over the indentations of the bark before picking Zo's sword from the floor near where Daniel had been lifted from, he was surprised at how heavy it was, it seemed to grow heavier every second he held it, almost as if it objected to his touch, Elly took it from him, balancing Daniel on her shoulder while she tucked it in her belt. He removed Elly's knife from his holder in his boot, he had been quiet surprised when she handed it to him as they walked away from the creature's corpse, but there was no point in wasting a good weapon, besides, it would come in handy. He made several cuts through the transparent bark before a translucent fluid split the remaining fragments of wood, he moved quickly, catching Acha as she fell forward. For some reason it seemed the forest wasn't fighting back, perhaps because it knew they would never escape. It was a strange plant, one that fixed itself into its prey's lungs forcing air into the capillaries as they body's needs demanded, this way, it ensured the body lived long enough to be of use to it nutritionally.

Eiji held Acha near the floor for a moment until her eyes shot open as she coughed the fluid from her lungs, followed by several long stands of some kind of green plant like substance Acha continued heaving until the last of the plant had been removed from her lungs.

"Where's Zo?" She whispered hoarsely. "I… she tried… to save me." She panted gasping for air, Elly passed Daniel across to Eiji, Daniel still being conscious felt like some kind of unwanted baggage being passed around, he watched as Elly disappeared. Moments later she appeared with Zo, he felt his heart give a relieved leap, like Acha she was soaked to the bone, but unlike her, she didn't move, she simply hung limp within Elly's arms, the expression on Elly's face scared him no end, she always masked her feelings so well, but now, now she looked truly terrified.

The trees began to stir once more Eiji took Zo from Elly as Daniel fought to stand, she hooked Daniel's arm around her shoulder to help him walk, even now she could see the concern for his friend was more than the concern for himself, this was helping them press on. She found herself surprised by Daniel's silence, wondering why he was failing to ask why they weren't helping her, but maybe the reason was clear, they had to get out of the forest quickly, for all their safety. While they remained in the forest its grip on Zo would strengthen, although she may no longer reside within the tree, it still controlled her, once out of the forest, she would be stronger, they could only hope once they were clear of its trees, she would wake.

"Acha… are you…" Elly started prepared to offer a hand.

"I'm fine… now." She looked at Zo cradled motionless in Eiji's arms. "Will she be ok?" Acha whispered walking besides Eiji looking to the ghastly shade of the figure he carried.

"None of us will be if we don't make haste out of this place." Elly pulled the string tight only to find it had been severed meters from the place she held.

"Great" Eiji sighed "How do we get out now?"

***

"So Seiken, I see you have still found a way to warn our friends." Seiken was thrown before Night's feet by a large troll guard. "I never expected anything less from you; you truly are a strong willed youngster. It's clear you have a soft spot for…"

"Enough, you didn't bring me here for idle chatter, make me your offer, so I may refuse already." Seiken forced himself to stand before him, although found the restraints he bore made it difficult, but his pride alone fought to stop him kneeling before him.

"Very well… but I think you will find this proposition more to your liking than my last." Night gave a smile.

"What do you mean?" Seiken questioned as the magic inhibitors vanished, he rubbed the places they had touched, even now the red marks made by them were fading.

"This time Seiken, I am offering you everything, your world, your people, your freedom." Night watched as Seiken adjusted to being free by stretching a few times, despite the fact they did not restrict movement as such, they were a heavy draining burden for any movements he should make, Night was not concerned about giving him this moments of freedom, even should he try to escape he could summon the inhibitors back before he had taken even a few steps.

"My world, my people, *our* freedom? Things would go back to the way they were... before?" He questioned in disbelief at what Night had placed on the bargaining table.

"Well not exactly, I'm sure there will be some damage here and there, the fixed points that have been liberated, will still be destroyed, but as close to before as possible."

"How do I know you will be true to your word?" Seiken eyed Night questioningly moving to sit at the chair he had been motioned to.

"If nothing else have I not proven myself to be noble and honourable? I promised not a single one of your race would be hurt, as a God I am bound by my word."

"True, but you are no longer a God, you lack some power still." Seiken said contemplating this information. "Night was renowned for being an honourable deity even in times past, I cannot see why one such as yourself, would fall so low to take hostages and for what?" He questioned

"My daughter, I would do anything to have her besides me... but I would be lying if I were to say this would be my only motive, can't you hear it Seiken? The cry of this world as the beings upon it drive it closer and closer to extinction, can't you hear the laboured breath of Gaea? I want to liberate her, return her to her former glory. Surely you of all people understand, would you not do the same for your world in my shoes? Where as you use the beings of this planet, their dreams and imagination to keep your world alive, using their thought patterns to replenish your world's resources, I too, must use my... methods to accomplish the same task." There was a long pause where neither spoke a word until Seiken finally asked what was expected.

"What is it I must do, in order to free my world forever? To free my people from your control?" Night smiled gently, leaning forwards speaking softly.

"You must first choose between those you love" Night produced a small gossip crystal from the air, upon it an image of Zodiac, not at this present point but at the point they had first come face to face it Knights-errent. Seiken looked at it carefully, that day, he remembered thinking how she was more stunning in person she was then than through any crystal or looking glass he had watched her through, there was something about her presence in his world that brought out her inner beauty, when last he saw her before this journeys start, she had been a budded flower, a flower that now blossomed into a perfect rose. "And those your loyalty binds you to." Another image overpowered the one of Zo, it was his race, his people. "Of course, I don't expect you to make your decision straight away, first eat; I believe the food the guards provided was not to your taste." A huge buffet appeared from air on the table before him, all delicacies from home.

'To choose between loyalty and love... will my choice make that much difference?' He questioned unable to eat, he simply stared at the food before him as he reasoned with himself. *'I have known Ume for a blink of an eye in the time of my people and have quested with her for but a fortnight or so, although true, I have watched and adored her much longer and aided her unseen by fate's eye. Yet compared to my people, to those who have faith in me, who believe in me, who look to me to guide them...'* He looked to Night having not touched a morsel of food on the table.

"Tell me of this proposition." He sighed, a wave of nausea washing over him.

"All in good time, first eat, build up your strength, let's toast to our new arrangement." Night raised a glass and drank from it; Seiken followed his motion an empty feeling building in his chest.

Chapter twenty

"There's no way to navigate these trees now." Eiji sighed, dodging the swipe from another tree as he looked desperately at the broken string in Elly's hand begging for it to be nothing more than a figment of his imagination. However, the harsh reality was that the trees had done their best to ensure they could never leave severing their life line to keep them here forever.

"You'll never get me twice, have you learnt nothing?" Elly sighed pulling a match from her pocket striking it as she did so; Eiji looked to her wondering if she was addressing them, or some unknown force such as the forest itself. "When I was searching for the legendary treasure of Phliomese, I learnt the true meaning of friends, there were those who would do anything to see you fail, even sever your lifeline. Well, I have my own trick." She smiled dropping the lit match to the floor where the few remaining feet of string rested among the undergrowth, as it touched the string it ignited with a hiss, as a small paper thin line, with a vivid purple flame moved slowly across the rope, continuing over the forest debris. "When they tried it a second time, I was ready, since then always cover my rope in simolneous phosphated essence, so when I needed to return, I just light the start of the rope, where the powder had touched will ignite and it always returned me and my team safely." Elly stood for a moment ensuring the flame passed over the rope onto the ground; the trees themselves seemed to howl at the flame passed over them moving slightly to avoid its touch. A reaction that would make their journey back easier and quicker.

"Elly..." Daniel asked quickening his pace best he could, luckily, the flame moved slowly as it lead the way. "Great story but the treasure of Phliomese, was recovered or so rumour says... over six centuries ago... it's all documented, it's said that treasure is that kept by the king." Daniel panted finding both talking and walking a difficult trial, Elly thought of warning him he should only attempt one, but had feared he would stop in favour of talking. She picked him up once more placing him over her shoulder, worrying now about how his movement was increasing the spread of the poison, at first she hadn't been too worried but now it seemed to be progressing quicker than she had first predicted, he had a moment where his walking had been impaired greatly, his balance faltered, but this passing, bought with it more serious concerns, it was nothing more than a moments relief before the poisons final victory.

"That explains why I couldn't find it." She smiled picking up the pace now she had no cause to worry about leaving anyone behind, she watched Acha in front of her she seemed fine considering, it seemed the effects of the trees were less server on a mortal than on one whose magic it can steal, she glanced to Zo still cradled in Eiji's arms as he pursued their guide, a few of the trees moved a little as they dodged the path of the wandering flame. This was one forest that would regret messing with her, one more step out of line and she swore she would burn the whole thing to the ground it knew her thoughts, it knew she meant it, last time she left this place, it had been lucky, that time, it had caught her off guard, but it knew now to heed her warning and thus the trees remained silent. What were a few possible escapees as long as it could continue to lore travellers?

"I'm surprised you didn't know…" Daniel started the conversation again after a moment of silence, a moment he had used to draw his weary breath, he found talking tiring, but it drew his attention from the pains of the poison. "It was found by a renowned female treasure hunter, rumour had it she once found the hidden knowledge of the Gods just before the great battle occurred, of course, time scale alone deemed such things impossible… Lain Chevalied D'indutrie, Larcenist extraordinaire." Elly smiled to herself as he spoke the name.

"Clever name though, Lain the thief." She translated.

They walked in silence following the flame, they had long passed the place where the creature's body should have lay, only now, there was no sign of it. Although Elly was sure there was no chance of it living through decapitation, she was more than certain that one of two things had become of it, firstly, maybe the magic trapped within the forest had return it to life, or the second more believable option was that even now the trees were ingesting its life-force.

Finally, they saw light, not of that inflicted by the forest's hypnosis but by reality, the true exit stood before them. They continued venturing further from the trees to Elly's peg post now burnt fiercely with flames until finally neither the cord nor post remained.

Elly placed Daniel down satisfied that this time they had not drifted into the forest's sleep, Eiji seeing this, placed Zo gently on the floor near him, rummaging through her bag until he found what he was looking for, he sat for nearly a minute holding a small mirror to her face to check her breath, nothing, he glanced to Elly who was at that moment adjusting Daniel to be more comfortable before rushing over.

"What do we do?" Eiji stood up pacing the ground. "Daniel needs a doctor, maybe we could make it in time to take her too?" He looked desperately at her, her pale features her lips slowly turning blue, everything pointed to once thing, time was running out, if they didn't do something soon they would both die, the mission would be a failure, the prophesies would not be fulfilled.

"There's not enough time… I won't go… not until Zo…" Daniel gasped pulling himself up from where Elly had lay him moving forwards towards Zo, almost collapsing as he lowered himself to sit beside her, he took her cold hand in his, she lay motionless, yet in her lifeless sleep there was a strange beauty to her gentle features, Daniel whispered her name over and over in his mind hoping that somehow it would reach her, hoping it would draw her back from wherever she was.

"I don't think a doctor could help… either of them." Elly paused. "Herbal poison needs herbal remedies, since the appearance of chemical compounds last decade; botany is very much a forgotten art… Missy here's a nature child, she possesses herbal lore, she'd know exactly what and how much to mix just looking at his symptoms." Elly paced, her normally calm exterior crumbling around her. "You hear that?" She leaned towards Zo whispering her words so not to be overheard. "Without your help, Daniel will die!" Her normal calm exterior began to faltering further; she stood up again pacing back and forth along side Zo. "Elisha?" She questioned in a low whisper, Acha and Eiji were deep in conversation, only Daniel through hazy eyes glanced to her curiously, but no answer came. "It's no use." She sighed. "Face it, no one has ever survived this forest, no one knows how to counter its sleep." Elly sat down silently calling for aid over and over as panic began to rise inside her. She tried to weigh up what could be done, something anything that would start her breathing, if not for the vines embedded in her lungs, she could have given mouth to mouth, but their presence did one thing and one thing only, they secured the water in her lungs ensuring no air could be forced through providing just enough air so the body would live until it had been fully ingested, but the vines were rooted too far in to allow removal and they, were the cause of the fluid being sealed within her lungs as the vines created a blockage in the windpipe.

"I... I could go into her mind... try to reach her... I mean... maybe I can reason with her?" Acha approached the others warily, aware this whole mess was her doing, she had never intended any of this, she just wanted to do what she had been told was right, she knew now how wrong she had been, maybe she could help put the whole thing right, or as close to as she could.

"Hmm yes." Elly snapped. "Talk to the one who betrayed you, I can see how that would work!" She gave a frustrated sigh knowing even now Elisha was rummaging through a pile of books in hope to aid, time and time again she came up with one word, hopeless.

"Elly." Eiji placed his hand on her shoulder finding himself surprised to feel her tremble beneath his touch, she always seemed so calm, so rational, regardless of the danger they faced, yet now, she was clearly afraid, Eiji felt his stomach churn at the sheer hopelessness he felt from her, if she felt so desperate, chances were really slim, he took a breath before continuing. "It's the only choice; she's the only one who can do it." Elly nodded, knowing this to be their only option, Acha sat watching as if waiting for her permission as this was granted she took a deep breath moving to kneel besides Zo, placing her hand on Zo's forehead, she waited... nothing. Acha ran her hands over one another as if to remove her gloves, only to remember she had left them in Knights-errent when she possessed the merchant, without drawing on her life-force, there was no way to enter her thoughts, to speak to her mind, she glanced from Zo to Daniel quickly as a sudden panic passed over her.

"It's not working!" Her voice filled with shock, fear and questions, it works on everyone, anything that possessed a life force, anything, trees animals, people, this was the first time her powers had failed her, now more than ever she needed them, for the first time she viewed her gift as not a curse, but a way to make things right, and now they chose to fail her.

"It never did on Zo..." Daniel gasped interrupting Acha's panic, he looked to her meaningfully. "Remember when she nursed you back to health?" Daniels shaking hand still gripped Zo's tightly as he spoke, Acha nodded, it all seemed so long ago now, although he spoke to her he never moved his gaze from Zo. "Acha, I remember the words she used, I wrote them down... maybe I can..." He gasped as he took Acha's hand placing it on Zo's, he knew there was no time to explain, using the gift he shared with Zo he tried to search for her, finding the walls constructed too powerful, even now he felt Acha's touch stifling his breath, he slowly began to say her words, the words Zo had whispered when she first healed Acha, the words she needed to pass the walls and barriers into her mind, he felt dizzy almost as if he was falling into the endless darkness that now surrounding his gaze, he felt two hands pull him sharply forcing him to release his grip that joined both Acha and Zo's hand leaving only those two touching.

Zo smiled pouring a small cup of tea from the beige teapot, stirring it gently she looked to her mum and smiled, words could not express how happy being there with her made her, a strange sensation of relief filled her at seeing her mother alive and well, her fears about her not being recognised, about her mother being angry at her for her disappearance, vanished as if they never were. The sun filtered gently through the window, dancing across the floor as its light passed through the leaves on the trees dancing its hypnotic dance across the wooden floor of the small cabin, even from inside Zo could smell the soothing aroma of the blooming roses and the fading smell of the falling plum blossom, she passed a cup to her mum before moving to sit besides her. She thought back to the old man in Collateral, he was right; never a gentler being had graced the earth with its presence.

Zo's heart was filled by such joy as she sat talking, the past years fading into oblivion, like a faint whisper passing on the wind, so the knock at the door came as a rude interruption, tearing her away from her happiness, breaking their new found peace, the cup fell from Zo's hand as she gripped her mother tightly, as it crashed to the floor, it seemed almost as if it fell in slow motion, the contents spilling over the floor as it shattered beyond all repair.

"Mum." She gasped. "Don't let them take me... not again please." She begged burying her head in her mother's shoulder; feeling calmed by her soft aroma, Kez simply smiled that reassuring smile only a mother can before moving to answer the door.

A brown haired girl stood at the door smiling nervously at Kez as she invited her in, hesitantly, she followed the familiar looking stranger to where Zo sat, Acha knew just by looking at them their relationship, it was so obvious, Zo was almost the spitting image of her mother, except for a few features she could only assume to be her fathers.

"Acha!" Zo frowned. "You are not invited." She didn't move from her position on the sofa, just turned slightly to remove her from view.

"Zo you have to listen to me." Acha's voice begged, filled with desperation as she pleaded for her to listen, but she was good at that, Zo thought to herself, good at making people believe what they want to.

"Get out of my house! You had your chance before... you have betrayed me for the last time." She snapped taking a breath before continuing rising to her feet propelled under the force of her anger. "Although without your betrayal I would never have found my mum, so we'll call it even, now go!" She stood walking slowly towards the door that lead to her bedroom, she stepped back opening the door, stopped only from passing its threshold by Acha's frightened tones.

"Zo, don't you understand!" She pleaded, glad to see she had stopped, what reaction had she expected? She had after all done everything she could do destroy her, time and time again testing her trust, turning on her, but this was different, she had learnt the hard way the error of her ways, this time more than any con she pulled, she had to believe her, there was too much at stake. "This... none of this is real!" She stated hoping to keep her attention.

"Have I missed something here?" She snapped. "You sold me to the enemy not once, not twice, but three times! Now I will forgive you if that is what you have come for, but only if you get out!" She screamed she slammed the door turning to face her, if Acha wanted a fight, then she would get one, she looked coldly at her, staring her down, waiting for her to leave, yet challenging her to stay.

"I can't... as much as I would like to ask your forgiveness, I can't, nor can I leave, not without you."

"Why?" Zo questioned almost sadly, why? Why couldn't she leave her alone? She was happy here... so happy.

"True I betrayed you... but I would be betraying you further to leave now." Acha went as if to approach her but the warning look she received made her second-guess the choice; she glanced to Kez who was watching silently.

"What's once more between friends?" Zo snapped bitterly, also looking to her mother who was standing still simply listening to the conversation passing between them, a strange expression crossed her gentle features, Zo knew what it meant, but wasn't ready to accept it, regardless of the magic of this place, the person that stood before her *was* her mother, she didn't care if staying meant dying, she hadn't seen her mother for so long, she missed their time together in her home, Zo felt her barriers weaken, seeing this Acha spoke again.

"I deserve that... but your friends don't, Daniel doesn't." Zo looked from her mum, to Acha, behind her in the door way stood the silhouette of Seiken, he watched them in silence, in that instant, Zo's anger vanished, she looked to Acha her piercing eyes meeting with the genuine concern in Acha's.

"Daniel can take care of himself." She sighed as she saw Seiken shake his head at her although he never entered the room, or spoke a single word, he didn't need to, he was already convincing her to leave, the look in his eyes was worth more than any words, she tried her best to ignore him, but found it quiet difficult, he was the kind of person that demanded full attention, but she had to concentrate she didn't want to lose this now, she had waited so long to see her mother again, regardless of the implications, she just wanted to be home.

"Really? Then tell me, how do you expect him to survive a back full of poison darts?" Acha watched Zo's expression change. "Darts he took to protect Elly and Eiji and he came looking for you, you can hate me all you want for what I did to you, but please, don't punish him because of my actions, don't do to Daniel what I did to you... Zo please." She begged Zo picked up a small picture from the side, within its frame was a picture of both her mother and father, it had been one she had seen many times, but only now did it hold any significance; she looked to her mother meaningfully.

"I told you your father was handsome." Kez walked to Zo embracing her tightly kissing her on the forehead as she pulled away. "It broke his heart to leave without ever having seen you, but if he hadn't... not to worry, I think you should go... you don't need me to remind you of the truth of eleven years ago... Really Zo, how can you still be here, knowing what you know? You know I'm not really her." Kez took the picture from her daughter's hand removing it from the frame and placing it in her hand tightly. "The mothering aspect of my character wants you to stay, wants to keep you forever, to protect you from the world outside, but it's also that instinct that drives me to let you go, I don't know perhaps…" She paused deciding her sentence was best left unsaid.

"It was nice to see you again… for one last time." She hugged her mum tightly, knowing now she had no choice but return, the house was already fading around them, as she looked to Seiken he smiled vanishing into nothing just as the house was, forcing herself to let go, she followed the one who betrayed her time and time again, knowing her words may be lies, but also knowing she couldn't afford to doubt her, not this time.

"When you next see your father, send my love." Kez whispered placing Zo's hand in Acha's.

***

Elly stopped pacing rushing to Zo pulling her to a sitting position in a tight embrace as she began to choke spitting up the same green vines Acha previously had, she had barley taken her first clear breath when she looked to Daniel, he greeted her with a smile dropping her hand as he threatened to lose consciousness. Glancing at Elly she pulled away, time was short.

"Daniel pay attention." It was meant to sound so harsh, but all that came out was a slight whisper her throat and lungs burning with every breath as her limbs stung with pins and needles her reality spun and twisted around her as she felt ready to collapse. "I need." She gasped closed her eyes and began to reel of a list of herbs and quantities he was to mix between pained breaths, Eiji tipped open the bag spilling its contents over the floor, surprised at the weight of the bag once more, he tossed it to one side fanning out the bags of herbs still trying to find the first one she had mentioned, Zo opened her eyes. "Two and a half hours?" She questioned looking to Elly who nodded just as Daniel's eyes closed. "Eiji… can you mix?" She whispered still gasping for breath, the beads of sweat hanging to her forehead as the signs of cyanosis grew faint on her pale skin, Daniel was the only person she had ever trusted, he was always so accurate, after all he was raised in an environment where he grew familiar with herbs and botany through his mother, she needed him now more than ever, there was no time to lose.

"I… can't." Eiji rummaged through the bags spread across the floor still looking for the first item she had mentioned, a task made more difficult without labels marking the bags, Acha grabbed a bag from the floor as Eiji's hand passed over it.

"I'll do it." Acha interrupted before Eiji could say he would try, she had picked the bowl from the floor as Elly tossed her a thin pair of leather gloves she had picked up from Collateral, although they were visible unlike the others, they would do they job just as well without causing confusion, she pulled them on, Zo looked to Eiji who tipped her bag upside down once more checking it just to ensure everything was out and spread across the floor as Acha moved to sit by the herbs, lining them up for quick grabbing. "I know how to, I was raised in that time remember." She looked to Zo, who never looked up from Daniel to her as she spoke.

"Ok… Acha." She sighed trying to steady her breath, trying to stop the fuzziness she felt within her mind, she tried to use magic to drain away the symptoms, to block that which she felt, but she was reminded by its failure that this place lay between worlds, Knights-errent, where her magic was formed by sacrifice and her own world, it seemed here, most of knights-errent's laws prevailed, she had little choice but to accept her help, she would have mixed herself, all the times she had let Daniel do it for her wasn't because she couldn't, but because he wanted to help, but now she knew she didn't have the strength for this session, she had no choice. Closing her eyes once more as she started to speak the herbs and amounts once more even stopping at the end of each one giving her time to mix it, although it seemed Acha barely needed it, occasionally, Zo would ask her to add a little more than the dose she had first stated. Finally, twenty minutes later it was done, Acha passed the bowl filled with a green powder to Zo who smiled, a small cloud appeared above the bowl raining down exactly thirty drops into the formula to make the powder into a thin fluid. She placed the bowl down empowering it with the spirits of light and dark, time was running out, she poured a small amount of the fluid into Daniel's mouth lifting his head to rest on her knee, all being well they had made more than enough should he cough out the first mouthful there would still be more than enough to treat the symptoms. "Elly time?" She questioned a slight panic rising in her voice, it was clear from her movement she was tried, her energy was at an end, Elly was amazed she had done so much after the forest had been feeding on her power.

"Thirty-two minutes exactly..." She looked to Eiji. "A record for this kind of thing." She added for his benefit.

Zo looked to her as she tried desperately to get Daniel to swallow the mixture, but he coughed weekly as it hit the back of his throat forcing it from his mouth in a dribble, on general this kind of potion took anything in the region of forty minutes to mix, to succeed with time to spare was more than she hoped for, only it seemed, there really hadn't been time to spare.

"I had a good mixer." Zo smiled briefly as she glanced from Daniel to Acha, before focussing her attention back to him.

"Zo..." Acha whispered as she watched her move to lean forwards on her hands gasping for breath, more fluid spilling from Daniel's mouth as he failed once more to swallow.

"Damn it Daniel, swallow."

"Zo you've done all you can..." Elly placed her hand on Zo's shoulder squeezing gently; it seemed they were too late, if he couldn't swallow the mixture there was nothing that could be done.

"Elly... do you still have those sleep berries?" Zo demanded in a sharp whisper, she nodded pulling them from her pocket almost fearful of why she would ask.

"What are you thinking?" She passed the small bag to her, Zo struggled with fatigue as she tried to open the loose knot Elly finally knelt down to help, Zo looked to her gratefully, she only hoped she was right about this, but as it stood now, this was the only way.

"I'm thinking, if Daniel can't swallow this potion..." She swallowed the berry holding the potion and Daniel's hand tightly, Elly, Eiji and Acha faded from around her, as they did so she felt a gentle hand on her shoulder, although when she looked, there was no one around. Other than the disappearance of her friends everything else remained the same, by general law they should have been elsewhere, she glanced around wondering how this could be so, but did not want to spend precious time contemplating this.

"My gift to you Umemi, as I said, this place is different." Seiken never actually appeared he spoke to her directly. Zo placed her trembling hand on Daniel's neck checking his thready pulse relieved that she was right in the thought he would follow her across, but wondered if it would have been possible without Seiken's intervention. Taking a deep breath she pushed back the fatigue as the silent words filled the air around her, she moved her hand over his clammy forehead as her other gripped her shoulder tightly, she felt the sting of thorns and the numbness of senses, as she began to heal him and then came the descending darkness. Poison was one thing in her own world she could not heal with magic, cuts and scrapes, minor ailments, but things like this needed remedies not magic, as the pain from Daniel subsided she drank the potion her hand falling from her shoulder to support the rest of her weight, she had to take it now, even if it meant a break in the healing, she continued once more fatigue and pain threatening to stop her before her actions complete.

They had been gone for about fifteen minutes, the others had began to worry that something would prevent them returning, they had already been warned about the dangers of Knights-errent, once night had fallen, it was deadly. Elly had prepared the berries and stood rolling them across her hand, just as she was about to follow, to their relief, they appeared, Zo sat breathless supporting her weight on her arms before lying back watching the dancing colours of the sky as Eiji and Acha rushed to Daniel, Elly however, hung back watching Zo curiously.

"His temperatures dropping." Eiji sat with his hand monitoring his temperature. "Pulse strengthening, breathing is less shallow." He continued tones of relief filling his every word.

"What did you do?" Acha whispered looking to Zo as she lay breathless watching the sky with little movement

"My... rune... is sacrifice." She gasped unable to force any more words into audible volume.

"What she means is..." Elly continued still monitoring her. "Although she could not heal this aliment by magic here, in Knights-errent should she even attempt to heal him, his wounds and aliments would be transferred to her, he would recover but instead of the wounds vanishing, it would simply transfer to her. Effectively she just poisoned herself, with a herbal poison taken from another's body moments before it would have killed him, a stupid and foolish thing to do... but..." Elly paused looking to Zo gently and smiled moving kneel besides where she lay; she stroked her hair affectionately as it clung to her clammy face.

"But..." Eiji continued. "It is that foolish act that saved his life." He moved around Daniel checking again his life signs. "In another few seconds his heart would have stopped."

"How are you feeling?" Elly moved closer besides her noticing the beads of sweat hanging to her pale skin. "You over exerted yourself, you should have caught your breath after waking from the trees slumber."

"Then... Daniel..." She gasped looking over to Eiji struggling to find the strength to speak.

"Okay..." Elly turned her face gently to look back at her. "Seriously, how are you? You took on yourself the same concentration that within moments would have stopped his heart." Zo gave a weak smile, touched that Elly seemed so concerned for her, yet still she had to wonder of it was truly her worried for, or did her concern lie with Marise?

"Cold." She shivered, although as Elly touched her she seemed to be burning up "Daniel?" She questioned again Eiji nodded at her meaningfully as Zo closed her eyes to rest a little, the voices faded into the darkness; she feared resting in case she would wake in Knights-errent, yet the next thing she heard through the darkness was Eiji's voice.

"Pulse returned to normal, breathing, normal... she's fine." Zo opened her eyes, the sun had moved to the final quarter of the sky, she had slept, or whatever it was for hours, Zo moved shakily, still tired and weak as the herbal medicine fought the remains of the poison, she looked to Daniel whose eyes were now open as he turned to look at her smiling weakly, as they had both lay there sleeping in a dreamless sleep, Eiji had ran between the two of them checking their vitals.

"You did it again." He whispered feeling energy rushing back to his body, within moments he felt almost as if he could believe nothing had happened, he moved to kneel besides her amazed how he could have misjudged that feeling as his head swam, yet at the same time knowing that within moments it would pass. "Zo, you're bleeding." Daniel pointed to her shoulder that not only the doppelganger's blade had pierced, but also the tail of the power demon she had fought, the wound had gone unnoticed to both Eiji and Acha, although Elly had noticed it, what she had needed more than anything at that moment was rest, not have someone fussing around her injury, no matter how much it bled, disturbing her sleep would have had no benefit whatsoever, the ground below her was stained with blood.

"I'm fine." She grabbed Elly's hand who now stood using it to pull her to her feet, steadying her as her balance failed her, she wrapped her arm around her waste supporting more of her weight than she would have hoped necessary. "We need to leave right?" Zo looked to her, in response she simply who nodded, she hadn't wanted to say anything, but the longer they stayed the more danger they were in, true they had escaped the forest interior but the land here was just as dangerous and now both of them were able to move, it was better they returned to Collateral to rest a while longer before returning to Knights-errent.

"You're sure..." Eiji began cut short by her answer.

"A little tired." She smiled placing her hand to cover her wound.

"What happened to your shoulder to start it off again?" Eiji questioned looking at her curiously, noticing her right hand also covered in blood from where she had been holding it, he looked to her in surprise.

"I needed to take my mind of the poison; amongst other things... it's a little sore." Elly smiled at Zo she had already known her reason, from the second she had returned the wound had been obvious, it was a skilled level Hectarian that knew their limits and worked to overcome them by placing a third factor into the equation something she could focus on so the true tasks would go smoother.

"How about I dress it for you when we arrive back at Collateral." Elly smiled, knowing that the damage she had inflicted would have easily torn the stitches, but this was not important, more than anything she was relieved that she would get the opportunity to help put it right. Eiji picked up Zo's satchel, now once more full of the herbs Eiji had previously scattered across the floor.

"Zo." Acha held something in her hand along with the small wooden box. "This was in your hand... when they pulled you out." She passed her the tattered, folded, slightly damp picture of her mother and father she had wondered exactly how it had came to be with her, especially since it seemed Kez had not handed it to her until they left, nothing about this place made sense, but she decided not to question it, nor had she decided to mention that the man on the photo was the one whose paths they had crossed in Abaddon, surely Zo knew this already. "Also..." She opened the small box given to her by the lady before.

"When did you..." Eiji glanced up seeing the rune passing Daniel the packed satchel.

"When I was trapped, I met a wise lady; she passed it to me along with her hope and wisdom... Zo... I know I have betrayed you, hurting you and turning on you without a thought or reason, I see now how wrong I was to trust anyone's word over yours. When Sofie told me those things, I thought, because she appeared like an angel, the words she spoke were true, I'm not asking for your forgiveness I don't deserve it... just for a chance to earn your trust, I will do anything, please just one more chance."

"You're right Acha, you had your chance." Zo sighed, Elly tightened her grip as she faltered slightly, the silence seemed to stretch on forever Eiji busied himself creating a new gate she simply looked at her a while as if in thought before she gave a gentle smile. "Acha, you came to get me from a place no one else could, you came with the only desire of helping those I care for, and you used my magic to get you there, you never gave up hope, and you rose to help Daniel without a thought. I never lost my belief in you; you just lost yourself along the way. Besides, if I had been honest with you from the start..." Zo doubted the words she spoke, she doubted being ever able to trust Acha again, how could she? Yet at the same time, if she didn't at least try she could never forgive herself, besides, there wasn't much time left, they had to complete their quest as soon as possible, hard feelings and distrust would only slow things down, for now, she could at least pretend to forgive her, after all, if not for her, Daniel would not have made it.

"Nothing would have changed." Acha sighed honestly. "Even if you had told me yourself... when Sofie came, I still would have..."

"Who is the Sofie you keep mentioning?" Zo questioned as Daniel came to stand besides her, now able to comfortably hold his own weight, where as Zo was relying on Elly to keep her upright at this moment in time.

"She was an angel, or so I thought, when she betrayed me I saw her true form, Aburamushi." Acha sighed, why had she been so ready to believe a stranger over anyone else? Why had she been so foolish?

"We have seen him too." Eiji interjected once the portal was finished, the time they had rested had allowed Elly to talk him through remapping the route Aburamushi had sealed, that was the other reason they had stayed so long, it had taken a few hours to replot the route. "He posed as Acha to lore us here, and as Seiken before in Knights-errent." Eiji groaned and looked to Zo. "That was it... I was meant to tell you, Night has taken Seiken." He stated.

"I know." Stated Zo as Elly helped her through the water door followed closely by the others.

Chapter twenty-one

"Sorry Miss Lain, I can't find any records of the forest other than those I have already provided." Elisha sat amongst a huge pile of books; slowly they began to file themselves away as she watched the mirror intensely. Then all at once the girl on the screen moved, Elisha breathed a sigh of relief. Over the last week or so she had become quite fond of the people whose lives she watched on the silver surface of the surrounding mirrors, she never imagined this job would work out as fun as it had so far, not only did she have a vast library at her call, but she also used the knowledge she gained to help those venturing on their quest.

Elisha stood slowly, dusting herself down as the last of the books filed themselves away.

"I have found out so much about you Miss Lain, who would have thought, in your age you accomplished so much." She glanced up to a nearby clock on the wall, as if on cue a knock echoed through the chambers. There was a slight pause before the door opened, she removed the wired helmet that linked her to the sleeping Lain and rose to meet him, the helmet was no longer a necessity, she had bonded with Lain now, but in times of intense concentration, she used it all the same..

"Elisha." Night smiled. "This is…"

"Seiken." She gasped. "I know you from here." She pointed to the mirrors which Seiken took the time to study, relief flooding him as he found Zo was breathing once more, this very second she fussed over Daniel, before starting concoction of a strange potion, despite the obvious fatigue her near asphyxiation caused, against what would have been his better judgement, he was also surprised to see she was letting Acha help.

"Very good." Night smiled. "Seiken has agreed to help us, the reason I tell you this, as this is knowledge not to be revealed to our travellers."

"Then my Lord, why do you present it to me?" She questioned.

"Well, you are part of Lain's knowledge, should Seiken say something you know not to be entirely correct…" A dawning realisation flickered in her eyes.

"I understand." She bowed. "Lain will not know any falsities that come from his words, but what should happen should she discover this deception of her own merit?" Elisha questioned, Miss Lain was intelligent after all, she still held within her conscious a lot of the knowledge taken from the Gods, the last thing she would want is for Night to think she had betrayed him should something go wrong.

"Try to dissuade her." Night smiled, he knew there could have been no better person for the job than Elisha, she had proved this time and time again.

"Very good my lord."

"I knew you were a fine choice." He smiled. "Now Seiken and I have some papers to sign, would you care to bare witness?" Night motioned her over to a table Seiken followed closely behind.

"Papers?" She questioned.

"Yes, for our piece of mind, where as Seiken does not trust my words, I do not trust his heart." He smiled at Seiken. "Signing our promise to these Grimitical papers, our word is bound to the completion of our contract." He smiled

"Grimitical papers?" Elisha questioned her eyes growing wide. "I thought they were merely legend. Signing one binds both parties to their vows written upon its surface… if they should betray it…"

"They pay the price, I see you are familiar with its workings, I took the liberty of drawing it up, if you would do the honours?" Elisha took the paper from him, passing it to Seiken so he could read it before the announcement. He nodded passing it back.

"By the law and judgement of these sacred parchment, so is it written, that in exchange for release of his world, the returning his people along with their freedom, Seiken son of Crystenia, is bound to Night by legal contract, to aid him where asked in the task of leading the chosen party, as needed, in order to achieve the desired goal leading ultimately to the retrieval of the final Grimoire. In exchange for all things offered above, Seiken son of Crystenia, must unquestioningly help Night fulfil the set tasks. Night must remain true to his word and not devise any way in which to take from parties involved, that which has been promised in return for cooperation. Just as Seiken son of Crystenia, must offer his complete service without betrayal to Night. Full cooperation of each parties is expected in each instant. Signing of this sacred parchment is an acknowledgement of agreement to the conditions, here upon its surface, and bind you through to contract completion. Until all debts are paid in full, upon this time this contract shall be absorbed binding neither of your names to its fate." Elisha took a breath placing the parchment on the table.

"I trust this is to your liking?" Night was the first to sign his name on the parchment the ink soaking deep into the paper, Seiken was elsewhere at this time taking in the vast library that seemed to stretch into infinity, he needed just a moment to concentrate on helping Ume, now he was no longer bound, he could offer her something she needed so desperately at this moment as she nursed over Daniel before attempting to cross into Knights-errent. Seiken walked forwards in the pretence of thinking over the contract, stopping only as his eyes falling upon a strange capsule, he was buying time as he thought over the wording and implications of the read agreement, it was then he saw her, a young lady suspended in sleep, a large skin tight suit covering her from head to toe covering all skin from her neck to her wrist and ankles, her long blue hair was about waist length much longer than the version of her he had seen walking with the 'chosen party' as Night called them.

"That's…" He gasped approaching for a closer look, Elisha grabbing the parchment from the table ran over preventing any further advancement towards Elly.

"Elaineor? Yes." Night answered still standing at the table in the centre of the room watching him carefully.

"But how?" He questioned pacing around the capsule noticing a small helmet wired to it, although other than that one piece of equipment, no wires or anything passed to it, yet, at the same time the capsule emitted a strange humming sound.

"All shall become clear." Night answered as Elisha passed Seiken the parchment encouraging him once more to approach the table. "But first, business." Night pulled the chair out for Seiken standing over him as he read the contract once more, his pen poised and ready to sign.

***

"So where now?" Daniel directed his question to Elly who had led them to this point; she had been guiding their movements for some time now without a hint as to where their target was.

"From here, you must venture through the cave of mysteries." Elly smiled at him "I shall wait at the exit." She raised her eyebrows waiting for the questions that were sure to follow.

"Can't we just cut through?" He questioned.

"You misunderstand." She smiled taking such pleasure in the words that followed. "I beat this cave, every riddle, every question and I, like any who can stake such a claim can step through to the exit, even in Knights-errent these rules still apply." She looked to Daniel who was beginning to feel pressured, what if he let them down? True enough Elly had told him much about this place, yet still, his confidence was lacking. "Don't worry, it will be an experience." She smiled patting him on the shoulder.

"Fine, what is this place exactly?" He questioned taking in the strange cave that stood before them, it seemed to be made of a rock like none he had seen.

"This place, was built by the Gods, it gave passage to those deemed worthy to pass through to the mountain of spirits, should you choose not to venture this way, you are looking at, at least a five day hike, one you may not survive to make, taking the chance on the caves always work out… less fatal, let's say." She smiled again about to enter the cave.

"How does it work?" Again Daniel as always was filled with questions.

"Well, each tunnel represents an answer, if you get it right or wrong the path you choose will open, the only difference being, the more mistakes you make, the closer you approach to your doom." Elly stepped into the cave vanishing before their sight.

Daniel hesitated a moment thinking over what had said before their arrival, he took a breath stepping in, the others followed mere seconds behind, the cave mouth sealed around them leaving them in a circular room with but three paths of exit none of which was the one they had come through. All around them old-fashioned wooden torches burnt filling the air with the sweet smell of rich wood. A large pedestal was the only object standing within the room, Daniel and the others slowly approached

"Speak." Boomed a voice as he approached the pedestal, he could just make out some of the words written upon it before the voice startled him. "Who dares to enter the passage of the Gods?" There was a pause Daniel thought back to Elly's words as she had briefed him on his task.

"I, Daniel Starfire accompanied by my fellow travellers, Zodiac Althea, Acha Night and Eiji Um…" Daniel looked to Eiji but the voice had already continued.

"For what purpose do you venture to our world?"

"We seek passage to the mountain of the spirits,"

"Then I trust you accept the rules of this passage?"

"Yes sir." He answered hoping he had understood all that Elly had told him of this challenge.

"Very well, begin." In the room a large hour glass tipped over the sand slowly filtering through as Daniel read the pedestal.

"Bird women, swine, ogre, I have faced many a beast, Scylla and Charybolis to name a few, I have sailed the kingdom of Hades, most in my time knew me, yet to some, I was nobody." Above each of the three corridors a name was written, to the far left, Odysseus, to the centre Sisyphus, to the right, Ulysses

"I guess we have to choose one but how do they open?" Eiji paced between them looking at the solid wall that blocked each path.

"Speak Daniel Starfire, make your choice and approach the door, it shall open before you." The voice resonated through the silence until it once more faded into nothing.

"My initial thought was Ulysses, he did all of those… but Odysseus and Ulysses are the same, before he left on his travels he was Odysseus, but as he travelled for ten years against the Gods who forced him from his way, they began then to call him Ulysses…"

"You can only choose one." Zo whispered looking at the draining hourglass that was embedded into the solid brick wall; it seemed to have appeared from nowhere as Daniel had read allowed the question which only he could voice the answer to.

"Odysseus then." He stated walking towards the wall as they approached it vanished as if it had been nothing more than an illusion closing once more behind them into a solid wall. Another pedestal stood before them the room they entered identical in every detail to the last, again Daniel approached the centre.

"By three golden apples I was forced to wed, but shifted to lions as we hurried to bed." He read aloud. "I know this one… Melanion made a bargain with Aphrodite… to marry this woman who refused to be wed; she was faster than any man alive but agreed to wed the one who could best her in a race." He smiled thinking of Zo. "The punishment for losing in this race was their life. Aphrodite gave Melanion three apples of gold to distract her from the race, curiosity making her stop for each apple, by these delays he won… But in his haste to bed his wife… he forgot to honour his side of the promise to the Goddess, so as punishment, Aphrodite turned them to lions…" He looked to the doors the name on the tip of his tongue as he studied the names carefully,

Athena, Atalanta or Minthe

"Atalanta." He pointed the others towards the central door, on and on the questions went as time speed through the hour glass until finally the last chamber stood before them.

"I have brief mention in old history, I was before Chronos and forgotten by Zeus, fear forgot me yet I live on, few mentions do I have in literature of past."

"That's easy." Daniel sighed; he knew this one from history, although history of the ancients dictated Night to be a Goddess who had set the very creation of the universe into motion. He learnt of him from Elly, he couldn't help but wonder if this was somehow warped with the passage of time, or if indeed sex had any relevance to a being such as he. The old world, the one said to come before theirs possessed the same cycles, his teacher had always been intrigued as to how one of the great Gods could have been forgotten back then, yet make a mark on this new land. Maybe in time, their world too would forget him, erasing him from their minds, but as yet, they still had to face him.

The final grains of sand began to filter through the hour glass.

"Night" He stated pushing the others through the opening door, outside the room, a small light was revealed, it was the exit, they had barely passed through when the final grain slipped into the bottom, the door closed heavily behind them.

"What took so long?" Elly leaned against the side of the cave as they emerged into the sun, it was clear from the suns rays they had not been as long as anticipated. The sun was still low in the sky, perhaps two hours had passed since entering Knights-errent, a good hour of that during their trail through the cave. "Personally, I would have chosen Ulysses, it was on his adventure after all… You got a few wrong but did far better than I anticipated, come on." Elly smiled warmly at Daniel, passing him a small gold coin he looked at her curiously. "That's your fast pass back." She stated, knowing that at some point in the future he would have a use for it.

"So how many times did you go through that to earn your free pass?" Daniel questioned quickening his pace to catch up to her; curiosity gripped him as he awaiting her answer.

"Until they ran you of questions." She smiled winking at Daniel; he went as if to reply but thought better of it.

"So this place we're heading, the mountain of spirits?… What do we expect to find there?" Acha questioned as the continued towards the mountains in the distance

"The final rune." Elly stated in a matter of fact tone.

Finally the rock terrain of their passage merged softly into the grassy field of the meadow they were to cross, in the distance, they could see the mighty mountain towering above all as it seemed to vanish into the sky itself to look down upon them.

"The mountain of spirits!" Eiji exclaimed seeing its silhouette just before them. "Even though you said it, I thought it to be nothing more than a rumour." He gasped. "A place of legend, never did I believe I would gaze upon it… it's the very home of the elemental spirits, deep within its core gnomes forge armour and weapons, in its clear streams and lakes the nymphs are said to play…" Eiji went to continue but was soon cut short.

"You only think of the good things, this place was once home to the Severaine not to mention the holding place of the star of Arshad, as such it attracts many creatures both good." She looked to Eiji then back to the mountain. "And evil, there are creatures sleeping in its depths that would freeze your blood if you were to so much as catch sight of them, creatures more terrifying than your worst nightmares could even begin to comprehend… Yet despite the dangers, somewhere up there the final rune rests awaiting our arrival, after this we head home before setting out on the final journey."

"Home?" Zo questioned a joyous lift to her voice as she looked to Elly.

"Yes… You do want to say goodbye, don't you?" Elly questioned quietly inaudible to the others in the group, Zo felt her stomach sink at her words, Daniel clearly felt this also as he stood staring at her questioningly. "Also there is something we need to collect before our journey is truly over."

"I would like that… Thank you." Zo smiled sadly, in her mind a single line reminded her of the truth, something she was told not long ago but with all that happened it seemed like a lifetime ago… *'To win… you must sacrifice everything.'* Zo looked at her friends each of them in turn and smiled, it was a warm smile that reached all the way to her eyes.

"I was beginning to wonder." Daniel slowed his pace placing his arm around her shoulders carefully, avoiding the wounded area.

"What?" She questioned turning to look at him as the others continued at their normal pace.

"If you had a genuine smile left." He thought back over the entirety of this journey, she had smiled so much over its course, a smile she used as nothing more than a shield for her true feelings, a smile to cover her fears, worries and pains, but this time was different, this time it reached her eyes making them shine brightly, he never realised how much he had missed it, until it was no longer there. "What were you thinking?" Daniel questioned, even now he had failed to capture what the thought that brought such joy to her eyes had been.

"Just… what great friends I have." They continued on towards the mountain.

"I never imagined it would be so…" Eiji paused at the bottom of the enormous mountain gazing on as it towered into the clouds. "High." He finished, the others stopped to view the sheer height of the lilac mountains. There was no way to estimate exactly how far above the clouds it rose, but its steeps sides would prove to be a challenge.

"Well, no time to dawdle." Elly stated approaching the first steep cliff face, although nearer the bottom it had started with a slight incline easy enough for them to climb, they soon found the almost vertical cliff faces a treacherous path. They had only been on its steep slopes for ten minutes when Acha stated the obvious as she paused on the vertical slant hanging tightly to the small rocks that provided her footing.

"I don't think this mountain wants to be climbed." She saw Zo's hand reach down for her giving her a lift to the small cliff face feet above aiding her in her struggle up. Once up she looked at Zo smiling as she did so, they all sat their catching their breath, resting for a while, Acha noticed Zo still clutching her shoulder tightly as she rummaged in her bag before pulling out a small root she began to chew on, it was a moment before she realised why, all this climbing wouldn't be helping her wound, yet still she had gone that extra mile to help her onto the cliff face, she scolded herself again, wondering how she could have been so blind as to not see her gentle heart, guilt filling her as she thought back over all the times she betrayed her. She did nothing but help those around her, regardless of the personal cost. Acha gave a sigh glancing down the path they had just climbed, although they seemed to be moving slowly, in the last hour they seemed to have made a lot of headway, climbing at least twice the distance than she had expected.

"It's a long climb to the opening at the top." Elly sighed. "We can't afford to wait around; spending a night on this mountain would *not* be a good idea." Elly looked to Zo who smiled, the root she had eaten would be slow in taking effect to relieve the pain she felt, but she knew there was no way they could wait around for it, but then again she hadn't planned to, she stood slowly ready to press on.

"Well actually." Seiken appeared before them. "You only need to climb to the next ledge." He pointed to a ledge not the one above them, but one far to the right, a ledge none of them had noticed before he had pointed it out. "There's an entrance there, from that point it's pretty easy travel." He looked to Zo a sadness in his eyes, she looked at him questioningly.

"I thought you were trapped?" She questioned lightly.

"I was… it's a long story, Night tried to get me to sign over to betray you in exchange for his withdrawal from my home and people, I was so close Umemi, so close to signing. In fact he was so sure I would agree he let his guard down giving me the second I needed to escape."

"To help him? How?" Zo questioned glancing at the others.

"He didn't say exactly, it involved betraying you though, all the time he was explaining I thought about the implications, I was so close Umemi, so close." He sighed " I had the pen in my hand ready to sign an agreement to aid him, but then, I started thinking, although it's true I want to save my people… how could I claim to be worthy of rule, knowing how I had gone about it? I have such faith in you Umemi, I know you won't let us down." He smiled the sadness vanishing from his eyes. "It won't be long until he finds me, I must keep moving… I will help all I can… But you *must* hurry!" His voice seemed to grow more desperate as he glanced around. "If you don't I fear not one of us will remain for you to save, I shall find a safer place and return, this mountain is treacherous." With those words he vanished leaving them to continue the steep climb up and across to the cave.

"Ok… so we just go through and our target is at the end?" Eiji questioned glancing into the pitch black hole that Seiken had directed them too, he was right, it would save time. "Ok… let's say we do get this other rune… then what? What are we meant to do with them?" He questioned glancing to Elly, until now they had been blindly following the map, retrieving the runes without a thought to what lay ahead, but as the journeys end drew closer, he was starting to focus on the unknown.

"Aren't they supposed to be some sort of key to release Seiken's people?" Daniel questioned glancing at the small pouch now held in Zo's hand as she examined them for clues.

"Well, if that's the case, where's the door? I mean, we've already been told their being held in Night's tower, if these were keys to get in… how could anyone else enter without them? And if they all had their own keys, wouldn't it be simpler just to jump them? I think the whole thing is crazy!" Eiji ranted, glancing at Elly occasionally, she seemed to be listening in silent amusement, again, Eiji had the feeling she was withholding valuable information.

"True but what else have we got?" Acha questioned looking to Elly sharing the same feeling as Eiji regarding information retention.

"We were told to find them, we found them end of story." She answered in reply to their looks.

"Well I know. But considering the 'eyes' were meant to be pursuing us, and Gods forgive me for saying this, the only things we have really had to content with in this place, are the troubles brought about by this world… It's almost as if they want us to succeed… If that's the case, then why?" Eiji wasn't sure if it was the cave itself, or the dark foreboding feeling he had about what lay ahead, but he knew one thing for sure, the longer he could stall, the longer he could try to pinpoint the morbid feeling radiating from the depths of the gaping mouth that stood before them.

"That's not strictly speaking true…" Daniel looked at the others there was a general air of discomfort surrounding everyone but Elly. "They got you, also I'm convinced behind everything that has happened will have been them manipulating events to suit their needs, manipulating this world to make it seem that way, to trick us into letting our guard down…"

"We have no other leads and us having the runes removed would not necessarily be a bad thing for them." Elly restarted the conversation just past, as she spoke; she made the first definite move towards the cave leaving the others unable to hesitate, knowing they had no choice but to follow her into its unmapped depths.

Zo hesitated outside the cave a small thought resting on the horizon of her mind, a thought she couldn't quite voice.

"Wait." She called entering the cave realising the others had already gone inside, she ran quickly following the figures just in front of her already immersed in darkness. "What do you mean?" She asked catching up with Elly, the lingering thought now forgotten.

"Well think about it, each time a rune has been located, it has been found in a place of magical power, a significant place in both our worlds, a place that linked by this power remains the same within the boundaries of this ever changing world, every sealed place on this map we have passed through or taken a rune from, we have been releasing the magic sealed in that area, we have passed now through every place since our journeys start."

"Except Crowley, it's no where near here, and remains the one place we have yet to visit." Eiji added, a slight smile crossed Elly's lips shadowed by the darkness of the cave, ahead there seemed to be lights of some kind providing relief from the complete darkness.

"So what you're saying is… that's where the door must be!" Daniel exclaimed Elly rolled her eyes turning back to face the others she smiled.

"Must be." She gave a sigh, there was no point whatsoever, if they weren't going to listen…

"You have to be careful here… It's their favourite hunting grounds… Their power is stronger here." Seiken's voice echoed around the cave, although they tried to locate him within the darkness it was as if he had never been there.

They stopped for a second noticing they had entered the pale area of light, it seemed to be generated from strange rocks embedded in the cave side and floor, shining by some strange power a strange shade of green, not too much to be overpowering, just the right amount to guide travellers on their way, ensuring they were able to see all around, Daniel stopped examining on of the rocks, occasionally they would pass a small water source bubbling through the ground to form a small pool, no doubt it worked its way free from the mighty mountain to create some of the vast streams and waterfalls that fell down its sides, they walked slowly, with the exception of the water the only sounds to echo its depths were those of their footsteps.

"How much further is this tunnel?" Acha answered surprised when Elly answered.

"About another half a mile." She stated speeding the pace a little Acha turned to look at Daniel freezing suddenly as she did so.

"Wait… where's Daniel?" Zo looked around quickly before Acha had even finished her sentence she was searching for his thoughts, nothing returned.

"When did you last see him?" She questioned looking to Acha who had been besides him just moments ago, or so she had thought, surely he knew better than to wander off and that's exactly what was concerning her, he did know better, yet at the same time he had done it before several times since this adventure began, but this time was different, surely he wouldn't dream of doing so in this place, and besides, it was a straight passage and he was no where to be seen. Zo squinted down the darkened passage hoping she could catch some glimpse of him, but there was nothing; it was almost as if he had vanished into thin air.

***

Daniel stopped briefly to examine the small rock, the others were only steps away when something grabbed him, it was almost as if the darkness itself reached from the wall wrapping around him silencing him with its shadow, seconds later he watched a small wisp of blue cloud shifting before him take his form moving to catch up with Acha, she scolded him slightly for falling behind, all the time he was being pulled towards the shadow he screamed their names over and over, but it was clear not a single one could hear him.

Then there was nothing but darkness, he felt almost as if he were floating through the air until his feet descended on solid ground everything was so black nothing at all could be distinguished walls, area, nothing.

'I wouldn't move too much if I were you.' The voice whispered, Daniel would have bet anything that had it not been so dark he would see the hunting eyes staring at him from all around, he moved his foot slightly feeling only air beneath the creatures laughed. *'It's a long way down.'* Daniel cursed to himself, the section he stood on was no larger than a stool, he had warned the others about letting their guard down, but he had done just that when he stopped to examine the glowing rock, he hadn't for a second considered there would be any danger, he had done it so often now without incident he was sure he would be safe, again he cursed his foolery. *'You're hoping they'll come back?'* One of the voices whispered. *'They wont come back for you… they can't.'* Everything grew silent Daniel felt alone, he reached to Zo with his mind, hoping someway to bridge the distance, but as hard as he tried he couldn't reach her, he swayed a bit, still weary from their previous adventure, the fatigue once more catching up to him.

Although Zo had succeeded in healing him once more, the sheer amount of times this had occurred and the closeness to the last two events was taking its toll, he hadn't wanted to worry anyone, but since that battle with Marise, he felt so exhausted, he had just dismissed it as blood loss and exhaustion, but thought now maybe he should have said something, then the incident with the poison just worsened things, besides, with Zo around he found other places to address his concerns, her shoulder wasn't healing and clearly causing large amounts of pain, he clutched her satchel tightly, hoping that whatever she had taken for the pain would last until they found him. He knew that they would be looking, and Zo would not rest until he was safe. A long time ago, she had made a promise to him, a promise to protect him. He wobbled slightly again through the darkness, he just hoped that she would be safe.

***

"Daniel!" Zo shouted her voice joined with the chorus of the others echoed through the cave, nothing but their own voices answered them back… at least, after the incident in the mine fields, they hope it was their own voices answering.

"Maybe he wandered off?" Eiji questioned, his cautious tone not convincing anyone, he had been there when he had caught up with them, Acha had scolded him for falling behind, that was only seconds before he vanished, you can't fall that far behind in just a few seconds. Eiji raised his arm silencing the others. "Something's wrong." He whispered only moments before the ground trembled with such force it shook them from their feet, a huge avalanche of rocks collapsed from the ceiling Eiji had barely managed to get to his feet in time to dive on Acha forcing her from where the remaining rocks had crashed to the earth protecting her until the last of the rocks had fallen, he blushed moving off her quickly.

When the dust cleared they looked in dismay of what remained of the only path they knew, they could only hope what lay before them was not only their success, but an exit. The tunnel was completely covered from top to bottom almost as if a perfectly constructed wall had descended. Zo knelt at the edge of the rocks moving them in hope to get through, in hope to find Daniel waiting at the other side, although she knew this was nothing more than wishful thinking she had to try, what if he was there? Waiting unable to catch them up, yet all the time she failed to make even the slightest headway. From time to time she paused clutching her shoulder before digging again, the others just watched her for a minute unsure exactly what to say, knowing that she blamed herself for not watching him closer, knowing she held herself responsible for his safety and knowing, she knew they had him.

It was Elly that approached her squeezing her bad shoulder just hard enough to make her stop, as she cowered away from the pressure Elly released it quickly, satisfied at gaining her attention.

"It's no use." She whispered softly. "We can't get through, even if we did you know as well as I do, we wouldn't find him, we could walk the path all day and still turn up nothing." Zo gave a defeated sigh at Elly's words, her hand still gripping her shoulder where Elly had triggered another painful spasm. "His best chance… is if we succeed." As she spoke Elly turned her away from the rubble, Zo glanced back once more as if expecting to see it vanish and Daniel standing in its place, she stood for just a moment longer before realising Elly was right, they had to move onwards.

'Daniel… I'll find you, whatever it takes.' She thought, a thought she put such power behind she hoped wherever he was he would hear it.

***

"Excellent." Night smiled at Seiken who sat at the table in Night's main room; to his right the prison cell, a cell now filled by complete darkness not a single ray of light entered the cell through his creature's field. "That was easier than I anticipated."

"What are you going to do with them?" Seiken glanced towards the cage, finding it odd that it had seemed to appear from nowhere and yet seemed to blend with the room as if it had always been there.

"That is not your concern… but… it can do no harm, I plan to use them as bargaining chips. You see my daughter would never aid me of her own free will, I learnt that just by watching her these last weeks, she is so much like her mother, although with her mother, I never felt the need to pursue what seemed like childish dreams, she was everything I needed, nothing else mattered as long as she was safe…" Night stopped realising he had drifted far from topic. "So I needed something in the way of persuasion a fair exchange, the Grimoire, for the lives of her friends." He finished the sentence as if he had never side tracked.

"But why go to all this? Why set up the fake runes, the quest, for something you could ultimately do yourself?" This had been bothering Seiken for some time, up to now Night had answered his questions without query; he wondered if this time he would have the same response, he did.

"On both counts there you are wrong, the runes were not fake, but true enough are useless now, they were key magical seals supporting the fields that restrain the Severaine, once removed the energy used to create the seal vanished, and on the second account, the Grimoire cannot be taken by my hands, the Idliod saw to that protecting it from my touch, but on the last book they placed a challenge, only one of my flesh with pure of heart could take the book from its final resting place, but their oversight on this was something that is limited knowledge, I have a daughter, you are possibly the fourth person I have entrusted with this information, but this is to go no further than these four walls, understand." Seiken nodded.

"But they already know this, one thing I don't understand though, why put your daughter through all this? Don't you have any consideration for her feelings at all, for the hardship you have forced upon her? For the dangers you have put her in?" He questioned, this entire situation was strange, he couldn't even being to think what was going through Night's mind.

"I watched every step of the way ensuring she was not in danger, but what you must understand, what I am doing is bigger than all of this, bigger than you, bigger than me, I love my daughter more than you could know, her mother too, was a remarkable woman, she alone could justify the salvation of human life, she was the one exception to that pitiful race, the one redeeming feature that made me forget my ambitions, my daughter is every bit the same as the woman I loved so dearly, but at the end of it, I did what I had to do to get here, when it comes down to it…" Night stopped again. What was it about this boy he found so easy to talk to? Maybe it was because they were of similar mind, they weren't too different, both would do what they had to, to obtain something they desired. They had both followed their paths, besides, the wisdom and knowledge exchanged in conversations with this boy, was unfailingly like with the ones he had shared with the great Gods of times past. "Enough of this, they are waiting for your guidance." Seiken nodded vanishing before his eyes. He glanced in the gossip crystal watching as Seiken appeared, he gave a sigh. "When it comes down to it, I wish there was another way."

**

As they continued down the passage it opened out without warning, they found themselves in a large room with an enormous chasm before them, stretching across the chasm's centre; a black cloud formed a single straight passage.

Eiji walked warily to the edge peering down the huge drop, it seemed to stretch to the very centre of the earth itself, the heat rising from it did little to disprove this theory.

"So what now?" Eiji questioned wondering if perhaps they were meant to somehow walk over the cloud, or perhaps it was nothing more than a lore to send them plummeting to their deaths.

"Once across the bridge of Obscurity, there is very little distance left." Seiken took Zo's hand in his, it was almost as if for a split second he hesitated, but as he looked at her now, he seemed his normal self once more, she smiled at him, again as always she found herself staring deep into his eyes as he did hers.

"There's a solid bridge under all this?" Eiji questioned, it made sense now he had heard it, although there was still in doubt whether or not it truly existed, the clouds surrounding it left him with a deep forbidding feeling, from where he stood, through the darkness of this open area, the top did seem to curve around as if descending leaving to reason there may be a ledge like this on the other side but still something about the bridge just didn't feel right.

"Another thing." Seiken continued releasing Zo's hand. "Once on the bridge, you must not look back, no matter what you think you hear, no matter what you think you see, do not stop, do not hesitate, if you want to live. The bridge here is constructed by magic, as you walk the magic forms a solid barriers beneath you, but only should you keep walking, if you were to hesitate just a little, you would plummet to your deaths, or perhaps worse." Seiken walked to the edge looking down into the vast empty space, feeling the heat from below warm his face. "One more thing, once across the other side, do not attempt to cross back using this route."

"Why?" Acha questioned pulling Eiji further from the edge of the chasm, to which he seemed to be getting closer and closer to as he tried to make out the bottom.

"This bridge, as I said, is constructed of magic, it was designed to work only one way, once you have crossed the bridge the magic that carries you resets to the entrance side, although the first few steps back into the darkness remain, you would never make it out, there is one entrance one exit, never do the two meet understand?" Before they could even answer Seiken vanished.

"There's something very strange about that guy... it is still him isn't it?" Eiji questioned approaching Zo, if anyone would be able to tell, surely she would, the way they spoke, the way they were together seemed almost as if they had known each other forever.

"Yes... he seems distracted... maybe it's because..." She paused for a second thinking of something she had heard long ago before pushing it from her mind and continuing. "He has a lot of burdens to carry now, the future of his people rest on our success, if his actions to try and help us haven't already cost him."

"Still, I don't recall anything like this at the top if we had entered there..." Elly paused as if waiting for some sort of confirmation, as they exchanged glances, none of them had been to this place before, how could they answer such a statement it was a while before she continued her mind seemingly made up. "Although I must admit it does seem to be a shortcut." She went to take the bag from Zo, before realising it was no longer within her possession, Daniel had been carrying it since the injury, and since he was now gone, so was it. She sighed slightly pulling the backpack from her own shoulder, a backpack Zo recognised as the one she had used to pack all the food and supplies when first coming on this journey. Zo looked to her, she had seen her carrying it although this must have been only the second or third time it had come to Knights-errent with them, definitely the first since obtaining the charms from the traveller in Abaddon, she couldn't help but wonder what had made her bring it this time, until she realised, with the exception of a few bits, this had been the place Elly had kept everything for their travels, if this was to be the final cross over, it stood to reason she would come prepared.

Elly pulled some smooth almost invisible thread from the bag, Zo knew it as the substance Elly had used to stitch her shoulder, she started to unravel it, first securing it around Acha, then Eiji, then Zo and finally herself, leaving enough slack between them so as to use the remaining thread and give them plenty of distance. "Well it's not rope, but it will do for what we need it for." She stated. "Well you heard him, we're nearly there, let's go." With that Elly began to lead the way across the bridge the others now strapped together had little choice but to follow.

As they first entered they found strange columns either side preventing anything more than single file passing using the walls either side for guidance, she set a slow pace as they began to walk across the pitch black bridge, Zo held the tight string in front and behind her unaware the others also mirrored her action in order to monitor the tightness in case any of them hit danger, of course, she wasn't sure what exactly she could do, but doing so gave her a small amount of comfort.

They had been on the bridge walking at the same steady pace for around ten minutes when she heard Daniel call her name, she continued putting one foot before the other finding it increasingly more difficult, his voice seemed to come from right behind her, yet she took to heart Seiken's warning, but still, what if he was trapped here? What if the force that stole him had imprisoned him here? She swore she could hear his footsteps as if he walked behind her, she tried to block out his conversation, his requests for her to wait just a second so he could catch up, she focused hard on the darkness before her.

Elly however, was enjoying the silence, but she knew it wouldn't last for long, she didn't need Elisha to tell her the dangers of this bridge, yet she knew she could face them, she had no guilt for her actions past, she had no reason why she should need to hesitate or reach for anything this bridge may tempt her with, they had been walking a while, and just as she began to think it wouldn't bother the voice started.

"I told you to go the other way but no, you were so fixated on getting the treasure, you sacrificed every one of us for your greed." A young anger filled a voice she knew from many centuries ago, filling the air around her.

"It was necessary." She stated coldly. "Besides, you would be dead now anyway, so get over it." Her step never slowed, although for some unknown reason, she found herself somewhat surprised at the accuracy of the voices from the past, she wondered for that split second if they truly were sharing this dark walk with her.

"But you killed us." A slightly older voice spoke now, Elly smiled remembering the owner of it, he had been wise for his age, at thirty-two he had already found various lost arts, solving the most tedious of clues, there was a man who could really use his brain, it was just a shame he hadn't used it on their final journey.

"No, I saved you, because of me, you lived that extra time until your death, you never would have lived to share my journeys and don't forget that, all of you, I took you all from certain death. True it cost your life in the end, but think of all the extra time you had, all the adventures and the living you would have missed if I hadn't. If your trying to make me feel guilty you can stop, I hold no remorse for what happened, I warned you of the danger, but your eyes were too filled with the gold to listen, besides, you lost your own lives with your greed, we went only for one item, one item that when I left I passed to the nymphs, an item that saved the life of one of the heroes of this world. It was your own greed when you lined your pockets with gold and treasure that signed your death warrant. I did warn you." Elly never realised she had stepped from the bridge until she opened her eyes, she walked at the same steady pace as Zo followed behind, then Eiji, the rope was still tight behind him, in a few more steps they would have made it without incident. Then the rope fell slack, Eiji grabbed it looking at the place it had been severed turning back he paused at the end of the bridge, remembering Seiken's warning he stopped short of his re-entry placing only his hand into the darkness, knowing even as he did it, it was a stupid thing to do, he waved it about for a second hoping to some in contact with her, it had been there mere seconds, when Elly pulled him back, the cloud shifted almost as if something had been charging stopped from exiting by the force of the cloud. Not a word passed between them as they undid the thread that attached them Elly wrapped it up placing it in the bag before they continued on their way.

***

Acha entered the bridge repeating to herself over and over to keep walking don't look back, then through the darkness she heard rushed footsteps behind her.

"Acha?" The voice questioned, it was a voice she knew at once.

"Daniel? You made it." She smiled she could hear his breath behind her as his pace slowed now to match hers.

"I thought I'd never catch up." He still seemed to be quite breathless as he spoke.

"Daniel this bridge is dangerous, you must not stop, nor must you look back." She warned repeating the words over and over in her mind.

"Thanks." His voice returned to normal, the fatigue previously displayed within it vanished, she felt his hand fall gently on her shoulder as she continued walking. "It's ok now though, can't you feel the stone beneath our feet? We made it." Acha smiled, it was true, the area she walked on now did share the same texture as that they left, she placed her hand on his looking to the hand to confirm he was really still there now they had reached the exit, her heart leapt as her stomach fell as she realised what she had done, the cloud was still so thick she could see nothing, no sooner had looked she felt the hand change beneath her glove, its once smooth texture became covered with hair, the hand itself growing, the rope before her severed as a giant beast took hold of her stabbing one of its long claws into the back of her neck, she felt herself grow weak as she fell forwards aware this creature had now lifted her to the air.

***

Daniel was unsure exactly the time that had passed since his captors had placed him on the raised area, he had once slowly turned ensuring void met his step everyway feeling with his foot for more ground through the darkness, he had hoped this was perhaps some elaborate trick, but found it was not. For each way he tried only air met his foot as he slid it a little towards any direction. His body had began to ache now from standing so very still, he had known for some time he would soon reach his limits as he tired, his legs had been shaking under the strain for some time. Then it happened, he knew it would, he had prepared for this moment, yet he screamed all the same, his balance failed , forcing him over the edge, he let out the terrified gasp as he began to fall though soon found it cut short as he fell to the floor, all around him the mocking laughter echoed as he lay dazed and somewhat relieved on the floor, light returned to the room, he found himself in a small cell, annoyed to find his first concept of the place he stood to be accurate, it wasn't that the ledge he found himself on was the size of a stool, it was a stool, well a stone raise in the cell designed to be sat on, there were three in total which he could now make out through the fading darkness, from nowhere a breeze swept past, hearing the thud he pulled himself up from the floor, finding Acha now lying not to far from him, he moved slowly to pull himself besides her, his body still aching from the hours of standing still.

"Acha." He shook her gently as he rose to his knees before her. "Acha?" She didn't move, he looked her over quickly finding no cause for her unconsciousness, then he saw it, a small drop of blood at the back of her neck, a place used by Bengaulds to induce sleep into their victims so they may carry them away, he remembered reading about them in class before the term end, although not that long ago, it seemed like years. It was a legendary beast that can project images into its victims mind, what ever is needed to steal a look from them, but once they look upon them they shift and change into a mighty beast, using their index claw, a long retractable spike to pierce the victims flesh rendering them unconscious, many people however mistook these for the nameless creatures from ancient mythology that would follow travellers after night, should they look back, they would kill them. Of course, they weren't always nameless, or at least so he thought, but it seemed fear had wiped their name from existence, but unlike Gods they were never forgotten, the lurking fear of the dark would always remain meaning they were immortalised, for as long as there is darkness there will always be the fear of that which resides within it. He looked to Acha, she seemed alright, the only thing he could do for now was leave her to sleep.

Daniel stood slowly approaching the bars of the cage. As he looked through he saw a rather large table before him, behind this table a window through with the pale light of the full moon gently caressed the room, looking harder he could just make out a large door to the left of where the cell was located, although anything to the right was completely invisible, try as he may he couldn't see what lay that way. Light filled the room, it was not a normal light like that you would expect in homes or buildings, it was a light created like magic, a door closed from somewhere to the right and a familiar voice greeted him.

"Welcome home." Daniel, from the lunar phase alone, knew they were no longer in Knights-errent, but the voice of the familiar stranger confirmed it. "Do not worry the others shall be joining you shortly." As the figure moved into sight Daniel felt his jaw drop.

"You?... But why?" He gazed upon the figure, his raven black hair fastened neatly back, although he no longer wore the clothes of a traveller, his identity was clear.

"Sorry to have deceived you, allow me to introduce myself, I am Night." Night gave a small bow; a long silence seemed to pass until it was finally broken by Acha who was now sitting, her hand rubbing the back of her neck where the creature's talon had induced her sleep.

"You're my father?" She questioned glancing out of the cell in disbelief the man that stood before her now bore no physical resemblance at all to her father of eras past. "You look so different now." The father she had known had brown hair and all in all looked fairly common place, exactly the opposite in regards to what could have been said about the figure standing before her now, he had about him, an unearthly beauty, it was then she placed the feeling back outside Abaddon, the feeling of familiarity around the stranger.

"Ah, Acha immortality does wonders, this is my true form, the one both you and your mother beheld was a disguise as I was forced to mortal flesh, anyway I have so much to do, after all I am expecting company, although what kind of host would I be to leave you without company."

"More monsters I suppose?" Daniel spat residing himself to the stone stool that he had been forced to stand on for hours.

"No, not at all, I need you unharmed." Night began to walk from view his footsteps stopping. "Ah, Seiken, I trust you shall take care of our visitors until the others arrive."

"But…" Seiken moved forwards to take a place at the table not far from the bars of the cage; he looked at Daniel and Acha as they glared at him. "I thought you wanted your daughter to find you?" He questioned looking again at Acha, Night's footsteps continued and the sound of an opening door was heard.

"That is not *my* daughter." He stated coldly before exiting.

"Traitor!" Daniel threw himself towards the bars hoping they would somehow give under his weight, he knew this to be impossible but if he could just get hold of him. "We trusted you!" Seiken did not meet his gaze; he simply pulled his chair closer to the cage.

"I did what I had to." He sighed still not looking at either of them, instead occupying himself by taking in strange patterns on the floor at his feet. Daniel suddenly realised as he looked Seiken must have been no older than he himself was, at this moment, as he sat in shame avoiding their challenging looks, he seemed so young, for some reason noting this cushioned his anger.

"I don't understand… Why?" He approached the bars looking out to Seiken.

"When I found out the runes were fake… I knew even with your help, there was no way to free my people… They're dying Daniel; they've been away from our world too long. Even should you have succeeded in collecting the runes, it would do no good. Night is the only person who can release them, don't you see? Can't you understand? The lives of my people rested on me, I had to make a deal. Don't you understand? The needs of the many must *always* outweigh those of the few." Seiken's voice although soft filled with desperate pleads for them to understand, despite how things turned out he truly hadn't wanted to betray them.

"Wait a minute… the runes are fake?" Acha raised her hand silencing Daniel's next comment.

"Yes, the runes were never a key to my people's freedom, I too was fooled by this pretence until the truth was told, the runes were seals to a great power, seals created by people as a protectional barrier, each one that you have removed, has weakened this protection in your world." He sighed

"Great power?" Daniel questioned, his stomach churning at the implications this conversation was leading to.

"I don't know the details." Seiken lied, this was one fact he was bound to keep secret, a last minute addition. "Just a great power was hidden somewhere in your world that he wanted... before, when I was trapped he offered me a deal, my world, my people, our freedom, if I aided him in obtaining this by leading you astray in the mountain of spirits, although true, they will soon reach the holding of the final rune, there was a much safer way to travel that would not have cost so dearly, I had no choice, my people are dying, as their heir I am responsible for them."

"Seiken, you should have had faith in us, in Zo, she gave her word to free your people somehow, no matter what, she has always been true to her word, regardless of the personal cost." He looked to Acha who nodded; this was something she had learned the hard way throughout their travels. Daniel continued the conversation from where Acha had previously cut him off. "What was it you were saying about his daughter?" He questioned

"He told me the entire purpose of your quest, was to get his daughter besides him, or something like that, only I don't think it was as straight forward as that, else why bring her here and not even attempt to acknowledge her?"

"Acha isn't his only daughter." Daniel answered looking to Acha who seemed as shocked as Seiken about this statement, he thought back to both times he had previously met Night, both times he only had one interest, one real interest that is. "What has Night told you of this game?" Daniel questioned sharply.

"Nothing really, only to live she must win, to win she must lose everything." Seiken glanced up to Daniel this time holding his gaze.

"Even herself?" Daniel questioned thinking back to something Zo had once said "All along..." He whispered. "All along she knew, to win, *she* had to lose."

Chapter twenty-two

They left the bridge, glancing back once more in the direction they had come from, the platform they had crossed from no longer visible across the chasm, before leaving the only way they could, through a small arch leading into yet another tunnel.

On entering this strange room they took a moment to look around. Not only was this place filled with natural light, there was something unnerving about the fact they had emerged on a giant circular floating rock, the floor, this one opening was entirely different from the rest of the caves they had walked through, for some unexplained reason it was covered with a fine layer of sand, sand they decided must have come from the large hole that leading outside which bathed the room in a pale sunlight, to the opposite side of this room was a small dark cave, the place they had entered this room through after crossing the bridge. The platform itself had a clear break all around the edges, a break they had jumped over in order to reach the small circular platform that seemed to be impossibly hovering in the room over rivers of molten lava about thirty foot down, occasionally the platform would drop a few feet, only to rise again, giving the impression, no matter how impossible, the rock was simply held in place by the rising heat of the lava below.

In the centre of this room they gathered around a central pedestal, within it, hovered it the final rune bathed in a strange silver light that seemed to be emitted from the peak of the mountain itself, Eiji's hand hovered level to the rune, he sighed lowering his hand, remembering all the dangers they had encountered so far in seizing runes.

"Is this it?" He questioned cautiously circling around the pedestal all in all it was less than a foot in diameter, the rune itself hovered a foot above its top bringing it to shoulder height his hand rose again towards the light closer this time before pulling back. "No corpses? No monsters? Can it be this easy?... Maybe the place will fall in, but I doubt this place repeats itself too often." Elly and Zo watched him cautiously as indecision gripped him; he looked to them for answers.

"Well... looking at it this is the rune of spirit." Elly for once offered no real help.

"Everything else we have encountered, its traps have always somehow been linked to its meaning, like sacrifice had the corpses of those sacrificed to Aburamushi. Balance, the falling building, maybe its trap is liked to its purpose." Zo continued, as Eiji began to examine the light again as if looking at it one more time would somehow provide him with all the answers.

"True... but what... what can be related to spirit? Do we summon the ghosts of a million dead to feed off our life-force?"

"Only one way to find out." Elly prompted, Eiji nodded raising his hand determination on his face. "But." His hand dropped again, relieved to hear the 'but' to the extent of heaving a sigh of relief. "Can you catch?" She questioned. "I'm not too convinced about the nature of the light used to suspend it." Elly fished in her pocket finding a handful of left over narca berries from when she had mixed the potion, she flicked one towards the light as it touched it seemed to shrivel and age before turning to dust having never penetrated the light. A look of horror reflected on Zo and Eiji's face as they noticed exactly how much dust surrounded them, dust they had previously mistaken for sand. Eiji snapped his hand back quickly holding it protectively as he took three large paces back.

"I nearly touched that!" He exclaimed taking another step away from it just to be sure. "We just need to dislodge it somehow... Without actually touching it." He glanced at Zo as if taking the hint, she summoned a small fireball to her aid launching it towards the rune, no sooner had it touched the light then it evaporated into ashes. There was just one other choice, it was clear it would have to be shoved loose, by something long enough to buy time as the light travelled to its user, Zo glanced to her sword and then to Elly.

"I don't know." She answered cautiously before Zo had even asked. "There's no guarantee... Perhaps if Eiji and I were to take some of the strain the light you would be hitting would not be as potent, then maybe, but..."

"Do we have any other option?" Zo questioned already snapping the fasten to release the sword and hilt from the belt. "We need all the keys to open this door, gate or whatever it is... and I just know Daniel and Acha are waiting somewhere on the other side." Zo readied her sword, holding it like she would a baseball bat.

"But if you misjudged even a millisecond..."

"I'm ready." Zo nodded to Eiji, Elly sighed passing him a handful of berries. "I'll create a life field around the blade using magic, hopefully that will satisfy the light leaving me with time to dislodge the rune."

"We'll have to make sure the berries hit at exactly the same time in order to draw enough energy... you ready?" Elly looked to Zo doubtingly she nodded raising the sword once more to the position of a baseball bat, as she did so she felt Daniel's arms wrap around her his voice whispering softly in her ear as she stood upon the grassy meadow

"Ok now head up, shift your weight a little this way, that's right, but you need to hold it a little more like this... now when I throw it, you need to keep your eye on the ball and swing." Daniel's image faded as the pop of the first two berries hit the field, Zo smiled to herself much to the questioning looks of Eiji and Elly.

She whispered softly, a life field similar to the ones she used in healing to push life from the elements to the person she healed, the spell formed in pale blue light around the sword, again the berries hit the field, by now, their timing was perfect but they were quickly running out of berries, she took a breath shifting position slightly watching as the berries left their hands, simultaneously Zo swung her sword hard timing it so that it would impact with the light the exact time the berries would, she felt the solid resistance of the light as it began to feed upon the life barrier, at that moment she cursed her stupidity.

Elly and Eiji could only stare in horror, time itself seemed to slow, as her sword stuck the barrier, her hair began to fade losing its vibrant shades to shine an aged silver, the pale blue aura surrounding her turned as black as night, the berries evaporating to dust as the sword grew closer and closer to the rune, then the rune was dislodged her sheath following in the same slowed time frame until it reached broke the barriers side, time suddenly returned with great vengeance, it seemed things were now, in fact, rushing now to correct the time distortion their minds had created Eiji moved quickly to catch it finding it quicker than he anticipated as it slipped through his fingers rolling across the floor towards the rock face, he tried to scramble to his feet but there was no way he could make it in time, he pursued it none the less but as it grew closer and closer to the edge he realised the truth, they were going to lose it, just as he had given up Elly's foot shifted in front of it stopping it in its path, he stumbled forward in what would have been his final attempt to grab it, their final chance if not for Elly's intervention, she moved her leg quickly avoiding the sliding figure that threatened to knock her from her feet.

They approached Zo cautiously as she clipped her hilt back onto her belt, unsure exactly what to expect as they approached her, she turned to look at them smiling brightly, she was the same as always, except her hair shone that ghastly white, she shook her head gently, as she did so it returned back to its original rich copper brown colour faded down from the roots almost like running water.

"Stupid me." She smiled, her voice holding tones of surprise left over from the shock. "Forgot my rune was sacrifice, luckily, I switched over to darkness just in time."

"Darkness?" Elly questioned

"Yes, although I chose to follow the path of nature, I am not as pure as you may think." Zo paused realising no one in this room would consider her pure, especially knowing her past she continued anyway. "I studied black magic for a long time as a child, before finally choosing my path when I was no older than eight. But before I could truly embrace my powers there was much I had to learn on that side of things, to heal I must also know the fundamental aspects of death, I drain the powers to heal from nature, thus taking their life force, but as I do it for good, it is viewed as white magic, but if I were to do it in reverse, that is for my own gain without asking…" She couldn't explain it, no matter how hard she tried, what she came out with was nothing more than a confusing mess, what she had done was basically healing, but in a reverse manner to that, which she would normally do, thus it was classed as black magic, a magic where the host must be willing to rip the life from something without its permission, willing to kill for a personal gain, that was the basic concept it and the laws on which this particular magic operated. Black magic was not only the summoning of dark masses and dark powers, but taking the life from something for a personal gain. The magic Zo generally used was far gentler and took only what powers the life around would offer, never taking more and always giving thanks and she would never dream of using those powers to call forth a being of pure evil, the power needed for such a thing may see her lose herself, not to the darkness, but to the power or even the being that she was calling.

"I don't understand." Eiji interrupted. "You created a life field by magic, to hold off effects of the light right? Taking life from around you to give to the field." Zo nodded. "As the rune of sacrifice is in your possession it took it from your life as your magic is linked directly to it, so what your saying is, if you cast a spell to take life force from yourself or something around it and transfer it to something else, under the runes powers you actually take its life-force?" Eiji frowned, confusing himself more as he tried to make sense of what had just occurred but he wasn't the only one Elly too seemed to wish to question this further, and why shouldn't she? Marise had never managed to grasp black magic, or charms, the magic she had used came naturally, she had an instinct for the spells she could use, but Zo, Zo seemed to have no boundaries, it seemed she could turn her hand to anything.

"Close enough." She smiled, it wasn't quite right but close enough, it would take too long to explain the basics behind it, it had taken her months of study before she herself finally had grasped the concept safely.

"I never knew you knew black magic." Elly stated, all the time in which she had known Marise, never once had she called on dark powers for anything more than Aburamushi, up to now she had thought her magic was the same as that used by Zo, of course, Zo seemed to be more proficient in healing, but the difference in their offensive power balanced any real power difference, she had always believed them to be the same, until just, this one demonstration left her filled with questions, Marise had never managed to call on the dark arts, it seemed there were a few more differences between the two than she had initially thought, it seemed to stretch deeper than she first thought, it seemed just as Zo could not use the sword to Marise's full ability, Marise could not use magic to Zo's. After all she had just switched between them instantly without hesitation, even those in neutral arts need the binding time to expire before recasting to call on other forces, but somehow, she had overlapped the expiry of one with the creation of another, it was unheard of, impossible, or so she believed until she had witnessed it. "Well." Said Elly finally after a few moments of silent contemplation. "There's just one place to head now." She stated as they walked from the cave. The others followed her quickly still feeling uneasy about the giant floating platform, once on the solid join Eiji stopped, the others hesitating, for possibly only the second time he opened his version of the map, surprised to find it now contained only a small island he knew to be Crowley.

"It seems the other places on this map have... vanished?" He turned it over in his hands once or twice just to make sure.

"That's because the magic that made them fixed points has been dispelled when we passed through or took the runes." Seiken placed his hand on Zo's shoulder as Elly spoke, for a second it seemed something around them changed, in that second he vanished, as she looked around she saw all was as it had been, she approached Elly who was busy glancing over Eiji's shoulder at the map, it seemed they were unaware that Seiken had even appeared before them, they exited quickly into the sunlight, by the position of the sun a few hours remained until they had to think about their return.

As they stepped out onto the ledge, Zo heard herself gasp, she glanced over the incredible view, against all odds they had appeared on the island of Crowley, they had appeared through, what looking back, seemed to be a solid wall of stone on the small mountain they had climbed, from where she stood now she could see her home.

"How did we get here?" Eiji questioned looking straight at Zo, as if he knew it was information she possessed, he was right.

"I think it was Seiken, he was here a minute ago." She answered, still unsure of exactly what had happened, yet relieved to find it had, it put them one large step closer to their goal.

"I never saw him." Eiji glanced past her as if he expected to see him hiding nearby, giving up on that idea he returned to his looking around, still unable to believe they actually stood so close to the place they needed, instead of half way around the world, he turned back to see the exit they had left only to find, as Zo had moments ago, there wasn't one, nor had it been concealed by magic, a discovery only made real, by him running his hands across the solid rock they had emerged from.

"You were too busy studying the maps, I think he's concerned about the time it is taking us, so where possible, he is aiding our travels." She didn't seem convinced, yet at the same time she was so relieved just for the sight of home.

"There's a few hours until sunset, how about we search for that door so we can return tomorrow." Elly turned to look at Zo finding she had already began to start her way down the mountain, she stopped turning back as she heard Elly's words.

"Tomorrow?" She exclaimed, waiting as they caught up. "But…"

"We don't know what may lie behind it; we can't risk getting caught in the dark. I know you're worried about your friends but there's no point rushing in, if something were to happen, there is *no one* to come for us, let's just settle with this head start. Besides, if it wasn't for your friend Seiken, it would possibly take us another few days to get here anyway, as yet I haven't located this worlds version of Collateral meaning we would be walking from the mountain of the spirits, these amulets work two ways you know, help and hinder." Elly smiled to herself, she knew neither of them would have considered reaching Crowley in their world and the *removing* the charm, it was something she had been going to suggest, but it was pointless now.

"I guess." She sighed some of her enthusiasm dying before they continued at a slower pace down the mountain.

As they entered the town the most striking thing, was that the dream Crowley, wasn't too dissimilar to the one she knew, she hadn't expected any difference, after all, the fixed points of this world were exactly the same as their counterpart, only the external environment seemed to change, but she was still surprised about how powerful the feelings, something she knew to be a copy could stir within her.

The buildings stood about two stories high, the houses constructed of a red brick found local only to the mountains of this country, the island itself was very small, just this one town was located on it, she thought back to how Daniel's father, while away on business, had tried so hard to find someone who knew her, yet it seemed all the time he turned up empty handed, Daniel had even brought her to sit in on a few of his lectures on Mainland, she never used her magic there, she knew better than to attract unwanted attention, but it seemed no one there knew her either. They would spend until the final boat back to Crowley searching the towns for the slightest bit of familiarity but without joy, everyone had tried so hard within a fortnight of her arrival to not only find her old home, but to provide her with a new one. She got a job working with Daniel's mum and soon she felt as if she could really have believed this was her home all along.

Looking over the town now, not a single person that resided within it was actually a member of the town she knew as home; sure the town itself was identical in every detail as was the surrounding area. It hadn't been that she had expected anything less, but seeing it now brought back all kinds of emotions, all throughout the adventure she had wanted nothing more than to return home, but this place wasn't her home, but just for this moment, it was enough, she smiled to herself knowing that when she woke, she would head back to that place she loved so much, the real location of this facsimile… she paused in mid step, knowing that when she did return she had to face Daniel's parents, a feeling of dread washed over her knowing she had to tell them the entire story, well most of it, they knew this town better than anyone, Angela walked it on a daily basis and Jack had been hands on around the village for as long as she knew him, there was nothing for it but honesty, well a level of honest she could afford, which given the situation, was very little.

"So how will we know this door?" Eiji questioned snapping Zo out of her daydream, she turned to join the conversation knowing they would call on her for an answer, in Daniel's absence she knew this town better than any, after all was her home too.

"I guess, it will be the one legend says that no one can pass through, that has perhaps a similar place in our reality." Elly looked to Zo who shook her head, in all the time she had spent in and around Crowley not once had she heard of such a legend.

"I can't say I have heard of a place like that, there are lots of underground ruins though, maybe we could ask around." She answered, it was after all only a small island, hearsay and legend would be easy to pick up on, and having Daniel around, no doubt they would have even visited the place once or twice, yet she had heard not so much as a whisper, about anything that seemed to fit the description, of what they now sought.

"Ask around? For what?" Zo turned to see a young boy who seemed to have been following them since they first entered the town, he was about three foot tall with a messy head of dirty blond hair, he stood now rocking back and forth on his heals as he waited for their answer.

"We're looking for a door." Eiji began, but before he could get any further the young boy jumped in his tone filled with excitement.

"Well there's plenty here, my pop Tony, maybe you've heard of him?" The boy rolled his eyes as they shook their heads but continued. "Anyway my pop can make anything." He stood proudly glancing between them excitedly.

"Not that kind of door, we aren't looking to buy one, we're after a door that has been around for years, one that doesn't open." Eiji finished what he was going to say before he was interrupted, the young boy laughed at them shouting back as he ran.

"What good's a door that doesn't open?" He laughed disappearing into a nearby house. Eiji gave a frustrated sigh,

"Maybe I can be of service?" Zo glanced towards the familiar voice, there before them stood the old man from the mining village, although he was no longer covered with soot, and was dressed differently, there was no doubt it was him.

"Isn't that the guy from the mining village?" Eiji questioned almost as if reading her thoughts.

"Mining village? Can't say I know of such a place." He smiled gently looking at the travellers, although he wasn't sure why he felt indebted to these people, for whatever reason he was compelled to help them.

"You think you can help us?" Elly questioned sceptically thinking back to the previous 'help' he had offered that resulted in them being trapped in the mines, and ultimately the kidnap of Eiji and by the look on Eiji's face, he also had the same unpleasant taste in his mouth that this particular recollection brought.

"Well I couldn't help hearing your dilemma, that little Tom is nothing but a loud mouth really. I was a renowned treasure hunter in my day, it just so happens there's quite a few ruins around here, one of which has never been excavated, you see it's sealed, not by a door though." He paused rubbing his clean shaven chin for a moment before continuing. "Maybe the door you seek is metaphoric?" Zo and Eiji exchanged glanced and smiled; Elly on the other hand did not seem too impressed by the interference of this man.

"What exactly do you mean?" Zo questioned wanting to grasp a clearer meaning of how this place was sealed, trying to determine, if there was anyway to break its seal, or at least give her time to think it over as they sought it out.

"They're sealed ruins, no one can enter, it's sealed by magic I suppose." He explained, he wasn't really sure if it was magic, after all magic had been dormant for twenty-three years, he had forgotten its power and appearance, but was sure that it had to be what sealed them, his gut told him so, besides, there was no other explanation, at least not one he was willing to consider.

***

"The old man said it was just past here." Eiji stated passing a large rock, the path, so far, had been exactly like the old man had described, Elly trod carefully watching the subtle change in texture of the ground around them, since arriving here she hadn't said a single word.

"Do you think he was telling the truth? I mean this place doesn't exactly go out of its way to help us." Eiji questioned, Elly, in the meantime had decided to rest for a while, settling herself in the shade of a nearby tree while the others wandered aimlessly across the field.

"I didn't…" Zo began cut off by the voice of the old man, as he approached Elly, "Young 'uns these days." He shook his head at Elly who smiled. "Can't you see it? Your friend had no trouble." He winked at her as she stood up, he stamped his foot near the ground where Elly had sat a tin sound resonated from the ground beneath. "Well I was thinking, if yer going to try break this seal, I at least want to watch, I've tried nearly all my life to unlock the mysteries of this place, I'd feel cheated if someone got there before me." Eiji helped him slide the grass from the top of a copper plate the old man grabbed the handle pulling Eiji was about to offer his aid when it opened almost like a trapdoor, the ground gave a hiss breathing out the warm stench of stale air.

The old man hurried inside following the steep stairs towards the bottom, after descending about ten foot the steps reduced to normal size. At the bottom he waited for the young travellers to catch up, for some reason they had seemed a little hesitant about entering, almost as if they questioned his motives, finally as they appeared he once more sprung off in youthful steps as he led the way, although it wasn't long before he stopped again. Elly and Eiji stepped aside letting Zo approach. "Well my dear, how do you propose on breaking the seal of the ancients?" He asked in a very straight forward, told you so, kind of tone, Zo stepped forwards, the field glittered all the colours of the elements, she closed her eyes resting her hand on the field.

"Earth." She whispered the field seemed to shimmer bronze at she called its name "Air." A clear blue wave rushed across to greet her hand. "Fire." A vivid red orange met her call. "Water." A sea green swept quickly past their vision. "Spirit" A brilliant white swirled around the colours. "Darkness." A foreboding black took its place in the circle. "Light." A clear area appeared over the coloured field, it seemed they sat now divided into their elements each one spanning out from her hand across the field in its own colour. "I release you." Her voice was filled with silent power, a few seconds passed before a sound like a hummingbirds wings echoed through the cave followed by a large pop as the field vanished into nothing, each section of the field retreating the way it faced in the circle.

"Well I'll be, that's quite a trick young lady." He smiled. "All those before you failed time and time again, but I said to myself, there's something special about these ones. Come, come, uncharted territory awaits!" Without waiting for them to move he rushed ahead but his fading silhouette soon came to a stop once more as he approached the dead-end, the place was empty, no treasure and very few carvings could be seen on the walls. But there was one carving in particular that attracted their attention.

"The door?" Eiji questioned approaching a six-foot carving in the shape of an intricately designed door.

"Perhaps..." Zo approached looking to the door running her hands over its surface. "Only there doesn't seem to be any indents for the keys to fit." She looked to Elly. "Hey where's the old guy go?" She questioned realising he had vanished.

"Seems he woke up." Elly stated finally having to speak to break the silence, Zo stood examining the carving closely. "We can explore further tomorrow." She turned leading them back down the short route they had walked. She knew the end was drawing closer, they all did, there was an unmistakable tense electricity in the air that always seemed to surround those near the end of an adventure. There was a part of her that hoped this adventure could last, just as the other part of her knew it would soon be over, as much as she had wanted this day, now that it came, she was filled with a strange emptiness.

"Unless the slots appear by magic... I don't see how much further we can go, there was nothing behind that door but solid rock." Zo sighed.

"Funny isn't it?" Eiji stated as they exited the building. "We travel all that way only to end up where we started... In fact, that first fairy ring we slept in is around here somewhere." Eiji pointed past the town into the distance, although the town Acha had pointed out when they first arrived was no longer there, the area, none the less, was the same. A further understanding of this world had come with them on their journey, although the world had several fixed locations, it also possessed fixed passages, places like fairy rings that would link the world to its counter part, like a fixed guideline between the two, a small area that's location would never change even though that area's surroundings would.

"It will be the safest place to rest tonight." Elly stated. "If we head back early maybe we can find out if the door exists in both worlds... or something, but you both saw, there were no holes, it was just a carving, not even a real door." Elly seemed to have worded that sentence very carefully, the others couldn't help but notice the lack of effort she placed in her carefully spoken words, Zo and Eiji exchanged glances before he decided to speak.

"Don't worry." Eiji looked at Elly. "We'll still find a way, after all that's what we're meant to do"

"And besides." Zo continued. "Maybe the key is back home." She looked up amazed to find they had reached the fairy ring already; she stepped over the mushrooms thinking back. "It's hard to believe, after those literal elements, this is the first place we slept." She sighed wondering what would have happened if perhaps they would have chosen another route, whatever the reason the route they chosen, led to the island of Crowley, perhaps this was fates way of guiding them to their final destination.

***

"How are they?" Acha questioned her back leaning against the bars; she knew that somehow Seiken knew everything that was happening.

"They just discovered the door that should lead them here... is a fake." Seiken sighed, sadness filling his voice, if only there had been another way, if the situations had been different, maybe Umemi would have been able to save them, but sadly, he would never know. He felt dirty having betrayed them like this, but ultimately no one would get hurt, Night would have the Grimoire, the Earth would be revitalised and they could all just carry on as normal... this line of reason brought him little comfort, something Rowmeow had said eleven years ago kept repeating over and over in his mind, he knew everything wouldn't go on as normal, there would be casualties.

"I don't believe this!" Daniel's voice was filled with silent rage. "We went through all that and for what? Nothing... What is the point, what's in it for him? Were we just some kind of entertainment? Does he enjoy sending people on wild goose chases just to watch them fail, because there's no chance they would ever win? Is that the nature of the game? Ooh you're doing so well, what a shame you'll never get past this final hurdle!" He gave a frustrated sigh as he paced within his cell, his ranting continued until the sound of Night's voice startled him.

"Now, now Mr Starfire." Night moved into view, he wasn't sure exactly when he had entered the room, but it couldn't have been too long ago. "I'm surprised one of your intelligence hasn't figured this out yet." He looked to Seiken. "Don't you have business to attend elsewhere?" He questioned, Seiken vanished from sight. "All this was merely a test, I had to make sure she was ready, she is the very image of her mother, her courage, her spirit and her heart." Night smiled with hidden meaning.

"Ready?" Daniel questioned abruptly. "Ready for what?" His voice filled with demand, what exactly was the plan? What was this really about? All were questions he wanted the answers to, if only to be able to warn Zo of his intentions if a chance was presented to do so, he had already ascertained their fixture in this prison was for the moment, permanent, but perhaps he could find another way to warn her? Perhaps he could force his thoughts upon her.

"To seizes the final Grimoire of course, that's what this entire thing has been about, each rune you seized destroyed not only the Grimoire resistance barriers, but the Severaine's protectional barriers too, this whole thing was an ingenious scheme to lead you here to the very moment that will be upon us shortly, I had to know she would make the right choice."

"Choice?" Daniel questioned grabbing the cold iron bars.

"In situations like these, one always likes to believe the choice to be made straight forwards, the needs of many always outweigh the needs of the few, the fate of the world versus those you care deeply for, it's a decision people so often cast judgement on, they say things like, I can't believe she would risk the lives of everyone to save one person, it is the choice of an idiot, what choice is their really? To save everything and lose one thing, or risk destroying everything to save it… I had to know which her choice would be when the time came, would she think the same as myself and Seiken?" Night smiled "She is so much like her mother."

"And her choice?" Acha questioned but in answer Night simply smiled.

***

Zo didn't wait for the others to arrive at Collateral, as the first rays of dawn flickered on the horizon she had already borrowed a horse from the dealer and had fled down the street she knew to lead home, she had much she needed to do before her and the others could open the final door, like firstly finding its location.

The sun had barley flickered past the mountains when she rode into Crowley. Dismounting quickly outside Daniel's home she slapped the horse on the rear sending it back to its master, she rushed in the house forgetting all the courtesy she would normally show.

"Angela? Jack?" She cried darting from one room to the next, as she entered the sitting room, Angela, was already standing to greet her, concern in her eyes regarding the desperation in her voice, Zo ran to her hugging her tightly wincing against the pain as Angela wrapped her arms around the trembling figure, Angela pulled back feeling this reaction before she pulled her top down to see the wound.

"By the God's Zo, what's happened? How'd you get in this state?" She went to sit her in a chair to better examine the mess, but she gently declined, it was all she could do to hold back the tears.

"I'm fine." She lied. "Something horrible has happened… they took Daniel!" Angela placed a hand on Zo's uninjured shoulder, concern flickering through her eyes as she realised her son had not accompanied her.

"Who? Who's taken him?"

"There's no time to explain, but you have to believe me, I'll get him back… but… there's some sealed ruins just outside town somewhere, I need to know where they are."

"The only ruins around the town are just north of your home Zo." Jack came through the door, alarmed at having found the door wide open, Zo looked at him and smiled sadly. Unaware that since his arrival a strange shadow had been watching through the window.

"Don't worry, they won't hurt them… Not if I get there in time, but I have to find that door." She looked back to Daniel's mum. "I promise, I won't let anything happen to him." Angela nodded; the words brought her a small amount of comfort.

"You sound as if you know these people." She questioned, wondering if maybe on their travels Zo had finally found someone she knew, a place to call home, and if that was the case, what trouble must she have gotten caught up in for this to be the result of those actions?

"She does." Elly appeared at the door knocking quietly before stepping into the lounge. "It's her father" All four of them looked at Elly as Zo's stomach sank to the floor.

"My father?" She questioned. "No, dad's the one that's been helping me all this time, he would never... mum told me he loved us more than anything and would never wish us harm." She looked to Elly her eyes searching for any hint that what she spoke was lies, but as always them remained unyielding to such emotion.

"If he loved you so much why did he leave and why now does he hold your friends?" Elly turned towards the door, of course, she knew the answer to both the proposed questions, but the fact Zo didn't, meant it was something she could use to her advantage, something to use to guide her actions. "Do you have the location?" She questioned realising Eiji seemed to be lingering outside possibly with the wish of not intruding.

"Yes." Zo sighed, how could it be true? How could the one behind this mess be her father? If what Elly spoke was really the truth, then the responsibility for this whole mess lay with her, if he was truly family, she shook her head pushing the thoughts aside, now was not the time to be lost in such thinking, now was not a time for thoughts, but for action, the anger and confusion this brought her would prove a useful spur to guide her forwards, she had to put this right while there was still time.

"Good, we can't afford to waste any more time." She hurried Zo towards the door; she glanced back at Angela and Jack before she left mouthing the words. 'I promise'

"What was that all about? Who were those people with Zo? Is everything Ok?" Jack asked taking his wife in his arms; he held her close as she seemed to be trembling.

"I'm sure it will be." She began to cry gently in his shoulder. "Someone has Daniel; they want a trade for something in the ruins." Angela explained, having not quite understood what Zo had meant about a door, Jack pulled back to look at his wife.

"The ruins? But they were excavated ages ago, I should know, I led the team, we took everything, it's all now in Mainland museum." He stated taking his wife by the hand. "I think we should talk with the elder, maybe he can help."

Chapter twenty-three

"It's not quite… what I was expecting." Eiji looked at the clearly marked mining tunnel leading underground into the ruins, they were neither concealed nor barricaded like the ones in Knights-errent had been, they were just about to enter when Zo heard someone calling.

"Jack!" She exclaimed waiting while the tall man with pepper coloured hair rushed towards them. "What are you…?"

"No one knows these underground ruins like me, I led the first expedition down here you know." He smiled his voice filled with pride as he moved to stand next to them while he caught his breath.

"You mean…" Zo stated sadly looking to him sadly her stomach dropping as she knew what was to follow.

"Yes, everything in here has been excavated to the museum in Mainland."

"I think we'll take a look around just in case Mr Starfire." Elly added in response to questioning looks from both Zo and Eiji.

"Very well Elaineor, now do you mind telling me exactly what kind of trouble you and my son have found yourselves in?" He rubbed his hand through his pepper grey hair looking at them questioningly.

"Talk and walk, you can guide us." Elly looked back from attaching a string to a nearby tree to look at Jack. "And you can explain." She glanced to Zo who nodded, Elly finished securing the string and they head deep into the mines.

***

"And that's it." Said Jack approaching a dead end, the ruin itself was no larger than the one in Knights-errent, although the carvings and designs were much clearer. "Sure there were odd bits of ancient technology here and there, but like I said they're all now in Mainland." Elly traced her hands around the wall knocking in various location as Jack stressed time and time again there was no exit, all the time he did so, he was reading to himself the carvings written in ancient tongue regarding magic, the life of Gods and how to achieve immortality.

"Here." Elly whispered grabbing Zo gently pulling her to the same carving of the door that was within Knights-errent, all the time Elly never took her eyes off Jack. Zo examined the door, again there were no indents where the runes could fit, but she knew what she had to do, in old shrines, the builders often carved a door on the wall to hide the location of a real door or passage, a passage that led to the tomb's greatest treasure. Even now she could feel the emptiness behind what should have been a solid wall, there was only one thing to do. Zo gave a sigh, she felt uncomfortable about doing this in front of Jack, especially, after trying so hard to keep her skills a secret from all those she encountered, he already tried to avoid her as much as possible, now he would have a reason, how could she ever hope to gain his trust, if all he sees in her are lies and the reckless endangerment of his son's life? She took a breath focusing her mind as she read the surrounding forces, as she did a gentle wind began to whip around her as she felt the energy race through her body she reached forwards placing her hand on the carving of the door forcing the energy she had received to the stone carving, she braced herself. It was a spell she knew and used even without incantations, something she had learnt now she could do, a spell that forced the large amount of pressure she took from the elements from her hand, it was something used a lot as a child, the last time she remembered using it, it was against some men she had found in her home, yet that was all she could remember, they were in her home and they shouldn't have been there, it was a memory she had fought to remember for so long, but something seemed to block it from her, almost as if her will to forget was stronger than her will to remember. She released the energy waiting for the wall to crumble, yet instead, it swung open as if she had merely pushed it, she looked sheepishly to Jack, waiting for him to speak, to say something, but he didn't even seem shocked, Elly raised her hand to the door she seemed to be feeling for something.

"Eiji, could you escort Mr Starfire home, from here it gets unpredictable." She gave Eiji a meaningful look unseen by Zo, Eiji nodded approaching Jack.

"I don't think I'll be able to catch up." He stated softly turning to escort the protesting Jack away, leaving only Zo and Elly standing at the door.

"Don't worry, there's a barrier protectional system here, one only maidens may pass through, it's an old rule for temples of Gods, as maidens were less likely to pilfer their goods, we'll come for you once we have what we came for." She watched until they left, there was a long drawn out silence as they waited by the door; Zo was the first to speak.

"Elly… will Eiji be alright?" She questioned sadly already knowing what would happen as he left the temple.

"Your father knows he's under my protection." She replied simply.

***

Eiji led Jack through the tunnels making idle conversation.

"It's a shame about the barrier, but its well known protection like Elly said, I would have loved to see what was behind those doors… so anyway Mr Starfire, how long has Zo been staying with you?" He followed Elly's string through the tunnel rolling it up as he did so knowing neither Elly nor Zo would need it to navigate back, he was unsure why she had even used it, after all it was just a straight forward run with one or two turns along the way.

"I don't remember now. It seems like she's always been there." He answered as they stepped outside, squinting against the brightness of the midday sun as they did so, Eiji glanced around the fields before summoning a water barrier over the mines entrance, at least this way he knew no one else would be able to enter, not that there was anyone now who would wish to.

"So how did you know we were coming here? What is it you really want?" Jack stopped in his tracks at Eiji's question he turned to look at him, surprise in his face.

"What do you mean? My wife told me you were after something in the North ruins, I wanted to help." He answered simply seeming outraged that his intentions were questioned.

"Look, quite simply I don't believe you, Mr Starfire has never met Elly, yet back there you called her Elaineor, nor can he read the magical writing of the ancients,

Daniel told me he was a great explorer, but as it stands not one person has worked out a translation for the writings. The only ones that knew it were Hectarians, and the language was forgotten when their powers were removed, you see they used their magic to decipher the codes into the language of magic, and from there into the words we speak, their magic of old let them read it, once that had left, not one of them could break the complex codes and finally, Mr Starfire, or anyone for that matter, doesn't know that Zo can use magic, yet when she used it to open the door you weren't even a little surprised. You thought since she used it freely before us and in Knights-errent it was common knowledge, you made only one mistake, you assumed." He sighed, he wasn't sure at all about any of what had just been spoken it was all based on hearsay, after all, he had arrived shortly after Elly, maybe she had introduced herself then, there was no reason why Zo could not have taught him to read the ancient scripts, her Hectarian blood had remained unaltered and there was no reason why Daniel's father wouldn't know Zo was Hectarian, but it seemed as if she had been waiting for some reaction, he was sure he was right, wasn't that why Elly had sent him out? There was no such thing as a maiden barrier, the Gods did not fear men looting their shrines, after all, they would rain down judgement should they be betrayed by any entering their shrines, thieves, were not something a God would have to fear.

"Well I guess my plan had a few oversights, I never did finish reading the section on immorality, I will have to leave that now to Night, in repayment for my favours. The last thing I want it that witch of yours remembering how to banish me, I refuse to be returned to Hades. But you see, there may have been a minor flaw in my plan, in that you saw through my disguise before I could finish gathering the information needed, but there was a fatal one in yours. You're mine." He stated coldly changing back to the form they had first set eyes upon in Knights-errent.

"True as that is, I am also under Elly's protection, something Night happens to respect." Eiji hoped that despite her betrayal to Night by trying to hide Zo from him, he would still respect it; otherwise, he was in deep trouble. His thoughts stopped suddenly as he realised something that he had over looked all this time. Elly, had not yet betrayed her master, only Blackwood, every word she had spoken since the time they met had been carefully worded. 'I'm not taking you back.' She had said when they first met Zo, but what if Zo happened to make her own way there? Or what if it wasn't Zo who returned? Eiji's heart leapt, his thoughts broken by Aburamushi's statement.

"Under Elaineor's protection?" He questioned glancing around. "Funny I don't see her anywhere. Besides, alive… is not unharmed." He threatened.

"Lead the way." Eiji smiled, he knew no matter the power of the fight he gave, the outcome would remain the same, at least if he went willingly he could leave some form of trial to aid Zo and Elly in the finding of Night's tower, although he doubted they would need it, nor would they be able to follow his path as he soon discovered as they vanished into the shadows.

***

"A barrier only maidens can pass?" Zo questioned slowly after they had vanished from sight and their footsteps were no longer audible. "Are you sure he'll be alright?" She questioned looking back over the darkness that lay behind them.

"I should think so." She answered

"Another thing, it's been bothering me for some time." Zo started, for some reason she seemed to be stalling. "How did Aburamushi get to be here anyway?"

"My guess is he crossed over with us one time, maybe he followed us or something, or perhaps, since Acha gave him the mark of boundaries, he can cross over as he wishes, like us." She answered simply.

"Is that possible?"

"Do you really have to ask? Don't tell me you have forgotten the creatures in the bushes on the first night? You've felt things cross over with us too. You've felt them here knowing that this is not their home." Elly saw Zo shudder as she thought about it.

"Elly." Zo paused taking a breath almost as if she feared the words she was about to speak. "There's no door is there?" It was something Zo had been wondering since their arrival in Knights-errent's Crowley, yet it had been a question she feared to ask.

"I never said there was, if you recall, I believe it was Daniel that made that assumption, I simply pointed out there was only one place we needed to go and the door I was referring to, you have just opened, besides it's not a door you're here for, although in some ways I must admit it is a key."

"Another one?" Zo questioned looking to the small pouch of runes.

"The only one, that is if you *want* to save your friends. There's only one thing you can use to bargain with, and you are the only person with the talent to get it."

"The Grimoire." Zo sighed with a sickening realisation as everything fell into place, it had been she herself who had obtained the other six, under the name of Marise Shi, and now, she was requested to finish the job. "This whole thing, it was never about Seiken, or his people."

"Not as such, no, we needed to get your attention, and break through the boundaries in order to release the seals. Now, step through the door, finish what you started all those years ago, it's the only way to save the lives of those you care for." Elly motioned for her to enter, she sighed doing as she was told, even now she knew there was very little choice.

Elly smiled to herself, it seemed so long ago when she first approached Marise with this quest, and now it was finally coming to and end…

…"Impressive, they no longer can draw the breath to scream." Elly smiled leading her assassin through a maze of corridors. This, like all rich men's housing had been built upon the ruins of old buildings, the workman ship was shoddy but some parts of the old house still remained intact, there was no way people of this time, of this skill, could yet even begin to grasp an understanding of how these places were built, they were by far sturdier than today, that is why they still stood. It was this very thing that made Elly's task, of showing Marise to a safe place, simple. Those that lived within its walls would have no concept of the secrets a place like this would hold.

"I saw no point for him to suffer; he did not annoy me like the others." Marise smiled at her as the door to the hidden chamber opened. Already, the world knew her name, she was feared for some of her more cruel and torturous killings. "Besides." She continued. "Tonight I don't have time to kill his guards; I want to hear this proposition." Elly smiled, Marise had become very apt at reading her, and her actions now.

Any second now, the guards of the Lord would enter his chamber to find their employer dead, but not a thing would be out of place, the invisible threads they used to secure the doors unbroken, it would be, as if no one had entered. They would not have the slightest idea that his assassin took shelter within the walls of his own home.

It no longer surprised Marise that Elly, or Lee as she called her, never failed to unearth every home's secrets, secrets so old most were not known by those who resided within them.

"Mari, we have spoken of this many times, after tonight, I will not ask again. What are your ties to Blackwood?" Elly moved to sit against the wall in the small stone room, they would be here for a while, it was best they were comfortable, searches like the one about to start, would often continue into the early hours of the morning.

It was not the fear of confrontation that made them take shelter, Marise had proven on several occasions her ability to conquer a large number of guards, but tonight, there were more pressing issues. It was finally time for her true purpose to be revealed. Everything depended on the answer she would receive, a question; Elly already felt she knew the answer to. A mission so secret, it had to be discussed away from listening walls of Blackwood's mansion.

"I have told you I have no ties to him, for now he keeps me amused. I grow bored of these high class assassinations, I want adventure, excitement, but if I was to leave to seek it, I would miss my master." She looked to Elly and smiled moving to take a seat besides her. She smiled, hearing Marise talk, it would be easy to mistake her for an adult, she was old and wise beyond her years, something many found most deceptive, especially considering she had not long passed into her teenage years.

"There is but one catch, Blackwood must never learn of this, you must continue to work as his assassin."

"I understand." She answered, it was true, for the past two years Blackwood had given her everything, she had been the realisation of an unhealthy obsession, one with power, and now with her, the person who gave him that which he desired. He wanted her to himself, he feared her time away from him and much to her annoyance would constantly interrupt her training with Elly. The only time she was really free, was when she was on a job, unknown to Blackwood, Elly, would always accompany her and watch from the shadows, he would sometimes send her with Marise, especially to the high class assassinations, but he was paranoid, afraid Marise would favour Elly over him, thus he enforced limits on their time together, doing this only made Marise more determined to spend time with her, but for now, she knew she had to play along with Blackwood's games, she had to obey his rules while in his sight.

"Very well, I shall start at the beginning. Before you were born, the God, Night, formed a group called the Idliod, they were the seven most skilled Hectarians across the world, each pair excelling in a certain form of magic and the seventh member excelled in all fields. Night chose to gather these minds as fate had said he would. He did not normally allow his actions to be dictated by hearsay, but this was one prophesy he could not ignore, in fact, he would do everything within his power to ensure it was fulfilled. He trained the Idliod to be the best, but then, as was written they rose up against him fearing the future he would create. They sealed his powers into seven books called the Grimoire, which were then banished to the four corners of the world. But a high cost came with their actions, to see the deed through, they not only sacrificed their lives, but the very source of Hectarian magic itself, all the magic that was, or ever would be born into this world, was sacrificed for this cause."

"Obviously not all of it." Marise began stopped by Elly next words.

"All of it." She answered firmly. "But you, you were different, you see, you had divine protection. Night is your father, he left only for your own and your mother's protection. A youth called Eryx had threatened your safety, if ever his true identity would be revealed, you would never have been safe, his punishment to Eryx was harsh, and once such a threat had been made, Night had no choice but to leave and so, he decided to return to the Idliod." Marise shifted position slightly as Elly spoke. "Your mother, always knew the truth about your father and kept his darkest secrets until the day she died, before he left, he cast a powerful spell on his sword, leaving it in your mother's care, it would protect both you, and her until the day I would come for you, but as long as you remained clear of Drevera, you would both be protected. The prophecies told of a maiden who would rise to restore Night to his throne, you are that maiden, I want us to locate and return the Grimoire in order to restore Night, but it won't be easy, especially hiding our mission from Blackwood."

"What exactly will this quest entail?" Marise questioned, a slight smiled crossing the edge of her lips at the thought of what was being offered to her.

"Danger, like you have never known, adventure, like you could never imagine." Elly answered simply, she was offering Marise not only what she wanted to hear, but the truth as well.

"And do we know the location of the Grimoire?"

"No, as yet, I know of but two of their resting places, but for each one that is removed, a new one shall make itself known to us."

"And you would travel alongside me?"

"Of course, the best adventures are shared by friends." She smiled, Marise's answer was already clear.

"And how will we explain our absence to Blackwood, I am guessing these wont be quick or easy tasks."

"We tell him nothing, I feel there is much our current terrain cannot offer with regards to training." Elly and Marise both stood knowing now the guards had abandoned their search, dusting the cobwebs from their clothes they walked to the sealed door. "Then you'll do it?"

"You knew my answer before you even asked." Marise replied searching for the brick to release the door.

"But still." Elly pressed, until she agreed, she could leave nothing to chance.

"Let me think, I can spend my days doing ten a penny assassinations, or I can do something fun for a change, something dangerous, exciting, of course I want to do it, when do we start?" Elly approached her, pressing the brick she had been searching for, the door silently moved, the outside air rushed in and around the room filling it with the scent of morning dew.

"Soon, but for now, let's head back." She took the document from Marise, this assassination had been more about the information, than the target, she placed it in her pocket before leading the way. Of course, even then she knew convincing Blackwood would be easy, she just had to press the right buttons, something she had become so good at recently.

"I don't understand." Lord Blackwood protested as Elly told him of her request. "What further training can be offered that these volcanoes do not already provide?" If she took her away from him now, where would that leave him? He hadn't even begun to build his empire; if she were to leave the entire place would be left unguarded. He steadied his breath wiping the beading sweat from his forehead, he was being stupid, he had other guards, but still, what she was suggesting was insane, he could not afford to be without his assassin. He rubbed his hand through his dark hair waiting for her response.

"Well, navigation for one, there are no areas of poor visibility around here, sure we practice it, but what it the use of it if she can just look up and check she is on course, then there's terrains…"

"Let me stop you there." Lord Blackwood interrupted. "My Marise has already performed battles in such conditions." But before he could continue he was interrupted.

"No, until now, her battle terrain has been the same, the inside of someone's house; we are not always going to be that fortunate. It is my job to train her, I just thought you wanted the best, I mean until now she has been lucky, the guards employed by most of your targets are little more than children with toy swords, but you forget, she is little more than a child herself. A mere distraction to a bounty hunter, you know as well as I they travel the world to train, how long until bounty hunters make the payroll of your next victims? What then? If she was to misjudge a single step, where would that leave you?" Another bead of sweat formed on his forehead as a wave of panic began to wash over him, he paced backwards and forwards thinking it over, he couldn't let her leave, no way, what if it was the last he saw of her? Elly turned away speaking as she reached the door. "Hey, if it bothers you that much, we can make do…" She turned to open the door, smiling secretly to herself as she pulled it towards her. She knew exactly what he was thinking; she could read him like a book. He was remembering how, at one point, Night would claim Marise for his own, his thoughts spiralled off in all directions, mainly that of doubt, if it was that time, surely Elaineor would not give up so easily, perhaps it was nothing more than what she said, training. She had scared him with her words of bounty hunters. Worse still, everything that Elly had said as true, his contacts had already discovered a few of his future targets had already added them to their payroll. After all, Marise had a bounty on her head, its value steadily increasing with every successful assassination, which over the last two years had been a fair number. The risk was becoming far higher than he thought; the thought of her not making it to an assassination had never even crossed his mind, let alone the possibility of her being beaten. He was beginning to realise how foolish he had been assuming things would go as planned just because of her origin, was it really possible for things to go so wrong? She had only been his for two years, and already there were few alive did not know her name. True enough, her skills were excellent, especially considering her age, but could she surpass one who had decades of training on top of her own? The only real advantage she had, was having Elaineor for a trainer, but would that be enough to tackle those that have already fought for a lifetime? If it wasn't, he would lose everything, his control on the country, his upcoming stature, everything.

"Wait!" His voice trembled with nerves as the word quickly left his mouth; Elly pushed the door closed slowly before turning to look at him. "This training, what will it be exactly?"

"Nothing sinister, all low profile really, I will take her to an area suitable, and teach her how to use the environment to her advantage, travelling using Collateral."

"How long? How long will my Marise be gone?" He questioned nervously.

"As long as it takes, surely you can understand that." She answered simply, how could he expect her to put a time on how long it would take her student to master terrain? Besides, if she *were* to give him a timescale, he would surely suspect something; he was not as stupid as he would try to have her believe. She glanced around the library, Blackwood had been sitting at a small central table looking at the court's recent progress, before her interruption he seemed to have been doing some research into parasites.

"Well…" He glanced around carefully as if wishing to avoid prying ears, surely he knew by now; the only people who listened around here were those he paid to spy. "Maybe… maybe it would be better if you were to say, do it all at once, would that not be easier?" An idea already forming in his mind as he asked.

"I would not be so selfish to suggest such things; it would upset your business, unless there was some way to get your wishes to us."

"It would be better wouldn't it?" He paused for a moment. "I can't stand the thought of her being beaten by some dirty hunter." He paused again. "I could always get my jobs to you by other means; I rarely need her in the observation room now." He paused again rubbing his finger across his chin in thought; it was a while until he spoke again. "Yes, thinking about it, some time away from here would be good, I wouldn't want people to talk about my inhospitality, I can't have leaders over as it stands, in case she were to arrive and it will only be a matter of time before talk starts. They already know that Knightsbridge is my second home; I could not do with them being suspicious. I guess… I would also keep more of my recruit intake without fear of her butchering them… I… no, it's a brilliant idea." He paced back and forth, this was the best solution, but at the same time he feared what not having his assassin close could mean, he loved the power she brought him, but ultimately she was his, she was loyal to him, he knew that she would never betray him for Elaineor and the more time he spent with Marise the more confident he became that when the time would come when Elaineor asked her to return with her to Night, that she would choose to stay.

"Does that mean I can make preparations?" Elly questioned before he had time to change his mind.

"Yes, stay in Collateral; I can always give you my instructions by this." He pulled a small stone from his pocket, Elly as if on cue, pulled her own from its concealed position on a chain around her neck.

"A gossip crystal, perfect." She answered; satisfied she had led him well.

"Then it's settled, you may leave at once, but I expect a full report on her progress, and my work is not to go unattended. Take what you require from my vault." He waved his hand towards an old full-length portrait on the wall, behind which was a door leading to his vault.

"No need." She smiled. "If it is all the same I would prefer to use my own, you wouldn't want someone tracing the funds back to you should we be discovered? I shall inform Marise to prepare, although, I am not sure how she will take the news." With these words she left, things had progressed exactly as she had planned. For the last twelve months she had been planting ideas deep into his mind, it was she herself who had given him the crystal on Marise's first mission, so should things change after their departure, he could contact them without worry.

"So where to?" Marise stood just outside the library, leaning on the wall besides the door waiting for her to emerge into the finely decorated hall.

"First, we head to Collateral, it's a three day walk to the portal we need to take this time, I can't risk taking the closer one until we are certain to have lost Blackwood's spies, so we may want to get some horses. I would have suggested hitching a ride, but it seems your reputation precedes you." Marise smiled meaningfully at Elly, still not moving from the wall. "No." Elly answered in reply to the unspoken words. "We have to travel incognito, the last thing we need is to draw unnecessary attention to ourselves in a stolen vehicle."

"Then horseback?" Marise sighed, her excitement vanishing.

"Yes, you arrange the horses, and I shall make necessary preparations, and make sure you look after the natives." Elly warned as she began to leave.

"You worry too much, I like the locals, they're... accommodating. Especially since I drove off the settlers on the other side of the rings." Marise smiled a mischievous gleam in her eyes. "In fact, I think it has been all too long since our last volcanic eruption, I've noticed they seem to be edging back, it could be a good way to conceal our exit." Elly nodded, she knew Marise well enough to know concealment had nothing to do with it, it was all about watching the small village panic as the skies rained fire and filled with volcanic ash.

Marise walked through the mansion, surely she had being playing the fool to Blackwood's spies long enough, even now they were watching, listening, reporting her every word to him. When she first discovered them, it was Elly who had stopped her killing them, secretly informing her that they would work to her advantage should she stay loyal and true to him while in their sights. However, for some reason, whenever she was in the vicinity of Blackwood, they dared not follow, that is why she had waited outside for Elly, their plans were something not to be overheard by anyone. They sat watching, following, thinking themselves great for not being discovered, but she saw them, she saw them all and one day, she would kill them, each and everyone, she would be walking one day, just like today, in a flash she would be gone and it would be they who found themselves stalked, she would pick them off one at a time until not one remained... but for now, this action had been forbidden by the only person whose ordered counted, Elly...

...As Zo walked the corridor, knowing what lay ahead, everything seemed to make so much sense, Elly had always seemed to know everything, was this because she had the inside information? Pretending all this time to want to help, where as all along she was leading them, guiding them towards this very moment, she followed the short corridor, her steps slow and hesitant as she feared what waited.

"Stand before me." A voice beckoned, Zo glanced around the room it was laced with all forms of treasures as far as the eyes could see, to one side of the room was another door, one Zo correctly assumed, would lead outside, Zo approached a statue that stood on the alter. "Zodiac Althea, you have entered now the chamber of the ancients, the library of hidden knowledge from times past, present and future, long has it been told of your coming, tell me, what do you seek? Tell me and I will grant it to you, if it is within my power... anything." The deep voice echoed around the chamber, Zo noted that Elly had yet to enter.

"Sir…" Her voice trembled a little as she spoke; she tried her best to steady it as she continued. "Then…" She glanced towards the door where Elly lurked in the shadows. "I wish my friends, Daniel, Acha and Eiji to be free and appear here alive and well before me." Elly smiled in the darkness impressed by her choice of words, after all, what use was her friends' freedom if they would still be trapped within Night's walls? Even now Zo refused to surrender. However this request was not something that concerned her, nor was it something unexpected, she now knew this girl better than she herself would even believe, it had been an essential part of the mission to learn about her, her thoughts and feelings, this information had been carefully reported to Night to help with the research on the mission.

"I am sorry." The voice answered. "That request is not something within my power, Night is a God, even I cannot penetrate the seals into his domain." Zo gave a sigh, knowing there was only one other thing she could ask.

"Then," she paused trying not to choke on the bile brought about by the words she would speak. "I seek the Grimoire that resides within you care." Zo sighed again, once she had this book, she could free her friends, at the same time liberate Seiken and his people by trading for its release, but the ultimate cost would be high, she knew this, and yet, despite this, she only had the one choice, she had promises to keep. There seemed to be a long silence before the voice spoke once more.

"Impossible." The voice stated much to her surprise, even Elly shifted in the shadows.

"But sir, you said anything, you don't understand, if I can't have it, he will kill all my friends, a whole world will die, ultimately bringing about the destruction of our own world… please." She begged falling to her knees before the statue.

"If it was still within my possession, I would not hesitate in granting your request." It was at this point Elly stepped through the door.

"What do you mean not in your possession?" Elly questioned moving to stand in the centre of the chamber her shadow covered the area in which Zo knelt as she stood behind her. "How can that be, only the blood of Night himself may remove that book, you are looking upon his daughter." She stated, Zo heard herself gasp, she had hoped there was just one flaw in Elly's plan, the seal of the book, but it seemed again she was mistaken, Zo felt herself begin to tremble, how could this be? Were Elly's words really the truth? She felt her throat close at the realisation of the situation, as she found it increasingly more difficult to breathe, she knew her father had her friends, but she had not linked the two together, not yet, if Night was her father, then… her thoughts were interrupted by the voice as it addressed Elly,

"Lain, have you learnt nothing, what is a book to distinguish blood line? Although they used their very life-force such a task is impossible but for the Gods, do you really think man would be granted such power? Although you were correct, the book should have dwelled here, yet it has never been to these walls." The voice admitted.

"But sir, how is that possible? What about the magic barriers that surrounds it?" Elly questioned as Zo shifted trying to force herself to stand but failing.

"The details are unimportant, did your hunting days teach you nothing, or in your slumber have you forgotten, there is always more than one solution to any problem. Lain return to your master, tell him what he seeks is no longer here." Elly turned on her heel before walking towards the wooden door, Zo watched as the scenery changed to a location outside of Crowley, there was a short lived silence once the door had closed.

"Sir…" She finally asked after a long stretch of silence. "What became of the book? Who has it now?" She questioned still kneeling before the statue, she spoke only once she was certain Elly had left completely, even then it took her a few moments to find her voice.

"Even I cannot answer that, many, many years ago, before you were even born I would guess, an adventurer did me a good turn, with no other way to repay him I gave him the only thing in my possession. I knew I could trust him to guard it, besides, as he went on to tell me of his many adventures, I knew, even should he say where the book originated, no one would believe him thus it would be safer within his possession than in this shrine."

"Yet you still guard this temple?" Zo questioned unclear on the reason, if the book was no longer here and he was to guard it in this wall, why did he remain still?

"Not only is it written that you would come for the book, I must also remain for those who shall trek this path after you. We are always provided with the beginnings and ends of our time, the interesting part is watching how people journey from A-B, it was written that you would arrive just as it is written that Night will regain his power." Zo smiled at his answer.

"Then I find the Grimoire?" She questioned hope filling her voice as she rose to stand before him.

"Find? You cannot find what isn't lost my child… but you will stand before your father shortly, take care of your business and when you are ready open this." A small box appeared before her on the floor, she glanced down to it, it was of simple design, no bigger than her palm. "It contains just enough magic to take you to his exact location… well into his tower anyway." The voice answered the unasked question. "I am sorry there is nothing more I can do to aid you."

***

"Night." Daniel, Eiji and Acha stood to the sound of a familiar voice moving themselves to the cage bars so they could see what was about to occur, Night rose to meet her.

"Ah Lain, you have returned." He glanced around. "Alone I see."

"Night." She started again. "The Grimoire never reached the shrine, the ancients themselves admit it!" She stopped bowing slightly as she stood before him; she glanced across to where Eiji and the others were held, before returning her attention to Night.

"Lain, your job, was to bring my daughter and the Grimoire, am I to assume you have failed on both accounts?" He questioned something about his tone made Daniel shudder.

"She will be arriving shortly, just tying up business I believe." Elly stated.

"Elaineor!" The power behind Acha's voice commanded complete attention from all around as she moved to the bars in order to look at the one who betrayed them. "You betrayed us! All this time you were working for him!" Elly slowly approached the bars just out of arms reach.

"With him." She corrected. "And who are you to talk about betrayal?" She questioned walking away again to address Night. "It seemed the rumours of the blood seal were nothing more than that, yet still, somewhere out there unknown to the idiot that should have been guarding it, the final Grimoire waits. I think now would be the best time to bring Marise back, she could locate it easily, I don't see why we should delay any longer." She smiled, soon Zodiac would be permanently removed from Marise, of course at the cost of her life, but as long as Marise survived what did it matter? Soon she and Marise would be together again, hunting treasure and killing all those that opposed them in their quest for victory. Yet, at the same time, she couldn't deny her feelings towards Zodiac, at first, she had just been in the way, but regardless of this Marise was her only concern, her best friend, she could not let fleeting moments of guilt, or feelings towards the girl destroy what she and Marise had, or what lay before them.

"A reaction I expected from you." Night smiled. "How long will she be?"

"My guess will be she will try to find the book, realise quickly she has no chance of doing so, then when she realises that…" Elly trailed off for the first time ever she did not seem too convinced with the answer she had provided.

"We shall see." Night smiled. "We shall see."

Chapter twenty-four

Zo sat alone in her hut, as she sat there she realised the place had never seemed so cold and empty, even before this adventure, when it was just her, it always seemed to fill with the anticipation of Daniel's visits, she sat scolding herself for the self pity she was in as she spoke to no one in particular holding the small musical ball in her hand, something was different now, it no longer played even a single melody. Only moments ago had she returned from Daniel's home for what she guessed to be the final time, now she should be preparing herself for what lay ahead, but instead she simply sat looking into the musical ball, talking to it gently.

"Umemi." Seiken sighed sadly his figure appearing in the doorway, for a moment she feared she had somehow drifted off to sleep, but then she remembered that he could cross over into their world, after all, the first time he appeared before her, it was in this very house.

"Seiken." She whispered. "Seiken am I glad to see you. It's terrible, Night has everyone, the only chance I had was lost... Seiken, I did as you told me, I gathered the runes, the keys, but... there is no door is there?" She questioned sadly on the verge of tears, she knew by now that Seiken would know the answer to this question, but still she felt the need to ask.

"Oh Umemi." Seiken pulled a chair to sit besides her. "I feel responsible; I brought you into all this." He touched her hand, his very touch was like ice on fire burning and cooling the places he touched.

"No. My father did, this whole thing was a set up from the start." She clenched her fists.

"At first..." Seiken sighed, he owed her an explanation, his role in the deal with Night had now finished, but for the release of his people, but how did he tell her? How could he tell her he was the one who betrayed them? "I knew something was going on, one by one my people seemed to disappear, mortals with the same marks as yourself, passed through to seek for something... I heard rumours of a game, it seemed people were betting their life for something, but with my people being free, before death could take them they would find themselves awake and the mark of the chosen would vanish."

"There have been people before? Tell me what did you learn of this game?" Zo questioned staring only out of the windows.

"I know you can't win." He sighed squeezing her hand trying to offer what little comfort he could, knowing the best thing for her would to stay where she was, but also knowing that was not the action she would choose, she had too many promises to keep, something Daniel had pointed out when he had first discovered his alliance with Night, she would not give up.

"I must." Her voice filled with determination as she stared at his hand on hers.

"Even if you win... you'll still lose, to win you must lose everything."

"I know that!" She snapped, blushing as she heard her own harsh tones, she pulled her hand free from his touch, her voice once more softening. "I knew that when I first agreed to play." Seiken looked at her in silence, she had changed so much since they first met, she was confident, alluring and dangerous, to him this made her even more irresistible than all the times he'd watched her. He pushed the thought from his mind as quickly as it had entered, now was not the time to contemplate his feelings for this mortal.

"I'm not talking about your friends." He stated

"I know." Her answer shocked him more than she had expected. "I made a promise to save your people, I made a promise to Daniel to protect him and his mum that I would see that he returned and I will do everything within my power to make sure I stick to those words, the promises I engraved on my heart."

"How? How could you know?" He questioned clearly understanding this time she knew the price of her words, yet at the same time wondering how she could know the cost of that never spoken of.

"I knew from the moment I saw you… I knew the first time we met in your world, it could only end one way. It started a long time ago, it seems like forever as I sit here now, I was about seven, the other children hated me because they knew I was different from them, they use to tease and bully me, mostly because I spent so much time with Amelia, she had been the village witch before Hectarian powers vanished, she had many books I would sit and read, and although *she* could not longer perform magic she taught me how I could use it. Step by step incantations, potions, charms, everything, that was why the children hated me. I remember one day she had been teaching me the theory behind herbal lore, I was so excited at the thought of trying it, when the lesson was over, I went straight to the forest, but the other children were already there, they teased me threw things at me and pushed me in the mud, I ran to the small lake at the other end of the island, it was only a small island, like here only having one town, but much smaller, I sat by the lake cleaning myself up. It broke my mum's heart to see what they did, but I had become good at hiding it by then, I hated to see her worry. I sat crying quietly into the lake, it was then I heard the gentlest voice, a voice so soft and pure it seemed to be that of the lake itself. 'Don't cry' it whispered. 'Eyes as pretty as those weren't made for tears.' I looked to the river to thank it for its kind words, yet as I looked up there was a clear circle upon its glass smooth surface, within it, I saw your face, exactly as you are now, you haven't aged a day, you seemed to be looking in a river, I saw a beautiful land behind you filled with bird song and trees, it seemed so peaceful."

"You could see me?" Seiken interrupted feeling himself blush, he had never realised he could be seen, his magic was to be as a one sided looking glass yet somehow, all this time she had seen him.

"That wasn't the only time, it seemed whenever I was sad or lonely, I would see your face, in the mirror, in the water…" She paused thinking back. "The last time, before we met in person, it was just after I had been taken to Blackwood." She stated unaware this had not in fact been the last time; they had had many brief meetings after that point, meetings shared by either her, or Marise. "I was so homesick and depressed, I missed my home, I missed the sweet scent of the trees outside, my mother's warming smile, I hated it there, I was so alone, I was studying all the time, and had no friends, as I had hoped. I seemed to be the only person studying in the entire place, with the exception of trainee guards. I sat in my room that evening brushing my hair over and over in the mirror, the next thing I knew I saw you, this time sitting in a large room with a huge bed in the background, through your window I could just make out the trees the next thing I knew a person, along with what I thought at that time to be his pet cat, entered the room, I tried to warn you, but you couldn't seem to hear me, then the hand fell on your shoulder. 'You spend to much time watching this mortal; your obsession has become unhealthy.' The voice seem angered. 'If ever your two paths were to cross in our world, she will lose everything, I forbid you using this kind of magic.' The small cat jumped upon the table before the mirror, although it spoke only in meows, for some unknown reason I understood every word that it spoke.

'Fates have told of the meeting of two, a mortal from the world of the Goddess Gaea and a prince from ours, the chosen, once met will be unable to escape their fates, one shall be lost to Night, the other'..." Zo paused looking at Seiken.

"Will lose everything to prevent it and be taken into the darkness." Seiken finished, back then he hadn't realised the 'Night' Rowmeow spoke of was a being, he thought he simply meant darkness, night time, but now reminded of these words, they scared him. He looked at her searchingly, knowing in fear of what lay ahead, why? Why had she agreed all the time knowing what the cost would be?

"Why did you watch me when I was sad?" She questioned gently as Seiken released his grip on her hand.

"I watched you always Umemi, I don't know why, I just found you intriguing I guess." Zo smiled at his words gently and passed him the bag containing the runes she they had collected.

"The door these will now open is not one that I can reach; it is a door that leads from our world to yours." She sealed his finger around the bag.

"Umemi, there is no door." Zo simply smiled at him taking a mirror from the table as she waved her hand over it the place Seiken's people were held appeared upon its surface.

"Seiken, magic is a wondrous thing, you have it yourself, yet for some reason you always used mine."

"After my father caught me, once more ignoring his wishes, he banned me from using magic, he passed it to Rowmeow who has guarded it since, he always told me he would know when the time to return it as right." He sighed. "I can only tap into other people's magic now, that's how I could help you all those…" He paused deciding not to continue, even if he did, he would doubt very much she would remember, after all, back then was not her time.

"I see, well take these runes and place them in these five points, I have empowered them with magic so they can link together to create a door for you, they must be placed in the exact order, have Rowmeow restore your powers, or if he will not simply speak the following words." She handed him a small piece of paper, on it was a small diagram and the incantation he would need. "This will invoke the pentagram which in turn will summon a door that will lead to your world."

"But how? How is that possible?" He questioned.

"Night's tower does not exist in this world or any; as such it has the potential to have an entrance in any world, just like Olympus. By using this, you're simply activating the dormant world by awakening the part of Night's tower that exists somewhere in the plains of your home." She watched Seiken, his eyes grew wide with shock.

"How do you know this?" He questioned rising to his feet.

"I read it once... any five objects could be used, but since we went to all the trouble of getting these..." She didn't continue, she didn't feel the need to. "Seiken, please tell my friends I am coming."

"I..." He lowered his gaze to the floor; she knew of his betrayal, he felt ashamed at having let her down after she had tried so hard.

"Seiken... It's ok, you did what you had to, what was expected and I must do the same." She smiled gently turning her gaze back to the parchment on the table, having expected Seiken to have vanished, she tapped the pen on it lightly wondering if indeed she should even write this, yet he stood still watching her, a questioning expression upon his face.

"My people... they thrive in your world's darkness, maybe I can visit you." Seiken spoke softly, sadness to his voice.

"That..." She began her sentence cut short by his cold hands touching her face as he leaned towards her, she felt his lips on hers with a gentle pressure on hers, he pulled away, tears hanging in his eyes, before her gaze he vanished.

She gave a sigh looking at the silver ball she had rested on the table thinking about what Seiken had said about visiting her, wondering if he knew that once Marise appeared this time, she would no longer exist, she would simply no longer be, the darkness she would be forced into would be the dark void of nothingness, she touched her lips blushing slightly, the letter she had written vanished from the table as she opened the box, a white cloud surrounded her, as it embraced her she heard the ancients voice.

"Did you find your answer?" It whispered.

"Yes, everything you said was right... I never did believe his stories." She smiled as a feeling of weightlessness drifting over her.

***

"Zodiac Althea." As Night spoke her name Daniel rose to see her enter the room through the bars of the cage, he sighed, Night was right, she came. She looked over to Acha, Eiji and Daniel all held in the small prison, before rushing to them touching Daniel's hand that rested on the bars. She cared little that Night and Elly stood awaiting her attention, first she had to ensure her friends were safe, not only that, she needed to buy time for Seiken, who even now would be placing the runes as she had instructed him, as long as Night was focused on her, it gave them a better chance of escaping.

"Zo... you came." He whispered sadly, he had known she would, yet that did not stop him hoping that she would not.

"Of course I did." He cringed to see her smile, again the smile she had used so often to cover her pain, yet under it all he felt her relief at finding them, alive and unharmed. Even through the walls of her mind he could feel her fear, her cold hand on his as he gripped the bar trembled slightly, he remembered something his father had said a long time ago, something he had never really seen until now, 'being brave is doing something, even though you're afraid,' and that was exactly what she was doing, he could feel how afraid she was, although she hid it well, yet at the same time there seemed to be more to her fear than just facing Night.

Night stood behind her waiting patiently, she turned to face him trying to extinguish the fear she now felt for the stranger that had helped them through their journey.

"I knew I knew you from somewhere." She said coldly wondering to herself how much her companions knew by this point, but regardless it didn't matter, this would all end now. "Mum had always told me such great stories about you, she told me my father too was a great magic user that he left in order to protect us. As a child I couldn't understand, I didn't know why I had to be the only child without a father; you can't imagine how difficult it was. Then, in the perpetual forest, I saw you when I met my mother, there you were in a frame, you, her and me, of course I wasn't born then." She pulled the tattered drawing Acha had handed her outside the forest from her pocket, upon it there they stood, Night smiled as he stood behind her mum, one arm around her the other on his unborn child. "There you were, the stranger that over the last few weeks always seemed to catch me, mum told me my father was filled with wonderful ideas, how wonderful do you think she'd find them now? Maybe I should have stopped by to tell her on the way, but I was scared, scared you would hurt her too!" She screwed the paper up throwing it at Night, he caught it, smiling as he looked at it before it vanished in his hands.

"Now there would be a trick worthy of Hades himself." Night stated coldly.

"What?" Zo challenged

"Well if you can bring her back from the grave, then I will gladly listen to anything you have to say."

"The... grave?" Zo questioned sadly her legs giving beneath her as she heard Daniel call her name.

"Oh, what's the matter, don't you remember?" He stated bitterly. "I remember it perfectly; you failed to protect her, just like you failed to protect your friends."

"Protect her? I don't understand." She whispered

"Don't listen Zo, he's lying, Mr Venrent would have told you when you asked of her, Zo he's just playing you."

"Mr Venrent, Eryx you mean, he would no more tell you, than he would help you."

"You're wrong, Mr Venrent loved my Mother, he'd do anything to help me."

"You're right, he did love your mother, so much so that he crossed from Knights-errent to be with her, threatening to reveal my identity and endanger your lives further. I did what I had to, to ensure that never happened, just as I bargained with him to give you the potion that brought your past back to haunt you, he didn't do it to help you, he did it to help himself, in return he got both his sight and youth returned." Night smiled. "Now as I was saying, you failed to save your mother, you failed to protect her; shall we see the same mistake repeated here?" Zo opened her mouth as if to speak only changed her mind about what she would say.

"If you loved my mother so much, why didn't you save her?" But before Night could answer Elly interrupted.

"I see you came empty handed." Elly approached Zo cautiously, already seeing surrender in her eyes, Night's tale had weakened her resistance, she would gladly do as they wished, Elly smiled triumphantly.

"No!" Zo stated soberly. "I had what *he* wanted all along, only I never realised it... I was given it years ago by an amazing guy, he was filled with such wondrous stories about everything, even his firewood was enchanted." She looked at Daniel meaningfully who clutched her satchel tighter, he understood completely, even if his life depended on it, he would not give it to Night, not if it meant losing her.

"Impossible, we would have known if it was in your possession." She snapped stepping forwards as if to challenge her, but her challenge was met only by Night's orders.

"Lain, leave us." Night commanded, Elly opened her mouth as if to object, but turned sharply leaving the room, what did it matter, whether she was buying time or truly did have what they sought, it would all finish the same way.

"So where is it?" Night questioned, Zo paused glancing to the window, upon its shiny surface she saw Seiken was helping the remaining few of his people through the door the runes had created, Night looked at her and smiled. "It turns out you could have helped them after all, although they would have been free in just a moment regardless, after all he did fulfil *his* part of the bargain. An ingenious plan of yours, if I must say so, I expected nothing more for my own flesh and blood, now about the Grimoire." He pressed wondering if it could truly be within her possession.

"There's one slight problem." She smiled glancing towards the cage. "You see it's in there." She pointed towards the cage much to the surprise of both Acha and Eiji... "now although I could ask for it to be handed to me, if I were to do that, there's no guarantee you would release my friends once you had it, so here's the condition. You have what I want, I have want you want, a fair trade, my friends go free and you are *not* to bother them, the same applies to Seiken and his people, in exchange, I will release the final Grimoire, that is what you want isn't it?" She questioned.

"Zo what are you doing?" Daniel objected, as Acha and Eiji exchanged puzzled glances, only Daniel understood the situation fully, what was she thinking? If she was to give him the final Grimoire then... she was doing exactly what Night had expected of her, choosing those she cared for most, over the needs of the many, that wasn't the way it was meant to be, once he had the Grimoire, then he would surely break the final two seals that restrained the Severaine, the world would be forced into peril.

"That seems fair, and you will release the Grimoire, you understand what that means?" He questioned knowing that she would, but still, he had to be sure she completely understood the situation.

"I know." She looked to the cage as its bars vanished leaving Acha, Eiji and Daniel free to join her which they did at great speed trying to place themselves between her and Night.

"You really are your mother's child!" Night smiled as Daniel took her in his arms squeezing her tightly as he did so.

"You stupid girl." He cried lovingly as he held her, as yet he had not fully grasped where this situation would lead, this was one small comfort to her at this moment, nor had he noticed the subtly movements she made to remove him from between her and Night.

"I have every faith in you Daniel." She smiled pulling away to remove the satchel from his grip.

"What did you mean by you would release the Grimoire for him?" He questioned, she looked to him smiling sadly, her arm quickly extended sending an invisible force to his chest pushing him and the others towards the door, as they rose to their feet eyes filled with questions, she erected a field identical to that used, to keep them out when Marise had previously fought both Daniel, and the power demon leaving them only one place to go, the exit, as Daniel caught his breath he approached the field in disbelief.

Night placed his hand on her shoulder encouragingly as she knelt on the floor.

"Every time a Grimoire is located, it must first be released before its power returns to me, now in the past, I have just had messengers bring it to me, reading the incantations written upon its surface, true their pronunciation wasn't all that good, yet it still worked, in every case the person who reads it is sacrificed for the cause, although I am not sure exactly how it will effect one who still possessions magic, but in layman's terms, my daughter has agreed to release the seal at the sacrifice of her existence. This is after all, the only way to release a spell formed by the sacrifice of another." Daniel banged against the barrier trying desperately to break its seals as Zo turned her back to him.

Is that what you've agreed to?' His voice screamed to her mind, not in anger but in fear. *Is it?*' He demanded

To win... I have to lose.' She simply replied, there was a sound of tearing as she tore open the bag.

"What's she doing, I emptied that back at the perpetual forest, there's nothing in there." Eiji stressed before recalling the weight of the empty bag, all too soon he realised what it meant.

"Daniel, you always said I would lose something in there." She pulled a small rectangular object from the bag covered in white cloth and she turned back slightly to look at him. "I left it there for safe keeping, and well, I guess I forgot about it." She stated, she had made a deliberate choice to bring it with her, stitching it inside the lining for safekeeping, so no matter where she went, it would be something to remind her of home, but never had she thought this item to be of any relevance.

"That's..." He gasped watching as his friend unwrapped it gently

"The book elder Robert gave me for saving his life? Yes." She smiled softly, turning to face Night as she rose to her feet.

"Damn it Zodiac!" Daniel snapped. "I made a promise, don't you make me out to be a lair." He warned, she looked to him sadly.

"Daniel, don't worry, you kept your word, I never lost myself."

"Damn it Zo... that's not..." He stopped, his words lost as she slowly she opened the book, as she stood there the once faded writing on the book's yellowed pages seemed to bleed onto the page forming words in the ancient text. Taking a breath she stood trembling before her father and began to read. There was only one spell within this book and that was the one to release the powers sealed within, a bright light encompassed her as it read, the foreign words sounding like poetry on those that listened, she paused turning back to look at her friends, she gave then a warm smile closing her eyes before saying two final words

"Shemiste Nilishatar." Which in the ancient words translated to mean, for this cause I will give my life, although there were many different interpretations on these words, all of which resulted in a vow of sacrifice for the one that spoke them, it was a vow spoken by those pledging their service to another, Daniel had never realised until now they had been words spoken from a Hectarian spell. Throughout the sound of whispers before the final words were spoken, all of them heard a gleeful sound, although but a whisper it called to their hearts.

'And that makes three.' Somewhere in the distance, the shrine of Geburah in both worlds, crumbled.

As the final words were spoken the light which surrounded Zodiac faded transferring through the air to Night, the words of the ancients whispered upon an imaginary breeze falling upon the ears of all those around as a strange smoke filled the air, in that spilt second Daniel swore he saw the silhouettes of three people standing before them, the new figure's hand seemed to plunge into Zo's chest she faltered a few steps as the hand drew back, the figure vanished and the air had cleared taking with it the field erected by Zo. Before them now the two figures turned to look upon them, Night and who now they knew would be Marise.

"Oh… I guess I should have mentioned." Night said in an artificial tone of forgetfulness. "Just a small thing really." Night smiled placing his arm around Marise. "I promised *I* wouldn't hurt you…" He smiled, Daniel felt himself gasp as Marise turned to look at them, unlike before not a trace of Zo remained. "But I never did mention anything about anyone else…" He looked from Marise to them meaningfully. "Are you still here?" He questioned smiling watching as the three of them began to run.

"I have just confirmed all five of the barriers both in Knights-errent and here were destroyed." Elly re-entered the room in time to see Zo's friends leave with haste. "Mari!" She exclaimed.

"Lee." Marise acknowledged her presence as she watched the space where Daniel had stood only moments ago.

"Does this mean…" Elly questioned placing her hands on Marise's uninjured shoulders

"She's gone for good." Marise smiled. "Zodiac is gone for good, Hades himself collected her." She stated raising her hand to the place Hades hand had penetrated.

"For a moment, I must admit I had my doubts." Elly smiled brightly before embracing Marise as Night picked the open Grimoire from the floor just to the side of where Marise stood eagerly awaiting her instructions, he was, after all, so much more imaginative than Blackwood ever was. Marise drew her sword she breathed a sigh of relief to find it still worked.

"Well." She stated her sword still drawn. "I think they have had a large enough head start."

"Before that." Night raised his hand before her preventing her from taking another step. "There is something else you need to attend to." He looked to Elly who nodded, understanding this wasn't over until one final task had been completed; linking Marise she escorted her from the room to prepare her.

***

Night stood at the window watching as his daughter's friends as they ran across the open field towards the entrance of Collateral, their adventure had been the most exciting yet, ending with his victory. The previous people he had sent to Knight-errent were merely test subjects, their missions nothing like the true goal, people were always so willing to ask the Gods for their help, he would have been more than happy to grant any of their requests had they succeeded, after all they were merely guinea pigs in, what had been, a fantastic game, but now there were more pressing matters to attend to, he had to pay a visit to an old friend.

Chapter twenty-five

They had scarcely made it to Zo's cabin from the entrance of Collateral when the tremors began. The ground shook with such unexpected force it knocked the three of them to the ground.

"What was that?" Acha gasped struggling to her feet before following Daniel into what had been Zo's home.

Since Zo's confrontation with Night he hadn't spoken a single word, he hesitated at the door, he could still see Zo rushing around bottling herbs and reading herself for the picnics they would so often have, she looked to him and smiled before vanishing into the air as another tremor struck.

"Eiji, what's happening?" Acha cried as the furniture began to walk across the floor of its own accord.

"I think..." He paused, it was better to explain the entire story. "A long time ago my master told me a story of the ancients, back then before our world was even as it was now, the races that came before us sealed away a magical power, this power was known as the Severaine. You see when this world was young, there was no dividing line between Hectarians and Elementalists, we all used the same powers, more or less, the Severaine was a raw magical energy that ran riot through the earth. It was us back then that served the earth, or so the story goes. One day the Gods decided to give us a chance, swayed by the words of Gaea and Hecate, allowed man to create a power that could seal the Severaine, somehow they created this stronghold, and seven seals were placed at key elemental locations across the world, five of which were said to be so strong, they crossed over into another world, the world of dreams, it was said because every person who roamed the earth at that time dreamt of this peaceful world, these were said to be the strongest barriers of all. Held not only by magic, but the people who believed in the world they were trying to create, each seal was home to a key aspect of the world itself, an aspect of nature contained within the Severaine. However, before they managed to seal it completely the Severaine sent forth a huge power changing the shape of the planet as we knew it, lands sunk and continents rose from the seas, volcanoes erupted killing almost all the people that resided upon its surface but for a few, from there it is said all human and demy human life evolved, they were said to be people who despite the age of technology still knew how to live with the earth, instead of listening to the technologies predictions of weather they devised by their own means and saw this coming and thus were able to survive, these people were known in their time as Elementalists, followers of Gaea, like myself, and Hectarians, those that worship Hecate, Goddess of witchcraft and the cross roads, and some who possessed no magic yet travelled with Elementalists and Hectarians also survived. When the Severaine was sealed, the power between the Elementalists and Hectarians began to alter, and due to Elementalists only being able to learn from another, when the world was destroyed a lot of the magic Elementalists used was destroyed with them meaning they could only use powers of the elements around them, earth, air, fire and water." Eiji knew all too well the story had been altered by time, but in time, he would come to learn the true story of the Severaine.

"What's this got to do with the tremors?" Acha questioned bracing herself as the next one struck.

"Well before, Seiken told us we had destroyed five of the barriers, I'm willing to bet, if the legend is correct the reason Marise didn't follow us, was so she could finish what we started by collapsing the final barriers, the problem being." Eiji found himself having to raise his voice over the volume of the earthquake. If the stories are true the Severaine has been sealed for aeons, now the runes we collected, spirit, sacrifice, innocence, balance, power, they all relate to attributes of nature, now its just a theory, but I bet they also acted as some form of cushion to prevent these powers welling up and getting out of hand, once we destroyed them the power will be returning straight to the Severaine and I think that is what is causing this shift in the elements." Eiji released the wall as the tremor subsided. "But if that is the case, it could mean the very end of existence, the Severaine is generally used by the Gods to purge the earth." He looked to Daniel desperately, if his theories were correct, the release of the Severaine meant the beginning of the end for everything. "Daniel were there any other theories? Please tell me I'm wrong, Daniel!" Daniel simply shook his head as he sat against the wall, just then a small silver ball rolled across to his hand, as he picked it up, it played a strange but sorrowful tune, he looked up to Eiji.

"Eiji… is there anything we can do to stop this?" Daniel's voice seemed horse and alien to their ears.

"Unless we knew…" The tremors stooped, Eiji lowered his voice. "Unless we knew where to find the final two seals and faced Marise, we have no chance… but…" Before he could continue Daniel had rose to his feet and was walking towards the door.

"Maybe we can find the answer in Knights-errent?" Acha questioned pulling her sleeve up sharply as if to demonstrate the point only to reveal where the mark should have been, but Daniel wasn't listening, he had his own ideas and was already about to leave.

"Brace yourself." Eiji called as he felt another tremor stirring deep within the earth, Daniel was already opening the door as the tremor hit.

"Daniel, you can't go out there… You don't even know where to look." Acha called out after him Eiji rushed to the door a violent wind whipped outside the house.

"Daniel." He called into the wind wondering if his cries had reached his ears, Eiji and Acha exchanged glances before heading out after him. "Daniel." He yelled again over the howling wind, he placed his hand on Daniel's shoulder stopping him in his tracks as the torrential downpour began. "Daniel." He said again, already soaked to the bone by the wall of water that awaited them as they left the shelter of the hut. "I was wrong, it's too late the final seals were broken, that's why this is happening… Can't you feel it? It's already too late." Eiji stated, he felt the great energy gathering around, gaining energy and strength as it stepped once more into their world.

"I… I can't just do nothing." Daniel's whisper was almost lost in the violent winds, the sky above them now completely black lit only by the flash of lightening; the thunder itself was so forceful the ground trembled

"You're right." Eiji shouted over the wind. "You need to help the people down there… help them secure against the storm, help the men build guards against the raging tides of the rivers and seas, Daniel, you need to help your family."

"But..." His protest was cut short by Eiji's angry interruption.

"But nothing! Zo promised your mother you would return, do you want to make her out to be a liar? Do you think she did everything she did, just so you could throw your life away?" He screamed, Daniel looked at him determination rising to his eyes.

"Let's go." He said, slowly his heart wanted to hunt down the people who had done this and make them suffer like he did now, but it also told him Eiji was correct, there was nothing he could do, he had faced her before, to go alone would be suicide, besides there were people down there right now that could use his help, he could always leave later, but for now Eiji was right, he had to show his mother she had been true to her word, he had to help save those that this whole journey started out to protect, the people of his home, if not for her love for them, she would have never left with Elly, none of this would have happened and to selfishly stand by and watch that which she had loved so much be reduced to nothing, for something such as revenge, well, it would make her angry. He could not lose sight of the things that were important and for now, it was to safe guard his home, protect those Zo had wished to with every inch the effort and determination she had place in their journey.

**

"Oh Daniel." Angela met him at the door throwing her arms around him hugging him tightly kissing him of the forehead before pulling him into an even tighter hug; she looked behind him seeing his friends had followed him home.

"Where's Zo?" She asked softly worry rising to her gentle features, there was something odd about the last time they met, something that made Angela fear for the situation they found themselves in, and the smile she gave before she left, it was so sad, so final, almost as if she was taking one last look around, a look to burn into her memory something she knew she would never see again.

"She chose to stay with her father Mrs Starfire." Eiji answered for Daniel as he and Acha walked through the door leaving a wet trail across the wooden floor, mentioning what had happen just now was not appropriate, he knew that much from watching Daniel's posture stiffen as she asked the question, they would not speak of what happened to his mother, at least not until Daniel was ready.

"Her father? The man that took Daniel? Why? Why would she do that?" She questioned persistently still holding Daniel tightly.

"Ah... she explained..." Eiji felt himself blush at having been found out in the lie, he had not thought that Zo had known this truth and from her reaction when she met with their captor, she hadn't found out until the last moment, possibly in this very place, then again, she had not expected to face Night, that was clear also as she approached the one who had been aiding her. "There really is no time to explain, we must secure the village barricade the river."

"You're right, Jack is already down there, but last I heard it was a losing battle, I'm sure they could use some more man power." She pulled away from Daniel who looked at her sadly and nodded. "I'm sure an Elementalist would prove useful as well." She added as she smiled softly at Eiji who nodded.

"Acha, you help mum gather supplies and evacuate to higher ground, leave something so we know which way you're heading." Daniel looked back to Acha from the door; he was trusting her with the most important task, protecting his mother Acha nodded to him, before he closed the door.

***

Finally the men returned praising each other for the hard work, Jack slapped Eiji on the back.

"Couldn't have done it without you kid." He smiled heartily slapping him on the back hard enough to wind him as he took a few staggered steps to regain his balance. "How you held back that water while we laid the first bunker, genius." Eiji felt himself blush Jack stopped in his tracks looking upon their home, considering everyone was meant to have left by now, their homes looked undisturbed, Angela opened the door waving to them.

"Mum... Acha, I thought you were evacuating!" Daniel scolded.

"Daniel, this is our home, there's not a person out there who doesn't feel the same, if we stay here we have more chance of surviving, the mountain cliffs are shaking and avalanching, and although the rivers are rising there is a long way for it to come before it reaches us... besides, with all the tremors, the old and the young of the village don't stand much chance, so we decided to stay." Daniel looked to Acha who shrugged, she had tried so hard to change their minds, even shown Daniel's mum the entrance to Collateral taking her in to show the ease of journey, but still they refused.

"We managed to barricade the river, put up several back up bunkers too for when it passes the first." Jack entered from the rain after thanking the men for their hard work. "How long do you think this will keep up for? Like it or not we may have to consider relocating to Mainland."

"Well..." Eiji began, embarrassed to find himself once more the centre of attention. "The Severaine will calm eventually when the stored energy is exhausted... the rivers will calm, the tremors will stop... but that's when the real trouble will begin. Mankind, if they survive the energetic burst, will fall once more to its power like it did before, the elemental creatures, creatures you believe only to be myth will waken once more from their slumber, you see without the Severaine they were forced into an eternal sleep leaving no trail of their existence even for those who look." Eiji paused wondering if perhaps these were the creatures that resided in Knights-errent he shuddered thinking back to the dragon they encountered, if beings such as that one were unleashed here, they would have an even slimier chance of survival.

"Why now?" Jack questioned drying himself on one of the towels Angela had handed out at the door. "Why after all this time has it happened?" Jack wasn't unfamiliar with the legends of the Severaine, after all, his son studied it and took great pleasure in telling them all about it.

"It was written on the tablets of the Gods that this would happen and also that Night would rise again."

"Daniel what are you talking about? Twenty-two years ago Night was sealed away, I don't know much but I know that, the Idliod saw to it that he could never return." Jack thought back, he would have been a little older than Daniel when all this occurred, yet even living through it the details given were so vague, almost as if it never happened.

"Twenty-three." Daniel corrected. "You don't have to believe me, if I were you I wouldn't believe me either, but I saw him, I saw him with my own eyes, we were there when he obtained the final Grimoire... the book that all the time had been kept in this village." Daniel's mum sat him down on the sofa trying her best not to fuss over him as concerns began to rise about what exactly had happened.

"Daniel... What exactly happened while you were away? And where is Zo?" Daniel rose to his feet and began silently up the stairs.

"Mrs Starfire." Eiji addressed her quietly as Daniel left.

"Angela." She corrected as her concerned features followed her son's trip to his room.

"Angela then." Eiji smiled. "It's a long and complicated story, one I don't think your son is ready to tell yet, give him time, when he is ready I am sure he will tell all, perhaps when he makes better sense of what happened himself." He phrased it carefully as Daniel looked down from the top of the stairs as another tremor shook the house, he thought of the last time he had seen her here, how she rushed through the house straight into the guest room where Acha had lay. He closed his bedroom door behind him and collapsed on his bed for what he knew had to be the last time.

Marise had made it clear she had a score to settle, if she did come searching for him, he would hate to endanger the lives of those around him, to stay would mean he would condemn those he loved, he understood now the choice Zo had made, he never really had until now, he was angry at her that day for sneaking out with that stranger from her past, he couldn't understand her decision to leave, but now he faced the same problem, he saw clearly, no matter who faced this decision, there was really but one choice, to protect those you cared for, to sacrifice your own happiness and comfort to keep them safe. He turned Zo's musical ball over and over in his hand as he listened to the melody it placed suddenly one of the carving shifted to line with another, almost knocking it from his hands as it rotated, the top opening slightly.

"Daniel..." An image of Zo appeared projected just above the ball. "I hope you enjoy this new toy, it's part of the ancient technology of those that came before us, those who were ultimately destroyed by the Severaine's power, if you're watching this we both know what this means... either I'm an idiot and left it out where you could play with it while I'm out..." Daniel smiled sadly. "Or you found it, but I guess we both know why really. It seems every millennia or so the world turns a complete cycle, then most of this technology is buried and long forgotten, you know the story about the Hectarians and Elementalists that survived, but what you may not know is it was said near the beginning of this cycle some of the Hectarians changed themselves to become part animal for the extra senses they would provide, so they could have more warning if ever this was to happen again, this is the theory behind why we have demi-humans, just something I thought you may enjoy, but that itself is not common knowledge compared to the other theories... Sorry I'm getting side tracked and I have very little time." She smiled gently. "Anyway, it seems Night found a way to bypass that cycle by sending us to Knights-errent he had us destroy five of the barriers, I'm still unclear on his motives... You probably know this already and I'm not sure how long this thing lasts, so to the point. The people that came before us developed many things, one of which you hold in your hand, now somewhere out there is the knowledge you need, every problem has a solution, the Severaine was contained once by these people and it can be done again, after all if the keys to sealing it were destroyed, the seals would have been broken, where as we had to remove a physical aspect in order to collapse them, so if you can reactivate the source, the barriers would reappear. Daniel, somewhere forgotten now by us, there is a vast library of information, if you can find that, you can find the answer… the staff I made you is written in their language, I know you can undo what I have done… There is so much I still have to tell you." She glanced away to what Daniel could only guess was the door before staring back down to the ball; she sat in silence for a moment looking deep into it

"Umemi." The sound of Seiken's voice filled the air and the image began to fade.

"I believe in you." She whispered before her image faded completely. He lay watching the ball for a moment before rotating the sphere back to its starting point.

"Eiji, Acha!" Daniel galloped down the stairs filled with a new energy. "There's a way to stop this thing… I have to find it." Eiji looked up from his cup of fresh chocolate surprised to hear the determination and anticipation filling his voice.

"Daniel, what make's you so sure?" He questioned, as nice as it was to see his friend enthusiastic, there was also that part of him that believed this may just be his way of coping with what happened, finding something else to occupy his attention, it was a common reaction to avoid facing grief.

"I have to get packing, there's so much to do, I just want you to look after my mum ok." He smiled at Eiji and Acha knowing neither of them had homes to go to so to speak.

"You're leaving again?" His mother sighed softly hugging him tightly. "Mum, somewhere out there, is the knowledge the ancients used to seal the Severaine in the first place… I have to find it." He went to rush together some things pulled back by his mother who stepped before him slowing his pace as she intervened to embrace him tightly once more.

"Okay." She smiled looking at him now he had grown up so much, she couldn't help wondering where her little boy had gone. "You do what you have to and when you are ready, come home." She said softly, clearly she had a similar feeling to that of Eiji's or her words would have been so different.

"You really believe there's a way to stop this?" Eiji questioned rising to his feet, hoping the growing feeling that this was more than just a coping mechanism wasn't a manifestation of what he wished to believe.

"Yes, but finding it wont be easy, that's why I only ask you stay here and look after my mum." He glanced from Eiji to his mum.

"We stand a better chance together." Acha smiled taking her gloves from her coat pocket pulling them on.

"It would be a shame to split up now." Eiji smiled. "You can tell us all about your plan as we pack." Eiji stated glancing around at their few possessions that littered the floor of Daniel's home.

"Better yet…" Daniel smiled. "While I grab some herbs, I'll show you." He pulled the small silver ball from his hands turning it until the image of Zo appeared, he stared at her image for but a moment before leaving them to watch it he approached his mother's study.

"Daniel." His mum met him at the door; in her hand she held a dark brown leather bag. "Zo left this when she came to the house before, she said she was on her way to get you and she wanted to leave it here, as a surprise, it seemed a little odd at the time but…" She stopped passing Daniel the bag, on the front she had sewn skilfully his name just on the corner of the right flap, the back like his staff was covered with writing, Daniel now knew, to be of the ancients, his mother left him to investigate its contents. As he peered in he smiled, there was hundreds of different herbs, each stored in the best way to preserve them, there were a few packets, labels detailing the contents and properties within and what aliments could be cured by it. There was also a leather belt, as he pulled it out he noticed the tiny grooves just big enough to hold some of the many glass phials that rested within the bag, as he fingered through them he noted only a third were actually beneficial to health, then he saw something that made him really smile. When they first met and her childhood memories began to return, she had told him how she had explored the fields of black magic, seeing this now he knew what she spoke nothing but the truth. Within the clearly label phials were poisons and drugs, each one carefully labelled again with content and effect, although there wasn't many of these, most of the phials, were in fact, for his protection, she had done things with herbs and chemicals he had never dreamed of, he tucked a few of the smoke screens in the belt along with some healing remedies and various other liquids to be used as self defence, there was one that caught his interest, fire in a bottle, she had called it, it was a yellow liquid, on the bottle it read. 'Explodes when induced to air, even without magic.' Daniel would sure have hated to cross her, even without her powers she would have proved to be deadly, the very thought she could create such things had never even began to speculate in his mind, he fastened the thin belt around his waist removing the old one, it had just enough holes to hold eight potions and a special hook for his staff, he folded the bag over tucking carefully into it, the list of herbs and uses she had written, it seemed that this had been prepared for a long time, he hugged it to himself still able to smelt the sweet aroma of plum blossom.

***

Finally, they were ready to leave. Daniel's mum stood at the door waving goodbye once more as her son departed on another adventure, he stopped turning back to take a final look, waving to her as she stood watching from his home, he wasn't sure exactly what he quested for, or how he would know when he found it, nor did he worry about not knowing the first place to look for this ancient knowledge, for now he had set off and that was all that was important, they head towards Collateral, knowing that by now, not even brave fools would try to sail the deadly waters. For just a second he paused, wondering if he was doing the right thing, with all his heart he believed he was and if they didn't succeed at least they tried. Collateral stood before them now, he took a final look back before they continued on their way.

***

In every generation of this world there are those we call the chosen, within their life they achieve many great things both predestined and unpredictable.

Three dark figures smiled as they watched over the tablets of the Gods that told the stories of the chosen, a never ending wall of stone tablets, stretched as far as the eye could see and beyond the earliest of which dated back to the beginning of time itself. They mounted the latest in its section in wall removing a blank stone placing it to lie before them, waiting for the next names to be selected from fates hands. These three had watched with interest since the dawn of man the journey of the chosen, but as they watched, waiting for their next journey they were unaware that three of the chosen now set out to do something none before them had done, they were on a mission to oppose destiny itself.

The three figures smiled to each other safe in the knowledge each of the chosen had a definite beginning and end, it was the watching them on their journey from A-B that proved to be more interesting than the outcome itself.

"Impossible." One of the voices exclaimed as the blank tablet shattered before them, they rushed to the tablet of the previous chosen; it seemed another story had begun. It seemed things were no longer as definite as they had first believed. Could it be the loop would finally stop with these? Something in the fates had shifted, something was different now… But what?

Printed in the United Kingdom
by Lightning Source UK Ltd.
117155UKS00001B/33